Hellbent Redemption

This is a work of fiction. Any names, characters, places, events, and incidents are a result of the author's pure storytelling to be used fictitiously, and any resemblance to actual persons, living or deceased, establishments, events is entirely coincidental.

To contact the author: ianramsayian3125@gmail.com

ISBN: 979-8-218-31291-6

Printed in the United States of America

† Table of Scriptures †

† DEAR HEAVENLY FATHER... †

Ian Ramsay

†

Holksdale

The more workers lost, the sooner they're replaced by another body. Most people desperately seek jobs and will not only settle with a low paying job but also the unjust behavior that's now a requirement.

There are many private schools located here. The tuition is very expensive, mostly high schools and there are two colleges there too.

These high schools usually are made up of Caucasian students who are privileged enough to attend. It also consists of minor kids of ethnic color whose parents work hard for them to go to school there where they believe it's a safer environment. But unfortunately, that's not always the case.

Some ethnic students have been bullied by upper-class students for being underprivileged compared to them. Some of them can attend through academic scholarships helping with their tuition. Having a lot on their plate academic wise and always being belittled by others is too much to take. The schools usually can't intervene due to it mostly being verbal harassment that never usually escalates to racial attacks.

After being repeatedly made fun of, belittled and feeling bad about themselves just for the other kids to gain a huge power trip, the ethnic kids retaliate in several ways. Few ethnic kids get expelled for causing a fight or bring a weapon to shoot up other people in the school. Others who are too overwhelmed with these ongoing parasites bothering them end up taking their lives through suicide. Lastly, those who refuse to put up with this end up

† History of Holksdale †

Holksdale is a large city. With all it inhabits, the feeling is diverse due to its three interwoven communities. The city covers many of its aspects of underlying problems with all types of propaganda of vast things that would influence no better. That strays us further from our creator.

Holksdale contains many unjustly issues affecting other people. From the selected privileged that's resulted in division, to the overtly offensive causing turmoil to the largely defensive. Citizens that almost gain pleasure in complaining over the most miniscule topics usually later escalates to a *HUGE* controversy.

The troubles could lead to word of mouth spreading to the next town over. Holksdale developed a status of many things: being overpopulated, hypergamous, hypocritical, racist and intolerant, including constant lust for greed. And yet the city's status doesn't link together the people located here. The three communities all share blame in either sin but refuse to be held accountable and blame each other instead. Consistent shaming of others but then retaliates when opposing sides slander back. Not one hierarchy ever fights to address the self-made issues within their community.

UPTOWN: Located here are the wealthiest of people that've derived from upper-class families. Or from other places that've settled here to work for the time being. The community is filled with many factors for economic and financial success. Also having the community to feel nice and secure. Whether it being successful bankers, higher privilege bestowed upon the lucky and fortunate, and many other prosperous professions. A wealthy family inheritance passed on to the next generation and of course being white. Uptown is populated by a mass of predominantly Caucasian people.

There are sights of minorities there, but it's very rare to find one who is in love with their own professions. They derive from downtown Holksdale to work here doing task that many residents here would find degrading. Many works as janitors, plumbers, construction of large buildings for upcoming stores or businesses. They come prepared for manual handmade labor. Some workers endure hardships of their own through constant disrespect while on the clock. This involves the looks of disdain expressed to them by formal employees at whatever workplace has hired them. Even blatantly expressing rude, mean, condescending comments since they're deemed as lesser than. Or just receiving an attitude of not being worthy enough to add in any input of value. Usually overlooked by employers believing these lower-class people aren't fully educated and do not know better. Making anyone feel less than human.

Most express many issues they have on the workforce to the usual human resources. Unfortunately, they aren't investigated any deeper or altered by any means. Being constantly disrespected on the job and the people responsible for these refuses to stop has led to a bitter

division of not just labor but of human decency. The po that be causing this disconnect are too stubborn to benc a little bit or are too focused on work to ever conside feelings of whom they see as less than human.

While most minorities instead keep their heads dov avoid confrontation, others refuse to tolerate this r They see it as nothing but unjustly acts, especially kno they get to return home to their well-off families, st paycheck and gated houses.

All these positives they flaunt off while these frust laborers not only having to work one or two jobs b make ends meet but also must encounter nonstop cont on top of that just further has workers irked.

This ongoing problem has led to reports of vio breaking out in the workplace. Mostly through ac terrorism, former employees who shoots up the c resulting in dead employees and the assailant us turning the gun on themselves. Or several protests exis to a combination of anger and being unstable by contempt placed on them and the propaganda use midtown Holksdale. This'll normally lead to either al conditions or policies in the workplace for them l denied for future ones or being arrested and fired from jobs.

Most police uptown are slightly prejudice, ca several altercations with minority people just pa through. Some have been killed after being pulled ov police, never making it back to their families downt transferring to another school somewhere midtown or downtown Holksdale. These problems have created a further disconnect amongst teens in this city.

There is a certain company here in competition with the ones from midtown. Consisting mostly of restaurants, fast food joints, and others who are in the same kind of business are at odds with each other. There is history of ongoing battles between similar businesses in the city that has lasted for years.

Uptown previously owned a Five star rated restaurant called Great Drakes that contained many workers of all ethnicities being chefs, dishwashers and of course waiters and waitresses. The food was perfection, extraordinary taste leading to higher word of mouth to the other two communities. Great Drakes was the one place uptown that catered to ethnic people's needs with their diverse food and respectful customer service.

The restaurant was the one exception keeping others from generalizing that whole community as intolerant. It had freshly prepared Caribbean food, Spanish food, including Indian food. The waiters of different races indulged the customers with friendly conversation. The restaurant had their customer service staff tend to whatever ethnic people that were alike to themselves. It made the environment more comfortable and coalesced with many diverse people from both two communities.

Great Drakes had been in competition with another well-known restaurant in midtown called Biggup, another place serving ethnic food. Biggup had a decent reputation for having good freshly cooked food. However, their business kept losing regular customers to Great Drakes due to their vast advertisements. Biggup couldn't afford to promote themselves too much other than setting up flyers. Yet it wasn't enough to draw in half the customers that their competitor had, they knew.

The owner of Biggup had an employee of his get a reservation there, everything payed for. The employee had been ordered an entrée of curry goat and rice. The employee had plant a rat head in the meat and reported it to the manager. To the manager, who was embarrassed to of come to this discovery, had brought the employee to the back to offer his full apology for everything and complementary food.

The next week, it was reported on the news that the employee had exposed the restaurant's incident that they'd try to cover up. He had taken pictures of the rat head in the food and worst of all, had recorded the manager's apology using it as pretty much a confession. The report had cost Great Drakes hundreds of their customers, smeared their credibility, and were under further investigation by the health department. Unfortunately, the health department had found a couple of hazards forcing them to shut down completely.

Yet there was a bridge to all of this.

The manager one day had seen the employee who'd reported that restaurant passing on the street. He followed him to his work and realized how he had worked at Biggup, a place that was always competing with them. He had pieced it all together that they had planned it and cost them all their jobs and customers. The former manager had zero proof of this but had been in the acquainted with other food joint runners within the community.

He'd warned the other business owners of this ethnic employee from midtown pulling stunts like this. They had taken his word for it, which led to them rejecting ethnic people from midtown and downtown who applied for there. This had led to racial tension and causing other food places to be at worse war with the other ethnic communities because of this.

This racial tension made it uncomfortable for the very few ethnic residents that shortly lived there. People of color who had moved in the nice, gated community where the houses were nicely designed with beautiful gardens that looked to of been tended to regularly. The houses were close enough together and everyone knew each other either by name or by face.

Few ethnic people who'd moved had felt the cold isolation in that community. Other residents never tried to hide it, they would overtly study whomever came through their window and seemed hesitant to greet them. Or worse, whatever neighbor who would try to introduce themselves were clearly somewhat scared to a little diversity. It was to the point where they came off like they had another agenda from the newcomers' perspective.

Only further alienating people from being a community.

MIDTOWN: Here in this part of the city lies the constant promotion of even the smallest things in order to move up in the world. Middle-class residents are here, people are always waiting for the next best thing to be advertised. Since most advertising comes from here, midtown catches the latest news and updates on future technologic materials, events and businesses.

There are many restaurants, theatres and shopping centers located around here. Always filled with people enjoying themselves with their families and friends. But had rivalries with similar businesses located uptown. The racial tension between the two were kept still, especially when word got out about the stunt midtown caused in bringing down Great Drakes. Uptown residents who normally planned their dinner parties there were furious and blamed this whole ordeal on them. Which soon resulted in crimes against certain places in midtown either being vandalized or fake reports of sanitary hazards by people uptown.

Residents here knew what they'd done, this was leading toward them making allegations, but weren't proven due to lack of any evidence. Including whatever suspect from uptown was brought in for questioning, they had expensive good lawyers getting them out of any possible scrap. The furious residents saw it as nothing but one of the perks of having white privilege. While certain leisure's of these people were being taken away by them. It later escalated to their movie theatres being vandalized and those in midtown soon retaliating worse to an uglier extent.

Midtown being a source for many media updates had become a key factor to their vindictive acts. It was no secret that employees from downtown Holksdale despised their superiors that they had worked for which included the uncivil work environment and ongoing mistreatment there. They'd always been aware of this, so they played off their emotions. Midtown was responsible for the creation of propaganda videos slandering most businesses uptown.

Their videos basically took any minor information about a particular place that had underprivileged employees and exaggerates the problems. Exaggerating the selective facts like being condescending and unjust hours to it coming from a place of racial hatred amongst these many elite superiors.

Playing off their emotions to influence these workers to cause problems by protesting for respect. The purpose of their propaganda videos was to instill the idea that efficacy would be possible by protesting. Knowing that it wouldn't happen, yet it would halt business production for them and create racial bias being affiliated with the company's name. This manipulative move had worked to their advantage, causing further uproars to certain businesses.

This included minority chefs to refuse to work, ceasing production in certain food joints for a while. Also, janitors and other cleaning staff protesting, creating an unsanitary hassle at other places as well. This constant protest resulted in many of them being arrested, removed off the area or fired. All the videos did was costs many citizens from downtown their jobs or had gotten them arrested instead. This caused not only businesses in uptown Holksdale to suffer at points but opened the eyes of the exploited employees.

Their realization of being nothing but a pawn in their competitive dispute just to give them an edge on the other made them feel dense to what was really happening. It also created this social disconnect with the other two communities. Believing that anyone who seems superior trying to give back to inspire change wasn't coming from a genuine place, it was viewed as nothing but an alternate agenda to further their interest.

Midtown is also known to of been in the middle of many white-collar crimes which originated from downtown Holksdale. Many criminals from downtown involved in drug dealing, narcotics trafficking and weapons dealing required their help and knowledge of ways to hide their proceeds. In agreement between criminals from both towns, midtown had helped for criminals to not only disguise their proceeds but had helped them to accumulate more of their wealth and fund further criminal activity.

While each side benefitted off this illegal exchange, the money launders from midtown grew more and more greedy. Resulting in them trying to steal more money from their partners but was exposed soon enough. This was revealed during the integration process of money laundering, where they're supposed to give back to the downtown community. To return their proceeds from what appeared to be professional sources in the public's eye.

However, they'd noticed they were being skimped on more than once.

This was a constant thing happening between the towns which led to violence amongst themselves. This fight for money created gangs representing both towns, the war between them had cost multiple deaths from both parties, including anyone unfortunate enough to be visible during their unannounced attacks. Each gang could travel to the other's town and kill them on sight.

Gangsters from midtown and downtown had started out with a good alliance in the criminal underworld. Yet greed had influenced an unfair power struggle and had impacted their authentic money laundering scheme. And created years of gang violence and division.

Even though midtown had inhabited different races of people including Caucasian folks, people are still progressive, and all races and lifestyles are respected within this community. Even regardless of whatever tension happens uptown. They're all usually coalesced at either one of the community colleges located there. Since it is less expensive compared to the schools located uptown, there are a sea of diverse students going there for a cheaper education. Unfortunately, the schools harbor some trespassers lurking around for female students. These trespassers usually creep from downtown Holksdale. Due to the many attractive younger females still in their prime beginning school, they search the campuses and try to blend in with other ethnic students. Since college consists of all ages higher than late teens and these community ones don't acquire people to have to present their I.D. It's impossible to differentiate actual students from ones that aren't. Usual trespassers could be late teens to grown men with a common lust. They normally approach and entice females to attain their phone numbers or have them lured to somewhere private on campus.

This normally leads to women being attacked or stalked. Or if the woman escapes, it'll get reported but always ends with no results. The person had left and can't at all be traced. Actual students who try to approach girls usually have no luck. This is due to the preconceived notions females have of any guy being a possible predator, resulting in them being already on their guard.

This had caused almost a divide between genders due to the possibility of being assaulted. Plus, while attending these community colleges, most people just want to get out. Not socialize or date, yet these known downtown trespassers make it difficult to let girls be in peace. This resulted in many sexually frustrated male students harboring anger towards these men from there.

DOWNTOWN: Lastly, here lies downtown Holksdale. This area of the city is where the most danger is, here is the catalyst of most narcotic activity, murders, and including corrupt police enforcements trying making matters worse. Many more illegal things fill up that atmosphere, making the crime rates there that much large.

Many murders have happened on Wrench Street, normally results in the victims suffered from multiple bullets due to being gang affiliated. There are many investigations that continue that street, always garnering the attention from few bystanders. No witnesses ever engage with the police, knowing the possible repercussions of talking to the authorities. There have been times where people, who've complied with the police, have been killed the very same day. Police are very on guard while on duty here, they're always seen to be cruising through the streets. Anyone on the streets, ranging from residents to homeless people, keep to themselves whenever hearing the warning of sirens sounding aloud.

Police have pulled over drivers and walkers to question them. A lot of times officers are unnecessarily aggressive when trying to investigate. By having an overtly dictatorship attitude when approaching people. Not all officers here are bad but the media, especially the news posted from midtown, would glamorize police as nothing but uncivil, corrupt and racist. There have been many reports of civilians being shot dead by officers downtown. Most victims were innocent, and some died through unwarranted police violence.

Many women fears walking down the block unaccompanied, due to the fear of being accompanied by a stranger. There are some perverts lurking all around downtown Holksdale. It's not uncommon for a few men to harass many women in this side.

Usually by catcalling from up-close or from across the street. By following a female for several blocks or engaging in unwanted sexual advances toward them. There are men who will grab them, give inappropriate hugs or just not respect their space.

As bad the police have been known for, they do take female safety very seriously. Many reports of street harassment, sexual assault and domestic violence usually gets handled yet it's taken care of unjustly so. Police usually pander towards the women here, usually ending in their favor. Causing many of them to feel embolden enough to become very nasty and vindictive towards many men they don't like.

Regardless of any creeps and stalkers around, here also inhabits genuine respectful young men. But some have been falsely identified or racially profiled to have assaulted a female and go to jail. These men fear either a woman giving a mean attitude or fears them taking their advances the wrong way then reporting them. A few of these men have been investigated or arrested due to a woman who lied about them harassing them. Some of them did this because of the guy standing up for himself or from her getting her feelings hurt. This constant female privilege had costed many women a chance of finding a decent man here. It also brought about more disrespect from men or having others lose further respect for women. But many women here try to date men from uptown who are well financially secured.

Downtown has a large diverse community, involving many to be familiar with each other. Not at all rare to see different races being shown together, ranging from Blacks, Hispanics, Indians, Caucasians and mixed races. A lot of interracial dating and couples are seen here. The public schools here contain many ethnic kids in this underprivileged school. Most of these public schools have had policing happen, including massive school shootings involved.

The blocks are filled with several homeless people resting near bus stops or anywhere free to not be disturbed. Many bums just lie down resting on the pavement or are drunkenly passed out. There are several delis side by side located all over here. Few of them conduct drug dealings or get robbed for their drugs and their profits in the cash register. The parks have many adults who're unemployed just hanging around there drinking or doing drugs. And teens quit sneaking there at night once the lights got put up, police also stroll pass there as well.

Many children here grow up without both their parents in the picture. Normally the father is absent in the family's lives from either being a deadbeat who spends most their days drinking or refusing accountability. Or from the mother refusing to let the father be a factor in the child's life. Fathers who try to get involved are either charged with unfair payments of alimony or child support. Most mothers choose to not work and solely rely on those payments to stay afloat.

There are a couple of churches that cater to different religions all around. There are Muslim churches, Hispanic churches and regular Christian churches. They're always crowded on Sundays and normally undisturbed. Most churches are close towards the woods. Even when passing by, there are many small houses that don't look to be more than one floor up. Most homes look like a better design is warranted or in need of better security due to many home invasions that transpire here. Yet those don't always happen to the many apartment buildings around. Here is pretty much ghetto in every sense yet the residents take pride in that. People do whatever is required to survive in this here city.

†

PART 1:

MIRACLE NOT TO CROSS

† Chapter 1: Hi, ma.

It's June 3rd, 2017 here in downtown Holksdale. Summer is here, having public schools finalize students' grades after their last exams. Coleman high school is in preparation for wrapping up the last semester. Many students took their last exams today and many underclassmen pack home their final books.

A young fourteen-year-old, black freshman named Larissa Sheppard had just about finished her first year of public high school. She leaves the school while on her phone. She's watching students spend their last day relaxing with friends. Some students are laughing with one another, girls are giving sweet hugs goodbye, and some are posting pictures for social media with their crew.

But Larissa's girlfriends were finished and had left beforehand. She's on the phone with one of them right now. Her bestie Lyric, had always contacted her through either call or text. Nicole LeRock Grace was her closest friend despite her many others. She still appears real cordial and affectionate whenever she's approached by other peers.

"Nah, girl." Lyric said. "Lemme tell you about that class, that shit was jokes."

"Oh yeah?" Larissa asks.

"I had to walk to and from school for some art critique type shit, and few had the nerve not to critique my shit. Girl, I can't."

"*OH NAH*, that's why I ain't take art."

"I swear, Livingston cannot teach worth shit." Lyric confirmed. "Ain't even half my class showed up, don't nobody respect that man! I checked out."

Lyric goes on about two fights that happened that day too. One of them occurred while she and her friends were waiting for her to cut class.

Lyric groaned. "You should've cut your last class. Girl, you missed the whole congregation."

Larissa felt a jolt of excitement. "Yo, did you hear that Woke Knee-Grow just dropped his new album?"

"Girl, you already know. Dropped another banger!"

Woke Knee-Grow is a famous rapper for this generation. He was raised in downtown Holksdale. Growing up struggling, he admits to being a gang member. He's these girls' favorite rap artist who lives a wild lifestyle. During his career, he's acquired seven baby mamas and conceived fourteen kids. The music he's produced is praised by many.

"Lyric, hold on, I got another call."

On the other line was her legal guardian, Essie Chu, a twenty-nine-year old, Vietnamese woman. She was calling while on call at her job at the hospital.

"Hi, Essie."

"Hey," Essie greeted. "You answered quickly. School's done, you got out of class yet?"

"Yeah, I finished the last of finals today."

"How'd it go, think you did alright?" Essie asks. "How'd the math portion go, I know math isn't your strong suit?"

"Eh, it went fine, I guess." Larissa replied.

"Where are you now, with your friends?"

"Nope, on my way home." Larissa replied, gazing at the bright sky. "It's gorgeous out today."

Essie agreed, then warns her to not stare up at the sun. Claims it's bad for her vision. "Believe me, I'm a doctor."

Larissa reminds Essie about their plans for later. Essie playfully tells her to be ready by the time she gets off work, incinuating there will be consequences.

"Be ready or it's my belt!"

Larissa giggles. "You a doctor. Your practice is to heal."

"Don't let this lab coat fool you, I'll whoop you."

"Ok, great. See ya soon, I got someone on the other line."

"Alright, I'll be home soon." Essie said.

Larissa took Lyric off hold, resuming their conversation. Lyric invites her out later to listen to the new album together and go for a swim. Larissa kindly declines because she already has plans. Without asking, Lyric already knew as to why. To spend some quality time with her mother.

"Well, then let's hang at my house in the meantime. I ain't seen you in a minute."

"*Can't.*" Larissa pouts. "Gotta get myself ready for later."

Lyric groans, "All these excuses but alright."

"I know, I know. I promise I'll pull up this summer."

"Ok, bet!" Lyric agreed. "Bye, girl."

†

Here in downtown Holksdale, on Kelvin's street lies many delis aligned perfectly together. Where many people come together to buying beer or eating out. But here has only one bar that's on the right-hand side, a small red colored bar called Richez Shrive that inhabits many men who day drink.

The bar isn't that bright inside, it has a dim brightness through the outer window glass. Being that is the start of summer, it should get a bit brighter inside. There is a pool table that is only accessed by customers willing to pay five bucks to play. There's a hanging lamp over the table to help out some. The few customers inside are men of all races, some who have day jobs that don't require returning back much sober. Other customers have high value market jobs and some remain unemployed.

The bathrooms are disgusting, most stalls are clogged with urine running past the next stall. Some have shit left behind from people not flushing, leaving others to see that they've defecated. Also, most drug deals take place in here as well, usually the exchange of cocaine, weed or edibles. The people in the bar are aware but remain jaded due to it never escalating to violence nor the police.

Most men in the bar talk shit about stuff happening in the news or complain about nonsensical things that most adults sober would see just how minuscule they are. Many customers in here are regulars, normally in here drinking, smoking, isolated or even conjoined around the bartender's table to be served straight away.

In this small franchised bar, there's a sign: IN GOD WE TRUST. EVERYONE ELSE SHOW I.D. where the words faded away then reappear every thirty seconds. The twenty-nine-year-old black bartender, Jovanny Gibbs. He normally indulges the customers not just with specific drinks but with meaningful conversational inputs. Men and few women there converse with him while he's working, expecting to hear his opinion on things. Jovanny appears as a light brown man with a well-built stature that's usually accentuated through his muscle shirts.

Right now he watches from behind the counter, few customers drinking mostly and then sees a group of men in suits just playing pool. Then he focuses on a young college Caucasian student, Rory Cambridge. After being here for a while he notice how depressing this kid looks. He's already been served three drinks and the alcohols affecting his poker face. Rory finishes his beer glass, his body began to slouch over more once engulfing it. He then looks Jovanny, politely requesting another.

"Rory, you good, bro?" Jovanny asks. "That's like your third one. And you ain't looking too hot, man."

"I'm fine, just got enough on my mind right now." He replied.

"Lemme guess, school right?" Jovanny asks. "I tell ya, student debts a bitch, fam! I see college kids go through this everytime."

"No man, not that really." He said confessing that he had to withdraw from two classes this semester. Upset that it's a waste of money right there. Might get cut off of financial aid because of this. And worse, his parents don't know yet.

"How you drop two classes? Hol' up, two outta what?"

"Three. Fuck me, right?!"

Rory starts to stress, his head begins to throb hard. He leans face first into his hand palm still hunched on over. Jovanny pours him another beer and sets it down. As soon as it's there, Rory starts to take a big gulp.

"That's tough!" Jovanny said.

Rory continued about being heartbroken over a girl he was distracted with all semester. Instead of studying or showing up to class, he was with her. She dumped him recently for another guy. They never slept together. Rory felt cheated after spending money on her clothes, drinks and dinners.

Jovanny Gibbs shook his head in disapproval. Laughing at Rory for not realizing he was being taken advantage of. Advising that he should've just kept it purely physical. That he should've focused on earning his degree instead.

"I was gonna take her to this restaurant nearby too."

"Stop feeding broke bitches, man." Jovanny said. "Let Jesus feed they souls then."

"What up, Gibby!" A loud, female voice happily announced from the entrance. Jovanny spots his friend. Yanie Juergens just emerged inside. She was twenty-eight-years-old with a brown skin complexion. Her ears and nose were pierced. Yanie's arm was written in tattoos.

"What up, clown." He replied, giving her a fist bump. Then Jovanny included her in the conversation. Divulging everything about Rory getting heartbroken.

"I'm getting real thirsty vibes." Yanie mocked.

"Fuck off, Juergens..." Rory hissed.

"I'm just playin', ok." Yanie said, advocating his decision to withdraw from his classes. "Go on, take the easy route. Life's hard enough."

"Especially with herpes too." Rory said, mocking the bump on her upper lip. Yanie reassures that it's a cold sore.

"Don't be upset you got played." She said, warning there girls who will take advantage of your kindness.

Yanie digs inside her pocket to pull out car keys to a grey Mercedes. She flashes it around for all to see, waving it up, purposely having it make a rattling noise for them all to witness. To the amazement of Jovanny and the few customers who acknowledge this, she reveals how she attained them.

Jovanny smiles. "Last month, a shitty Honda Prius. Now you out flossin' a Mercedes. Nice lil come-up, I see you."

"Thank you, and it wasn't as hard as you'd think."

"Well, come on with it!" Montrez said.

"Alright, sure but before any of that—"

"Uh, no." Jovanny firmly says, refusing to serve her a drink. Being how Yanie hasn't paid her tab in months and can no longer tolerate that. She pulls out a stack of money it appearance of large twenties and fifties rolled in her hand. Jovanny, now astounded by what he sees, pours her a drink.

She starts proudly gulping up as they await the story of how she had this car. She knows this, Yanie takes an extra couple of sips just to further tease them a little more by her prolonged drinking.

"Well?!" Jovanny said impatiently.

"OK, ok." Yanie said after leaving her cup half empty. "So I'm at Midtown community college, yeah? Welp, first off, I was assigned a Mercedes for about a month now. And a few weeks ago, I cruised a bit, searching and then it hit me. Why not try a college campus for once. I mean anyone can just walk in there."

Everyone around the bartender's quarters were listening in on this. Yanie has this way of capturing your attention through her sanguine energy alone. She recalls the day she'd been walking around on campus during the daytime, she described how it was during classes transitioning with all the young students walking. And how she met a guy who was sitting on the grass just on his phone with his earbuds in, and his Mercedes keys lying down too.

The guy was Hispanic, seemed very reserved especially sitting alone while everyone was passing by together. The thing that stood out to her mostly was this sadden look on his face. He might have had some distress going on lately. She focused in on him and made her way through the crowd to the shady guy.

Yanie describes how she went up to him, acting all concerned whether or not he was alright. She described the guy as trying to act like everything seemed okay, but she didn't let up. After her addressing how he defeated he looked, then asked him if it was about finals. He confessed about having his heart broken by being cheated on again.

The more they talked, the more he admitted to of been cheated on by every girl he's dated. Each relationship, he's told them how the last girl had cheated and how on guard he was when entering a new relationship. Yanie realized how him complaining and still hurt over the last, kept getting him cheated on. He kept shooting himself in the foot and that people don't want to hear about that. She explained that confiding too much in young girls who are focused on themselves will just drive them away.

He was hesitant into fully believing that but Yanie persuaded him to believe it. Mostly by acknowledging that she's a girl who knows what she's talking about. Then she said she's a different kind of woman, since she didn't take off running once he'd opened up. And how she'll break down the steps to helping him out. The guy thought she was funny and really appreciated it. He saw someone from one of his classes walking from afar, and was going to ask them something. He asked Yanie to just watch his stuff for a second and she agreed.

She could've easily swiped his keys to his Mercedes and left. But then he could easily suspect it, giving a description to campus police. Instead she wanted to make him believe he misplaced it. Wanting for there to be no traces of her at all left to behind. He finally came back and then talked a little more. The guy seemed really into her. He realized he would've had to be in class soon but wanted to know her more. She urged him to not be late and picked up his books on the grass along with everything else and helped stuff it in his bag. He even admitted to never knowing her name. Then offered to give him her number, then she put it in his phone after talking for almost an hour.

They hugged each other goodbye then he left. He left with a number for the midtown restaurant 'Biggup' under her alias, Miranda. While she left with the keys to his Mercedes in her hands that she swiped after him letting his guard down. Yanie went straight for the parking lot, searching for this Mercedes. Which wasn't heard finding, being that it stood out at this cheap community college lot, surrounded by these kids regular cars. It was a grey Mercedes that's lights blinked as she messed with the keys. She hopped inside as soon as no one else was around and took off.

"*Congrats,*" Jovanny said, as he poured her another glass.

"Get a real job!" Rory said.

"Jacking cars don't involve her following regular workplace standards."

"Like being in uniform." Yanie agreed. Talking about having any attire on, showing off her tattoos, wearing her waist trainer.

"Denise." Jovanny chuckled, remembers the name Yanie calls her black, latex, curve sculpting bodysuit.

Rory finally gets up and left.

Yanie scoffed. "His whole energy just exudes simp."

"I should've told him to chase you next."

Yanie dismissed that. Letting Jovanny know that she'd rather go for that veteran who sometimes come here watching films on his phone while drinking. Jovanny reminds her his name is Chet Lopresti. She praises him for being handsome, muscular and tall.

"I bet he wants me. Hope I don't catch feelings though."

"You can't even catch a cold. But can catch a cold sore."

"*Nigga!*" Yanie hissed.

"I'm just playin'. Here, get some medicine up in you." He poured her a drink.

Jovanny asks if she's still coming tonight to hangout. Yanie nodded, as if it wasn't obvious. Then plan on buying some drinks for the night.

†

Essie Chu and Larissa Sheppard drove togther, heading to visit her mom. Larissa's on her phone listening to music with her headphones in. Essie, peeking over at her, sees Larissa observes all the passing delis through the window. Seeing all these men standing around the corner talking with a bottle paper bag. Most guys are shirtless out on these streets, while most women are wearing tight legging pants.

They were in midtown, they could tell by the passing fast food shops, stores and malls. There were coffee shops with wide glass windows where you could see customers sitting together at tables. You could smell the scent of food, the aroma of barbeque roams the sidewalks for pedestrians to catch a whiff of. There are lines of people extended outside a particular barbeque spot called "Fried Thighs" that had a steady amount of customers.

Larissa looked out, wanting to maybe try some. But the more they drove, the faster she loses interest. As they keep looking out, they witness a group of what appears to be young Christians, they looked to be in their early twenties. It seemed like they were handing out flyers to ongoing people. But they were mostly ignored, yet they never appeared affected by it. They were dressed thoroughly, cleaned from head-to-toe. The group consists of men of color with short haircuts, dressed in plaid blue shirts and in beige colored pants held by a belt. All of them were matching, even with their welcoming smile advertised to every person they approached.

This astonished Larissa due to almost every guy from where she's from, being downtown Holksdale. Based on how those guys around that age are usually walking with their pants sagging with no belt keeping them aligned. Or how they're even shirtless half of the time wearing a durag on their heads. Especially how these guys weren't catcalling the passing females either, but being respectful still got them ignored. She always heard these kind of men exists but always imagined them as a fallacy overseas.

As Larissa got distracted by that, Essie tapped her, letting her know they're at their stop. They both got off and finally walked to where Ms. Sheppard was… at Holksdale Midtown penitentiary. It was guarded high with wide barbwires overlooking on both sides, the outside having civilians and the inside caging female inmates.

After being searched first by security, they are escorted to her mother's window. Larissa sits still awaiting for her mother to be brought out. Essie hovers over her, patiently waiting too.

"See you've been looking forward to this all day." Essie said.

"Mm-hmm, but sometimes not. I'm always scared that there could be something up in here happening with her. That either she'll come through with bruises or not come through at all."

"Larissa, don't worry, she's fine." Essie comforts her.

Upcoming to them was the sight of a caramel-skinned, inmate woman being escorted by prison guards. Her mother, Danielle Sheppard, she had a very skinny appearance like figure. Both her wrists are handcuffed. Adapting to prison life and their conditions had left her looking extremely undernourished. As she drew closer and closer, a smile appeared on her daughter's face. Her black hair was all long down to her back. She appears a mess yet shamelessly embraces herself, and Larissa hopes to get that exact affection.

The guards uncuffed Danielle. They both are seated across the glass barrier on each side. Each picks up the phone to greet each other.

"Hi, ma." Larissa enthusiastically said.

"Hey baby," she replied. "You gettin' big, girl. How you been?"

"Alright, just got outta school today, tests went fine."

"Ok, I see you. You a sophmore, right?"

"Nah, freshman. Could've been better though *but oh well.*"

There was a brief moment of silence shared between them, with Larissa awaiting for her mom to show interest. Even from when her mother was outside of bars, she wasn't as close to Larissa as she was now. Danielle was very self-absorbed, mostly focused on her wants, her desires even with a responsibility to take care of. Usually gone out drinking and experimenting with drugs as if she was a young, curious girl trying to find herself without any second thought about the repercussions.

"How's it going in here?" Larissa cautiously asks, hesitant of whatever the answer would be.

"Girl, believe me," Danielle began. "You don't ever want to be in here, you'll think of never seeing the light of day. It can feel like forever being cooped up in a cell or being forced with hundreds of goofy tasks to do. Locked with people you'd normally ain't fuck with."

"You ever get lonely?" she asks, hoping her mom would share that she missed her.

Danielle shook her head, snickering. Mocking other women who are bitter that their boyfriends ceased contact while they're in here. Or husbands cheating with someone else they knew.

"I don't be sittin' praying for no rich and prosperous man. Just for health and longevity. Won't catch me in here lookin' goofy. Don't nobody need that, even if I do sometimes feel caged. Don't get locked down."

"Ok, I promise." Larissa genuinely agreed.

"Here, let me talk to Essie right quick!" Danielle said.

Essie took Larissa's place and held up the phone to talk face to face. They always talked when it came to Danielle receiving some money in her commissary. She wasn't too concerned about Larissa being taking care of under Essie's supervision. Essie normally informs her of Larissa's well-being. Other than that, Essie didn't have much enthusiasm towards speaking with her. Larissa waits a few feet away letting the grown-ups talk.

Essie assured her that she put one hundred dollars inside of her commissary account.

"Alright, 'cause I ain't trippin' in them showers with no damn sandals on, ya feel me." Danielle said, continuing about needing some tampons. It's to the point where she's using napkins, praying that they help keep her clean. Praying she won't catch any infections in here! "It gets tedious awaiting the end of my period as much as having to serve up this damn sentence."

"Alright, times up!" the prison guard announced, now further setting them apart. Larissa quickly turned her attention to her again, wanting to tell her mother goodbye one last time.

Danielle turns her head off facing them despite her body

facing forward back to her cell. Her wrists now in handcuffs.

"Mama, I love you." Larissa instantly yells, as she waves to her.

Danielle is brought away, Larissa watches her still. Lastly, she hangs up the phone. Essie, knowing Larissa better than her mom, can tell she's hurting a bit. Being separated from her mother by a dangerous place like this. Essie draws close to her, Larissa feels her presence more in now from behind.

She wraps both her arms around Larissa, steadily rocking her back and forth.

"She'll be okay, sweetie." Essie consoles her. "Come on, let's go." Both walk out of prison together on their way to the car. These visits always leave Larissa a little depressed like, having to be in that type of environment. Being able to walk out without her mom at hand routinely clashes her mind each jail visit. Essie wants to lift up her spirits, so as always, she'll treat her with what she knows Larissa likes.

"You hungry?"

"Mm-hmm."

"Well hey, how's about we order in tonight, huh? Chinese special?" Essie suggests.

"Sure." Larissa nonchalantly says. "What'll we get?"

"Whatever it is you want."

"Boneless spare ribs smothered in barbeque sauce…" she instantly replied.

"…with pork fried rice." They both said.

"Alright, sounds like a plan." Essie agreed.

"And a small iced tea, *please?*" Larissa politely asked.

"You know all that sweets not good for you. And no, I'm not diluting it with water. *Believe me, I'm a doctor.*"

As for Essie, she calls ordering herself sesame chicken with pork-fried rice. Then followed up with Larissa's order. The imagery of the food sends a warm, craving smile on Larissa's face. Larissa asks to pay inside the restaurant, Essie agreed. After ordering, Essie told Larissa she's not eating in the car. Both get in the Essie's car, then took off.

†

In the dining room of Essie's apartment, the table is filled with Chinese food for both Essie Chu and Larissa Sheppard. Larissa ordered boneless spare ribs with pork fried rice; with fried chicken wings added. Essie ordered sesame chicken with pork fried rice. The food is being mauled down by Larissa. This prompts Essie to mock her about eating her meal too fast.

"Here, Essie." Larissa offered a napkin, seeing rice grains down her chin.

"Thanks. I was saving this for later but thanks."

Larissa began snickering as Essie playfully tries grabbing some food. She dramatically pulls her food closer towards her, playfully sticking her tongue out. There was an unopened fortune cookie near her guardian.

"You not about to open that, Essie?"

"Why because I'm Asian?!" Essie jokes.

She opened up the fortune cookie. It reads: *Living unfulfilled is considered daydreaming. Dying with your dreams is your wakeup call.* Lucky numbers: *227, 121, 600.*

This looked profound to Essie by the way her eyebrows raised. She kept it on the table. Larissa wanted to know but Essie kept it private. Essie swiped Larissa's fortune cookie.

"I'm being nosy." Essie childishly gasps.

It reads: *Loss shouldn't mean you lose yourself. You'll gain more within in the aftermath.* Lucky numbers: *242, 433, 23.*

This had Larissa perplexed as to what this meant. This is obvious to Essie.

Maybe Larissa will have to experience this once she's older. Larissa returns back to eating her food.

Knowing how she feels about her friends, Essie informs her that Jovanny Gibbs and Yanie Juergens are coming over later tonight. Larissa loved seeing them. They're both fun to be around; considers them both wild. Also, they're both African Americans she's grown up with. Larissa isn't around many people who share the same race *(besides Lyric)*.

As Larissa's face lit up, Essie knew she'd be happy. Even though she loved Essie, it was nice having two other adults who felt like guardians.

Two hours had passed, Larissa was in her room. Essie was watching TV. Now she's in the kitchen washing dishes. Her phone vibrates with a text from Yanie that they'll be over soon. The sound of the fridge door opening had frightened Essie. Her heart went oomph.

"You good?" Larissa laughed. "I scare you again?"

"No. I just didn't want you stumbling across my gentleman friend."

Larissa nodded. "Jovanny. My fault. I forgot y'all—"

"Oh, say, can, you, see, by, the, dawn's, early, light," Essie comically sings. She normally sung "The Star-Spangled Banner" to cut off someone or in attempt to deflect. This always made Larissa smirk. *"What, so, proudly, we, hailed, at, the, twilight's, last, gleaming."*

"That ain't the Chinese national anthem." Larissa laughs.

Larissa pulls the leftover Chinese food from the refrigerator. Then put it in the microwave. Essie got the Uno cards prepared on the coffee table. Sets down a bowl of chips with salsa. Essie knows that either Yanie or Jovanny will bring over liquor.

Essie buzzes them inside; then opens the door. Yanie and Jovanny lively dances inside.

"Choo-Choo!" Yanie happily hollers, giving Essie a hug. She has two liquor bottles in her hands. This was her nickname for Essie based on her last name.

Jovanny Gibbs hugs her next. "Essie, where the hoes at?"

"Right here." Essie gestures to Yanie.

Yanie's nickname for him was Gibby. Her nickname for Larissa was La-la. Yanie's eyes searched for Larissa. She spots her smiling as she drew close.

Yanie hugged her, smiling. *"What you doin' walking lookin' lost and stupid?!"*

Larissa chuckles, then spots the liquor. "Ok, I see you. Y'all about to get lit tonight, huh?"

"Nah, bible study." Yanie flatly said, then gleefully announced: "La-la, you already know what time it is!"

Jovanny nodded. "If I want, I can always get right with the lord come Sunday."

After a few minutes, Larissa roams back upstairs to her room. The adults get to the living room. All huddled by the coffee table now accompanied with glasses for the drinks. Jovanny started playing soothing music from his phone. Yanie starts pouring drinks for everyone. Essie began dealing three stacks of cards.

They made a bet like they usually do (*no money involved since Jovanny argues)*. Whoever is the last person still playing has to either do something embarrassing or unlock their phone to be explored for two minutes. Essie tells them to choose a deck on the table. Yanie and Jovanny snatches any random card deck. Lastly, Essie theatrically claps her hand on the final deck; slowly drawing it in. The others laughed.

"No cheating. I'm watching those slant eyes, Choo-Choo." Yanie jokingly said. Essie skips Yanie. "Wow."

"You still owe me for that pizza." Essie reminded. Last time, Yanie was intoxicated to the point where she ordered two pepperoni pizzas off Essie's credit card. Yanie promises to repay her. Essie skeptically implies she'll use the money she get paid for stealing cars. Yanie dismissively shrugged.

Jovanny already picked up four more cards. Yanie had to draw eight cards. This still had Essie on the edge.

"Your go, Essie." Jovanny said.

"Yes, ma'am." Essie changed the color from green to blue.

This had Yanie suck her teeth. Then she drew a card. Jovanny was munching the chips with salsa. The game went on for a while. They started talking about supernatural topics such as spirit animals. Jovanny claims he would be a lion living in the amazon.

"I'm a lion almighty, nigga. Fuckin' savage out these streets." Jovanny proudly roars. This prompt Essie to include his girlfriend as his lioness. "Nah, let's not get it twisted now." His mind conjured another comparison. "I'm lobster, she's salmon."

Yanie shook her head. "Nigga, you're tuna."

Essie snickered. "Man, you're fucking anchovies."

They looked at Essie, waiting for her response. She took a moment to think of an animal resembling her. The best answer she conjures to make herself look good was a dove.

Yanie began: "I'm sure I'd be a…"

"Cockroach." Jovanny blurted. "Can't get rid of your ass."

"Nah, Gibby. Fuck off. I'm a—"

"Leech," Essie laughs. "Because you stole my money."

"That's crazy." Yanie said, as the others laughed. A brief silence came as she couldn't think of anything.

"Cockroaches outlive us all." Jovanny mocks.

"Gibby, you a rat!"

Thus far, Essie is almost done with this round. Yanie has three cards left. Then began drinking. Jovanny was taking his time since he had the most cards. It was now his turn. Impatient Yanie began gloating about almost winning. Jovanny tried focusing.

"Wakey-wakey, nigga." Yanie said. "What's the moves?"

"Alright, say less." Jovanny said, determined. Fiercely dropping down a draw four card. Then watches Yanie pick up four more.

Essie asks Yanie how her date went last week. This made Yanie laugh about not actually liking the guy. However, he was consistent for two months. She hardly responded to his texts, never was intimate with him, never kissed him either. The guy took her to a ranch restaurant. Their meal was paid for by him. And he paid for her to ride the mechanical bull. Yanie played the video for them. The audio plays several noises to cowboy music, Yanie's hyper yells, and customers cheering as Yanie kept hanging on the spiraling bull. The thrilling feeling ran through Yanie. She was smiling wide as she almost collapsed off.

Jovanny gritted his teeth. *"Damn, bitch!"*

"Who you talkin' to?"

"Shut up, hoe!"

Yanie nods. "That's more like it." The video kept playing. She could tell Essie would've wanted to try it. "Best believe, I've rode dick better."

"I could tell." Jovanny said, looking at her lip. Teasingly reminding her of that bump. Yanie knew he thought she was being overly sexually active. She turned to Essie only to see her staring at it. Essie couldn't conceal her giggles. Yanie dismisses it by placing down her cards. Yanie won first. Her friends started joking about it though.

"Y'all play too much." Yanie said, stating that it's a cold sore. "On God, I ain't been fucking."

"That's cap!" Jovanny said, in disbelief. "You can't bury your past, Yanie. Your body count's too vast to cover up."

Essie teasingly implies that it looks infected. Then bragged about knowing diseases since she's a doctor.

"Then use your medical expertise to help treat it."

"It may possibly be sexually transmitted."

"Bitch, pray for me then!"

"I'm just kidding." Essie laughed. Then followed with how she should practice safe sex. And to engage with a trusting partner.

Jovanny nods. "She right, that's why I always get a girl's

consent first."

"Atta-girl." Essie mocked him. Knowing that Jovanny always insists females sign his consent form.

Now it was Essie's turn. However, she kept glimpsing over at Yanie's bump.

"Why you keep staring at it?" Yanie asked Essie sounding slightly irritated.

"Because it's staring back at me." Essie replied. "Your turn, Jovanny."

Jovanny was down to three cards; Essie held five cards. Yanie kept eating chips and salsa. Jovanny looked secure in this round. The anxious look on Essie was obvious. This had Jovanny tease her about catching her breath. Then Yanie went to the kitchen and came back with a can of ginger ale.

Essie notices. "May I take a quick sip?"

"No, you don't want mine."

"How come? What's wrong with it?"

"My lip."

"Yeah, you don't want to hurt the can but what's wrong with it?"

All three erupted with buffoonish laughter. Yanie withheld her soda still. Then they resumed the game with Jovanny down to two cards. Then Essie hopefully gasped as she placed down all five green cards. Essie cheering with Yanie, both hopping around him.

Jovanny threw in the remainder of his cards. "That's bogus as fuck."

While unlocking his phone, Essie stopped him. She had a funnier idea involving her phone. She actually wants him to throw on a wig for them to take a picture. Essie took a glass shot then ran to her closet. Essie came back, placing a reddish curly wig on Jovanny. He shook his head, smirking. Yanie's laughing with the urge to call down Larissa. Yanie and Essie leaned on Jovanny, smiling at the camera. Then took the picture. The photo has Jovanny looking moody. Yanie's head was placed on his shoulder holding the soda. Essie's head placed on his other shoulder holding the 'bunny ears' over the wig.

"We all good?" Jovanny pleads to remove it.

Essie laughs. "Yes, ma'am."

Jovanny flung it on the couch. "Great. Back to being a man again."

"Sure, if that's what you call it."

Yanie reminded him of how wearing the wig reminded her of that story from last week. That had Jovanny smiling. Essie urges him to elaborate. The joyous energy has Jovanny begrudgingly agree. Two glasses of liquor get poured. Both women huddled by him as if he's about to deliver a sermon.

About a week prior, Jovanny's girlfriend invites over a woman she met at the club. Her name was Taylor. She was tall with long black hair. Her skin color was peach-colored. Taylor seemed easygoing with them. They were planning to have a threesome. Jovanny was on his way to get his consent form for Taylor to sign. Once he returned, she stood naked with a flaccid dick.

That reveal had Essie hysterically laughing. Yanie urged for him to continue preaching.

His girlfriend was shocked. Jovanny was internally petrified but refused to express it. Instead, he masquerades it with anger. Yelling for Taylor to get out. Taylor nonchalantly reveals that she's transgender. She wanted to still engage. Requesting for Jovanny to give a blowjob. Jovanny kicked her out. As Taylor left, her wig had almost fallen off. She ranted about how Jovanny's not considered a man. Trying to demonize him into considering becoming intimate.

Retelling this sent shivers through him.

"I still remember how he caressed his weave ever so majestically." He sarcastically said. "Our queens."

Yanie laughs. "My boy was down bad."

"Down on his knees bad." Essie mockingly chimed in, seeing Jovanny playfully disgusted, Yanie laughing. "Oh, was that a dick move? Sorry, was that a low blow?!"

"Can't believe he showed me his dick."

"You just gotta look pass that."

"Yea, at the balls." Yanie added.

Jovanny then complained that Taylor had the nerve to criticize himself on being a man. Then gloats about kicking him out.

"Atta-girl." Essie sarcastically said. "Self-proclaimed man for the win." Then she turns to Yanie. "That'll be his new rule of thumb: Signing his consent form and to reveal their birth certificates." Everyone started laughing. "If they can't adhere to these rules, then it's a deal breaker."

Yanie nods. "Yea, it's a wrap."

Jovanny shook his head. "Any man who fled from being

a man can't hold my feet to the fire over what it takes to being a man."

Yanie's phone began to vibrate. It was some guy trying to take her on a date. He texted her trying to initiate an expensive dinner date. She claimed he was unattractive. The vibrating sound irritated her nonstop. This had her give Essie the phone instead for their usual protocol. Essie answers in the most stereotypical Asian accent. Stating a cliché sounding Chinese food restaurant. There was this stiff confusion in his voice. He asks if Yanie Juergens was there. Essie repeats the introduction. The man repeats his request. An awkward silence fell. Yanie concealed her laugh; Jovanny blatantly looked annoyed. The man asks again, sounding like a petulant child. Essie insists on sesame chicken instead. The guy then hung-up. Essie then insists that Yanie shouldn't lead men on if she's not interested. Yanie dismisses it entirely.

They went back to having fun. Essie and Yanie kept laughing about the picture. The music was blazing. Everyone kept drinking; then plays drinking games. Yanie was dancing and rapping. Soon, they watched movies.

Essie returns to her room, she's sprawled on the bed staring at her window. She watches rain pelting the glass, followed with continuous flashes up lightning. She's amazed by how strong this storm was tonight. Yet it's loud, breezing sound made her feel more tranquil on top and enjoyed a good night's slumber. Yet none of them, including the world, could predict what was to come tomorrow.

† Chapter 2: That shit's called freewill.

The next morning on June 4th, the weather had completely changed from last night. Its seventy-six degrees outside with no trace of decaying mess left behind from last night. No aftermath of fallen tree branches or trees themselves, everything is still in place.

Essie still feeling the effects of last night was still exhausted in bed. Eyes barely can hold themselves open but the light piercing through the bedroom window helped her awaken some more. She turned to rest on her side. Still didn't feel that comfortable but remained still due to being too tired to move, let alone think. Her brain was already hard trying to start up again.

She finally rests flat on her stomach and reaches for her phone to check the time. It was 9:49 a.m. and to find a text from Yanie sent in about an hour ago. It read: *gurl we out, last nite was lit. ttyl* :)

The sounds of pots turning, and the sounds of the TV are heard from the living room. Larissa's probably looking for something to eat yet she didn't hear the microwave.

As much as her head hurts, her confusion to what's taking her so long adds on to the pain a bit: "*Geez Larissa, all that clanging when there's leftovers still.*"

Essie, too exhausted still to make it downstairs, dials up Larissa and waits for an answer.

"Morning Essie."

"Larissa, hey, what're you looking for, food?"

"Yea, what happened to my Chinese?"

"Jovanny had some I think, sorry."

"Oh my god."

"Just check on the bottom shelf, there's a pack of noodles there, help yourself. And try not to set the apartment on fire."

"Alright, bye." She said then hung up. Essie's head was still spinning so she rests it back down and goes back to sleep. She ignores the continuing clattering pots downstairs and prays she won't spill nothing or start a fire.

Jovanny's place

Jovanny is at his place after dropping Yanie back home. His truck is parked outside, he makes his way up the stairs of the apartment building. His stomach pains grow more and more inward to a twirling, sour-like discomfort. Slowly climbing up, he finally gets to his door and lets himself in.

He flops forward to the couch and tries to sleep it off some more. His head throbs worse yet all he focuses on, while pinned on his back, is his inability to succumb to his nausea and the spinning ceiling fan. Then his head turns slightly over to his girlfriend's footsteps creeping over.

His girlfriend, Solanda Wright, was a slim twenty-eight-year-old. Her blonde hair was long to her lower back. Solanda had green eyes and teeny freckles across her nose. Tattoos were on her creamy, white skin. There was a heartbroken tattoo between her upheld breasts.

Solanda joined with him on the couch.

"Where've you been?" Solanda said sounding concerned. "I was up for a bit waiting on you."

"Ugh," he replied with agony. "Was kicking it with Essie and Yanie, we we're at her crib last night, you ain't get my text?"

"Mm-hmm, must've thought you sent that after getting smashed last night." She said as she handed him a small bottle of water.

"Good looks."

"Smell like weed too. Plus, I was calling you 'cause in case you were wondering, I ended up making over three grand last night." She proudly said.

Jovanny opened his eyes quick, seemingly confused though. Intrigued as to how this was possible. She sat down up close, putting his legs over hers and gets cozy up on his chest.

"Now explain to me, how in the hell did you make three grand in one night? I don't care how cool your boss is, ain't no way he finna let that shit slide unless his fat ass all a sudden pulled a *180* with the rest of y'all on them damn stripper poles."

"Believe me, Daniel's the last person who'd know of this shit." She spoke that she was giving the casual lap dances and there was this guy who was sprung on her all night. Wouldn't stop watching, calling, nor flashing money at her. She finally got to him, and he requested a private booth. His stomach was still pounding but kept gulping down the water. It was hard getting comfortable with Solanda all up on him, but he was curious as to what transpired next.

"So, then this guy got his dance, requesting at the beginning of almost every club song playing." Solanda said. "Wouldn't stop waving around that cash. I swear, on his lap, I made this dude cum after the first pop song."

Then after hearing him constantly bragging about being a successful banker, he begged her to leave the club with him to his hotel.

"Hotel?"

"Mm-hmm, 'cause he's just here for the weekend and thought he could buy me with that much, as if I'm not worth more. So, I'm like ok, you gotta pay me upfront, so he did. Then I pocketed his shit and called it a night."

Jovanny started laughing then pulled it back when his nausea almost increased. Then gave her a kiss. She pulled the stack of money from her skirt, waving it before him.

"*YOOOOOO,*" he said. "…that's O.D."

"I know right, *SAVAGE!*"

"And you ain't scared this fool's gonna pop back up?"

Solanda reminds him that he was here for the weekend, thinking he was going to get lucky.

"Nice, my baby's smart." He said as he kissed her.

"This dude was drunk, I ain't even tell him my real name." she chuckles. "I told him a name. Hilary."

The two laughs about it, then he rests back his head on the edge of the couch. She turns on the TV and gets up to the kitchen. She comes back to hand him another bottle of water. Then kisses him and allows him to sleep off his hangover. Jovanny gets some more rest.

Back at Essie's apartment, she awakens to her phone alarm. She's somewhat feeling more clearheaded and began making her way downstairs. Still feeling a little hungover but can move down to the kitchen. As she comes down, she spots Larissa eating cereal wearing her brown, furry, wolf onesie. Essie smiles at how childish Larissa appears. She sits cozily watching TV. Then puts some tea in the microwave.

Essie makes a playful, skeptical face. "Young lady, did you sneak yourself some of our liquor last night?"

"Nah?" Larissa answered, confused.

"Oh, you were sober when you chose to sleep in that. Ok." She mocked, watching Larissa smiling.

"Oh, you got jokes." She snickers, watching Essie slowly handling the tea from the microwave. "Look at you struggling. *Need some help cooling it off too?!"*

Essie teasingly scoffs. "I don't need your morning breath near my tea."

"On my mama, I brushed. Don't play with me."

They sat together watching TV. Essie went to the bathroom, splashing her face with cool water.

"ESSIE, ESSIE!" Larissa hollers. *"COME SEE THIS!"*

"Wait, what? See what?" Essie rushed out.

Larissa turns up the TV news channel. Essie stares at the TV. Larissa peeks to see if she's paying any attention to the news but she noticed her discomfort. Essie catches her and regardless of her headache, she entertained whatever it is Larissa had mentioned.

Taking a spot on the couch next to her, first thing she saw was *BREAKING NEWS!!!*

It had been footage of a huge circular depression, as wide as the eye can see. The clip was recorded from a news helicopter, it helped advertise the entire deepened surface of this episode. What was also captured was the hundreds of citizens circulating it, including the sight of police vehicles preventing them from coming closer.

Essie, who had been hunched back on the couch, had tilted forward with her eyes glued to the screen. The news anchor had popped up with many adults seen either catching sight of this event or trying to seem visible in the background on camera.

"Good morning, everyone." the news anchor said. "This is Marisol Hernandez, and I am here in downtown Holksdale, with what people are calling behind me… a miracle. And there are those who're claiming it's the End Times. However, it appears to be mostly a warning."

"What is this?" Essie asked.

The camera reverts to the crater formed in the ground with a close-up. Inside of this was a vast variety of names formed deep into the dirt. It appeared from the sight broadcasted, have been caused by lightning. Multiple strikes of lightning with careful precision to this exact spot. This was no accident, the lightning strikes scripted names, first and last. The names were placed in alphabetical order but there was a purpose organized to illustrate the deepen meaning behind this.

"It appears that last night's thunderstorm had resulted in this unbelievable event being viewed not just here… but throughout the city of Holksdale. Lightning struck all three towns here and reports are saying it's become visible all around the world!"

"We're getting view of it up here to be a list of real residential names struck here, Marisol." The helicopter reporter confirmed. "Marisol, I can't believe my eyes… they appear to be categorized in order of all who're, I guess, worthy of going to heaven."

Essie realized her tea was still on the table. Then gets up to get it, yet still focused on what they're informing everyone on the news. She raises it to Larissa, gesturing that she'll pour her a cup. Larissa didn't feel for any. Essie came back with her tea in hand, then went back to watching again.

The reporter informs that within each mark around the world, especially here in Holksdale, lightning strikes had imprinted a list. A scripture is there from what is rumored to have derived from the Lord Almighty himself.

The camera goes back to the names but features an additional clip of the names under the words dividing them apart. With each of portion rationed as either HEAVEN or HELL. With heaven, being the biggest component zoomed in on screen. Regardless of which side the names were placed, everyone's last name had been blurred while broadcasted. Lightning formed a deep line separating heaven and hell.

"The sight of this is astounding." Marisol said. "Actual words that we as people can interpret and comprehend."

The words had been viewed on TV with the inscription telling the meaning behind this:

THE ACTIONS OF YOUR PAST HAST DETERMINED WHERE THY SOUL SHALL REST SOON AFTER DEATH STRIKES UPON THEE. FOR THE LORD CAN SEE MISPLACED POWER BESTOWED ON THE APEX HIERARCHY WHO SINS UNJUSTIFIABLE HARDSHIP AMONGST THE WEAK. FOR THOSE WHO SEEK BALANCE ARE THOSE WORTHY IN REACH OF THE PROMISE LAND. ALL CAN BE FORGIVEN FOR THOSE WHO REPENT AND SEEK SALVATION FOR ALL WRONG DOINGS. THOSE ABOVE WHO REFUSE WILL FALL DOWN TO AN ETERNAL PIT INHABITING INNER DEMONS THAT SPILLETH INTO THE SOUL.

Both Essie and Larissa were glued to the channel. Larissa was amazed as to how this was possible. Essie was in disbelief, trying to register everything whilst hungover.

Larissa already knows her friend Lyric will post this on social media and soon call her about this. This trending news has Essie more annoyed because it is nonsense.

It appears the scripture is stating that it is our chance to possibly reflect and rectify all our sins. The lightning is approximately five hundred yards. Filled with several names, in alphabetical order, either heaven or hell. The news shows many people having all types of reactions to this. People are holding banners high in the sky, others remained in circle groups praying together holding hands. The cameraman focused on a pack of women repeatedly bowing down in worship of the Lord. Then Marisol the reporter began to interact with the crowd of people, hoping to get an interview with these witnesses.

On the other hand, there are many stubborn people who're opposed to what's happening. These protestors are chanting on how this is phoney. Many are restrained from getting closer by on sight police officers. The camera captures the visible disgust these protestors share. All are loud, spewing blasphemous chants aloud. Marisol sought and interviews several different opinions in the crowd.

Olivia:

"Words cannot describe how my family's prayers have been answered, knowing there's somewhere to be placed after here. God is good."

Felicia:

"I've tried my entire life to better myself."

"So, is your name placed to reach eternal bliss?"

"Oh, heaven's no."

Cedric:

"I don't get why I'm headin' to hell. I don't cheat on my girl no more. I only got three friends now. The father, the son and the holy spirit. Actually, erase that other part. I rebuke that last statement, in Jesus' name, amen."

Julia:

"No surprise I'm going to hell. I've cheated on my husband so many times. He knows who's in charge. I've snatched more souls than Satan himself."

All these footages are of people expressing how they feel about this. Most are sensitive on the subject matter. There are banners advocating Satan in despise of God's judgement. A lot of phone cameras out, documenting this. Everyone's posting this up on social media too.

"We are witnessing all different reactions from the crowd out here." Marisol said.

Marisol acknowledges those citizens on their knees having a candle lit sermon. Others with banners praising Jesus dressed in their religious attire. But of course, there are those who're outraged by their name placement. In attempt to interview protestors, she gets report of chaos going on.

The camera shows the people growing more aggressive behind the police holding them back. They erupted by throwing beer bottles far at the deepened hole. Being filled with rage and stubbornness, many others wasn't respecting the officer's space. Coming off as potentially aggressive with their constant shouting, cops began pressing them back with their nightsticks.

Both opinionated sides were screaming at each other about whether this seemed legit. The footage showed them even spitting afar at each other. Eventually a fight had broken out for it to be caught on TV.

A vicious brawl broke out, a pile of adults fighting each other. Throwing punches, no matter what gender. Bystanders trying to escape unexpectedly being tackled by an unknown stranger. Just ruthlessly having them plummet to the ground. Police began to break up the fight as best they could, but these people were still at it.

"This is and will be the most controversial topic of the year." Marisol said to her news anchor partner, John. "This is an unbelievably amazing sight. Back to you John."

"Well, maybe you should believe," John laughed. *"This miracle sure is groundbreaking."*

"I feel we've barely scratched the surface to all this."

"There's deeper layers to this phenomenon."

Both reporters start to laugh at their forced jokes. Essie rolled her eyes, then turned the volume down.

"Fuck you!" Essie scoffed, forgetting Larissa's presence.

"Nah, it's good. Apparently, every newscaster forgets they not at the Apollo." Larissa adds. "I think this is no joke. They even went and said actual lightning caused this, actual strikes."

"Over exaggerating. A lot of news reports do this."

Larissa shook her head. "Aw nah, the hype on this thing ain't all for nothing. It's a miracle."

Essie went for a bottle of water after finishing her tea. With her head still not entirely sure yet, she pours herself a cup slowly. Then starts to sip a bit.

All those names carved on a huge plain field dictating our future. "I think that was on the outskirts near that downtown here, Figure Pines. Think we can go?"

"I don't think so, you saw what's happening out there. A live fight literally broke out. And I know you wanna believe in this but it's not possible."

Larissa detests that nobody's got time to pull off that in one night, plus it's done by lightning strikes. And not just here, but everywhere. She continues watching protestors being aggressive on TV.

"Look at all these struggle sinners getting all triggered. God just be out here creating anybody nowadays, huh?"

"Geez." Essie said. "The world's trying to find divinity all around and someone's already pulling this mess. Just a way for leaders to gain control over citizens probably, especially to broadcast reactions like the ones we'd just seen."

"Ok, I'm finna keep away from you before the lord strikes you down up in here." Larissa mocks. "Know what, I think you're afraid where God placed you."

Essie gulps her water. Then makes her way to Larissa, scaring her thinking they both may possibly get struck by a lightning strike. Larissa shuts off the TV then looks back to her on the couch. Essie momentarily ponders on the accuracy behind this. Larissa stared gleefully, feeling this.

"Put the fear of God in you, huh?" Larissa teased.

"I tell you what, if my full name ends up somewhere without my consent, I'm reporting—"

"To who? Ain't no one higher than God almighty who created this!"

"Alright, now I digress. Believe what you want." Essie said as she went back upstairs.

† *Richez Shrive, 1:34 P.M.*

Here where most scum resides, who normally either drinks or engages in illegal activity, all give in their input on what's been trending all on the news and social media today. The TV is set on another channel going in more depth on how 'this miracle' has everyone all riled up.

Many more customers, male and female, are dropping by. The place is packed with so many adults. It's clear that these people have checked where they are placed and coming here is the result. They're probably here in celebration of their confirmation into eternal bliss. Or they slithered here to drown their sorrows from their negative results and contemplating their past behavior that's brought them to this fate.

Unable to accept how they could rectify this; they ease their nerves with liquor. Most are in a drunken stupor at this point, outright confessing their sins to anyone who'll listen. Some men appear isolated to themselves with nothing but their thoughts and beer. They are tormented by personal troubles created by them with such a hopeless aim for change. What scares them all most is what unknown evil awaits them in the afterlife.

Will it bring about their most deepened fears to the surface once buried six feet under? Will it be an everlasting pit of vulnerability that God has created just for YOU? There's paranoia of any entity that could pierce right through whatever barrier you've built up for yourself, just to sense exactly what makes your skin crawl.

The uncertainty of whatever evil lurks deep down there would awaken even the hardest, most dethatched of humans on earth. Jovanny keeps hearing people talk about their role in all of this, he keeps serving drinks to those who'll pay still.

"What're you so damn happy about?" Montrez said, a normal large, bald customer.

"How can I not?!" Jovanny said. "Lo and behold, all these incoming sad fucks up in here buying into all this '*have you been holier than thou shit-list*'. Jesus, God, Satan—whatever demonic entity responsible for all this, my prayers go out to you."

Jovanny pours him another drink. Montrez observes the crowded bar of saints and sinners coalesced together. More are coming inside but these people are with their friends.

"Like, it's embarrassing enough to fall for this but y'all missing work to fill your sorrows here 'cause of that?"

"Says you!" Montrez said.

"Think about it, y'all done spent y'alls whole lives not knowing what's to come once you die. And now there's a bit sighting with your names and that's it? Fuck outta here with that!"

Montrez expressed how some folks are becoming suicidal now.

"Wait a second." A regular customer, Donny Bedford chimes in. "So, you're practically at the mercy of the devil if you commit any of the seven deadly sins, right? But you're still at the mercy of the lord who'll be up there judging you still whether or not you are good?"

Jovanny, Montrez and a few more who caught word of this were all in agreement or at least could see it from this Donny's perspective. What made them not completely dismiss him was the fact that unlike others, he didn't seem at all affected by it and that he appears to handle his liquor.

"I'm 'bout to search that shit up right now." Rory said as he's on his phone. He researched to find sloth, gluttony, lust, greed, pride, wrath and envy. "And in case y'all are wondering, apparently I'm going down too for four out of seven so far."

Jovanny mocked at Rory's effort to research this.

Rory shrugged. "Well, I bet the increase of people in here is a result from all this. I'd include you guys but y'all are in here almost every day, drinking. There! Right there, the sin of greed."

"That's gluttony, alcoholic!" Donny blurts.

The men looked like they were contemplating that. Some just ignored what they perceived as his dumbass input. Jovanny pours Rory another glass while he stands before the customers. The things he's overheard them say and years of what he knows about them helps him have a more concrete opinion.

"Well, I ain't claiming I believe in this shit or even saying I'm a saint neither…" Jovanny began. "But a lot of y'all, like I've seen some y'all been up to no good. Hell, couple of y'all even paid for me to be y'all alibi. Like, I ain't no snitch but I kept my receipts on all y'all niggas up in here."

Some customers remained silent, guilty of some illicit acts. And hoping for nothing too personal coming out about them that they'd completely buried.

"Erin, nigga, ain't you been involved in all kinds of domestic abuse?"

"Bro, miss me with that shit!" he said. "I ain't never hit anyone of my exes,"

"Oh, thank God." Rory said.

"… with my fists."

"Bruh." Jovanny said unimpressed.

"However, on the other hand I've struck 'em with the truth, the harsh-ass truth at that. Petty fights, petty attitudes just to top it all off with a backhanded compliment. Except them bitches weren't having it and done ran off to the police."

Jovanny scans the rest of them, prepared to call another out. Many of them weren't visibly scared, that from having an inflated sense of pride, though were internally self-conscious of what's next to come out of Jovanny's big mouth. Jovanny finally makes up his mind and ponders on calling out Icarus McGrew.

Icarus was a very sketchy-looking, pasty, white guy, from the sight of him. Always had zero control of his shifty eyes, he would most likely study you as you pass by his way. You'd notice his eyes just moving around nonstop at first until he catches a sense of a figure before him, even if they're not blocking his path onward. His eyes regularly trail off. Not at all budging or acting to look elsewhere to the point where a person would feel unease with this.

The strangers unfortunate enough to cross his path would unnaturally force their heads down until hopefully hearing his footsteps pass forth with no interaction by Icarus whatsoever. This was a normal feeling for him, even to carrying this to the bar. Normally Jovanny's only interaction with him is serving drinks but he could've even felt his pupils on him from a moment's notice.

Once Jovanny choose him, he felt a bit of buyer's remorse. Noticing Icarus' deadpan eyes to have appeared staring up at him like he'd been observing his entirety even while others were talking. So instead, he quickly bypassed this to engage with Jeff Smith.

"And Jeff, you ain't no saint either." Rory said.

"*FURTHEST SHIT FROM!*" Montrez yelled.

"There's been times I've given back." Jeff detests. "I bought drinks for people out of the kindness of my heart."

Jovanny interjects to clarify that it is for solely women. "Just to get some ass outta it, ain't no blessed act of it neither, nigga. Plus, I done seen you add a bit of Satan's concoction to them damn drinks, bruh."

Jeff, stepping in his victims' shoes for once, now choose to keep his mouth shut. Not wanting to waste any more energy making excuses for himself. Especially knowing these guys won't let up or hear him out. His attention went to his phone, acting like anything else was more interesting to pull him away from this. Keeping up a straight face.

Jovanny called out Donny too, noticing him pretending to be on his phone. Donny already could sense his focus on him but still didn't feel like being on trial right now. Revealing that Donny has been unfaithful to most of his past girlfriends. Including not being around in his kids' lives.

"Ain't no guarantee those two are mine." Donny said.

"Absence from your children's lives, that's a hell sentence right there." Rory said. "I'm sure somewhere in the bible you gotta be there for your flesh and show compassion."

Montrez agreed. Then claims that every child needs their father in the household.

"I do take care of my flesh when I be laying that pipe game up in your mom's house. All in her walls! Plus, adultery's not a sin when we're not already married."

"Welp, premarital intercourse still is though." Jovanny adds.

Donny seemed slightly annoyed. Getting unexpectedly more silent. Gathering his thoughts to better defend his case. He was the type of guy to always justify his own irresponsible shortcomings. Donny doesn't ever take accountability for his actions like a man should and he knew this. Maybe that's why he refused to get involved in those kids' lives, from not being a man himself. Or perhaps his pride was too large to want to accept that his actions had brought them here in the first place. He'd finally figured what he needed to say and had a whole way of thinking behind it.

Donny begun: "See, now if I wanna part the legs of some easy, low-grade, dumpster slut to make something biblical happen, at the end of the day it's her tempting me. See, now that's a sin."

"How so?" Rory asked with his voice going high pitched from across the table.

"Any man would get lost in the devil's legs himself." Donny said. "And what's with that shit of sex prior to marriage is a sin? If anything, the girl's Satan, who's opening the gates to temptation by herself."

Jovanny nodded his head, entertaining his logic. Others continue to drink yet also remained intrigued by this perspective of his. Him coming off so passionately about his own nonsense was entertaining within itself. It amazed Montrez how far he was stretching this thing out to make it seem normal.

"Now say a man forcibly pried them gates open… *JEFF!* Then that ain't wholeheartedly her fault. However, if they're shining that spotlight of seduction upon the flesh, especially with all these dumb mind games they like playing, then who am I to resist?!"

"Is that right?!" Rory taunts.

"If my flesh gets tricked to stumble towards what I believe to be the floodgates of heaven then guide my soul the fuck elsewhere!"

It was at that moment, after that excessive speech of rubbish to justify his stubborn nature, all the men sarcastically applauded him away. Whether they were sober or not, they all cheered, cackling aloud at him. Even Jovanny treated him with another drink just for that good relief there. Of course, Donny gladly accepted it and went back to his phone.

"That shit's called freewill." Jovanny said. "Ain't God's fault you can't control yourself. See, now you got me defending God like the nigga exist."

Montrez pays for his drinks then leaves the bar. Jovanny continues serving drinks and notices many more people entering the bar. He realized Yanie never showed up there, she was probably still out of it. As the news keeps up with the latest info on this most recent event, Jovanny turns up the volume. They announce that people are still there, now camping in tents outside near this deepen miracle.

The regular customers are discussing how this may seem plausible. Showing each other videos of online streamers' reactions. Discussions of celebrities giving their input on this and searching for other related information.

† *Greynard's Junkyard, 2:48 P.M.*

Yanie's absence from the bar is due to her being at her second favorite place, the junkyard. She would've been called out by Jovanny for her flaws which includes stealing cars, also could've added her input on this recent event. But she's here for work.

Greynard's Junkyard is located here in downtown Holksdale. It is located near Figure Pines, far from many apartments and homes here. It's gated tightly, with nothing but illegal activity transpiring here. The sight of garbage is piled at its highest over the guarding gates. Here is where employees not only bring in trash from the town but also inhabits stolen vehicles to be later altered and sold on the black market.

Franklin Burrows is the pioneer of this business, orchestrating all of this here. He watches over everyone coming in and out, giving his workers many tasks of what type of vehicles he is willing to pay them for. Never ripping off his crew who are risking their necks out doing this for money. He'll either assign two people to recruit a specific vehicle and whoever finds it first gets a higher pay, usually for the latest vehicles.

He always gets great results when having these workers compete like that. He instructs his crew to be extremely careful, never wanting any trace of them leading police back to these headquarters. Usually, he'll give them black masks in case any cameras are around and cannot urge them enough to return the car here as if it's in mint condition.

Meaning no breaking any window trying to get it, nor causing any dents to form outside of it.

Since Franklin sells each of these cars, he gets specific orders for his customers. This could vary from what type of car is wanted or what color or any additional modifications. Whenever they bring him cars, he has his other crew alter it to the best of the consumer's request. This crew does professional paint jobs, can put on rims, remove glass, and they'll always remove each license plate.

Yanie normally brings in what is ordered but tries to get as much work from Franklin as she can. With the many workers he has, she's always been the most persistent. She always adds her input on what cars they should get, especially knowing what's the latest people want. Or alternative ways of doing business. One of her plans was to break into a car, search it for anything illegal, then snap pictures as leverage. Blackmailing the owner to keeping them silent with a note and copies of the evidence. Then paying them off by leaving the money in a specific area yet never knowing their identity. But Franklin always dismissed that idea and similar ones due to them being incredibly dangerous and not wanting to change patterns from their usual business plan.

Yanie's even tried persuading her co-workers to attempt this with any car, even would let them keep any profits out of it if they show Franklin that her idea was effective. But they don't want to bring any more attention trying to pull a plan that may not even work.

Including the fact that these workers don't owe anyone of them any favors, so it's not just because of her personally. This crew don't need to go out of their way for each other just because they're affiliated here. So, they'd either refuse or scoff at her ideas.

She even had another idea of them just stealing parked cars to remove and sell any motor parts or extract it for gasoline. They could've sold the motor parts or install them inside the stolen cars still there if customers refused to buy. This causes her frustration, especially with them poking holes in her ideas. Having many rational reasons for what could go wrong but Yanie labels them as nothing but excuses. Sometimes this ongoing thing has Franklin consider her a possible liability. It does nothing but make her feel underutilized and ignored. Even with this, she's brought Franklin some requested cars she's been assigned, just not always in great shape. However, he doesn't even know her real name. She claimed it was Beverly Chase, in case of anyone here turning on them to the police.

Yanie heads to Franklin's office. Passing through the junkyard, of course she smells rancid garbage, but she's used to it by now. Also watches other workers parking in stolen cars. She catches some removing license plates and replacing them with new ones. She arrives at his office, which is filled with his desktop and used car parts. Also written call-ins for any cars and when to expect them. He's always caught forming arrangements on the phone. Despite it being an illegal business, he always has a professional agenda when he sets these up. Yanie sees him on the phone and waits for him to get off.

He is getting an order for a possible black Toyota jeep, and says it'll come here in about a week. Yanie's here waiting for her money, but he signals he'll get off in one minute. He smiles thanking the caller and hangs up.

"Hello, Beverly." Franklin greets her. "Just who I wanted to see."

"Hey Frank, what you got for me?"

"Your cut for that Mercedes." He said as he handed her a paper envelope of money. "Been a while since you brought in something of this much worth. Figured it be a nice little come-up."

"Great, it's been a minute." Yanie said.

"Now head with me outside really quick."

The two walks outside his office, she catches some of the other workers huddled around. Franklin leads her to them; she can't tell what's happening there. By the time they're up close, she sees a black Mercedes parked with the thief proudly sitting on the hood, Johnathan. He was a young, muscular, Caucasian, blonde who was in his early twenties. Johnathan always impressed everyone with how fast he could acquire these cars, especially when Franklin has others compete with him on who could bring it here first. He locks eyes with his boss, and Franklin gives him a simple nod of appreciation.

"So, what you got for me?" Yanie said.

"License plates."

"Huh?"

"Remove, stamp, and stick on some of the new incoming cars, including Johnathan's." he ordered. Then mentioned that there's freshly made plates back in his office located in the drawer.

"You serious? Man, how the hell he be getting shit this fast?!" she groaned.

"Because he puts in more hours than most of y'all here."

"I fetch cars good too. I be putting in that work."

Franklin checks his phone for anything. He starts texting the woman who ordered the Mercedes that it's arrived and should be ready soon. As he walks further, Yanie tries catching up to him. He doesn't seem at all interested by Yanie's rambling with his eyes still on screen.

"Sure, but not nearly as much or even of the same maintenance as he does. You caught us a prius, supposedly the safest car there is, with the back window shot out."

"Hard to steal low-key when you gotta hot wire it with no key." She replied defensively. "And I told you, wrong wire, alarm went off first, owner came out guns a blazing. You tell me how a car safe for the environment be in that toxic one. I could've been killed!"

"And yet you're still here."

Nothing she says is getting through to him. Then she peeks over at the others going through the car, checking for anything worth taking. Franklin would be alright with them keeping any souvenirs for themselves since their taking the risks. However, the rest of them keep things individually for themselves except Johnathan. He always lets them keep any loose change in the seats, air fresheners, or anything they could find. Yanie rolled her eyes at the sight of Johnathan.

She reminds Franklin of the Mercedes she brought in. Franklin told her that the order was for a black one, not her grey one. However, he'll pay her for using parts out of that vehicle she had brought.

"Next thing you need, I could get it exactly how you want it. You just gotta give me something."

Franklin silently contemplates if he should. He likes how she's not just suggesting one of her insane plans again. This time it was different. Maybe she finally took a hint. He is getting more orders, so he may need her help anyway.

"I just got a call before for a green Camper." Franklin said. Following with a lot of those located in midtown. It needs to be here by Thursday. He'll refuse to pay her if there are bullet holes, broken mirrors, or cracked windows. "I don't even wanna see any spilt coffee stains from riding over any speedbumps. Mint condition, green Camper. Understood?"

"Ok, bet!"

"Alright." he reluctantly said, reminding her to bring it by Thursday. Then promises her to talk about getting you more jobs. "Now go help them with the license plates."

Franklin walks off. Yanie's relieved to have finally got another shot. She hops up, being startled by the honk of the Mercedes. It was creeping behind her, with Johnathan steering it to mess with her. She sees him cackling inside, she flips him off. She tries walking off, he blocks her path. Frustrated Yanie storms in front of it, she jumps again the moment he honks at her passing the hood.

† Chapter 3: I know, it's crazy out here.

This miracle that's made its way all around the world, has been the latest thing consistently discussed amongst all Holksdale. Not just in the city but in the news, on the internet and all over social media. There has been some good to have come out of this. Many more adults have been attending church twice a week and are even donating to the church. People feel more compelled to not only say grace, showing how grateful for whatever they're about to eat, but are praying long before they go to bed.

Others are showing actual kindness to strangers passing the street. They're acknowledging young church goers handing out flyers. Either they'll take one or give them their time to hear more about their church. Some are helping people on the streets who're down on their luck by giving them change for the bus or for food. Instead of just disregarding them completely. And some people's good deeds have made the news too.

There are reports of some wealthy people from uptown Holksdale who have helped donate towards not only the church but to underprivileged charitable foundations for younger youths in both midtown and downtown. This has been much accepted and appreciated by both parts. These had been funded by uptown bankers, and wealthy folks. They've even been interviewed as to why they'd do this, they just wanted to give back to lesser privileged communities. Everyone can clearly see it's simply a maneuver to gain access into heaven. Most people born privileged have grown up with the notion that they can buy their way through life, so why not the afterlife.

Regardless of their other agenda, it's giving somewhat back to the urban parts of Holksdale at least. Social media has gotten constant uploads of their reactions to this too. In the form of videos exposing to the world their past sins and how they'll make up for them. Mainly teenagers and people in their twenties are doing this whilst stating what position they're in. Or pictures of them doing positive things such as going to church or volunteering at the soup kitchen. Even photos of them having a good Sunday church meal, since people always love posting the food they eat. Also, people are posting and sharing other followers' status of morning bible verses.

All these recent changes all because of how they're reacting to this. Hoping they'll elevate their chances of living a beautiful eternity. But as far as people who aren't pleased with their results, their reactions were the complete opposite. Instead of them trying to reflect on their life and change their actions, each town in Holksdale has had negative consequences. And not just here but even around the world.

Unable to accept their fate of going to hell, crime in each town has increased more. Dealings have increased, human trafficking has too, and street harassment has grown rapid. And that's just downtown. There aren't just uploads of people shamefully confessing their sins to the world. But there are idiots posting videos of them beating up people, vandalizing property and uploads of stolen property. Most of these are items of shoes and freshly shipped in shirts. Photos of their illegal arsenal have been up there too. These are causing more arrests, especially since many of their faces are exposed in the footage.

This has happened in both midtown and downtown. Midtown has many stores that have these desired items in stock. People downtown ranging from young men to adults have a need to want to show off having the most impressive stuff. This leads to petty thefts and illegal trades. It's even worse at night, especially uptown. Some minority workers who'd suppressed their years of never-ending abuse have now acted out. Many who have realized their depressing life has a depressing end just lost all sense of morality at that point. By cursing out their bosses or vandalizing employee's cars. Just doing nothing but wreaking havoc for the people at the workplace.

It isn't that safe to be walking the streets lately. However, that hasn't stopped Larissa walking back home from a frozen yogurt store. Enjoying her vanilla, chocolate cookie dough, pumpkin patch and strawberry flavors. As she is walking across the street, she noticed a bunch of church people and it wasn't even Sunday. Larissa observes a large portion of adults including some kids around her age doing various activities there.

They appear to be doing almost volunteer work on the church garden. Teens digging into the dirt with tiny garden shovels, adults using pitchforks to do the same. Then setting in different flowers inside afterwards from the flower van parked upfront. Some of the teens seem frustrated by the annoying mosquitoes since they keep clapping their arms and legs. She then asks the mailman passing by.

"Excuse me." She said, he halts in front of her. "Do you know what's going on over there?"

"Oh, kid, it's ridiculous." He scoffed. Telling that ever since that profound list, these folks come out bringing their kids out in this heat doing work around the church.

"Ridiculous? You don't think that's a good thing?"

"Yes, it is. When people are out acting like this 'cause they believe they're going to hell. And even so, it's for their own self-interest. Not really out of genuine kindness."

"Wait, I think I've seen some of them before. Aren't some of them already church people?"

They both watch over there some more, with him recognizing some people he's seen before.

"Yes, some are." He said. "See that's why I don't trust most church-goers. So, either they've done some shady shit they've now gotta make up for, or their greedy selves are doing this because they believe they deserve more than just heaven itself."

"And ain't 'greed' one of the seven deadly sins too?!"

"I see you've got your head on straight, I can tell."

"Thanks."

He continues to the house in front of them.

Larissa stands there watching still. Then he comes passing by again.

"Understand, they can't make a deal with God almighty himself, alright? Only the devil."

"You don't think it may come from a wholesome place?" she sheepishly asks.

He condescendingly shook his head. "Hell, the fact that God's control has them following his command, like some sort of dictatorship, he may as well be Satan himself instead. Then in that sense, you can bargain with him."

After his rant, he gets back in his mail truck about to leave. Then looks to her before he drives off.

"Don't appease like these idiots." He urges.

"Bye." She politely said.

He drove off and she watched him turn the corner. Larissa leaves to, still eating her frozen yogurt before it melts. As she walks around, she always looks around, taking in the things she sees. She enjoys watching the different people outside on a hot summer day.

Even with this heat, she still feels a warm breeze continuously blowing in her face. Also, from the speeding cars and buses too. On the streets are mostly adults doing their own thing. On Newly Avenue are many convenience stores aligned together. She spots men standing outside of them loudly talking. Then one of them jogs quickly for the upcoming bus. There are a few Hispanic people waiting for it too.

She kept scooping in her mouthful of yogurt.

Then sees an elderly white woman pushing a cart with nothing but plastic bags attached to it. Three bags with visible tiny water bottles in them all, each one smacking against each other the more the cart moves. Then she stopped and proceeded to digging inside the trash can, a bright light emitted out. Shielding her eyes, she manages to pull out two bottles with her bare hands. Then goes on about her day because that's the norm for her.

There are men riding bikes fast on the side of the street, risking getting into an accident. She evens sees women outside wearing scarfs on their heads and headphones looking overtly mean. Like they don't want to be bothered or deterred from reaching their destination. Larissa isn't keen on being approached often but doesn't like projecting that image out on these streets either.

And again, across the streets she sees another Christian handing out more flyers for their church. At least many people are accepting them. She reaches the end of the avenue, there's this grassy landscape where the sidewalk she passes by is. Tall weeds and grass that if you were to drop your phone in, you would never see it again. But the one recurring person she always sees is this elderly man in his mid-sixties that owns a truck. His truck is always parked there, and in the back, there are watermelons he attracts people with.

Like clockwork, everyday around two o'clock he's there with those melons. He wasn't strange or anything to her, didn't appear to be struggling either. Just seemed to be making his living off these melons. He gets off his phone when he noticed her passing through.

"Excuse me, young lady." He calls out. Larissa stopped with her frozen yogurt still. He sees what she's eating and then introduced his melons. Then begins to cut a thin layer out of one of them.

"I just got these melons in today, ya see here? These are healthy instead of what you got there. All that sugar, not good for you. Frozen yogurt, right?"

She nods as he finished cutting off a piece then hands it to her. She notices the inner yellowish color as she takes it.

"That is better for you, enjoy."

She walks off taking in a taste. It wasn't sweet or sour, just good. She kept biting into it until she was finished. Then threw the rest in the garbage can with the frozen yogurt container. She left to go home, as she walked, she heard someone yell out her name from afar.

"*LARISSA!*" the person called out.

Larissa turned around quickly to recognize the person was someone from her school. A boy she had met last semester named Elijah Atwood, they had freshman bio together. He had approached her when she was in afterschool once waiting to be picked up. Immediately after her friends left, he introduced himself as she already recognized him from class every day. He came off very upbeat and sweet, liked talking a lot.

The thing that made him stand out the most was how wide he smiled. Always making jokes or attempting to keep the conversation flowing. It was almost like he was animated, kind of trying too hard to come off entertaining but she never called him out on that. He asked her for her snapchat once she was ready to leave. Larissa gave it to him to be nice then added him later. Ever since then he sees all her stories, even messaged her a couple times.

Even though he jogged to her, she plastered a smile and waved to him.

"Hey, thought that was you." He said, sounding lively. "How'd finals go?"

"Hey, they were fine. Yours?"

"That biology final though… probably the hardest." Elijah said while folding his fingers into a gun and playfully blows at his head. "But I managed to pull through."

"That's good."

Larissa wanted to listen to her music on her phone as she fidgets with her tangled headphones. But Elijah kept giving his input on last semester. He talks about how his experience was hard at first but really adapted to the school last semester. He also talked about the classes he's taking in the fall. Larissa normally doesn't mind being outside enjoying a nice warm day. However, standing in one spot having the heat all over her accompanied by her own sweat was an exception. Especially, when she was just trying to be polite. Elijah asks how her freshman year was.

"Was good, teachers were alright. I'm actually heading back to my place, so I'll catch you in the fall, ok?" she said as she was about to leave.

"Oh, by the way, did you see that link from this whole miracle going on?" Elijah quickly blurts.

Larissa paused for a second, then gave him a bit more of her attention. She didn't know anything about a link regarding this whole phenomenon. Throughout the whole interaction, this was the one thing that genuinely got her invested.

"Ain't there hundreds of links trending on this though? Which link you talking about?"

Elijah explains how someone from their school shared a link to this website revolving around this newfound marvel. On it, people can search up any names from anywhere around the world to locate where they're placed.

"Just about anyone?"

"There's no profile or picture of them. But it'll have on your location and say which side you're on for all the world to see." He said as he scrolls through his phone then shows her the link. The website popped up showcasing the sight of the deepened crater formed. It shows the one there in their town since it goes by location.

"So, I just type in, search any name I want, and it'll show where they're fate is, right?"

"Mm-hmm."

"Ok, good looks."

Larissa was about to leave.

Despite feeling trapped at that spot, since he suggested something of importance and showed much interest in her, she decided to ask him something solely about him. Something she probably already knew, regardless of her feeling stuck longer.

"So where do you see yourself on that list?"

"I'm glad you asked, I'm on my way up. Going to reach the clouds when my time comes. Only time can tell now."

"I hope it does. Later." Larissa said sweetly.

She walked off after he said goodbye. Stuffed her headphones in and listened to music on her way, through this heat, back home.

MIDTOWN: Hart's Daily 6:14 P.M.

Yanie got off the bus from downtown all the way to here. She received a text from Franklin on her burner about a particular area that's rumored to of had a Camper. It was an area called Hart's Daily, a gated community of middle-class houses that most resembled each other.

She arrives to the open gate, scouting out the area. It seemed to her like a more suburban rural area compared to downtown. She throws over her hood and walks around normally still. Just observing and distinguishing how different things had appeared here than where she is. The houses being houses and not locked together or locked down from banks kicking families out of there. A small empty pool that looked to be safe and not guarded by perverts. And as glad as she felt not being spotted, the absence of attention from catcallers got her the most. She came closer to the gated pool, watching and hearing it stream. There was a plastic volleyball rolling towards her after being blown close. In the near end of it were different colored long pool noodles. She turned to see those other houses from across the pool. The sight of people could be detected from the windows. Grown-ups with their families, there was a particular one she'd seen. A little girl being hauled up by her mother, twirling her around with her child's feet gleefully swinging. The father in his suit had come up behind and kissed her cheek.

To her amazement, two parents in the same household. Not one who's possibly a deadbeat and no signs of domestic violence. Just a normal environment for a child. Normal families, safely grounded area, including some nice cars parked upfront. People here didn't always have to worry about any lurking figures possibly trying to break in the windows nor slash their tires. All these positives surrounded her.

She snapped out of it, reminding herself she came here to do a job. It was getting a little dark outside, she left from the pool and strolled the middle road which led one way for residents to leave. Yanie peeked at each house she passed by, hoping no one would recognize her or unrecognized her questioning what a stranger was doing trespassing here. She never even knew if this was a neighborhood watch community. The breeze was hitting her face more to where she looked down.

Each car she passed wasn't fitting the description. There wasn't a hint of a green Camper parked outside yet. Yanie kept lurking around, and she sensed that she was coming close to the end of the gate. As she turned the corner, trying not to look at all suspicious, she'd spotted it.

A green Camper car parked upfront at the house. She turned to the window to see its curtain was down. Yanie halted for a moment, hesitant to whether the curtains would be drawn back at any time. From the sight of it, two shadowy figures appear facing each other. She couldn't make out what gender they were or race, nothing was identified. Hopefully for her, the same exchange would be returned.

She jogs forward to it, noticing another vehicle parked before it. It was a brown, pickup truck, the two were in front of the house. Yanie stood looking around there, then pretending to be on her phone so it doesn't seem strange. Contemplating to herself what her next move should be and how long it could take. There was no exact estimate on how much longer she had, which drove her more. Yanie passed the green Camper, making her way to the pickup truck. She kept glancing around taking a huge risk, getting open the door. To her surprise, the door was already unlocked.

Then she makes her way to the back, connecting the chain to the bumper of the Camper. Yanie runs to the driver's seat of the truck and proceeds to put it in drive. Through its silence, just as she expected, the engine ran. As soon as the sound could be heard she pulled out the parked space. She could see the Camper being hauled with her through the rear view mirror. Her pockets are being felt, detecting her wallet, realizing no trace of her was left behind.

Yanie leaves Hart's Daily, but the same thought that crossed her mind during the theft was still there. Her having an almost outer body experience back there. She doesn't know if it was from feeling nervous about being caught or wishing herself was a resident there instead. But the thought of why someone would just leave their doors unlocked had baffled her. However, an accomplished wave soared through her after proving her idea worked.

MIDTOWN Hospital: 6:23 P.M.

Here at Mercy Naomi Hospital, Essie is doing her residency in medicine here. She's just finished doing rounds and now she goes to the nurse's desk quarters where she sees a nurse, Beatrice Phillips. Beatrice had been there longer and had guided Essie during her internship. Comforting her with support and instilling confidence in her to better treat patients.

Every now and then she'll make conversation with Beatrice, as gratitude to reliving her stress back then. Beatrice treated her with respect that her instructor didn't really have for her or his other student interns. Every round she had with him seemed to be more and more stressful with his stern teachings. Luckily her ability to keep up, the guidance of Beatrice and her love for treating patients motivated her to push forward in her career.

Beatrice had approached her looking annoyed.

"Ugh, God help me." She muttered, sounding more irked. "Kids don't need to be out without a proper diagnosis."

"Another scared parent, huh?"

"YES!" Beatrice complains about a late-night shift for this recurring mother who obsesses over her son's well-being. The mother assumed her kid had early symptoms of the cold flu. Her child was fine.

Essie assumes it was her concern for the child's health. However, it unfolds that the mother became paranoid over her kid's fate due to this newfound spectacle. Beatrice questions Essie about her future.

"Whether I'm going to hell or not?!" Essie arrogantly said. "I'm a decent person, and a doctor. So, I've got an okay idea where my fate lies without this hoax."

As they're relaxing by the front desk, a sudden feeling struck Essie Chu. Unsteadily looming over her, slowly deepened at her focus. This indescribable blotch expands the more she tries to deviate from it. Her eyes gravitated at the entrance. This sight was too familiar. As if she subconsciously knew what was to come. Thirty seconds had passed with her eyes fastened at this direction.

Doctors' pagers were going off. Many began to get equipped with incoming patients that burst through the door. The sight of some men being rushed in here while doctors on call are quick to respond. Incoming patients appear unconscious while on the stretchers. Each man is about to be attended by nurses, including Beatrice as well.

Essie Chu immediately gets involved instructing nurses on which person to attend to. None of these guys are responsive. They're being rushed to any beds. Essie has two nurses following, operating respirators to keep them stable. Following any of Dr. Chu's orders.

†

After the influx of injured patients in the hospital, doctors were attentive to everyone. Most of these patients were ecstatic about allegedly heading to heaven. People went out celebrating. Going out being uncultivated. They either became susceptible to alcohol poisoning or drug overdoses. Many were in car collisions, fist fights, or engaged in the crucifixion challenge.

Another form of self-harm were the attempted suicides. A few patients had slit their wrists, hung themselves or tried overdosing. Their crushed faith of not being validated to reach heaven had some patients suicidal. Knowing that hell awaits had them accept that they weren't above this. Some patients weren't revived. Unfortunately, the others that could were still lost.

Essie Chu, exasperated, had returned to another patient being treated. Keith Parker, a sixteen-year-old with a cast on his left leg and neck. Her intern had just informed Essie that he fell from a third-floor building.

"Keith Parker. How are you feeling today?" Essie asks.

"Parkour." Keith corrects. "Keith Parkour."

Essie was confused. Keith explains that he is a content creator for online videos. His videos show him performing flips over obstacles. Leaping from somewhere to grapple onto objects. Using walls as leverage to hop uplift himself onto different floors. These videos garnered him over sixteen thousand subscribers.

Keith reveals how he was destined to reach heaven. This slightly irked Essie. Keith, overjoyed about this, promised his subscribers a video of him performing a somersault while attempting to jump from one building to the other.

As a former gymnast while knowing his fate, Keith overestimated his abilities to make it to the other side. The stretch was too vast. This had Keith plummet onto a dumpster. Then lastly, onto the cold concrete. A pedestrian passing by had spotted Keith screaming in agony. They called for an ambulance.

"You put yourself in this predicament because of that?" Essie asks, sounding irritated.

"Guess I just took a leap of faith." Keith playfully said. Essie's detached face had him feel embarrassed. "Well, I thought it was funny."

"And just like yourself, that joke fell completely flat."

Despite his outcome, Keith admits it was worth the wild experience. His main reasoning was to live his best life to the fullest. Essie told him that her intern will monitor him. Tells Keith that she will return periodically to check in on him. Now she arrived to check a woman who engaged in the crucifixion challenge. Mandy Morris, twenty-one-year-old, had two pierced hands. A nurse was struggling to give her stitches because Mandy kept being combative. Only one hand was wrapped thus far.

"Mandy Morris? How are we doing today?" Essie asks.

"What do you think!" Mandy hissed. Complaining over not receiving painkillers nor anesthetic. The nurse refused to give Mandy more from her past medical records. They show multiple incidents of Mandy's past drug abuse.

Knowing the catalyst behind Mandy doing this had irked Essie Chu even more. The nurse was annoyed arguing with Mandy still. Essie intervened, explaining that Mandy's had enough already.

"You must be used to those private practices where you receive that coddle treatment." The nurse laughed.

"You mean a hospital?!" Mandy scoffed.

Essie tries to console Mandy. It doesn't work, Mandy continues to be rude to them both. This does not affect Essie since she has dealt with those types of patients before.

Mandy began complaining about her circumstances that drove her to do this. Disclosing that she stole money from her friends to help support her drug habit. That her parents kept advising she checks into rehab. Mandy kept promising until her parents eventually had lost faith for her recovery. Her drug addiction led to pawning materials owned by her parents. They severed contact with Mandy after numerous warnings to cease her stealing.

The nurse finally finished her stitches in both her palms. Mandy kept complaining about needing more pain relievers.

"I'm in pain still, I need more." Mandy yelled.

The nurse shook her head. *"What you need is medication, a session with our hospital's Chaplin and Jesus himself."*

There was a brief internal relief for Essie Chu. That most of these patients survived.

DOWNTOWN HOLKSDALE: 8:34 P.M.

While awaiting for her guardian to return back home as usual, Larissa Sheppard sat down on the steps outside her apartment while on her phone. Watching cars drive by, seeing people walking too. She sees a kid from down the street on her front yard throwing up and repeatedly catching a plastic volleyball. The road is cracked with all sorts of debris scattered out everywhere.

At this point, there's only a cool breeze hitting her cheeks. She could feel the shade of the hovering clouds as well. The darkness of certain big things that projected shadows always comforts her. It always gives her this inexplicable tranquil feeling, especially when it's summer. The shade enables her to have a clearer mind to focus or just reflect on things such as her mother. Plus, she can always save up on her phone battery with the screen being always dim in the shade.

As she waited for Essie to come home, she browsed through her social media. Most of her followers' posts have to do with this miracle, from them making video confessions or pictures of them performing a good deed. As she scrolls through social media, she sees a post by her friend Lyric. It was a full selfie of her alone in church posing in a bright yellow sundress. She had a sweet smile with her hair straightened too. Under the picture was this caption: *ain't never took part in no crucifixion and I still slay ;)*

It never crossed her mind of where Lyric would've ended up, guess she assumed good. Lyric didn't seem like she'd have to supplicate to God so she could go to heaven neither. Though she does like social media attention. Her post had over one hundred likes and many comments. Of course, Larissa added on with another. She felt like messaging her about it but didn't feel like reaching out.

Suddenly, she thought back to that link Elijah informed her of. She searched up the link and found it. The website popped up showing of the one nearest her. Each second there was a comment from someone popping up. Most of these are blasphemous comments by these people going to hell. Others are defending the miracle as a legitimate thing and there's a section where these two parties get argumentative. Instead of having a civilized debate, the arguments go from trying to poke holes in their logic to just being merciless. The arguing has evolved to being racists or ignorant from both ends. To Larissa, it is almost hard to differentiate who's going to hell and who's not. Especially with both sides coming off as almost trolling each other.

Larissa typed in her friend's full name, Nicole LeRock Grace, into the website. Her name automatically appeared. As her name came, the screen zoomed into the deepened crater showing off an image of her name. The results state she's going to heaven. Larissa felt a small relief for her friend. So, it was official, Lyric was only doing it for attention. She then searched some more names while on there, people in her neighborhood, from her freshman year classes and so on. After a while, Essie had finally come back home.

"Evening." Larissa greets.

"Hey, what're you doing out here so late?"

"I'm only on the steps, and its summer. I ain't got no curfew."

"Regardless, it's getting late, come on inside."

"Ok but can I show you something though?"

Essie, feeling tired and reluctant to whatever it was, still acknowledged her interest. She put sat close to show some curiosity. Larissa showed her phone, the screen showed more of comments coming up. It didn't explain what Essie was looking at.

"It's a website." Essie states.

"Not just any, an official website showcasing everyone's fate—"

"Oh, not this again. *Oh, say, can, you, see—*"

"Showcasing everyone's fate… for now. Until they get woke and start repenting. See, over a billion comments on it still. People are debating, yea. But some say they've found God, or they been saved. Others are being narrow-minded… like some people." She playfully hints at Essie. "But everybody, all around the world, is getting now put on blast."

"It's called being realistic, sweetheart." Essie said.

"Well forget the trolls, there have been actual informative chats on here on whether or not it's real." Larissa scrolls to a civilized discussion thread. "Some folks are dropping some knowledge on this. Say what you want but this miracle's brought more people together than religion itself ever has."

"That's a unique way of looking at it." Essie kindly said.

Seeing Larissa's attitude with this was surprisingly cute. All invested in something trending like most millennials nowadays. To Essie, she is very young and has been through a lot with her mother. So, seeing her spirits uplift no matter what nonsense it's based on, wasn't too bad. Essie still pretends to be infatuated by peeking at the screen for Larissa to see. Larissa tells her of the people that they've met, where their eternal soul will go.

"There go people we know on the list too, but I only caught a few of 'em."

"Like whom?"

"Remember Mrs. Torres, my mother's public attorney? Yea, she going to hell."

"Alright, okay, who else?"

"Angel Gregory… HELL!" Larissa confirmed.

Angel Gregory was a previous tenant in their apartment who was accused of allegedly abusing his wife and children. He got arrested but released shortly after without it being confirmed. After that incident, he moved away.

Essie shrugged. "Well, I hope he finds Jesus."

Essie wondered how far this nonsense would go. She had seen the site zoom in on those individual names as they appeared with the results. It seemed strange to her how whoever's behind this hoax went through such great measures to make it seem authentic. The names being so carved in deep to look like its source might've come from actual lightning strikes.

Out of curiosity, Larissa typed in a name of someone on their block. Raheem Carter. It confirmed he was going to heaven, but he was on the threshold line separating both sides. Raheem had committed crimes in order to financially support his wife's desires. The last crime he did was attempt to rob a bank. The police had caught and arrested him shortly after. His wife divorced him while incarcerated. Once he'd gotten released, he met a man who helped turn his life around. Offered him a job, introduced him to new people, taught him not to be so dependent on a woman, and taught Raheem more about himself. The two men married and are still holding up.

"Well, what do you know," Essie said. "…being gay helped set him straight."

Essie decided to indulge this some more. Larissa seemed to keep typing in names of people she'd known. Each result repeatedly popped up. It was getting darker out, and she didn't like for Larissa to even be out on the steps around this time. That's how dangerous downtown can be at times, to where she's concerned with her well-being even knowing Larissa's right outside. She figured to entertain one last time before they go back inside.

"Now tell me, where does your name place?"

Larissa's face lit. "Glad you asked. Both our names, and I checked this twice…"

"And?"

"We're both going to heaven, aye!" Larissa merrily said.

At first glance, Essie was shocked that her full name was displayed online.

Larissa showed her name being showcased on screen. Her first and last name appearing seemed spooky to her. To the point where Larissa showed her the location stating it was downtown.

"Honestly, I don't feel comfortable having my name engraved in the damn ground." Essie said. "My info's not posted, is it?"

"No." Larissa chuckled. "Your address, credit and social ain't shown here. God sees everything but I doubt he'd get that personal."

"Right, because showcasing how we'll all end up once we're dead and buried isn't personal enough?!"

"Won't ever have to worry about dying, knowing there's a source for the afterlife."

"Alright, you can keep an open mind to death if you want." Essie said as she playfully made Larissa flinch. Pretending to hit her and kept making her flinch back some more.

"Know who else's name I searched up?! Mom's."

Essie's face dropped a bit, luckily Larissa wasn't looking. Acting unbeknownst to what she could already expect, she asks as to where she'd be.

"So, where'd her name fall?"

"Hell, where else you think?" she said as she keeps scrolling on her phone. Essie and she shared some silence as all they could hear were the sounds of cars speeding by. Even could feel some itchy feelings on her ankles, probably done by mosquitoes.

Essie could sense Larissa's disappointment, even if it is over something as ridiculous as this.

"It's okay since at the end of the day… that list doesn't mean a thing." Essie said. "You know why?"

"Why, 'cause jail's better than hell, that it?!" Larissa said, irked.

"Might be. All those prisoners believing death rows an easy scapegoat, not no more." Essie jokingly said. There's this badly concealed attempt Larissa has by turning the other cheek, which has her try hiding her smirk.

Essie even tries convincing her that she's not the only one with relatives who'll go to hell. Larissa is already in disbelief because she knows Essie hasn't searched their names yet. This doesn't deter Essie from saying her experiences knowing them is enough verification to know. Larissa then indulges her.

Starting off with her cousin Jenny. Revealing that she's been unfaithful to every man she's been involved with. She's been pregnant with another man's child. Jenny is married in her thirties and is still committing adultery. "You know how my name's spelled C-H-U?" Larissa nods. "Well, hers is spelled H-O." This prompts Essie to show Larissa a picture of this Jezebel.

As dark as it gets, she decides to tell her about another relative before they go in. "Then there's my aunt Karen, the name says it all." About her aunt who lacks the capability to be civil or flexible with opposing opinions or individuals. Always causes an unnecessary scene in public, no matter if it was simple miscommunication, an accident or caused by her lack of accountability. Essie's mother called her recently telling her how she had just witnessed Karen get argumentative with a stranger at the supermarket over the plausibility over this miracle.

Larissa gradually smiles then leans upon Essie's side. Her guardian let's her nest upon her lap, like a mother should. It was quiet again but without any awkwardness behind it. All but a serene feeling shared between the two. Listening to cars passing through still and feeling that cool breeze hit yet again. Then the silence finally breaks.

"C'mon, let's head inside." Essie softly said.

The two got up and secured inside they stayed.

Richez Shrive, 2:23 P.M.

The next day Essie sits at the bar conversing with Jovanny on his shift. She discusses what happened at the hospital yesterday. The bizarre injuries each young patient had. She is drinking a glass of water while Jovanny pours himself a shot of whiskey.

"I just couldn't believe how stupid these people were acting," Essie said. "I mean parkour just from good news originating from rubbish?"

"Well look around." Jovanny gladly said. Most recent customers are in here getting drunk off their good news. Or downpouring their gloom with alcohol. It was evident to them both that many people take this seriously.

Essie mentions that adults and teens have been rushed in due to hand injuries.

This made Jovanny laugh. "Ugh, these fuckin' kids with these trends today."

Jovanny pulls out his phone and goes on his social media. He brings up this video page with hundreds of uploads from kids with the same similar injuries. "Ever heard of kids getting hurt off these challenges?" he asked.

Essie looked perplexed. "I like to have faith that Larissa's too smart to do that stupid stuff."

Since this phenomenon has occurred all over the world, people have also come up with creative forms of entertainment that pertains to it. Most are posted online; some have made the news. The most recent was the crucifixion challenge.

Jovanny puts on a video on his phone, it's buffering. As it's loading, Essie expressed a look of confusion as to what else could've evolved from this nonsense. Then she watches as she sees a teenage black boy in the video. On camera, there is him behind a desk with a cross necklace on. On the table is a long piece of flat wood with each end having the bottom of two nails exposed and in the center is a bible.

"YO EVERYONE!" The boy hollered. "It's your boy, Jace here. Shout out to all my subscribers watching this. Now as y'all already know, this new miracle that's come through. We're all up here repenting and shit, hoping to expose ourselves so don't nobody put us on blast. 'Cause y'all already know… salvations where it's at!"

"Just keep watching." Jovanny said as Essie was unimpressed.

"Nah but real talk," Jace said. "I've struggled in the past with addiction, clinical depression and even opening up in general. But today, I'm here to drop some truth. Something I struggled to come to terms with since… so here we go."

"He's gay." Jovanny blurts. Essie shooshed him.

Jace began with a long time ago, when he was in junior high, because he's a high school senior now. But then, there was this girl Jace had class with, Jalisa. Now Jalisa was sweet, well-liked, and Christian at that too. "She was a good girl… but boy, she was bad! She had flawless-ass skin and a beautiful smile. She knew I was feeling her and soon we dated." While they were together at the time, he was writing a book to be published. "So, I admit, I was trying to finesse her out her draws back then. Of course, being a Christian and all… she wasn't havin' it. And knowing this I kept pressing her but no luck." Jace labeled her having low self-esteem despite her having many friends and her other positive attributes. Always feeling overshadowed by others, not believing she was most important.

Essie still seemed engaged with this video. She tapped the screen seeing she had six more minutes left of this. Yet she wasn't bored but doesn't see where this would lead. She glanced at Jovanny, seeing him give her that look. The look that this long buildup will all pay off. So, she keeps watching.

Jace continues about Jalisa getting comfortable opening

herself up to him. "I felt for her, I did. But at the time, I was thinkin' down here." Jace said, gesturing at his groin. Once he finished his book and had it in the editing stage, he caught an idea. "How could I prove myself to her? So, I dedicated the book to her." His book called Flare Empress. So, he showed her the page dedicated towards her and she was so excited. She felt so appreciated that to Jalisa, her name was the foundation of it all. "And that night, I confessed my love for her. Then that night, she and I made love at my crib." It was their first time.

Jace's eyes started welling up. He looked away from the camera and had taken in a deep breath. You could see his throat muscles clenching in. The video abruptly cut to him talking again. This time with his eyes clear and voice sterner than before. Now his eyes focused in on the camera.

"Ok, I'm back. Now we, as time passed, we had been fine but then I started talking to other girls. Jalisa got all in her feelings and told me she wasn't havin' that." Jace kept doing it until she broke up with him. He was heartbroken, could picture her laughing at his pain with all her friends. By the time his book was published, he sent her a copy. She accepted it and when she opened it, her name was gone. "Replaced with it being dedicated to another girl I stayed talking to. Then I told her straight up that she never meant anything to me and walked off." Jace told his friends that they had sex since he manipulated her. Word got around. Everyone in their grade labeled her a hoe for a whole semester. Eventually it became too much for Jalisa and was found by her parents in the garage with the car engine running. "Our teacher told us what she did, but I felt like she knew I was the prime cause, and she was right." Jace unfolded. "That night, her parents came to my place. Jalisa, the night she took her life, decided to have her suicide note dedicated to me."

Her parents tried to make sense of how Jace handled their breakup from what they read. After everything spiraled downhill, he lied. Instead, Jace said he just didn't see a future together. And he never got in trouble for it. "So, if they see this, I just want her folks to know I'm sorry. I ain't never wanted it to come to that, I swear. I want for all my subscribers and lurkers and the whole world to know what I did. 'Cause God knows, and Jalisa knew. And I just hope she ends up in a better place, and I do to."

Jace holds the bible to his chest and rocks a little bit. His eyes aren't teary, but he seems to be contemplating something. Essie has a look of sorrow for the boy in the video. Then the boy lifts both arms and quickly clapped his hands down on the sticking nails with all his might. Piercing the palms of both his hands, leaving each individual finger of his trembling. Essie's eyes widened; her jaw dropped.

Jace was screaming in anguish, he pounced up off his desk causing for the camera to fall on the ground. All that was seen was the carpet with the sounds of strong hollering echoed as high pitch squealing made by either himself or the messed audio from the fall. The footage was still going. Essie was locked in but then Jovanny pulled away his phone.

She wanted to see the rest of the two minutes left but he ended it.

"What else happens, it's still playing." she said. "Is the boy alright?"

"I don't know, and only reason it's still playing 'cause his hands are friggin' preoccupied."

"My God!" she said. "So what? That's the crucifixion challenge, tearing the flesh of your hands?"

"Yerp, almost an allegory to Jesus' hands being nailed to the cross. The shit is ridiculous. I swear, kids will do anything for the hell of it. Just for some clout."

As they were talking, an emergency news was broadcasted on the TV for all to see. The news anchor Tim Brush appeared. Jovanny turned up the volume, Essie ingested the rest of her Shirley Temple as she watched too. The screen says whatever is going on is taking place in New Jersey.

The news anchor announced an outbreak of protest erupting around the world with thousands of people in the streets. Protestors voicing their bitter concerns and opinions regarding the future of this miracle also known as 'the list'. Footage broadcasts hundreds of citizens, who may or may not be going to hell, using blasphemous overtones and outrage to have their voices heard. These protests have been going on for days since this was first discovered, out on the streets, outside businesses and it is suspected that more crimes will emerge. Many adults gathered with signs, posters with lines slowly forming of the cross being marked with a fat, red **X**. There are signs that read: *"FUCK GOD!"*

"HELL IS A MADEUP CONCEPT!"

The camera zooms in on a man exposing his bare chest with tattoos freshly made, marking *666*. The man is shamelessly adrenalized while broadcasted.

Essie shakes her head; Jovanny pours himself another shot. Then a scene of police officers coming plays, many cruisers pull up to the scene.

A police officer interviewed informs that protest had now escalated into riots in certain areas, they deployed flash bang grenades to break up the crowds. More than two hundred people were placed under arrest.

Now it started out as a peaceful protest but then it escalated throughout the night. There have been over one hundred protestors in midtown for police to say that it went from peaceful to a riot. Ninety-six people have been arrested and to disperse the crowd, police turned to lethal force. Such as flash bang grenades and tear gas. One police officer referring to people as anarchists, those who were among the crowd vandalizing property, breaking windows, throwing blunt objects as well.

Another video appeared of people causing havoc in the streets. Doing everything that was described in the video. Blocking up traffic and gathered in groups.

"Once they all arrived, police called it extensive danger criminal behavior in an unlawful protest." The news anchor said. Including riots and fights endangering civilian life. "There are also reports of protest in Philadelphia, Baltimore, Portland and Oakland. Here we have had multiple arrest for gathering around the listed site in this area, vandalizing and engaging in blasphemous protest."

Footage of people disguised in hoodies are seen throwing in broken bottles. Some are lighting trash and tossing that in there too. Then police are seen rolling into the scene causing them all to run.

Others are arrested for blocking roads, including minors being taken in for breaking curfew. In Portland, over five hundred people protest police officers preventing further entrance near the list. Thirty-six others were arrested for trying to vandalize this sacred landmark with graffiti and M-80 firecrackers that were being throw in and threatening police.

Essie couldn't believe how insane everyone acted in those videos. Police being forced to resort to such measures, and with how seriously everyone was taking this based on her patients, it was only a matter of time before around her area is consumed with barbarity. Jovanny had picked up a worrisome vibe from her and poured her another water.

"My God!" Essie said.

"Yup, apparently he the reason this shits happening!"

"No, it's these lunatics out here. Society's that sensitive to where we're this easily triggered? The thing isn't miraculous!"

"I know, it's crazy out here."

Essie gets skeptical as to some of them being intoxicated before they go out causing mayhem like this. Jovanny simply shrugs it off.

"You ever keep track of how much you serve your customers?"

"They all adults, that's why I don't be supervising 'em." Jovanny said, goes on about how it brought more business.

Montrez listening in began chuckling to himself with his drink in his hand. Jovanny criticizes Montrez, believing he's taking this seriously.

"Fuck no!" Montrez said. "Even though you were going in on all of us a few days back." He brought up incidents of people vandalizing areas he does construction on. It doesn't help his boss is a religious fanatic. "Yeah, soon me and my coworkers will be building fucking North Korean walls up protecting this miracle. I guarantee it!"

"What do you think it is?" Essie asked Montrez. She was hoping that even though he seemed like a casual customer to Jovanny, he would have rational thinking. Unless in her eyes, she'd have to categorize him with the other degenerates surrounding herself in the bar.

Montrez sums up his thoughts. "To me, it's a bit of a conspiracy. And if it is real, then all of us out doing construction to keep this shit intact deserve angel wings. I'd never embrace Catholicism with more gusto."

Essie couldn't really label him after that. But she could figure not to get into it with someone going on possible conjecture rather than facts. Yet it's been weeks, and no one has come up with legitimate resources as to what had created these all around the world.

"A drink on the house, for my input?" Montrez asks.

"I wouldn't give one free on the top of the cathedral church, ya heard?"

Besides his laughing, Jovanny brought up how people are attempting to alter their fate through volunteer work, donating to the church and the salvation.

"Good for them." Essie said. "All desperately trying to gain access through a fictitious gateway to heaven."

"What, you saying you don't believe they'll make it?"

"Yes, ma'am. I believe there is a heaven but not one to be bargained for."

The fact that she must break down how illogical sounding this notion is for people to have has been frustrating alone. And on top of that, it's bringing about more violence from something with no concrete evidence of the afterlife. News like this worries Essie about Larissa roaming the streets by herself.

"Wait…" Essie said. "So, if good equates to heaven and bad doesn't, then where on earth do bystanders fall?"

Jovanny doesn't see where they should. People pray for God to save 'em all the time. But he theorized that they'd be sent to this oblivion called purgatory. Left to forever walk the earth for all of eternity. And that's a hell we all must live until we eventually die. Jovanny mocks of the idea of getting reincarnated with the same exact mentality just to again fuck up.

"Repeating life over and over again, a reset option basically." She said.

Jovanny laughed. "Ain't no option if I ain't got no say."

This has Jovanny conjure a ridiculous scenario of Essie dying, then going from a Vietnamese girl turn white boy, turn spirit animal. Or himself to a Hispanic boy or Arabic man. Or Yanie into some Asian woman. "Just God pretty much fucking with us at that point. It's all an endless eternal cycle."

"Well speak for yourself because I'm not going there." Essie said. "From what Larissa showed me, both her and I are heading to heaven together."

"Bet you feel good about that."

Even with her not taking it at all seriously, it was somewhat satisfying to have Larissa believe she was going there with her. Not just for Larissa's sake but to have her think even more highly of her. So even some good came out of this list but Essie wouldn't overtly revel in this.

Essie mentioned her mother incarcerated still. Larissa upset from believing Danielle's heading to hell. Jovanny argues that she should be smart enough to know this is a hoax.

"At least she's not out breaking the law like these idiots out here. I blame the internet, people having access to all kinds of info. Leading to new ways of thinking and anything against their beliefs, suddenly they get offended."

"Yea, all in they feelings still." Jovanny said.

"Then they demand for those outliers to be either eradicated or to be conformed to whatever they believe."

Essie was surprised by that response. By how she'd always weigh in her two cents on how this to her seems like nonsense. She argues that she's not getting overtly aggressive with people opposed to the truth behind this. That she's not out breaking the law, dealing with police, nothing of that sort.

They took a moment away from this as a customer was coming. Jovanny saw this woman approaching with an empty glass. He refilled her glass and then she took a seat close to the bar. She seemed irritated and in need of this drink. He assumed she was probably going through hell in her head, stressing herself over this too.

"Ma'am, are you alright?" Essie asked.

"I will be once I get this liquor up in me." She confessed. "There's some guy back there annoying me, trying to get my number."

Essie turned around to see exactly what this guy looked like. It appeared to be Icarus McGrew. He was in all black just drinking at a table alone now. She automatically recognized him as the guy her friends had told her about but couldn't recall his name.

"What was that guy's name again?" Essie asked.

"Icarus." Both Jovanny and the lady said.

"Wait, so what was he doing?" she asked the lady.

He came up to the lady talking about how lovely she looked. Then started to ask a bunch of random questions to know her better. But she was annoyed still. Then he went on to offering her a drink.

"I don't know what this fucker could dose me with, so I came here to buy one myself."

The woman turned her head to the side pretending to look out the window. She was peeking to see if Icarus would emerge from his seat to bother her again. All she could see is him looking at his drink then at her. That's when she turned around facing Jovanny again. He didn't wish to look at him over there, so he resumed to Essie.

"Wait, I just thought of something." Essie said. "Say this thing really is legitimate in terms of God's perspective."

"Mm-hmm?"

"I figure all those monsters throughout history most likely have been suffering the same fate they brought on themselves. From dictators to now deceased criminals."

"All of them past serial rapist, pigs and savages… they gonna learn today." Jovanny gloats. "And it does those poor fuckers justice."

"All those slave's souls can rest in a now safe haven."

"Can they really?!" he scoffed. "It's just dictated and redlined by a higher entity, the same way he done categorized everyone now. Sets up this huge threshold based on who he wants in."

"It's better than hell, I'll say that."

Jovanny brought up plantation owners back in their hay day, everlasting slaves. Abducting Africans and making them slaves. Having to work to death out in the sun while hardly ever fed. "If that were me, I'd have to discuss some of these working conditions."

"With whom?!" Essie said. "Only time they'll climb up off their high horse is unless it's to beat you!"

Essie sets up a playful scenario of a slave filing a discrimination complaint. *"Jim-Bob keeps calling me the n word. Is there a human resource on this plantation?"*

"There are but niggers ain't human!" Jovanny adds in a hillbilly accent. Then compares the slave with outraged, triggered people. *"Easily offended by every little thing under the sun, boy."*

MIDTOWN 10:26 P.M.

At this time of night, patroling the areas become more draining due to dealing with the amount of drivers under the influence of alcohol behind the wheel.

Tonight two Caucasian officers Cliff Lambeth and Declan Colthirst had drove their regular patrol routes. Nothing out the ordinary thus far. It has been so crazy recently that tonight feels almost like a relief.

A black Mercedes ahead of them began moving across the lane to the opposite side. Then quickly swerves then returned to the proper side. Indicator wasn't blinking. The screeching was heard from a mile away. Both officers unspokenly agreed that the driver must have been drunk. Their siren went on, flashing lights had the car slow down. Time went on for about five minutes before they officially pulling over to the far side of the road.

Colthirst seemed frustrated that it took this long to get to this point. His hand cupped his forehead. Lambeth seemed suspicious as he monitored the driver through the back window. The car was rocking. Lambeth chuckles, Colthirst observes next.

The driver was accompanied by someone in the passenger seat. They scramble trying to switch spots before being confronted. Each of their arms stretched to the opposite seat. The two officers shook their heads cackling at this miserable display. In minutes, they had finally reached their destinations.

Both unaware of being watched.

Prior to changing seats, the driver was a dark-skinned man. His friend was an olive-skinned man.

"Trans-racial." Lambeth arrogantly said.

Colthirst nodded, smirking. Knowing this protocal that they've playfully executed before. "You got driver?"

"Sure. You handle the pretend one."

Both officers nonchalantly walk towards the black, luxury vehicle. As Colthirst drew closer, the driver's window came down unannounced.

His eyes latched with the driver. Behind the wheel, he held a stern look. Keeping his trembly hands on the steering wheel. Lambeth observed the real driver who kept averting his eyes. The guy was chewing gum, possibly to mask his breath. The two men looked to be in their early twenties.

"What seems to be the problem, officer?" the guy behind the wheel asked.

Officer Colthirst informs him about them swerving into the other lane. Also mentioning that they took a while to pull over. The guy in the passenger seat kept silent.

His friend calmly nodding his head.

"May I ask," Colthirst began, with a plafully, suspicious look. "Do you have any African in your heritage?" the guy shook his head slowly in confusion. "No black ancestry in your lineage of any sorts? No?"

"Why?" the guy sneered. "Are you implying young black men can't afford a Mercedes?"

The atmosphere was briefly silent. His friend in the passenger seat seemed worried. Looking at both officers.

Colthirst snickered. "Oh, I'm sure they can. Because the driver we pulled over was black. That's why I'm confused as to what you're doing behind the wheel?"

The guy's eyes bulged out, eyebrows elevated high.

"So unless you're now dressed in white-face, I'll have to ask to see the real driver's license."

"Perhaps he is." Lambeth playfully added. "Probably wearing a full pasty bodysuit. God only knows what else he's got concealed."

"Right, I heard of those down at the station. Might need for him to strip down in the middle of the road and give him a good ol' cavity search."

"Including his friend here too." Lambeth's eyes hunt for him. "You know, since we don't discriminate."

"IT WAS ME! I WAS THE ONE DRIVING!" the guy erupts from the passenger seat.

He presented his license to officer Lambeth. Colthirst instructs for them to step out the car. Both young men comply without hesitation.

They're both forced to take a breathalyzer test. The actual driver was Malik, his friend was Nate. Malik's blood alcohol content was greater than 0.08%. Nate passed his breathalyzer test due to him being sober.

In the most polite tone, Nate explained that Malik found out he was destined for heaven. The two went out to celebrate with friends at the bar. Nate states he only had water. Malik proclaimed he was sober enough to drive them home since they're roommates. Once the sirens were heard, Malik had grew anxious.

Claiming he didn't want to end up shot nor in the news. Exposing that it was Malik's idea to switch seats. Nate apologetically admits he should have been the designated driver from the beginning.

The desperate plea in Nate's voice was enough for them to talk privately. Nate nervously paces around the Mercedes. They escorted Malik to sit in the back of their patrol car.

After a quick discussion amongst themselves, both officers made a decision. They kept Nate on edge a little longer due to his earlier attitude. Especially, since the catalyst was because of this ridiculous miracle hoax. Then both decided to simply write Malik a ticket and that Nate will drive them back home. Officer Lambeth helped escort Malik to the Mercedes and gave him a pat on his back. Everyone agreed that was fair. The young guys escaped at the exact speed limit. Officer Lambeth and Colthirst mocked them as they continue their patrol routes for the night.

†

Woke Knee-Grow had made news for his charitable donation to the public park in downtown Holksdale. He announced this after his fate was destined for hell. Also, has recently paid child support for his fourteen kids. Claiming that this donation was preconceived before this miracle. His actual name is Bryce Wiggins.

Prior to now, this rapper was a self-proclaimed gang member who's allegedly been connected to murders. He's covered in a pletheora of tattoos all over his body and face. Normally claimed he would give back to his community while flaunting gold chains, watches and custom grill teeth whenever he promotes his new albums. His gangsta rap music influenced the urban youth to engage in gang violence, doing drugs and mistreating women. Usually took advantage of his position with young aspiring female artists in his music videos. Even impregnating one of them (*twice*).

He gained notoriety for his altercations with a famous rapper, E-Lit Lyfe (*Lamar Beasley*). Believing he was part of the elitist lifestyle. He donated to charitable organizations, was faithful, was a dedicated father, and made dope music. All prior before hearing that he's heading to heaven. Had multiple verbal altercations initiated by Woke Knee-Grow (*Even to go as far as antagonizing his devout fans online*).

A lot of these stories about him unfolding to the public didn't faze him due to his thrill of clout-chasing. However, he never believed (*despite his blasphemous lyrics*) it would ever gain worldwide attention from his own Creator.

† Chapter 4: I don't have money on me like that.

Later that day at the bar, Jovanny was still on the clock. Essie was gone to cook dinner for Larissa. Customers had left and came in. It wasn't as noisy as earlier, just people enjoying their drinks. Icarus McGrew was wandering around the bar, then he nested by the pool table.

He noticed Donny Bedford in here still, he's been sitting at a table alone for a few hours now. He wasn't on his phone or conversing with anyone. There wasn't a hint of sadness on his face, he just seemed blank to Jovanny. The sight of him looked like he was deep in thought, unable to emote anything. His glass was finally finished as he got up. Jovanny took a shot for himself since he's not serving now.

Eventually Donny came to him requesting another glass. He served him, not a word was exchanged between the two as he was pouring him another refill. Jovanny knows it must be from him calling him out the other day. To him it was all fun and games to just banter with the customers. Apparently, he must have been impacted by it despite Donny's rationalization. Which seemed to be strange since Donny was not even close to as bad as other men in there. Lastly, he serves him his drink.

"Donny!" Jovanny called. "Yo, you good?"

"I'm just sitting here thinking, is all."

Donny took in some of his drink. Appeared to be difficult to explain or maybe he'd fear of Jovanny running his mouth again. Regardless, he didn't care about before.

"It about that bullshit list?"

"Yeah, it is. I don't know if it's real or what, but I know I can't get it outta my head. It's from my kids, not being in their lives."

"How many you got again, two?"

"Yeah, they're at their mom's place."

"Man, that thing's not real." Jovanny said. "Maybe I was outta pocket talking shit, but I was just fucking with you. There is no hell, this shit ain't affecting our lives. Ok?"

Donny's confession didn't make him feel any greater, just made him feel worse. His absence of their lives not only affected theirs but could've affected him in the afterlife. He pulls out his phone and shows him a picture of his son. His mother sent it to him, but he never responded to her. He has rosy cheeks with curly, brown hair and his blue eyes were as wide as his smile. Donny never had a picture of his daughter; he figured the mother would've felt like she was wasting her time.

"How old are they?"

"He's seven, she's nine…" Donny said with uncertainty. "Their mom takes care of them. Ain't seen 'em in years."

"Welp, if it's got you stressing, go see 'em then." Jovanny said. "Be in their lives, at least your son's. Trust me, a woman can't teach a boy to be a man."

"I could help keep him off these streets."

"Or instill in him some goddamn common sense so he don't be running around doing no crucifixion challenge. It's crazy out on these streets, bruh."

Donny was contemplating it as he pulled out his phone. The mother of his children, Taivy, wasn't even in his contacts. Thus, having him go scroll through multiple recent texts. He had her text saved still with an unanswered one from her. She had messaged him apparently about being free to take them off her hands for the weekend. That was last seen years ago.

"If you want it bad enough, you'll make it happen."

"Being able to reach the promise land, we'll see."

"Ok, I meant fighting to be with your kids but ok nigga, you do you. Go handle your business."

Donny waits for Jovanny to serve another customer when some guy approached there. He took in some of his beer then went to the bathroom. There was nobody inside the stalls from how it seemed. Inside the stall, he calls Taivy whilst on the toilet. There's this small pause, then the phone proceeds to ring.

As the lines ringing, all that's going through his head now are thoughts he hadn't reminisced of in years. Him interacting with Taivy or her kids, her pushing him to introduce her kids to his parents or even the kids themselves. Ending things on his own terms as far as avoiding the stress as far as parenting goes. Or feeling tied down to a woman who he'd never loved. The realization of him reverting to her, almost crawling back in her life, made him have somewhat second-thoughts. But the more the phone continuously rung, he figured it was too late. Then the rings stopped, and he went straight to voicemail. Her voice had been heard, heard to him for the first time in years. Just a simple voice recording played, giving him an even worse realization. Taivy either deleted him from her phone or kept him in and refused anything more to do with him. The recording still went on until frustrated Donny finally hung up. He didn't see no point in calling twice, she already got him once.

He got out the stall and felt his phone buzz in his hand. Donny checked at it quick, nothing but an update suggestion for a game he downloaded. Jovanny was seen serving more incoming customers as he made his way back for his drink. The more sips he took, the sooner he figured Jovanny would ask how it went or if he'd call her; he didn't. Guess Jovanny already told him what to do and moved on serving his customers. Exactly like Taivy doing the same, caring for their responsibilities, and forgotten about him.

Donny again checked his phone for anything, he kept drinking still. The crowd getting louder from these drunken buffoons. He kept at his phone until he finally finished his beverage then he left before it became more crowded.

Greynard's Junkyard, 3:56 P.M.

Yanie drove there in the pickup truck with her pulling behind the requested Camper. Other workers noticed and watched to see her driving in. She had brought it out in front of his office. Franklin hears the sound of a vehicle parked outside; he opens up to witness this. Yanie honks at him, seeming extremely pleased with herself. So much that the muddled look of Franklin didn't even faze her.

Franklin studies the pickup truck before him and that it was connected to his desired vehicle. He waves over the other workers to help to disconnect the chain. Yanie sees them emerging and automatically unhooks the green Camper. She already cleaned out the Camper for anything of value. All she found was a corkscrew, metro cards and fast-food receipts.

The others browsed inside anyway. Yanie hadn't searched the pickup truck yet. Franklin hints for her to come with him to his office. She follows behind as she sees them pulling the truck to the usual adjustment spot. Franklin closed the door to his office, Yanie sat down waiting to get her money for this job.

"Guess y'all ain't never think I'd pull this shit off, huh?" Yanie bragged. "Hook, line—"

"Beverly!" he firmly said. "Didn't I tell you I just needed a green Camper, hmmm? What the hell else is that you've brought me?"

"Uh, an investment… to help us boost more cars."

She knew Franklin never really was thrilled about her ideas. Though with her acquiring what he needed, she thought he'd be glad about the Camper more than upset about this addition. His face seemed a little red, reframing from further frustration.

Franklin yells. "I told you one thing, that's all I asked of you. I bet this is another damn scheme you've conjured up."

"It's perfect! We use this to boost more cars out in the open. No more having to low-key break in or be out here lookin' sus'."

"Y'know how much attention the sight of these things get when even getting that hook connected to someone else's car? You could've been tailed and might've led them straight here. This is worse than that time you stole me that hearse still accompanied with a dead passenger."

"Don't worry, I wasn't." she reassured. "And next time I won't."

"I can't risk that." He said. "I won't jeopardize my own, our entire crew's and including your own safety for whatever you want. It's not happening!"

Knowing Franklin, she figured he wouldn't have another score for her now. Probably back to replacing license plates and changing wheels or anything to do with them.

"You're done here, Beverly." He firmly said.

"Done where…" her nonchalant attitude fled as Franklin gave her this stern look that didn't look like it could be tampered at all with. "Frank, c'mon fam, you can't be serious?!"

"Mr. Burrows." One of the other workers said but felt the tension between both parties in the room. "I can come back."

"Yes Harold?"

Harold says they ran through the pickup truck and found a phone and charger.

"Just leave it here." Franklin said as Harold did and left.

Franklin shut back the office door. Yanie sat there, not cracking jokes or making any smart comments. She's even regretting in her head how she'd not checked that pickup truck beforehand. He focused back at her still face a bit red and a small hint of concern.

"Frank, c'mon… I'm the best you got."

"No, you're not actually." Franklin proclaimed. The best he's got here ranges from people like Johnathan who can do as instructed. No more, no less. What constitutes the best are the one's here who aren't at all greedy to where they'll get everyone here pinched by the cops. Nor are anywhere near as stubborn not to realize that their ideas to everyone else here are nothing but a nonentity.

Yanie was getting fed up with him. Not only was herself terminated but to her, he's gloating about it. Basically, rubbing in her face that all her past ideas including this one brought into action. That feeling of being underutilized had her feel as her time here boosting cars for him had been wasted. All those successes that might've resulted in her arrest meant zero and now has nothing to show for it. This awareness drove itself deep in her core.

He instructed her to leave the junkyard and not to come back. Then left his office. Yanie sat there still, feeling cheated of her time and talents wasted here. She kept doing these weird hand movements, fidgeting inside her pockets still. Enough time passed until she finally got up and forced herself outside where the truck was. She could see those ungrateful workers adjusting the Camper there. Yanie didn't even care if they saw her, she hopped inside the pickup truck and raced out of there.

As she drove out the junkyard, her hands scavenge through the bottom of the driver's seat in search of anything the others may have missed. Her hand had hit something, from grazing it, to firmly feeling a leathery foldable wallet. She checked it on her lap, without checking for I.D. she discovered credit cards, cash filled in and a condom.

Killip's Quarter's, 5:23 P.M.

Located downtown is Killip's Quarter's, a lucrative strip club where Solanda Wright works weekly. She usually performs up on stage or provides her customers a lap dance. The main room is a dark atmosphere with purple lighting flashing around. There's a decorative design of stars displayed high up that get highlighted for the customers to see. Levitating stars moving above. There are a few dancers who perform on all poles on each side of the entrances.

Around here are a variety of people ranging from men to women but being outweighed by men. There are some at the bar paying for expensive drinks or getting ripped off by taking thirty percent if wanting to acquire change. The girls are of course half naked, most in black bikinis and black laced high heels. Many of them are throwing their weight around the pole. Either that or approaching guys.

These strippers here throughout being employed have been involved in sketchy activities. Other than just performing for hundreds, most here entertain customers with ulterior motives. Either in hopes of snatching their credit cards, exchanging drugs within a more private setting, or blackmail them for commitment of adultery. Many of them seduce men into the Cognac room backstage.

In the Cognac room, strippers not only give off lap dances but with the right amount of money… they will engage in full on intercourse. The usual ones are either drunk or schmucks or both. They're the easiest to tempt, even without those playing any factor, most strippers can detect certain types of men that crawl in there.

Most men are either lonely, desperate for the touch of a female or in general cannot get a woman. The lonely ones are at the bar drinking, seeming like they don't want to be here yet still check out the strippers walking around. Many hopeless ones constantly entertain them almost as much as the strippers' performance there by tossing dollar bills up for them. Some reach out for the dancers on stage to possibly cross that threshold away from professionalism. The ones who aren't getting women always try sweet talking many of them to, a more private setting, as they would put it. Unfortunately, if they're drunk enough, they'll feel summoned to the Cognac room for them to be tricked into having unprotected sex, especially if they're seen tossing hundreds on stage. This leads strippers here to have full leverage over them.

This can be done by requesting money for an abortion if the father doesn't want to be locked down or them keeping the money and still having the child. Many of the pregnant girls perform still. Some customers are aroused by the sight of them on stage even if it's a safety and health hazard. There are some who engage in indulging in their customer's strange fetishes as well.

A lot of the girls here spend their money on getting enhanced injections, mostly butt injections being common there. They come with this mentality of feeling superior to these customers even though they're a pawn for a business sexually objectifying woman. These women believe that sex equates power, especially being the desired source there. Even knowing this and they would rather take any other options.

Killip's possess many self-hating strippers who've done some disgraceful things to themselves just for the sake of getting by and have left their values down the pole. Some got caught up in a crazy, reckless lifestyle. Solanda on the other hand doesn't take it to that extent. She's always prided herself not doing what she's seen and a lot of times making more money than the average stripper there. All she's doing is trying to make enough money to pay for school.

Recently like at her boyfriend's job, there has been an incoming of people lately motivated by that list. Some who're just trying to live every day like it's their last before meeting Satan. They come to express their perverse sexual nature there by asking for the most grotesque things imaginable. Or spend so much on drinks that they either pass out or get themselves tossed out. The girls however, don't at all take that seriously being they've got bigger things to worry about.

Solanda's with a few of the other strippers on break. Her regular co-workers are changing with her. Olivia and Tammy just finished with their clients. They discuss how more and more men are coming because of the circumstance.

"Girl, I'm telling you…" Tammy groans. "…this dude will not let up. It's to the point where I'm 'bout to quit putting in this work."

"Mm-hmm, over here with that fire coochie." Solanda said. "Ayeeee, got these dudes sprung over you."

"Girl, you already know. Like, that's why I got in all these men, they stay having wet dreams about me. I mean, I already know I can grind 'cause bitches who grind stay making niggas nut. And when I'm on they lap, I feel like I'm on a grass of morning dew!"

"Like check out these baddies!"

Solanda's lights up a cigarette. Then lotions her creamy legs. Other women are around the area. Some are changing into tighter bras and different heels then go out to work.

"Solanda, who you been avoiding out there?" Olivia asked.

"No one, I'm on break." She replied. "We got mad men coming in here recently. Don't they got work?!"

"I know right, a lot of these fools are drunk. Idiots I'm grinding on, praising God."

"Girl I get it, your pussy's on point."

Olivia smirks. "*No, no, no…* I mean these men in here are confessing their sins to me. *That they shouldn't be up in here.*"

"All up in this!" Solanda said as she playfully caresses her body.

"Exactly, you know what I'm talkin' about." Olivia said. "You wanna find Jesus? Go to fucking church mass. Not up in Killip's talking 'bout you messed up when you stay doing the same shit. I mean c'mon, miss me with that praying for forgiveness-ass shit."

"Nah, I don't mind them coming through." Solanda said. "They should be up on my lap, the way I'm having them expose themselves. I drop all kinds of knowledge and I have 'em come out their pockets just for that. I get more success simply talking to people."

"You must hear some weird shit then?" Tammy said.

"The usual… *'I'm bad with money.'* Probably be tossing it here! *'I hurt all these people in college, I cheated on my wife…'* bet'cha with these bitches here!"

"I had some fool practically spend all night here once trying to wife me up." Olivia laughed. Adding that he'd got on his knee and proposed. The bouncers had to get this guy out.

"Alright, my time's now." Tammy said as she went back to work.

Solanda knew what she meant by that. She saw Tammy off to approach a guy just drinking by himself. He was watching every other girl walking around until she came. Tammy sat up on him, whispering something in his ear. The man's face had lit up, nods his head then follows her off to the Cognac room.

Olivia asks what Solanda thinks of this miracle. Solanda doesn't believe in it whatsoever. She tells about how her boyfriend experiences the same thing at work with his customers.

Solanda put out her cigarette then went back out. She walked out half naked with attitude in her high heels. Then came up on stage to perform on the pole. The guys were flinging money up at her as she twerked hard while balanced on her heels. All these moves she performed up there intrigued the audience. Solanda crossed her legs around the pole and twirled upside down.

As she hung there still, the money kept flying around. From her flipped position, she sees (*another stripper she knows*) Latoya, coming from the Cognac room after being turned out. She walked out looking frustrated whilst the man was seemingly relieved. Maybe the situation didn't work in her favor because her whole attitude looked like it got deflated. However, she continued entertaining everyone still.

Kental Avenue, 7:15 P.M.

Here on Kental is where there's a cul-de-sac filled with houses. Not much crime happens here due to the police having leverage of residents' inability to escape. Illegal activities ceased from the cops having higher ground whenever they roll in the only ingoing outlet. Even so, a police cruiser will tour here every day unannounced.

But what else lies here is Donny's kids and the mother of his children. He doesn't need to search her up online since he remembers the house she lived in still. Taivy never had much money to move away from here, he never tried to contribute either so finding her was no problem. He parked in front of her house; the street was silent. Taivy's home was small and wide, from the outside it looked like there appeared only one floor. The yard had weeds overreaching its dead grass. The house itself was decorated in dry, chipped away grey paint.

Donny reluctantly got from his car and opened the gate. As he went, he watched the upcoming window to see if any heads would've peeked through first. At the door, hesitantly rung that bell, resulting in the sound of a buzzer. Donny waited there for a few seconds until he heard steps behind the door. It didn't open because whoever was behind the door must've been checking through the peep hole.

"H-Hello?" Donny said. "Taivy, that you?"

"What are you doing here?" She yelled from behind the door.

"I—" Donny said startled, as to how long it was to hear her voice. "Just thought I'd drop by. I tried calling. I haven't seen you and the kids in a while."

"YEARS!" Taivy flung open the door with her hair all tied in a bun. She looked frustrated enough already but having kids will do that to you. He couldn't believe how little she's aged since after all these years.

"Taivy…" he muttered. "…you—"

"All these years you've been absent, talking about '*I ain't seen you and the kids in a while*', are you serious, Donny?!"

"Look..." he politely began. "I tried calling you to see how everything's been, but I see you sent me straight to voicemail. And you've got your phone on you I see."

"Donny, I texted you asking for pampers, you left me on read for all these years!" She yelled.

"I know, I know. I'm here now, I'm not even trying to argue with you neither, alright? Just wanted to know—"

"Know what! Know how I've been managing here still without your help?! Or why I'm even entertaining this bullshit?!"

"*All due to you, just you.*" Donny quickly said. "Come on, how you been?"

"You're unbelievable, can't even ask about your own kids!" Taivy firmly said. "Or you already forgot you left me here alone to watch after your responsibilities?!"

Donny tries calming her down as her hollering wasn't about to provoke him into lashing out at her. Then it came to an abrupt stop from the sudden sound coming from inside. There was the noise of clanging pots from the kitchen. Taivy hurries back in to handle it, leaving the door open. Donny slowly crept in, inside was bright from the sunlight shining in. Taivy screams again but at her kid for making a mess, her loud voice can be detected down the hall in the kitchen. He noticed the pictures of her and the kids on the wall in passing. There were separate ones of her parents too.

The kids were in their school uniforms in one of them. Donny could feel just how small this place was. It gave him a sense of relief with the notion of any more people living here would feel too stuffed. Perhaps him abandoning them helped trim the fat. He could hear little Aiden's voice telling his mom what happened. Donny kept moving forward then cautiously emerged in the kitchen.

Her misplaced frustration projected on her son was soon placed back on Donny as he was spotted by them both in here. Taivy got more fed up that he came in while their son was trying to recognize him. He waved to Aiden; he gave a cautious *"hello"* as he drew closer to his mom. Donny noticed the pot spilled eggs on the ground then picked it up, tossed it in the sink.

"And who let you in?"

"Just heard you scream from outside." Donny clarifies that she had left the door wide open.

"Donny, I haven't got time for this—"

"You're not gonna introduce us?" Donny said hinting at Aiden, the boy kept peeking at Donny.

"Y'all would've been better acquainted the day I introduced him to the world, but you dipped off elsewhere."

Biggest mistake I ever made was dipping up inside said open legs. Introduced us both to your crazy world of bullshit. Annoyed Donny thought to himself.

"Sweetie," Taivy reluctantly began as she looked to him then back to her son. "This is you and Lauren's father, Donny Bedford."

Aiden finally came off his mom and studied him a bit. There was no look of surprise or anything resembling that. Just a neutral expression, zero trace of recognition to be had. Donny studied his son too, the boy appeared very small and thin. His skin was peach-colored. Aiden said nothing but still look at both his parents with his big innocent eyes. Taivy took a rag from the sink to clean the spilt eggs.

Taivy softly tells Aiden to not worry over this mess and go play in his room. Aiden nodded, looking perplexed.

"See ya', pal." Donny sweetly said. Watching his son warily wave his hand.

Taivy bent over to clean it up. Donny was about to help until she visibly rejected it. He grabbed a seat at the counter, watching her down there clean up. She finished then rinsed off the rag.

"He's gotten big." Donny said, also compliments his haircut.

"My friend does his hair, and Lauren's too." Taivy said.

"Yea, tell me about her, how's she doing?"

"They're both fine, Donny. They've been fine with me since. Plus, she's at her friend's house."

Taivy lights her cigarette and opens the kitchen window, Donny sits still wondering if this will go well. He can hear Aiden playing games from his room.

Donny smiles. "You've really done right by these kids, Taivy."

"All without you. And I see you're doing quite well for yourself." Taivy calmly replied, knowing Aiden is most likely eavesdropping in on their discussion. She compliments his nice car parked out front. Her and Donny both know that money spent on his car could've gone to supporting their kids. Donny humbly says the car wasn't expensive.

Donny thought of offering money but wasn't sure if he'd even be allowed alone near his children first. He asks Taivy how life has treated her since his departure. She goes on about working as a waitress but refused to disclose where. Donny insists that if he were to take the kids off her hands he would need to know.

"With whom?!" Taivy condescendingly asks. Reminding Donny that it's been years since he last kept in contact. "I don't know you; my kids don't know you! I'm not leaving them with you to do God knows what."

"Our kids!" he firmly states.

Taivy tells him to offer money in order to help.

"I don't have money on me like that."

"You're lying" she said. "You're out driving that fucking car but couldn't spend a dime for your kids."

"My kids?! Oh, before you said they were your kids. So now to get me to pay for shit… now they're our kids?"

"You didn't contribute shit after all these years, and you're the one begging to come back—"

"Nobody's begging!" Donny yells, enraged at that idea. "I was gonna take them out, spend time with them but you're making it difficult! If anyone's begging for shit, it's you trying to get more money—"

"*MORE?* I don't receive any from you! Be glad I never reported your name to the state." Taivy yelled.

"If I wish to spend money on them, I'll do it when I take them out for food, or games."

"You're not taking them out for shit! Not on my watch, not my kids!"

"See there you go with that 'yours' shit again. Admit it, you just want my money all for yourself."

"And what, I don't deserve to be reimbursed somehow?"

"Motherhood's a blessing in itself, didn't think there was no greater feeling, just saying." Donny said.

Taivy began to regret even engaging with him. This constant back and forth was just like it was between them years ago. The smoking wasn't helping her tolerance level with him neither. She put it out, then looked to see if Aiden was coming to poke his curious little head in to be nosy.

"You need to leave. Get out my house right now."

There was a brief silence between them. Donny finally said: "Taivy, I said I ain't come here to fight."

"I don't care what brought you back up in here. Get away from me and my kids! We don't need nothing from you. And not no more stress and heartache you've already caused."

"How's that? Kids barely know me." Donny said. And to his own surprise he was right. His kids barely even remember him so who else could've been hurt? Then tries not to not be any more of a hassle after realizing why else she's mad. Projecting both anger of him not contributing, refusing and arguing about it, now seeing the damage he'd done leaving on top of that… it might escalate.

Donny calmly offers money for school supplies, groceries, toys. Narrating why he should be paying for Aiden's next haircut for—

"Donny, you aren't hearing me, we don't need you here."

"C'mon, just relax!" he said as she started to shove him away. She had been fed up enough and forcibly tried again, he stood his ground still. He wasn't going to let her provoke him into hitting her back.

"Taivy, quit putting your hands on me!" Donny asserts as he peeks over at his son's room.

"GET OUT!" she screamed.

Taivy couldn't call the police, or shove Donny again, nor even stomach another outburst. She took a step back, Donny got caught off guard by her sudden attitude adjustment, hoping it wasn't a trick. Then he faced the opposite direction to see Aiden standing still watching them again. He wasn't stupid so they weren't about to act sweetly towards each other now.

"Donny, please just leave. Go on." She said as politely as possible. Donny wasn't trying to startle this boy by staying there any longer. Begrudgingly so, Donny once again took off to his car and left his family behind.

†

Midtown 9:40 P.M.

Around this time of night, officer Cliff Lambeth and officer Declan Colthirst were nearing the end of their shift. Patrolling the streets, not much had transpired yet. The two just came from a convenient store. They both purchased teriyaki beef jerky. Lambeth bought an energy drink, Colthirst bought himself a can of *Dazzle Me*. A sparkling water where the visible twinkles are afloat.

They cruised pass a large movie theatre parking lot. It was filled with mainly empty cars except one with two teenagers seen through the windshield. Both male behind the steering wheel and female in the passenger seat just sitting eating fries and nuggets. Then their vehicle slightly shook. That movement caught officer Colthirst's attention. He pointed it out to his partner. The car suspiciously shook again. Both teens weren't fazed by it.

After detecting this, they drove into the parking lot. This scene continues. Both officers emerged towards the vehicle with it still rocking. Officer Lambeth cautiously waves to the teens in the front. These teens were expressionless, still focused on their meal. Officer Colthirst shines his flashlight at them and was about to emerge. Neither is startled by the bright light. Lambeth finally realized what it was. He silently warns his partner to keep back. Then cautiously moves toward the windshield. The vehicle's rocking ceased.

His fingers peeled the edges off, realizing this is a customized windshield sunshade. The sunshade is used as a blockage, visually depicting two teens enjoying food. Lambeth tore it off entirely once the rocking commenced. Both officers simultaneously flashed their lights inside.

Two teenagers having missionary sex in the backseat. Each one was shirtless, sweaty and in disbelief. Their heads clicked at the cops. The girl's scream soared as she pushed the guy off her. Colthirst orders for them to get dressed and come outside.

After a few minutes, these kids slowly drew from the car. The girl was fixing her long, brunette hair. The boy was adjusting his belt still. Her eyes averted away from them; his fingers began trembling. Both trying not to look guilty. As Colthirst was monitoring these two, his partner investigates the vehicle. There are two empty liquor cans in the backseat with a few unopened ones. A phone still playing pornography with this young girl's panties laid underneath.

Lambeth asks if they've been drinking tonight. Both glanced at each other, then shamefully nods their heads. He asked what they were doing exactly. The girl swelled with fear, unable to speak. The boy reveals they were aiming to have intercourse somewhere private. He admitted that he was the only one drinking, this was his idea, and she was hesitant to engage. Lambeth reminds them that they shouldn't be underage drinking. His girlfriend whimpered something while nodding to that statement.

This led to him asking if there were any drugs in their car. They claimed there weren't any. Colthirst adds that they shouldn't be having safe sex. The boy claims he had a condom, but it ripped as he tried it on. To prove it, he slowly whipped out the condom wrapper from his pocket. Colthirst recognized that brand. He knows they tear easily, especially if someone really doesn't know what they're doing.

"You know how to put one on, kid?" Colthirst skeptically asks.

"Yea, officer." The boy instantly nods, then commenced to unzipping his pants.

"Nobody's asking for you to demonstrate, son. We aren't dick policing here. Just explain the process step-by-step."

The boy began with blowing air inside it like a balloon. Exhale in more if you need a magnum. Have your partner holding it steady for you to strap it on by firmly tying it around the shaft. The officers looked perplexed. Their eyes turn to his girlfriend who rolled her eyes in embarrassment. The boy sounded so self-assured. Then he concludes with: "Then when you're done, just flip that bitch inside out for round two."

There was a brief silence as everyone stared at this boy. Then his girlfriend finally spoke with the correct explanation. Both officers excuse themselves to their cruiser. These teens are ordered not to move and to remain silent. Officer Lambeth and officer Colthirst discuss how to handle this situation while trying not to laugh after hearing this kid's explanation. A few minutes went when they finally came to an agreement. The young couple were quietly bickering towards their car. She sounded like she was on the verge of panic. Her boyfriend tries calming her down. She keeps swatting at him out of frustration.

"This is all your fault!" she said. "I knew I heard something outside. We should've wrapped this up."

"Wrap what up, girl?!" Colthirst mocked. "Boyfriend here can't even strap on a rubber."

The teens stood motionless. Their eyes locked on these officers, waiting for whatever comes next. Lambeth approached them nicely, expressing a soft smile.

"My partner and I were thinking this," Lambeth began. "We'll confiscate your alcohol. Your girlfriend will drive since you've been drinking. And you'll go to the nearest convenient store to buy stronger contraceptive. There's no need to drag this out."

Colthirst, with his arms crossed, asks the girl if she's on any birth control. She shook her head. He insists she purchases a Plan B pill. Her boyfriend doesn't know what that is. Colthirst agrees with his partner, urging these two to buy stronger condoms.

"What next? An STD test saying I'm positive or negative too?" the boy snarks. "What if there's none that fits me?"

Officer Colthirst dangles his handcuffs. "I'm positive these will fit you."

"Yes, officer."

Officer Lambeth turns to the girl. "Help him."

"To find his size or to properly strap it on?"

"Both." Both officers blurts.

After confiscating their alcohol, the teens are granted permission to leave. Officer Lambeth, with a look of pity, gave the boy a pat on his back. The girl gets behind the wheel with her swatting her boyfriend once more. Then drove off into the street.

The cops returned to their vehicle, laughing at that oblivious boy. They stayed parked while eating their beef jerky. These two knew it wasn't worth escalating the situation. Lambeth commended the boy for not being dumb enough nor drunk enough to stir problems. Colthirst acknowledged how annoyed his girlfriend looked. Then begrudgingly admits it was noble of him to come honest about everything.

"*Christ!*" Colthirst groaned. "This is what generation these kids are in now? Almost as worse as that guy we caught getting his dick sucked in his car last month. No tinted windows or nothing."

"*Windows?!*" Lambeth scoffed. "That man drove around with no hood."

They began to leave the parking lot after monitoring around one last time. Then patrolled the streets.

Richez Shrive, 7:50 P.M.

Yanie is drinking here with Jovanny still on the clock. They discussed the miracle before that Yanie wasn't informed about. She didn't believe in it either, he told her about the others in the bar who probably would end up there. There are many other people drinking that they know because of this, they both just criticize them on how ridiculous they're being.

"I'm glad you don't take this shit to heart." Jovanny said.

"Uh, yea! 'Cause I know fucking better, that's why."

"I meant 'cause you a damn car thief, that's why. And you'd be here bitching too. At least you and I see it ain't nothin'. Essie thinks that way too."

Yanie's not surprised, knowing Essie's too smart for that. Yet not so much about Larissa though.

"She ain't piercing her damn hands so props to that. And for my petty theft days… my nigga, them days are dead."

Yanie tells Jovanny that her boss let her go.

Jovanny began chuckling as he pours himself up another shot. Yanie shot him a look of not wanting to be criticized like how she'd know he would. He listened but was smiling still. He poured her another drink. Unbeknownst to her, he was treating his friend.

"Sorry to hear."

"Yo, good looks." Yanie said as she accepted the glass. "Fuck am I supposed to do now? I'm screwed."

"Just pray on it." Jovanny laughed.

More people came in with their friends laughing in groups. It was a group of white college students approaching Jovanny's work post. They were posing together taking selfies in the bar too. Jovanny and Yanie both exchanged looks of annoyance. Them knowing each other well, she can sense his already impatience once serving these kids. They were laughing about how they made it to heaven and finally got together to celebrate.

Yanie hints that she'll move somewhere else, him already knowing she doesn't want to deal with their loud, pesky mouths in their ears. She takes her drink with her and seeks for an empty small table, but most are filled with sorrows and isolation. Yanie sees a small table with an open seat across from Donny Bedford appearing closed off. She heads over and gestures to sit, he nods and then takes a seat. They both were quietly drinking together, Yanie pretends to scroll for importance on her social media to avoid conversation. However, she noticed he was oblivious of her presence. Donny appeared locked in his own headspace. He wasn't browsing his phone nor looking around the bar, Donny had simply stared off into space while every now and then sipping his drink. Yanie finally stopped pretending and acknowledged him even from what little she knows about him.

"Glad we both had the same idea coming here from these college kids, huh?" Yanie said.

"Nah, I been at this spot for like twenty something minutes now. I was gonna come here earlier but something popped up."

"I bet, guess it kept you busy. Look like you got something on your mind."

"Yea, kinda." Donny said. "What about you?"

"Uh, actually my day's not been too good neither, so." She confessed. "I got let go from my job."

"You not out boosting cars no more?" Donny said.

Yanie's face looked shocked. "You been ear hustling on me talking to Jovanny, huh?"

"Not eavesdropping." Donny corrects, he reminded her of how loud she is when talking about it to Jovanny Gibbs.

She shrugged. "Well, the guy who put me on let me go."

"That sucks, sorry to hear."

"Thanks. But least I got a free beer outta it." Yanie said.

"What, you caught a pity drink?" Donny jokingly said.

"Pretty much." Yanie plays along. Then brags about how guys have offered her drinks in the past.

"Welp, I ain't got dudes throwing shots my way."

"Nah, that ain't what I heard. Jovanny was flaming all y'alls asses a while back."

Donny remembered Jovanny calling everyone out for their sinful behavior. He asks her if she knew what Jovanny said. Yanie couldn't recall.

Donny contemplated telling her, but she seemed alright. Yanie kept drinking trying to block out the background noise still. She glanced over at Jovanny to see him still entertaining but having on a fake smile.

Donny felt the urge to confess.

"Well, I stayed busy today to see the mother of my kids."

Donny confides. "I went over to try and settle things out between us. At most, try to get more time with my kids but shit escalated still."

"Escalated?! What, like she wanted to square up?"

"Yup, and I wasn't having it. Then my son, Aiden…" Donny continues as he pulls up a picture of him on his phone to show her. "…he came in outta nowhere and that's when I left."

Yanie smiled and nodded. "Smart, bet she still feeling salty that y'all ain't work out. Best believe, us women are petty and vindictive as hell."

Donny then admits that he should've tried rectifying things way beforehand, but he did today. And didn't get any recognition.

"Yea, I feel you. Cute kid too."

"Thanks."

The two kept overhearing them chanting still. Donny felt for another beer, but he kept to his seat. Jovanny was already crowded serving drinks, the two were visibly annoyed by them. Then watched them start taking videos on their phones. Especially with drinks added, they'll get even louder.

Donny mocks about them taking photos for social media in celebration of getting into heaven. Yanie shares that she's got a gram of weed on her if Donny wishes to partake. He gladly accepts.

Both Yanie and Donny headed to the back smoking weed that she rolled. She and he were talking for a half hour then decided to hot box in his car. Yanie bragged about the stolen truck and how she left her job. More time passed from a half hour to another, them talking about stuff and agreeing on a lot as well. A more comfortable vibe was soon developed, Yanie and Donny eventually moved to kissing. Yanie wasn't certain whether this was from her recent beers or the high of weed but had found herself lost in his mystique.

The two were going at it in his car. Then led to more physical contact to where it escalates to the backseat for extra space. Both were naked in the back, thrusting up on each other. They'd almost seemed passionate if they weren't high. That car was rocking well back and forth, both had started sweating from repeated fixation of each other's pelvis. Locked legs around Donny's waist until the two of them both got off. Lastly satisfied, both just slumped on top of each other feeling nothing but bliss.

† Chapter 5: Begone George!

Richez Shrive, 11:23 A.M.

Yanie and Donny are still parked behind the bar, both are hardly awake but are aware of what happened. Her eyelids difficult to keep wide, her temples furiously constricting together tight. The sunlight through the glass shines bright in their faces setting them back to reality. She feels his warm, bare chest as she still refuses to get up. Feeling him reach for something in the car door, believing it's for another condom but in fact for a water bottle.

Donny digs in his pants pocket that was under the seat for a packet of Advil. Then offers her one and they both engulf a tablet and share the water. It was silent until they both gazed into each other's eyes with the sunshine exposing all on their faces, including the shock of how fast they escalated last night. Donny smirked, Yanie began to snicker, the two laugh at themselves.

They looked out each window on both ends, nothing was detected. He handed her some of her clothes and she returned the favor. He checked to see how late it was on his phone, then stepped out the car to light a cigarette. She checked herself with her phone, appearing disoriented with her short hair messy with strands all in her face. Donny was just outside without a shirt on, still smoking. Yanie gets barely dressed and comes join him.

"Got another one of those?" she said, he handed her one.

"You, okay?" Donny asks.

"It's all goody. Believe me, you not the first dude I been in a car with."

Both just lean up against the car smoking, Yanie's on her phone while he just thinks to himself. No one is in sight of these two, yet they still causally glance to check just in case. Yanie hopes he's not considering her to be his girlfriend or even a possible model figure to introduce to his kids. She can't tell what's on his mind, so she breaks the ice.

"So, you know this wasn't, like, nothing serious, right?"

"Uh-huh, don't worry."

"Oh, ok." Yanie seemed surprised. "Cool."

Donny shared that he's just thinking of his kids. That he doesn't have any urge to date anyone anyway.

Yanie shrugs. "Can't blame you, ain't nothing loyal about these thots out here, checking for a dude on the next come up. Marriage ain't on these hoes' minds. Shit, it ain't on mine. Least you straight with it, not out here running no games."

This has Donny reveal that he hates mind games. Or having to tolerate nonsense to get what he desires. His job already keeps himself busy enough. Yanie asks about his profession, only to find out he's a car salesman. He usually uses his charm to rip-off buyers or scam people into debt with his vehicles.

"*Oh.* So, you and me both be sneaky with these cars, huh?" Yanie gloats while cheerfully nodding. "You sneaky on them prices, I'm sneaky on the whip. Ok now, I see you." Then she took a drag of his cigarette.

"To this day, I still got it." Donny proudly said. He's done this for over a decade, had major promotions and has made a lot of money. Then expressed he should've made more time for his kids.

It started to get quiet as they leaned on the car still.

"Last night was fun." Donny began. "That sucks about your 'job' but you're cool. I know you'll eventually get into something where the world will see your potential."

"Yea, real talk. You a real one."

Yanie heard him out. Didn't think he was criticizing her like almost everyone else. He seemed genuinely pleased with her to where she heard actual admiration. Sure, it wasn't for stealing cars but for something better: herself. Unable to completely conceal her smile, she looked to the side mirror, pretending to fix up her hair. Then she looks down at her phone too.

Donny looked over to her. "I'm not pressing you or nothing…" he softly said, then reminds Yanie of him not really looking for anything right now. Starting to uncomfortably feel like he's giving her the power. "You could loan me your number."

Yanie sweetly smiles, extending her hand for his phone. "I'll loan you that over a down payment any day. I know how you be cheating motherfuckers."

"Yeah, back at you."

"Nah, nah. See I go about it behind people's backs. You a different breed, Don." Yanie mocks.

This then prompts Yanie to urge him to just keep it basic,

no jealousy. Donny agrees, feeling minor relief.

The two get everything out of the car and help each other get completely dressed. He tossed her another bottle he had in the car and then exchange numbers. He starts his engine, about to leave while Yanie heads inside. He honks at her, startled Yanie turns around.

"Forget your panties?" Donny asked.

"For real?" she said as she checks her pants. She sees her purple panties attached still.

"Made you look." He said as he honked.

"Forget about your kids?" she quickly taunts.

She heads in the bar, Jovanny's already here with a few more customers. He noticed her almost dragging herself in, then automatically puts down a beer out for her.

"What up with it?" Jovanny said.

"It's all goody, you?"

"Lemme tell you, last night was lit." He announced. Beginning with how he trudged home exhausted. "The second I get up to my bed, to my gaze, there's this white bitch up in the crib. Then Solanda comes from the closet dressed both in lingerie looking like two baddies."

Apparently, the lady was an older stripper who used worked with Solanda Wright. They coincidentally ran into each other in a beauty store, Purity, at the mall. She wished to see Solanda again since her schedule was cleared.

"Got her to finesse up out them draws and had me wait to come through. This girl's tongue game was on point, even had my ass speaking in tongues by the end of it."

"That's wassup." Yanie said, smiling.

Jovanny asks her about what happened with Donny Bedford after seeing them leave together yesterday. Yanie told him how they were intimate in his car. Jovanny mocks her for being having a threesome with waist-trainer Denise. Yanie gloats about him wanting her phone number. She knew he loved what he'd gotten himself into last night.

"Not gonna lie. The dick was bomb." She laughed. Yanie was shocked he could keep up since she wore men out. Jovanny dismisses that, claiming she's exaggerating.

"Girl, you a damn lie. Acting like you got the holy grail of coochie on you."

"Nah, fool. I do. Got on me that holy pussy." Yanie said, then reminds him of her old friend, Phebe.

Told how men Phebe had blessed told all their friends, they soon labeled her as Pho-bie. Jovanny seemed perplexed. He assumes it's because Phebe was so attached that she had latched onto these men. Making them claustrophobic. Yanie shook her head, hinting he was close.

"It was because every time dudes would hit it from the back, no matter when or where, they'd always feel her walls closing in."

Jovanny cackled, finally recalling who she was. "The one phobia any man would squeeze himself into. Ok, your Holiness. I see you."

As they talk, Jovanny averts his eyes from the man passing in pursuit of the exit. Once he leaves, Jovanny goes on to tell Yanie about him. He saw him leave out the bathroom with another customer, Kyle, late last night. The guy was quickly buckling his pants; Kyle was pulling up his pants. Both had left the same stall. Claiming Kyle lied about just using the urinal.

"This fool's balls were practically exposed." Jovanny said in disgust. Quickly adding he's not intolerant. Just not able to understand how men get aroused by other men. "Like, make it make sense to me. I just can't put two-and-two together."

"Why not, they did." Yanie snickered.

The two still talked about their past week. Jovanny still joyous of his experience last night. Yanie drinking her beer while watching some people come inside. Today wasn't as filled as it's been lately, only a few people had been in here. George Nate was one of them, but he was moving around the bar. He was at a table drinking and now at a pool table conversing with people. Montrez now walks in looking like he's come off the morning shift all sweaty and tiresome. Jovanny serves him a drink then pours himself a shot.

"Y'all here from George lately?" Montrez asked them.

"No, what of it?" Jovanny asks.

"This idiot's out apologizing to people in the bar he's done wrong. See him over there!"

"What for?"

"To try and make amends to get a one way shot into heaven."

"Christ, this bullshit again?" Jovanny groaned.

Montrez told how George had apologized to him last week. George had vandalized his crew's construction site once because gentrification in low-income areas to him was wrong. Causing more work for Montrez's crew to clean up.

"*I can't.*" Yanie scoffed. "Oh wow, here he comes."

George was seen approaching them most likely to make amends. Montrez instantly turned around leaving Yanie and Jovanny visibly standoffish. Yet that hadn't deterred him from still coming forth appearing friendly. Jovanny had hoped he just wanted a drink instead.

"Blessed morning, everyone." George politely greets despite no one answering. He begins that he's been going around town recently making amends for all my wrongdoings."

"Man, I know you not drunk this early?" Jovanny asked.

"Sober as can be, Mr. barkeep. Hell, I already made amends to some people." A few men in the bar, my exes and Mrs. Campbell yesterday for hitting her car while under the influence."

"I ain't know all that. What, with your car?"

"Nope, with myself." George flatly answered. Wandering aimlessly into traffic drunk once on her way home, suddenly crashed into him. Nearly gave her and her children in the backseat a heart attack. Then fled afterwards.

George's whole demeanor was different. Not just from what he was saying but the vibe he was giving out. Prior to now, he'd gave off unwanted attention that'll turn away any cautious person. His presence was still unwanted now, however, it wasn't as painful as they assumed. George displayed this almost naïve, simpleton persona. Almost as if he was pure with his more toned-down attitude and calm voice.

"Jovanny, I actually want to confess my sins and make amends to you personally."

"Say what?" Jovanny said. "George, you sure you good, bruh? Man, you ain't done nothin' to me. Come have a drink."

George refuses to drink. He reminds Jovanny of this woman he once knew, Kennedy. Jovanny remembered she had cut contact with him. George confessed it was his fault. Yanie and Montrez turned to George, and casually peeking back to Jovanny. They could tell by his reaction before sounded seemingly aggressive. Yanie with her eyes all widely attentive on the adults talking, seemingly like a child eavesdropping, then takes a sip of her drink. Everyone waits for George to break hesitation and continue.

Long ago, Jovanny and Kennedy used to date after meeting her as a customer. Jovanny was unfaithful with other women and bragged about his conquests at work. George had always overheard.

"George, come with it!" Jovanny impatiently said.

Kennedy's aunt Clove had died while they were together. George overheard their conversation about how she was coping. Kennedy knew beforehand that Jovanny was never fond of her aunt, jokingly called her a 'belligerent bitch' while she lived, but he pretended to be consoling.

George held in a steady breath before continuing. "Long story short, as soon as her auntie passed—"

"May that belligerent bitch rest in peace." Jovanny said.

"As soon as her aunt died, I desecrated her aunt's grave with those exact words that just came out your mouth. I did it with graffiti."

Everyone within earshot, including Jovanny, was speechless at this confession. George had told her it was Jovanny all along. That he had overheard Jovanny in the bar. Knowing she would break-up with Jovanny while simultaneously pursuing her knowing how vulnerable she felt. Thus, killing two birds with one stone.

Rage cycled through Jovanny but contains himself for the sake of his job. He calmly tells George to go away. This had forced George to add that Kennedy thought he was a creep for trying to pursue her as she was grieving. Even admitting he was an extreme scumbag trying to change for the better.

"MAN, MISS ME WITH THAT DUMB SHIT!" Jovanny hollered, dismissing all rationales.

Some other customers were watching as the bartender was yelling loud at George from afar. The customers had never seen Jovanny this way so hearing him like this made it more alarming.

"I get that you're angry. I completely regretted this."

"The fuck you have, your bitch-ass way of trying to go to heaven." Jovanny yelled. "Y'know everyone you believe you owe apologies to knows this shit ain't genuine. Desperately seeking forgiveness, not from us but the lord. Guess what, he not buying it!"

"God will forgive me for all transgressions." George calmly said.

Everyone seemed irked.

Yanie chimed in, agreeing that he just proved that he doesn't care that Jovanny doesn't forgive him.

"Well, I was the bigger man here." George said, almost sounding passive aggressive. Almost taunting how he wishes Jovanny will one day find it in his heart to forgive him. "Actually… let us all hold hands in Jesus' name."

"Nah, I'm good." Yanie declines.

George extended out both hands for Montrez and Yanie to grab on but the two refused. Montrez turns his back to him and continues drinking still. George places his hand on Yanie's rested one on the counter. She flinched quickly then saw his eyes closed.

"Dear lord and savior, let us rejoice—"

"Begone George!" she calmly said.

"…in repentance of our sins."

"Nigga!"

"Ok, ok. Have a good day, y'all. Stay blessed." George softly gave a farewell.

Yanie swiped her hand back then rests it on her lap until hearing George's footsteps away. Jovanny poured them both a drink, him visibly annoyed still. Montrez began chuckling to himself as he watched George from across the bar getting ignored by others.

"Wonder if people who ever did me wrong will come at me like this?" Yanie said in disbelief.

"Better repent yourself, your Holiness." Jovanny said.

As Jovanny went back to serving more customers, the sound of a police siren was passing through. It seemed to of not only been sounding louder but pulling up closer too.

Dealers usually lurking in the stalls had scurried out quickly along other men involved in the transaction. One guy drew to the bar with his body erect, attempting to seem unfazed.

Yanie glimpsed out the door to check if any police cars were parked in front of Richez Shrive. All she'd seen were the flickering red and blue lights seemingly zoomed in her face. Dazzling now inside the bar that's normally somewhat dark. Fewer customers began emerging towards the window, from what transpired outside had eased their worries now.

Two police officers stepped outside their vehicle, both trying to get through the crowd of people causing a commotion. Not one soul could tell what exactly brought them here but were relieved to see their attention away from the bar. There were people out watching and recording something happening. As more people were moving around, Yanie was able to make out a strange figure from the distance. It didn't make any sense but all she could witness was a man apparently digging a hole shirtless.

He was a scrawny black man in a pit continuously digging with his rail-pipe arms whilst remaining in the small pit himself. The man's look of determination to keep on forward was captured through all the sweat caught in his brow and beard. He appeared to be on drugs, his body movements were very odd especially the constant rotation of his upper body.

The nodding of his head as if he'd move to the exact beat of music but all to be heard were sirens and no headphones were present.

People were surrounding him and capturing it on their phones. You could hear the increasing laughter and younger folk mocking his current state. The man ignored them all including the presence of authority that finally came. It's like the red and blue colored flashes reflecting of his sweaty, slender body made no impact whatsoever. His eyes zeroed in on each pile being shoveled up, carefree as to wherever it's being flung off.

"Travis!" a pedestrian yelled. "Bro, what is you doing?"

That familiar voice had brought the man digging a little bit back to earth. Travis finally took a quick recess from digging so much then turned his head over to the crowd. Stretching his neck, in search through all the faces seen through his wide reddish eyes.

Travis finally sees his friend but still looks completely baffled. He waves to him with one hand as he rests the shovel up on his shoulder with the other. He begins to stretch his back without breaking at all eye contact.

"What the fuck, man?" said his friend.

"Oh nah," Travis laughs. "Bro, it's all goody. I'll be out on my way soon."

"What, to where?"

"The abyss, son!" Travis said. "Y'all seen my shit up on that fuckin' list. I'm going to hell when I die... fine! But I ain't waiting no more, I ain't giving God no satisfaction in sending me once I'm out. I'm 'bout to head straight the fuck down to Satan myself."

"Nigga?! Man, what is you on? You in another world."

"Yo, what of it? Ain't none of that shit matter." Travis then commenced back to shoveling nonstop.

"Man, you gotta stop! Nigga, you'll get locked up."

"I STOP NOW, NIGGA, I'M FINNA BE IN CHINA AT THIS POINT."

Travis, before complaining about his falling pants, begins to sag them more. People start making room for the police to come through and some civilians show their contempt aloud. The officers move in completely aware of all their surroundings present. Officer Cliff Lambeth, appeared stern and prepared for whatever was to happen. His partner officer Declan Colthirst, seemed a muscular guy who didn't seem like he couldn't take on his own, unwilling to tolerate further problems from this individual.

Witnesses verbally demonize them for intervening.

Travis keeps digging as his friend warns him of the upcoming police. Men in the crowd cackle louder as both officers close in. Officer Lambeth keeps a far enough distance in case he tries to flee. The two exchange glances meaning Lambeth will engage closer. Colthirst orders people to back away as they work, Lambeth takes his time coming inside the pit.

He placed his hand near his holster, unaware of how the man to him will react. As he silently comes in, Travis continues to dig and dig. It seemed frightening how focused his wide eyes were to an extent to where he may impair anyone in his way with that shovel.

"Hello sir!" Officer Lambeth said. As soon as he spoke, Travis abruptly halts with dirt and some gravel still piled in the shovel. His whole body frozen as he's hovering down. Lambeth repeats himself. Travis then slightly turns it over letting it all collapse back down, those wide eyes of his quickly shifts to officer Lambeth. Travis slowly faces him with his body remained in the same digging position. Officer Lambeth noticed his grip on the shovel handle had grown tighter, yet his face remained blank.

"Alright now sir, tell me your name."

"Yo, don't front like you don't already know." Travis said. "Everyone already done seen my name and know I'm going to hell."

"I don't know you, but I—" Lambeth softly said as he studies his body language still within the exact same position. "...but we can get to know one another, sound good? I'm officer Lambeth."

Travis skeptically nods his head, body still slouched over.

"Ok, now how's about you tell me yours?" Officer Lambeth suggests.

"Depends, you finna switch places?"

"I don't follow? You want to be an officer?"

"Fuck off! I wanna be an angel!" Travis hollered.

It was strange that he was clearly angered yet his face couldn't emote that at all whatsoever.

Travis could just pounce on him using the shovel as leverage. Especially since Travis automatically resumes back to digging. The two officers know he's on drugs and Lambeth hesitantly creeps up to him. He's trying not to have him at all on edge or as uncomfortable as he feels moving in on him. It's like Travis doesn't at all sense his presence, the crowd is silently anticipating for mayhem to ensue. Travis tosses another pile out the pit but can't dig now, Lambeth is now grabbing the end of the shovel.

Travis stares at him momentarily then tries to pull it away. The officer wouldn't ease on his grip. Travis releases it then moves back fast with him studying the cop still. He keeps flinching even though neither officer presents themselves as a threat. Once Lambeth throws down the shovel, Travis gallops around the pit. His expression finally changed, he looked alarmed and kept circling around inside, desperately attempting an escape. Officer Colthirst, on the upper hand, sprints around wherever Travis lands.

The crowd is cheering aloud, most chant for Travis to run free. His chest gets increasingly sweaty, his shifty eyes look all around for a way out of this hellhole. He almost resembles a petrified child resisting anymore trouble. Officer Colthirst jumps inside to finally settle him down. Both officers grab his arms then forces him down to lying on his chest. Travis keeps swinging up his legs, but officer Lambeth firmly pinned them flat. His partner attempts to now cuff him, Travis screams hard. He's finally handcuffed and hears the ambulance pulling up.

They're both trying to calm him down, understanding his current state. His breathing gets heavier now and the ambulance parks upfront. The medics are preparing to bring him in and getting everything set up. The officers slowly help him to get up, his legs are as loose as freshly cooked spaghetti noodles. Both officers are now supporting him up, helping him out of this hell he's dug himself into.

"Just relax, you're gonna be fine. Understand?" Colthirst said.

"Listen to him, the ambulance is gonna help you."

"Really?" Travis desperately sought.

"Yes, you're heading to a good place, a safe haven." Lambeth said, consoling him. "And officer Colthirst and I will help escort you there ourselves."

"Good looks." Travis said, relived. "We all need our guardian angels that be holdin' us down since day one."

Everyone watched them help strap Travis on a medical stretcher into the ambulance to take him to the hospital. Everyone in the bar saw it all and resumed to their normal routine after the cops drove away.

Killip's Quarter's, 5:23 P.M.

Solanda is giving a man a lap dance now, she performs in tight blue outfit exposing her fully fleshed white legs being rubbed by the customer. This guy was talking about his problems with Solanda, who appeared mighty interested, held direct eye contact the whole time. Her arms wrapped around behind his neck, caressing his wavy, black hair with her long nails. She had up a genuinely looking smile that occasionally turned to glimpse of concern.

He was a tall black man who had been here for a while but wasn't engaging with anyone. Solanda noticed him looking isolated, especially with him seeming upset for a handsome face. She approached him, he causally accepted her invite. He gave off this "go with the flow" feeling since how easygoing this whole interaction had gone and he was tipping her. Though Solanda had money worth making from this young guy who looked a bit irked.

She casually eased the conversation of his daily schedule to what had brought him inside Killip's Quarter's today. The man admitted to needing a drink from the closest bar near his place and then decided to check out the women here as a way to make him feel better. The more she conversed with him, it turns out he has been having recent problems with his girlfriend. Everything from how she doesn't respect his manhood nor take him at all seriously with her unmoved attitude to him suspecting that she may possibly be cheating.

They're constant bickering at one another leaves him with nothing but a headache. He tells of letting her even walk away as victor from a lot of their arguments just so she won't leave him. Solanda sees him almost as the woman in these relationships that desperately want to resolve their issues but has no luck. But doesn't admit that since he's sensitive about his masculinity. All that crosses his mind is whether she'll leave him or is she out cheating.

"Like real talk, I know I'm buggin'." He said. "But she be out always. Not all out at night, no shit like that. But she ain't got no job neither and still ain't rid herself of her old apartment."

"Oh really?" Solanda said.

"Hell yea. And every time I'm on her about it, she wants to play me like I'm stupid or ignore me. Like, I ain't try'na be all clingy and shit but she's tryin' me."

"Look love, take it from a woman, ok? You hearing me, right?"

"What's up?" he said.

"She needs to go, kicked to the curb. 'Cause this chick isn't respecting the relationship and shows no sign of change."

"Nah, but—"

"But you'll keep stressing over her when nobody is looking out for you, hun. If you keep pressing her, she'll do nothing but resent you more than she already has. I know you wanna be taken seriously as a man but sometimes you've gotta distance yourself… at least for now."

"I just don't want her to be out all day not answering her phone. Or be all up on some other nigga's dick."

"Tell me this… you haven't gone through her phone yet, right?"

"I thought about it but no." he said. "Bitch always got her phone on her. Probably not when she sleep but *we ain't*—we ain't smashed in a while so she be at her own place. So I can't even catch her slippin'. And I can't imagine who's there at her apartment. I mean other than our kid."

"Y'all have a kid together?"

"Yerp and that's a big issue. Like, don't get it twisted, I love my son but his momma makes shit mad difficult. When and where I can see him and if I bring up this *'where you at'* shit… she be on some petty shit, makes it difficult for me to see him. Or *'who you be bringing around my son?'* too."

"First off, that's irresponsible and dangerous."

"FACTS!" he said as he tipped her some money. "Like, I picked my kid up from his mom's once. He in the backseat muttering all these guy names. *Alex, Vic, Jake*… like who the fuck's Jake? My son seemed nervous answering. And I ain't wanna ruin our limited time together pressing him like he his mother. I swear, I can't."

"No, it's understandable." Solanda said. "Baby mama got all the grip."

"Up on my balls, yea!" he adds.

"Nah, I got you. Has all the advantage over your kid, got her own place driving you insane. And I bet she got you on child support?"

The guy was amazed how Solanda could read him like a book and easily piece all those facts together. She felt good knowing she was right, it was evident on the man's face. Though she concealed her prideful look by seeming more concerned, Solanda really wanted to help him out. He seemed like a good guy in her eyes compared to the scum usually in here, even in his wretched state. Only flaw she could really make out was him being seemingly too obsessed with his girlfriend's whereabouts. Even him mentioning to not want to scare his son. Maybe it was a bit try hard since his masculinity was in question not only to his girl but to himself. Most likely to assert his dominance. But given the circumstance with his child possibly affected, she understood.

"I bet you think I'm wild'in but who knows what goes on behind my back? And she got other options, not just with men but my son. Can't be on her like that 'cause she ain't having it."

"The way I see it… yes, as a woman she's got options. Probably got niggas blowing up her phone always. So show her you do too, stop hittin' her up for a bit."

"Alright, maybe?"

"And since she just shows up to your place, kick her out if she rude to you. Show her you got options too and you ain't havin' it! Make her worry about losing you. That shit'll set her ass straight. Real talk! Like, don't have her thinking she's got all the power."

"Bet!" he said sounding appreciative.

The guy had seemed more hopeful of his relationship after his and Solanda's talk. He tipped her an extra twenty dollar bill before he decided to go on his phone.

"Yo, what's your name?" he asked.

"Ariel. Yours?"

"Deon."

"Alright, take care, love."

She cruised around the club in search of another customer. Pleased with herself on how much money she's made just fuels her enough to accompany and guy feeling helpless. She watches her co-workers doing their job. She can't help but overhear the men complain to these girls in hopes of an answer. Some of these girls pretend to show interest, some are visibly not invested at all in whatever they're saying. However, neither of them can give decent feedback like Solanda can.

Solanda makes her way to the backroom, some girls are counting their money. Others are checking in the mirror, to adjust themselves being their leggings or newly implants. Solanda checks around and sees Latoya again. Latoya has been acting very standoffish lately, she's rarely talking with the other girls here. When she is on break, she goes outside alone for a smoke. Latoya's on her phone now sitting near the backdoor. Solanda heads over to catch up.

"Latoya!" she said.

"Hey."

"Hey, everything alright?" Solanda asks. "Look like someone out there's been trolling you."

"Trust me, ain't nobody out there fucking with me today. I'm all good."

"You know I normally go on about my business but I don't just hear out customers. So, I could pick your brain without being on your lap. So c'mon, what's wrong?"

Latoya put her phone away and seemed on guard for herself. She peeks at the other strippers, making sure they're not at all eavesdropping in on them. Then Solanda comes close to see what's going on.

"Solanda, I'm pregnant, have no clue who the father is."

"Nooooo, aww, c'mere." Solanda gave her a hug, consoling her. "Girl, don't even worry. It's not the end of the world."

"How not?! Some fool here had to of done it. Ain't had no other dick recent outside the Cognac room these past two months."

"Hun, listen to me… it's not like you'll get let go 'cause of this."

"You think I don't know that?! The club can't fire you if you started 'fore you got pregnant. And plus them nasty fucks up in here crave over bare showing strippers anyway. Getting all hyped off our bodies. Don't matter a fetus in our sac or silicon enhancements through our racks."

"You sure you'd wanna dance here still?" Solanda said.

"I gotta support myself somehow. And I can't keep whoring out here for money, might fuck up the baby. Just don't wanna end up like Jocelyn."

"Mm-hmm, heard she took some weird turns on her course to motherhood. Poor girl."

"Uh, yea." Latoya said. "She was giving into these mama boy's milk deprived fetish issues by doing lactating tricks for 'em."

"Seriously?"

"Yassss, ain't even had the decency to go back in the Cognac room instead pulled that shit in the bathroom."

"Honey, we will get through this." Solanda reassures her.

She gives Latoya a long hug, resting her friend's head on her breast. Upset still but feeling some relieve getting it off her chest, Latoya returns the love. Both of them hugging in their skimpy outfits.

"There, doesn't that feel good getting it off your chest, hmmm?" Solanda softly said.

"Real issue's getting it out my stomach."

"Whoa, I—"

"Girl, you know I'm playin'." Latoya laughs.

Solanda finally returned back to the customers. Latoya, now feeling more hopeful, contemplates her big changes that are to come in her life.

Kental Avenue, 6:56 P.M.

Taivy is at home relaxing on the couch. She was cooking some ribs for her kids, waiting for them to settle in the oven. Aiden is playing his video games while his sister's playing on her phone in her room. Taivy hasn't told her daughter of her father arriving and warned Aiden to not bring him up to her either.

Aiden was curious to know more about him especially since he hasn't come back. However, he knows better than to frustrate his mother with those kind of questions that Taivy classifies to both her kids as "grown-up business". Taivy sits scrolling her social media on her phone, seeing more updates pop-up on the miracle gaining more notoriety still. Updates claim that groups of people, early twenties and up, are increasing in numbers of suicide. All articles claim the suicide notes found at the scenes reveals a common reason. Everyone's loss of will to live due to them knowing where they'll end up come judgement day.

Taivy sees her friend posted a video on her social media of her walking around looking clean in her white church dress. Her friend leaves a description under the video describing how she's going to heaven and how she's feeling blessed to be where she is in life. Her screen lights up with a call from an unknown number. She figures it's probably one of the many men who she's gave out her number to but hasn't saved them as a contact yet.

"Hello?" she answers.

"Taivy, its Donny. Don't hang up!"

"Whose number are you calling me from?"

"Doesn't matter. I just had to talk really quick, weren't sure you'd pick up."

"Donny, I don't have time for this—"

"Three hundred!" he said instantly. "I'll get you that much to help out with the kids."

"I should hang up this phone right as we speak, you're offering me three hundred a month?! I know you're not—"

"A week." He overrode her. "I'll pay you weekly."

Taivy got unexpectedly silent, to both Donny and herself. She wasn't sure how serious he was or if he be consistent and stick by his word. Donny wasn't sure if she hanged up the phone believing he wasn't being genuine. He knew that she had the advantage whether to cut him off, killing his chance to know his kids. And is seemingly glad yet nervous that this is over the phone since he can feel his face looking agitated. Knowing how bitter Taivy rightfully feels, if she could see him right now she'd probably push him for more than he's offered. He fears that if it comes to that and he refuse, she might take him to court and let the child support system take him for more. Donny knows she's got all the advantage here but talks cordial to not remind her of this.

"Hello? Taivy, you there still?" he said trying to not sound desperate.

"Three hundred a week? You're serious?"

"I am. I want to spend time with them."

"For what?" she asks. "Just to take 'em out, out where?"

"Anywhere, I dunno. Around here I guess?" he said.

"You're joking right? Think I want my kids roaming around downtown Holksdale? Like things aren't crazy enough out here already?! Especially when they don't know you?"

"I'll try getting to know 'em."

"Where I barely know you?! I don't even really know what you do. How I know this ain't no drug money, huh?"

"It's clean, alright." Donny said, annoyed.

"How do I know you're not bullshitting about this so-called money you promise then?" she said. "No telling if you'll be consistent not just—"

"It'll keep coming every Sunday!"

"…not just the money but the kids. They don't need you getting them attached to you then suddenly something comes up and you don't show up anymore."

"Taivy…"

Donny stops himself, understanding her misgivings about whatever positive relationship they might form. He hopes that if he lets her express herself, not being interrupted or being told she's wrong, that she might even sense something has changed. Maybe she won't fall to her second thoughts about granting him time. Or maybe she'll hear herself out loud and refuse. Donny was really risking his chance but Donny just sat back and listened.

"I don't want you making them feel like they're not a priority in your life." Taivy said. "They're not that young anymore, alright? They weren't born yesterday to just forget all a sudden you came into their lives. I don't need no one hurting my babies."

Donny heard her express true genuine concern, he could hear it in her voice. It was so large she could've been in the room right close to him. He knew he'd have to choose his next words very carefully to really assure her that everything would be fine. To let him get a chance to make up for years of hell she probably struggled through to feed their kids.

"Aiden plays games, right? I'll get him some games, we'll play together always. I don't know much when it comes to Lauren but we'll get there. I'll get involved whenever you or they need me. You've got my number so—"

"No I don't."

"I'll text you my number and you can dial my phone if anything urgent pops up. I'll get involved as much as you allow me but it's up to you."

"Mm-hmm."

Hoping after he made a convincing plan and reminding her it all comes down to her, maybe she'd feel a little more respected. Maybe she'll believe he takes her seriously now yet he still awaits her answer.

"One more thing…" she says before fully making up her mind. "…why?"

"Why what?"

"Why after all these years, you now wanna get involved, huh? You feeling ill?! Out trying impress these sluts?! Why now?"

"I'm their dad and their both my angels, honest-to-god."

Taivy suddenly realized the ribs were in the oven still. Quickly she rushed to put on a kitchen mitten then pulls out the tray of barbecue smothered ribs out. She sets the food down on the counter for her kids.

"KIDSSSSSS, COME GET SOME FOOD!"

"Taivy, you there still?"

"Alright look…" Taivy hesitantly began. "I'm about to go but I work a double shift next Friday." She doesn't feel like paying her neighbors to watch over them. Then offers a chance to prove that he can be responsible enough to supervise them for a few hours Friday.

†

York Avenue 6:36 P.M.

Another ordeal from the hospital had Essie exhausted. She wanted to relax with Larissa, but Yanie Juergens had called to come over. Then they invite Jovanny Gibbs. Essie wasn't too eager to have anyone else, but Larissa would've liked seeing them. The four hang out in the living room. Essie's flopped on the couch with Yanie. Larissa sat on the floor besides them with Yanie fiddling with her braids. Jovanny's on a soft armchair.

They're all watching TV.

As they sat in silence, Essie began talking about the craziness at work. Jovanny laughed since coincidently enough him and Essie discussed the crucifixion challenge. Then she brought up Keith Parkour. Belittling Keith's logic about living his life to the fullest. On the other hand, Yanie shrugged about the declaration of her eternal damnation.

This prompts Yanie to bring up that random woman complaining to them a few days ago. Her name was Lisa. Lisa just wanted to open up about her going to hell. She claimed that she was a pure person. Essie and Yanie were confused as to why she's trying so hard to convince them. Then whipped out her phone showing the website where her name was placed. Essie was perplexed by this. Lisa's name was under heaven on the opposite side of hell. Essie showed it on her phone; Yanie prayed for this lady to just leave. Once Lisa realized it, she confesses that she's dyslexic and just couldn't read it right. Once she left, Essie could read the irritation on Yanie's face.

"It's a shame she couldn't read the room either." Essie said.

"*RIGHT!*" Yanie agreed. "Don't nobody wanna hear this shit. I would've lost what little religion I have if she ain't leave. On God, she stayed pissing me off."

Larissa smiled, looking at Essie. "I told you, it's a miracle for this generation. *Let's GOOOOOO!*" she merrily said.

Essie drily groaned. "Yes, ma'am. I guess I'm just too old and cantankerous for this nonsense." She mentions how God was once viewed as a worldwide judge that people worshipped and helped bring self-reflection. "Now The Lord's seen as this great omnipresence to witness all types of human foolishness."

"Preach." Jovanny agreed. Then reminds Larissa of these awful decisions people are making because of this. The crucifixion challenge, being hospitalized and Lisa. "As for Lisa. What she took, I'll spell it out for her, was a huge L."

Larissa shrugged. "I get it. My generation's all backwards now. But I ain't lose faith in humanity just yet."

"I have." Essie bluntly said, bringing up the crucifixion challenge. "People aren't gonna learn unless they get hospitalized or end up taking that dirt nap challenge."

That statement didn't bring any response from Larissa. She simply dismisses it, retaining her beliefs. Then began munching on her bag of chips.

"La-la." Yanie called, watching her eat. "You sharing?"

"These hands." Larissa playfully said, bawling up her fist. Then pours her some chips. "You still jacking cars?"

This question annoyed Essie since she wants Yanie to keep those illegal acts private. Silence dropped. Yanie was hesitant to tell Larissa about it.

"It's all good." Larissa smiled. "If you still out jacking cars, that's between you and God."

"Well, I just got you to come up out them chips." Yanie said, playfully tickling Larissa with her foot.

Despite what impact this miracle has on society, Yanie dismisses the existence of God. Everyone's overreactions are ridiculous since she claims there is no heaven or hell. Then brings up Catholic people she's known that don't adhere to every teaching in the bible.

"Shit, don't let me be our lord and savior." Yanie laughed. "Best believe I'll turn to the entire world and yell out '*deuces*' before I block off the sun."

Essie laughs. "All of mankind now just plunged into darkness."

"Just making the ultimate sacrifice as a loving God."

"As a shady God at that." Larissa adds.

"You can't even bargain with the lord. You could bargain with Yanie's self-righteous ass." Jovanny said.

"You can't con your way for amends. That would be cheap." Essie said.

Yanie looks to Larissa. "You can easily get absolved."

"But at what cost?" Larissa asks.

"A bunch of hardened confessions."

"Say less." Larissa agreed.

Jovanny went to the kitchen and came back with a bowl of popcorn. A loud crunching sound is made by him when they're watching TV. Yanie asked for some popcorn. Jovanny jokingly ignores her since it irritates her.

"Jovanny, let me get some." Yanie groans.

"*Say please.*" Jovanny smiled.

"Nigga, what?"

"*Say please.*"

"Man, please these nuts."

"Close enough." Jovanny shrugs, pouring her some popcorn. Then passes the bowl around for everyone.

Essie recalls Yanie being treated by a guy who asked her out to pizza earlier. Then ate some snacks from her kitchen and now wanting popcorn. Yanie shrugs it off.

"I wonder what Denise has to say about that." Essie mocks. All of them explode with laughter.

†

Given the circumstances of citizens acting crazy, police have been more on the lookout for potential incidents that may occur in the city. Officer Lambeth and officer Colthirst are on their regular patrol route. They had just arrested a drunken man for masturbating in a public park. The bearded man is passed out in the back with handcuffs on.

In the meantime, the officers are playing a game they conjured up on their time working together. It's called Belt Check. While their cruising around, the driver pulls close to any random driver who isn't wearing their seatbelt. The driver stares at them until they eventually are scared enough to put their seatbelt on. If the driver doesn't within thirty seconds than that officer loses that round. This game always emphasized their power and made them laugh.

Officer Colthirst is behind the wheel this time. He drives closely towards a black jeep driven by a teenage girl. They're slowly driving together. Colthirst's head is facing her with a neutral facial expression. Her frail eyes flickers towards him. Both her hands are holding the wheel. However, her seatbelt was on. The cops had trailed towards another vehicle. A grey Honda suspiciously at the speed limit driven by a thirty-year-old man.

The man noticed officer Colthirst's eyes sternly locked on him. His seatbelt wasn't fastened. Officer Lambeth commenced the time limit. The man in the vehicle tries looking normal but keeps contemplating why he's watched. Ten seconds have elapsed. Officer Lambeth gladly announcing this drives officer Colthirst to get annoyed. Not by his partner but from this driver not realizing the most simple safety precaution. Twenty seconds have now elapsed. The sirens suddenly start alarming. This causes the man to realize his mistake. His head shot downward, struggling to put two and two together, until he finally snapped his seatbelt on. Then officer Colthirst smiled and sped forth.

"Man, that's cheating." Lambeth hissed.

"Nope. Still counts." Colthirst said, sounding satisfied.

This man eventually started waking up.

This quickly annoys officer Colthirst, making him groan. Officer Lambeth instantly ignores whatever is to come. Once he's conscious enough, he instantly starts ranting about how he's innocent. He kept repeating how he was framed for this. Then announced that the women were lying on him. As he's being ignored, he starts talking about how all police officers are going to hell.

"I KNOW MY RIGHTS! MY BODY, MY CHOICE!"

"I can't believe you had me cuff him." Colthirst groaned.

Lambeth shook his head. "I could've had you collect the evidence instead."

His hollering from the backseat grew irritating. Promising that he was being framed. Officer Colthirst snapped about him being caught masturbating.

"You tried to lie when we arrested you." Colthirst said. "You just beat around the bush, no pun intended."

"As God as my witness, the lord sees everything." He arrogantly yelled.

"You think that shit will hold any ground to testify in court." Colthirst hissed as his partner began snickering.

"When your time comes, you'll have to answer to God."

"And your judgement day will be set before a judge and juror a week from today." Lambeth calmly states.

As they're driving, the man in cuffs continues to cry about this whole ordeal still.

† Chapter 6: Shut up, Lauren!

On Kelvin's Street, there are people walking on the sidewalk late this evening. At night, there are various noises being heard. The acceleration of honking cars, the crowd of many people and the occasional police sirens patrolling here. Some people passing by heard a loud commotion from inside one of the many delis. The sound kept having passing adults either turn their heads or peek over to the right side of the deli.

And this disturbance had come from a small deli called Quarter Likes. All that mysterious uproar was heard from outside, the sound of people hollering at each other. Including shattering glass, or objects clashing resulting from falling on the ground. Then the abrupt ruckus progressed with a smoke detector sounding off, momentarily causing the screaming inside to halt but then it resumed shortly after.

More adults begin to slow down, recording the deli from outside. Through the recording are of shadows that're detected from inside. One shadow remains still on the left while the opposite side moves in an eccentric motion. The shadow appears as a bigger, widen grown man waving his arms around. The shadow keeps circling still as the other shadow observes from a distance.

The yelling from in there grows louder and louder, now attracting a few more people recording from different angles for a better view posted for social media. Whatever is happening inside had apparently became the most interesting thing that night. But like most people who post seemingly cool things wanting to garner more views, the actuality of what can't be seen despite the outer view, may in fact be nothing special and can ruin it. None fear of possibly getting harmed, at least not from their slanted point of view. Yet all are too afraid to get a different perspective by investigating inside. However, what settled their uncertainty of how to know what's going on behind this wall, was the presence of someone in a higher position: the police.

Officer Colthirst and officer Lambeth had pulled up by the curve with their siren loud and alerting. The two come out the car. Everyone observes them as well; some even through their phones. Both men appeared stern and mindful of what transpires through the deli window. Officer Lambeth knows they all desire the full scope of what's happening as evidence for their phones. Even though it's his job, him and his partner's knowledge of what they can't have boosts up his own value. Lambeth would take any small grace while on the job. Especially something like this since most citizens disrespect officers; feeling stereotyped out as being corrupt or racist like some others patrolling Holksdale. Officer Colthirst is fully aware too of what's happening and how this might escalate into hurting other people. He begins to gesture for everyone to keep a clear distance away from Quarter Likes and his partner follows behind him. Seeing citizens obey and not question his authority had officer Colthirst exhilarated with himself.

Once everyone is secured away, the two head inside; Colthirst cautious and Lambeth being completely alert. The door opens making a *ding-ding* noise as it closed, alerting the two men arguing inside. The man on the left of them is the cashier behind the counter who remains still. He might've been considered calm had they not noticed the wooden bat lied flat on the counter. Than the other on the right was an overweight Hispanic man dressed in a black, flat wig while in a glittered, yellow dress. He must have been transgender but besides that, he acted stranger.

The man was spiraling around where an aisle was separated with foods prior to all of this. He had knocked over the shelves of merchandise leaving on the floor; shattered glass oozing salsa, candy bars, packets of chips and oatmeal filled cookies. Both men turned all their attention to the officers. Lambeth and Colthirst turned to the cashier to question how this all started.

"Sir," Officer Colthirst began. "What exactly ha—"

The sound of a packet bursting like gunfire scattering plenty chips everywhere startled the two. The Hispanic man stepped hard on a few packets as he stared at everyone with his widen eyes, showing off a genuine look of confusion. His body language kept slightly rocking, unable to hold still for a second.

Officer Colthirst tries to resume but is interrupted yet again by him crushing a bag of candy on the ground. Colthirst is visibly irritated, Lambeth remains patient. He gestures for his partner to handle him and Lambeth nods. As he starts coming toward him, the man gets antsy now.

Lambeth halts as he slowly raised his hands, gesturing that he is no threat. The man lifts up his glittered dress and scurries around behind the shelf on to the next aisle. Aggravated Lambeth screams: *"Shit!"* Then dashes for him as his partner gets involved.

"Sir, stop right there!" Colthirst said. "We're here to—"

"Don't call me 'sir'!" he demanded.

"We don't know your na—"

"I AM A WOMAN!"

"There he goes again with that shit." the cashier screamed. Continuing about him entering with not enough money. "Claims he misplaced his wallet."

"PURSE!" he screamed as he sprints from the cops.

"Whatever… claimed he had it in his dress. Then starts acting crazy when I tell him to leave."

"Just like God himself… telling me where to go. Just like cops telling me to stand still. I ain't heading to jail or hell!" he said as he pushed down a whole shelf of food, causing a bigger mess.

"Fuckin' shit!" the cashier groaned.

"He made fun of me." The man explained in a fast yet high pitched voice. "He made fun of my dress, my fate, my weave! I'll have you cancelled!"

"He didn't have any money then went off about going to hell!"

"And you flamed me 'cause of that!"

"Who the hell comes in here dressed like that? Hell yeah, I'ma roast you, bro!"

"Enough out of you!" Colthirst yells at the cashier.

The man had been caught in an aisle with Officer Colthirst and Lambeth blocking opposite ends. The man mirrored Lambeth's on-guard movements. His head kept turning all around the store hoping to find an escape.

"Sir—" Officer Colthirst slipped up. "Ma'am, I'll need for you to get on the ground!"

"Listen to us, okay?" Lambeth reassures him: "Remain calm. Everything'll be alright."

"No, no, no." he frantically said then with no way out, he drops to his knees. "Please lord give me the strength to overcome these pigs in my time—"

"*GO!*" Lambeth screams.

Both officers tussle over him. Disrupting his prayer by seizing both arms. Shelves are pushed forward with Officer Colthirst colliding into them, spilling bottles of pills, more food and his wig caught up. The man groans loud for God as he struggles to break free. He gets pinned face down to the ground; they both can see he has taken some drugs.

"Ma'am, what've you taken?" Officer Colthirst asks.

"Bet'cha hormonal pills with his crossdressing ass!"

"Not enough…" the man groaned.

"Enough what?" Lambeth asked.

"Jesus!" he screams. "I ain't took enough Jesus in my heart."

"Alright, but what have you ingested?" Lambeth clarified.

"Praise Jesus!"

"*PREACH GIRL!*" the cashier mocked him.

"Shut your mouth!" Colthirst yelled at the cashier. Once he did, they didn't hear another peep out of him.

"I'm on fire." He said sounding scared. "I'm going to hell for everything Carlos did."

"Carlos who? W-who's that?" Lambeth asks.

"Me," he somberly confessed. "He's who I was before I became Carlotta."

Both can feel how he went from extremely tense to slowly unfolding. Not just his muscles but from the sound of his tone too. What began as a masculine tone screaming from what could be heard from outside, to sounding as an effeminate somewhat voluptuous woman, to a now regressed, jittering voice.

"Carlos wasn't nothing but scum to everyone. I wanted to be better than he ever was, so Carlotta wouldn't suffer for his sins. *N-now look at me.* That dick will always be a part of me and there's no severing that… *it's hopeless.*" She begun to weep.

Officer Colthirst look to his partner and Lambeth looks back. Both understand the factors that brought her here. They can see through her, that inside was someone who was ashamed of their past and wanted to evolve into someone better who removed all ties from oneself that trailed with her. Lambeth offers a pitiful pat on her back.

They simultaneously helped Carlotta up to her feet. Her head was still sulking down, staring down to her dress. All hope to be a better person had deflated especially from her position. And the two can sense that while they had her by each hand. Officer Lambeth picked up her wig and placed it steadily on her head. While Officer Colthirst on the other hand, had stared directly back at the cashier. Hinting for him to keep quiet still and the cashier silently looked down.

Carlotta appeared to be coming down off whatever she was on but was still placed in the back of the cop car. People were recording the whole walkthrough. Both officers who normally take glee in detaining someone but not this time. Carlotta wasn't scum or a criminal, just an unfortunate circumstance that brought them together tonight on Kelvin's Street.

†

The next day on the news, recent reports have come out about a certain fast-food place located in midtown. Open Saws had been a small food restaurant serving the unhealthiest foods in all of midtown Holksdale. Fries basically covered in salt, nuggets not even made from actual chicken, most of the grease used to enhance the flavor. It was really advertising their ice cream sundaes as their 'summertime munch specials.' However, there had been many allegations of health hazards reported by certain customers who'd gotten sick from leaving there. But most customers who weren't giving bad reviews had outweighed the others.

This restaurant had been one of the most popular places to dine at in midtown. With headlines recently not advertising any food nor toys or better deals, but for an incident caused by one of their employees that impacted their business. Their employee who made the news, a twenty-two-year-old Caucasian male named Timofey Souvenir. The news came out that this man who worked here as a cashier, part-time cook with all the other employees had admitted to certain things he'd done there that made big notoriety in this online video that has gone viral.

Timofey Souvenir had admitted in a video that he filmed himself of his disgusting behavior while handling food at Open Saws. He isn't just an employee but a resident from uptown Holksdale. It is reported that his intentions working there wasn't to just flip burgers and cook fries. Souvenir was a former employee of a popular uptown restaurant called Great Drakes, that had been shut down years ago. He washed dishes in the kitchen as his ethnic co-workers cooked food and served it.

Souvenir had lost his job due to the false health hazard made by an ethnic person working at a rival midtown restaurant: Biggup. This was the hugest factor keeping that town from being seen as racist thanks to their large ethnic workers and vast variety of cultural foods. However, having this ethnic person cause the loss of multiple jobs there; many fast-food businesses refused to hire minorities.

Great Drakes, seething many uptown residents from it being gone, had brought people from all three parts in Holksdale together. Without it being there and midtown being too stubborn to hold any accountability; it began an ongoing war between the towns to ruin each other's business. After Timofey had seen the aftermath of what midtown started, he along with many citizens from uptown, hated their town. Especially as they had denounced businesses located there with their midtown propaganda videos. Leading to minorities protesting and slandering the town as ignorant; even with Timofey seeing why, to him it was justifiably so.

This further proved his point when he was hired as a cashier at a bakery located uptown. Timofey had worked there for not even a full month before it had been torched on fire one night. The next day, surveillance had revealed that it was three men who had broken in pouring gasoline everywhere. They set the place on fire and were arrested the same day. In the news, the three were identified as residential men from midtown. Footage revealed a confession from the court that it was in retaliation to uptown folks vandalizing their movie theatre.

Timofey confessed in the video that he was enraged by everything midtown had caused and how they still had their many businesses while the best one in uptown was forever gone. He decided to attack them from the inside by applying to Open Saws. Souvenir said during the interview that he lied about being ashamed of how his town had been violating parts of midtown and exploiting his white privilege. He knew people there labeled uptown folks intolerant with no care for ethnic people's plight in life. Basically, telling the head manager interviewing him what she wanted to hear.

As the video revealed his plan, it led up to him laying out his tactics on working there. His intent was to have this place (*the most popular fast-food joints in Midtown*) to have its reputation tarnished not just there but all over Holksdale. He revealed him spitting in every order he had to make. To masturbating his semen into customer's shakes; having recommended it for half price. Leaving dead animals and insects near dining tables. People were complaining to management about unsanitary environment here, but it wasn't loud enough to shut it down or be inspected.

Timofey Souvenir has been fired by the restaurant since this video leaked. Open Saws is making a lawsuit against him and questioning employees who worked with him. And he admits to coming forward with all of this as his way of repentance into heaven. Then claims he wasn't in a proper mindset when he committed the offense. Even without apologizing for any of this.

At Jovanny's place, he's in the living room watching all of this on the news. He sits there on the couch drinking some beer, gleeful that he's never ate there himself. The news shows clips of people who've eaten there being interviewed and many protesting for that place to now be shut down. Solanda comes home from work with some coffee, she sees him on the couch.

Holksdale Midtown Penitentiary 2:36 P.M.

Larissa Sheppard and Essie Chu came to pay Danielle another visit. Essie's shadow hovers over her as she awaits her mom. She notices Larissa's slight disappointment of being separated again by glass, having to speak to her over the phone.

To Larissa, it was almost unfair how each gap between their visits just led up to a minimum of playing catch-up through glass. She tries to request a sit down so she could hug her mother but Danielle herself prefers these instead. She never gave neither Essie nor Larissa an explanation as to why, but Larissa speculated many reasonable excuses: *she probably doesn't want me catching anything; can't nobody be seen showing no love in prison walls; she'll probably break down hugging up on me.*

In fact, she couldn't really recall the last her mom hugged her by choice. That clouded her thoughts even more. She'd barely ever got one when her mother was free and isn't getting one now. Larissa can picture it in her head, but it just made her desire it more. What upset her most was knowing the only thing in the way of her and her mother hugging it out wasn't the glass itself. But the answer was perfectly clear through glass: her mother. Essie can see her face seemingly more saddened, as if she's got a lot on her mind. However, Larissa herself is a forgiving soul who's mature enough to not let that hinder them from communicating.

Essie decides it's probably best to let Danielle be alone with her child. She knows once she's here, she'll spend some time talking about her commissary money for a little instead. Essie tells Larissa she'll wait outside and to tell her mother that her funds are secured. Larissa's concealed her joy of them being left alone and nodded. Essie left and immediately, afterwards she could see her mom being brought forth.

"Hi ma." Larissa happily said.

"Hey, baby." Danielle greets as she searched around. "Everything good?"

"Uh-huh. Essie's outside by the way, said your commissary's all taken care of."

"Aw, good." Danielle said sounding relieved. "That's wassup."

"Ma, are you ok? You've got marks on your arms."

Larissa had noticed heroin scarring on Danielle's fragile, shaky arms. Though Larissa wasn't exactly sure what caused it she had hoped no one hurt her since. Danielle shook her head, brushing it off like it's nothing. However, it was a genuine response Larissa picked up on since she'd done it plenty before outside of jail. That worried Larissa more, being left with the open option of it being self-inflicted. She prayed her mom wasn't contemplating suicide in there. Danielle can see on her face that she remained worried still and had that keeping her from conversing still. Essie wasn't exactly sure what it was but had assumed it was drug related.

"Baby, I just got my check-up in here." She lied. "Just the regular flu shots 'cause up in there's dirty, alright? So, tell me what you been up to? How you been?"

"Ok, I guess…" She mumbled. "I just miss you a lot, just be thinking about you a lot. Hoping you're alright."

"Don't nobody gotta worry, I'm good."

Larissa knew her mom wasn't keen on having her time wasted especially with her not saying much. She didn't want to remind her of her situation by caring about the ins and outs of prison. And she had already felt like nothing but a burden on her mother sometimes. So instead brought up a more interesting topic.

"You hear about that whole second coming miraculous sign worldwide?"

"I have, that's all these bitches up in here be talking about nowadays. Hell, to the point where gangs of inmates join in on a circle out on the yard. And not to cheer on no fights or kick off no riot but to drop to they knees and pray. Praying for forgiveness of their sins and shit."

Danielle goes on a whole rant on how ridiculous it is seeing that all around the world. She and many inmates were aware of it through the televised news in the T.V. room. Then begins talking about how prisoners had turned themselves in recently and how many others here are reacting to their fate revealed.

"I guess you're not praying for forgiveness then?"

"No, baby." Danielle scoffs. "Larissa, I pray you don't believe in such stupid mess."

"I see it more of an eye opener to enlightenment."

"Only eye-opener of use in here is to watch yo' back." Danielle said. "Not have it turned while on your knees with yo' eyes shut. Best way having yo' head caved in. Like, we done had a crowd of apparently guilty newcomers who turned themselves in."

"That's good, one way to repent, I guess." Larissa added sounding not too confident. "Face the consequences of their actions?"

"Consequences dispense to those unfortunate enough to suffer them, like myself." Danielle groaned. "Not to those who damn well choose whenever they please to endure through them."

"Ma, your name is under hell on that placement." Larissa shamefully said. From how her mom talks, she feels more fearful for her mother's fate. She sounds no different than Essie. Their time together is limited (*and while hesitant to annoy her with this still*), Larissa hopes that she'll try to repent for forgiveness for her.

"Ma, I don't mean to keep pressin' you..." Larissa said in a lower uncertain voice. "But it would do you good, especially up in here. Maybe on your way back to your cell or before you eat dinner."

"I'll pray this place blesses me with a decent-ass meal."

"Or we could do it here together." Larissa hopefully said.

"So, we finna pretend this fuckin' glass ain't here then, huh?! And hold hands praying to get me up in God's good graces. Baby, mama's alright."

"I don't think you are." Larissa said, her voice regressing.

She confessed on already hating seeing her mother in this hellhole every chance she gets. Plus, I'm heading to heaven, and I just can't bear the thought of a whole afterlife without you there neither. "I wanna see you long after I'm dead and buried. So please… for me, ma?"

"LARISSA, QUIT ACTIN' STUPID!" Danielle hollered as she looked around for any guards closing in. "Miss me with this bullshit about the afterlife and rekindled spirits and shit! Look at you, all delicate over some damn, fool-ass shit like this. *AND FIX YOUR DAMN FACE UP!"*

With all her might, Larissa tried keeping a straight face, not to let her emotions get the best of her. Danielle always had this way (ever since Larissa was a kid) of making her daughter always feel mistaken. From her point of view as a child, Danielle seemed always sure of herself with almost everything she was talking about. If Larissa ever made a small mistake or wasn't too sure of something, Danielle would always contradict her. She'd broadcast to her how wrong she was, no matter how miniscule.

She always knew her mother was smart; Danielle had excelled greatly academically back in high school and somewhat in college. There were certificates proving how intelligent she was. There was that notion ingrained deeply inside Larissa that would always have her second-guessing herself. She'd never felt mentally superior nor assertive enough to be in the same intelligence bracket of even arguing with her mom. Larissa wasn't an academic prodigy which made her feel even less than; since she was not up to par to fill in her mother's shoes.

Her mom's dominant presence had overshadowed her, feeling inferior to Danielle's concrete opinion, like always. Of course, Danielle's criticism of her made Larissa withdraw back from sticking to her beliefs. She draws back to this recurring thought that has stuck with her since she was a child and became too her belief: *Mama knows best!*

"Goddamn, how old is you?!" Danielle groans. "Shit, I'd say '*don't make me get my belt*' if most bitches weren't up in here hanging themselves with 'em. Especially due to the lord's sacred list."

Danielle pulls herself together before the guard enters to escort her out.

"Can't believe I done wasted the last couple minutes hearin' this shit—*see this is why I don't be bringing your ass to church!*" Danielle snapped as she got up. "Ugh, lord give me strength."

Alright ma, that's a start: Larissa thought to herself.

Danielle returned, "no goodbye nor I love you". Larissa would've initiated first but she feels that she's provoked her mother enough for today. It was hopeless for Danielle to self-reflect on her actions (*even if in front of a glass with her daughter*) and her surroundings wouldn't help. Despite letting her mom get the last word, God still has the final say. Larissa momentarily fell back to the idea of them together in heaven. Even with her mom constantly being right from the past, her past actions had brought them both here. Yet feeling wrong all the time, it could have been a pleasant surprise to her mom if she was right.

Kental Avenue, 5:03 P.M.

The next day, Donny drove to Taivy's place to pick up Aiden and Lauren. He got out of his car and texted Taivy that he's arrived. He lit up a cigarette, hoping to get a good smoke before the kids come outside.

The door opens, Donny automatically stomps out his cigarette. He watches as Taivy comes out in her waitress uniform with her kids alongside. He expected them to be arguing or coming out loud but that wasn't the case. Lauren had been on her phone with her earbuds in and Aiden was close by his mother talking to her. Donny just studied them all together; observing his family how they interact on the daily.

"Hey, so we're good?" Donny asked Taivy.

"I hope so, where are y'all going?"

Donny informed her that he's driving them around midtown because there's many stores. They'll probably grab some food.

"WE'RE HEADING TO MIDTOWN… THEY GOT PREVIEWS FOR NEW CONSOLES COMING SOON!" Aiden enthusiastically yelled.

"Baby, baby, enough of all that yelling. Don't you see grown-ups are talking?!" Taivy sweetly said.

"Sorry mom…" Aiden said as he gained back his composure.

"No, sweat little man," Donny said. "We could head by the nearest game shop there."

His son's face lit up once more.

Donny then looks over to his daughter who's still locked on her phone. "And you must be Lauren."

"Uh-huh, hi." She nonchalantly replied as she took out one earbud.

"Put the phone down!" Taivy firmly said.

"Nah, it's fine. Let her be on it. I ain't got much to say."

"Really? Donny, don't undermine me in front of my kids."

"No one's undermining anyone in front of OUR kids, I'm just saying it's all good, that's it."

"Just trying to get them to know their father." Taivy said.

"Like you said, 'grown folks are talking', I don't mind her headphones. We've got a whole evening for us to reconnect."

"Reconnect?! Nobody but me knows you here."

"And we're gonna get better acquainted once we pull outta here."

"Pull out in what?!" Taivy said as she approached his car. Peeking inside, checking its safety for her kids. Both parents beginning to get frustrated with each other. Donny sees that Lauren's finally off her phone to watch, Aiden moves around unable to keep still. Taivy seems skeptical of any possible substances inhabited inside there prior to now but finds nothing.

"You done?" Donny asks. "I already wrapped up the evidence."

"Everything checks out." Taivy begrudgingly expressed.

"You're not planning on keeping them for the night, right? Not going to introduce them to no unsavory characters, am I right?"

"Taivy, for Christ's sake, can I spend some time with our goddamn kids. You're overthinking things."

"Don't fucking swear at me in front of them and there's no overthinking, not when it comes to my kids."

"OUR KIDS!" Donny reminds her. Including that it's hot out. They've got these kids standing out in the hot sun. Except for Aiden, moving all around. "Look at him, he's trying to leave too."

"You're lucky I gotta head to work." Taivy said as she turned to her kids. "Y'all are gonna be out today with your father, least until I get off work. Call me if anything, because best believe I'll call to check in."

"Call my cell if you want, ain't nothing bad gonna happen." Donny added.

"Love you, love you." Taivy says as she hugs them both. Then gives Donny that look of '*you will be held accountable if anything bad were to happen on your watch*' and went to her car. Donny playfully extends out his hands for a hug as she pulls out the driveway, annoying her more. Donny puts on a friendly face to make his kids more comfortable. The two were exuding sweat, waiting to leave in his car. Donny unlocks it open with his keys. As soon as the sound happened, Aiden and Lauren immediately went for the doors and climbed in.

Donny got in the driver's seat and drove off. Aiden and Lauren are both in the backseat. Her on her phone, him checking out the window and occasionally peeking at Donny. The car was quiet, neither kid initiated any sort of interaction with him. The sound of the car moving was all to be heard. Through Donny's mind was how to move their relationship forward. Maybe with his first-born Lauren, but she had her earbuds in, so he focuses on his son.

"Aiden, you been good?"

"Mm-hmm." Aiden answered innocently.

"How's school been?"

"We're out for the summer."

"Right, right, ok. Glad you're not in summer school."

"Lauren is though."

"Don't go telling him my business!" Lauren said as she slaps his arm.

"Ain't nothing to be embarrassed about." Donny said. Admitting he had to go at the worse time of school, his senior year. Kept skipping classes, not knowing how much absences add up. Couldn't walk the aisle to receive his diploma like everyone else. "Instead, I had to make up economics and health during summer then I was eligible to get my diploma."

"So, mom graduated before you?" Aiden asks.

"Maybe. I ain't ever knew what year she was in."

"So, how'd y'all meet then?"

"A long time ago, I met your mother. Then something happened that had us together for a good while."

"But y'all two are apart, so must've not been that great." Lauren said in a snobbish tone.

"Looking back at it now, you're right… it ain't." Donny said, as his eyes dart at her through the rear-view.

The silence came again. Lauren had music from her earbuds so loud that Donny could hear it upfront.

"So, son, tell me what you've been up to this summer."

Aiden happily expressed him going to the carnival last week, hanging out with friends, and playing video games.

"You play any games?" Aiden asks.

"Oh yeah," Donny said. Revealing he plays multiplayer first-person shooter games mostly. He's got it set up on his flat-screen and theatre stereo.

"YOU DO?!" Aiden ecstatically said.

"Great, got him all hyped up." Lauren flatly said.

"I be wanting to play them shooter games, but mom won't ever let me. All I can do is watch the gameplay channels online."

Donny understandably nods. Sharing that he does, that sometimes, but most of those content creators are annoying with their stupid, loud, unfunny commentary. Donny names a few of his favorite games like Arsenal Heavy 2, Ferocity Road: Apocalyptic Tales. And he just recently pre-ordered Lucifer's Blade Shed Gory.

"I want that game so bad!" Aiden said. "The updates I hear are pretty lit, I hear."

"I know your mom forbids you but maybe one day I'll let you watch the gameplay on my flat-screen. Minus the annoying commentary. As long as you can come?"

"If Aiden's there it'll be nothing but annoying commentary." Lauren mocks, elaborating on how she often overhears him playing in his room with his friends. *"Go this way, head back that way, fallback, fallback!"*

"Shut up, Lauren!" Aiden squealed.

"You're always doing that when I'm playing games on my phone!"

"Hey y'all two, c'mon. Chill out back there."

Donny was glad to be building at least some rapport with his son. Lauren went back to her phone. Aiden to be seemed more comfortable back there. Donny felt Lauren's absence though and there's no point of ignoring her.

"Lauren, I hear you're always at your friend's house?"

"Uh-huh or just out with mom shopping." She flatly said.

"Ok, cool. And you're in summer school?"

"Yeah, for math. Had a bad teacher."

"God, I hated math coming up. You not on your phone during class, huh?" Donny jokingly asks.

"Nope, mom just bought it for my birthday."

Donny felt a little embarrassed for not remembering her birthday passed nor that being able to recall when it was. She had this kind of reserved attitude of divulging what little she felt only if asked. Lauren doesn't even make eye contact with him; she answers each question while on her phone. She finally broke focus with her phone by glimpsing outside, the area was unrecognizable to her. There were coffee shops with wide glass windows where you could see customers sitting together at tables.

"Y'all don't recognize midtown?!" Donny asks. "Thought you went with your mama to buy your phone?"

"No, I said she bought it for me, I barely go shopping with her. And it was a surprise gift… I wasn't there."

"Welp, we're in midtown." Donny announced, clarifies here is much safer than traveling around all of creation.

"What we got planned?" Aiden asked. "Can we go eat first?"

"Yea, I'm hungry." Lauren added.

"Don't worry kids, I got you." Donny assured them. "I know just the spot."

Donny accelerates around the corner, nearest to their destination. He pulled up, the sight of both his kids' faces lit up, their hungry prayers soon to be answered.

Inside the place, Donny, Aiden and Lauren each carry their own food to an empty table. They watch as their dad scanned the table first for any sauce stains, spilt liquid or prior crumbs left behind. The table was clear, now covered in food bought by Donny.

Lauren had herself small fries with a packet of honey mustard along with small nuggets. Aiden, sitting close next to him, had a large fry with chili barbeque glazed tenders, lastly topped off with a big cheeseburger he'd already bit into before they reached the table. The cheeseburger covered in teeny bite marks all over, like a malnourished mouse finally having stumbled across food and indulged quickly in it. Aiden also digs deeper in his bag and his skinny fingers brushed on something.

"Cool." Aiden said in a surprised child-based tone. He pulled out a toy airplane from the bag. It took up his whole tiny palm as Aiden grasped it, held it up near the window.

Donny glimpsed to his daughter, where they both share a smile to Aiden's adorable innocence. So childlike that he's oblivious to them and everything else; just lost in his imaginary realm of being in the clouds.

"You ain't get a toy, Lauren?" Donny asked seeming concerned.

"I did." She said as she shows off plastic sunglasses. Then shrugs it off, suggests probably handing them over to Aiden to play with.

"That's nice." Donny mumbles as he chews into his corn.

"You sure love corn huh?" his daughter said.

"Yup. Especially on a cob. Can't stand it though when they touch on my potatoes." He said as he brushes corn alone to the side of his plate with his spoon.

"Same." Lauren agrees. "It's better when you get to bite into it, but ma does it different." Taivy has all the corn in a bowl for them to pour into her kids' plates because Aiden can barely eat them off the cob. He'll just fidget with it in his mouth. She separates it from the rest of food on his plate.

"Ah, picky eater. Gets it from me."

"Do all picky eaters groan when they eat." Lauren teases Aiden on his odd sounds when chewing and drinking. "Aiden sits at the end of the table sounding like a bum when he eats. Either his food's touching and he complains, or he suggests on how to rearrange his plate." Her eyes trail over at him. "Beggars can't be choosers."

"And closed mouths don't get fed." Donny protests. "He's a growing boy. Can't you see how skinny he is?"

"Yeesssss!" Lauren agreed. Including the amount of food he already eats. Multiple fruit snacks, bags of chips, vanilla ice cream, popsicles, and sodas. Lauren mentions how much Taivy loves to cook for them too.

"I remember your mother's cooking." Donny said. Telling of how he'd have her cook for him a bunch back then. Used to broil chicken with all these different spices. Baked macaroni and cheese. Baking brownies, chocolate cake, muffins and cupcakes. Couldn't get enough of her ribs too. The aroma of food being prepared always made him try foods he'd never on his own.

"Hey, next time I see y'all, bring over some brownies in a container for your dad, eh?"

"I got you." Lauren nicely agrees.

They all return to eating their food, Aiden still playing with his toy. Lauren on her phone while finishing her meal. She spots her brother peeking at her remaining nuggets and she blesses him one. Donny comes back from getting a refill; he watches how well-behaved his kids are. Both beautiful kids, Taivy raised them right. Which had Donny feel like he missed out all these years. He was glad they were getting along but so far most of their conversations only had his kids engaged if the topic somehow revolved around them. Donny knew he couldn't be mad since he was selfish first for leaving them. Even doing all of this had been for his own gain and he knew it. These thoughts crossing his mind led him to something to discuss with them that was fascinating.

On the other side of the restaurant, there had been a line of customers. The employees had been seen from over the counter in the kitchen, preparing their meals back there. A Puerto Rican employee was the cashier taking orders. She wore glasses and is in her twenties. She wears a reddish short sleeve uniform accompanied by a red hat. An older black woman was next in line, she approached the cashier with her plate of served food.

"Hello?" the employee asked seemingly confused. "Ma'am are you enjoying everything so far?"

"NO!" the customer rudely said. "I'd prefer my money back."

"Excuse me, ma'am? Why would you need a refund? I don't understand."

"Well, how's 'bout you take a good look!"

The woman blatantly drops the orange tray on the cashier counter. Crumbs of chicken sprinkled on the tray; the woman crossed her arms awaiting her money. On the tray were two chicken bones with skin behind, remnants of mashed potatoes and some bits of corn sprinkled on a dead rat's head. The employee's eyes widen from being grossly shocked. She looked at some customers behind the woman, in hopes that no other customers suspected anything up here.

"Ma'am, I checked this plate of food before I gave it to you. I always do when customers want their food to stay—"

"So, you can give me my money back!" she demanded. "Next time, do a better fuckin' job or have someone else up in here do it… 'cause this ain't it."

The employee remained calm while anger was stirring.

"No, no, no." the employee politely responds. "There was not a trace of this nastiness anywhere on that tray. Ma'am, I do my job, ok?"

"Clearly not well enough."

"Why'd you eat it?! If you were that disgusted to a rat's head that somehow appeared. Why'd you eat up the food?"

"It must've been under my unseasoned corn."

"You know what I think?" the employee boldly said. "I think you somehow obtained a rat's head for reasons I don't even want to know."

"Hey, lil' girl—"

"And *I KNOW* for a fact that I didn't see no rat's head."

"EXACTLY!" the woman asserts. "You ain't see it!"

"I can't see what's not there!" the employee said aloud which garnered some attention from the customers way, way in the back. The closer ones had been awaiting to be served. A man right behind the black woman who'd been overhearing this had walked away. The employee's eyes follow him escaping fast.

The sight of that had her a lot more frustrated. This woman barking in her face and now costing them customers as well. The more the woman orders: *"You fucked up my order, I expect my money now."* She begins demanding it in a smug way. A way of having this already strong notion of expecting to get away with this. Taking that "customer's always right" motto to an over extent. The woman's small silent smirk, from her glossed upper lip to her filled outer bottom lip, aggravates her more and more.

"I'm not refunding you your money back."

"Say what?"

"*NEXT!*" the employee announced.

†

Oblivious to the small uproar at the counter, Donny wants to talk more to his kids. He catches his kids both trying to see what's transpiring too. It must've been that impactful since it took Aiden from his imagination, and he transfixed as well.

"So, kids…" Donny announced that got their attentions. "What y'all think about this marvel all around the world huh?"

"You mean that 'miracle' trending everywhere still?!" Lauren skeptically asks. "Mom says it's not real."

"Yea, and that we shouldn't worry about it 'cause it's a hoax." Aiden added.

"Well, y'all believe in God, right?"

"Uh-huh." His kids simultaneously said.

"Then don't listen to your mother. It's ok to believe in miracles even if they're seemingly suspect."

"Really?" Aiden cautiously asks, his voice beginning to croak.

"Yes. It speaks truth, alright? Honest-to-god."

Aiden's eyes start to tear up to Donny's astonishment. His son began to cry, Aiden's head rocked hard down. Frustrated Lauren got from up her seat and wrapped her skinny arms around her brother's skinny body. *"It's alright."*

She softly said. Donny was still confused, waiting for his daughter to explain.

"Mom's on that list, heading to hell." Lauren said.

"Oh no, I ain't know little man." Donny softly said. "No, my bad."

Aiden was still sniffling and bawling his eyes out. Donny thought maybe he should hug him but refused. His daughter shot him a familiar look, the same look she gets from her mother: *"you've already done enough."*

†

The employee and customer still bicker both at each other over this meal. The line is being held up and more customers proceed to leave.

"Y'all fools be fuckin' up people's orders here. Shit, I seen the news on this place."

"Then you decide to come here still?!" the employee charged back. "What sense does that make?"

"Tried giving this place the benefit of the doubt, my bad!" the woman sarcastically shouts. "Y'all got nasty-ass employees up—"

"MA'AM, MA'AM!" the employee interrupted, trying once more to resolve this. She reassures her that Mr. Souvenir was immediately terminated after his public confession. Reminding this lady that this was announced in the news. "So, we don't employ no other people like him. He came out that he'd be the only one up here doing shit like this, as a desperate plead hoping to repent."

"Terminated?!" the woman said. "You actin' like he got let go of some prestigious-ass firm. Open Saws ain't nothing but a half-ass, fast food joint. Y'all ain't shit, y'all can burn in hell, *NATALIA!*" the woman mocks as she finally saw this employee's name tag.

Natalia gets quiet now, her frustration worsens. The sight of the remaining customers peeking behind this woman are captured as she contemplates something. Pondering whether or not to just grant this belligerent woman her money back. She's a stubborn customer halting their business and she'll be gone. As her palm drew close to the register; there was that smug smirk on her face again. Direct eye contact solely for Natalia, and it went from smaller to wider this time. She places her hand back.

"You right, customer's always right." Natalia said.

"Good, now co—"

"Because let me tell you something… just like Mr. Souvenir, I'm heading to hell too."

"*What*?" the woman murmured.

"That's right, real talk." Natalia boldly states. "But I ain't see no difference really. I been in hell since the first day I clocked up in here. Working like a slave over a broiling hot-ass stove or having people like you throwing shade nonstop over bullshit!"

"And who you mean people like me? Let me speak with your manager, I can't with you."

Natalia scoffed. "Oh, you wish to speak with the devil himself instead?! Well, he's not here."

†

"Well, speak of the devil." Donny playfully said, seeing Taivy calling his phone. The continuous rings go as Aiden cries nonstop. Lauren was consoling him still; frustrated Donny wanted him to be quiet but couldn't yell at him. To him, he didn't really do anything wrong and believed he's overreacting.

"I think that's your phone." Lauren bluntly said. He could tell by how she acknowledged this meant she wanted him to get up and take the call outside, leaving them both alone. Donny instead refuses to leave and tries to console his poor son Aiden.

"It's just your mother, I'll call her back." He told his daughter with a mocking sneer. "Son, listen to me, you and your mother will both be in heaven."

"What about Lauren?" Aiden hopefully asked.

"Let's focus on you two first, huh?"

"Wow." Lauren dryly replies. "Know what Aiden it's cool, it's cool. Just let him cut me off. Like he's been doing this whole drive up here, like he's been doing all our lives."

"Hold on, hold on!" Donny said, sounding annoyed. "I have spent time and money on both y'all. Nobody's getting cut off."

†

"YES MA'AM, YES! Can you wrap this shit up so I could soon take my heavenly break?!" Natalia said.

"I WANT BACK MY MONEY YOU DONE FUCKED UP MY ORDER!"

"AIN'T NOBODY DROP THAT FUCKIN' RAT HEAD IN THAT FUCKIN' TRAY!" Natalia Yells. *"YOU A LYING FUCK!"*

"FUCK YOU, YOU A DAMN LIE!" The women yelled. *"I DON'T GOTTA LIE, YOU DON'T KNOW ME!"*

†

"Son, son c'mon..." Donny pleaded with him. "You know your dad."

"Not really." Aiden moaned.

"Well, I was just messing with you, bud. Your mom's right. It ain't real, I ain't mean to upset you."

"Seriously?!" Lauren condescendingly said.

"What, it ain't like he'd be seeing her there anyway."

"W-we won't be together in the end?" Aiden asks.

"No son, because in the end you'll both be dead."

His son sobs some more, simultaneously frustrating Donny and Lauren. Donny grows more and more impatient with Aiden, along with the chaos he overhears in line and now by his cell ringtone from Taivy calling him to check in on the kids. He gestures for Aiden to lower it down then answers the phone sounding very cordial.

"Hi, how is everything?" Taivy asks, being pleasant.

"CUSTOMER SERVICE HERE'S BULLSHIT!" yelled a customer in the background.

"Donny?"

Donny explains that employees here are getting complaints over messing up orders. Then he goes on to tell them where they are and him and the kids are having lunch. However, there was a dropped pause on the opposite end. He knew that silence, he understood it was Taivy seething about something in mind. But couldn't understand what made her upset, Aiden hadn't made a peep either. Donny sets her on speaker phone.

"Donny," Taivy begun, sounding frustrated. "Don't you know they're spitting and doing vile shit in people's food there?"

Aiden and Lauren simultaneously spit out their chewed food. He quickly took her off speaker. Taivy goes on a rant about him taking her kids to that disgusting Open Saws restaurant. Donny defends by acknowledging their children aren't at all sick. Aiden starts sniffling again, Taivy detects this sound over the phone. She asks if he'd been crying, acknowledging that those sniffles are made after her baby's long cry. Donny gestured for him to remain silent as he lies.

"Mom, I don't want you in hell." Aiden screeched.

"WHAT?"

"Taivy, we're fine. Everything's fine on our end."

"No, because I'm not there to see for myself."

†

"Ok, I see you." Natalia condescendingly said, nodding her head, completely sure of herself. The customer awaits to hear what she's about to preach next. "All a sudden since you been out living your best life and is guaranteed eternal bliss, you now forgot how to act. Believing you out here better than everybody else but your broke ass finna start up shit over three dollars and change. You won a fuckin' fortune and now you want more, you greedy bitch. Comin' up in here sinning. You're a damn joke!"

"WHO THE FUCK IS YOU TALKIN' SHIT?!" the woman screams.

†

"WHO THE FUCK ARE YOU TALKING TO?" Taivy yelled over the phone.

"Taivy, it's getting too loud in here. I'll call you back." Donny quickly blurts as he hung up. His attention turns to Aiden as his eyes begun swelling up once more. "Son, please quit acting like such a baby."

Lauren's eyes darted at him. "What'd you just call him?"

†

"HOE!" the black woman hollered as she threw her drink in Natalia's face. Natalia's high-pitched scream was completely heard everywhere in the restaurant. The pent-up anger from dealing with this verbal dysfunction, thoughts of her constant submission to prior disrespectful customers and now being assaulted by someone who

doesn't deserve to die and go to heaven had reached its boiling peak.

Natalia swiped that rat's head, gripped the woman's shirt and firmly bashed it down her cleavage. It resulted in a horrific scream, instantly pulling away from her. She maneuvered enough to have it fall out, then she slid over the counter powered by rage. The customers recorded these women grabbing at each one's hair whilst throwing random swings hoping to hit each other. The other employees come to her aid. Donny grabs his kids, who both enjoy the show, and brings them out of there.

† Chapter 7: Continue on, my child.

On York Avenue, Essie notices Larissa over to the corner nearest the window. Larissa gets off her phone, observing outside the window. Essie wonders if she's upset about her mother in prison still. It perplexed her since Larissa would normally seem reserved for just that day. But she'd been so quiet that to Essie, it felt like a lifetime since hearing Larissa's joking, positive attitude. Larissa scrolls on her phone and Essie leaves her be.

Later that evening, Essie went to Larissa's room. She still looks aloof, not even on her phone. It's almost like she pretended to occupy herself on it earlier by sensing Essie's presence. However, now she just lies on her bed, even when hearing her guardian push open the door.

"Larissa, everything okay?"

"*Mm-hmm…*" she lowly responds.

"No, you aren't." Essie states. "What's the matter?"

"You're just gonna get annoyed."

"I won't." Essie promised as she sits with her on the bed.

"Well, it's about the list."

Larissa confides in her guardian about her last visit with her mother. She tells about her unwillingness to show any remorse for her actions and how frustrated she became as by the end of their visit. Of course, Essie feels slightly irritated again hearing this topic not only at home but at work.

However, she masquerades this and engages with Larissa without any judgement at all.

"She just be thinking I'm nothing but stupid." Larissa confessed, her voice trembles. "I probably am but either way, she's not havin' it."

"She shouldn't have said that. She's gonna get chewed out by the wrong person. There's nothing wrong with being concerned and if she can't see that, then that's on her. Danielle's where she needs to be."

"Locked up is the last place I want her to be."

"That's not on you. Danielle is grown enough to choose her own direction in life."

"Alright but what about the afterlife?!" she debates. "Ain't no one got no say about that. God has the final say. Like, I been thinkin' of a way to help her."

"How so?"

"Like, I could go to church and repent in the name of her sins."

"Honey, I don't think that's how that works. You cannot repent over someone else's transgressions in life."

"I could try, just pull up to church and repent for my moms, that's all."

Despite how ridiculous this sounds, there was just something different with Larissa this time. Essie could feel how passionate she was about this. Larissa had clearly put some thought into this, and sounds determined enough to follow through with it. Essie figures that maybe a priest would perhaps play along and finally ease her nerves.

"I tell you what," Essie gently said. "Perhaps we could head to one of the churches around here to do this."

"Can't, mad people be there Sundays now. And not just here but almost every church downtown. How's about some other church Saturday instead?"

"Somewhere else?! If you want, you and I both can head up midtown if that works for you?" Essie said.

"Ok, thanks Essie." Larissa said sounding genuinely grateful.

"Just remind me Saturday and have yourself together by then."

Left alone in her room, Larissa felt uplifted. Essie knows there's no hope of Danielle ever redeeming herself. She couldn't denounce her mother without hurting Larissa. Of all the opinions she's had, that's the one she hopes Larissa grasps on her own.

Kental Avenue, 8:23 P.M.

Donny Bedford drove his children home after all the havoc back at Open Saws. It was nothing but silent during the drive back. Lauren had watched outside the window with her earbuds in, getting familiarized with other parts of downtown that their mother never introduced them to. She'd even seen a group of men on Wrench Street outside circled around a car holding beer in a paper bag this late at time. Aiden was asleep, his shaved head rested on his sister's shoulder the whole ride back.

He was still holding the toy plane on his buckled lap.

Donny himself had been thinking of Taivy's reaction this whole time. Not knowing if she was going to curse him out, refuse anymore visitation with these two or would charge him with child endangerment. All these troublesome thoughts really came to the surface when he saw her open the door as they pulled up to her house. He even refused to honk the horn to let her know they arrived in hopes of not further aggravating her. Both parents locked eyes, one of them feeling agitated. Aiden had slowly woken up off his sister. Donny turns to them both quickly to address what had happened today on their small venture.

"Ok kids, I'ma need for y'all to act as if nothing insane happened at that place." Donny urged.

"You mean that brawl with the cashier?" Aiden asked.

"Yes."

"I thought you meant that trash food we had." Lauren said.

"Nobody ate any trash food there, alright? Weren't no mouths running when I paid for it neither! Know why, because both y'all mouths were enjoying it."

"So don't mention that lady's weave getting yanked out?"

"NO!"

Everyone inside abruptly ceased speaking at the frequent tap at the driver seat window. Taivy had alarmed her kids and their father as she silently waits for him to roll down his window. Donny could tell from the look of her crossed arms and deadpan face that she wasn't in any mood for more nonsense. He rolls his window down giving her a greeting nod.

"What are you telling them back there?" Taivy asked.

"That I love them, dearly."

"You both ok?" she asks them both as she hugs them. "No one's feeling at all sick?"

"Nah, mom. I ain't eat much. And look, dad got me a plane."

"Yea mom, we've been good." Lauren agreed.

"C'mon in, there's dinner inside."

"Oh. What you cook 'em?" Donny excitedly asked.

"Food!" Taivy stated.

Aiden and Lauren race inside for the enticing aroma of freshly made mac & cheese with fried steak too. Lauren beats her brother inside as Aiden turned back to wave goodbye to Donny with his airplane in hand. Donny waved back then got out his car knowing Taivy would want to discuss today. He pulled out a cigarette and offered her one, but she refused. After lighting his cigarette, he made sure to exhale far from Taivy by stretching his neck away. While trying to not aggravate her, he felt slightly relieved and proud of both his kids for playing along. Taivy peeks back at the house to ensure that Aiden wasn't being nosy as always.

"Welp, what I tell you?!" Donny arrogantly said. "We had a blast."

"Next time, be careful what you feed our kids." Taivy calmly demands.

"I didn't know about no shit li—" Donny said as he paused to confirm something. "Wait… 'OURS' you say?"

"Don't make me regret saying that."

"Nah, it's just nice."

"They seemed fine; I get you didn't know. So, we'll see about next time."

"Alright."

Taivy heads back to her front steps. Donny's glad that there was no bickering with each other whatsoever. He recognized the face she had when he arrived resembled the exact same look, she's shot him years ago whenever she was enraged. As many times he'd witnessed it, especially when he stayed around, had made it deeply embedded inside his head.

Even with it seemingly sad that she alone is getting left with the kids to look after again, he justifies it with it all being upon her. Donny is well aware that she's got the choice to contact him whenever she needs help, including the money he even now contributes. She even dictates his visitation rights and can cut him off at any time she please. To him, she's in control to where if she still feels overwhelmed then that's her own problem. Taivy recoiled back inside wearing a stretched plain shirt with her hair wrapped in a bun. He sits in his car exhaling the smoke out the window.

Later that night around 10:00, the family was doing their own separate things. Taivy was loudly talking to her girlfriend on the phone, Aiden was playing with his toy plane; pretend crashing it into the wall. Lastly Lauren was in her room listening to music on her phone while relaxed on her bed. She's downloading an app as the music blasts in her ears. As the loading bar slowly goes, an incoming call happens. She's perplexed as to who could possibly be calling her this late on a Friday night.

"Hello?"

"Hey, it's dad." Donny answers.

"Oh, hi." She replied confusingly.

"Why're you up this late?"

"Summer times no curfew."

"Huh, your mom gives me one though. To haul y'all asses back home at a certain time." He jokingly said.

"Mm-hmm. Look, if you called to see if we snitched—"

"No, it's not even like that. If you did, your mom would be calling my phone as we speak. I just called to check up on you."

"Ok?" Lauren asked, not knowing what this man could possibly need that's so urgent at this time of night. She peeks out her door to see if her mom or Aiden can overhear any of this but detects no one.

"At that restaurant earlier, you said I had cut you off on the drive there and your whole life. What was that about?"

"Oh…" Lauren muttered sounding embarrassed. "I mean, you ain't say much to me in the car. Instead, you were laughing with Aiden."

"We talked some while we we're eating though."

"Only 'cause Aiden was in his own little world, you got stuck with me."

"That's why you were more upset with me when Aiden was crying." Donny stated.

Lauren was silent on the other end of the line. To her, he sounds so sure of himself that she momentarily couldn't deny it. Lauren silence said it all.

"Baby, listen…" Donny said softly. "I get you wanted me to talk to you more but with me driving up and you on your phone... that makes it all the more difficult. I wanna get to know both my kids, so you gotta give back at least ten percent by not always being on your phone and talk more. Seriously."

Lauren had dropped her guard down the more he had gone on. She had already felt wearier after him telling her and her brother to hide from their mother what happened earlier; almost having him come off sketchy to her. *How often did he lie to our mom? I bet this man always has another agenda.* These thoughts were boggling her mind when he kept pressing them to keep quiet. That's the impression she'd gotten from her father.

There was brief silence.

However, this time felt different. Hearing him point out how she didn't make their time together any easier made her understand where he was coming from. She never knew if it was him giving constructive criticism or just him unable to ever hold himself accountable. Lauren hardly knows this man, being that he wasn't ever really involved in her life by choice. But from how he spoke so natural and calm, without seeming like there was any ulterior motive, to her it came off more as positive. Donny spoke in a sense like he genuinely wanted to be more involved, and the only barrier to that was no one to blame but herself.

She felt that responsibility, Lauren began questioning maybe she should've had a better attitude. Yet she couldn't bring herself to confess this aloud.

"I'm not trying to make you feel bad or admit any shame 'cause I'm the same way. Like back when everybody got their own diplomas while I was sitting in summer school. I didn't have no one to blame but myself."

"You did summer school?"

"Yup, said it in the car. See you weren't listening." Donny jokingly said. "Like when Aiden mentioned you in summer school and you blamed the teacher instead. Used to be the same way."

Lauren couldn't believe the parallels between her and her father. She'd completely forgotten about telling that in the car earlier today. That to Lauren was like mentioning something in passing, almost like he could dig deep in the depths of even the most unimportant stuff to her. But it mattered to him because she was important to him. And at that exact moment, she felt that.

"I'm here to stay, ok?" Donny said. "As long as I am around, I swear no one's gonna harm you, your brother or your mother."

"Ok." Lauren said sounding hopeful.

With all that being said, with Lauren expecting him to hang up, Donny said one more thing: "Oh, before I forget, how was your birthday? I ain't ask back in the car."

Lauren smiled so wide to where she was relieved that both were over the phone. She told him all about her day involving the cake, gifts and friends. And Donny just sat back and listened, counting his blessings.

†

On Saturday morning, Larissa is early awake getting herself ready to head to church in midtown, getting all gussied up all for her mom. Essie is downstairs already dressed in black, brushing her long black hair hanging to her back. She hears Larissa's footsteps coming down. Larissa had walked down in a blue dress, a white vest slipped on around it with the front buttons open. Her hair was tied in a bun, she had worn dark blue shoes, and lastly did her own make-up. Larissa hardly ever wore make-up; Essie bought her a set for her birthday but always convinced her that Larissa's natural dark skin was glamourous in itself. However, even Essie noticed how much it had enhanced her looks, Larissa's face was glowing the more she came downstairs.

"Of all the times you've cleaned up for your mom, I never would've pictured you like this." Essie acknowledged.

"Well, this time we ain't in no courtrooms. If I'ma do this, I'ma do it right!"

Essie teases. "You pulled yourself together nicely. *No provocative clothing, no odd piercings, no mismatched church socks.* Nope, today you look quite presentable."

The two leave together for the terminal to take into midtown Holksdale. They'd normally drive there but being the circumstances of having to get to a further destination outside of prison, they make an exception. Both arrived to the train station and got on the first one departing.

Today was reported to not only be a scorcher out but had even a greater increase in crimes escalating in Holksdale since yesterday. Essie had gotten news updates on her phone and shows it to Larissa. There are reports of people robbing delis, especially downtown. Police having to arrest people out looting during more of these riots with the catalyst to all this havoc being from the miracle again.

"See that's why I don't like you traveling far without me, ok?" Essie sternly said.

"*Ugh…*" Larissa groaned.

"Larissa, did you hear me?"

"Yes, it's just hot, that's it. I can feel it through that glass."

Larissa in general doesn't mind the heat during her walks around but it really struck her today in her church dress. Her chest and down her neck drenched sweat, with some soaked down her armpits. She hoped no stains would be present through her dress but was certain her make-up would remain the same. Essie dug in her bag and gave her a water bottle.

As the train went on, they both were quiet. Larissa on her phone passing the time and Essie staring out the window. It was beautifully bright out, she can only imagine how much hotter it'll be later. There appeared so many more adults on the train looking to enjoy themselves with their company. Though there is this young man she spots from afar who's coming their way. He was a young kid around Larissa's age wearing sunglasses, and sweet apple cologne. His skin was creamy white with a short haircut. Despite Essie not seeing his eyes, she can tell his direction is for Larissa who is locked to her phone.

"Hey, excuse me?" the boy politely said.

"Hmmm?" Larissa replied as she pulls out one earbud.

"You look like you're headin' to church." He said as he hovers still.

"I am. Guess you could tell by my dress."

"Yea, I like it."

"*Thank you.*" She said sounding flattered. "I'm just here with my guardian."

"Hello, I'm Essie."

"Chase." He responds as they shook hands. "Nice to meet you."

"Likewise, here have a seat." Essie said as she scoots over.

"So what's your name?" As he sits revealing his yellow highlight strands in his brown hair.

"Larissa. You said you're Chase?"

"Yep. I'm just heading to buy some games in midtown."

"Oh cool. I don't really be on consoles like that but I get you."

"Mm-hmm, really to sell some old games." Chase said. "Trying to make more money."

"What kinda games?"

Chase tells her shooter games, sports games, games from his old consoles. Essie could sense the chemistry between them and remains pleasantly silent.

"Ok, I see you." Larissa encouraged as she chuckles.

"Welp, I get off here." Chase said. "But you're pretty cool to talk to, how's about I get your number or something?"

Even with Larissa enjoying their small chit-chat, in the back of her mind she hoped he wouldn't ask her that. She had a small smile that slightly trembled on the opposite side of this boy. She knew she couldn't lie about forgetting her number since he caught her on her phone. Larissa politely replies: "I don't really give out my number like that."

"Alright." He calmly responds. Then suggests he adds her on social media instead.

"Ok." Larissa agrees. She gave him her phone so he types in his social media. She promised she'll add him back and he leaves.

"He was sweet." Essie said.

"He was, I'll maybe add him back."

"What's your age range use again?"

"Man, you're old." Larissa teased.

"I'm old-fashioned, get it right." Essie playfully said. "I'd give out my number and question his intentions. In fact, I should've told him yours."

"Nooooooo!"

"Hell, why not?! I pay your phone bill so it's basically my number."

"Oh, is that it?!" Larissa mocks. "I see how it is."

Essie and Larissa finally arrive at their stop. Both in pursuit of the nearest cathedral in midtown. They soon arrive to one that wasn't too far from the terminal. Larissa is in gaze of the tall cross statue upon the church roof glistening with sunlight. The two walk together inside.

They emerge into this sanctum to witness over a hundred people formed in a line. These church goers were dressed in suits, men and women are here to unload their sins in the confessional booth. Essie and Larissa exchange a frustrated glance of how long this is going to take. The two joins in line behind a grown bald man in a grey suit. Larissa watches many of the adults kneeling as they're praying on line. It was apparent way upfront of a domino effect of church goers on their knees, eyes closed, and hands clapped in asking for forgiveness. However, it ends somewhere up in the middle of the line. She plugs earbuds to her phone then listens to music, knowing this will be a long wait.

Her guardian on the other hand is tired but doesn't mind doing this favor. She raises her head trying to keep awake which becomes harder when they're slowly moving from just one spot. Then reminds herself that compared to that broiling weather they had to endure outside, slowly waiting inside with it feeling much cooler was better. And as she glanced up, she notices the church's stained-glass window. It was of a depicted brown cross with a bright yellow painted sun hovered behind. The background appears dark red, the surrounding edged layers give off a dark reddish colored shine from the blazing sun outside reflecting it. Essie just studies it momentarily trying to detect some deeper meaning to take away from it, yet nothing comes to mind. However, there's a tethered familiarity about it. Then finally looks forward to seeing how much far until Larissa gets there. The doors behind them open and more people arrive inside for the same purpose. The bald man in front of them had seen this and mouthed out "fuck" in frustration. Since Larissa stayed on her phone, Essie spoke to him.

"Excuse me, did you come here to confess your sins too?"

"Mm-hmm." He replied. "Just like you and everyone else."

"Not me, I'm here for my kid. I'm her guardian." Essie adds quickly due to his perplexed look of her kid being a black girl. "We're here for her mom really."

"Her mother couldn't make it, ok. I'm Kurt." He introduced.

"Essie introduces herself and Larissa. She asks if the man placed on the hell category.

"Yes, I have. And I pray I'm repenting for the right one otherwise I'll be wasting time on line all day."

"Right one?" Essie asks.

"I'm sure it's either because I work for an agency that forecloses homes…"

"Alright, not too bad."

"Or because I possibly killed someone last black Friday. Almost chocked some poor other customer to death at a clothing store. We were both jonesing for some holiday attire."

"So, uh, was it over winter boots or earmuffs maybe?"

"Turtleneck."

"Well, seemed a bit excessive but I'm sure the other guy survived."

"Was a woman." Kurt coldly replied.

Essie simply nodded, hoping he wouldn't be offended since he had no qualms about hurting women. For all she knows, he could really be here to repent for that but his monotone voice not hinting any at all remorse showed otherwise. Including that this happened during the holidays, he had a large time frame between then and now to have done this. He must have detected her nonverbal judgement because the man turned his head back forward after a shared awkward silence. She was just relieved that Larissa hadn't paid that man any mind.

That just made Essie actually more impatient, not from being here for Larissa, but for the extent it takes to do this. To Essie, these people were all like Kurt. People who never gave a damn about their godawful decisions to where the only time they gave it a second-thought was over some stupidity like this here. A trend she never believed in brought her here. Neither her nor Larissa are damned to hell but are still in place along these other assholes here. Everyone else here sees this as nothing but a quick bargaining exchange then just go on without worrying how the aftermath of their actions may have impacted other people. Then she watches Larissa, so innocent and pure in her church dress, even knowing her being here is no different. However, her actions came from a bona-fide place of slight ignorance and immaturity. It made her that much more pure in Essie's eyes, and even brings frustration to her mind since it is all for her ungrateful, convict mother. Moments like this make Essie wish she could just grow up to see Danielle for exactly who she is. But at the same time, moments like this have her more appreciative of their quality time together. It even has her supportive of how pure-minded and pure-hearted Larissa can be, not being yet exposed to the coldness of the world. Essie never would fear of showing her that; while her mother does nothing but confines any glimmer of sincerity.

Larissa begins to rock around back and forth a bit, putting her phone down to just listen to music alone instead. The line doesn't move much as Essie hints to her with a sympathetic headshake. She can feel how cool inside was and how tired she was from standing as Larissa gently rests her head under her guardian's skinny arm. Then is held in more, radiating each other's warmth.

Kental Avenue, 1:03 P.M.

Donny Bedford made plans to take out his kids to the carnival happening this weekend. Taivy seemed alright with the idea, especially with her plans on cleaning the house today. Unfortunate enough, his car had been vandalized last night. The windshield had gotten smashed as a result of criminal activity being increased. His car is being repaired now, so he called Yanie Juregens instead.

Yanie's driving him to pick his kids up and take them to and from the carnival in that stolen truck still. She's agreed to tolerate his kids for a couple hours in exchange for him going down on her with his special tongue flicker that's gets her off always. Donny warns her about meeting his baby momma and both agree it will go smoothly if they label themselves to Taivy as just friends, and hopefully his kids will have too much fun to care enough.

They pulled up to Taivy's house, except she wasn't out sitting on the steps. The kids weren't rushing out like he'd expect, especially with him and Lauren now being cool too. Yanie was glad to not have to be introduced to Taivy yet.

"Dammit Taivy, you ain't have 'em ready yet?!" Donny said to himself.

"And if you get here like an hour late, she gonna give you shit." Yanie added.

"With my car getting fixed and I still get here late, I'd blame you. Yanie, that shit's on you."

"Oh, really?!" Yanie jokingly said. "Alright, bet. Try explaining it to the courts. Y'know don't nobody give a fuck about men's rights in these courts."

"That's true. Makes me glad I ain't never married first."

"Oh, facts! You couldn't even afford a whip. All that cash would be solely going to her. Not these kids, her!"

"I'd be paying alimony on top of child support. And mind you, I could still be brought up in court if she or these kids get upset. So, be cool with them, alright?"

"I'm good with kids, don't worry." Yanie reassured him. "My girl, Essie, I'm cool with her adopted kid."

The door opens, Donny's the first to pick up on this.

Lauren is the first to come out as she holds the door for her brother to follow out. Then closed the door behind her; having both Yanie and Donny relieved to not have to explain to their mother who's this stranger her kids are getting in a car with. Both are hurrying to the car, dressed down in shorts with sunglasses.

"Aiden and Lauren, right?" Yanie asked.

"Yea, there they go right there."

The door opens fast with his son hoping quickly inside first. Lauren came in after. She bickered about him getting a head start to the car since she closed the door behind them. They both greeted him as they were already loud in the back. Unbeknownst to him being in the passenger seat, they noticed Yanie instead behind the wheel. Donny can tell their confusion based on how silent they became, neither one of his kids had the courage to ask who she was. He faces them before they leave.

"Kids, this is my friend, Yanie."

"Hey, y'all." Yanie greets with a warm smile.

"Something happened to my car, so she'll be driving us today."

"What, it got stolen?" Lauren asks.

"If so, it'd be ironic." Yanie murmurs.

"Chill with that." Donny replied. His windshield got smashed but it's getting repaired. He asks about Taivy.

"Mom got us ready then said she was taking a nap before she has to clean." Lauren said.

"Alright, we should be there in like ten minutes if we go now."

Aiden's little face lit up as he became gleeful in his seat. Lauren scoots close to him, helping to get her brother adjusted in his seatbelt. Then sees Aiden through the corner of her eye, again playing with his toy plane. Her face was visibly irritated since she is used to him annoying her enough with that at home. Not even pulling out of the driveway yet and her brother loudly commenced to making flying sounds.

Lauren blocks out his noise with her earbuds turned full volume now. Yanie was so relieved to have complete confirmation to their mother's absence that she wasn't at all vexed by Donny's son's noise. She even peeked at Aiden through the mirror before pulling out. Then her eyes quickly glared at him as he was crashing the plane into his dad's back seat. Donny didn't mind but Aiden was trying to dig the plane into the backseat pocket. In those pockets were a plastic bag of three and a half edibles that weren't to be detected by anyone, including their father.

Without hesitation, Yanie's arm stretched back to swat away Aiden's tiny hand. His hand zipped back to his chest, resulting in his plane striking the ground hard with his seatbelt restricting him back. Yanie picked it up then hands it back with apologetic eyes. Aiden's mouth dropped open as his muscles still stiffened. He cautiously accepted it back and understood it as a warning to not play inside of there. Donny saw what happened but didn't give much care to it since no one was crying. No words between Aiden and

Yanie were exchanged but he could see that she wasn't doing it to be mean then went back to flying his plane.

The ignition started as Yanie reversed the truck out. Donny surfs on his phone on their way out the cul-de-sac. Then Donny texts Taivy that he'll have them both back this evening. He tries to roll his window down after feeling how powerful the heat was. Yanie locks the windows and has the air conditioner blowing everywhere inside.

†

Back at the church, for the past hour, the line has moved up significantly with more adults joining in from the entrance. Larissa checks her phone it sees it down to thirty percent but still just listens to music. She and Essie check forward to see that the next one in line appears to be a young black girl in her late teens.

The confessional booth is a wooden structure with a small compartment, and there the young girl entered. Inside through a curtain in which the priest sits and, on each side, there is a latticed opening for the penitents to speak through and step on which to kneel. By this arrangement, the priest is hidden but the penitents are visible. The young girl represents what many girls aspire to be, a light skinned queen with straightened hair. She worn a purple church dress that rose as she kneeled then looked through the opening before the priest.

"Afternoon father." The girl greeted.

"Greetings my child, for who do I owe the pleasure of speaking with?"

"I'm a college student and this is my first ever time going to confessional."

"Hello, and what brings you hear today?" the priest gently asks, sounding tolerant.

"Father, I am here before you to receive sacrament of reconciliation." She said sounding as if she'd rehearsed that prior to coming here. "Pretty much to relieve out my sins."

"Ok, let us begin."

"Bless me father for I have sinned in the act of trolling."

"Pardon, my child?"

This girl had elaborated on what exactly she meant by trolling. She tells of back when she was a high school junior on the track team. There was a new student who joined the team who wasn't as fit as the other track members. She wasn't exactly overweight, but she had some fat on her that was more exposed by her belly and arms. Yet, she was the fastest sprinter on the team. Even hadn't struggled when they had to practice afterschool. The girl seeing this newcomer having a good track infuriated her. Already having looked at her with disdain for not resembling anything at all to a track fit star; just to surpass her and her track friends with nothing but ease was even worse. Like she couldn't measure up even though it was all superficial based.

She felt triggered to where she and her friends spread rumors about her health to their class peers. Pretended to befriend her one day and alter their attitude towards her without notice. Just to screw with her head and self-esteem, having her believe she must've done something to turn them off. Once she confided to her fellow teammates that she was trying to lose weight so she could look better. They had orchestrated this plan of having their guy friends to comment under her social media pictures by exaggerating about her weight. Then admits that she and the other track girls created fake accounts to message her, claiming to of watched her at track practice. Insulting her for being overweight and how it affects her during practice.

After constant comments of this, she had lost a lot of weight but was mainly due to having an eating disorder. It started small to just believing that she was more overweight than she was. Even when gaining clear results, she was still incapable of seeing it. She developed a mental disorder from being berated constantly online. The other girls could detect this state she was in, but they didn't care to stop. It only became evident by their last practice of how it went to an over extent, with her passed out from starvation that was self-inflicted.

By that time, she was extremely skinny by only consuming the bare minimum of food and had been rushed to the hospital to be treated. Everyone on the track team disabled their fake accounts and had never come forward to their coach or this poor victim. Then again, she never gained enough strength to practice with them again.

"Like father, I saw just how vulnerable she was about her weight. Hell, we all did but took advantage anyway."

"Was she now?"

"Mm-hmm, you could see just all ribs." She said. "You could hang her lil' boney-self in Jesus' place up on that cross and won't nobody know no difference."

"I can see you genuinely wish to seek forgiveness for breaking your commitment with God. Young lady, may you come around to see me?"

"Yes father." She said making her way to his side.

The priest appears to be a tall, average looking, balding Caucasian man wearing glasses. His glasses make clear his brown eyes to her as she sits across from him, face to face. He holds a bible in his lap.

"Father, do we recite something together?"

"Yes, we will soon recite the act of contrition, my child… within a moment."

They discuss more about what transpired and the aftermath of it all. She didn't question transitioning before him because she figured that he wasn't gullible. The copious number of sinners he's had to encounter today must've had him detect that we're all here just for ourselves instead. Her divulging out more about how much of an impact her actions had begun to have her feel more vulnerable. The priest can tell by her repeated pauses, especially whenever she referenced the victim herself. She felt that he wanted to see an actual look of remorse and then she did.

"Continue on, my child." He encouraged.

"I be trying not to think about it but now I can't help it."

She feels her eyes becoming sensitive, almost close to shedding tears. Then closes them momentarily to resist temptation. Once opened, the priest scoots in closer, sensing her distress. He asks her for her name to make her feel comfortable. Ivorie, she confides to him which makes her finally breakdown in tears. The number of times she acknowledged the girl was hard enough but having to disclose who she was hadn't helped either. Her teammate's critical condition, the one who orchestrated all of it and the coward who never held themselves accountable was all tied to that one name: Ivorie. All to be opened by this loose end, making her feel like even more of a coward.

"Now Ivorie, only I can bless you with absolution."

"I understand, father."

"And to avoid being subject to the devil, you must devote on behalf of thyself to endure full obedience to be relieved of all sins."

"Father?"

Larissa checks on her phone again to see her friend Lyric had posted a recent selfie. It is of her in church with her wearing a wig, dressed in another church dress. The sunlight had hit her face, showing off her clear light-skin complexion. The tagline read: *No filter needed. God's shining his light watching over me.*

Just as she was going to like it, a scream had been heard. Everyone in the church heard it and all heads checked forward straightaway. Young Ivorie had bolted out of the confessional booth, the next sound heard was of the priest collapsing onto the floor. She deviated from there but remained confrontational.

"THE FUCK IS YOU DOIN', HUH?!" Ivorie hollered.

The priest is slowly crawling from around the confessional booth, one hand caressing his private parts, the other pulling him along. Everyone is perplexed as to what's happened. She's now hovered over him, screaming ten times louder.

"What'chu lying for?!" Ivorie said as he gestures that it's all a misunderstanding. "You stay here lying though!"

"*No, no, no*." The priest pleaded in agony.

"This pervert here tryin' to finesse me… in church!" Ivorie announced to the whole crowd. "I just curved this fool."

The adults all go in a frenzy while the priest can't even defend himself from desperately trying to catch his breath. People are in an uproar but not because of what had just transpired. Everyone awaiting in line all this time including the remaining ones who just confessed their sins was angered by their time being wasted. The people begun to get aggressive inside the church. Some men went to confront the priest while other women pulled their kids away to safety. The church once filled with nothing, but tranquility is now drenched in animosity.

Essie yanks Larissa by the arm to a corner somewhere until the exit wasn't blocked. Five men led by Kurt himself were kicking the priest, keeping him in place. Then other people went near the fountain outside filled with several diverse colored rocks. They'd taken a handful of rocks one by one and had brought them inside. The priest is all disoriented whilst covered in blood from his runny nose,

Ivorie cheers for the men in the background. Essie holds Larissa in tighter by her head and back. Larissa's compressed too deep in her breasts to where her racing heartbeat echoes into her ear. She turns her head to see the priest cowardly scattered in the corner as everyone's closing in. All angry faces zeroed in on him, screaming "pedophile, pervert" that grows more and more powerful to the ears. Their screams in addition to the rocks brought out had crumbled the final barrier that borderlines his vulnerable state against their concrete hostility, resulting in him urinating himself.

"They're gonna kill him!" Larissa cries. *"Stop!"*

"You're not getting involved, stay here!"

"Essie—"

"You are my first priority right now," Essie said as her head instantly flicks around, desperately seeks for another exit. "We need to slip out the back!"

Larissa had vanished once she turned back around. Essie frantically looks everywhere around for her, screaming for her. All she sees are adults scattering as much as her in distress right now. Suddenly it dawns on her about her whereabouts, almost in a sense of mental enlightenment. But from what she suspects, for Larissa's sake, Essie hopes she's miraculously wrong. Essie faced the priest way ahead; Larissa is closer upfront as she forces her way to the man's aid.

Essie dashed into the crowd, attempting to break through as much as she could. Larissa finally broke through the sea of protestors to become this man's barrier. Everyone sees this then takes a quick hiatus. Essie sees this mostly as her not knowing the full story of what happened and could get herself harmed. Although they stopped moving, they're all still yelling: *MOVE GIRL! THIS IS GROWN FOLKS' BUSINESS! KEEP AWAY FROM HIM!*

"NO!" Larissa sternly said. "This is the home of the lord, and this is how we act?! About to kill him?! Who are we to play God?! We are joined here today despite our sins to seek repentance for 'em. He's exploiting his power of the church by doing stuff like this to young girls and look where he at. Some of us may have done worse, so ain't nobody got no right to pelt him with no rocks. Put his name on blast, exile him from the church but don't nobody hurt him!"

The room immediately died down once she was done, and Essie hadn't expected this neither. All eyes on a fourteen-year-old standing before them all. Larissa, body posture straight in her church dress, stares directly at the crowd to show she'd not back down. Poor girl's adrenaline was racing as to what might happen next. Yet not a single rock was flung, not one camera phone was out, just everyone having a shocked facial expression.

Then Kurt in the crowd announced: *Bitch, you better kick rocks 'fore you catch one upside your head!*

And all adults were fueled up again, Essie charged up to her, afraid to have been struck by an incoming rock. Larissa froze at the possibility of death; Essie's shadow came over her as she was scooped away from the priest. As they escape, the priest's cries for help are overheard as he gets hit by rocks coming from all angles as the crowd's sadistic rage builds. A rock flew straight into his stomach, making him drop to his side. He barely crept open his eyes after a rock bashed his face directly. This left dark blood trickling from the open wound revealing white bone that succumbed exposure.

Everyone halts once more from the sound of sirens outside. Essie and Larissa had managed to elude this widespread pandemic by then. The priest, however, was manhandled off to a secluded area behind the church. There were three police cruisers surrounding the church with sirens flashing lights everywhere. As police came close, people from inside began attacking them. Some had flung rocks from the open door, smashing their windshields. Officers took cover behind their cars; the aggressors inside had broken the painted stain glass church windows from more rocks hurled forward. Shattered, sharp remnants of glass landed on some officers and an incoming rock struck an officer right in her scalp. She collapsed on impact; her partner attended to her aid. The following cops held their own and charged inside the church with their weapons set.

Essie still ran, pulling Larissa's arm. More incoming sirens were heard on their way. Paranoid Essie quickly believed for a moment that police would pull them over, assuming they were affiliated with that chaos. Both finally arrived at the station, yearning to leave back to downtown Holksdale. Both arrived at the train station and got on the first one departing.

†

Later that day at Greynard's Junkyard, Franklin is there with an employee named Alan Rohrer. A recruit who replaced Beverly after quitting. Alan removes license plates off other cars, then must clear some cockroaches from the last floor. Franklin sits in his office returning missed phone calls of customers trying to acquire specified vehicles.

All the noise from the tools Alan uses overpowers the approaching sound of unknown footsteps. Unbeknownst to him, Alan continued his job. These steps marched forth to Franklin's office. This stranger was undetected thus far. As they're waiting for Franklin to finish his call. Once he laughed then hung up, a soft knock was made.

Franklin turns to his door already open. To the presence of a woman standing there. He studies this young, white woman. She was thirty-two-years-old with blonde hair wrapped in a bun. Her cheeks were rosy, with brown freckles around her small nose. Her green eyes were alluring, (*flattered by black eyeliner*) holding a gracious expression. There were multiple piercings in both ears.

"Good morning." She kindly began. "I'd seen you on the phone, thought I'd stand by."

"That's fine." Franklin replied with a warm smile. Admiring her skirt accentuating her tight waist and slim curves. Her chest flares out, highlighted more by her elegant, straightened back. Tattoos covered her whole right arm. Different colors with scriptures down her forearm. She appeared bold.

"Nice tats. What're they?"

"You're the proprietor of this place, right?" she deflects.

"You mean the junkyard." He laughed. "Yes, how may I help you today, ma'am?"

"Where do I begin…" she began, her voice was angelic. Explaining that recently her pickup truck had been stolen. This had Franklin's smile slowly descend into a neutral expression. That the police have not found a trace of evidence yet. Just the mention of the police sent overwhelming chills through Franklin. She mentions her phone was in the truck along with money. There was this app she used to locate her phone which led her here.

"Ma'am," His startled voice begins, attempting to maintain a sturdier tone. "I'm sorry about your truck but it's not here." He said in the most professional tone he could.

Her gracious eyes fixes on him. Franklin's uncertain body language, his facial expression's failed attempt to remain stoic, and his shakily breaths he tried to conceal. This lady knows he is scheming.

Silence struck the office. Franklin senses that she knows something based off her vague expression. He tries to deflect by offering her a cup of water from his office water dispenser. She simply nods. An unsettling smile came as he quickly pours her a cup, showering her with complements. He promises to keep her in his prayers. As the cup is filling, the evidence downpours. This chorus ringtone is heard from his desk. Franklin's head flickers back at her. She had a prepaid phone on display, calling her own phone.

"You aren't gonna answer my prayers?!" she said flatly.

His whole body froze as the deafening ringtone amplified in his ears. A deteriorating twisted unsteadiness overtakes his body. Franklin staggers over to his desk. His chest heaves, her focus itched at him still.

Pulling out her phone had his hand trembling. Franklin buckles into his seat. The ringtone ceased. Silence consumed the office. His eyes steer off. Her eyes still trained on him.

"See, we—"

"My phone!" she demands, extending out her hand. Having Franklin anxiously handing it over, like a petulant child. "Care to explain this to me?"

Words struggle to bubble up his throat. The dominant energy this lady exudes is looming over him. Franklin's entire being felt stiff at the possible outcomes from getting caught. Tense inhales ripped in and out. His mouth finally formed a word but was abruptly cut off by her. She states that she received texts from others about her truck's whereabouts around this area before.

Anger slowly brews as Franklin knows that Beverly is responsible for this. Especially for defying his orders. Franklin decides to take control of this situation. Him and his workers' livelihoods depend on this job. He says that someone possibly might have stolen her vehicle and crossed his path. Going on about them leaving behind what he thought was their phone. Promising her that no trucks are located here.

"Where is my truck?" she asks, unconvinced by this.

"Just because you traced your phone here doesn't mean we're behind any of this." He warily said. "I swear to God."

"On one hand, phones are traceable." She taunts. Then pulls out a pistol, Franklin jerked back. "Unregistered guns on the other hand, not so much."

Fear gripped at his throat. Both eyes bulging at the gun being waved around. This reaction drove a demonic look of triumph on her face. Now directing her gun at him. She firmly asks again about her truck, expecting an honest-to-God answer.

"NNEKA?" a voice shrieked from the door. It was Alan Rohrer, who watches in disbelief. "H-How'd you find me?"

"Rohrer? You're in on this too?" Nneka replied.

Franklin stared off at Alan trying to figure out exactly how he knows her. Nneka gave Alan the opportunity to properly introduce her. Alan's eyes warily flowed along with her gun. His tone went shrill as he carefully picks his words. Alan introduces Nneka Barshak, an illegal arms dealer, well known on the streets. She'll mercilessly wipe out any rival dealers around midtown and downtown Holksdale. Either through robbing them or obliterating them entirely. Nneka has people around the city that update her of any activity.

"She's got eyes and ears everywhere." Alan admits.

"Because I'm God." Nneka declares. Her eyes detected Franklin's expression of disbelief. "Do you disagree?"

"No ma'am."

"NO WHAT?" she barked. *"SOUND OFF!"*

"N-No, goddess." Franklin's words turned skittish, his eyes still on the gun.

"GOD!" she corrects. Then irritably asks if he believes that God is supposed to be a male entity. Watching his words go inaudible had her answer for him. *"FOR SHE WHO SEES ALL TRANSGRESSIONS, BIRTHED THE CREATION FOR ALL OF MANKIND THROUGH HER SEVEN DAY CYCLE PERIOD!"*

Nneka explains that Alan owed her money two years ago. He paid her back with interest six months ago. What perplexed Alan the most was why Nneka was here then. Her gun now directed at Alan; she demands to know what operation they are running. Alan staggered back. The truth gushes out of his mouth. Telling her about stealing and selling vehicles to shady customers.

"Where is my truck then?"

Not knowing anything about this left his mind blank. Knowing her reaction sent this inflow of helpless fear to engulf him entirely. So powerful it began to have Alan's words rattle. Forming low, jumbled words to flush out.

Nneka began mimicking him. "What the fuck are you speaking in tongues for, Rohrer?!"

"I don't know." Alan timidly said. *"I swear I don't."*

That unsatisfying reply left her straight-faced. Her predatory eyes flickered at Franklin. He averts her stare. Then she looks back at Alan.

"That vehicle means a lot to me. It's like a child of my own." Nneka said, staring down Alan. A powerful gunshot goes off into Alan's ankle. The fierce noise echoes in Franklin's ears. His body is completely stiffened. Alan crumbled onto the floor. This strained, deafening scream teared out Alan's throat. Warm tears had escaped Franklin's eyes. His breathing became very rocky.

As Alan desperately tries crawling away; Nneka continues her child analogy. "When they forget their place," She watched him crawl off. Then stomps on his leg, ceasing movement. "I put them in park!" Nneka drew out her switchblade, flickering it open. "When there's gunk on their face, I wipe down it's windshield." Cupping Alan's face. His grunts then turn into screams as she slid the blade down his cheek. Hot blood pours to his chin. Alan's head trembles then flickered helplessly. "Rocky path you've chosen." She taunts, withdrawing the blade from him. Still clutching onto his cheeks. This hollow, defeatist expression drifts across Alan's face. "And like any good parent, I make sure you watch your mouth." Nneka forcefully lodges the gun barrel into his mouth. Alan's lips quiver, his bleeding cheek grew numb. This dragging moan amplifies as he helplessly looks at Franklin.

"Please don't kill him." Franklin pleads. *"He do—"*

"Don't tell me how to raise my child!" She hissed.

There was no hint of when exactly. A bullet could launch at any moment now. Alan bawled as he clapped both hands together, praying for a miracle. The gun gets pried in more causing a dragging, gagging noise. Franklin's mind scrambles for what to do. His incoherent thoughts increased at the horrifying possible aftermath of Alan's predicament. Alan's throat dries like stained glass.

"Who took it?" she asks. Prompting Alan to try pleading with Franklin. The gun deepened down his clenching throat left this clotted, unsteadying, gargle to escape. Her eyes flicker at him. "Don't talk with your mouth full!"

Drool seeped from Alan's bottom lip. His body was overflowing with this tingling, shivering sensation. Franklin scavenged for any other alterative than to disclose this information. However, Nneka's looming energy consumes him. Nneka glides her switchblade down Alan's genitals. The sharp feel had hot urine downpour his leg.

"I'm waiting." She said impatiently. *"So, chop-chop."* Then lodged the gun deeper. *"Or bang-bang."*

"Beverly." He hurriedly said. Following up with a lie about her being Asian. Franklin writes down a fake address.

Nneka reads this. Then slides out the gun from Alan's mouth. A rush of saliva gushed out his mouth. Alan took in a gust of breath. Witnessing Alan struggling had left a grin on Nneka's face.

"Just be grateful I didn't stuff this down the trunk instead." She sharply said.

As she left the office, Franklin rushed to Alan's aid. Performing a tourniquet on his ankle. Alan screamed in agony as he is being treated. Franklin looks outside his office for any sign of her. He knows that he has limited time until she realizes that address was fake. Having to leave in order to avoid the second coming of Nneka Barshak.

† Chapter 8: YOU REMEMBER ME?!

Donny and Yanie brought them back to Taivy's house. They spent all that time at the carnival playing games, walking around, recording performances and carrying collectibles. Both his kids were asleep in the back, tuckered out from a long day. Aiden was heard slowly exhaling, Lauren was drowning in an oversized princess shirt. She also had a plastic bag of candy, glow in the dark vampire teeth and a small puzzle arranging game rested between her skinny legs. Aiden had eaten all his candy but can sleep peacefully knowing his sister would bless him with some of hers. Both Aiden and Lauren wore a Lei, (*a Hawaiian garland of flowers around on their heads*) with both their faces covered in red face paint.

Donny peeked back at them to see if they were waking up but they're so serene in the backseat. Yanie pretends to honk the steering wheel as a joke to waking them up and scaring Donny when he faced her. The two chuckles at the thought, then he slowly shook his daughter's shoulder to wake her up. Lauren groans a little as her head turned to the window, then took off her sunglasses to confirm if they were home since outside is dark.

Donny nods to her, implying that we're back. Lauren rubs her eyes, but they look tiresome still with her slightly falling to the side. She recovers fast, then checked the time on her phone. Aiden slowly awoke from Lauren calling his name, then shook him. Donny unfastened his seatbelt and gently poked him, tickling his son to where he couldn't pretend to still sleep. His scrawny, little body soared up with his cheeks coiled up, now cackling to himself. Lauren and Aiden both make sure nothing has dropped behind out their pockets. Donny stretched behind in between both front seats to wish them goodbye. Then to his surprise, Lauren wraps her skinny arms around his neck and rests her warm head on his shoulder. Her brother follows behind hugging him as well. Donny feeling both pieces of himself that for years were apart from him, were what recently had him scared of burning in hell. Yet, this moment had him pull himself together, joyous that they finally embraced a part of him.

He gave them a firm hug back, getting some of their face paint on him but didn't care. Then both leave the truck and race back inside. Yanie mocked him for the paint on his cheeks and pulled away from the house before Taivy comes out.

†

DOWNTOWN HOLKSDALE: 8:34 P.M.

Essie and Larissa finally arrive back home. Her guardian being mentally drained from such those distressing circumstances early on that she flops down on the couch. Completely sprawled out on the cushions, eyes shut appearing exhausted. Larissa first went to the kitchen covered in her own sweat, grabs a water bottle and gulps down half of it. Then opens the refrigerator again, staring inside to try deciding exactly what she wants.

Essie could hear her messing around in the fridge, wasting electricity. Where she would normally say something, Essie was too worn out, unable to muster up any energy to even retrieve anything from the fridge herself. She asks Larissa to grab her the bottle of wine in the bottom draw and Larissa does so. Larissa brought both the bottle and glass, but Essie tells her to put back the glass.

A loud yawn was heard from Larissa across the room, then goes to her room upstairs with another water bottle. Upstairs she wipes the make-up off her face and changes her clothes. Essie can already tell that Larissa is laying on her bed surfing her phone. Essie's face is flat on the cushion just staring at the wall. All she focuses on is how crazy everything escalated today. The fact that the church was overpowered by sinners themselves who sought forgiveness and she was there to witness that, almost had her lose faith in humanity. Then wondered about the aftermath of the police showing there, Essie turns on the news to see if there's any mention of this.

The evening News covers what has transpired at that church, she watches and sips some wine. They report acts of violence, declaring that the homicide of the priest had happened by five unknown suspects. The priest was found brutally nailed on the wooden cross inside the church. He had bleed to death, with autopsy reports showing evidence that he suffered internal bleeding from his main artery being ruptured by rocks. Reports had claimed that Father Brandon Lucas had attempted sexual assault on younger female church goers behind closed doors.

Police had raided the church after officer Viana Castillo had died shortly from a skull fracture caused by a flung rock. The assailant has been taken to custody and many others were detained. This sent a cold, paralyzing fear up Essie's spine at how awful the situation had become as they rushed out from church. However, what really had her affected were the unpleasant scenarios of how those animals would've impacted Larissa. She recalled back to how they threatened her from preventing their sadistic fun. They weren't going to show her no love, and Essie felt this self-inflicted anger at that. Once Larissa spoke out, Essie honestly believed for a brief second that these sinners would've complied. But now felt as stupid as they would've looked being seemingly controlled by a fourteen-year-old girl. That immature portion of her mindset could've costed the life of someone she loves dearly. This frustrates her more; all this overthinking began overpowering her. More gulps of wine were had to help ease her nerves, made her feel less like herself, but begins reflecting on herself. The unknown of Larissa's fate if her guardian had been bashed in the head by a rock. At the same time, she worried about the circumstance of the average life she's lived with her ongoing routine of responsibilities, including Larissa. If they hadn't escaped, that would've been the extent of the life Essie Chu has to show for. Being fully aware of this has Essie ingest more liquor, finishing herself off.

†

Donny and Yanie were back at his place for the night. As promised, he's eating her pussy out to orgasmic climax. Yanie gripped the sheets tight as she hollered aloud, ceasing with a prolonged moan. Donny uses her released squirt to glaze her sensitive clit making her quiver more. She groans it's too much to handle but then teases that that's what she wanted. Lucky for Yanie, his phone ringtone comes between them. He digs for his pants underneath the sheets and pulls out his phone to see Taivy calling.

"Shit, am I bleeding?" Yanie panics as she noticed red marks between her legs. "No wait, it's that paint shit from your cheeks still."

"Keep talking shit, it'll be all on your cheeks once I eat that ass soon."

Donny answered and held it to his ear, Taivy was yelling from the other end of the line. Donny was shocked, like her vocals brought him from his tranquil state back to reality. Yanie hearing her somewhat didn't care as she was still recovering in bed. Donny takes to the bathroom half nude and rinses the paint off his face. He's boggled as to what's going on, the kids had a blast, they left on a high note, but he tries hearing her out first. Taivy is more angered by him not knowing what's going on involving their kids. Taivy reveals how angry she is about a stranger he's involved with laying their hands on her son. Donny's mind completely went blank as to how of all things that went well today, that's what infuriated her. This to him was something so miniscule that it wasn't anything worth giving a second thought into. He tries to explain that Aiden just was playing around too much and was about to invade her stuff. He explains Aiden wasn't harmed anyhow but felt interrogated as she confronts him about what stranger he introduced Aiden and Lauren to, where did he really go with her kids and why he didn't do anything.

Taivy wasn't willing to listen, she wanted to express how upset she was. Donny didn't feel or sound ashamed over the phone to her which had her more irritated. From what he knows about Taivy, she'll usually project whatever else she's angry about onto some other issue as a coping mechanism and sometimes combine the two. After all these years from being absent, believing things have changed, he still sees her carrying on this childlike behavior. He can't take this seriously, especially with him feeling disrespected by her excessive screaming as he's trying to peacefully resolve this. Donny starts raising his voice too as he now has her on speaker. He can tell she must still be upset over their history together, about them not working out and him ending their relationship on his terms instead of hers. It just shows how immature she's acting towards him, resulting in an intense argument from both stubborn parties.

Taivy threatens letting him be alone with them anymore. Donny paused at the reminder that at any moment she can terminate his rights, he could tell she's serious and ponders carefully on what next to say. They had discussed through text about possibly letting him take them out for the fourth of July to watch fireworks. It may not happen now and Taivy can sense he knows this by the joyous silence from his end over the line. He composed himself, he promises that he won't have them around his friend again. But that wasn't enough for her, Taivy then demands he contributes more money to her now.

Donny argues that he already pays her enough as it is. Taivy mockingly reminds him of how he should be paying twice as much after all these years. She warns him to think it through, then hangs up on Donny as he tries to come to an understanding. After hanging up on his end, Donny deflates on the toilet seat. Taivy got the best of him, he knew it wasn't Aiden's fault since she has all the advantage. His head is crammed with their recent argument, on repeat again and again like a meme on a loop. What boggles his mind the most was her gloating, acknowledging him being in a vulnerable position. Donny alone felt stuck in this perpetual, helpless state with only Taivy being fully in control. Now all he can do is be left seething on the toilet.

Donny finally came back to his bedroom appearing frustrated still. Yanie checks over her shoulder to see him at the end of the bed remaining silent.

"Baby moms salty still, huh?" She mockingly said. "Yo, you good?"

"Baby moms got pissed about you hitting my kid. She just called my phone screaming."

"Oh, fuck. You dead-ass?" she asked, shocked. Remembering when she did it. Then led to follow-up with:

"Now she trying to have you come up out your pockets for more child support than you be already paying?"

"And if I refuse then no more quality time, so…"

"Goddamn, all over me keeping him up off my edibles?"

"What, not like this shit's my fault. She's obviously the one being petty over nothing, really. No one got traumatized."

Donny found out that Lauren told her what transpired after being confronted by Taivy.

"So close, too damn close."

"To what? Getting into heaven? Nigga, you still on that shit?!" She rebuked.

"That's not the point! Shit between us was getting good then your ass had to fuck it all up!"

"My ass brought y'all together up in my truck—"

"That you stole." Donny overrode her.

"Ok but you still had 'em up in there though, pops! Plus, who's the one that needed my help? How 'bout you blame you? Who the one got up out their lives just to show up over some dumb shit? Exactly… crickets."

"I can't with you." Donny said sounding irritated.

"It ain't on me that she still salty over y'all not working out, Donny."

As aggravated as he was, Donny felt some sort of relief that he had someone agree with what he believed to be the core problem. Even better to him that it was opposed by someone of the opposite sex. Even with Yanie getting upset at him too, she knew this was something he needed to hear. She's known from her many experiences of stealing cars was on how to manipulate someone by giving them bits of what they want to hear so she can get all she wants. Although she does believe what she's saying, he had nothing she necessarily wanted. This had Yanie feeling the most honest, especially with herself, realizing she just wants nothing more but for him to stick around.

"It's like she knows I'm just trying to do right but still being uncooperative." He complained.

"That's how it be sometimes, you left her a single mother, she not letting that shit slide. But real talk, she needs to quit finessing you still. You don't even give me bread in exchange like that. But the way Lauren was hugging up on you before seemed genuine. Almost like she ain't wanna tell and knew that it might come back to you, like an apology. So now, don't get it twisted. Plus, I'd be salty if someone touched one of my siblings too!"

Killip's Quarter's, 12:23 A.M.

Solanda is outside smoking her last cigarette before her break had ceased. The cheers of drunken fools can be heard from there as well, but it doesn't bother her compared to being in the belly of the beast. Or in her case, grinding on one man's lap while another yammers in her ear. However, a sense of her felt good that she had the ability to persuade men into offering her copious amounts of money by simply just talking. Her social skills being that good, revealing more about her than her body ever could. The proud ownership that she was more than just a pretty face or a hot body. There have been certain dudes who've singled her out just off her personality alone, and it never gets tedious to her. At first it seemed ridiculous for men to confide in her, scared of going to hell; but with them valuing her opinion alone, had almost equated the follow-up money afterward.

She checks her phone to see that she's back on. As she walks back out there, Latoya is heard barging in. Solanda seemed concerned but Latoya sprinted to the bathroom with a look of nausea on her face. The loud sound of a stripper vomiting before her next performance was nothing new here; Solanda however, knew Latoya was bearing a child and didn't advocate her even working still.

"Latoya, baby, you all good in there?" Solanda gently asks.

"Mm-hmm…" Latoya groaned.

Solanda wanted to dash in the stall to hold back her hair at least but reluctantly had to go out. She headed back out observing the newcomers sitting around. The sight of men laughing together while carelessly tossing money up to a stripper performing on a pole. Then saw the men getting lap dances who appeared miserable. In her high heels, she explored for a customer without service.

She'd seen one man in the corner on his phone as her possible chance. Then another stripper had approached him just as she was halfway there. Solanda turned around to catch a shadow figure of a man in the corner. The flashing lights in the center made it hard to put the spotlight on him. There's no telling if he was looking at her or what direction his head was facing as he appeared as a visual silhouette. Her curiosity raised as she moved forward but was cut-off by on passing strippers.

The figure before her had vanished as her path cleared up. Solanda walked back as a man emerged from behind her. He was a furious dark-skinned man with a big, hairy belly had her stop, his intent presence held Solanda momentarily. Most times, strippers here wouldn't recognize a man who's only popped in once, but that once for Solanda was enough.

This was the man who paid her three thousand dollars to come home with him and she never did. The whole uncomfortable pleading he made suddenly struck her mind hard. She never imagined ever seeing him again.

"YOU REMEMBER ME?!" the man shouts.

"No, and I got cust—"

"I paid for you to leave up out this bitch with me and you dipped! You fuckin' dipped and pocketed my shit!"

Solanda could tell how other people might soon intervene with him lashing out right now. This man started closing in more with his belly almost pressed up against hers. His jaw was clenched to such extreme that it was visible through his left cheek. His heated exhales radiate out his enlarged nostrils, like the sound of a steam engine, brought discomfort blows down her lower chin. The crusty outer shell of his bottom lip seemed like it was at its cracking peak the more tightly pursed together his lips became.

Eye contact with his outraged, coal-black pupils were really highlighted as his neck stretches at her more.

"Sir," She calmly said as she took one step back. "I'm not obligated to come straight home with you."

"So where the fuck my money at then?"

"You need to back up!" Solanda asserts. "Nobody cares about you feelin' duped."

"You had me waiting outside this piece of shit place for an hour looking goofy! All that for quick sex from some stripper, that's all you good for! And you couldn't even come through!"

"I'm not gettin' you that money back." Frustrated Solanda said as she walks away from him.

The man kept screaming his head off as he follows her. Him feeling cheated out his money, outwitted by who he deemed less than and to be ignored by her on top of that had enraged him ten times more. Repeatedly hearing him call her over and over, Solanda held her composure. She sees the other customers start to watch this through the corner of her eye. Then walks the path of one of the security guards as the man's forceful footsteps keep pressing at her closer and closer. Her back faces the man as she keeps moving forward, completely unfazed by him. The black outfit she has on accentuates her whole body. It is harshly evident to him when her curvaceous ass that slightly jiggled, especially the more she moves on ignoring him, was the thing that squeezed him out of all his money.

He dashed forward at her.

Solanda hears his steps increase then turns quick at him. Her head yanked down as he forcefully grasped down her hair. Solanda's horrid screams are echoed inside the club, so loud it briefly overlapped the music. The stripper on stage froze stiffened on the pole. Two security guards rush to Solanda's aid as the man hissed down her right ear. Solanda's back is arched sideways in such discomfort that a painful sensation ran through her spine the more she moved. However, she couldn't help but put up as much a futile defense by swinging at him with one arm that just grazes his neck at most.

As her head faced down, a fist blindsided her, bashing her nose in. He sees the guards drawing in closer but gets a few more hits in. Solanda is tossed to the ground like a used stripper, then the man flees the club, never to be seen again.

Kental Avenue, 2:03 P.M.

The next day, Donny Bedford awaits up the cul-de-sac, parked behind another car by the sidewalk. His vehicle had been repaired; he sits in there with the radio on. The sight of a police cruiser circling down there has him more reserved. He gets frustrated that it's been five minutes with the cop car there, especially with Donny's intent on confronting Taivy. All he ponders is how this will end and is it possible to rectify this. Once the cop drove towards his direction, Donny looked down to his phone. The car's acceleration had intensified past his side then turns around the corner. Donny pulled from the sidewalk and had driven to Taivy's home.

The car pulled up in front of her house. Donny dialed Taivy up, lowering the radio as his phone rung. Her phone went to voicemail automatically. He draws out the driver's seat and storms to the front door. Taivy opens it fast the moment he's pressed on the front step. She looks at him with an impatient attitude. Her arms crossed, eyebrow raised and a condescending sneer. Donny clearly saw that she expected more child support which vexed him more.

"Donny," Taivy calmly greets. "You got something for me, don't you?"

"Not really. Just came for my kids, that's it."

"What about what we discussed?"

"There's nothing more to discuss, ok? We both said some shit, both were out of line. I just wanted to pull up, take 'em to the movies or something."

"They're not here." She coldly replied.

"What, where are they at?"

"Where the fuck's my money at?"

Her stubbornness continues to annoy Donny. Even knowing prior that she'd most likely act this way still didn't instill in him enough patience to tolerate her loud tone. Then checks around the other houses to detect any neighbors watching. Donny reminds himself why he's here and composes himself.

"Taivy, do you know where our children are?" he politely asks.

"Yes, I do know where my kids are. I'm the good parent."

"So, it would've been nice to give me a heads-up so—"

"For what?

"I had plans with Aiden and Lauren!" Donny's voice raised. "Then you haul 'em off wherever, using them to get back at me! For whatever reason—"

"Whatever reason… you're leaving sluts alone with my kids, smacking my son around.

"It wasn't like that! I don't know if Lauren exaggerated or you're exaggerating but—"

"Now you're saying Lauren can't see or I can't hear?!"

"Well, clearly you aren't hearing me 'cause I already told you I was there!"

"Nice, nice, Donny… you were there and you ain't think to intervene." Taivy sneers.

Taivy then begrudgingly informs him that her friend has them for the day. He offered to take Aiden and Lauren for a couple hours for Taivy to have time to herself. This has Donny seething, especially since they had already planned prior for today's visitation. Taivy senses his frustration. She then begins bragging about relaxing in the bedroom, watching TV while baking cupcakes.

This prompts Donny to asks exactly who is watching them. She ignored the question, showcasing this arrogant, devilish smile. Donny demands she puts him on the phone. Taivy swipes out her phone and dialed up the person supervising her kids. Donny's heavily breathing is overheard and increased by waiting for the prolonged ringing on speaker to cease. Taivy boldly holds the phone up in his face which further annoys him. Then the ringing stops and someone answers: *"Hey?"* Donny was distraught by the masculine tone of voice expecting for Taivy to speak on their end.

"Hey bae, I got someone who's trying to speak with you." She responds.

"Hello, who's this?" Donny sounded perplexed.

"Nigga, who this?" the man responds. *"I know you, bruh?"*

Donny introduces himself as Aiden and Lauren's father. Softly explains that he was supposed to have his kids today and requests for this guy to drop them back.

"Well Donny…" he said condescendingly. *"You should talk to they moms about that. Plus, I been known these two. They ain't never told me anything about no dad."*

"Wonder why?!" Taivy snobbishly adds.

Donny not knowing this man's name nor much about him led him to wanting to detect more information. He was trying to seem understanding until he saw Taivy facing him. Her smug, arrogant look had gotten worse the more he appeared submissive to not just her but this stranger over the line that she's in control of.

"Do me a favor. Put one of my kids on the line."

"Nah son. I ain't finna do that." The man bluntly said.

"I'm asking you nicely. Just wanna see—"

"Talk to their moms then! I'm carrying 'em back to their mother, not some stranger—"

"I'M THEIR FATHER!" Donny yells, his anger boils more. *"WHO THE HELL ARE YOU THOUGH?"*

"Someone who's known them kids far longer than you." The guy quickly replied.

Being fueled with anger had Donny loudly repeats the question. The guy over the phone refuses to disclose his identity. Buffoonish cackling is heard as Donny demands to know who his kids are with. Not just from this guy but from Taivy herself. Her gloating laughter enrages him more. Donny then threatens that he'll find this man's address.

"Taivy, who mans is this?!" the man said, annoyed. *"Nigga, I wish you'd pull up at my crib, son!"*

"Oh yeah!" Donny yelled as he tried to grab her phone.

Taivy waves it away. "Relax alright! You better contain yourself."

"Don't pull up at my crib lackin', son!" the man threatened. *"Trying to act all hard, you not about that life. She told me all about you."*

The guy mockingly details how he abandoned her and the kids years ago. Had cut contact. Taunted Donny about him desperately resurrecting in their lives to form a bond with these kids.

Donny argues that he's willing to financially support and buy gifts for his kids.

The man laughed. *"Bribing with expensive gifts ain't finna get you closer to them. You got a greater chance getting closer to God, playboy."*

"I can't even bargain with the devil incarnate herself here."

"WHO THE HELL DO YOU THINK YOU ARE?" Taivy snapped. She rants about raising Aiden and Lauren with good morals. Mentioning that she even takes them to church on occasion.

"I could take them off your hands and bring them to church." Donny urged. "Where we'll all rejoice—"

"Rejoice these nuts, motherfucker!" the guy overrode him on the phone. *"You ain't having them. Not today, not easter Sunday, communal Wednesday."*

"YOU DON'T DICTATE WHEN I CAN SEE THEM."

"Pull up! Pull up! Pull up!"

Taivy ended the call as Donny continued screaming over the phone. Her laughing intensifies as she watches Donny pacing back and forth. Despite their varying emotions, the two share the same idea: Donny has zero control over this situation. The two argue again without any consideration of the neighbors who may overhear. Taivy wants him to leave and keeps closing distance between them both the more she gets in his face screaming.

During the argument, the sound of a vehicle pulls up to the house. The sound of that vehicle caught both their attention, Taivy thought that an undercover officer was coming to intervene. Donny had recognized that vehicle, it was Yanie Juergens driving in that truck. The sound of the engine stopped, as the truck remained there momentarily. Yanie rolled down her window, puts on a neutral expression to hint at Taivy that she's neither dangerous nor lost.

"Can we help you?" Taivy said sounding skeptical.

"I know you don't know me. I'm a friend of Donny's."

"No, no, no, don't tell me." Taivy said as she looks at Donny. "She's the one who hit my son?"

"It wasn't like that." Donny assured.

"Nah, ain't no shit went on like that, don't get it twisted. Just came–"

"Woah, woah! Who is are to come to my house and tell me how I should react to something like that?! Laying your hands on my son?"

"I get it, not my place to discipline your kid who probably ain't used to that."

"Excuse you? I discipline my kids. I don't know what mess Donny's said—"

"Yes, yes. Fairly disciplined. Your son not knowing you don't go through stranger's things. Just to overreact when said person puts 'em in they place."

"Bitch, I should fight you right now." Taivy threatens as she draws closer. "Get the fuck off my property!"

"Donny, get your baby moms, alright!" Yanie mocked. "I ain't about fucking more of your fam up than I already know I could."

Taivy and Yanie began screaming at each other, their argument is more extreme than the one with Donny. Taivy just expressed her anger that was getting more boiled as stubborn Yanie began provoking her more on her property. After ignoring Taivy's final warning to leave immediately, she yanked open the door and pulls her out from the driver's seat. Taivy, completely enraged, commenced to dragging her by the hair. Not able to firmly grasp entirely on her short hair, Yanie swings at her head. Slapping Taivy's face causing her to fallback a few steps, then she tackles Yanie onto her lawn. Both women holler as they roll around the front lawn.

Repeated hits are being thrown at Yanie as she shielded her face with her forearms. Yanie caught the upper-hand as she flips Taivy lickety-split flat on her back. Piling her entire body weight to prevent Taivy from moving. Yanie got off once Donny grapples her by the arms and flings her away from them both. He blocks Taivy's eager path, cursing and threatening each other with Donny caught in the middle of this. Their arguing ceased as Donny had overrode them both by solely confronting Yanie. He blames her for trespassing, and instigating this entire altercation.

"My nigga, you deadass right now?!" Yanie said. "Who came at who wanting to square up, huh?!"

"No but who pulled up at her house?!"

"Your whip already been parked here, then you see this bitch come at me like—"

"Leave!" Donny demands. "Leave her property! I shouldn't even be involved with you. Just came here causing a disturbance."

To her eyes, Taivy was stunned at how this whole situation was being resolved. Donny came to her defense despite their constant bickering prior to now. She gleefully watches Yanie argue as she slowly recoiled to her vehicle, still hurling insults at them both. She pulled off their property and accelerates from there while she flips them off.

Donny checks to see if Taivy's alright, she nodded with appreciation. He apologized for her showing up and acknowledge the dirt stained on her shirt by brushing some off. With not much left to say, Taivy suggests that this situation involving their kids shouldn't continue on like this. Donny agrees and requests that they both discuss his future with Aiden and Lauren. Taivy mentions she has to clean herself off inside and invites him to come along. Donny emerged inside feeling relieved that it hadn't been worse.

†

Back at Jovanny's place, Solanda awaits for him to come home on the couch. She flopped on the cushions reflecting on the aftermath of today's whole ordeal. After the man fled, she collapsed on her back, a bloody mess. Sprawled on the ground with her arms spread apart, barely conscious after repeated hits to her head. Her right eye became swollen, with a blood vessel which appeared to burst. There was an extreme burning feeling from the sharpened sting of rushed blood flowed out her right nostril. Fluid gushed out nonstop while the other nostril somehow withstood any blood loss. The opposite nostril felt inflamed with an irritation breeze the more it slowly intakes air.

Within that hour, Solanda regained enough consciousness to recall what transpired to security and the owner in his office. Her nose now covered in a dried blooded ring now pressed down with a moist rag. The pounding in her head won't cease, especially the more her mind focused on that traumatic assault. She kept resting her head down in her palms. Unfortunately, there weren't cameras there to prevent any evidence of all shady activities there. Solanda doesn't want to reveal the large amount of money she withheld from this place, so she labeled him a hurt customer.

Her boss, Daniel, had apologized about this and sent her home early. Solanda had been anxious leaving her job. She constantly felt unease wondering where this guy was. In the back of her mind was the thought of him watching her travel to her car and possibly following her travelling home. Solanda kept checking her mirrors to detect any familiar cars driving her path any more than usual. She made it back with no trace of that lurker behind. Despite not seeing him since, the image of his disgruntled face had penetrated deep in her mind.

On the couch still, she's locked on her phone trying to detach from everything else that should matter: her wounds, fear and mood. There isn't anything about this that drives her to post this on her social media, it is more of a private matter. Jovanny is heard from behind the door from the sound of the knob. As her enters in, Solanda calls him over where he discovers her injuries. He's shocked as to her condition, he caresses her face. Her chin cupped in his left palm while his right hand rubs her right cheek. They're both on the couch as she tells him what happened at work.

Solanda recalls the guy she ripped-off and how he confronted her then got assaulted as she tried to stray away.

"Well?" Solanda asks, eagerly awaiting his response.

"I don't know… I'm not sure what to tell you."

"What?!"

"C'mon Solanda, you clowned this dude, left off with his money and ain't catch his name. What'd you expect to happen?!"

"THIS GUY RAN UP ON ME, RAN UP ON YOUR GIRL AND THAT'S THE SHIT YOU SAY?" Solanda said as her voice started to crack but retained it fast. *"LOOK AT MY FACE!"*

"And I hate to see you like this but yo—"

"YOU KNOW WHAT, IT'S FINE. LET'S DROP IT!" Solanda hissed as she left to the bedroom.

The door slammed leaving a clear threshold for Jovanny not to cross. He lies back on the cushions, nonchalantly watching TV.

†

Back at Donny's place, he sits at his kitchen counter smoking weed as he reflects on today. He just relaxed there until the sound of this loud pound on his front door. It continued repeatedly, forcing him to walk faster to the door. The door opens to reveal Yanie Juergens impatiently waiting in the hall. Her cold stare and arms crossed, Donny can feel her fierce presence.

"Well?" Yanie said.

Her frustrated scowl disappeared, replaced with confusion. She was concerned whether Taivy had called the police afterwards. Yanie had conjured this plan of having Donny confront Taivy, getting her so aggravated that she would transfer that anger towards her. Donny watches them fight, capturing Taivy starting it on his phone. He made sure Yanie never officially came onto her property. Once she invites him in after standing up for her, both parents discussed a compromise. Donny pays the amount he had done before and still sees his kids soon. Donny compliments her on being so strategic with this. Yanie was so enthralled by his appreciation until he resumed talking. Donny continued about how after they made a future plan about their kids' well-being, she insisted he'd stay longer for some drinks. Yanie sat next to him fully grasped into this story but not from seeming intrigued but for the hope of it not leading to them officially becoming a family.

He continued on how Taivy recalled the time they first met when Donny first approached her. The two were in a good place, sitting amongst one another on Taivy's couch drinking and cackling about how much time has evolved. On how the kids had grown up under her supervision and how things are elevating for them and glad that Donny isn't holding them down. The more time had passed in the story and in present time, the more Yanie was eager to getting to however this concluded. More liquor was flowing as Donny informed her on his life as he was making a life for himself and wanted to include the children in it as well. Which led to Taivy wanting to hear more of why he returned again.

Donny had told Taivy about the whole list that came to earth. She said how Aiden was extremely concerned about her placing. Donny then continued on about how he was worried about his fate as well to where he wanted to make amends to his children and become more involved. Donny then paused momentarily as Yanie automatically picked up what may've transpired next, and she was right. Taivy's sweet, happy drunken bliss had vanished as she became stunned.

Taivy's whole demeanor changed, the man who she'd admired that evening hadn't been the man she thought he was earlier. The one who selflessly intervened and came to her defense seemed so genuine. She even snapped out of that childish fantasy since he was just on her property not truly for her at least, nor her kids but for himself. Donny tells Yanie how she was furious about his true motive for exposing himself after all these years without revealing why from the beginning. He mentioned how Taivy had this glimmer in her eyes before she found out. Almost like she had vision them all being an actual family again out of love brewing deep inside between them.

Donny knew her too well to know that Taivy wouldn't ever expose her true feelings for him, especially since he didn't return back for her. So he believed her cursing him out and saying he's no "true parent" was her way of concealing her bruised ego. To him, her letting him return into their lives again over unresolved feelings felt like that was her ulterior motive. Yanie listened to the rest of the story of him and Taivy going at each other's throats and how she said that she'd take him to court to settle this once and for all.

Yanie wrapped her arms around his shoulders consoling him. Donny removed them both, not out of anger or annoyance but from knowing the stress he'll have to endure soon. Yanie reminds him of the video of her being attacked to gain some leverage. He felt a small bit of relief yet it still wasn't enough with the thought of how much impact this will have on both Aiden and Lauren. He walks Yanie to his door.

"I really appreciate today but this really don't involve you." Donny said. "I got all this shit happening that—"

"It's all good, I get it." Yanie begrudgingly said even though she didn't mean it one bit. She wanted to try persuading him into not letting her go but not only would she feel like she'd be stringed along but she couldn't. Yanie couldn't bear the thought of her trying to manipulate him into letting her into his life just to be turned away. He just pulled that with Taivy so he knew all the tricks. She wants to feel better in comparison to him for not doing that but it doesn't surpass the weight of not only unspoken truths but by also being strung of feelings that had her moved by him, like a puppet. Almost like he was the one manipulating her to be around and she didn't mind that until now where he cuts off all ties together.

She couldn't express how upset she was, knowing that not only won't it change anything but he'll just see her exactly as Taivy, someone upset over unresolved feelings on his terms. Yet he not abandoning her like he had Taivy and his kids years ago was Donny being nice, at least in his eyes. So Yanie held on a straight face and left. As she's leaving the building, she thinks of all those past schmucks she's played into getting what she wanted, their cars. Though the thought of Donny Bedford, the one guy who was equally on her tactic bracket, had surpassed her and left her to navigate her own path alone.

† Chapter 9: How may I help you, sir?

Officer Lambeth and Colthirst are cruising through downtown after just dealing with a complaint reported midtown. A Caucasian woman had spotted four minority kids between the age range of eleven and twelve. The four who she'd never seen on her block before were near her house in a formed circle. Their activity appeared felonious to her as she reported to the cops what she'd witnessed. After officer Lambeth having the kids explain what really transpired, him and his partner had told them that they weren't in any trouble. Officer Colthirst recommended they take it under a shady tree that's apart from the lady's house since today was so hot. But it was mostly to prevent the women from harassing the kids any further. Lambeth even gave each a dollar, not only to get an ice cream cone but to relinquish any fear they may have towards them as cops.

They discussed the havoc at that church with the priest getting attacked by church-goers.

The two were irritated over these ridiculous emergencies this summer. Colthirst recalls the urgent call over to report on a supposed group of gang affiliated adults surrounding a church, on a Sunday of all days. When all they were was church-goers. And his excuse was they're all wearing the same color.

"Yea, black!" Lambeth added, then recollects over that obese woman who was a compulsive hoarder. She had reported a home invasion. Being robbed of many valuable possessions. The victim had showed photos of the multiple objects scattered around her house. And surveillance of every room cluttered with items.

"I swear I thought she was a kleptomaniac. *Could've got arrested herself from the state of that house."* Colthirst said.

Lambeth nodded. "Exactly. They cleaned her out."

"I guess they sealed their fate." Colthirst said.

His partner was perplexed for a second until he realized he meant the miracle that's still being theorized that's had everyone acting crazy. Lambeth showed his annoyance by this event since not only did he not believe in it whatsoever, but it was the driving force for people he's dealt with on the force recently.

"Don't tell me you fell for—"

"No. I'm untouchable." Colthirst arrogantly laughed. "Everyone else we've come across has been overreacting to the point where now my fate is sealed watching over these buffoons is an issue."

"Buffoons I wish to claim are mentally developed adults."

Officer Lambeth believed that his time on the job was too valuable to waste on people acting crazy over something that's meaningless. Nonsense keeping him preoccupied from real crimes happening that request his assistance. Lambeth felt accomplished arresting actual criminals and further preventing future mayhem. He felt bold to know that he could withstand real threats from escalating to where he's self-assured enough to believe he solely can protect everything around him, from regular pedestrians to his wife.

To him, patrolling for citizens deluding themselves over this hoax was an enormous burden.

What aggravated Lambeth worse was how other officers he's dealt with are responding to this. Throughout his career he's been exposed to officers who're corrupt or blatantly racists that've been introduced to his department. Through the many years of being in Holksdale, he's met police officers who ruthlessly enforce down the law through brutality. Many unarmed minorities had been racially profiled, arrested or shot to death on sight due to a certain police officer's preconceived notion that they were dangerous. It even sickened him to see how other officers would welcome them back after they return from temporary leave with zero consequences after their trial.

He had met an officer twelve years ago who had responded to a report of alleged child abuse from the neighbor between a father and daughter in downtown Holksdale. The mother had left the house for groceries and there was noises of screaming heard from there shortly soon afterwards. The officer went to investigate only to discover a black male who claimed to have been watching scary movies on loud stereos with his twelve-year-old Caucasian daughter. The officer didn't believe him and requested to come inside. The officer refused to believe she was his child as he ordered her to wait in another room. More noise came from inside as an argument between the men had ensued that this was a misunderstanding and for him to leave. The man had felt threatened and attempted to flee from there;

resulting in him catching four bullets in his back once he escaped outside on the grass.

The cop got all charges dropped due to him claiming that the guy came off as a hazard; even when a paternity test revealed that the man was in actuality her biological father. Lambeth had been bombarded by proud officers bragging about taking down minorities; lacking any empathy over the expense of their families. It however doesn't help that most officers that reside in Holksdale throughout are seen under the ***Hell*** category on that list for their past injustices. Many of them either turn a blind eye to it or have engaged in more illegal acts since they believe they've got nothing to lose. This has increased the number of ethnic citizens losing their lives this past recent summer.

Lambeth has always kept this story in mind to where he knows to never go overboard, especially with people's ignorant bias on all cops. This helps for him to keep his cool to where he feels he can defuse literally any situation at hand and felt much more superior in comparison.

"But I see what you're saying though." Colthirst said. "I only be seeing crazy shit these days. And when we come to help, a lot of people wanna throw shade, thinking we're about to shoot somebody. Or the people who need help wanna start acting belligerent and shit."

"*See…*" Lambeth snears. "That's why I just step back, let them go off and then settle them down. 'Cause I already know I'm gonna handle it so I let them put on a good show before I haul their asses off to jail. Get it all out their system.

The residents already think we're bad, then attempt to provoke us. I ain't gonna give them that."

"Nah, I'm not the one. I'll tell you that right now." Colthirst said. "These folks act all tough, causing shit that I go outta my way to fix up. I could give a fuck less what they think. None of these citizens are gonna walk all over me!"

Similar to his partner, Officer Declan Colthirst was just as good at his job. Throughout his time on duty, he's faced many adults who've done unspeakable acts. As bad as Holksdale is, it's hard not to cross paths with these certain individuals weekly. He had made multiple arrests long before they were partners. And had done so with no racial bias needed; although another one had manifested. All of these interactions led him to have a warped view on many people he's come across to where they're mostly just bad.

As simplistic as that sounds, it's been what he's exposed to constantly. Most people here disrespects cops or just overlooks the decent ones as well. He knows what he's up against and always asserts his dominance above them. Even deluded to believe they're inferior as opposed to himself.

"These people know when to fallback when I tell them to. Like this couple who lost their kid at the carnival, ain't nowhere to be found for hours."

"Uh-huh?" Lambeth replies.

"And I tell them that they gotta go over the story with me again about what happened exactly, right? Then the dad wants to get all big raising his voice, *'you should be out looking for my son, you're wasting time!'* and I flat out told him, in his own house, I told him to sit his ass back down. And he did. Then I found their kid that same day."

"Mm-hmm, gotta keep everyone level-headed."

"More like don't raise your voice at me." Colthirst said.

†

Donny Bedford had resumed his life after him and Yanie were finished. The following week, Taivy had informed the kids as to why their father really returned back into their lives. Contact between him and his kids were cut off. Donny had expected this but didn't beg. He also knew that eventually he'd be taken to a small family court and it happened the same week. He and Taivy had to decide on the welfare of their children. Taivy would've preferred for him to leave them again and to never come back. But after feeling years of stress raising their kids alone, she felt she deserved to be compensated with child support. Donny had hired a lawyer as well and came with his head held high.

It was evident how much Taivy wanted for him to give her a copious amount of money as a way to gloat in his face. However, he wasn't just going there to let her have that notion of being squeezed for just his money's worth. The two fought for their kids but not over Aiden or Lauren; they were at odds over their pride.

After much discussion, the small court decided for joint physical custody between the two. This arrangement will have both Donny and Taivy involved in their children's upbringing. Aiden and Lauren will also be spending time between both their parent's residencies. Donny gets them on weekends which infuriated Taivy to no end. She just wanted for him to vanish after the court settled this, not to share her kids. Donny knows that this will lead to more tension.

Especially with the focus on Aiden and Lauren split between, sending his kids from hell and back.

The first weekend after this was settled, Taivy was supposed to let Donny have them over at his place. Instead she let them go to their grandma's house. This led to Taivy explaining they'll possibly return back by that evening and shut the door on him. Donny knew that this would continue if he lets this slide once more. Hours passed when Taivy received a text from Donny but refused to open it until an hour later just to frustrate him more for not responding sooner. Once she opened it… she wished she hadn't.

It was a video of her attacking Yanie on her front lawn. Her eyes widened, it felt so unreal. There was no detection of Donny even having his phone out. There was another text that followed up after the video was done: *I'm done with your childish shit, using my kids against me whenever I wanna see them. I'm not having it. Either have my kids ready by the next time I come up or the girl in the video will press charges over you attacking her.*

Taivy sat on her couch frozen, in complete disbelief to what she just read. The fact that he's got leverage over her that can get her into legal trouble had escalated her paranoia. But what kept being drilled in her head was the fact that once again, Donny had gotten the best of her, and he knows that she knows. She swipes her couch pillow and bashes her face in it hollering. Almost sixty seconds of pure roaring uttered into her pillow. Alas, now evolved to tears and childlike sniveling at the ongoing emotional turmoil that she's succumbed to. Taivy's whole body crumbles knowing that there is only one choice left; to give in.

Two days later after really contemplating her options and discussing with her therapist and male friends, Taivy had texted to meet with Donny at a small restaurant in midtown. This was one of the few places not vandalized by any residents from uptown. Donny agreed to meet with her to discuss the future involving the kids, he was pleased for once since he doesn't have to play any more games with her.

Donny had arrived to the restaurant as the employee escorts him to Taivy's table in the back. As he got close, he seemed surprised to see not only her but Aiden and Lauren sitting on her side. He finally gets there to a warmer welcome from the employee than his own family. They all sit together with Donny facing across from them all at the table. The kids remain silent with his son seemingly wanting to say something. Donny probably knows that they know about his fate bringing them all together. Either from Taivy blabbing her mouth to them or over the phone. Regardless of how they knew, this whole matter between them was supposed to be discreet.

He smiles at his kids and offers to buy them something off the menu but Taivy says they ordered already for takeout. Hearing this meant that this discussion wouldn't be long. Donny wonders why she wouldn't just do this over the phone instead until she digs in her pocketbook. She pulls out some papers and settles it on the table. Taivy goes on about how she and the kids were happy before he came into their lives causing problems for them, now she wants to have a fresh start elsewhere, especially with how chaotic everyone is acting now. She explains how she has family further away in Memphis, Tennessee. They can get her a job and a better, safer life for their kids. This whole meeting was for him to sign these papers to relinquish his parental rights.

This was all too much for Donny to take in. The look on his children's faces hadn't changed, it was apparent to him that she must've went over this with them already. Donny still called her out for doing this in front of the kids and not in private. Taivy can tell by his reaction that of course he wasn't happy to sign off on this. She glanced at both her kids to see them still watching their father, silently on her side.

"Donny, I appreciate you spending time getting to know your kids," she calmly said. "However, I need to think of their safety as a priority first."

"I'm their father, I'm here to protect 'em both."

"No, you've been here this whole time to save yourself and ain't nobody can save you but you." Taivy firmly said. "Now you played 'daddy' with them for a bit, they got to know their father despite it being over some nonsense."

Donny was getting aggravated at how calm she was behaving since he knows that this whole thing was planned to have him look bad. Right now she seems like the one considerate of the kids justified by a different agenda. The waiter finally brings Taivy and the kids her food all stacked inside a plastic bag. Donny orders a glass of water, Taivy gives her kids permission to eat, implying they'll be here for a while due to their father's stubbornness.

"Know what kids, don't fill up before dessert. We're about to be here for a while."

"Oh Jesus, Donny!" Taivy said. "Why you gotta make things so difficult?! You already got to know 'em, right?"

"I see your games! Acting all civil as if I'm crazy for wanting to be a part of these kids' lives."

"You had two chances when our kids were born and you ain't even want the first chance."

"All in your feelings now 'cause I won and now you ain't havin' it."

"I'm just trying to turn the other cheek is all."

"*Awwww*, need some help?!"

Taivy was getting annoyed with his uncompromising position and being taunted too. Aiden and Lauren remained quiet still hoping this wouldn't escalate in a full-blown argument. Taivy began looking around hoping they wouldn't garner any unwanted attention. Donny still feeling upset begins to rant on how her being immature over the courts not favoring her but for *the man who got her hopes up again* instead had just sealed his fate.

"You love your children so much but you were furious when I refused to schedule an abortion!" Taivy hissed.

The entire table was quiet, everyone except Aiden knew exactly what that meant. Lauren's face switched from her dad to her mom, hoping that wasn't true. Lauren finally faces her dad asking in an innocent tone: *"You wanted us aborted?"*

"Lauren, baby, now don't get it confused…" Donny softly replies. "At the time, your mother used you as—"

"You're lying!" Taivy overrode him then faces Lauren. "But no, I didn't."

"Yea, did that shit back then just to spite me. Just to have me stick around."

"You barely ever were!"

"Well jokes on you, I left."

"I see, such glee to be a deadbeat."

"Not anymore. You keep bringing up old shit!"

"Really?! You came into our lives over bullshit but I'm who's fucked up?"

"Know what else's fucked up, I see you kept that money years ago, I'd like that shit back."

"That's what you're concerned about?"

"Hell yeah, I want my goddamn money back."

"Money that was to abort your daughter?!"

"You ain't even follow through with it so if you don't mind?!"

The waiter finally came with Donny's order and politely asked for them to tone it down out of consideration for the other customers. Both of them nodded and noticed some people peeking at them. Aiden and Lauren weren't eating anymore, Lauren just stared down to her phone. Tension was still there, Taivy demanded as quietly as she could for him to sign those papers.

"Taivy, when are you ever gonna quit using these kids to get what you want?!" Donny said with a smug attitude. "It ain't work in court, ain't work when you gave birth to them and it ain't working now."

Taivy, after being fed up with Donny's constant bullshit behavior from impregnating and abandoning her to being manipulative to now playing on her emotions again. Taivy forcefully hit over Donny's water glass, the freezing sensation had him leap up out his seat. His cursing had other customers stretch their necks back at them. At that point, Taivy didn't care who looked. She knew she could get away with it, no one watching is going to let her get beaten by a man. Both parents knew this; their kids however did not.

As Donny was cursing at Taivy, she took a used napkin from Aiden's meal that had ketchup on it and smeared it across Donny's face. Enraged so much, his yell soared through the whole restaurant, drawing him to get intense right up in Taivy's unfazed face.

Seeing the frontal of his hot-tempered face made her smirk, then she swipes his face again. Taivy glanced at the kids that witnessed her making Donny look foolish, the same way he's made their mother look since the start of this summer. Acting as if he had a change of heart, her giving him another chance; all this rushing through her head made her slap him again.

Aiden and Lauren felt glued to their seats, not from their mom telling them to stay, but from being in the mix of their parents' arguments. They brought him back here it felt like, both adults shouting and having others staring sent such volumes of internal discomfort that no child should ever experience. They both especially noticed that their dad kept glimpsing back at them. Both could not comprehend Donny, being a grown man, just allowing this to simply go on in front of them all. Donny himself seeing Taivy take glee in demeaning him not just in front of mixed company but also his children especially just had him seething. He hadn't appeared furious still because his face was visibly sad. Shamed by how he promised his daughter before: *As long as I am around, ain't no one's gonna harm you, your brother or your mother*.

There's no way she could ever take him seriously now, he could feel it from her distressed look. And how could his own son respect his authority as his father's getting unapologetically slapped repeatedly again and again. However, Taivy's proud body language, having her back erect with her robust tits puffed out, exemplified how no one will intervene because she's a female. Donny had this slapped more in his face, which had him seething more after everyone witnessed him scream aloud. Not being taken seriously as a man had him look and feel no different than a child around Aiden and Lauren's age who'd just thrown a tantrum. Not only did he feel beneath Taivy but now beneath his children too.

That realization had him block out the rest of the restaurant with the thought of his promise to Lauren in his head again: *As long as I am around. . .*

Taivy watched him standing still, she believes he's paralyzed knowing all eyes were on him. She tells both kids to pack your food now since she's now done. The kids had hesitantly got up, trying not to make more eye contact with their father. Donny slapped their mother's cheek fast with her papers, having her whole face turn. The other customers gasped, women in there were in utter shock. But no one was in more shocked than Taivy herself and her kids. Both Aiden and Lauren were paralyzed in fear. Taivy started screaming and furiously rushed from around the table only to be slapped again. Three male employees ran out to get between the two. Donny heard the race of their footsteps, gives them an intense look, not afraid to have a whole brawl take place here. Two rush to the her aid, the other spreads his arms to block Donny from escalating this further.

Taivy was knelt down with her face covered. She didn't want Donny to see her sorrow look, but that hadn't mattered to him. Her hand slowly trembled away from the feeling of something slimy spread across her cheek.

"By the way…" Donny gloats. "I spit in that!"

The other two men turned their heads at Donny with a look of disgust. He never noticed due to observing Taivy's hurt reaction. Her hands clapped in her face as she sheds tears into her saliva-stricken palms. Aiden and Lauren raced to their mother, hugging her tight while her daughter tried wiping her face with a clear napkin. Donny saw the two kids staring at him, this was a man who just harmed their mother, making her sob before their eyes after rubbing it in her face. Donny watched Aiden hold her tighter and began crying while Lauren scorned at him. Donny steps forth to console his kids but employees intervene by threatening to call the police. He fled from his kids again.

Kental Avenue, 12:15 P.M.

Five days had now passed since the whole dispute at the restaurant. Donny's phone calls to his kids were ignored and he didn't even try bothering Taivy. He was really paranoid about the police showing up to his place after fleeing the restaurant, especially with all the witnesses there. It was confusing since Taivy was normally vindictive as hell towards him, yet nothing happened. However, today was his day to take his kids. Donny pulled up to her house not knowing exactly how she'll react knowing she's forced by law to deal with him. Once he parked, Donny honked twice but no one came out to the front steps.

Finally, he dials Taivy's phone only for the number to be unavailable. Frustrated Donny leaves out his car to the front door, the screen door was locked. He ringed their doorbell repeatedly after being fed up with being ignored. Taivy's car is parked outside and she knows Donny can easily blackmail her, but she's still causing problems. The door finally opened revealing only his daughter.

"Lauren, where's your mother at?" he asked.

"Her room." She replied flatly.

"Well, get you and your brother ready since apparently she couldn't."

His daughter just stood at the door watching him from behind the locked screen door. She just studied this man with a serious look as to wonder how he's got the audacity to show his face around here again. Donny knocked on that screen door, implying for her to unlock it. Lauren had just remained still, testing her father's patience.

"Alright, I know y'all are still upset from before but I need for you to open the door."

"I have. How may I help you, sir?!"

"I meant the damn screen door!" Donny demands. "I'm not in the mood."

"Mom doesn't wanna see you."

"That's fine, I'm here for you and your brother."

Lauren started smiling and shaking her head. Donny looks confused. "What's so funny?" he asks.

"What makes you think we wanna fuck with you too?" Lauren hissed. "Nobody wants you here."

Donny's face dropped at his daughter's response. She had a stern face with a screen door for her own protection. He raised his voice demanding her to show respect and to get her brother. Donny caught himself for a moment and checked to see if any other neighbors were watching, but no one was in sight. Once he turned back, he saw Lauren recording him on her phone.

"Excuse you, young lady?" Donny said.

"Capturing this moment," Lauren calmly said. "How's about you tell everyone watching why you're here?"

"Lauren, that's enough! I'm here to pick up you and your bro—"

"Nope, nope, I mean why you're really here!" she said. "I mean what really brought you here was 'cause you're too scared to die and meet Satan since you lived your life as a deadbeat who don't give a shit about his kids."

"That's not even it, I'm here—"

"Admit it! This all 'cause you're scared."

Lauren went on about how he'd just been using her this whole time and how Aiden had got attached. She brought up how he was blackmailing their mom. Donny doesn't want to overreact since he's on camera.

"You promised as long as you were around, nothing bad would happen to us. Then you go outta your way to hurt mom."

"She wanted to assault your poor daddy."

"All she wanted you to do was put us first for once in your life. It's getting crazy out here and she just wants to protect us. No more parental rights means you actually got a legit excuse to ghost us this time."

Donny tries to justify it being more than just that miracle bringing them back together but Lauren didn't believe it. Then tries to explain how their mother is using them to get back at him and justify it as being responsible. Once he blames Taivy, Lauren dismissed it completely. Then she recalled the incident again but how he wasn't driven by the list or out of love to fight for his kids.

Every word furiously ejects from Lauren's mouth.

"Know what I think?! I think it's all just outta pride. Always blaming our mom, just trying to get us against her. You can't handle being pushed out our lives so you gotta force yourself in, even if it means driving a wedge between us. Just sign those papers and get outta here! You ain't ever love us anyway, so just go. *GO TO HELL, DONNY!"*

The door slammed hard followed with the sounds of each lock turning. Donny stood there perplexed as to everything that had just transpired. He walked on over to his car until he heard both the door and screen door open, it was his son. Donny stared at his son with open arms but his son stood there on the steps. Aiden had an innocent look from afar, almost like he appeared remorseful. The boy placed something on the step and returned back inside.

Donny walked back to the steps only for his son to express his last farewell. Left outside was what Donny bought for him during his quality time with the kids; Aiden put down his toy airplane. Not only that but also the papers to relinquish his paternal rights were under it. He picked it up and held it firm. His fingers fiddled with the wings, remembering how much Aiden embraced this toy.

He returned to the car with the toy stuffed inside the glove compartment. Donny sat there watching the house, feeling like a stranger from the outside wondering about the life they could have without him in it. He realized that Taivy had won at the expense of his kids' respect being loss. All that raced through his mind was what his daughter had said and how Aiden's silence spoke volumes. Then he rest the papers on his lap. The engine ran as he drove out of there.

As Donny was driving, he remembered that promise he made to Lauren and how he could understand how she feels different now. Then reflects on how Taivy has turned their kids against him by exposing why he returned and how she escalated the fight. He just can't handle not being involved.

Hours since Donny came, Taivy has been in bed after ordering Chinese food for the kids. She finally came to the kitchen to get some water, it was getting too warm in her room. She noticed a flashing red light near the house phone, one new message was left on the answering machine. Taivy hoped it wasn't Donny but it was. The voicemail starts with him admitting that both of them were wrong to act like that around their kids. Her head starts to ache at the sound of his tone. Donny also went on about how he knows they all want him out their lives for good. However, he politely refuses to terminate his parental rights still and is taking this to the family court again to enforce his rights to see his kids.

Taivy's headache strengthened by the end of that voicemail. Then goes in the cabinet and has herself a drink. The thought of his presence irks her and it doesn't help that the incident at the restaurant keeps playing in her head. His proud feeling of slapping the shit out of her and still coming out on top. Everyone seeing her mortified, including Donny. It didn't even matter whether or not his message was supposed to hint at an apology. To Taivy, it's just another reminder of his acknowledgment over hurting her.

Later that night, she arranged an emergency meeting with her therapist, a fifty-year-old woman named Evelyn Claudette. They discussed everything about him which was a huge release since Taivy's never brought him up before. It wasn't until that session where she vocalized exactly how much pain he's inflicted on her. Taivy's talked bad about him to her friends and in front of her kids but never delved to the core of how vulnerable he's made her (*after her therapist picked at her brain a little bit*). She left her therapist feeling somewhat better but it wasn't enough to resolve it entirely. Then Taivy called up two of her friends and had a three-way call. One was a man who was an effeminate, slightly overweight black male from her job and the other was the man who argued with Donny over the phone the day he had his kids.

Taivy expressed how tight of a predicament she's in with her baby father. How he's relentless and keeps getting involved even when she gave him an easy out. The kids refuse to see him and he wants to remain here still. Her friends could see how much it's affecting Taivy by her voice growing shriller as she confided in them. Taivy finally cleared her throat trying to compose herself again. Though she made it clear that she wants nothing more but to rid herself of Donny Bedford.

Richez Shrive, 6:34 P.M.

During that evening, it was getting darker outside. He is leaving the bar after a few drinks. Inside he confided in Jovanny Gibbs about everything from the restaurant fiasco to both his children cutting him off. Jovanny recommended that Donny should just sign over his rights to prevent financial turmoil from child support. Donny wasn't concerned about that really, he just can't help but zero in on how his children both harshly rejected him away. At least when he abandoned them, he didn't permanently scar them one bit. Jovanny agreed with him on how he handled Taivy at the restaurant but thought he shouldn't had given her any closure through voicemail. Leaving the bar tipsy, he was on his way to his car.

Everything his daughter told him sounded like she was so self-assured about this man that she actually got to know, who actually had gotten involved by choice. From how she spoke with such conviction in her voice with only one motive, to get him to terminate his rights, it came off more as the truth. Donny reflects during his drunken state on how he spoke like he genuinely wanted to be more involved, and the only barrier to that was no one to blame but himself.

Lauren analyzed him in a way where it was like she could see into the depths of Donny Bedford. Where he never held himself accountable and no one's opinion has ever gotten through to him, like it was mentioning something to him in passing. This mattered to him because she was important to him. Unfortunately, at this point his daughter firmly established this to him because he wasn't important to her. And at that exact moment, he felt that.

Soon as Donny wobbled to his car door, he dug in his pockets to whip out little Aiden's airplane. He held it even firmer as he teetered back and forth like he was experiencing some type of turbulence. The scrape of a footstep followed behind him, two shadows appeared before his car. Two men covered in black tackled Donny to the concrete. His slow reactions impeded his escape as they temporarily incapacitated him then dragged away his body.

† Chapter 10: *Heaven… God, is this feeling heaven?*

Everything really began collapsing around the city of Holksdale. Days later in the small court, Taivy was there feeling anxious about how this may all result. Donny has that video still, the thought of all negative scenarios from that race through her head. Thoughts on Aiden and Lauren's well-being crosses her mind too, she wouldn't want to go to jail and lose custody over them. He wasn't here yet, she contemplated him taking his time to have her distressed to the point where she's internally suffering.

The door had opened, everyone's heads turned fast, including Taivy's. The father of her children appeared in the room dressed in a suit. The whole arrangement today was based on him calling for one since Taivy refused to comply with him seeing his kids. Donny himself had requested to speak for a moment. "Good morning, everyone." Donny politely greeted. "I have come here today to do right by my kids. They are my world to me, always have been."

It was making Taivy more worrisome as to what will transpire now. Donny declared how much of a positive influence Taivy has on Aiden and Lauren, and how she wants to have them be somewhere safer than Holksdale.

"See, I didn't want custody just because I felt they needed me. I desperately needed them, all over an irrational fear of something completely irrelevant. They're my children, not my props to resolve any type of issues I may have had with myself nor their mother."

Donny digs in his folder and holds out the papers Taivy had mentioned. He's signed over his parental rights, to further solidify granting full custody to their mother.

Taivy has become utterly flabbergasted, all scenarios of how tragic this could've gone has vanished from her head. Not just from what he did but how he's speaking. His tone is so gentle and soft, his demeanor seems extremely passive and his eyes were widen as if he couldn't believe what he's saying. However, the court agreed and they finished early.

"Donny!" Taivy calls to him as she made sure they were secluded. "What about that damn footage you've got?"

"All deleted." He said remorsefully. "I apologize for taking it this far."

"What?" she asked. "So, you're okay if we leave?"

"Anything to secure the well-being of your children."

Donny spoke so differently that Taivy had studied him momentarily. His whole face was serene to where he didn't seem to be at all fazed by her ending this all on her own terms. He even had on a gracious smile too while remaining completely statue-like.

"Hmmm, don't even give a shit about ever seeing your kids again, ok." She condescendingly adds. "Aiden and Lauren will elevate just fine without you."

"I'm glad." Donny nicely said.

Taivy had took flight, leaving him there, no goodbye or any polite exchange. She ensures that the kids leave directly left with her.

Richez Shrive, 3:56 P.M.

Essie Chu talks to Jovanny Gibbs about Larissa's persistence with getting a heavenly pass for her ungrateful mother. She recalls how Larissa constantly insists on another church somewhere else. Essie reminds her of how they could've been possibly killed by those crazy folks but Larissa is just hopeful that they'll be able to repent for Danielle's sins. Almost like she's oblivious to what harm may transpire. Essie's excuse she's been using for two weeks is that she has to work or she's too tired.

"Like she can't comprehend the extent of how far these lunatics will go." Essie complained. "As if people weren't arrested, detained and killed."

"Ain't no prayer strong enough to save Danielle. Bitch been a lost cause since her body count quadrupled up in the pen." Jovanny said. "Know what, you stay enabling her."

"Not according to her it's not."

"Have me talk to her. Hell, I'll tell her straight-up her crazy-ass mama not—"

"No, you won't. That'll only hurt her, I can't have that."

"But real talk, that priest really tried to finesse his way up in them draws, huh?" he asked.

"Yes, that sick bastard taking advantage of his positon like that."

Jovanny brings up something relatively familiar. In the news lately, many allegations have come out about a lot of Hollywood celebrities. There have been many news reports on how self-destructive actors and producers can be. Multiple celebrities have gotten notoriety for causing conflict on set, recorded confessions of racial opinions especially if posted on social media, admittedly attending rehab for years of substance abuse or engaging in multiple infidelities. Including plenty more issues whether it being caught on footage or not.

Recently there have been more exposures though, from celebrities themselves. Many actors, actresses, models, screenwriters, producers, even stunt doubles have come out to the public that they have done amoral things in their past. Most were illegal activities, paying people to keep things concealed and much more. These recent scandals have been fueled by the *"**Hell**"* section confirming each of their destinies. The miracle is engraved in the huge area under the Hollywood sign.

However, they weren't truly understanding that most were destined not just for sinning but more internally. Several of them have this preconceived belief that they are superior compared to the average man. Their fame, achievements and higher status elevated their inflated egos but lowered their core virtues. Many had become privileged and greedy creating entitlement issues, especially when courts granted leniency for many involved in felonious acts. Even those who donated money to give back to their communities had done it just to boost their reputation to the public. Although, there were very few public figures that donated out of genuine acts of kindness.

The sole purpose for these confessions coming out were in hopes of receiving providence. Either from them holding big press conferences or by posting viral videos for all the world to see, or for their sake, to go beyond globally.

Of all these revelations, the most common one was inappropriate sexual advances being taken place on and off set. Male celebrities had exposed themselves for taking advantage of their positions with lesser-known actresses who relied on them solely for guidance. Or a chain of women came out with these allegations on certain men who refused to lie about it. A few arrests were made due to actors who knowingly previously engaged with underage girls. There were issues unfolded of some harassment caused by being under the influence.

Jovanny went down the list of those celebrities that were going through this, almost sounding sympathetic, and brought up the most relevant actor: Grant Critchfield. Jovanny went on about how Grant's recently facing a sexual assault allegation and how he refuses to respond to this.

"What is it with these men in Hollywood today?" Essie asked sounding frustrated. "Just like those maniacs at that church that had no remorse whatsoever for what they did. But now their moral compass exists from being caused by the wrong direction. And I bet these were one of those scandals that had crept and concealed all throughout Hollywood itself. They had already known."

"Maybe but think of it like this," Jovanny said. "You an actor with all this clout, especially if you a dude of color on the come-up. I get why they moral judgement done got clouded. If my career was dead-ass on the line and I'd seen some shit, I ain't coming out to nobody neither!"

"Even so, just remaining within the same proximity on set with not only the assailant but the victim as well, it's uncomfortable. I would have eventually called them out."

Jovanny adds how celebrities are also now taking sides exposing certain actors that they worked with. Whether they want to get in God's good graces or just want to boost their career.

"These self-righteous figures already knew this; they could've intervened prior to now. Just exploiting this recent opportunity. Not one person can just come out and express that they were scared."

"Nah, it's all 'cause people be quick to jump on ya ass that you done fucked up, especially the internet. Like, I try to be honest and y'all finna show me no love?! Nah, son."

Essie goes on about how it's all a business move in attempts to protect their self-interests and Jovanny criticizes some men coming out crying during their confessions.

"Plus, these dudes caught up in all this, I wish they kept it one hunnid at least. Sure, you pressed up on some chick you worked with but at least admit you were just following the trend."

Essie's face showed some confusion. Not that she couldn't comprehend but that she hoped it wasn't what she thinks he meant.

"Just be all like the self-indulgence, non-sanctimonious,

thrill of Hollywood glamour crept up inside my veins. That whole aura had y'all forgot how to act."

"I thought you weren't snitching." she skeptically said.

"Don't have to name drop. Besides, most of Hollywood could be categorized as one entity that instills they uppity beliefs. Just could admit that their surroundings led 'em to act out and they ended up doing too much."

"Because that makes it any better?!"

"Nah, 'cause the atmospheric pressure of how people be boasting you, the success you receive plus all that paper you make, you would feel a bit of a pompous-ass too. No lie. Ain't sayin' shit's right but it's understandable."

"*No, ma'am.* Regardless of what thrills, men are still able to express self-control." Essie states. "So fanboys, fuckboys or whoever else influenced by their idols enough to try this whole '*casting couch*' shit should think twice!"

"I swear, people are so quick to blame the men." A strong voice emerging from the counter announced. It came from a tall Caucasian man who had a tan and short brown hair. His stance was upright for someone who's been drinking and was well-built. He was a soldier, now veteran, named Chet Lopresti.

"Excuse me?" Essie responds seemingly annoyed.

"A lot of these females knew exactly what the fuck they were doing. These girls in their early twenties who came out with these allegations aren't too far to blame. They put themselves in certain positions linking up with these men because in all those stories, they met with them somewhere private. They did it in hopes of attaining that money and since it didn't work out, now they wanna cry harassment or unprofessional workplace conditions."

"Even with being tempted by someone young who's not fully mentally developed yet, those actors could have refused." Essie said.

"They could've been going through a dry spell for all we know. Plus, females can get it easier."

"Well, females know dry spells don't last forever."

"Yeah, not when they're wet all the time." Chet states. This continuous debate between them had Jovanny just sit back observing. Essie would normally ignore someone, especially in a bar where they're probably drunk, but she's seething by how his responses either logically contradict her or how his narrow-minded viewpoints aren't fazed by her. Chet elaborates more on how the actors initiated but never coerced those women. The participants knew there was an ulterior motive for going out of their way for that interaction off set. Essie tries to meet him with some middle ground since he's seemingly that close-minded.

"Possibly some women may see this as an opportunity to be equal to men."

Chet tells how women have been indoctrinated to wanting more power than they already have. Ranting on how society's molded female's minds into thinking the world owes them something. He believes females can't be upset over not being viewed as true leaders because women act most off irrational emotions. Essie can't believe just how bold this man is to declare this with full conviction. He explains how men are the creators and builders that contribute more to the world than women ever do. Also how women keep resisting serving men, believing that's suppressive and that they suppose they equate to a man.

"We men are in a higher position in the world, take it from a veteran like myself. We can watch over the earth no more than the lord almighty himself and I don't even believe in God."

"Firstly, women running the world wouldn't be a detriment to mankind whatsoever. For all we know even God may be a female entity." Essie suggests.

"It has always been a man's world." Chet asserts. "Now let's say God was a broad spirit then, it just means she's putting all of mother earth in ruins. Since everyone's going crazy over her spreading her wonder all around the world, then things are escalating due to female nature. A woman of the highest power now exploiting it, might I add. In that case, the world should revert to what it was before, as a man's world."

Chet could sense the aggravation in Essie by how she sings the Star-Spangled banner while surfing on her phone to deviate herself from this. He couldn't care less though, and thought it was cute. Then he watches clips on his phone.

Jovanny begins to ponder whether or not this might be somewhat of a phenomenon. Perhaps with all the reactions consistently showcased in his face, there is some truth to this creation. He even reminds Essie of his placement.

"We that lost that we deserve to be judged?" he asks.

"Maybe because whenever God looks down on us, it's to not catch us looking down on our knees in repentance of our sins but in meander at our phones instead." Essie bluntly said.

Essie finishes her drink and tells how she's visiting Danielle to drop off some food. She then leaves the bar. Then time passes by while Jovanny serves more incoming customers including Yanie Juergens, who sits talking with Jovanny.

Soon after Yanie comes in, a pastor walks into the bar. It sounds like a joke but he immediately came in garnering some attention for stumbling into a place like this. He was a big dark-skinned man with an oversized belly. The man was bald with a smooth clean shaven face. He wore a black long-sleeved clergy shirt with a white collar wrapped around his jumbo neck. Then he stood in the center of the bar and announced: *"BAM! GOOD AFTERNOON, EVERYONE! HOLY SUNDAY, PEOPLE!"*

Customers, including Jovanny, had all stared at him in annoyance as if he was drunk or worse, about to give a daily dose of an unrequested sermon. Not one soul responded to his greeting and some others turned back to their drinks, ignoring him. He first acknowledges that this generation had been blessed by a sign from God.

"The fuck is this shit?" Jovanny groans. Yanie just watches to hear what this man's stupid analysis on this miracle could possibly be.

"All of y'all stay wondering, even questioning the miraculous insight we have now been blessed with last month. Well, God's world is filled with sinners. Apparently everywhere that God's struck, bein' all over HIS world, lurks sinners." The pastor said.

As he preached that, some customers had opened their ears again.

"People ask me, *'Marques?'* I say, yes? *'How do I make it to heaven when I be in the hell category?'* Well I say, how is your relationship with your superiors?"

Everyone listening became perplexed to what he meant by "superiors" since the most common question is "how is your relationship with God?" However, this man spoke with such an attitude that it had some customers engaged. He recited a part of the message God had sent down everywhere: Misplaced power bestowed on the apex hierarchy whom sins unjustifiable hardship upon the weak. For those who seek balance are those who seek balance are those worthy in reach of the promise land.

"Ergo, the hierarchy, all of them crackers responsible for yo' checks, promotions and current living conditions. Them folks determine if you gon' break the law to feed yo' kids." Pastor Marques states.

Some patrons began nodding their heads while other heads start to turn towards him.

"If you finna hold up a liquor store to pay yo' bills 'cause your boss don't give you that raise you been working for. If y'all killed y'all cellmate in self-defense 'cause guards ain't about protecting yo' ass. If the cops be the ones who got yo' ass at gunpoint when you get pulled over. Whatever they do will dictate whether you outta pull out yo' gun or intentionally kill an innocent bystander in a getaway chase. And on top of that, including their position towards y'all, they're actions predicate whether or not y'all going to hell! It's not all on y'all. It's 'cause of yo' relationship, not with God, but with the people above you."

"What kinda ridiculous-ass shit is this?" Yanie said and Rory shushed her. Jovanny was even listening.

"The lord claims to seek balance to make it to heaven, right? Welp, sometimes you outta tip the scale a bit in order to ration out both sides. In today's age, it's ok to play the race card to survive in this life 'cause God made us in his image. Don't let yourselves be the victims, people."

More customers agreed, engaging with one another about what they hear. Yanie and Jovanny were shocked. This pastor's voice had such self-assurance, he linked with how vulnerable they must have felt with living and being brought up in this rural part of town. How unfair life itself has already been since the day they were born and how it being a long struggle with nothing to live for once they die.

"At least the white man forcing y'all misfortune is going to hell too. Slavery ain't end after post-civil war, we all in 'white hell'. Even low-income white people are here."

Customers drunkenly cheer for what they hear except Yanie and Jovanny. Patrons raised their glasses up in the air with high hopes and more drinking circulating. Even to the point where Jovanny almost momentarily had the urge to cut some off. The drunken vibe was contagious and then a voice in the corner arises: "Excuse me, hello? How's about your God?"

The man was Muslim, sitting by himself drinking water. As soon as he asked that, all the cheering and hollering had come to an abrupt stop.

"Excuse me, sir?" Pastor Marques replied baffled.

"If the hierarchy is your detriment, responsible for all this erratic behavior… then what about your God then? Last I hear, all this loitering, protesting and vandalism had increased from God, the lord almighty himself."

It took a minute to let that all register in yet didn't let that deter him. "*God makes no mistakes.*" He replies fast.

"But God dictating everyone's destiny had caused y'all to act even crazier than before. It is his fault, he's the superior deciding YOUR placement for your eternal fate."

"All this critiquing." Marques mocks. "Where on earth do you place then?"

"*PAKISTAN!*" Montrez yells. The other people laugh.

"I am from Istanbul and have not wasted time on this. I have not checked the one that showed up here or Istanbul."

"Then shut yo' know-it-all ass up then, Aashif!" Marques hollers.

People in the bar sprung in a loud cheer again, holding their drinks up to him and applauding him as well. The pastor nods at his listeners, embracing them.

"No!" the Muslim man protests. "No God would promote a miracle for all his followers like this."

"And Allah-Ababa telling them Muslims to kill us Americans is so much better?!"

The man detests to this, dismissing all other reactions of the crowd. He defends that most Muslims aren't terrorists and that he worships Allah.

"Now that's yo' first problem right there. You going to hell until you convert to Christianity! You are worshipping Allah yet not the right God." Marques said as he recites the sermon of Leviticus 26 that enforces not to idolize anyone else as God.

"Leviticus my ass, you Christian extremist!" the man snarled.

"See, he exactly like all y'all bosses, people." Marques announced. "Its people like him believing he some nice Islamic gentleman amongst all us '*American Barbarians*'. You fucks out here terrorizing good ol' American folk."

Everyone had got louder, the atmosphere was filled with cheers and laughter. All drunk and sober patrons on the pastor's side.

"Good ol' American Folk?!" the man scoffed. "Most of you in here cheering believe you're going to hell."

"And again, y'all blowing us up will only get us there faster!" Marques said.

Seething by all this racist antagonizing, idiots cheering and his opinion not being accepted even when valid. Yanie was begrudgingly pleased by how this ignorant pastor had gained all this support and admiration. She didn't even care for this miracle and yet she was engaged by his views. Jovanny was just silent, hoping everyone won't get out of hand.

The frustrated man made one last argument involving something from his personal life. He admit that his wife and daughter had died but had practiced Islam when they were alive. Claiming they both were not only good people but are in a better place and no list had to reassure him of that.

"They blew themselves up!" Chet Lopresti yelled.

"That's a lie, don't you dare disgrace my family like that!"

"What family?!" Chet mocks.

The man reveals his daughter died of a heat stroke from wearing her hijab during the summer two years ago. His wife had died in a car accident.

"You ain't never love your daughter or else why the fuck else would you make her dress like that in blazing weather?" Chet said. "But don't worry, you'll feel real heat soon down under with that wife of yours."

"What!" the man yelled.

"She just as bad for making her wear that hijab."

"My Priyanka was a good woman."

"Oh, then I guess you won't rekindle with wifey's spirit in heaven then, huh?"

The man resists responding and turns around.

"No wait, my bad." Chet said. "Deceased wifey."

The Muslim man bursts forth out his seat roaring at the

top of his lungs at him. Chet's condescending sneer just pisses him off ten times more. Pastor Marques began provoking him, claiming how they already want to attack customers. That remark just provoked him to where he's about to fight him. The guy has his fist bawled in aggression until some drunken men intervene.

Jovanny dashed down under the counter to pull out a bat to break it up. Three men have their arms grappled around him. The man is struggling, bawling curses and for them to release him. Then Jovanny finally intervenes by yelling out: "Take this shit outside!"

The men had viciously dragged him to the exit. As they're moving, a woman tosses her drink in the Muslim guy's face, resulting in him coughing to excess, damn near choking off the unexpected slash to the face. They kicked the door open and threw him to the pavement. His coughing died down, but he spit up some of it to the ground. He was kneeled still trying to catch his breath. Then the bar door is slammed shut with sounds of all others from inside applauding and hollering away.

Kelvin Street, 5:45 P.M.

Essie is at the bus stop with a container of food for Danielle Sheppard. It contains fried rice and curry goat cuisine she had just bought from a corner Caribbean store. She's still feeling annoyed about Chet's relentless opinions but tries to not focus on it.

There's several delis in the vicinity of here, including many people she observes walking pass by. It wasn't until she rests still, feeling the warmth under the glowing sun that reminded her of that relaxation of it being summer. With all her responsibilities tending to Larissa, her job and the mundane tasks of adulthood, she forgets this sometimes.

Besides the people and stores, she observes the aftermath of the miracle still. On this street was vandalism of red graffiti marks of blasphemy stating: TO HELL WITH GOD! HAIL SATAN! FUCK CHRISTIANS. 666 BITCH! All these markings on deli windows, concrete walls and plenty more.

What also had caught her eye was what looked to be a scrappy teddy across the street. It was stapled onto a light pole bombarded with tulips, wrapped bouquets and a poster of a child's face. She realized it was a roadside memorial. Being too far to read clearly, there was an arrangement of post-it notes shaped into a wreath reading positive messages. However, she kept studying the large poster of the deceased child, a young Hispanic boy that looked to seem no more than eight-years-old.

A man walking had come to wait too by the bus stop.

"Excuse me." Essie called out, the man turned. "Sorry but someone died over there, right?"

"Yes." He replies, somewhat somber. "He was eight and got shot near there last week by some crazy guy."

He could see the change of look on her face.

"This guy kept screaming about going to hell and not being good enough. Then he sees an incoming mother with her kid and shoots at them both. Asshole hit the mother in the shoulder and her son in the face. Then the coward turned the gun on himself before the police arrived at the scene. Kid's name was Hernandez Felix."

Essie started feeling aggravated hearing this. The man sensed this but unlike Chet Lopresti, he wasn't going to instigate it further. He just ceases it by acknowledging how unfortunate it is for the mother to now be living her own personal hell while the shooter had taken the easy way out. The man turns to his phone as Essie sits there silently.

This whole pandemic of ongoing violence and anarchy happening out on these streets resulting in the death of a child just left her seething on that bus bench. That child could've been Larissa out roaming around Holksdale. Once Larissa crossed her mind, her anger turned into sadness, especially realizing who she was holding this container for. Her ungracious, detestable mother who doesn't even deserve a visit and how Larissa refuses to let her just rot alone in prison. Sadden by how poor, starry-eyed Larissa can't accept the reality that her mother won't ever change and how embarrassing it is to get her hopes up for nothing.

The bus is slowly pulling up. A woman crosses the street and quickly asks Essie for change while holding two dollars. Essie hands her some and tells her to hold on to her money. The woman expressed some gratitude then the bus finally stopped. They all climbed aboard. Essie got herself a seat and gravitated towards looking out the window at that pole which grew smaller and smaller as the bus pulls away.

Ian Ramsay

Numerical Airlines, 5:49 P.M.

This airport are many people constantly in motion. Cars, taxis and trucks all honking at each other. People outside carrying their luggage with a line of people weighing their suitcases. The sound of airplanes take off, being seen in the sky. Here at numerical are a group of people outside handing out flyers to visit the church in downtown Holksdale. The group is made up of youngsters in their twenties with plastered smiles and gleeful eyes approaching people to come represent at their barbeque.

In preparation of the flight to Tennessee, two pilot captains are behind the controlling station. Pilot Sean Kimble, a light-skin short guy with a black goatee in his thirties, prepares for takeoff. The main air pilot was the Muslim man prior from the bar named Rashid Bhalla. Sean announced to all the passenger over the intercom to turn off their devices and wishes everyone a safe flight.

"How you feeling today?" Sean asks. "You arrived on board looking frustrated. You alright?"

"I'm fine, just got caught in traffic." Rashid said. "And yourself?"

"Eh, can't complain. Ready to take off."

The plane had caught speed, gradually picked up and took up flight. Numerical flight 227 had took off.

Passengers are relaxed in their seats as the stewardess roams up and down the aisle checking on people. She had been requested to get a granola bar for one of the passengers in the back. So far it's quiet on the flight with people distracted by the airline movies provided on the tiny installed televisions with the headsets. Others are browsing through the magazines and are enjoying the small meals they had asked for. The stewardess finally comes out with the granola bar for this little boy. His mother reminds him of what he should say.

"*Thank you.*" Said Aiden sitting next to Lauren while Taivy sits in a seat in the front. The stewardess would've asked if Lauren preferred something but she was busy listening to music on her phone. The whole family got packed for Memphis after Donny relinquished his rights two days ago. Their luggage containing all clothes and other things being transported through airline services. Taivy didn't call their father to give him a warning in advance that they were leaving. Lauren had no urge to wish him goodbye and Aiden had mixed feelings but kept his mouth shut.

Back in the control room, Sean and Rashid aren't talking like they normally would. Rashid seemed deep in thought and Sean detects this.

"What'cha thinking about?" Sean nonchalantly asks.

"I've been thinking about this so-called worldwide phenomenon."

"Oh yeah, it's all everyone's talking about. Still trending, last I hear. At least it confirms I'm heading to heaven. What about it?"

Rashid elaborates on how it's engraved on a huge plain surface where he's from. He discusses how people found it offensive. He told his partner that people label many Muslims as terrorists, Muslim extremists or affiliates of ISIS and a list of his people's names stating most of them are destined for hell is disgraceful. Rashid had checked on his phone on the website with the list in Istanbul before the flight to see this for himself.

"I had even got into an altercation earlier over that exact same religious persecution nonsense." Rashid confessed, sounding somber.

"You're kidding?" Sean expressed in shock. "Where, here?"

"No, at some bar. They not only disrespected my religion but my family as well. These drunk, repugnant, intolerant fools labeled my wife and daughter as terrorists."

"Don't let 'em get to you, Rashid."

"I cannot help it." Rashid said. "My people in Istanbul were furious to this message vandalizing our land. We believe Allah had created humankind with the purpose of worshipping him. Allah would send messengers to guide people in fulfilling the sole purpose of worshipping him. Not send my people this discriminatory list of who's worthy enough to make it to live eternal bliss."

"Then who do you believe did this?"

"Well, many Muslims in Istanbul believe that this act on our land was made by American soil. Thinking now that the U.S. government is accountable for all of this."

"Rashid," Sean spoke softly. "I guarantee we had nothing to do with this. I promise you."

Rashid acknowledges just how powerful this country is with its politicians, police officers, including how they mistreat their own citizens. So, he can't imagine why not his own people. Then rants on how this country can barely keep in accordance with the legality of crimes that transpire. Sean nods in understanding where Rashid's coming from but feels anxious by what he'll follow up with next. All this disgust with Americans has Sean feeling tense and almost wanting to go back and forth with him but refuses. He is his partner whom he must spend hours with during each flight. They're both normally untroubled by each other in the serene sky and wishes to keep it that way. So, he let Rashid unfold as a chance for him to clear the air.

"I mean," Sean cautiously said. "No countries perfect."

However, that did not faze him and went on about how this country besmirched not just his home but everywhere else as well. Literally nowhere on earth was safe. Sean was tenser, looking directly out into the sky. Fidgeting with his belt, acting like it had to be attended to more. Furious Rashid had noticed his partner's detached presence and finally stopped. The control room remained in silence. Lastly, Sean excused himself to the bathroom.

Rashid looking out at the clouds couldn't help but picture his family. *"No wait, my fault. Deceased wifey!"* Had played itself in his mind like a broken record. He was still boiling about feeling shamed by that bar. All focus locked on that pastor who evoked all tender feelings towards his past wife and daughter. From the taunting, to the laughing at this expense, to that drink striking his face leaving backwash behind. His breathing grew more intense, especially recalling pastor Marques. *"Shut yo' know-it-all ass up then, Aashif!"* Everyone denouncing Muslims and claiming his family's fate. Every time he'd fly in the sky, Rashid carried a small hope of getting some miraculous sign in the clouds that his wife and daughter's soul was somehow in a better place. This was the first flight where that hope had slowly faded, there was nothing to see. Nothing but a widespread of clouds and brightness.

As he piloted the plane, a shadow casts itself momentarily, leaving everywhere dark. Rashid's eyes glimmered with hope once more, stretching his neck to detect what this sign meant. Then the sun came out again. It was just simply a cloud hovered over him that passed. All traces of yearning for a sign of sorts had changed to now doubt. Any hope that pertained to his family that had got him out of bed in the morning, that pushed him to move forward, that kept him afloat… had completely obliterated.

Rashid had dug for his wallet, pulling out a picture of his past life, with him and his family. He stares at the faces of his wife and daughter both covered in their black hijabs. Nothing will have him relive that moment again, this feeling all encapsulated in this last picture of them together. Rashid gets up from the pilot's seat, approached the bathroom door where his partner is still in. Sean is inside on the toilet reading a magazine, then noticed a strange noise from behind the door. He brushes it off. Rashid then sets the picture of his family on his lap as he returned to his seat. Inhales deeply and exhales as he slowly pushes the plane down.

Passengers detects the sudden shift in feel which became more evident since it hasn't even been an hour since their departure. The plane was gradually heading down. Little Aiden had looked out the window to see the sideways angle of the sky. He shuddered convulsively by how everywhere outside went blank by the clouds. Lauren yanks her earbuds out to hear the crowd's extreme worry. Taivy was trying to peek behind at them but couldn't by the shaking of the plane. People were perplexed, looking at each other, up waiting for the pilot's announcement for reassurance, as well as up at the sky for answers.

"Mom?" Aiden and Lauren both simultaneously muttered in their shivered tones. Taivy consoles them by claiming it's nothing too serious. Aiden grappled onto his big sister, stuffing his face in Lauren's side trying to conceal his high-pitched squeals. Lauren wrapped her arms, closing her brother in tighter. She buried her head on top of Aiden's, begrudgingly missing her ears being popped by the air pressure instead of the filling of passengers' screams. In the control room, Sean leaps off the toilet, pulling up his pants and calling for his partner. He can't open the door which blew his mind. Sean's fixating with the knob, yelling for Rashid. There is a chair blocking Sean's outer path.

"RASHID!" Sean hollered at the top of his lungs. *"WHAT THE HELL?! LET ME OUT!"* Sean's heart began to

race the more they progressively slope down. Rashid ignores him, buckles himself up. The stewardess tries to settle everyone down over the intercom. Passengers are barely listening to her forced tranquil tone above them. Then everyone's heads were held attentively up as the plane nosedived down. The plane has lost vertical control.

"BRACE POSITION, PEOPLE!" the stewardess shouted with a quiver in her voice but swallowed her fear and resumed. *"HEADS DOWN, ARMS FORWARD! HEADS DOWN, ARMS FORWARD!"*

She repeats this again until everyone executed this perfectly. Aiden and Lauren were horrified but both kids separated and fulfilled her demands. Regardless of the trouble, Taivy stretched her neck to check on them. The kids respond to her yelling their names. The vibrations disrupt the secured suitcases, causing all to spill out from above out around the aisle. A dashing blue suitcase bashes Taivy upside her head, knocking her unconscious. Lauren wails at her mother's unresponsive body being levitated just inches above hitting the ground.

As the plane descends from over thousands of feet, the stewardess tries making it to the pilot's headquarters. The plane viciously shakes causing her to slam her neck into a corner. The passenger that witnessed this cringed at the cricket sound that was heard. Her neck was broken, turning her head all around facing her right as her body is sprawled down the aisle… *DEAD.*

Sean had slammed head first into the mirror. He broke

the glass resulting in it sprinkling remnants of glass upon himself. Sean slammed his mouth that agapes open, leading to his two front teeth normally in front of his bottom teeth to be clipped upon impact.

Sean was out cold with his mouth and nose drizzling blood. As the plane descends further, Rashid can see the sighting of buildings, and so can everyone else. This just sends adults screaming and kids bawling. The body of the stewardess flows down the aisle in passing of passengers. The sight of her ongoing corpse, including the turmoil, forces Aiden to urinate all over himself. Her body travels downward to the front of the plane. The stewardess had finally made it to the pilot's headquarters.

The plane comes forth past buildings. People from below looked upward to the sound of the plane drawing down further and further. Citizens draw out their phones, posting on social media for all to see. Others are pointing up high. It is coming towards midtown Holksdale. Essie Chu looks outside her window over the bridge they're passing. The same bridge where the plane is landing. The bus driver detects this and the traffic on the bridge ahead. It came to an abrupt stop as all travelers, including Essie, looks to see exactly what's happening.

The moment everyone realized where that plane was headed, the bus intercom announced: STOP REQUESTED. The bells had repeatedly gone off, people yanking hard on that yellow cord in attempts to dive off. The bus gets crashed into by a car from behind while on the bridge. The people onboard were thrown forward and were all distorted. An ongoing collision happens further behind, all frightened drivers focused on the plane above. The plane is about to crash into the bridge's tower up above.

Back on the plane, some passengers unbuckle themselves. Others hold themselves and their kids to strap in. The free ones rushed for the emergency latch. As it opens, the rapid suction of air dispenses out people from the plane. Their loud prolonged howl out the plane horrified Aiden and Lauren as they too make their way all the way down to the bridge deck. Taivy's unconscious body could be held down by the seat belt no more. Her kids witness their mother be blown out just to get sucked into a propeller. Everyone is screaming harder than before. Rashid gazed into the approaching bridge tower. He glimpses at that picture again then closes his eyes and begins to smile. Most passengers believing all might come to an end, many for their own sake had held hands, and soon begun to pray.

All drivers jump out their vehicles when the sight of a man crashes into the roof of a church shuttle bus. More bodies rain down into traffic. Essie remains locked inside the bus while others trample over each other trying to run outside. Her teeth clenched shut, toes curled inward and her mind puzzled as to what to do next. The bus driver is trying to calm passengers down, announcing how dangerous it is out there right now. A body clashes into the vehicle close to them. Everyone swerved their heads quick at this. The roof deeply dented, windows busted and the car alarm went off. Blood was oozing out the cracked parts of the lower half of the car. Essie shuddered to the uncertainty of the blood being from either the passenger or the driver she crashed into. Paranoid at the thought of the bus being next, the bus driver open the doors releasing everybody out.

The plane's left wing collides with the bridge tower. People halted at the deafening sound of that striking. The tower comes down directly to the cars. The huge tumbling tower hits the deck causing everybody to feel the ground had rapidly shook, resulting in screams and smoke. White smoke fills the air, blinding everyone. After all the noise, now the screams had Essie frozen in her seat still. She couldn't make out anything outside the window, being fogged with white smoke. All that could be heard was the roaring sound of the plane slashing into the sea. This separates the above cable wire to clash down with others.

It begun to clear up, revealing to Essie why more people are screaming. The downward wire, sparkling with electricity, swings across back and forth killing people. It slashes some people in half, decapitating them alive or electrocutes them. Essie bends forward to her knees to avoid seeing more. The inner bridge deck crumbles down, thus tipping the bus forward. The three aboard wrap themselves to the bus poles and seats. This bus is on the ledge, rocking itself back and forth above the ocean, startling them all.

Essie witnesses the man and woman so distraught to the reality of this circumstance that they looked unbalanced.

"Quick, climb to the back!" Essie demands, finally taking control. "Put all your weight back here. Let's go!"

The man tries but the bus dropped back, sending him off to crash through the glass windshield. Essie watched as he fell to his death. The other woman was bawling her eyes out, holding on still to that pole. Fast-paced vibrations from the bus sent her into a frantic state of mind. Determined Essie stretched her arms close to the woman, they lock arms, and then Essie uses all her might to help haul her up. Relived to be in a safer position, the woman almost cries some more. Essie kicks in the back window. Shattered glass remnants falls at them as the bus rocked again. Essie throws the woman under herself to avoid her getting cut. Then brushed teeny broken glass out her hair and pursues forth.

"You first!" Essie urged. The woman was boosted out the window with Essie's help. She made it out on the ledge crying of relief while Essie is slowly crawling outward. Her arm extended out to be pulled up. The woman dashed away to freedom, leaving Essie dangling on the ledge above sea. She began coughing intensely, her worries of death are pulling her down, and several decapitated adults get shown on the upper level. Her skinny arms were starting to tremble, feeling feebler. Legs that were swinging to latch onto something had slowed down. All that went on in her head was the mundane extent of her existence.

Not many amazing moments she could hopelessly recall. It strikes her mind how she never had a huge impact on the world. She spent most of her college life preparing to get into medicine. *"Maybe the people I treated in the hospital will become legends someday."* Essie thought as her body went numb.

Then that was it, it all comes crashing in her head. All that desire to care for people and making the world a better place. *"It's what's kept me motivated for all these years."* She recollected as her petrified feelings lessened a bit, sending again sensation to swing her legs forward.

"Larissa…" Essie's breathing intensified. She swallowed a little to help clear her throat. *"She needs me, without me who'll she have? Who… carjacker Yanie?!"* Essie regained some muscle in her arms but could only sustain herself still. Her groans can be heard from the end of the bridge, no one was around. She let out a yell filled of distress and even a cry for help. It's almost as if that energy driving her to pull herself back up just wasn't enough to keep her fulfilled. Then subconsciously, strength reached Essie's bare arm muscles, persisting on keeping her levitated. Larissa consumed her head once more. Her well-being, their memories together and her love for that poor girl. *"She needs me, not her mother. She needs me!"*

Groaning as she scrapes her stomach being dragged up the sharp ledge, smoke from the sea rises at her. Ignoring the clouded smoke, she enriched her mind with memories of Larissa, her <u>number one priority</u>. Essie's upper body was coming forward more, but her legs weren't quite there yet. She kept gasping for air, as much as she could. All noises were made from her bellowing in agony, to snorting out of convulsion. *"I can't leave her behind with Danielle. Her mother's no good!"* Essie drilled in her head. Her hands desperately lurked around for any support to haul herself up. Then momentarily held still, exasperated with repeatedly doing this, afraid she could possibly lose a tug on her grip. Essie was so used to assisting others, having no need for any kind of symbiotic relationship whatsoever that now the one time she's involved in a life-threatening situation… no one's around. All those years of non-stop care had culminated for this exact crisis, she put all her capability into herself.

"Danielle will mistreat her like some dog if she ever gets out." It's what races through her head. *"She can't appreciate her like I do."* Essie Chu single-handedly hauled herself upright with every ounce of strength in both her bare arms. *"I need you."* Her thoughts unclogged as she made it over the ledge, then rolled onto her back, releasing a huge breath. She made it. Her face appeared to be in stunned disbelief as to pulling herself out of this, followed by a gaze in awe up at the sky. Essie lays still, eyelids barely open but something catches her eye. A glowing light of sorts spotlights upon her. She couldn't move and with what little strength in her left, she widened her eyes to the radiance being emitted. This shining light hit her bruised skin, Essie's now henceforth stripped and exposed. With her headspace this clear, no list of things to take care of in mind, she couldn't help but become stimulated by this dazzling light.

"Heaven… God, is this feeling heaven?" she ponders to herself while marveling at this newfound wonder.

†

Part 2:

Chastity Era

† Chapter 11: I'm not leaving here for a while.

Temperatures having risen amongst citizens within each town.

Holksdale has been the center of worldwide news today. Multiple news channels have broadcasted this tragedy but the first to do so was of course midtown, being that here is where the latest news updates happens.

Every resident in midtown can see the huge cloud of smoke polluting the hot air. There are helicopters hovered all around the collapsed bridge. The plane itself had separated in the sea with a rescue team now involved. Within that area lies multiple bodies on cars, split in half on the bridge or deceased passengers from the crash.

Several abandoned cars are still aligned on the bridge indicating a lot of people had fled. The sirens of many are still active. The crash has very few survivors leaving eighty-one dead. Only four people had survived: two teenage boys, one Hispanic woman and pilot Rashid Bhalla.

Crowds of people are witnessing the aftermath of all this here. As far as the bodies piled on the bridge, there are no survivors from this gruesome incident.

York Avenue 7:23 P.M.

Larissa sits outside under the shade as normal. She's listening to music while wondering how else she'll help her mother. Then her phone vibrates.

"Hello?"

"Hello, is this Larissa Sheppard?"

"This is she." Larissa answered cautiously.

"This is nurse Melrose from Sacred Bond hospital. Are you in relation to Essie Chu?"

"Yes…" her voice quivers sounding very hesitant. *"She's my guardian, is everything alright?"*

"We are treating her, she apparently had got involved in that accident caused by Numerical flights this afternoon."

"HUH?" Larissa blurted out. "She never got on no flight."

The nurse informs her of the accident and how many people haven't survived and the few that were are now being treated. She explains how a rescue helicopter had flown to her aid. Larissa was frozen, her whole body constricted of fear and whatever would come out of this nurse's mouth next. Her pulse felt more intense, she stood upright, wide eyed. Pounding from her heart races more too where Larissa's almost unable to bear all of this crashing down.

"Is… she ok?" Larissa's voice began to crack eagerly awaiting for an answer. "Sacred Bond hospital, right?"

"Yes." The nurse reassured. "And she's being treated."

"Ok," Larissa exhales a huge breath of relief. "Ok, I'll be there."

Larissa scrolls fast through every contact in her phone searching for Yanie then calls her straight away.

"C'mon…" she impatiently muttered as it rung. *"Yanie, please come through."*

"LA-LA!" Yanie gleefully answered.

Sacred Bond Hospital 7:47 P.M.

Essie Chu is now in a hospital bed in a patient room with another patient being seperated by a grey curtain. She had been in here for a while in silence with the misfortune of the only sound being the patient close by having his catheter removed.

Her right arm has a needle inserted, helping replenish her body with fluids. The cooling sensation runs through her veins, like an inner icy pad felt through her chest. This kept her awake as she stares off at the ceiling, just lying on her pillow. Even while being treated, she still is traumatized after this whole ordeal.

All that raced in her head at this brief point in time was the aftermath of that plane crash. The uproar of everyone on that bus screaming and scattered in chaos. That passenger who had fell to his death in the bus. Essie's breathing begins to increase as she scrunched up her face, her eyelids shut as she sensed herself tearing up. The crash of bodies hitting certain cars with that loud, damn car alarm blasting non-stop. Her neck constricts as she remembers the bodies of people who'd been severed, having blood ooze whilst she climbed to freedom. Essie impulsively squeezed together her toes at the dread of her legs swinging off the edge, hanging for dear life. Despite her now being replenished, she still felt entirely drained.

She's starts to groan to herself, frustrated how she can't just ease up. When beginning rushed to Sacred Bonds, there were a few patients injured. They were from the bridge who survived and was unlucky enough to leave in their cars. She was on a stroller with a oxygen mask being pumped in her mouth. Everything moved so fast, the speed of ceiling lights kept flashing as doctors charged through the halls. There was a Hispanic woman from the crash who miraculously made it. Essie remembers her burnt flesh being treated out in the lobby. Her crisp outer layer skin stuck out like a sensitive cuticle near a fingernail. There were two teenage boys too. One had kept coughing viciously and his body ached in agony. The other boy was in shock, cradling back and forth repeatedly reciting a bible verse. There was no peace for her or anything.

The worst thing out of this whole ordeal was for that small moment when she saw into the light. While lying there so weakened she couldn't move. That light from up above, that glow had her believe that she was miraculously saved or at least chosen to be in a better place. Her mind was clearer than ever from her responsibilities by falling for this optical illusion. Instead, it was the rescue helicopter shining their spotlight checking for any survivors. She recalls how the sound of the propeller disrupted her serene oasis. Essie had never been more disappointed than by how those men came to her aid.

It had her feel extremely foolish, especially where she lies down now. The only light above her is now a teeny circular one enforced into the ceiling. Now Essie is more helpless and isolated that the best treatment cannot cure.

Meanwhile, Yanie sped through the highway trying to get there as soon as possible. Larissa isn't worried by her driving since her mind is more focused on her guardian's condition. Larissa's reading directions off her phone, each part Yanie swerves or cuts traffic lights to reach Essie sooner. They are five minutes away from the hospital. Larissa felt a little relieved that they haven't encountered any police which cleared her head enough to notice something.

"You stole this, didn't you?" Larissa skeptically asked.

"Nah."

"Lies. Plus, Essie's not gonna wanna ride up in no stolen truck."

"Ain't nobody finna pull up in no stolen whip, alright?"

Yanie parked in front of the hospital, the two dashed out the truck. Yanie heads in first to the lobby then straight for the nurse's desk. She spoke loudly for all other passing doctors and patients to overhear. Yanie explains they're here for Essie Chu who had just been admitted. The nurse searches on her computer for information on what room Essie's in.

"Listen," Yanie said to Larissa. "I want you to wait up in here while I check on her."

"Uh, no!" Larissa defied. "I wanna see her."

"Ain't no telling what her current condition even is yet? Plus, you too young."

"I'm not no lil' kid. Quit treating me like one!"

"Excuse me." The nurse interjects, stating that Essie's in

room 202 on the second floor.

"Oh, good looks." Yanie responds then turns back to Larissa. "Lobby now! Don't make me say it again."

"Lemme see Essie or I tell her you drove me in a stolen truck."

Yanie gave her a serious glare. "You brat-faced bastard. Bring yo' ass on, c'mon!"

They raced to the second floor up the stairwell. Larissa spots room 202 then opens. Larissa's heart raced and her skin begins to crawl. As for Yanie, she stood paralyzed by doubt as to the sight of her condition. Essie was laid down on the bed with a hospital IV hooked to her arm. Her black long hair strands were scattered making her appear all discombobulated. Her head was facing the opposite side of the room so neither one knew she was even semi-conscious. Essie slowly turns her head to the door expecting a nurse, but she observes both Yanie and Larissa together. Essie smiles and Larissa sprints over, giving her a huge hug.

Once again, she felt Larissa's reassuring warmth combat against the biting cold inside her. Her trembling arm wrapped itself around Larissa. Essie can feel the bruises stretch when moving around her arm. However, this little pain is nothing compared to the noise of Larissa breathing heavily to withstand her shedding tears. Essie caresses her back pulling her in more, binding them close together.

Yanie studies the bruises on her arm and watches them both. Essie locks eyes with Yanie, reassuring that everything is okay by a simple nod.

"Yanie, you brought her here?"

"Yea, but how this happen?" Yanie said. "Girl, you ok?"

Essie takes a quick glimpse at Larissa. "I'll live."

"The hell went down out there? Larissa said there was an accident?"

"Plane crash." Larissa added.

"Off coarse collision onto the bridge I had to take."

"Jesus!" Yanie shrieked.

Essie explained how the bridge had many people who hadn't survived. Goes on about the helicopter saving her. She refused to elaborate anymore about the people electrocuted or being sliced apart since Larissa was here.

"I'm just glad that I'm alive." She begrudgingly said.

The room stayed silent. Both of them looked towards innocent Larissa, then at each other, noting that the deeper parts aren't need to be said.

"They bring you up something to eat?" Yanie asks.

"They've got other patients to tend to."

"Naw, how they gon' dub you like that?!" Yanie snarled.

"It's alright, Yanie." Essie gently replied, not wanting her to upset Larissa more. She feels Larissa rest her head on her leg as she massages her head.

"Sorry I couldn't get to your mother."

"It's ok, Essie." Larissa softly said.

"So how's it?" Yanie asked.

"Hopefully I'll be able to leave soon."

"Nah, I mean being up in here as a patient instead of always checking charts?" Yanie mocks.

A small grin grew on Essie's face as the two laughed.

"It's worse when I have to bathe them." Essie laughed.

The doctor emerged in their room. He apologized for interrupting and introduces himself. Larissa leaped upright awaiting for whatever he had to say. He talks about running more tests.

"Say less, doc." Yanie said. "Let's go, Larissa. We out."

Larissa looks to her guardian for confirmation for them both to leave. Essie struggles but puts up a gracious smile and nods at her.

"Don't worry, I'll be home soon, ok?"

"*Mm-hmm.*" Larissa murmurs not eager to leave.

"Yanie, I'll need you to stay with her in the apartment tonight."

"Alright, bet." Yanie replied. "I'll hit up Jovanny, tell him what happened."

Yanie is at the door, relieved that she's alive. Larissa hugged her one last time as Essie soothes her nerves that she'll be alright. Larissa headed out with Yanie.

Jovanny's place 9:04 P.M.

Solanda had arranged for a caramel black woman to come over to indulge in her and Jovanny's sexual acts. So far, the three have been at it for over an hour now. The woman named Tania, had been riding on top of Jovanny's dick whilst his girlfriend sits upon his face receiving oral from him. Solanda passionately moans as Jovanny persistently teased her clitoris while simultaneously thrusting his pelvis. Jovanny was always an exceptional lover, regardless of if it was his girl's vagina or someone else's. Tania's eyes are closed as she pursed her lips in expecting a huge climax to follow along with their flow. Now with her sparkly nails, she dug into his sweaty chest. The build-up sensation grows intense and evident as Jovanny gyrated more. Tania's lower body could detect through small movements that he was close to orgasm. Including the way Jovanny's thrusting rhythm would change her reaction, he knew he'd help her reach this tipping point. The three consciously knew each were at that pinnacle point if they glide into this continuous motion.

A stream bursts in Jovanny's face causing Solanda herself to slide right off, collapsing onto the edge of the bed, barely able to utter a word. Tania on the other hand, had an enormous outburst orally by the rush that escapes her mouth and vaginally by the copious amounts of outflowed juices that gushed out. His last pump led Jovanny to spurt out, resulting in his body to spasm from this intense wave.

Tania, sweaty and exhilarated, noticed this eruption then commences to blowing his erect dick. Her veering tongue had him squeal in excitement, the persistence had almost made him bawl. After devouring his whole cock, Tania sat upright, stared him directly in his eyes and swallowed up his sperm. Then a seductive smile popped on her face as she knows how they both share the flavorful pleasure of tasting cum. She then slowly rests down on him chest-to-chest. Her bosoms so massive, the cleavage hits his chin as she kisses him. Jovanny, lied on his bare back with both arms widely separated, went into raptured ecstasy. All there was to see was both a smile and a cascade of mouth-watering juices gushed onto his face.

"Daddy, you like that shit?" Tania seductively asks.

"Shit was fire…" he exhales out.

"Which part of us was the most luscious?"

"You're lips."

"Awww, ok. What about our bodies though?"

"Y'all bottom lips."

Both Solanda and Tania laugh while twiddling with each other's soft hands, fingering with one another's nails. Jovanny continues to kiss Tania's cheeks then makes his way to her face. He grabbed a handful of her breasts and suckles on both her swelled nipples.

Solanda reached from under the bed, pulling out (not no dildo) two small water bottles. She and Tania shared one while Jovanny swiped one for himself. Tania's excessive gulps almost had him flashback as she was ready for round two.

She began kissing Solanda now, swapping spit with Solanda pulling her face in deep. Jovanny stretched for his phone and watched them go at it. Moments like these are amazing for him to embrace. Solanda had never before been open-minded to exploring her sexuality with girls and various sexual acts either. Jovanny had insisted that she'd find pleasure in this. However, this has been for a while.

Two years ago, Solanda had been by the train station smoking a cigarette. She was listening to music with her headphones in. Then she saw a man approach her general direction from a far. She first peeked at him but he locked eyes with her. Jovanny walked in a way that stood out to her, he expressed good posture. His back was straight with his shoulders back. His arms swung freely and he had a tranquil facial expression. Solanda had put her phone away to see what he wants.

"Excuse me," Jovanny gently said. "You ain't got no other loosie on you?"

She nods her head and hands out one. He lit it and stood standing by her still.

"You 'bout to hop on the train?" Jovanny asked.

"Nah, just got off actually." Solanda replied as she took out both headphones. "Just came from the city."

"Huh… I ain't never been."

Her whole head faced him. "You never been?"

"Just ain't never had the time. Y'know, with work and usually just too busy. Or just be chillin' at the crib."

"It be like that sometimes." She agreed as she puffs out

more smoke. "I'm a introvert too most times."

"So why you went to the city then?" he asked. Then he just sits back enjoying his smoke as she goes on about having an aunt living there. Solanda went on about taking her out for her birthday. She took her aunt to a restaurant, to Madison Square Park and had spent last night reminiscing of family barbeques. She flicks her cigarette; he notices her small tattoo behind her left ear. It was of a tiny scale with two separate ends aligned perfectly.

"Nice tattoo."

"Thank you." She sweetly replies.

"What is it?"

She reveals it is a scale tattoo and explains that it pertains to her zodiac sign of being Libra-born. Jovanny invests in asking if she actually relates to any Libra traits. She claims that she's fair, social, and even a bit indecisive as well. It's evident by her open attitude that she likes talking about herself. Jovanny reveals that he's a Gemini without the tattoos.

"We both air signs." He added. "You, me and Aquarius. I ain't really into astrology signs like that, but at least you live up to yours. So when your birthday?"

"October 6th. Wait, how old are you?"

"Twenty-seven. June 1st." he said.

The two got quiet for a moment as Solanda pulled out another cigarette. Jovanny pulled out his phone. "Yo, you pretty cool to talk to, let me get your number."

"Let me get yours." She replied.

She punched in his number in her phone then calls it, he saves her as a contact. She then asks Jovanny what he was doing around here anyway. He talked about buying a gram of marijuana from a guy who lived by here.

"You smoke bud?"

"Yup." He proudly replies as he finished his smoke.

"I ain't smoke in a while." She confessed. "My last dealer just got caught with some drug charges."

"I tell you what, since you came through with that loosie. You can come pull up at my crib and smoke with me sometime. I don't live too far from here."

"Ok." She graciously said. "I'll message you."

Ever since that first encounter, the two had kept in touch with a relationship progressing. He initiated first with getting to know her more through text. Solanda had eventually felt comfortable enough to come smoke weed at his place. During the time, hours had passed of them both just joking around and learning more about each other on an intimate level. She had leaned in to kiss him and that's all they did. As time went on, they kept seeing each other every week. Jovanny was fun and laid back towards her but what really kept her invested was more about interest. There were a variety of aspects about Jovanny Gibbs that kept them together.

Solanda had been in plenty of relationships prior but the men were so similar that they could've been categorized as just one ex. These men shared the same traits of giving her excessive complements, putting her on a pedestal, being close to needy with certain texts such as *"good morning, beautiful"* or *"sweet dreams, lovely"* after almost each date. The past men didn't have much going on in their lives. One was a bum with no ambition whatsoever that led to a toxic relationship. Other guys had their whole world just revolved around Solanda Wright. Including the fact that they weren't that much of a pleasure to be involved with. Most even tip-toed around how or what they said to avoid offending her, causing them to come off as very lamblike and submissive. Jovanny appeared the exact opposite.

He was strongly opinionated about whatever he believed in, not once could she remember proving him wrong. Solanda had never felt pressured by him contacting her since there were several times she wasn't sure if he would. From her knowledge, he had exciting things happening to where it kept him busy instead. This was to the point where she'd initiate contact with him first. Unlike the other men who had always picked and dropped her off home, Jovanny barely did. He had a truck but insisted she comes to him. Solanda had to go out her way to getting a ride or walking to his place and she had to bring snacks for whenever he'd gain the munchies. Eventually, she started cooking for him at his place, he enjoyed her meals but rarely ever verbally expressed it.

That was the biggest part of it all, it was very rare that Jovanny had ever validated her looks or efforts that she took to be involved. It confused her since she invested so much time with him. This hadn't pleased her which compelled her to do more to receive some sort of acknowledgement. She never called him out on it because she knew he complained about "crazy girlfriends" and didn't want that label. Also, she genuinely liked him and wanted them to last. Jovanny had received constant sex, delicious food, and her permission to involve other into the equation. He pushed for her to approach the type of females that fit his desired standards. After their threesome with a Hispanic woman, he had blessed her with: *"Good thing you brought her."*

Solanda still fulfilled his wants and loving him as much as she could. To this day, she still is loyal to him. They had patched things up about how he reacted to her being assaulted, then celebrated with Tania, someone they both found irresistible. Jovanny continued to watch these stunning beauties as he goes on his phone. Once his screen showed the time, his face had a look of shock as to how much time had passed since they engaged. Also, the four missed calls and six unread messages all from Yanie Juergens.

He read each text explaining that there was a plane crash that involved Essie. This sudden bombshell had his mind go in shock, almost hesitant to open the next text. He excused himself to the living room completely nude. Pacing around the living room, dick and balls flopping about, followed up with the other texts telling her condition. Then how she and Larissa saw her and the doctors are running more tests. Jovanny had the urge to dial up Yanie but he decided to stay back on target and returned to the bed.

Sacred Bond Hospital 11:47 P.M.

Essie Chu cannot sleep after the long day she's had. All things that she's endured today, just thinking about it had her muscles tighten again. After running their tests to check for further internal injuries, she was relieved that nothing was extreme. The hospital would discharge her within the next two days. All she could do is watch the small television in her room broadcasting the news. They are still discussing the aftermath of this plane incident. The pilot Rashid Bhalla had been arrested under several different charges of manslaughter. There weren't many images of this accident in its entirety but Essie can still see them. The news highlights a birds-eye view of the plane in the sea. The decapitated bodies of adults sprawled out on the semi-bridge flashed before her eyes. Clashing sounds of people falling onto cars made her bruised shoulders tremor with discomfort. The prolonged noise of the bridge crumbling into the ocean ruptured her ears.

The news confirms that paramedics are recovering bodies in body bags. Vehicles that weren't damaged are abandoned on the bridge still. The nurse came in to check up on Essie. She asks to turn the TV off, the nurse shut it off and left the room. Essie's mind gradually resumed back to normal, then her muscles loosened up once more. The male patient close to her hadn't moved an inch at all tonight. He was extremely skinny and had apppeared malnourished. The doctors were overheard by her earlier, discussing how this man has stage three lung cancer that's getting worse. He was a scrawny, white man who's neck was veiny along with his forearms. Then his eyes slowly opened and looks back at her.

"You were in that accident?" he muttered out. "The plane crash, right?"

"*Kind of...*" Essie confessed, her voice cracked having to recall it but regains herself. "I had crossed paths with the bridge it clashed into."

"Oh, ok. That's all everyone in the hospital has been talking about. So how bad are your injuries then?"

"Not too harsh." She said. "In fact, I'll be able to leave sooner than expected." Essie knew his condition was terminal but asked when he'd leave out of consideration.

"I don't see me leaving here to be honest." The man said. "Doctors said it's pretty bad, stage three lung cancer."

"I'm sorry." Essie wholeheartedly said. "I've treated cancer patients as well. I had a patient last year struggle from pancreatic cancer."

The man was surprised to be in the presence of another doctor treated as a patient. Then went on about being isolated here for almost a month without much interaction.

"You don't have family that'll come visit you?"

"My wife and I don't talk anymore." He confessed. "My children on the other hand, they refuse to drop by."

Essie was surprised by how nonchalant he had responded. She assumed it was possible for him to conceal his hurt emotions from a complete stranger. There wasn't a point in trying to psychoanalyze him; so she refrained from asking for more explicit details.

"So being a doctor, I assume you spend so much time tending to patients that it's hard to make time for yourself?"

She stared at him momentarily, almost like she wasn't sure if she'd given off that sign. Regardless whether or not his cancer wouldn't end him to where she'd see him again; Essie calmly replied: "No. I have time to myself even with a teenager under my guardianship."

"You mean the girl from earlier." He said. "I could overhear from before, how long have you looked after her?"

Essie elaborates on watching over her for a few years now and how her mother was incarcerated at the time. Even while sounding gracious about having Larissa in her life; he could detect that she wasn't completely fulfilled with life. The man's face turned into a sight of pity. Essie ceased talking anymore about her life.

"You know, regardless how much care that you invest in your patients and how much love you shower your kid, make sure you always have time reserved for yourself. If I could reset time, things would be different for me now. When my daughters, Jessica and Tori were born, my entire existence revolved around them. I stayed attentive, especially during my wife's postpartum depression stage soon after they were born. All I ever blessed my family with was love and affection. Any spare time I had, instead of writing my novel or doing my art, it was spent contributing to my family's happiness."

"You did all you could do." She added.

"Yes, yes I did. But I never prepared them for this world. I spoiled them to no end even when they misbehaved. So once when they were in their mid-teens, because they're both grown-up now. But years ago, they thought it'd be cool to entertain some boys over some boys in my house during my absence. I came home early and kicked their guests out after I screamed at them in front of their friends. And from that day forward, my kids never wanted to be bothered with me again. They had gravitated more towards their mother. I tried to buy them things to have them ease their way back but nothing worked. Once they turned eighteen, they got legally emancipated. Then my wife left too with half my assets, after everything I did for her. It took me years to understand why this was, what I did wrong."

"Did you ever find an answer?" she hesitantly asked.

"I did. They never respected me, not as a parent, as a man, nothing. That's why they couldn't accept that their father finally disciplined them. It's almost like when someone you deemed low of finally gets the best of you."

"And you can't just live that down."

"Exactly." He agreed, maintaining his tone. "I never lived my life to the fullest, even when I had chance after chance to do so. Now look at me, I've got nothing and no one to show for it. I just sit here alone with memories of people who could care less about my well-being. Isolated with ideas that'll now die inside my head. My advice to you ma'am, take as much time to enjoy any leisure for yourself. Before you get to my age."

Essie felt the genuine meaning from all his words. She could tell her face had melt by how nothing had worked for this man in the end. A pitiful grief ached her stomach realizing that being in the hospital was the most private time she's had for herself. Then she remembered Larissa and how much time invested raising her takes. She turned to the man with a smile and said: *"How old are you?"*

The man smiles answering: "I'm two-hundred-and-twenty-years old."

Two Days Later 1:39 P.M.

Yanie and Larissa had picked up Essie from the hospital after she was officially discharged. Essie is so eager to get back home that she doesn't even question her friend about the vehicle she's driving her in. They all arrive back to the apartment. Yanie gives her goodbyes and heads back out. Essie rests on the couch drinking a glass of water.

"Larissa," she called. "You said there was something you wanted to talk to me about in the car?"

Larissa observes how comfortable Essie looks right now, especially after the whole ordeal she's been through.

"Nah, it ain't nothing big."

"You sure? Wait, it's about helping your mom again, isn't it?"

Larissa hesitantly nods her head. Essie tells her to come join her on the couch. She sat down close.

"Look, these ways of trying to get Danielle into heaven are kind of dangerous at the moment."

"I know, I know." Larissa said sounding patient. "We had a few setbacks but there's a Methodist church up a few blocks over I thought we might try. Y'know, once you get better."

"I don't—"

"I mean, I don't know how they worship, might seem a lil' unorthodox but we—"

"It's not that." Essie firmly said. "It's that outside is getting more and more chaotic now. And I can't risk you getting hurt."

"But you'll keep me safe though, right?"

Essie shows a look of disappointment but has to stick with the reality of their circumstance. Then replies: "No."

She explains how everyone is acting crazy to the point where they're harming others and how it didn't really unfold until now. The extent of that bridge collapsing had opened her eyes to how much more worse this will eventually progress. She even reinforces her strong belief of how this isn't an actual miracle itself.

"This so-called 'marvel' doesn't mean anything. But I'll take that mayhem from the other day as a sign of what's to come."

A slow frustration piles up as Larissa blurts: "But you gonna head up out of here eventually so what's the point of staying closed off?!"

"I'm not leaving here for a while." Essie admits. "I'll be taking some sick days off, I've got enough food for us both."

"What about ma?"

"From what you've told me before…" she said irritatedly. "If she chooses not to change then nothing you do will alter whatever ficticious fate there is for her, alright? If she dosen't want to repent, pray for forgiveness, if Danielle's pride is that thick then that's on her. I won't be contributing to this nonsense anymore need be."

"She just needs someone to show her a lil' faith, that's it!" Larissa complained.

Aggravated Essie tells her this phenomenon is a farce. That it isn't worth getting fixated about and how it's not safe for a fourteen-year-old girl to be alone outside. She expressed how scared she is for Larissa to be harmed and is fuming by how much she just ignores all the havoc that has transpired. Larissa charged off the couch and goes upstairs to her room.

Richez Shrive, 2:26 P.M.

Jovanny gets the insight on everything about Essie's condition up to this point. Yanie elaborates more on how Larissa was practically heartbroken seeing her like that. Jovanny appeared somewhat glad and ponders whether he should call her or not.

Yanie urged him not to, he should probably let her have a bit more time to cope. Then he decides to pour himself a drink and poured her a glass too. The bar wasn't as crowded today as it normally was. Just a few men inside talking, this prompts for Jovanny to tell Yanie about how inside here has been more empty and how he hasn't seen Donny Bedford in a while. Yanie takes a sip of her drink looking unfazed. Her phone starts to vibrate, she checked it.

"God, leave me alone, man." She muttered.

"What, some other thirsty dude you ghosted again?"

"It's my ex punk-ass boss. He been blowing up my phone for days now. Been texting me '*we really need to talk, can't explain over the phone*' like bruh, don't nobody wanna talk to you."

"Probably changed his mind and wants you back."

"Nah, he ain't like that. Sounds mad sus' too. I just dub his calls now. Ain't like he giving me my last check neither so the fuck's there to talk about?!"

"Sounds serious though." Jovanny adds. "Like it almost involves five-o or some shit."

"Then we definitely ain't finna talk." Yanie vowed. "Gibby, I swear to God if this fool trying to pull some shit, 'cause I hate to admit but they are professionals. So I doubt no one got pinched."

"You not scared they'll just search for you or pull up at your crib?"

"Alright, full disclosure… I ain't never gave 'em my real name." She said as she elaborated more telling them she was from outside of Holksdale. She never fully trusted them working at a sketchy business.

"He got your number though."

"*Aaaaannnnd?!*" she said. "Just for my burner phone not my other one. Actually, I'ma block him."

Yanie blocked his number, Jovanny turned on the TV over the bar counter. He turns it to the news station channel where they're discussing more on the damage the airplane collision had caused. The news anchor then suggests that people have started speculating that this may have supposedly been a terrorist attack. A mugshot of the pilot responsible had been projected on screen. Jovanny's eyes widened at the sight of this.

"Yo, you remember that dude a few days back?" he asks. "The one who got tossed up out this place."

Yanie took a moment to recall then looked at the TV and it all came to her. "*...Boy!*" Yanie said looking stunned. "Oh shit, that's him. Goddamn, all 'cause these fools were flaming him and this dude just snaps? That's a bit of a huge over-fucking-reaction."

She gulped down the rest of her drink then just shook her head.

"Plus, he's made religious tensions higher now." Montrez said.

Both of them looked at him confused. Montrez mentions how some citizens are now harassing Muslims and other Islamic folks in Holksdale ever since that crash. Very shortly after the news revealed a Muslim pilot had intentionally crashed into that bridge, everyone had fallen back to their prejudices of them. There was group of men that jumped a Muslim couple, resulting in stomping his wife to death and leaving the husband in critical condition the other night in midtown. It had been caught on camera.

A Muslim restaurant had its windows busted earlier today. Many adults have inflicted hate crimes on their property, almost in attempts to have all Muslim folks exiled from Holksdale.

"Shit, my neighbor is planning on packing his shit 'cause people wanna start vandalizing his place now."

"Damn." Yanie said. "Where he gonna go?"

"Bangladesh, probably." Montrez said.

"That where he from?" Jovanny asks.

"I doubt that, but they kept spray painting for him to go back there up on his fucking house."

York Avenue 3:12 P.M.

Larissa is curled in her bed still seething after what happened before. She's been on her phone for the past half hour texting the boy she met on the train. The guy had initiated the conversation at the perfect time. He asked her what she was doing. It took a moment for it to register in her head who this was until she remembered his name, Chase. She decided to tell him about the church that she went to and how everyone went crazy. They both were engaged in the conversation to the point where she opened up a little for him to try to get to know her. Turns out they're both from downtown as well.

As she kept replying, a knock came to her door. Her guardian asked if she could come inside for a minute. Larissa texts Chase that she'll talk to him later and rests her phone down to charge.

"Mm-hmm." Larissa answered.

Essie comes in and sits on the bed, Larissa still looks upset but acknowledges Essie's presence.

"Listen," Essie said gently. "I know we were both upset and could have ended that discussion downstairs a lot better if you hadn't have left. I don't want for us to off like that again, ok?"

Larissa begrudgingly nods back.

"Now tell me, sweetpea, is this determined goal of yours really something to adhere to? Truly worth possibly losing your life over?"

It was quiet as Larissa figures a way to explain herself. Then she musters up the words to speak up.

"Ma ever tell you I had a sister?"

Essie looks perplexed. "No? She didn't."

"She was my half-sister, different dads. Her name was Rennita Sheppard but she went by 'Ren'. She was a few years older than me and she died when I was seven."

Larissa recalls of a contagious flu epidemic in Holksdale a few years ago. Around that time, her mother sometimes couldn't be found so she was mainly around her sister. Ren at the time was looking after her especially when Larissa became infected and was bed ridden.

Larissa's knees fold up to her chest and wraps her arms around her legs. She then resumes her story.

Her sister pretty much couldn't afford the medication to help because they were way too expensive for the people in downtown Holksdale. Since her sister never graduated high-school to help raise Larissa, she couldn't afford it either. Ren told her that she had a way of getting her medicine through certain connections. However, it was all a lie. Ren and a group of guys she knew had broken into a pharmacy to steal whatever they can get. They came with all types of weapons. Unfortunately, they were killed during combat when the police had arrived. Ren and her gang of thugs ended up taking lives in the process. A full-on massacre leaving many officers and their back-up dead. Larissa's mom was able to obtain the medicine through the help of a guy she knew.

"I was devastated and ma," Larissa confessed. "I think she was just too proud to show it, but I believe she was hurting too." Larissa paused momentarily. These series of thoughts coming back, having been bottled up inside this whole time had her exhale a huge breath of relief. Having her throat tremble as she continued. "Our family was already breaking with ma and Ren steady at each other's throats. Now with Ren gone, and ma and I alone, there was no family left, just us."

"I don't understand." Essie patiently said. "What're you saying?"

"I'm saying that I believed Ren was fighting for me to get better but just went about it the wrong way. And it don't matter just how close or as good a person I knew she was, she burning in hell as we know it." Larissa peeks up starry-eyed. "All 'cause of what the Almighty sees. Like it doesn't matter just how bad a parent everyone says my mom is, all that matters is what God thinks. Plus, she ain't never kill no one, so she not as bad as Ren. Ma was even able to legally buy me the drugs I needed for treatment. She's still alive to repent for her sins."

"HER!" Essie asserts, unable to understand why Larissa still somehow justifies her mother even when implying that Danielle's not the perfect parent.

"She's my mother and I'll go above and beyond for her, because she's in a position where she can't."

Where she can't?! Essie pessimistically thought. Not understanding whether Larissa meant that Danielle's incarceration prevented change or by hoping she wasn't blinded enough to believe her mother ever capably could.

"Ren's soul is in a bad place, probably was long before she died. I'm not going to hell when I die, *so I'll never see her again.* And it's a shame I gotta live with that. Essie, when our family died, I would've done anything for us all to rekindle again. Even now, if that only means through death. Ma's the only family I got left and if I go through with this then she'll be grateful and turn her life around. Our two souls will spend eternity together, away from this crazy world as you know it. Way above 'cause we're better than all this."

Larissa could feel her eyes tingling with tears, Essie knew she hated acknowledging whenever she felt sad, lonely or isolated but none of that mattered. Essie drew closer and wrapped her arms around Larissa still curled with her legs up against her chest, until Larissa completely unfolded and hugs her back. Warm tears squeezed from her eyes as she kept them shut. Her guardian's head softly nested on top of Larissa's, a warm, sweet hug filled with something that wouldn't want to make Larissa leave the apartment no more than Essie would: *A hug full of love.*

Yet full of sorrow, knowing that she'd break Larissa's heart following up with this: "You know I love you but I'm sorry. It's gonna take time for me to recover from all of this, I need space. You understand, don't you?"

Larissa releases her and begrudgingly nods her head. Then recoiled back to her phone. Essie leaves her room then takes a nap back in her own.

An hour later, Larissa sits outside on the front steps trying to bask in the sun, but it was hard to with everything racing through her head. Thoughts of her guardian, her mother's future once she's dead just weighing down on her completely. Larissa tries to distract herself by surfing the web on her phone, then scrolls through her social media. The sound of footsteps are passing by, she looked up to see it was Chase. She just stares at him walking until he detects her sitting there.

"Larissa?" He greets sounding surprised. "What up?"

"Hi. What you doin' here?"

"Told you I'm from downtown. Right now I just been walking for a bit, nice out today."

Chase sits with her on the steps. Larissa is somewhat glad to have company over. He gives her a piece of gum from the pack he has.

While they're talking, she smells his juicy apple fragrance cologne.

Chase had sensed that something was troubling her and even asked about it. This felt abnormal for her to converse more with him in person instead of text but she decides to open up. She tells him about wanting to help her mother, how her guardian feels nervous about leaving but refused to mention Ren. It felt too personal, knowing her sister now suffers in hell and how it was out her control was too much to bring up. After revealing this she hoped he wouldn't look at her like she's stupid or take pity on her.

"Shit." he shockingly replied. "Sorry to hear that."

"It's all good. Like, I can't vent to my homegirl without getting clowned by how ridiculous this shit sounds."

"I get it."

"And what's worse is I can't find no other church in this area that don't got no long line or have some fight break out. So there's that."

"Does it have to be Sunday?" he asks.

"No. Even if I wanted, them damn lines inside extend to the next day."

"Actually, I think I might know one."

Chase recalls of a church in uptown Holksdale that was rarely ever packed. The people who even believe in this aren't acting crazy like around here. This gives Larissa a little relief and listens more. He tells her the name of the church and then concludes with how his grandmother used to take him and his sister there.

"I dunno how to get there or what buses to take." She said not sounding too confident about going solo.

Chase checks his phone for a moment as the two sat there quietly on the steps. Then he turns to her, sees her trying to masquerade her concerned face with being calm.

"I got you." He reassures her. "I'll guide you there bus-to-bus. Have us transfer hand-to-hand til' we get up there."

"Foreal?"

"Yeah. I'll come by. When you wanna go?"

"Tomorrow afternoon. I'll hit you up." Larissa said.

"Got it!"

Even with a new guide, Larissa was having second thoughts about roaming with some guy she had just met. She talks to him, trying to know him more as they both watch the construction going on their street a few houses down. The men are wrapping up to go home. The workers were adding a new coding layer of cement spread to the sidewalk, it is still wet.

"Why they redoing the pavement?" Chase asked.

"The pavement itself needed to be fixed. All kinds of cracks and crackheads and all that other ghetto shit be up on it. So they been redoing it for about three weeks now."

Chase looks to her then smirks. She looked back confused, especially as he bolted at the wet cement. Larissa jogs on over to him.

"You gonna imprint on that, huh?" she asks.

"Yerp."

"Lemme guess, both our names together up inside a heart with an arrow shot through."

Chase didn't answer as he's still bent over touching the cement. This led Larissa to peek over his shoulder more but couldn't detect anything still.

"What is you doin'?" She asks.

He finally finishes then takes a step back for her to see. Larissa's eyebrows raised high in surprise, she bent over to observe it more clearly. It wasn't a handprint, nor their names in a heart; and yet, it was still art.

It was a horizontal line with the word HEAVEN stated above it, with the name Danielle Sheppard smeared under it.

Larissa grew a sweet, lamblike smile and then looks towards Chase.

"To hell with that other list!" he said. "Once this shit hardens, it'll be official. So, follow the word of me!"

He looks at her, assured that they will make this happen together. Almost all traces of uncertainty were fading. Now relieved that she now has someone else to depend on.

† Chapter 12: Sir, maintain yourself!

Larissa had prepared for this small venture, eager to be by Chase. The next day, Larissa is accompanied by Chase at the terminal to catch the bus headed uptown. Chase checks up at the monitor indicating that their bus arrives in twenty-eight minutes. Larissa views around the whole terminal, there are many adults crowded inside. Outside has people standing or bench sitting, waiting for their ride. Most men that are recognizable are usually here every day to hangout. They could be spotted individually or coalesced together; just talking aloud, laughing, smoking and drinking. They're the men who don't have jobs nor any ambitions, other than approaching multiple decent appearing women.

Larissa notices a few odd things apart from what she's heard that transpires here. Outside through the wide glass are people reading their bibles on the bench. At first, she assumed they were hunched over on their phones but they were flipping through their thin, handheld bible.

Men, who are usually seen catcalling females were barely even peeking at their backsides nor saying a word to them in passing. Adults that normally appear mean and extremely off-putting are acknowledge these religious folks roaming around handing out pamphlets. Everybody was civil, well-mannered and even ladylike.

Chase saw one of the religious people walking in his direction. Larissa then noticed the guy too.

"Hello." The guy pleasantly greeted.

"Oh, hey." Larissa calmly replies as Chase simply waves, not really in the mood to converse with him.

"My name is Andy, I am involved with a Christian enlightenment group in midtown. As you can see, my associates and myself are going around handing flyers to gather others to our upcoming church barbeque."

Andy was an overweight Caucasian guy who looked to be in his late teens. His eyelids were wide, exposing his blackened eyeball pupils. His smile was large and was dressed in a plaid white shirt with jeans held up by a belt, including everyone else in his group handing flyers. Andy had a larger-than-normal smile stamped across his face. He hands them both a flyer advertising the midtown church and explaining how crowded it is today.

"We will be serving food there." Andy said.

"Churches fried chicken?" Chase asked.

"Mm-hmm. We'll hand you a menu once you arrive."

"Wait, so y'all just go out handin' flyers?"

"Yup."

"In this heat? It's a scorcher, bro." Chase adds.

"Yup." He graciously said. "Our group doesn't just consume us. There are many other members located all amongst town engaging with the public to help enrich people's minds like yourselves. All ran by Evelyn Claudette, she helped finance our entire shindig. And if you lose that flyer, don't worry. We're located around here, the grocery stores, train stations, airports and especially hospitals to show forth a sparkle of hope. The information's on the pamphlet. It'd be nice of you to come."

Without being completely sure if they would, both of them agree to think about it. Larissa expressed a friendly, serene smile. Chase held up a vague expression.

"Great!" Andy gleefully said. "It's good to open your mind and try new things. I hope to see you both because I do not forget faces. Have a good day."

Andy walks away to another passenger on the other side of the terminal.

"It'd be funny if he comes back, completely forget our faces." Chase said, chuckling.

"Nah, don't be mean, c'mon. You gonna pull up?"

"To what, this?!" he sarcastically said while tapping her flyer. "I might come for a plate of food, that's it."

"It may be low-key fun though." Larissa said. "It's next August on the 22nd. Essie should be woke by then and may come through with me."

Chase checks the monitor again to see only fourteen minutes left for their bus. The two are on their phones. The sound of people moving around the terminal is outweighed by the sudden voice for everyone's attention. It didn't come from the intercom, but from a passenger himself.

"HELLO!" A large Hispanic man said while holding his girlfriend's hand. His black hair is thinning on the top, his hairy belly meanders down through his white tank top. He was light-skinned and sweating from the outside heat. Despite this, he shamelessly halts in the middle of the terminal, the main spot where people usually avoid waiting due to the blinding, shining heat that's emitted through the

glass window. Many passengers ignore him but that doesn't deter the man from continuing.

"ATTENTION, ATTENTION, EVERYONE!" the man announced. He caught the eyes from a few people, including the religious people. Security guards are slowly emerging to the sides with their hands by their holsters. His Dominican girlfriend looks perplexed as to where this is going. If people acknowledge them for anything else, it would be for their blatant age difference. This man appeared to be within his late forties; his girlfriend on the other hand looked to be in her mid-twenties.

"This woman whose hand I'm holding," he proudly states. "She's been my lovely girlfriend of three years now. Her name is Claudia."

Claudia looked around as people listening began to multiply. She scrunched her thin eyebrows, sucked in her bottom lip and casually nods her head to the crowd. Like Claudia, everyone was curious as to where this would lead.

"At first glance, she was all on her phone, didn't even notice me walking down her path. I remember I was so nervous she'd ignore me in front of the other passengers bombarded by us, who I don't even remember what they looked like. That's how unimportant they were. I normally wasn't that shy but the moment I saw her… I became self-conscious."

Larissa was really engaged with this sweet little tale. Chase notices this then decides to put away his phone and listen. Larissa has a hopeless romantic glimmer in her eyes as she smiles at them both.

"I remember I approached her at this exact spot and said 'excuse me'. She raised her head and so did the nearby passengers waiting but I didn't care." The man faces his girlfriend. "And do you remember what I said, hun?"

Claudia, ignoring all their surroundings, gladly recalls their first encounter and replies: "You asked, 'what made me smile so big?' And I told you I got the job I interviewed for."

"I did, right?!" he playfully said then he turns to the crowd. "We talked that afternoon until her bus came, exchanged digits, and now we're here. Three years strong. Claudia Annabelle Gutierrez, you are the love of my life and I want everyone here to know this."

Claudia drops her head down trying to hide her blushed cheeks. Then without any hesitation, the man emerged down to one knee. Claudia's eyes widened as if she'd seen a ghost, both her hands clap to her mouth in shock. The crowd grew reinvigorated as to what they were now witnessing. Others began to applaud the couple, while people started recording once he holds her hand.

"Oh my God..." Larissa genuinely idolized.

Claudia looks up, batting her eyes trying to hold back her tears. She then looks eyes with her man.

"Claudia Annabelle Gutierrez, will you do me the honor of-"

"YES!" Claudia loudly favors. "Yes, yes, I love you."

The couple both scream in excitement and hug each other tightly. Everybody cheers as the man uplifts his fiancée off the floor, joyously swinging her around in rejoice. Passengers cheer, security guards whistle, everyone applauds for the newly engaged couple. Larissa wrapped her arms around Chase, who nods his head in admiration for the couple. Then rests his head on her to mock just how much taller he is than her. The pair smiles.

Claudia gave her fiancé a long kiss, both their eyes closed, cherishing this moment together. People were still clapping in excitement.

"Ok, ok, people." The man said sounding appreciative. "I got another announcement to make."

Everyone started to ease up. There were some folks who purposely missed their bus at the curiosity of where else this beautiful moment would lead to.

"Now everyone, we are all aware of the so-called phenomenon this summer in regard to our destinies, right? Well, not to put out all our business but I have been blessed enough to make it to heaven. Unfortunately, my beloved fiancée won't be joining with me."

The people had seemed somewhat sorry for their misfortune but were a little confused as to how any of this pertained. Claudia had a minor look of annoyance on her face as she pursed her lips but changed it to a teeny smile. Almost if this isn't the first time she's heard this from him.

"Honey," Claudia patiently said. "You know that thing around the world ain't nothing but a hoax."

"Claudia, please let me finish. Now you're all probably thinking, *'marry each other now so we can spend the rest of our lives together.'* And I do cherish you, baby. Till death do us part, right? But after death, our souls will for never intertwine with each again. And I can't imagine living even a moment whether it be here on earth or in nirvana without you. So I propose this…"

The crowd is in awe listening to his genuine speech. He digs inside his baggy pants pocket. Everyone watches as they expect for him to pull out and slip a ring on her finger. Their excitement slowly has them electrified again, then the entire terminal got still. Larissa's jaw dropped as she releases Chase. He himself had took two steps back.

Claudia's fiancé had just casually whipped out a pistol.

"Sebastian, what is this?" Claudia had muttered completely stunned. She struggles to pull away her shaky hand but he grasps onto it tighter, all adrenalized.

"Don't worry." Sebastian reassures her. "Everything's gonna be ok. I'm just gonna shoot us both—"

"WHAT THE FUCK?" a passenger from afar yells. "Girl you better get the fuck up outta here!"

"QUIET, PLEASE!" Sebastian demands as he freely waved the gun causing some people to be frightened. Everyone in the terminal remained silent, all traces of glee gone, and now switched by a dread for Claudia that they all now shared.

Claudia rapidly moves her arms, trying to break off his grip. Her sight goes back and forth from Sebastian's merrily face then at the gun. Each wave from the gun has the crowd react. Some duck down, full frontal spread on the ground. Women and their kids began sniveling while huddled amongst themselves. Security all lacked guns and they remained still, pressed up to the glass. Chase holds in Larissa with his body, shielding her. He wraps his arms around her tightly. He could hear Larissa's tiny whimpers.

"I'm gonna kill you, you'll go straight to hell." He sees that his fiancée's scared as hell. "Then I'll shoot myself, resulting in a suicide. Which means hell, where we both can spend eternal bliss together… forever."

Claudia hollers for her life to where people from outside the terminal turned to see. The frightened ones outside dashed away and the others took cover while recording on their phones.

"Sebastian, pleeeeaaassse." Claudia begs as she dropped to her knees. *"Baby, please don't do this."*

"Oh, honey." He said. "It's my proposal. I'm the one that should be on my knees. Come here!"

Sebastian hoists her back up then had her in a chokehold. Claudia's begging the crowd for help as she struggles by kicking around her legs. The people are screaming for Sebastian to let her go.

"Everyone shut up!" Sebastian yelled as he raised the gun to Claudia's temple. "Now baby, I love you."

"GO TO HELL, PSYCHO!"

"See you there, hun." He enthusiastically said as he gave her a peak on the cheek, this had her blood draw cold.

Claudia's so petrified that hot urine runs past her thigh. She furiously screams, squirming in his sharp grip. He takes the safety off and fires.

The crowd begins to sprint out the terminal. Claudia's blood is spread is splattered all over Sebastian's face. A reddish, fluid, phlegm-like gush of blood smeared upon his bulbous cheeks. He commences on slurping the drizzle of blood. Sebastian's so obsessed with her that even when dead, he still can't get enough of her. She's now lifeless, he starts caressing his fiancée's now corpse. The guard holds the doors open, ordering everyone to get out! Chase pulls Larissa up with him, shielding her eyes as the two head for the door.

Someone must have tipped off the cops because the police sirens roar from a few streets away. Sebastian detects this. He looked at Claudia sprawled out on the floor, tears run from his eyes, then positions the barrel under his chin. Once the police pulled up to the terminal, they could be spotted through the window getting out their cars. Sebastian pulled the trigger, resulting in a straight bullet through the head. Both now dead and collapsed there together. Larissa and Chase never made it uptown that day.

Richez Shrive, 2:26 P.M.

The bar hasn't been as crowded lately as it was in the start of the summer. Only a few customers are here while Jovanny sees Montrez from behind the counter. He notices Montrez is pretty quiet, like he's in deep serious thought right now.

"You good, bro?" Jovanny asks.

"Man..." Monterz said sounding frustrated. "My wife's been on me lately about my health."

"Good! You be up in here every damn day."

"Plus, it don't help that ever since that list, she's not hoping for me to die anytime soon."

"Thought you weren't falling for this shit, Montrez."

"I'm not but she did."

"So what, you headin' to hell?" Jovanny asks.

"Nope, she just don't want me dying on her so I can quote on quote, *'be upheaved to live a safe haven frolicking with all these heifers.'* So we're getting healthy together."

Montrez elaborates on how they're both working out together, going on long walks, eating fruits and vegetables. Jovanny protests on how he's letting his wife order him around and pours him another drink. Montrez brings up how his wife made them cut ties with another couple since they were destined for hell. Claiming they were a bad influence and that she didn't really know them at all. Then even confides on how this whole ordeal has had her too depressed lately to even want to engage in sex.

"Well, glad I can't say the same." Jovanny gloats then brags about his recent threesome. Montrez raises a glass to him. "That shit was crazy. I had my girl swipe through her dating app for any thick, robust bitch. Big, fat ass and beautiful arousing feet."

"This like the sixth bitch your girl let you smash. Don't you wanna take it down some soon?"

"Nope. Couldn't pull this shit when I was back home living with my moms. Black moms ain't havin' it."

"Your mother raised you right." Montrez said.

"No." Jovanny firmly said. "Mama raised her boys forcing us to believe all women are God's greatest gift to mankind, which is arguable, 'cause these bitches ain't bringing nothing much else. But she wanted me and my brothers to cherish 'em."

"Got you."

"One thing I low-key agree on is to worship a women's feet 'cause shit, I likes me some feet."

"What if her face ugly though?"

"Bruh, I mean, she ain't gotta be no model from head to toe. But you best believe those toes gotta be on point! Ya feel me?!"

Montrez looks like he's about to head out. Jovanny insists he stays more for a few drinks since his wife's on his case. He tells Jovanny that he has a second job later as a security guard and should get some rest. Jovanny pours him another drink anyway persuading him to since it'll just be him on the clock unsupervised. So Montrez then stays.

York Avenue 2:49 P.M.

Larissa walks with Chase back to her place talking about the madness they just witnessed. Even though Larissa is a little disappointed to miss their bus, she still had someone to take her mind off it.

"That dude just fuckin' shot her." Chase said. "Scared I could've been deleted back there too."

"Like, no one would accept his proposal, if you can even call it that now? And he knew that. That's why he low-key planned this shit."

"Yup." Chase agreed. "Man, but I actually thought him professing his love for her was at first actually genuine. Then he brought out that gun. All over some stupid shit. Is this what it's all come down to… people suddenly forgot how to act?"

"Yea, like how crazy is it knowing that people headin' to heaven are capable of pulling that exact shit?"

"Larissa, c'mon." he mocks. "People are capable of all sorts of shit. They probably feel bolder now than ever."

Larissa didn't disagree. As sure as he sounded, she just accepted it. She was just relieved that neither of them were hurt. The thought of her guardian's concern had creeped in her head. Certain areas are getting crazier and even verbalizes it.

"Damn," Chase said. "Your guardian is still inside. The hell is she now, a cat lady?"

She shoots him a dirty look. He quits mocking her.

"My bad." He apologized. "You said she was caught on the bridge, right?"

"Yea," she muttered. "She was on the bus that almost fell with her inside."

"How it feel?"

"She had a near death experience, I imagine she—"

"Nah, I meant you. How are you holdin' up?"

Larissa felt a bit embarrassed. Not because she misunderstood but because she wasn't used to having her feelings usually accounted for. Essie was the only exception to that; but she's so used to it from solely her.

"I mean, I feel for her that she's just stuck in this place in her life. Even going out today, I felt kinda bad just leaving her there. Plus, I ain't text her or nothing yet since I dipped."

"Well, you're back." He said as they made it to her apartment stairs. And to the amazement of Larissa, she hadn't realized they walked all those blocks back home.

"Keep her company then." Chase encouraged. She nodded and at waved him. As she heads up the stairs, she suddenly halts and turned back to him. She felt a comforting bliss to see him there waiting still, checking for her to get back safely inside.

"Hey." She calls out, Chase quickly turned. "Good looks watching over me today."

"I mean, how else would you get to the terminal?!"

"Not that." she chuckles. "I meant hovering over me during that whole situation, tryin' to keep me safe. You're a real one, y'know that?"

Chase smiled at her as she comes back down. Larissa kissed his cheek and could feel his smile grow bigger. They hugged and then she went inside.

Richez Shrive 10:45 P.M.

Montrez is still on his bar stool, laughing with Jovanny. Both talking about customers, his wife and how chaotic Holksdale has been. They were the last ones left here.

Jovanny then checked the clock to see how late it was getting. Montrez has had more drinks than he could count. His shoulders kept shifting around, his eyelids shielded most of his pupils and his speech was slow.

"Yo, I'm afraid it's time to bounce." Jovanny said.

"What?!" Montrez protested. *"Nah man, one more shot, huh? C'mon, don't make me beg."*

"Nah bro. Don't you gotta work?"

"Right, the museum Midtown. Fuck, I gotta hop on the bus. But seriously though, you're cutting me off, guy?"

Jovanny sees he's refusing and firmly said: "Yes."

"Welp, I'ma just seek somewhere else then… I swear, while the night is young, I will get my next shot!"

Montrez left the bar, rocking around while Jovanny locked up. He watches him get inside his truck and drive off. Montrez gives him a thumbs up as he hardly holds his composure still, then he heads off to the bus stop. On his way, he's singing and hollering late at night. He makes it to the nearest stop and rests on the bus bench. Heavy breaths and laughter can be heard. Montrez commenced to singing choir tunes whilst clapping his hands as if he's in church. He's so loud that someone peeked out through their apartment window at him. The sight of a black women with a scarf wrapped around her head stared intently at him, he watched her back and sung aloud. Then she moves from the window. His singing gets louder and he gets the attention from other people which is indicated by their lights coming on. Montrez takes this as his own audience, then he goes on. Only other noise to back up his singing were the sounds of oncoming sirens. The cop car traced down his irksome singing.

A Caucasian police officer approached from his vehicle up to drunken Montrez. The officer sees him rotating his body while sensing a strange aura by him.

"Night officer." Montrez said. *"T-there a problem here?"*

"There was a noise complaint." The cop informed as he shines his flashlight at him. "Are you waiting for someone?"

"Nada, Just the bus."

"Where to?"

"Work. Gotta get paid."

The officer studies him some more. Montrez head goes all around, body can't retain still.

"Sir, have you been drinking tonight?" the officer asked. He placed both hands on his hips. Montrez spots his hand near his holster, and zeroed in on his gun. Montrez blinks like crazy, trying to sober up.

"You know we've had a lot of crimes happening recently this summer? That's even including at night. So I find it hard to believe any boss of yours letting you clock in in your current state. I know this miracle's embolden a lot of you to be out causing trouble. Because I know you aren't out here praying."

Montrez hops up quickly, this agitates the cop.

"Sir, maintain yourself!"

This sends Montrez to wobble, he inexplicably feels as if he can't get a grip. His face seems frustrated while getting aggressive with himself, trying in order to save his soul. As

Montrez nervously stumbles, the cop focuses on him still. He's ordered to sit down, this slips through Montrez's ears once he sees that the bus from afar is pulling up.

"L-look officer…" He muttered as politely as possible. *"I got work and there go my bus right there. My work shift, I-I got my work shit up on me."*

The bus slowly stops there, passengers begin to look out there windows, caught by the flashing colored lights from the cop car. Montrez digs in his pocket for his work ID card. The officer sensed a strange underlying vibe from him, having him transfixed. Unexpected to the cop, the sound of the bus doors open. A fierce gunshot has everyone hold still.

Residents watching from a distance had jumped a few feet back screaming. People on the bus had ducked down, in fear of another one. Montrez had been shot in his chest, his blood sprayed on the bus bench. Montrez now has a new audience with him sprawled out, now pronounced *DEAD*.

MIDTOWN HOLKSDALE: 10:34 A.M.

Of all the customers within Richez Shrive, the most consistent one and familiar face that popped up every day of the week was Icarus McGrew. He was a scrawny thirty-year-old Caucasian pale-skinned man with a lot of black hair strands stretched out brushing over his forehead. With arms and legs as boney as a twig, Icarus appeared extremely malnourished. His facial hair wasn't ever in the form of a fully connected beard, just several teeny strands of black hair protruding all over his chin, cheeks and upper lip.

However, his distinct look never deterred him from going out, especially exploring out on a nice summer day. He was an author who'd written a couple novels, none of which were famous of course, yet it paid the bills. Though his creativity should have him writing more, Icarus had spent a majority of his time approaching women. He was single, always has been. Meeting women whenever he pleased was what had pulled him out of bed in the morning. It didn't matter the weather being too cold or broiling hot, even though he would prefer approaching during the spring. This summer was perfect since many women in Holksdale had worn more revealing clothing to his liking.

Richez Shrive wasn't the only place where he'd try picking up girls but was the most common place located in Holksdale. His alternative place to pursuit was the Midtown mall that brought everyone in Holksdale together. Solely he'd drive there and spend hours cruising around to scope out any attractive women, which there were several. Icarus was quite odd, not in a disturbing way but more of a standout in a crowd of people (*whether you were approached by him or had seen him in passing*). He usually spoke in a fully expressive way, revealing what he had truly thought about anything. His eyes would be widen with life, both pupils just bulging out exposing his dark brown eyes. Despite his several encounters with the opposite sex, he had achieved little to no results. There were times where he would strike up a conversation to appeal to them, mostly by revealing his true intent followed up with trying to obtain their number.

Though Icarus would never go out his way to harass a woman, several of them would feel somewhat awkward or a bit uncomfortable. Having this complete stranger drawn to you initiating conversations had seemed pretty random. This normally led to many of his interactions to be brief. A few were flattered though, even with some willing to divulge their information out. However, a majority of numbers he'd gotten were either fake; or they were legit but that particular woman refused to text or call him back. If females refused to give him a chance, their excuse would be that they're taken, in a rush or just not comfortable giving their numbers out.

Overhearing Icarus flirting with women out in the open wouldn't faze him whatsoever unlike most other men who scan the area before engaging. Normally when people converse with others, their eye contact may shift away from that person's face then turns back towards them. Not Icarus McGrew, he doesn't turn away. He didn't acknowledge the society that bombarded him whenever he spoke to women. His complete attention was on her entirely, zeroing in on her to where he would rarely blink.

At times he would be at the food court and would hop in line behind a beautiful woman to strike up a conversation. Or he would aim after a single woman at a table eating and pull up a chair with her. If they weren't in the mood to converse with him, either portrayed by their body language or facial expression, he would just politely leave.

As he walks around the mall for hours straight, Icarus wouldn't ever get tired. He would walk in the crowd checking store windows for anyone worth it. As soon as he did, he'd halt and go inside. This not only applied at the mall either. Icarus lives in a small house in midtown across the street from a gas station. At this gas station was a convenient store where many drivers pulled up to. Across from there was his home with a wide clear window revealing him to be just staring outside. It didn't matter if any drivers had detected him while pumping their gas since they'll just leave soon afterwards. All he aimed for were the unaware enticing females who would buy something inside (*whether it was cigarettes, liquor, lottery tickets or corn chips*). As soon as they came, he'd vamoose from his house right across the street.

Today was one of those days he chose to not drive out so early but to just watch from his window, awaiting for any opportunity. Icarus was attracted to several women, it didn't matter any particular race. Especially being exposed to different ethnic ones crossing his path daily. Though, the most consistent ones that tempted him were either mixed women or Caucasian women. The ones whose breasts were perfect for their body frame. Icarus did lust after those stupendous shaped breasts too natural to dismiss. Yet, there was something arousing to him about the right sized ones molded for that particular female. Even if she was small, the fact that her bosoms weren't too vast for her fragile, tender body little body would please him. Also, he liked girl's asses as well. The most magnetic thing about them to him was not only when they're bare but when they're both concealed. The majority would cover them in skirts, yoga pants, or leggings and whenever they walk, the cheeks would shake. That jiggle from both buns squeezed together would have him compelled to wanting the sight of them, and the fact that he couldn't had him craving it.

While most men didn't want to be ignored by the opposite sex, Icarus didn't necessarily mind it. He liked that most girls whom explored across the gas station could never detect him. So when he introduces himself, it'll seem like fate. Or if they didn't catch him at the mall, he would follow them momentarily while walking lickety-split up to them going the opposite direction. But as indifferent as he was, he was cautious about making a woman uncomfortable and had sworn never to take it as far as the parking lot.

Icarus would always wear his glasses while watching across the street. As he watches, sometimes he'd listen to online videos on how to pick-up girls to further enhance his skill. Sometimes he'd try implementing what he's learned but not gain much success.

As he pondered about leaving from the window, an attractive women drew from the corner of his eye. A black female walks in such a self-assured way. Her back fully erect in a white t-shirt with her cleavage slightly jiggling, to the degree of occasionally tapping her bottom chin without interfering her motion which made it sexier. She was a short brunette who wore black sunglasses. It looked like she just got out of bed since she wore pajama bottoms which weren't baggy enough; they still accentuate her firm ass, underlining her lace panties.

Icarus was already out the front door headed across the street. The door opens making a ringing sound. He looked down the aisle to find her by the fridges in the back pulling herself out a soda. She turned around for Icarus to be revealed. They looked at each other.

"Excuse me." He politely said. "You're looking quite nice today."

"Oh, thank you." She responds sounding bubbly as a big smile came up.

She went past to the cashier upfront. Icarus then went to the door expecting for her to not take too long paying. He held open the door and she thanked him. Three feet away he calls out to her: "Hey, what's your name by the way?"

The girl halts for a second with her head turned facing him, then hesitantly replied sounding confused: *"Alexis?"*

"Oh cool," Icarus lively replied. "I can see you're in a bit of a rush but is it okay if I can get your number?"

Alexis pondered for a moment then asks how old he is.

"Thirty."

"Oh nah, son. I'm nineteen. You too old for me!" Then she sped off.

Icarus recoils back to his house, sitting on the front steps on his phone. More cars drive pass, he just looks of into space thinking about going to the bar to better his chances there. Regardless of being rejected, it wasn't anything that really brought down his spirits. He had been through a lot worse with girls when he was coming up in high school.

As a senior in high school years ago, he hadn't had himself a great reputation. Prior to his final year, Icarus hadn't had much of one to begin with his first three years. He had been mainly an introvert, very self-conscious of how he presented himself towards his peers. Other students knew of him but weren't personally involved with him except one friend, Lori Timmerman, who transferred to his school after his freshman year. She had introduced herself to him when they were both sophomores that had geometry class, the two sat close by the windows.

Lori seemed sweet and approachable, that's why she made more friends her first semester there than Icarus had his entire freshman year. After their first interaction, the two had become more intimate a week later when they were doing a review sheet for their upcoming test. Lori who seemed confused turned to Icarus to have him explain it. He helped her gain a better understanding of it and was able to pass her test. During that time, she got to know Icarus McGrew who seemed very sweet yet shy. The more they talked outside of class, she saw him as a very mature, calm, insightful guy. He gave out that peaceful vibe that would make him appear older than his time. Like a formal guy who seems to have been blessed with a calming demeanor.

Reserved Icarus hadn't had a close friend such as her before and always made sure to never do anything to mess that up. Lori herself was a delicate darling who appeared very pretty as a Caucasian redhead who was lusted after by many boys in their grade, including some upperclassman. Icarus made sure to never overstep that unspoken boundary set between them, especially when she confided in him on how many of her "guy friends" would inevitably make a pass at her, either directly or indirectly.

So Icarus knew better. By their senior year, he had become infatuated by another senior girl named Kimberly Boyd. She became good friends with Lori junior year and hadn't really been acquainted with Icarus until senior year. Kimberly was a tall, brunette girl who was light-skinned. She was very nice to Icarus since she could tell he hadn't been much of a social butterfly. Lori had confessed this to him but told him to not be upset about that since they were fine with each other. This was shortly after Icarus confessed his feelings to Kimberly a month after knowing her, hoping she would go out with him. Unfortunately, she wasn't interested and was already dating a college freshman at the time. Lori felt somewhat bad because she knew he had never dated before and Kimberly wasn't the only friend of hers that he liked.

Another friend of Lori's was a cheerleader in their grade named Helen Fair. She had a reputation of being the school slut who had sex with many of the school athletes, college guys and was rumored to be involved with the head of the science department at their school. However, Icarus wasn't ever open to rumors, especially those revolving around girls he'd fancy. Even though her reputation for the most part was true, Icarus either wouldn't believe it or would make excuses rationalizing any possible peculiar behavior (*such as she's young, we all make mistakes, don't know her personally*). But as open and honest as Icarus and Lori were with each other, she couldn't reveal how Helen truly felt about him.

Helen would slander almost everyone behind their backs, including some of her friends, but she targeted Icarus the most. She admitted to Lori that he always gave her an uneasy feeling since she'd seen him mostly alone or walking the halls alone (*if he wasn't already with Lori or Kimberly*). Almost like a creeper just in his head plotting. Lori would try defending him but never persisted to avoid causing friction between her and Helen. Plus, Icarus wasn't ever around Helen so it wouldn't serve any real purpose.

So soon after Icarus had been rejected by Kimberly, he never asked her out again. It didn't deter him though from being constantly present throughout the semester, having a somewhat symbiotic relationship. Having Icarus wake up earlier for school just to run into Kimberly in the library either studying or relaxing right before her class. He would always converse with her about his life or be fully invested in how hers was going. Or he would constantly urge for them both to get together afterschool to just hangout. She was more comfortable with him being the third wheel whenever she and Lori hung out instead.

Kimberly noticed a change within him whenever they were alone. Icarus wasn't shy or calm anymore but more excited. Not "exciting" but excited to be around her. He spoke more different. His soft-spoken voice was altered with a chirpier one. She never verbalized this to him, only to Lori. Lori excused it as just him being a little happier; Icarus saw it as that and more. Throughout most of his high school career, he'd never felt this lively dynamic shared with anyone before. It was good for him that Kimberly's presence always uplifted his spirits without judgement.

Although to her, this dynamic he had with her was so overwhelming, having Icarus constantly tethered to her like a python had her feeling drained. It felt like a parasitism relationship to where she wish she could isolate herself by graduating already. She couldn't label him as a pervert but he was still flattering her with compliments. At least other boys in her grade would be more direct with their intentions towards her. Icarus on the other hand, wasn't outright with why he wanted to be around other than seeming infatuated. Kimberly wasn't sure what his agenda was and had to distance herself from him. She told Lori this, then Kimberly bluntly ignored him afterwards. Never making eye contact in the halls or when she said hi to Lori around him.

Icarus felt hurt and foolish being ignored. It didn't get any better soon after when Kimberly alongside with Helen talked about him being a creep with sketchy intentions. This was rumored all around his peers causing for girls to beware of him. These girls were blatantly obvious with their discomfort around him. Some would jog pass him if they saw him in the hallway. If they saw him around Lori, they'd wait for him to leave before coming around her. This had him feeling more insecure than ever before.

Lori was the only one who knew him personally which made her opinion appear the most fragile at the time. However, it didn't improve how much he was seething internally from Kimberly or on how other students perceived him. But he eventually came to the conclusion that they're talking about how upbeat he had become around her. He truly saw himself as being genuinely happy around her and shouldn't let them ruin his bliss. It didn't matter just how closed off he was before, this is how he'll be remembered. Icarus now knowing that their misplaced judgment was targeted at his changes for his own benefit (*happiness*) somehow uplifted the weight of criticism and shame off of him.

Despite there being an end to his suffering, Icarus still remembered that his high school experience didn't end well. By his freshman year in college, he became more cautious when it came to the opposite sex, especially at the time he had lived with them on campus. He didn't want to repeat having future girls look down upon him but still wanted to be around the large variety of girls. So he became very subdued during school.

He was as normal and passive as you could imagine. Even though he reached out more to girls, he was still extremely hesitant when it came to move things further with any girls he desired. Introducing himself wasn't as hard but he felt weak-kneed whenever the urge to escalate things sexually (*whether asking for numbers, out on dates or by simply flirting*) crossed his mind. This led Icarus to never getting laid at school and to reside to pornography instead.

When he graduated, witnessing his whole class toss up their caps in the air feeling euphoric led to this realization. The fact that everyone lived out their wildest experiences without judgement from their peers had struck him like the incoming graduation caps. All had memorable college moments and he wasn't a part of any of them. This had aroused his suppressed urges, galvanizing Icarus McGrew into expressing his past self (*how he felt with Kimberly*) and taking the necessary risks to obtaining women.

After high school and college, all these years of being turned down had never really compared. Icarus then left from his house to drive to Richez Shrive.

† Chapter 13: Noted.

Richez Shrive 11:23 A.M.

Icarus McGrew walks inside to see some customers raising a glass. He grew accustomed to the sad faces over this miracle still. However, he had overheard them talking about Montrez being killed two days ago. It was apparent that many patrons here knew him so he decided to try approaching women elsewhere.

Yanie being told what happened from the last person in the bar to see him shared a drink with Jovanny.

"How you feel about all this?" she sincerely asked.

Jovanny shook his head. "Awful. Like, he's gone just like that. And the way they making him out to sound too."

Yanie automatically knew he meant the news that announced that he was under the influence. Reporters implied he was aggressive with the cop. They both know that cops in Holksdale have been only getting worse due to most going straight to hell, they believe this cop was no exception. Jovanny pours himself another drink.

"Yanie, I been a real piece of shit, real talk." He admits. "I talked him into drinking that much. I just wanted to make some more bread for the bar, even at his expense."

Jovanny goes on about them discussing his wife and sexless marriage. Even on how his wife wouldn't let him drink and that he planned on arriving at work sober. Jovanny gulped his drink before he confessed about kicking Montrez out while intoxicated.

"Bro, bro," Yanie comforts. "This ain't your fault."

Jovanny could see through the corner of his eye that a few customers were beginning to stare. He then goes to pouring himself another glass and turns to the customers.

"Attention y'all." He said while maintaining himself. "I know this is tragic. Montrez was a good guy, been up on this stool for years. We lost a good customer today, even though last time he was here drunk, this fool still forgot to pay his tab."

Customers began cackling and started nodding.

"A shame what happened to him. Leaving wifey behind. I know y'all been up in here drinking 'cause of this phenomenon that's trended longer than it should, so we can all agree that man is in a better place."

He raises his glass in the air before them all: "To Montrez." The rest of them repeat out of respect for the deceased. Yanie's the last to do so then she drinks down the rest. All attention on them from everyone else has been diverted, leaving them both be.

"Jovanny." Yanie called to him. "You really believe he in a better place?"

Jovanny who afterwards appeared unconvinced simply replied: "Who the hell knows?!"

York Avenue 12:22 P.M.

Essie went back to sleep in her room after making Larissa some oatmeal. Larissa, while watching TV, received a phone call. It was a collect call from Midtown penitentiary. Larissa is overjoyed and quickly accepts this call.

"Hello, ma?"

"Hey baby." Danielle replies in a gracious tone. "Where you been? Ain't heard from y'all in a minute."

"Sorry, we been busy lately. But are you ok?"

"Yea, peachy." she replied in an annoyed tone. "Where Essie at? She was supposed to pull up with some food a week ago."

Larissa explains that Essie's been indisposed and was just in an accident. Without any real concern for her child's guardian she quickly asks: "Well, how soon til' she's fixed?"

"I won't hold you, maybe a lil' while." Larissa replied sounding fearful, especially feeling Danielle's long pause.

Danielle sensing her daughter's concern asks: "Well, how you been?"

"I've been good, keeping you in our prayers."

"Mm-hmm." Danielle replied sounding skeptical. "See you talking this holy shit again, huh?"

Larissa feeling hesitant to bring it up again, mentions how she did some research on how her prison has group therapy weekly.

"I done already known this." she said sounding smug. "Been involved in it to get outta laundry duty."

"I thought," Larissa hesitates. "Thought maybe it'd be good for you, before you get too far gone."

"To do what?! Open up to a bunch of convicts, disclosing my business for them to judge me up in here?!"

"Not like you'd not like the attention." Larissa hissed.

"Girl, don't you forget yourself!"

Larissa takes a moment to let her mom relax. "I'm just saying that admitting to prior sins before prison, no matter where you are, would help you repent. I'm concerned about you ma 'cause I love you." Both mother and daughter know that the call is about to end. "Think about it please."

The call ceased with no closure off the other end. Essie emerged downstairs from her slumber. Larissa changes the channel to the news, knowing her guardian normally watches it; then she heads to her room.

Essie slouches on the couch facing the TV. There have been updates on the current issues transpiring in Holksdale. Four robberies happened these past two days. Citizens have been harassing several Muslim residents and categorizing other Indian, Guyanese and Pakistan people with them. Targeting their homes, small businesses and property with vandalism; the tragic aftermath escalating ever since the plane incident.

Her shoulder muscles began to tense up once they mentioned the plane crash. An enormous exhale is released only to have more toxicity refueled into her system; further solidifying her nervy, uncertainty towards the future. Any vessel of positivity goes out the window.

Jovanny's place 11:00 P.M.

After a long day at work, exhausted Jovanny opens the door to his apartment. Solanda's not present in the living room so he just heads to their bedroom. Behind the door was an Indian woman spread on the center of their bed. Jovanny was shocked by the sight of this voluptuous female smiling at him. She bites her bottom lip in a seductive manner.

"Hello?" he initiates with a nonchalant tone.

"I guess you're Jovanny." She said sounding pleased as she rubs her thick thigh tempting him more. "I'm B. Your girlfriend approached me this evening telling me you two were looking for some fun tonight."

He remembered telling Solanda about Montrez being killed yesterday. This was her way of making him feel better, especially since B fits his physical desirable criteria. He simply nods then responds: "Where she find you at?"

"She caught me waiting by the bus stop and gave me a ride here. I had just left church."

B bats her long eyelashes enticing him over. She reveals Solanda getting ready in the bathroom. Jovanny quickly dismisses it and sits on the bed, they start kissing. Her prolonged moaning gives him a hard-on. Her smooth hand slid down his cock then flicked the tip with her sultry fingertips.

Jovanny pulls back with great excitement. B lies on her back, takes off her shirt that reveals her robust chest so filled inside her black bra that each is practically begging to bust out. B slowly slid off her pants while making a flirtatious face the whole time. Jovanny spots what appears between her legs, a black metallic chastity belt. Its design consists of leathery interior padding that's covered by dark glossy metal. The waist of each side is held together by drilled in silver screws. The frontier of this has a gold-coded gate illustration with a keyhole placed in the center of its gates. He noticed from the sight of pubic hair protruding to the point where if they were stretched any longer, they could unfasten the gates themselves.

She digs in her bra and toss him the key. It was a teeny, black thin key molded in the form of Satan's trident.

Jovanny's eager to engage, B awaits for him as she lays her head on his pillow, stretching apart her legs. He leans forward towards her face. As she expects for a kiss, she feels him feeling for something behind his pillow. A brown clipboard is presented to B.

"Wh-what's this?" B asks looking perplexed.

"Don't worry, it ain't nothing too deep. Just a consent form for you to sign."

B appeared really confused, her eyebrows raised up becoming wide-eyed as well: *"Excuse me?"*

"Just need you to sign your name here saying we good." He explains. "You could read it over if you want."

"I thought you were going for protection. Where's the rubber at? Under your pillow?"

"Nah, that's where the pen be at."

"No baby, c'mon." B pleads, trying to kiss him. Jovanny halts this with the form in her face. He shook his head, insisting she signs first. B seems to be frustrated. "Look, this is a one night stand. I'm not trying to put my name out like that, especially on some creepy documents. And, I just gave you the key to my belt, all my consent's right there."

"This is for my own protection, that's all."

B gestures her hand out for the key back. He flicks it to her, appearing unfazed. "If you not with it then I can't stop you from leaving." He said in an emotionless voice.

"I'm not leaving," B said while inserting the key inside, unlocking her belt. The sound of undoing this resembles thumb-bolt lock gears turning. Once it clicks, she sets apart both her legs. Graciously opening up herself; a gleaming light is slowly released. Cautiously unsure whether to release anymore after how stubborn he was being, she noticed how transfixed he was by this. "You know, I usually don't do this. It is a sin, so consider you and your girlfriend blessed." B admits as she gave into her demons and completely flashed him. The flare released from inside lit Jovanny's face, he stared into this mesmeric blaze that B soon awaits for him to burst.

"Yup, no kids neither." B said. "You feel better, babe?"

Jovanny shields his face with the clipboard, they weren't engaging any further without his consent.

"This is ridiculous." B roars. "You don't need my signature, I'm not gonna report rape or nothing of the sort. Plus, we don't even need a condom since I'm on the pill."

"GET OUT!" he demands. *"Fuck outta here!"*

B reapplied her belt and got dressed and slammed the door as she left. Solanda came out in tight lingerie wondering what that noise was and where B went.

Jovanny explains to her what happened. He noticed the aggravated look on his girlfriend's face.

"Really, Jovanny?!" Solanda spoke in an upset yet hesitant voice and then sat on the bed. "That's such a huge turnoff. Like, we getting it, vibe is there and shit; then all of a sudden you finna put on yo' reading glasses then present me some clipboard to sign for consent. We come to a shitty halt 'cause you're over-reacting."

"I'm buggin'? This church-goer bitch over here lying about being on the pill. Next thing I get her pregnant and it's a wrap. And she refused the consent form, so she could be down to fuck now then just switch-up and claim rape. She ain't no exception. Thinking just 'cause she got a wet box so hypnotic that I'll be caught slippin' so she can secure the bag. Fuck outta here!"

"Baby," she consoles him. "She would've been with it. We done been through this shit before. Not all these girls can't be trusted."

"Half these hoes you brought up in here ain't even loyal to they own man."

Solanda wasn't trying to argue with him but wanted for him to understand at least from her position. "I get that you think they might be on bullshit but what about what I want? You not the only one getting pleasure outta it."

Jovanny sat on the bed rubbing his girlfriend's lap.

"I ever tell you about when I was in college?" he asked.

She shook her head.

"Well, when I was coming up all pimply-faced and simple and shit… I used to dorm on campus. Used to be in this advertising club that had a few guys but was mostly bombarded with girls. I wasn't bold enough to ever take a chance and risk it all. So whenever they'd give me a chance to make a move, I'd always act like I ain't know what's up. Like my mom always told me and my brothers to be treatin' females right. That all women are deserving of respect. No hitting 'em back, no offending and of course… 'No means no'. So all my childhood, I been submissive towards females."

He confides about how he wouldn't say vulgar jokes, always catered to their feelings before his and valued their opinion over his very own. Solanda concealed her shocked look with a mundane, understanding look. Jovanny talks about how his older brother, Lestroy, who was getting girls and had broken out of their mother's authoritative principles. His brother tried motivating him to break out of that cycle and approach more girls.

So Jovanny felt embolden enough to pursue a girl in that club named Kira. She was a sophomore and had dated multiple boys there since her freshman year. He introduced himself and they shortly became friends. Kira would often confide in him about the boys she's dated and how they'd all mistreat her. The campus had its share of boys who were expelled or put on probation for sexual misconduct. He came off as the perfect gentleman, Jovanny tried to get inside her head. Always feeling cautious around her, initiating considerate conversations to know her more intimately, constantly second-guessing himself whenever trying to advance any further and non-stop concern over how she perceives him.

He would sometimes assist her when they had advertising projects to work on. Offering her ideas of his and encouraging her that she can be creative herself. The ads that she was influenced to create were presented to the club then posted around campus with her name solely printed as well. The many posters from her earned Kira to be the poster face of advertising the club on the school website and on the school bulletin board. Jovanny's ideas helped her to prosper in that club; instilling confidence in her that outweighed the impact that ex-boyfriends inflicted.

Despite seeing her blossom and the club praising her work, Jovanny had still felt underappreciated. They were friends but not in a relationship. He decided to persist a little further by inviting her to his dorm one evening since she's never been there, especially being a commuter.

"So, I low-key wanted to see where this could go since I gassed her up to that point." He said sounding regretful, taking a moment to continue. "Anyway, we were alone and she got things a little twisted. So she dipped and the next day she reported me for harassment and shit. Now mind you, I ain't ever touch her and the school dropped me from advertising club, dropped my classes and couldn't live on campus no more. Lost my disciplinary hearing too, couldn't finish."

"Oh baby, I'm so sorry." She genuinely said as she reached for a hug.

"And the big motherfucker… I ended up serving this cunt drinks last year. I recognized her with an advertising agency in celebration of an ad they pushed through. And she recognized me too. No apology, no remorse, just took her drink and went back to her co-workers that I had to end up serving each like some bitch. And the idea I overheard her pitching to them was for peace on earth, replicating the exact same scenario I told her in college."

His girlfriend can detect the anger fueling inside him and the trembling sound in his voice.

"Like, after all the shit I did for her and you do me like this?! Baby, advertisers' main goal is to create something memorable to be praised and my shit was out promoted under someone else's name. But not just that, I was nothing more but a bad memory. So since then, I decluttered out all that simp shit from up inside my head. And not just her but a lot of women be actin' the same damn way. Nothing changed no matter how conscious I was, so I may as well just end shit on my own terms."

"Not all women are that way, ok?" Solanda gently said. She curls up on him, arms wrapped around his chest. "And you're all memorable to me."

"I know." Jovanny said.

† *Hollywood: Los Angeles, California 2:45 P.M.*

Constant allegations have surfaced and increased since the miracle happened. The belief of suffering eternal damnation had fueled many actors to confess their sins to the public; their inappropriate sexual misconduct with other celebrities. More women (*whether they're actresses, fans or interns*) were coming out exposing everyone. Another famous actor caught in this scandal was Grant Critchfield.

Grant was accused of sexual assault recently from a woman who wishes to remain unknown. Reports reveal her statement of this incident transpiring the night she came over to his mansion for a dinner date. The victim claimed that Grant had forced himself onto her and she later fled that night after the assault. After this was announced to the public, he has been denied future projects from other directors, he's been constantly pursued by the paparazzi, and most people's allegiance was towards the accuser. Yet, the actor still refused to make a public response about this allegation still.

He is now discussing his circumstances and any alternatives with his agent, Joy Pluss. A thirty-five-year old cream-skinned lady with red hair and a skinny frame. Joy has always been understanding with all of her clients and has dealt with Grant's issues for most of her career now. Grant has gotten a lot of notoriety throughout the years for public intoxication, altercations with other actors on set, drug possession, offensive responses for movie interviews, disrespectful posts on his social media ranting on sensitive topics and a whole lot more. Joy has viewed his many antics as a challenge for herself but always miraculously rectified these situations. However, this situation's harder to resolve.

"This doesn't look good, Grant." Joy said shaking her head in annoyance. "This is not good one bit. People have been calling, having second thoughts on you."

Grant starts chuckling with a slight sneer and his arms crossed. "Uh-huh. Unable to be casted in such repetitive reboots of classics from the 90's… real great loss there. I got let go from some role in a remake they're doing of this horror film where the male protagonist is now switched to some demonic non-binary beast."

Joy gets annoyed by his dismissive demeanor. Grant is a tall, forty-four-year-old Caucasian male with a little tan. He has brown straight hair, his body is pretty slim with some muscle in his arms and a handsome face as well. His eyes were bright green and were staring down at his phone instead of Joy.

"Always with the arguing." She said sounding irked. "Either it being on set or with paparazzi, even with fans, Grant. Directors too!"

"These writers and directors don't know how to write fleshed out well-written characters. Claiming they wanted to make their traits revealed in subtle hints. Then I just disprove them in front of the other cast members and they'll rewrite some things. If I'm starring in a film, it better be up to my standards. So I'm well within my rights to do so."

"Then they don't ever wanna work with you again! It's either your way or the highway, even if it's to your own detriment. Especially with that little stunt you pulled last week, pissed a lot of people off, Grant."

Joy was able to set up a press conference for her client to inform people and reporters about this allegation. It was an ongoing effect with these actors making public apologies for their behavior. Though everyone (*whether they were his fans or just wanting to crucify him off whatever he confesses)* awaited for his statement since he's one of the few actors who never gave a hint about anything.

Grant seemed very reluctant to do this but he decided to shed some light on what may've possibly happened that night. Despite his usual indifference towards the general public's opinions.

He came out in a white button-front shirt along with a nice suit and wearing brown sunglasses. His brown hair sleeked down; looking entirely professional. Grant knew a few actors who either teared up or sounded *weakly*; like they were supplicating to everyone watching. The idea of actors having to pander to their own fans who'd once praise them, giving them that option to value them again, just disgusts Grant. However, his agent urged for him to come out.

Once he exposed himself on stage to the public, the whole crowd of people were in a frenzy and split between two camps. Many of his fans held white banners advocating his innocence; the other were a group of men and women who booed and hissed at him. Holding up signs stating how he's a *"disgrace to God"* or *"he should be forsaken from Hollywood"*. There were many raging women there being supported by these accompanied "males" who seemed to be hopping on the bandwagon. What made these women standout more was their attire but really a lack thereof that filled up the crowd. These females were completely nude and proud of it. Their topless breasts concealed in paint and their undergarments painted over as well.

A Caucasian female in her mid-twenties who seemed to have led them had both breasts covered in bright red paint, including her low-cut hair. Her waists was smeared with a black painted line stretched all around to her ass-crack. A black female (*who you'd never guess*) was livid and doused in orange from head to toe. Her afro was left black. Another girl was completely painted in gold with white even around her mouth. Her lips in gold too. She had black strips across both her ribs and around her thick thighs. There was an obese redhead girl who seemed ecstatic to be included in this group. Large white wings and dark lines covering each sagging bosom. One of her meaty legs were drenched in green, her belly rolls splashed with silver with everywhere else on her body in red. Grant noticed a twirling freakishly thin, anorexic-looking girl revolving around the crowd. She had her firm buttocks smeared in yellowish-orange; dark thin lines traced up through her veins.

Unfortunately, nothing had concealed the vulgarity spouting from out their mouths. The excessive barking of colorful language had overshadowed their enticing bodies.

Their fierce screams lit up inside his head. He leaned towards the microphone which sparked up stronger feelings from the crowd. Grant couldn't focus on the fans who praised him over everything else. "**PERVERT**!" which soared to the stage he was on. Other criticisms were ripping noises that began to make his headache. People just refused to simmer down by his presence. Grant Critchfield held up a straight face but was seething inside, his exhales get harsher the more he feels enraged. He pulled away from the microphone to prevent it from spreading out the force of his wrath. The more he contemplates giving out any insight, the more intense the protestors grow.

The constant name-calling, ridiculing, and yelling to provoke him into reacting was persistently gnawing at him. Then he recalled in his head every past actor visibly crippled for all to witness. Grant almost didn't want to step down; feeling like they'll have that notion of pressuring him off the stage. Then he remembered what brought them all here today, his statement to this. This reminder emboldened him to take a step back from the microphone. His head held high, shoulders back and said: *"Buh-bye."* Turned his back to the crowd and walks off. Their growling had torn louder onward to the stage, and a grin widened upon Grant's face.

"Those people already had their minds set." Grant said firmly. "Exactly why I rarely acknowledge these reporters or critics. Even these fans opinions aren't concrete."

Grant Critchfield was financially well-off. His status and movie roles over these past twenty years has made him insanely wealthy. He wasn't ever fixated on the opinions of his fans or any bad kind of publicity. Though, Grant does love to hear their praise of him; to the point where the few selfless acts he'll perform are autographs and pictures. He even wasn't surprised by the number of trolls making videos bashing him on social media or other actors against him when interviewed about their experiences working with him. Even though he had money, Grant loved to act. Believing his main performance outshines all else's and requested more scenes.

"This whole attempt of trying to pander to my 'supposed' fans out there seems quite trivial at this point. Also, the copious amount of women I've had inside my home and now this bitch wants to claim rape."

"Listen, I know you'd never do this but they don't know what you or anyone else in Hollywood's capable of. Plus, there were many actresses interviewed who said you were sometimes around the same actors who harassed them. That's not a good look."

Grant looked irritated. "Of course, I've worked with some of these 'actresses'… if you can even call them that. A lot of them seem disingenuous like they're reading off a teleprompter or something. No emoting whatsoever."

"It's called staying strong for the camera." Joy suggests.

"Or could just be lying, hopping on this cock-assault-train bandwagon."

"So let me understand this, you're saying every actress interviewed about you and other men are lying, that it?"

"Not all, Joy. Just the underrated ones exploiting this opportunity to earn sympathy in attempts to garner more publicity. 'Cause I've seen these girls act on set. Most fuck up their lines knowing fully well they won't get as much recognition as me. Now suddenly when it comes to this stardom, they're all rehearsed and able to repeat the exact same shit about us all in sync."

"Ok, Grant. I see." Joy replied sounding restless. "All these actresses are conspiring against you men who—"

"NO!" he overrode her. "Don't categorize me with men actually involved in this. I'm not affiliated with them."

"Understand there's been a gender imbalance in the film industry for quite some time now, you know how it is. These women now feel empowered to overcome the internal struggles pressured on them by superficial factors."

"*Right…*" he sarcastically said. "Because a large portion of these young actresses have that much substance deep within. That's why they all crave attention as a form of sustenance to fulfill their superficial, empty calorie stricken lives."

Another actor who had faced allegations from over fifty women was Calvin Harris, a fifty-six-year-old Caucasian man who was fat, balding and had a huge name in the industry. He was one of the men that Grant was seen being around. Calvin confessed to these accusations all being true at a press conference as he made a teary-eyed apology, seeking forgiveness; not just from the public but from God Almighty himself.

"I'm sure he mentioned God as a maneuver to act like he's pleading to be redeemed. Plus, this industry will make you do things you'd never imagine just to maintain your credibility. Because they all knew what he's been doing in private. It's all to keep up his past legacy as an actor."

"You sure about that?" she asks, skeptically.

"Hollywood will exploit you out to the general public. They don't even require you under film contracts anymore, Joy. Just need to trace your fingerprints breaking the 'I refuse to possess girls as my God-given right' clause. This also explains what leverage they held over him to have Calvin do those shitty voiceover direct-to-DVD and live action kids films."

"Well, it's more complex than that and this applies to you too, Grant." Joy said patiently. She explains how his name was under the *'HELL'* section, leading for some fans any others to have this preconceived notion that he's legitimately a godawful human being.

Grant snorted, his arms crossed as he leaned back in his chair cross-legged. "Joy…" he said with a grin. "You don't honestly think this has any bearing on anything in my life whatsoever now, do you?!"

"Yes, I do." She said, frustrated. "This has been trending literally all around the world. People have the wrong idea about you now."

"Unbelievable. And I've heard people embarrassing themselves over how strong they fell for this, like Audrey Bavaro."

Audrey Bavaro was a Hollywood executive who was facing accusations from actor, Reggie Burton. He had identified her for having allegedly groped his genitals at an industry party. Bavaro recently came out to the public confessing that this was true, acknowledging her fate for heading to hell and hoping to save her soul. Burton was an extremely muscular black man, his veins just protruding out his arm, calves and neck, starring in many hood films and was a well-known wrestler of his time. It would've looked bad for him to retaliate in a physical altercation against this white woman at the time.

"You see what I mean. She gave a statement to try to save her career. They met, it was supposed to be a simple meet and greet—"

"*Yes, it was a meat-and-greet*." He mocked. Joy paused to shoot him a serious look. Grant wiped away his grin.

"—we've seen how far this has gone to where even some females are now exposed."

"Yes, anyone's now up for grabs." He admits. "Reggie's practically an Adonis molded in the flesh by God himself who could easily beat anyone's ass and even she attacked him by his low-hanging fruit."

"Well since you're too stubborn to give any statement to the press, I propose this then. Keep a low-profile for a bit. No paparazzi. Don't post nothing on your page. Perhaps do some good for an organization by donating money or just anything positive, understand me? I'm serious, Grant."

Grant begrudgingly nods his head. "Noted."

MIDTOWN HOLKSDALE: 6:30 P.M.

Around town were some flyers promoting an upcoming event for women all throughout Holksdale to attend to. This event took place in this building usually hosting several different venues. Solanda Wright was invited by her friend Latoya to accommodate her. Latoya has been guided by her on how to handle her pregnancy by giving her books, advice and the occasional supervision. However, Solanda didn't mind, she liked how dependent her friend was on her especially since she followed. Latoya felt like she needed to become stronger since she'll be raising this kid on her own. It was advertised as a way of uplifting females especially living within low-income areas.

"This the place, this where it's at?" Solanda asks.

"Yea, said it on the flyer." Latoya reassures her. "No but girl, you'll love this. The hostess, she a spokeswoman, women activist. Plus, this bitch I hear is from the state."

"I bet, what's her name again?" she asks skeptically, but Latoya couldn't recall. She makes an evaluation of where they are. The entirety of this cubic room that was rented is a spacious, functional meeting room with no windows. Multiple women of various backgrounds (*black, white, Hispanic, Indian*) are here conversing with each other. More importantly, they're from different areas of Holksdale. A few Caucasian women from uptown are here and many ethnic women from midtown and downtown are conjoined here as well. Where Holksdale is normally divided amongst everyone in these three communities, this gathering today was to unify women with the food, drinks and soon… *the facts.* There was a long white table filled with food (*donuts, fried wings, soft fries, chips, nachos with salsa and guacamole)* and drinks (*soda, coffee, energy drinks)* that most of them were already digging into. A large amount of black seats aligned together row by row all facing the stage with a wooden podium and microphone.

Latoya looks over to the table of drinks but is unsure if Solanda would allow it so decides to sit down. Solanda soon joins her, handing over a small plate with two glazed donuts with sprinkles. As for Solanda, she had her own bottle of water.

Five minutes later, a woman emerges onto the stage. To inform them that it's time she then taps on the microphone. Every woman automatically finds a seat, all attentive to the stage. This woman was a pencil-thin, tanned, brunette Caucasian spokeswoman with short hair snipped to her shoulders. She was dressed in an extremely professional (*black blazer with buttoned inserts outside the sleeves, slim black skirt revealing her boney legs, black high heels*) attire with brown sunglasses fused on.

She remained still momentarily with a wooden stare at her audience (*she could've been fused with the podium*) then leans to the microphone: "Ladies and ladies, my name is Lorell St. Louis and welcome to this event honoring you all." Everyone's clapping. Solanda could hear the excessive sounds of food and drinks being munched and gulped too.

Lorell St. Louis introduced herself as a journalist, an American social political activist, and a feminist. She has held these events around the world mostly in urban communities to help unify and empower women to the best of their femininity. This is to inform women that reside in places where the education of this is scarce while welcoming other women who may already know. Then she brings up the miracle that's been all over earth.

"See ladies, as a Christian myself, I was astounded to see the number of women in Holksdale enlisted to be doomed to damnation." She said in disgust. "And not just being judged by the lord almighty but there's this general consensus claiming that the females of today across-the-board are a headache, nothing but unbearable. That we're not worth settling down with and are the catalyst as to why the 'dating scene' has gone significantly downhill."

The crowd was nodding, and some had shook their heads by the reality of this.

"Women of today's generation endures so many hardships only to be topped-off with us heading to hell. Isn't this, excuse my French, complete and utter bullshit?!"

An uproar of applause begins to extend.

"We've sacrificed our time, our hearts and our youth to appease to the male gaze. Are they grateful? No! Men conjure up these creepy tactics in attempts to pick-up us. They engage us discussing nonsensical things with their creeper agenda, then get upset when we sense it and refuse to entertain them further. Both parties know that you didn't introduce yourself just to exchange pleasantries. A complete stranger popped up to us out of nowhere, who's been eyeing us down from afar. WE NOTICE! Even when men thus commence to stalking. And it doesn't cease there."

The whole room was silent, her scenario seemed too familiar for all of them, even Solanda (*strip club assault*).

"We now have our well-known platonic male friends starting to fall into this category. They too have become convinced that we are just taking them for granted just for attention. That from our perspective, they're viewed as nothing to us but an emotional scapegoat instead of just friends we genuinely open ourselves up to. Because that's what friends are for." Lorell asserts. "Now granted, perhaps when we grow older and become more mature then we may decide to give them a chance. But then they'll harshly dismiss us. Pretty much revealing their true colors, that the basis of our entire friendship was solely them wanting to get us in bed when we're in our prime."

"HELL YEAH!" a woman in the crowd yelled. "They all of a sudden got this high and mighty attitude once we're a little older, 'cause now you don't like what you fuckin' see!"

Women were applauding while consuming more donuts. The cheers died down, eager to hear more.

"Today's 'males' generalize us as selfish children who they choose to oppress. Men overtly shame our bodies as a maneuver for us to fit a certain standard for them to simply just lust after. Labeling females as just a piece of meat, regardless of how the media tries uplifting us all into feeling more comfortable the way God made us, in our own skin." Lorell pauses momentarily. Observing the crowd's reaction, the look on these ladies' faces by how maddened they were. Not against her but towards how accurate this all was and by how powerless and vulnerable it had them recoil. *"INSTEAD, THEY WANT TO MOLD US TO APPEASE TO THEIR OWN SEXUAL GRATIFICATION!"* she said, enraged. The women verbally commence to coming into agreement with each other.

"Today's men not only objectify us as sex objects but also lack chivalry. Most resent us for having more rights and project their misogynistic views to help justify it as us becoming overly privileged. Their bitterness and hatred radiates so strong that they overlook our intrinsic values. That we contribute more to society than to just cook, sweep and letting men's selfish desires to take precedence over our livelihoods. All men commit the cardinal sin of consistently placing the onus on us when it comes to dating, assuming we hold all the cards. When in actuality, they're normally the dictators of the relationship. A lot of them refuse to take us out on dates yet puts in maximum effort into bringing us back to their place."

"FACTS!" a black woman upfront agreed. Lorell gestures for her to continue. "Like, I was talking to this guy, right, and his text game was so weak. Not even a whole day passed once he got my number, he tried to send out a bubble trail to lure me back to his spot. So I ask him what he's got planned for me there… zero response. Like, that ain't sus'."

"YES!" Lorell proudly agreed. "They don't take our comfort level into consideration, which brings me to the conclusion as to how this has influenced your eternal fates."

The audience had absorbed her entire presence, awaiting to become more enlightened by this. Solanda checked for her friend's reaction, Latoya was fully engaged.

"Ladies," Lorell said solemnly. "For generations, men have mistreated us as second-class citizens. The majority of women in the urban community are single mothers after being abandoned by ne'er-do-well males who impregnated us. They've done nothing to merit our time and possibly our virginities. Most mothers have had kids by becoming intimate before marriage, which is a sin, only for the father to later discard you and your children afterwards."

It became so uncomfortably silent inside that there was no trace of anyone eating the served junk food. It was evident how this was a sensitive topic the women didn't want for this spokeswoman to delve into.

"These men promise to protect us, to forever love us and to forever refrain from hurting us, just to have sex with us. Now see where that's gotten us." Lorell observed the room, all eyes upon her with many of them keeping a straight face. There's this ongoing aura circulating the room that Solanda and Lorell detects, the one of pent-up aggression that's been repressed for too damn long, now finally having an alternative outlet. That if someone were to fidget with this while still somehow being fueled, all hell could break loose. Lorell St. Louis calmly asks her audience: "Now, a show of hands before God and be truthful, how many women in this room are and will soon be single mothers?"

Multiple hands slowly raised up from most of them. Lorell assumed some were holding back then crossed her arms and waited. Seconds later, more hands went up. Latoya's hand shamefully went up, both eyes checking around her area. It irked Solanda in her seat seeing how her friend was getting self-conscious now, especially seeing right through what this feminist was doing.

"Now you've got no man grounded in the picture and you're destined to burn down in hell."

If she had persisted, they may soon become unhinged. However, she was willing to take the risk: "And these males get to live in bliss."

Everyone without hesitation went berserk. The "ladies" in the back raised up quick from their seats. The ones upfront were screaming while uncontrollably chugging down soda. *"Shit, I gotta protect mine's!"* a woman announced while having had her infant child strapped to her chest.

"Settle down, everyone. Let's settle down." Lorell said. The women were slowly regaining their composure. "So, we now see the problem, it's not us, it's on them. Men believe they've got the upper hand due to their careers, gender and superior physicality." She said indignantly. "They'll always look down on us as the weaker sex. We need to remind them that we aren't inferior."

A round of applause brings a grin on Lorell's face. Her words resonates with them.

"You all are beautiful just the way you are which should suffice, so you need to exercise your femininity to your advantage. Men need to provide for us... solely. Engage with those who are worth your time because we deserve no less. Extract the best of the best resources from him. Then cut off ties and move forth to another who provides better."

"I got mad dudes that blow up my phone." a white woman yelled from the back.

"GOOD!" Lorell encouraged. "You make each and every last soul in your phone treat you out to restaurants, concerts, vacations—all of those gems until we personally feel ready to escalate things more. And if they refuse to follow or try steering you to go in his direction, ignore his future texts until he gets the damn message. And we cannot just stop there!"

Lorell factors in the other advantages that help women already: the court systems, the police, and social media dating apps. But reminds them that those aren't enough. Then urges for them to take drastic measures to acquire more power and the top-tier men.

"At whatever jobs you're at now, let it be known that men are supposed to remain professional on the clock. Make an example of any male who even winks in your general direction again by reporting any discomfort to the company. Or any guy who trains their eyes on you out in public, you be stern enough to dismiss them. You shall only entertain the top-tier quality men. Remember, *WE ARE THE PRIZE, LADIES!"*

This spokeswoman knew she seized the audience. Women here were electrified. They either were recording this, eating more treats or drinking more soda, or so lively that they thrust back their arms only to almost fall out their chairs. Either way, this was the spark of an uprising.

"Now everyone, I also propose this." she adds. "We need to be committed, so we'll need to go on a sex strike."

They began to settle down again with a perplexed look.

"I know this is the sexual liberation period for us now so it'll be hard to refrain from temptation, but we must. Men only crave sex and they've already had their fun using us. You must have him marry you before, which will behoove you still. You'll be entwined to his resources even if there's a divorce, you won't be orbited around by many men just for his pleasure and you'll be redeemed in the lord's eyes."

The women seem a little unsure whether to engage in this or even advocate it. Some turn to each other, most are silent, Solanda sat there stupefied.

"If we wish to feel fulfilled here on earth and alter our fates to reach heaven… then ladies, we must hold ourselves to a higher standard." Lorell announced with full conviction.

"I'M WITH IT!" Latoya said in a manic outburst. Solanda's head snaps to her and so did everyone else. Then the others each galloped on. The verdict was in. An uproarious applause filled the room. Solanda sat there motionless, observing this buffoonery whilst she gulps down her water bottle.

Lorell embraced the affection from them all. However, their praise had only slightly tinctured her sense of self-importance. Despite this, she simply smiled and then turns her head behind the curtains, summoning out someone.

The curtains drew back revealing someone. A midget in a loincloth came teetering out, he stops right next to Lorell. He was an ashy-pale, bald white man with reddish, scrappy beard. Shirtless on stage only to have his thin waist wrapped tight in a white cloth and in high-heel sandals.

He keeps stretching his neck up at her as if to seek her permission to allow anything. Then he stares at the crowd, arms at his side, remaining still.

"Now everyone, here's my sweet little angel." She said as she presents out an odd belt. The belt was black leather with a combination lock in the front. "This belt symbolizes our unity to our mission, our purpose to restrain from the opposite sex. It's a godsend for you all and my little helper aid here will now demonstrate."

Unbeknownst to him, Lorell clicked it around his waist, almost having him topple off stage. He regains his balance quickly then used his teeny hands to fidget and unlock the belt. "It's easy to manage as seen on stage." Lorell claimed as he clicked it back around his waist. "And my assistant has something he'd like to add."

"Hello ladies." The man greeted, soft-spoken. *"I agree with Ms. Lorell wholeheartedly. My gender has got to hop off this pedestal and show more gratitude to you all for the many blessings and struggles that women must endure."*

Solanda detects the insincerity in this man's voice. Even with them aligned together, they didn't share the same value. His accommodating tone shows how even he can't convince himself. Just regurgitating the exact same mess this spokeswoman said. The sound of his voice is uncertain, but everyone listens to him advocating it. His submissive speech doesn't require any genuine care as long as he goes above and beyond telling them what they want to hear.

"Sometimes we men generalize when it comes to dating out of being rejected. The solution is for us men to step up. Men have got to quit trying to assert their dominance as an attempt to overcompensate in soc—"

"Yes, thank you." Lorell firmly said. "You all heard him testify, the opposite sex needs to take notes from him. Too much 'manliness' is causing a rift in our society. And before I forget, I have something for you all." The midget scurried behind the curtains then he came back hauling out a huge plastic bag. Lorell was handed a white, type of loose garment by him to present for everyone.

"What I have here in my hand will help to assist you ladies out on these streets." She said as she comes from behind the podium. Lorell throws on the garment like an overcoat; she then vanishes off stage.

The whole audience applauded; some women gasped with a baffled stare in their faces. Her whole being was now invisible. More of the curtain behind her was revealed through her see-through clothing. Her voice wasn't heard, no movements were either.

THEN LORELL'S HEAD ONLY APPEARS.

They all went into a frenzy. Her entire body isn't there still, just a levitating hardheaded woman.

"This attire I've got on is called the 'Ghost Cloak'." She said nonchalantly. "For whenever any man that you've grown tired of wants to keep pursuing, this will help for you to camouflage within the immediate vicinity, you'll just disappear. Or aimed at any male who wants to approach you too. And this is my gift for you to combat these me—in fact, I refuse to keep repeating it, empowering that word and neither should you."

"Ame—" Latoya hesitates. "Get 'em, girl!"

Her assistant tossed out each one of the cloaking sheets and black metallic chastity belts to the crowd. Each one leaped out their chairs trying to catch one. More were dispersed to the crowd. Latoya had caught herself an orange one, she gleefully tossed the hoodie over her head.

Solanda refused to budge an inch from her seat. She watched as Latoya made her head disappear then observed how crazy everyone else is. Seeing the midget on stage almost seeming validated by the crowd of females being ecstatic to have gained one. Observing them proudly wearing them and advocating all this. All were amazed by Lorell's magic act on stage; yet they still couldn't see-through this spokeswoman's performance.

This seminar was coming to an end. Now with Lorell's guidance, the help of the chastity belt and cloak sheets, the men of Holksdale won't see this coming.

† Chapter 14: Guess, a lot of bad dates, huh?

Yanie Juergens is on her way to the bar, she's steering around the corner listening to some music. Even with the radio blasting, it just gets outweighed by her thoughts over Essie. She contemplates whether to call her while scrolling through her contacts. On her way further down the street she catches flashing siren lights up ahead. There were officers behind yellow police investigation crime scene tape. It was bizarre, especially being in front of a church. An ambulance awaits outside the tape including other people gathered.

An officer instructs the crowd to keep further back. She slowly cruises by to detect the medics zipping up bodies. Then accelerates away to the bar.

At the bar, Yanie grabs a seat at the counter where Jovanny's waiting around. She asked him if he knew anything about the incident nearby.

"Yea, seven people got shot." Jovanny replied.

"Damn, seven and in front of a church too?" Yanie said. "You see who did it?"

"Nope. Plus, even if I did, I dunno shit! Cops been questioning folks around here too, no cap."

"It's the Satan Cliques." Chet Lopresti adds. "The S.C. gang has struck again."

Yanie stared at him eyebrows raised in confusion. This has Chet explain how this gang of guys who're predominately going to hell, they swarm around Holksdale doing drive-by shootings. They'll murder any random person on sight unexpectedly. They target everyone but anyone going to heaven are usually on their radar. The Satan Cliques would strike at churches, hospitals or volunteer sites such as soup kitchens or Salvation Army donation spots.

Chet tells them that there's a video posted with footage of the attack. He whips his phone out searching for the video. Jovanny pours Yanie and himself a drink. The video's starting, he makes it full-screen and they all huddle up. It starts with a wobbly footage staring down at the concrete, then the camera rises from behind a parked car to capture people gathered outside the church. The video appears to have been captured from afar. The sound of gunfire continues. A purple Bugatti vehicle does a sharp turn blocking other church-goers. The gunshots start blazing from the sound of a machine gun. *"HOLY FUCK!"* screamed an unknown source. The footage lowers back down to the ground in fear. The whole screen went dark; the driver and passengers are undetected in the video. There were people screaming in terror. The gunfire ceased, then the assailant announced: *"SATAN CLIQUE, BITCH!"* Then the sound of the car accelerates away.

Footage pans over on the aftermath of the attack. People are sprawled on the ground injured and some dead. Blood was seen everywhere, screams of agony were heard. Other survivors cautiously emerged from their hiding spaces. Then the video ended, leaving Yanie and Jovanny shook.

"Goddamn…" Yanie said flatly as she took a huge gulp of her drink.

"I've seen this shit twice already." Chet expressed nonchalantly. "The comments are something else too." He scrolls through some outlandish comments posted:

• *Wrong day to praise Jesus.*

• *And then the earth shook as Satan hast cast bullets from a new Bugatti. As bullets spilleth onto the earth, I say unto thee, thou shalt stop trippin' over cold blood.*

• *#HAVEMYMONEYCOMEHOLYSUNDAY.*

Chet snickers at these ongoing comments. Jovanny sees Yanie drinking more getting progressively quiet.

"Man, we've got some savages posting shit now." He said as he took a sip of his beer. Then he went away to play pool.

"Yo, pour me another!" Yanie demands.

"*Ok, cool out.*" Jovanny said, implying for her to relax.

"Sorry, just that shit got me thinking. Maybe Essie got a point. About being closed off, like she got an ankle monitor on now and shit."

Jovanny nods his head. "When's the last you seen her?"

Yanie says she hasn't contacted her for a week. She hasn't heard from Larissa either.

York Avenue 2:49 P.M.

Essie Chu has not left her apartment since she was brought back home. She's washing the dishes left in the sink from yesterday.

Essie's been keeping herself occupied while inside either with cooking, laundry, sleeping and excessively cleaning every square inch of this place. Whenever she tries to sleep peacefully, it barely lasts. There's times where she's experienced nightmares, mainly at night. However, it's rare for her to have them during her daily naps since she's asleep for an hour at best. Her nightmares consists of being in that rocky bus dangling for dear life, the noise of the man who crashed through the bus windshield or the screams for help. She'll suddenly wake up feeling pellets of sweat doused on her with a compressing sting in her chest.

The last of the dishes are stacked on the dish drainer by the window. As she hovers over the sink wondering what to attend to next, the brightness cuts in the corner of her eye. Through the shades by the window is a gleam creeping in, today is gradually getting brighter. Essie pulls the blinds up to brighten the kitchen. Outside is such a magnificent glow that beams directly in her eyes. A flash of foggy smoke filled her vision elevating into the sky with a quick loud impact shot in her ears. This prompted her whole being to scurry away from the window. She let out a huge shout, her eyes bulging and her head turning. There's severed lifeless bodies scattered within sight, the car alarm sound rises causing her to be alarmed. Her thigh collides into Larissa.

"ESSIE!" Larissa howls. *"ESSIE, IT'S ME! IT'S ME!"*

"WHAT!" Essie frantically said as she waves her head everywhere. Larissa seized both her arms, reassures to Essie

that they're just inside still. Essie snaps out of it, observing the refrigerator, dripping sink; but what had really made her conscious was young Larissa Sheppard herself consoling her face-to-face still. Heavy breathing is still heard but her guardian's muscles stop tensing up. "It's ok, it's ok." Larissa calmly repeats. Essie pulls away and closed the blinds. Larissa watches as she collapsed on the couch. Normally during this time, Larissa would sit outside enjoying the shade, but she wholeheartedly embraced the darkness inside as she accompanied her guardian upon the couch.

About an hour passed, Larissa made her a cup of warm shrimp noodles soup. Essie graciously accepted and felt more secure. They placed an order for Chinese delivery twenty-minutes ago. They both silently knew it was best for Essie to not cook for later. She blew it, then proceeds to eating some.

"Essie," Larissa hesitantly began. "What happened?"

While sipping into the soup, letting the taste of shrimp soup soak in her mouth, she pondered on how to explain this to her. Essie hardly knew how to identify it herself. "It's nothing too serious, okay? Just had a minor freak out, is all."

"Nah, that ain't seem like nothing." She claimed. "Was it something to do with what went on a few weeks ago?"

That feeling of anxiousness started brewing again. Essie stares down and sings The Star-Spangled Banner. She refuses to have Larissa worry about her when she's already focused on one parent. Essie goes for her yearbook sitting under the coffee table.

"So, you just gonna hide up in here still wrapped in a blanket, eating ramen and watching TV?"

Essie flips through her yearbook. "Hmmm, all those things as opposed to what's happening out there? I'll just count my blessings." Larissa scouts over to her. "All this got me thinking of all these people I went to school with. I hadn't seen this in years, all these alumni graduates."

"So, you finally believe this list is legit, huh?"

Essie shook her head. "*Please.* I never said that, but I'll play along for the sake of reminiscing in the past. You're about to be a sophomore next year, right?" Larissa nodded. "See you got the hardest year out the way and you didn't do too badly."

The yearbook cover said Saint Mary Diocesan High School in bold letters. Essie attended a private catholic school; where almost every student wasn't catholic. In fact, it was viewed by students as a regular school that would accept literally anyone who could afford it. Essie reveals that most kids did drugs, were underage drinking, got into fights and some girls had gotten themselves pregnant.

"Same at my school." Larissa said. "Sophomore girl I knew kept getting in fights in my gym class, got pregnant the first semester then wasn't there for the next."

"Well, these kids were worse." Essie adds, she points to a Hispanic girl on the page, Gabrielle Nunez. "She beat the holy hell out of an Indian girl on the second floor, witnessed it by my locker, and then threw her to the first floor."

Larissa's eyes widen, she looks at the girl again.

"Man, she ain't have to do her like that. What she do?"

"I heard she snitched on her over something I can't remember which resulted in her in handcuffs. And she was a senior at the time and couldn't walk down the aisle for graduation. As for the Indian girl, I believe she got a concussion, never saw her after that. So you know if she died, young Gabby here would burn for that."

She flips through more pages and introduces a senior, Christian Phillips. He got detention for spraying silly string all over the hallway stairs the last month as a senior prank. Then Larissa points to a picture of a miserable white boy with long black hair. In the news, it turns out he shot up his community college, he took a few lives before turning the gun on himself. Essie mentions how she'd remember seeing him isolated in the halls or in the guidance counselor's office. "So, you can imagine where he is now." Essie said.

"Yea, be glad he never pulled this at your school."

Essie studies the faces on page, remembering most of them without ever having read their names.

Larissa notices that she's almost in another visceral state this time, one of tranquility. She asks out of curiosity. "How was school for you?" Essie's head turned to her. There was a brief silence, unable to search for the right words to describe it. "That bad, huh?"

She shook her head. "No, no, just… unmemorable. Nothing bad or all that great, just not worth looking back on." She shuts her book and rests it on the coffee table.

"For real?" Larissa asks. "No homecoming at least?"

"Nope, no homecoming, no prom, hardly ever stayed for afterschool either. Didn't even date, just did what I had to do academically." Essie detects the minor pity on Larissa's face. "Enjoy high school while you're young. Don't spend time worrying over nonsensical things, ok?"

Larissa hesitantly nods, knowing who Essie was referring to. "Can we go more down memory lane, 'cause I wanna know how young you looked."

Essie had on a grin. "I'm still young-looking. Never have to worry about my youth." She flips her hair at Larissa. Then Larissa hands her the yearbook. "Let's see if you'll find me."

"Mm-hmm," Larissa skeptically said. "Yea, we'll see." Then she spots her. She even admits that the resemblance was still evident, she looked the same with the exception of glasses. Then the delivery guy called to bring their food.

Larissa raced downstairs to pay the man and came back shortly to dig in. I was the usual boneless spare ribs with pork-fried rice, a side order of fried wings and a large iced tea. Essie continued with her ramen knowing it was cooler by now.

"You're not going to wash your hands?" Essie asks.

"They're clean." Larissa said impatiently.

"After you just handled money? I suppose the fried wings will burn the germs then."

The two eat together while still flipping through the yearbook.

† *Hollywood: Los Angeles, California 3:38 P.M.*

At the Critchfield residence, it is a large, spacious house accommodating just one. The backyard is big with a tennis court, a pool, and a wooden gazebo with a fireplace. The front yard has a fountain with a statue at its core in the form of Grant Critchfield himself placed above the circulating water. The statue has him gazing at the sky, both hands placed on his hips with his back erect. His three flashy cars are parked up front for all to see.

Inside his home is decorated with beautiful paintings. His favorite one is a huge self-portrait of himself gazing into the sky with a serene look painted on. It hangs over his fireplace. There's also a wide glass window which stretches from the fireplace to the opposite end of the house, a whole view of the backyard and the sunshine glistens on the glass. His bedroom dresser is filled with awards he's won; two Golden Globe awards, four Emmy awards and one Oscar award. Grant proudly sits these accolades for guests to see, even knowing they've seen him accept them on TV. Or as a conversation starter for whenever he brought home a date.

Grant sits on his couch in the living room watching TV. He could be detected in that spot with his eyebrows arched down, his forehead wrinkled, and a scowl look on his face. He could be in deep thought in front of the screen, but that's how he's seen most of the time. Mostly he'll watch old movies while drinking the most expensive, exquisite types of liquor he can afford.

His agent, Joy Pluss, comes to the door. Grant had completely forgotten he was scheduled to meet with her today. She wanted to discuss more options about his career.

"Afternoon." She greets with a smile, they sit in the living room. Grant pours himself a drink. "I'm good, thanks for offering." She said sarcastically. He gets her a bottle of water to drink. "Well, firstly, I'm glad to know you've kept a low-profile for yourself."

"Yay." Grant flatly said, raising a drink for himself. "No matter, I'm not getting work anytime soon." He gulped down the remainder of his drink, then refilled his glass.

"By the way, I contacted two producers writing small independent films that were contemplating—"

"Forget it." he bluntly said. "I refuse to waste my talents doing some generic, indie project accompanied by a few talentless hacks and some mediocre script. Besides, they'll want to use my notoriety to gain publicity for their flick."

Joy releases an exasperated exhale. "You know most indie films are getting better, right?" she studies his stern face then decides to move on. "Ok, I tell them you can't."

"And don't tell them my schedule's filled with better projects. Lord knows they won't believe that."

"Also, I contacted another producer who refused to cast you due to a past dispute with one of the stars of his upcoming film, Craig Willis? He's the nicest, why?"

Grant took a brief second to realize exactly why. "That's right…" He tells her about having lunch with the screenwriter of an action film that Craig Willis was let go of two years ago because of him. The movie was a sequel to the film about a martial arts expert accompanied by his monkey sidekick. "Anyway, his pet primate died before the film was fully-written. I mentioned how miscasting Craig, a gargantuan black man, as the star's sidekick was the equivalent of making his ass a monkey and that it would piss audiences everywhere off, so he should cast a star like me in his place instead. The screenwriter considered it before having finalized any contract with Craig. Craig found out, tried to confront me and got kicked off set."

Joy was silent in disbelief and buried her face in her hands. "I can't believe this."

"I can't believe I didn't get nominated for that performance. Anyway, you want a stronger drink?"

"*Please.*" She groaned. Grant pours her one and they both relax on his couch. The TV news goes on about the plane crash aftermath from Holksdale. "Isn't that just awful. I know you're from Holksdale originally, right?"

Grant sips his drink. "Not proud of it but yeah. And I suppose it's bad but I'm here. And my mother lives there still but nowhere in the proximity of that wreckage, so…"

Joy sits there thinking. "Let me ask you… have you ever given back to your community before? I mean, after your career took off?" Grant nonchalantly shook his head. "It would've probably done people some good there." He shrugged it off. "Grant, I may have an alternative solution that would bring about good publicity for you."

He faces her, wide-eyed, turning the volume down.

MIDTOWN HOLKSDALE: 5:44 P.M.

Around this time, Icarus is spying across the street for an opportunity to soon strike. Cars keep pulling up to pump for gas, mainly men are getting out of their cars. Icarus has his glasses on whilst listening to pick-up videos online on improving his chances. Then a car pulls to the side of the deli store revealing a young white woman wearing shades going in the store. She parked besides the air pumper, then goes inside to possibly make change for the machine to pump her tires.

Icarus sprung up then raced to the door. He crossed the street, the girl had come out, headed to her car. The sound of the machine could be heard running from afar, the woman was detected fastening the pump into one tire only. Unbeknownst to her as she waited for it to fill, Icarus popped up. "Excuse me," She shrieked and flinched simultaneously, her neck snaps towards him, eyes widened. Her confused expression however didn't faze Icarus whatsoever. "Hi, just saw you passing by, I thought you looked nice today." He sweetly expressed.

The woman had a brief silence, registering this whole introduction still, then replied: "*Ah, ok, thanks.*" Then the machine stops. She hesitantly bends down to unfasten the pump, sensing him hovered over her still.

"So, what's your name by the way? Mine's Icarus."

"Why do you need to know my name?" she asked with

caution, not locking eyes with him, struggling to unfasten it still.

"Because I wanted to know who I'm talking to." He said.

Finally after getting it off her now filled tire, she raised up. Without looking at him with a straight face, she walks to the driver's seat and bluntly answered: "Mia." She quickly checked behind her.

Icarus just laughs it off. He couldn't tell if it was from her wondering if he'd sneak up or her concern when reversing. Then he goes in the store to buy a coffee.

"Hey, come here, chief!" the cashier calls out to him. His name was Happy, all customers knew of him. Happy was an upbeat, middle-eastern man who was balding. He was always joking and verbally bantering to mess with known customers. Icarus sometimes wondered what his exact ethnicity was but never cared enough to ever ask. "You got girlfriend yet?" he announced with a huge smile.

"Nope…" Icarus nonchalantly said. He walks to the counter, indulging him a bit. "Why, why you've got someone for me, Happy?"

Happy nods. "I tell you, always tell you, there's a girl up the street always come in here checking for you. Asks about you all the time while you're at home patrolling."

"Uh-huh, uh-huh. What's she look like?"

"You know, same girl you hit on before. Always asking for you? Can't keep dodging her calls, man."

Icarus grins hard, shaking his head. "I wish," he laughed. "I wish." Then fixed himself a small cup of coffee.

Once he comes to pay at the counter, Happy gestures for him to take it. They were cool like that for years now. Happy and his co-workers had always witnessed him approach certain women here. He never scared off any female customers and had regularly bought something.

Icarus came outside and saw another woman by her parked car. It was a black woman leaning on her door with her head down at her phone. The first thing he noticed was her busty breasts cupped by her forearms while holding her phone, her cleavage compressed under her neck. He could see her smile, completely oblivious of her surroundings. Icarus walks on over. "Excuse me," he politely said. She raised her head. The closer he got, the first thing he noticed was her distinct belt. A black leather with a combination lock in the front. "I like your belt, I've never seen one like that before."

"PLEASE GET AWAY FROM ME!" she roared, loud enough for anyone near to overhear. Icarus fled away to the opposite direction. Her eyes bulged out, pursed lips and pencil drawn eyebrows almost brought close together knocked him back.

Icarus commenced to the other direction still, his mind was processing exactly what just transpired. He then checks over his shoulder to see her back on her phone smiling as if nothing came about. That fistful uproar out her mouth still rattles his brain. He then crossed back to his house while trying to sip coffee. His hands now shaky but tries playing it off, then locked away back in the confines of his sanctuary.

York Avenue 12:49 A.M.

As usual, Essie can't get a good night's sleep, she had one of her nightmares. She's alone on the couch silently on her phone scrolling online, then she sets it down to collect her thoughts. Alcohol is flowing, she's also been drinking for an hour since, hoping to not wake up Larissa upstairs. She thinks about them both talking about high school. Her eyes shut as she cradled back and forth on the cushion. One thought that keeps popping up was the brightness from the accident, it kept flickering in her head. It was too unique to dismiss. Her neck snaps back to just gaze up at the ceiling fan. Her thoughts wrestle with each other nonstop.

"Essie?" Larissa calls from across the room. Essie stretched her neck to see hesitant Larissa still standing there, she smiles at her to try to seem okay. "You good?" she sees the liquor bottle on the coffee table. Essie gestures for her to sit with her. Larissa came over. "Mind if I—"

"Not a chance." Essie laughed as she swipes the liquor bottle away. She refrains from drinking more in front of her.

Larissa remembered how crazy she has been recently. Her guardian knows that she's never awake this late at night especially once she's asleep. Even in her drunken stupor, Essie knows this. Larissa probably figured Essie thought she'd be fast asleep so she couldn't be caught seen like this. At least she had a good enough excuse that wouldn't upset her.

"I heard you somewhere downstairs, just wanted to make sure everything's all good?"

Essie nodded at her, patted her leg. *"I'm fine, little one."* She grabs her yearbook and tries to change the subject. *"I was thinking of our little talk before. About—when I was about your age… could hardly remember—think of anything fun when sober… still can't."* she clears her throat. *"All I could recall were the things I refused to do. Never approached my crush, nor joined any clubs…"* Essie's eyes shut then began to rock. She chuckled. *"Just did work, work, frickin' work! There were even friends who sought out friendship but instead—just sat around watching students have their fun. Hell, I spent college on academics and then med school right then."*

Larissa tries to avoid the awkward silence. She doesn't want to take it seriously since she's drunk but senses some honesty here. "You made something out yourself." she encouraged. "Helping patients, saving lives." Essie's eyes looked dreary yet she felt proud by that which showed in her smile.

"I do, I do don't I?!" she said. *"I love treating people, being of aid whenever. Like, look at Yanie and Jovanny. I love these two but they'd never take a sec to be of help to anyone."* Essie's grin widened. *"I see my worth but it can overwhelm you at times. Because the funny thing is, it wasn't ever my decision to get into medicine. My dad urged for this."*

"Really?" Larissa asked.

"Yes. You even sound like my first roommate." She said as she showed her in the yearbook, a white girl named Jane Pears. *"She'd always go 'Why not tell your dad you don't want to be a doctor?' Like, woooow, you are so white. He paid for it all,*

so I can't just branch out like that."

Making herself more comfortable, knowing she'll be here for a while, Larissa listens to Essie discuss more about her college experience. She remembered the start of her freshman year when the sun was so bright out. Students hauling large boxes into their dorms, waving to each other and at her. But on campus at night was livelier. Many students attending were commuters. The residential ones could be heard in groups flocking at night laughing, hollering, and drunk. Or just playing late-night games out in the courtyard. Essie could overhear from her dorm every time and was always entertained. Sometimes she'd recognize students from her class out there and would contemplate joining up with them but refused.

Essie would spend most of her time in her building. Either doing schoolwork, sleeping, watching TV in the lounge or spending time with her roommate. Jane would always invite her out with her to join her friends around campus or encourage her to procrastinate on certain assignments just to keep her company. She wasn't a horrible roommate but she was a good reminder for her. Essie knew Jane wasn't a great student. Jane had withdrawn from some classes, hardly showed up to all her classes and relied on Essie's homework and notes. It made Essie feel good to know she could be of help and wasn't ever caught in Jane's position.

During her first semester, Essie got invited to accompany Jane and her friends to a Homecoming party by the school.

She didn't deny because she honestly lacked a legitimate reason not to. Also, Jane's birthday was that same week and thought it would be courteous to.

The campus parties were usually wild at night, taken place in one building. Music was blazing, the room was wide and had flashy lights and there was a professional DJ stereo. Essie had seen people drinking and grinding on each other. She was enjoying the atmosphere, especially feeling safe around Jane's girlfriends. They were all huddled in a group dancing together.

After a few hours, the students had brought the party out onto the courtyard. Music was playing off some students' stereos, people smoking weed and drinking as well. Essie had seen some guys approaching them. Each one danced with Jane and her friends but Essie had abstained. She hadn't felt uncomfortable but just instinctively held back. There was a skinny guy who tried to persuade her, Jane even insisted she should but Essie politely declined. She also rejected any alcohol offered by Jane's friends. Trying to loosen up a bit, she explored around watching everyone acting out. Most guys were being too buffoonish or girls were seen intoxicated or thriving off other guys gazing up at them.

While cruising, Essie had met a guy who introduced himself. The two had been making eye contact on and off prior to that, she even felt like dancing on him. However, she hadn't due to Jane explaining that men are to pursue first. He was sweet and had a friendly demeanor. These two talked for a while that night, getting to know each other. Her guard was taken down, she hadn't been this engaged with talking to someone her age like this before. He soon invited her to keep him company in his dorm. Essie was seriously enticed by this boy. His smile and being so well-spoken too. Yet, she choose to get back to her friends. Before she left, they exchanged numbers.

Later that night, a few fights broke out. There were people who didn't even go to this school who showed up causing problems and some guys couldn't take a hint from some girls who didn't want to be bothered. Essie couldn't locate Jane or her group anywhere in the madness of students scrambling. Instead, she rushed back to her room. Campus security had come causing everyone to leave. It wasn't until the next day that students had faced disciplinary action for the night before. Many guys were expelled for sexual assault or brawling. Some females were in trouble for being caught smuggling in alcohol. Essie had found out one of Jane's friends went to the hospital for alcohol poisoning after she had strayed away with a few other guys. Essie had felt an uplifting satisfaction knowing her record was clean as opposed to them.

Larissa had slouched with her on the couch, Essie still withheld that liquor bottle. She's hunched over with her face buried in her hands. Then ran her fingers through her hair. All that was seen on her face were regrets.

"What ever happened with that boy?" Larissa asks.

Essie groaned. *"He wanted to take me out on a date. I really wanted to too, even Jane was amazed someone had interest."* She hesitated for a moment, her throat clenched. *"I-I just never took any initiative back then. S-So that was that."* Essie confessed then tossed the yearbook back under the coffee table. *"College was a time for me to branch out—delve into new experiences. I've been cooped in here for weeks, not just here..."* she taps her forehead. *"But up here. The biggest impacts I've had in life were pushed by helping people. I love helping patients but that path was chosen for me. Or compelled to give your mother money while she's inside. The only recent choice I've made all on my own—that I stick by—that's been best for me... is keeping here. Searching and searching and still can't find what I want that truly drives my soul. Now I just sit at home still in question with all the time in the world and still nothing comes to mind. I just don't want to look back at my life and get crushed by how seemingly routine my life was. No unpredictability, nothing."*

Just from sitting still, she could detect Larissa's self-conscious face even without looking at her based on how silent she became. Essie knew Larissa already felt inadequate when it came to her own mother and refused to let Larissa have this notion that she was a burden on her too.

"See, I feel, I'm only destined t-to contribute to another's fate a lot at times. But it wasn't all bad, because I got you out of it."

All traces of inferiority dissolves off Larissa's face. She faces her guardian now relaxed from all that. "You say that life for you feels nothing but a routine, maybe average. But that's what I love most about you. Not just that you take after me as your own but I love that you are predictable."

Essie's eyebrows raised in confusion. She listens still.

"I already been through what it's like to have a mama who never makes it clear if she'll be home every night. Or will low-key show me love when you least expecting. Already had a sister I'd depend on that did a complete 180, *then to just up and leave me.*" Her voice croaked. "With you, there ain't none of that, no second thoughts not one bit. I don't worry if you'll keep your promises or appreciate me for me… *or if you'll be here.*" they both snicker. "Never have to fret when it comes to you coming through. You always a reliable source."

Her sincere words were loving. However, Essie knew Larissa wasn't mature enough to truly understand the harsh reality of looking back at living life not living. Without skipping a beat, Essie graciously nods her head, reassuring her that it meant a lot.

A large yawn escapes from Essie's mouth, she began to doze off. She placed the bottle on the floor then slouched the rest of her body on the couch, Larissa leaped up. She drew the small covers over Essie, tucked her bare feet in and adjusts the pillow under her neck.

"Oh yeah, how's that boy of yours? Your gentleman friend?"

Larissa smirks. "Chase is good, we all good. Thanks for asking."

"T-That's good." Essie yawns. *"Goodnight."* She turns around on the couch and proceeds to fall asleep. Quietly, Larissa retreats to her room.

Richez Shrive 1:45 P.M.

Jovanny Gibbs is serving drinks as usual, pretty small crowd today. He thinks about Essie trying to cope with her current circumstance and how Larissa is handling this. Yanie has given him some updates but part of him feels guilty for not calling or texting her still.

Icarus McGrew comes in and pulled up a seat at the counter and orders a strawberry daiquiri. To Jovanny's surprise, it wasn't to slip to another female in here, Icarus just wanted this all for himself. He sees Icarus just sitting there silent, Jovanny normally never wants to lock eyes with this guy but he senses he's in deep thought.

Without Yanie, Donny, Montrez or the usual circle in here, Jovanny settles towards Icarus. "What up, killer." he greets politely.

Icarus breaks from his train of thought. "I'm fine. Nothing new really. Not buying anyone drinks today."

"Yea, trying to pick up girls. Ok, I see you. But to be straight with you, getting 'em drinks ain't the way to go."

"Maybe," Icarus replied uncertain. "But I've got other tactics though, got separate tricks up my sleeve." He gestures at the door. "Not just here but out and about out there." He goes on about approaching women at the mall or at stores. Jovanny's engaged even with the notion that Icarus probably isn't sleeping with any single one of them.

"So you cuff anyone yet?"

"Nope." Icarus said quickly. "But who knows, could be

lucky today or someday this week. Maybe if I shoot a text that hopefully one'll reply back."

Jovanny nods. "Yea, the struggle of seeking answers."

"Uh-huh, gotten a lot of those lately."

"Well, you better than most dudes too afraid to speak to bitches out here."

Icarus gets quiet for a moment, takes a gulp of his drink. "I mean, I can't blame some. I even ran into some rude one this week." He confides to Jovanny about getting screamed at by a woman and walking off fast.

Chet walked over with his drink. "Man, that fuckin' sucks, *goddamn!*" he said as Jovanny serves him another. "Hell, I don't have to worry about that myself. Usually, I get women flocking at me. Don't even gotta pursue, unless I get the average choosing signals."

"This dude don't know the struggle." Jovanny said to Icarus then turns to Chet. "Bro, you a top-tier male. Technically, you ain't gotta do shit. Regular guys like Icarus ain't built like that."

"I'd say I'm pretty average in the looks department to say the least." Icarus humbly adds. "Plus, I'm a nice guy."

"See, these hoes today, no matter how much they say they want that guy, they want an alpha male. Even if they got a mans already, women always wanna level up to a man with status, looks and money."

Chet raises his glass in agreement. "Yup. Why do you think I don't commit to not a single one of them?! Just 'cause I can. I'll just switch them like they'd switch me. You think they'd outgrow that shit in high school." He looks at

Jovanny, getting confirmation that that's true. "I don't even have to take them out. Just come to my house, put on a movie and smash soon after. And the big motherfucker… these girls usually come by after a date."

"Guess, a lot of bad dates, huh?" Icarus asks.

"No, just be using these guys for free meals or movies then brag to me about it. Sometimes while I throw their backs out, I pity those poor nice guys a little bit." Chet shrugs it off. "*Oh well*, better them than me though. Not like these women know what a good man is anymore."

Icarus can't even imagine what it's like going out on a date. He's glad he doesn't after hearing all of this. This is the liveliest interaction he's had with really anybody in the longest time. Better than his ones with other females.

"Like, they really don't." Jovanny agreed. "They crave an alpha male but don't all at once." He acknowledges the confused look Icarus has. "Like, these black chicks be having these bastard kids with these no-good-ass dudes out here 'cause they easy to control, easily submissive over pussy. Thinking that's what a real man is but then can't handle an actual alpha male who don't play they games. But at the same time, lust over him since he got bread like that."

"Because those men have themselves some self-respect."

"It radiates off 'em, that's why these tricks know better than to fuck with me." Jovanny proudly said.

Chet laughs. Leaving Icarus confused.

"Man, you don't got no money or power. What's your excuse?"

"It be because I ain't out chasing for no bitches or tolerate the fuckery they come with like some bitch."

Chet looks over at Icarus. "Unlike our man, Icarus here." he mocks. "I see you buying women here drinks just to get curved afterwards. And not just you, I see other dudes do the same. I spot these ladies just laughing on their way to the restroom. They just get off on chumps like them."

Icarus chuckles a little, not feeling embarrassed but surprised that anyone besides the bartender could detect him doing that. He gulps more of his beer.

"Facts." Jovanny said. "The amount of drinks I've served to each bitch that be getting off on y'all expense almost has me wanna cut y'all off. Just see them repeat this shit over and over, having me caught in the middle of it."

Icarus nodded. "I'd honestly prefer girls like that instead of that woman I came across who wasn't so pleasant herself." He elaborates more about the women at the gas station who screamed her head off at him. Then told them that all he'd done was compliment her on her belt. Jovanny asks him to describe the belt. "The belt was of black leather with a combination lock in the front of it."

Jovanny knew exactly what he was talking about. Chet on the other hand didn't.

"My girl told me about that. It was from some feminist meeting to unite women all over Holksdale to keep from fucking. To regain their purity against us men."

"Are you serious?" Chet asks, then smiled. "Well, that hasn't kept girls from dropping hints at me still."

"It's all because they claim men fucked up their lives since most been pumped and dumped before marriage or had a kid outta wedlock. So, since they're going to hell, now they wanna take it out on men."

Icarus seemed confused. "But I thought Holksdale was divided by hate. Why would they come together like this?"

"Women are always drawn to the next best thing 'cause they not leaders." Jovanny said. "They all flock like sheep even if that means getting played by some feminist or being more difficult for men. Flaking, using guys for free stuff, playing games, not giving up the sex. Like, there's this ongoing chain of closed legs interlocked between these bitches out here, man. They all be on the same bullshit."

Jovanny also mentions that the women were told to only acknowledge alpha men, embrace their bodies just as they are, that men kept oppressing them and they were given an invisible cloak by a midget. He sounded slightly proud when he tells how annoyed his girlfriend was and refused any of their stuff.

"So, can't we as men counteract this somehow?" Icarus asks sounding hopeful.

Jovanny smirks. "*How?!* What, these simp-ass dudes gonna cop a chastity belt like they're rompers now?! Nah bih, miss me with that bullshit." He said then poured himself a drink. "Men are too damn thirsty that they crave females' bath water, that's crazy. Acting like its pure baptismal coochie juice, like this bitch ain't never been ran through her whole life."

"I can attest to that. He's right, Icarus." Chet said. "It's very risky behavior for some guys to pursue these ladies today. Hell, most don't even act like ladies anyway."

"Facts. Got these butch lookin' girls out here walking all swole and shit, all 'em built like lumberjacks. Back then women were all effeminate and sweet. Now they all mad masculine to where some even identify as men."

"Yea, man." Chet laughs. "Especially when they're on their period too, just exude masculinity. They're like overly aggressive linebackers without the pads."

Icarus just absorbs everything being said. He never knew it was this bad out here and almost feels isolated that everyone else seems familiar to this but him. All those approaches he's initiated in the past cross his mind; all accumulated towards nothing. However, this doesn't deter him from wanting to be intimate with a woman. Times have changed this bad; he realizes he'll have to adapt as well.

"So, what do you guys suggest for your everyday, garden-variety type guy on how to meet a woman then?"

The two could sense that Icarus means help for himself but is probably too self-conscious about it, so they play along. Jovanny even pours him another strawberry daiquiri.

"Well, my girl be pulling bitches up off these dating apps. Like, I don't fuck with those myself, but it's worked." Jovanny said.

"Nah man." Chet protests. "Women mainly use those for attention from guys. They won't ever want to go meet you in person or even respond back unless your pictures turn her on, that's it. Just nothing but an ego-boost. Plus, there's all types of freaks on those things."

"That can't be all..." Icarus said with uncertainty.

"It's all, trust me. She's got unlimited options on top of messages too."

Chet brought up a new dating app called Souls Rejoice that's now popular. Its shows that all members signed up who are destined for either heaven or hell. People are also given the choice to abstain from disclosing their fate. Depending on where you go, if you scroll down for hell, you can meet plenty of doomed, damaged souls to date or hook-up with. Or if you scroll up for heaven, you could possibly meet Christians, sweet loyal members, or a future husband or wife. A match made in heaven. And it's free.

"Also, the dating game is rigged." Jovanny adds. "It's all in a woman's favor. Girls ghost dudes after being treated out on dates. So, it's in your favor, in your best interest, to not pay for no dates. Better to just invite her to the park, chill at the mall or better yet—over at your crib."

"Don't you think that's a bit of an overgeneralization?"

"See Icarus, women know men want the pussy." Jovanny states. "They don't have much else to offer. They not that fun to talk to, can't cook or clean for shit and don't offer you much else but sex. Females can't give shit but feel like they deserve the world and might give up the sex to the best bidder. She could be willing to go out on a date with you till she meets a guy who'll take her somewhere more expensive, then it's a wrap. The only real viable asset a bitch has nowadays is between her legs."

There were no dating apps on Icarus' phone and was proud to admit it. He couldn't begin to figure out how to invite a woman back to his house without coming off as creepy. In his phone were a few texts he sent females that refused to respond.

Jovanny suggests a few options on approaching them. He talked about making conversation on their surroundings or ask questions. "One thing that worked for me is to ask a girl what ethnicity she is. You best believe that shit works every time. All they go on about is themselves."

"Or to just not bother them." Chet adds.

"That's a fact. Ignoring 'em does help."

"I mean actually focusing on yourself. Not as a tactic to lure them because girls are always here. If you do your own thing, you'll be at a point where attaining a girlfriend won't even matter. Trust me when I tell you way too many guys are out here craving women and wasting their lives."

There was real sincerity that Icarus could spot in Chet's voice. Jovanny didn't dismiss what he said despite his tips. Icarus honestly didn't want to ruin the moment by seeking more answers, so he graciously appreciated it. It even had Icarus reflect about how he casually spends most days pursing women but not making progress in his book or really contribute towards other goals. All three guys talked about other stuff with Icarus genuinely enjoying their company with nothing to gain.

† Chapter 15: *Hellooo.*

After a long discussion, Joy Pluss was able to convince Grant Critchfield to come back to his hometown, Holksdale. Joy's plan to help make her client appear good in the eyes of the public was for him to give back to the community.

A press conference was set up for Grant to announce his charitable donation to the destroyed bridge from the plane crash. During this planning, Joy had researched any other current issues within the city. She urged him to discuss the issues he had with Muslims now being targeted by citizens. Also, to not disclose anything involving this allegation. But to say that he keeps the alleged victim in his prayers.

During the actual press conference, there were many reporters. Many fans showed support while there were many outraged protestors. Grant had approached the podium with the intent to do so. Once on stage, there were a mixture of responses. His fans were cheering with banners wishing him well. The protestors (*who showed support for the alleged victim were both envious of his fame*) had booed him once he makes his image known. These people were yelling unholy names: *RAPIST! LIAR! IMMORAL! EVIL!*

Despite his detached expression, there was this sizzling anger that latched onto him. The words slowly ignited this fiery, settling rush. He tried to get the written speech to rise out his throat but couldn't bypass this. Joy could tell this would not go well. His head held high, shoulders back, posture aligned. Grant refused to speak and walked off.

Grant left the press conference altogether. After a minute of uproar, Joy substituted with the speech that her client was supposed to give.

Now they are both discussing his schedule at Joy's hotel room. Joy, exasperated after scolding him over the press conference, reminds him that he must be civil while he is here. That she is doing everything to orchestrate ways for him to appear good for the public. Grant silently listens, smoking his cigarette, trying not to be combative. Joy set up an upcoming visit with a fan in the hospital. She reminds Grant that she still has faith in him.

Grant agreed, then left for the parking lot. He notices a women dressed in nursing scrubs next to a man in a wheelchair. The man's eyes fixed on Grant. This made Grant think that he's just being recognized.

"Excuse me!" the man called.

"Yes, I'm Grant Critchfield. No time for autographs."

"I don't want one. You stole my spot." The man clarifies, pointing at the parking space Grant's vehicle's in.

This left Grant perplexed. His car was parked in a regular parking spot. Grant told him it was not handicapped parking. It didn't matter to him. His nurse was going for it while she was driving. Then apparently Grant took it without noticing them.

The man's reasoning had slightly irked Grant. However, remembering what Joy said, he politely suggested that they take the open handicapped spots nearby. The nurse looks timid. She remained silent but looked as if she didn't really wish to confront Grant over something so minor. The man wouldn't be flexible. Despite internal anger slowly brewing, Grant kept advising they go to the other spot. She finally interjects, suggesting they leave for the handicapped spot.

"Bernard," The nurse softly began. "It's not a huge deal."

"No. These celebrities are all the same."

"Excuse you?" Grant said, trying to maintain his tone, in attempts to keep his wrath from gushing out.

Bernard ranted about famous people always feeling entitled to things. That they see themselves as superior compared to regular people. Rage swelled inside Grant the more he listens to Bernard. Grant's exhales shakily grew more. Bernard continues about celebrities getting exposed on how horrible they are. Then still instigates with Grant by repeating that this was his spot.

"YOU'RE NO FUCKING BETTER!" Grant snapped. Claiming that Bernard feels entitled to misbehave due to him being disabled. *"YOU THINK BEING HANDICAPPED GIVES YOU A LEG UP IN TALKING SHIT!"*

A flabbergasted look swept across Bernard's face. He wasn't used to anyone talking to him like this. His throat felt teary at this grisly roar.

"We we're aiming for that spot." Bernard choked out.

"Jesus! I must coddle you now?! You're not even special needs, Bernard."

"I never said I was."

"And yet you desire special treatment still."

The yelling amplified between them in the parking lot. It

had Grant bellowing about Bernard subconsciously knowing that there won't be any harsh repercussions. That nobody wants to be exposed for getting in a physical altercation with a disabled person. Bernard justifies his attitude by accusing Grant of intentionally swiping his spot. Grant hollered over Bernard being entitled not only to handicapped parking but regular parking as well. This infuriated Bernard. The nurse politely tried explaining that Bernard just felt cheated out of his space. That annoying reminder had Grant yell for him to go to the empty eligible parking. Bernard stood his ground.

"You're a terrible person." Bernard yells. "No wonder you're going to hell."

"You see this?" Grant taunts, while mockingly stretching out both his legs. "You see that? I'm still more of an upstanding citizen than you, man."

"I guarantee that allegation with you is true!" Bernard yelled as he rolls himself backwards. Gripping eye contact with Grant, while furiously gripping onto his wheels. His rage increased knowing Grant wouldn't move his car. Still yelling about Grant being a rapist. "Burn in hell!"

"That's right, Bernard. Put it in reverse!" Grant gloats, tauntingly waving at him. *"Buh-bye."*

After that argument, Bernard got to his car, with the nurse behind the wheel. Grant returned to his car. He refused to leave because he knew Bernard was waiting to take that spot. Bernard's car honks at him. This prompts Grant to flip him off. They waited for an hour until Bernard left.

†

Since Lorell St. Louis came spreading her events in Holksdale garnering females' attention throughout, there has been a shift in dating and interactions between genders. Women have become more embolden to request more and to feel more entitled to the values provided by men. A lot of them wish to redeem themselves after their fate was sealed to damnation for premarital sex. Instead of holding themselves somewhat accountable for their past sins, the vast majority have been brainwashed into blaming men entirely.

Many have their own agenda after having been approached by men. They've followed Lorell's advice of extracting men's resources for their own personal gain. While out on dates, some have confided that their ex-boyfriend or the father of their child had mistreated them, causing for them to be weary of moving too fast. This also manipulates these guys to guilt them into treating them out more or to prove that he's different in her eyes. After these women get bored of that particular guy, they'll just cut off all ties. Ignoring his calls or texts then onto the next guy.

Others who've been approached will never go out with them but willfully absorbs their attention or will be overtly disrespectful to any unattractive ones. Lorell has also ingrained in their heads that men are potential superficial predators and there is no incentive to being polite to a stranger. Men have detected this ongoing shift in dating but this realization hasn't altered anything. Multiple guys have become so sex-deprived that they're willing to endure females' games while also trying to fulfill a woman's unrealistic expectations in fear of losing them. This has happened mostly in downtown and midtown Holksdale.

Within the midtown community, Lorell St. Louis had petitioned for their media access to promote more female empowering messages. The petition itself gained so much social traction that led midtown to comply. There were commercials broadcasted that christened females as beloved with many positive traits and messages. They even simultaneously promoted this narrative to demonize masculinity. This manipulation tactic has labeled natural masculine traits and behaviors as toxic and aggressive. This programming has females becoming more self-entitled and encouraged to behave however they please; while men have become cautious and passive to this new social dynamic.

The worst case of this has been a recent incident downtown. Justin Feed, thirty-eight-year-old, had been dating Courtney Noel, twenty-three-year-old. They weren't too serious at the time. Nonetheless, Justin has taken her out to three restaurants in Holksdale. Two in midtown and an expensive place uptown, he paid for her and everything. After the third date, Justin reached out to her again through text, requesting to treat her out somewhere else. He hadn't gotten any reply for over a week. Justin even tried again through social media that she had him on. Not only did he get no response but had quickly been blocked off her page.

Courtney had cut off all contact with him. He was entirely confused, they never had a fight, had great chemistry and he wasn't constantly texting her. No explanation, no apology, nothing. Unfortunately, Courtney had been engineered by the recent fluff that the media and Lorell had been promoting. She had even been approached by another man who'd offered to treat her out to better places instead.

One day while at the terminal, Justin just so happens to see Courtney sitting alone on her phone. She didn't see him coming until he called out to her. The moment they locked eyes, she froze as if she'd been possessed, then delved her head to her phone. Justin had confronted her as understanding as possible. She bluntly ignored him, never rose her head from her phone. He persisted for an excuse or apology or for at least some acknowledgement.

Frustrated Courtney yelled for him to leave her alone. Other people had witnessed this, she repeatedly screamed for him to leave. This gained the attention of more people, Justin could feel all eyes watching him, and he then veered off. Justin rushed to the bathroom where he could be in quick solitude, he locked himself in a stall and sat there enraged. All that investment of his time, money and himself into her accumulated to that. Justin searched in his bag and left the bathroom. His presence had people observing him again which only irritated him more. Courtney had remained in the exact spot; Justin walked her path. She could detect him and stared at him walking, in preparation to tell him off. Justin sprayed a bottle of acid into her face.

Downtown Holksdale 1:46 P.M.

Larissa had been out on her daily walk enjoying the warm weather out today. She got another watermelon from the same guy always selling, then sat at the empty bus bench. While scrolling through her phone, she saw a video link about the whole Justin situation.

The video was captured and posted online by a witness at the terminal. Its shaky footage of Courtney staring him down as he casually sprays liquid in her face. Her whole body plummets to the ground, through audio are her cries of agony as she covers her face. Larissa's fully immersed in the video. Adults rushed to her aid, some blocking the footage then the video ends. She quickly scrolls down to the article attachment detailing everything.

In the article, Justin had been shortly detained after civilian men held him down until police arrived. Courtney had survived the attack. Her injuries were severe: horrible burns to both her face and hands, including loss of sight in her right eye. When reports came out to why he did this, Justin responded: *"I don't know what possessed me to target her like this. I am so sorry."* There were reports from witnesses claiming he had harassed Courtney prior to the attack.

Larissa shook her head in disgust, this makes her almost glad about the recent advancements uplifting women that she's seen. As she sits there, Elijah Atwood comes by. He has a large smile on his face and gives a wide wave, too open to ignore. Larissa gladly welcomes him but still looked troubled, Elijah asks what bothering her. She unloads the whole story on him. It troubled her that the assailant's excuse was so generic to where she didn't believe his apology. It baffled her that he would overreact because Courtney simply lost interest. There's this awkward silence, she could sense Elijah had some input to say as his face showed him contemplating something. Being so sure of herself, Larissa's curious as to what it is.

"Like, from what you said..." Elijah hesitantly began. "It's kind of karma, I guess." Larissa stared at him perplexed, he quickly elaborates more. "It's an overreaction for sure but enough women are pulling stuff like this now. It ain't right."

"No." Larissa sternly said. "She had every right to dub him if she lost interest, especially since he's the type of guy that switched-up like that. And what'chu mean women be pulling stuff like this now?"

Elijah gives her his take on how women are taking advantage of guys for free stuff and their being influenced by the recent propaganda. Even though this annoyed her, Larissa patiently let him finish. This slightly offended her as he classified women as a whole engaging in this.

"Y'know that what you're saying is a generalization, right? Sure, there's some women like that but that ain't all." She calmly responds. Then recalls the situation of how it's not clear if this was Courtney's intent. Larissa implied that she maybe got uncomfortable being with him and uses the assault to further her point. "And as far as this 'propaganda' you said, it's only to elevate us. It ain't even that deep!"

Elijah urged more, he even adds how women are feeling superior to men. "Maybe not all but kinda a lot. Like, I know it sounds sexist a bit and I'm willing to hear you out but a lot of it is kinda true what I'm saying."

"Well look at everything women been through, how they been treated by men. It's not that women think they better than y'all. Just that everyone's now woke and seeing that we just rising up to a man's level. I think the thing is you see men being dropped down but that ain't it. Since it's something pushed that affects your current position."

There were more reasons he brought up. The benefits of being a female to where they have people automatically pandering on a women's side. Timid Elijah believes everything he's saying but doesn't deliver it with full conviction. Instead, the more he looks at Larissa's pretty face, the more he sounds uncertain as he explains all this, almost as if he's asking. This led to him explaining how females now have a bad attitude when dealing with men.

"Only reason people support it is 'cause they see the good in it, not just since it's a trend." She protests. "Plus, how would you know they got an attitude from this?! It could've been from whatever these guys be sayin'."

"Maybe." He admits. "But sometimes females, they'll reject a guy, right? But then years later, they'll want them after they had plenty of hook-ups or things didn't work out with their ex or the father of their child. And get all bent out of shape if she gets rejected." Larissa's face looks somewhat annoyed. Elijah feels like he's getting on her bad side, he withdrew beginning to feel like a burden. Especially since Larissa's mom is a single mother which struck her further.

"The thing is that they've matured." She said. "They got older and wanted to change for the better like everyone else that wanna better themselves. Ain't nothing wrong with that, better late than never." She's trying to not sound upset. "Everyone deserves a second chance. If anything, that shows off how us ladies had grown and this movement is empowering us to believe that." Larissa asks him where he's getting this information from. Elijah admits from online forums. "People be posting anything online, Elijah." She smirked. "Like how they claim all females want attention."

"But they do though, they dress all nic—"

"Because we tryin' to look good for ourselves. Plus, you be thinkin' we give attitudes to guys. So then why would we dress to draw them in if we not trying to be bothered from the jump?" she said. Elijah couldn't come up with an answer. "We not out for attention just 'cause our make-up be on point and we got a nice fit on."

There was a self-assured feeling she gained, like a jolt of energy knowing that he didn't have anything to back it up and was open to her perception instead.

"And miss me with that stuff about women being influenced to be bad, 'cause what about the online forums that slanders us? Not all things posted online is valid." She said sounding patronizing.

Elijah had more reasons. However, he rarely sees Larissa since they're out of school. She's been so busy with her own life that he didn't want to ruin the little time they had now. And despite his reasons, there was this subconscious feeling that he wouldn't win. That there wouldn't much use arguing with her. "My fault." He politely said.

Larissa accepted his apology and dropped it. This was one of the reasons that she liked Elijah Atwood. He seemed open to her point of view, was always enlightened.

"So did you ever visit that website?" Elijah asks.

Larissa tells him about scrolling through it and how legitimate it seemed.

Richez Shrive 2:10 P.M.

The time is slow, Jovanny is serving Icarus McGrew another strawberry daiquiri. They eventually discussed the acid attack that's made the news, Jovanny shows him the video of the entire incident. Icarus looked shocked once it ended and was baffled that he'd overreact as such.

"*Geez.*" Icarus says, aghast. "The guy didn't have to attack her like that. Poor girl, hope she's ok." He stares at the final shot of Courtney collapsed in agony.

Jovanny has no trace of empathy shown. "I get why he did though, bitch ghosted him. See Icarus, a lot of these guys been through the gauntlet with these hoes, bro. Notice how many of these men committing these crimes ain't never had no prior criminal record of hostility. Then women take advantage of they kindness like he weak." Icarus isn't sure how to respond and kept quiet. "So, then the guy's like, *'alright, bet!'* after getting fed up with how y'all just switched-up, so then he start kidnappin' hoes! Then people be wondering why y'all females come up missing. How this girl's limbs be sprinkled out in the ocean, why her severed head be locked up in some dude's attic, ran over by cars or how y'all end up buried alive. Females think men not gonna do shit, be thinking we sweet!"

Icarus, even without ever knowing the feeling of forming an attachment like that, recalled a similar situation recently. At the deli by his house, he met a recently divorced woman. They exchanged numbers and admitted it was the best natural interaction he's shared with a woman. Icarus was very cautious when texting her, hoping there'd be a response. She actually texted him back. Jovanny can see how happy he was by the gleeful tone of his voice. Icarus was getting to know her but was extremely cautious as to what he was texting back and felt relieved each time he heard back. Last weekend they had planned on a date at the midtown mall, he was ecstatic when she agreed. Icarus had showed up at noon as they agreed to meet.

Once he was there, Icarus messaged her that he's arrived precisely on time, and he'll wait by the coffee kiosk. There was no response, but he just waited, then a half hour passed and he ordered hot chocolate still awaiting for her. He still seemed optimistic, suspecting that she was held up in heavy traffic or some excuse. Forty-five minutes passed to where he was losing hope that she'd come. He didn't want to come off as desperate, but he texted her again asking how close she was. Then he dialed her up after a whole hour passed with no hint of a response. As the phone rings, he got automatically sent to voicemail.

Alas, Icarus begrudgingly accepts that she's not making their date. He remembered what Jovanny told him about women skipping out on dates and was hoping that wouldn't apply to this woman. Still grasping onto hope, he continuously checks his phone to see any missed calls or texts from her. It was a pity that she still hadn't and that he scrolled through their whole conversation thread trying to decipher anything wrong with how he messaged her. There was nothing he could figure out, then everything Chet advised to him circulated back. Him saying that he shouldn't waste time approaching women like many other guys. That stings him more since he just sits by the kiosk still alone. Icarus watches as groups of people are walking together and notices some females walking around the mall unescorted. Instead of heading home, he decides to browse the mall approaching women since he's already here.

Jovanny shook his head. "Man, I'm sorry but consider this shit's a blessing in disguise. You don't wanna break bread on these hoes no how."

Icarus remembered that he planned on walking together for a while at the mall, buying her a meal at the food court and would've spent money for movie tickets. He decided to keep this all to himself. It even felt like a waste. He showed Jovanny the message thread in his phone for him to detect maybe if he initiated wrong.

"I see you be hitting her back real quick." Jovanny said.

"But don't fret though, it ain't like you sent her no weird shit so that ain't on you. Bro, Stay up."

His clouded thoughts were now relived yet Icarus decided to not show it, instead he simply shrugged it off.

"I get what you mean about my replies, some people claim that you have to wait a little while before texting back but I really prefer to not play games. Not like it matters now since most don't respond or refuse to show up like this one."

"I feel you but females love absorbing your attention, feel they deserve it but don't never wanna come through in the end. They just make that shit a regimen or as I call it… ha-bitch-ual, treacherous, disloyal-ass tendencies with a false sense of fuckin' entitlement! Like, I'd rather y'all bitches just give out a bum-ass number or say you taken."

Icarus gulps down the rest of his drink. "You still get that excuse, huh?" he laughed. "I'm long passed that excuse, my friend. I've gotten *'Oh, I have work, I don't give out my number.'* Oh, oh or my personal favorite, *'let me take your number down instead.'* Just to never call or text me back."

Despite having Jovanny's confirmation, Icarus still has that perplexed look as to why she changed her mind, second-guessing himself.

Jovanny pours him another drink. "Here's how bitches operate. All of 'em be extremely emotional, ain't no sort of reasoning with the opposite sex. They not capable of giving sympathy ever, even though they claim to be emotional. Bitches' irrational feelings stay skyrocketing, always supersedes any ground logic. That's why they get rid of men real quick, leave you wondering. So don't get sprung on no female out here."

"I'm sure they've got some kind of reason as to why."

"They all like this." Jovanny said. "That's why you can't ever rely on a woman's word 'cause she'll just switch-up. That's why you gotta accept that a woman's not yours, it's just your turn."

Icarus nods. "Well, I'm not still fixated on her because I engaged with some women afterwards." Jovanny smiles at him. "I recently ran into this woman in my neighborhood, but she refused to respond too." He elaborates on how he was looking out his window to discover this attractive woman walking pass. Icarus ejected out his house, he didn't want to frighten her by rushing her. She had stopped to check her phone, he almost reached her until she began to jog. He halts afterwards, contemplating whether or not to pursue her still. By the time he made up his mind she was far down the road. Icarus jogged a bit then slowed down once she became clearer on his radar; he didn't want her to get suspicious of his pounding footsteps. She stopped for a moment on the sidewalk just to stretch. He began to walk with speed then stops.

"Hold up, hold up!" Jovanny blurts out. "You reached her but stopped? You ain't want her to see you comin'?"

"It was so I wouldn't scare her with me speeding up from behind." Icarus clarifies.

"Ok, I see you. Go on."

"Oh, believe me, I did." He said, then calmly continues. "So then she started walking, then I started walking. Then

she started jogging, and I started jogging. *Then she started running, so I started running!"*

Jovanny groaned. "So you chased this girl—"

"Nope." Icarus protests. "Just tried to catch up. Then we caught up. Texted a bit but guess she caught the wrong idea."

"Probably caught that creeper vibe of you on her trail. And what'chu mean she caught the wrong idea."

Icarus yanks out his phone and showed the texts between them. He initiated and they were talking for a day. It seemed pretty normal, then she asked him when he noticed her. Icarus replied that unsure as to what she meant. She wondered where exactly he came from since she didn't detect him prior to that.

"I just explained I was passing too and got the idea of stopping her." Icarus said. "Then she quits replying?"

"I just got the idea of stalking you." Jovanny read his text bubble. Observing Icarus' eyes widened. "You didn't type '*stopping you*'. And if you did, autocorrect fucked you up."

"Oh..." Icarus mutters. "Guess this one had a reason."

"Bro, just be glad you didn't get caught up over this. But women always leave for better options. Like, my girl for instance, if she leaves then that's that. It don't mean nothing 'cause she would've dipped off on me regardless and won't care. Only check for themselves and their offspring, it's in their nature. Just how evolution's ran. So stop worrying over them when y'all not gonna last from the jump. And stop lurking for these bitches down, ok?" Jovanny mocks.

Icarus spirits uplift and laughs. "See, the thing when it comes to stalking is you've gotta always keep two steps ahead while having let them believe they've got more steps away." The two are laughing. Icarus is left feeling more relieved looking back now. No heartbreak, no petty games, no jealousy. "Anyway, I don't really plan on getting attached." He confides. "I'd rather just settle for sex."

"We in a time where women are now sexually liberated and yet they're too damn fickle still. You not the only one, got mad dudes out here dick be just bone-dry. That's why dudes don't be courteous towards these females today."

"Plus, I hear they denounce men's help too."

Jovanny sneers. *"Thank God I don't endorse chivalry."* He informs Icarus that most women are mentally ill from constant fornication with multiple guys, impairing them from connecting with one man. "They body count is way too high 'cause women are whores. These thots can't bond with no man after taking so many dicks. They're sluts and whores, and that's all thanks to this sexual liberation. They can't even handle being disciplined, bro. Like once you put your foot down, they just ghost your ass. Then settle for these simps who always be blowin' up they phone instead."

Icarus wasn't entirely content with this advice despite how much conviction Jovanny speaks, he's silently hesitant.

"You just gotta lie to women." Jovanny adds. "Like my girl, Solanda. I just tell her what she needs to hear so she don't get it twisted." Jovanny mentions how he lied when they had first met. He lied to her about never being in the city just to escalate the conversation and also lied about having a job to keep him busy so she'd believe he was making money at the time. He tells how he's lied to her about other things. "You don't wanna get in an argument with no women 'cause they can't accept reality for what it is and go off on emotions, they'll just run they mouth to drive us crazy. Can't never do no fact-check with a bitch!"

"With all this knowledge you got, you can help build society." Icarus encouraged.

"I ain't try'na change no damn society with the wisdom I been blessed with. I been opted out. Just gonna look out for my own and get mine."

While they're talking, a commercial began to play on TV. It was a feminist commercial for a popular cologne company. Jovanny groans at the sight, Icarus hasn't seen this before. On screen, multiple men are shown acting overboard when approaching women. One Caucasian guy tries to approach one until another man in an angel robe attire prevents him. Another scene is a women leaving from church with the sound of men catcalling her in the background. A direct sunlight beams in their faces making them cease, shining a spotlight on what men are now being. Then the clouds clear a bright pathway for that church-goer. The final scene has a woman silently going up an escalator while reading a book, while a group of unsavory men going down the escalator try to get her attention by extending their hands. The actress ignores them and reaches the top as opposed to the frustrated guys slowly descending to the depths of hell with an unconvincing visual effect of fire below them. The commercial ends with *"WE REFUSE TO PLAY DEVIL'S ADVOCATE, RESPECT ALL WOMEN…"*

Jovanny is visually annoyed. Icarus keeps enjoying his drink, not wanting to instigate anything. Another customer comes in, Jovanny goes to serve him.

Icarus goes to his phone and searches for that woman's number to delete. *"Ah, autocorrect… out here sending the wrong messages."* He mumbles to himself while deleting her contact: Nneka Barshak.

York Avenue 3:12 P.M.

Larissa and Chase are together on her front steps after getting frozen yogurt. She's enjoying her strawberry flavored one; he's stuffing his pumpkin and vanilla flavored one in his mouth before it melts.

As they're settled there still, Larissa tells him about the video of Courtney's assault. Chase admitted he already knew from the news but never saw the video. They're watching it from her phone, Chase, fully aware of the story, wasn't affected by the video. After it finished, Larissa tells him about what Elijah had told him. He listens to her go on about how she proved him wrong and detects the pride in herself for enlightening him to the positivity of this movement. Chase smirked.

"What's good?" she asks.

"The fact that you defending this bitch's flakiness. And how you not see what Elijah's sayin'? How this movement ain't done us no good?" Larissa looked confused. "Like how would you feel if I ain't pulled up today like we planned?"

"Ok, ok but you ain't pay for my frozen yogurt though." She protests.

"But my boy in this story had broke bread for all their dates. So you admit that that's fucked up, still ghosted him."

There was a moment she had to gather her thoughts. Chase agrees that Elijah was right about women having higher standards and irrational behavior when it comes to men. His stern voice echoed without leniency yet completely certainty. Larissa started to deflate, unable to cloak her doubt.

"Well, how would you know how females be acting like, huh? You ain't up in their house. Where your facts at? Like, what info you got on you?" she said defensive.

Chase snickered and shook his head in a way that made him sound more aware than her. Almost in a pitiful way by how whatever his answer is, just like his patronizing attitude, it should be evident to her.

"You're asking '*where your info at?*'" he mocks. "I don't need a textbook when I got people experience. I hear from guys around our age and from older guys that be around the corner stores talk about how life works."

"You can't generalize all of us." She huffed.

"Ain't nobody say '*all y'all*', I said most." He states, Larissa looked awkward then recoiled. "It be a large majority that stay outweighing the ones who don't. Like statistical data will always have outliers, sure. But we take the data that be clearest to us, and that's a fact! And besides, me being exposed to all these different avenues of dudes out here is more than I need to get a strong enough basis. Who needs to carry around some textbook when you could meet guys with a chip on they shoulder instead?! Ain't nobody got time for that…"

"But see—"

"I be interacting with people more than you do. Try being a man about to approach a woman today. Y'all be closed off, foul as hell, or ignore us like it ain't nothin'."

"Bro, we don't know y'all intentions from the jump."

Chase groaned. "Fine. But to have up this whole bitch shield instead of being sweet and see what's up… y'all wrong for that. Women see dudes as beneath them, and how can y'all not?!" he begrudgingly admits that society be putting women up on a pedestal, how people don't truly hold females accountable and how guys act inferior in general. "So I get it, anyone in your shoes would feel like they could do no wrong."

Larissa is feeling self-conscious like he spotlights her second-guessing herself. "Like, take me for instance… I be a fair person and I see it after all women have been through with men, we deserve this. Even if it is a bit of an edge."

"But don't you think we should learn from our history?" he asks as if the answer is obvious. "That we shouldn't let one gender have so much power that they feel superior over the other. But real talk, this why men can't take y'all seriously. Like, it's clear how much power our woke, misandry, gynocentric-ass society blesses y'all females with, and instead of trying to make shit fair for both parties, don't nobody care."

Chase brings up many advantages women in society had now gained from this movement. Larissa's impenetrable stance from before is slowly breaking down.

"And you claim you a nice, fair person but you cool with this movement that favors women more knowing it be a detriment to men's livelihoods?! Then you not no fair person then."

"Well, regardless how we be acting..." she begrudgingly said, her voice quavers. "*... what that fool got caught on video doing ain't right*."

"I never said that neither. This dude deserves whatever he gets, he was fucked up. Just saying you can't be out talking crazy and not expect any repercussions, unaware of this man's snapping points."

Larissa felt some sense of relief. He refused to rub it in her face and she didn't feel beneath him. "Oh, ok. I got you." She expressed. "Least we on the same page."

Chase leaned in for a kiss, she gracefully accepts it. To him, it was youthful enjoyment. To her, it was reassurance that they were okay.

Midtown Mall 4:00 P.M

Icarus McGrew is on his normal routine of searching out for girls. He's been there for an hour now, sitting at a table alone in the food court. Many females there are with somebody else, he would hate to interrupt. At the table, Icarus munched his fries and pizza down and gulped more soda. Then he spots a white woman on her phone alone in the corner. Before she decides to leave he walks over to her table, she doesn't even notice him yet.

"Hello." He announced, she raised her head spiraled upward, her eyes wide. "Excuse me, sorry. Just passing by, thought you were looking cute today."

"Thank you." She replied then proceeds back to her phone. Icarus asks for her name. "Sorry, I've got a man." She politely said while still focused on her screen.

Icarus left feeling pretty hopeful still. While walking through the food court he scanned the area in pursuit for another. Through the crowd of adults, he detects a small Hispanic female waiting outside the restrooms. Heading forward he passes by teens huddled at a table, adults in line for their meals by separate different food spots, facing multiple people minding their business. The women sees him coming but thinks nothing of it. Icarus thinks she probably assumes he'll head to the bathroom. She's wearing a tight attire, exposing her bare arms and smooth legs; she resembled a dancer. He remembers what Jovanny said about asking women questions on themselves.

"Excuse me," he began. "I noticed your attire there. Do you dance or something like that?"

She smiles and shakes her head. "*Oh,* ok. Thank you, thank you." She took two steps away.

He seemed confused; he didn't even compliment her. "Wait, what do you mean 'thank you?' I don't—"

"Sorry, I'm not interested." She laughed as her female friend came out the restroom, the two left together.

A chuckle escapes from him with a huge grin. Then sees another woman passing. He waves, she turns her face to him but kept on moving forward slowly. She sees him over her shoulder to where she could've broken her neck. As he began to speak, her head turned back forward.

There's not a trace of a woman by her lonesome from what he sees as he slurped the remainder of his soda. Mostly couples, ones with their girlfriends or underage girls. He goes back to his table to toss his garbage out and left the food court. Another woman passes by him. She wore brown sunglasses and was slim with her earbuds in.

He speed walks, complete tunnel vision on her backside, disregarding any passing people or kiosks. At the pace he's at, he gradually slowed down and approached from behind to her side. She noticed through her peripheral and faced him, eyebrows raised and removed one earbud.

"Hey there." He greets.

"Yes?"

"Oh, nothing really, you just look good today."

She seemed speechless for a second. "Uh-huh? Ok?"

"I'm Icarus, what about you?" he said, as they're moving together. She dryly expressed her name was Anna while facing forward. Icarus could've just left but he figures it'll be more awkward if he just took her name alone. Besides, he already came this far. "I get it, a bit awkward." He laughed. "Sorry, if you're a little uncomfortable."

She gives a fake laugh while slowly nodding, lips pursed.

"So which store are you heading into?" he asked, seeming interested.

"Just," she hesitantly began. "Just browsing for now."

"Cool." He responds then realized this wasn't going anywhere. "Well, I think I'll go now. Have a good day." Icarus turned to the opposite direction.

Through the incoming crowd, Icarus made his way to the sorted couches for people to rest. His eyes gaze into space, watching adults, teenagers and occasionally security walk by. The realization that he hasn't gotten any numbers as of yet prevents him from leaving still. He blankly stares into a clothing store window of a female mannequin displaying a purple sundress with red polka dots on it. He remembered that was the store where a girl gave him her number and agreed to meet for drinks one day; yet she ignored his text.

There's an Indian woman approaching who sat by the couches. She relaxes there while staring off. Icarus noticed her long eyelashes through her glasses, her skin looked smooth as butter. She had an owl tattoo on her left arm. He walked in her direction and gave a friendly wave. She gave a tiny wave exchange while remaining tranquil.

"Hey, nice tattoo there." Icarus said in a friendly tone. "An owl, right?" she nods with a blank expression still. "*Nice, nice*. Always thought of getting one myself, maybe of a crow. Who knows…" she nodded then got up and left.

Icarus simply nodded as he watched her leave, he noticed an older black woman who watched the whole thing and he didn't care.

"I see you trying, it's ok." She encouraged. "Rejection's no big deal."

Icarus smiled. "Yup, I mean, I'm fine though. Thanks."

"See, times are different." She continues, Icarus urge to leave died down. "Women have many choices today, especially on our phones. But you don't give up." he nodded. "How old are you?"

"I'm thirty."

"You're my oldest son's age. He'll be thirty-one soon and still single. I tell him the same thing, to just not give up and continue trying."

"Thank you." Icarus politely said. "Maybe I'll get lucky." He finally gets up. "Have a good day."

"You too." she responds.

Icarus decides to try the usual store where he's had more luck attaining phone numbers. Before he goes, he buys two churros then goes up the escalator. Down on the first floor are so many people moving around as he watched from above. Here on the second floor lies this beauty supply store called Purity. It is always filled with women of all races that're more cordial inside. Icarus has patrolled in there many times, he's a familiar face to the staff, especially the tall man stocking shelves. Icarus goes in while eating half of his churro. There's a small line of women by the cashier, a man carrying a crate of incoming products to the back aisle. He goes down an aisle with several wigs on separate mannequin heads.

There's nobody in sight, he delved into the skin care aisle where there is a young black women. Her skin complexion was light and she seemed of mixed ethnic decent. She looked over at him as she heard the biting sound of his churro. Then went back to examining the lotions in her hands.

"Excuse me." He said, she moved in to let him pass through. "Oh no, no, I saw you passing by, was wondering what ethnicity you were?"

"Hmmm, what's my ethnicity, you said?"

"Mm-hmm."

She replied in a monotone voice. "Black."

"That's all? I thought you were mixed."

"Yea, I get that a lot." She admits, then decided on which lotion to get. "Have a good day." She said as she walked off.

He explored throughout the store, nothing attracted him. Then he waits a few minutes longer eating his churro in case anyone new emerged but nobody else entered. Icarus decides to wander around this aisle.

On his way out the store, Icarus looked around at the crowd of incoming people. Still eating his churro, keeping up an optimistic spirit. Suddenly someone familiar had caught his eye from over the balcony. He couldn't believe it; it was the woman he was talking to that stood him up.

She was a brunette, white woman holding a child's hand. It appears to be her child.

He thought of that interaction they had together and how natural it went during their texts. Maybe he could convince her into giving him another chance. He deleted her number along with the other ones who refused to reply, so it would give him an excuse for it again. Icarus bolts down the escalator, keeping sight out for her. She's at a slower pace to let the kid observe the toy store through the window. Icarus finally caught up from behind.

"Hey you," he happily greets. She turned around in complete shock, the little boy faces him too. "How're you?"

"*Hi…*" she responds with a surprised tone. "I'm good."

"Cool, cool. I just came from upstairs, haven't really found anything yet." Icarus looks over at the kid. "*Hellooo.*"

"I'm just with my son."

"You never mentioned you had any kids. That's good though." He adds.

She started to sway forward. "Alright, bye now."

Icarus kept up before she walked. "Actually, I'm not with anyone. We didn't really get together last time, now lo and behold, we're here together now… plus one."

"Yeah," she bluntly said, they're walking together with her son squeezing her hand, staring at this man. "Guess I had something come up that day."

Icarus shrugged it off. "Yeah, things happen." He pulled out his phone from his pocket. She noticed his movement through her peripheral vision. "I was thinking perhaps we could hangout, keep me some company."

Silence was shared amongsts the three.

"I actually gotta head back home, cook my son something to eat."

Icarus remembered her mentioning where she's from through text. "Right, by Kental avenue, right?" she skeptically nodded. "That's right, you messaged me that." he said, the two walked near the coffee kiosk. "Well, how's about I get your number again?"

"LOOK!" she hissed, they both halted at the kiosk. *"I'M GOOD, I DON'T* WANT *TO GIVE MY NUMBER OUT!"*

People passing looked over at them. Everyone in line for coffee spotted them too, overhearing her voice thunder at him.

"I don't need you near my son."

"Ok," his tone quavered. "I'll just head out, I guess."

"GOOD, YOU GO THEN!" she said, her tone sharp. Icarus retreated his phone in his pocket then swayed in the other direction. Her scream ripped through him. Everyone in the proximity of this are looking at him. Everyone's judgement targeting him has him swell up inside. Being surrounded by a heap of sour looks settled on him, having him manage to move shaky. There's a white guy focused on him with intensity. Nothing but a scowl look on his face that Icarus choose to ignore as they're passing each other. Forcing himself to tunnel forward while this man's fierce intensity is detected from the right; sensing that thick ocular grip pressured against him until he's finally gone.

Several feet away from there, he still was weighed down by the trail of exposure slugged behind. Icarus McGrew decided to go home with a zero-success rate today.

†

Uptown Holksdale 7:39 P.M.

Days after the announcement of his donation, Grant Critchfield and Joy Pluss arrived at his childhood home in a black limousine. It was a regular three floor house. On his way there, Grant thought about his mother's reaction. By now she knew about the alleged assault. The last thing he wanted was to disappoint his mother. They have had disagreements regarding some of his life choices during his acting career. However, she didn't like to pry too much in his business. She always understood that he may have been going through something. Always supporting him that he will get through any issues. Whether it involved a public dispute, or drunk driving or anything seen about him in the news or tabloid magazines. Both Grant's parents were his emotional backbone.

Unfortunately, his father, Thomas Critchfield, had passed away a few years into his career. His mother, Violet Moore, struggled with her grief. Violet had retaken her maiden name. Grant tried to console his mother but didn't fully commit as much time as he could have. He had coped with his loss by drinking, drug use, countless intercourse and mostly his career. Thomas Critchfield was a devoted father and husband who always put his family first. Grant hardly ever brought up Thomas when conversing with his mother. Normally, Violet would bring him up when it came to Grant's achievements (*From gaining a role from his audition, to starring in great films, to winning his first Emmy and Oscar)*, anything pertaining to his acting career had Violet proudly say: "I know your father looking down would be so proud."

Hopefully, his mother would understand from his perspective what really transpired between him and that young actress. Scenarios plummet his mind on how to explain to his mother this situation. Then reports from the news whirled through his brain. An intense nervousness cycles through Grant. He pulls out a cigarette, lit it up, and began puffing away. Joy encourages him that he should talk to his mother. Grant hasn't even given the entire story to his own agent. Despite this, Joy reminds him that she has faith in him. Not just that he's innocent but that he'll rectify his career if her listens to her.

Joy leaves in the limo back to her hotel. Grant continued smoking at the front yard. Once done, he stomped it out on the concrete. Then rings the doorbell. Grant waited. His heart began rumbling, his breathing intensifies (*especially having just smoked*), and two suitcase handles are latched tighter within his hands. Grant's vision just hooked to the front door. The sound of the door crept open causing a wave of tenseness to course through him.

As expected, Violet Moore cautiously opens the door. Her appearance struck Grant, sending this nervous internal trembling outward, resulting with his lips forcing an unfamiliar smile now fastened to his face. His tone fell frail but was able to pry out: *"Good evening, mom."*

Violet Moore appeared shorter than her son. Eye-level to his neck. Her brown tiresome eyes stared back at Grant nonresponsive. Her skin was a bit wrinkled, her hair was mostly long brown with some grey strands in the forefront. Violet had already anticipated his arrival.

Without any response from her, Grant wrapped his arms around her thin body, giving his mother a warm hug. Violet remained still; both arms remained at her waist. His arms unfolded as the two go inside. Violet sprays the air with perfume, masking the cigarette scent. Grant's eye trace around the house. Things appear exactly where he left off. Pictures of him and his parents remained on the wall. The walls were still white, the huge mirror still in the living room, a huge portrait of Thomas Critchfield stayed above the fireplace.

No words were exchanged between them yet. His eyes glanced at his side, only to see his mother had left for the couch. The back of her head was seen across the room, facing the TV. As she sat there, Grant announced that he'll unpack in his room. There's no response to be heard. This sunken feeling began to flow in him. While walking to his room, his eyes began wandering at the walls. Checking if anything was different. The same photos were there, the wall was painted the same, and everything was clean.

Grant enters his room to find everything intact still. From the TV on the dresser, his computer by the door, the window closed, his bed sheets the same, and the yellow carpet still clean.

He sat on his bed leaving his suitcases by the wall. Now slouched forward, his hand cupped his face. Violet's silence had him wondering how she must feel that her son is facing this allegation. Thoughts of how she'll react to everything puzzles him due to her silence. Wondering if she'll yell, cry, console him began itching his mind.

After a half hour apart, Grant emerged into the living room. His mother still glued in that same spot on the couch. This interior crackling quickly forms in him as he ponders if he should bring up his situation. Grant's throat clogged lumpy the more he thinks about it. Instead, he decides to let go of his pride and initiate a conversation with her.

His footsteps warily cross over to the couch. He sits on the opposite end of the couch. Violet remained still on her side. Her arms were crossed, legs coldly buckled on the cushion. Both brown eyes were pinned onto the TV screen. Grant's mind raced for anything to discuss, then it comes.

"Where's Ingrid, mom?" Grant gently asks. Knowing his mother was fond of their housekeeper that he hired after his father died. "She normally has dinner prepared around this hour."

"She did." Violet replied, her eyes remained fixed on the TV still. "We had baked macaroni and grilled chicken together. Then I sent her home."

"Ingrid's a live-in maid."

"Not anymore." Violet flatly said. After informing Ingrid of his arrival, she began getting nervous. Violet rearranged her schedule to come in early in the morning, staying all day until she finishes cooking in the evening.

The room fell silent once she finished. Only sound that escaped was from the TV. Grant sat there numbly. This blank expression had still orbited her face. As Grant glances over at her, Violet's focus maintained on the screen. This disconnect was shared between mother and son on the couch. A stuffed bubbling of shame cycles through him, wishing to burst loose. Grant struggles to find the words expressing how he'd never want her to be distant like this. Trying to shine any clarity about his current situation.

Violet gets up from the couch, saying she'll be in her room. Grant stretches his neck behind him, encouraging her to stay and watch TV. Violet didn't respond.

"I love you, mom." These words gushed out Grant's mouth. His eyes trail on his mother's back soullessly steering across the room.

"Goodnight, Noah." She coldly replied.

That dry response reminds him of how his mother never approved of his stage name: Grant Critchfield. Along with every transgression that's now attached with it.

Time passes as Grant sits lonesome on the couch. He then searches the dresser for a film that he's starred in. His parents always kept those around (*no matter how violent, raunchy or vulgar it was*) in support of his career. He pops one inside. A movie where he played an undercover cop infiltrating a drug kingpin and tunes into only his scenes.

Grant's spirits began to uplift watching his performance, idolizing himself, becoming his own biggest fan.

York Avenue 2:49 P.M.

The next day, Larissa invites her friend Nicole LeRock Grace over to hangout. Her friend's been reaching out to her for a while now so Lyric's ecstatic since they haven't seen each other since the school year ended. They're both sitting outside under the shade, talking on Larissa's front steps. Larissa refused to invite her in because of Essie's current state. Instead, she lied claiming Essie had the flu and was contagious. Larissa informs her about meeting Chase, mostly just trying to relax. Lyric was happy for her. Normally, she has boys at school lusting after her. Not just freshman but upperclassman as well, even requesting to follow her social media. Nicole LeRock Grace appears pretty to the world as beautifully mixed girl whose skin complexion blurs between a unique yellow and white skin tone. Her hazel eyes and her curly long natural hair has her seem exotic. It stood out the most to Larissa whose darker self-image varies more when they're both alone.

Lyric tells her about the guys she's been talking to. It wasn't any surprise to hear but Larissa was still interested.

"We been talking for a week, right." Lyric began. "So tell me why this boy tries to finesse me out my house just to meet up at his spot. Like, you not tryin' to at least pretend to court a bitch out first?!"

Larissa nods. "Exactly. Actually Chase was on this shit about men ain't wanting to take us out now. Sayin' women got special privilege." She brings up the story of Courtney.

"He got a point." Lyric said. "Can't nobody tell me nothin'. Like bitch, I ain't trying to hear it. Remember Brandon from homeroom? Bro, I almost went off on this kid arguing that all bitches do is play games, play with our emotions. I'm like *'everybody be out here playin' games.'* You not special. Like, I be shit-testing dudes all the time."

"Why?" Larissa asked.

"Well, 'cause these niggas be sweet as fuck. I wanna see who'll actually take charge. Girl, don't nobody want they back blown out by no spineless-ass nigga! But I'll let y'all take me out for food." She laughs. "Plus, they always be blowing up my phone wanting for me to slide over their spot. I'm like, what for? Then they go ghost or send nudes."

Larissa shook her head in disbelief.

"You think I'm playing?!" Lyric said, pulling out her phone. "Bitch, I'll pull up my receipts." She shows Larissa messages of penises. "And some of these be from college guys. Then they get mad when I don't wanna shoot some back. Like, y'all can suck my dick on that!"

Lyric mentions this older guy she's been dating. They went to restaurants and concerts that he's paid for. However, she's been entertaining other guys' that she'd forgotten to reply to him after a while. Then he wanted to go for simple walks in the park instead and she then cut off contact with him.

"He'd been blowing up my phone every now and then." She laughed, then shows Larissa his messages. "I just leave him on read. Ain't nobody told him to catch feelings. And I pray Chase ain't like this."

"*Nuh-uh.*" Larissa mutters. "He don't even seem like he'd care if we were done. Like, when we last talked, calling me out that I'm not fair 'cause of a minor double standard. It's like he almost didn't care about what I thought from the jump, unlike Elijah."

The mention of Elijah has Lyric roll her eyes, as if she's supposed to believe that.

"Elijah's sprung on you, *boo-boo.*" Lyric said. "Whenever we at school and I be seeing him wave you down in the halls. He probably listens to anything you say."

"Maybe." Larissa just shrugged, not wanting to seem arrogant. "But let's say he didn't like me like that, he at least heard me out to where I had him come on my side. 'Cause before, he was talking crazy, then I changed his mind. Not with Chase though."

"Guess Elijah outta give him some tips."

"Nah, like," Larissa began, trying to be nice. "Elijah sometimes be doing too much. Blowing up my inbox wanting to hangout." She sees Lyric encourage her. "Don't get me wrong, he's nice and I don't mind him liking my posts but still. He even catches me around town a few times since school let out."

"You be seeing him more than you be seeing me, ain't that a bitch?!" Lyric groans.

"It ain't even like that. He messaged me to come with him to that miracle's at but I told him I was already going with Chase." She continues that his friends are going to be there and it would be at night.

"Elijah said he was finna use up all of his silly string spray on it as a joke."

"Yo, tell me how I dead-ass forgot about that."

Larissa tells her how Chase offered to guide her to a church in order to help her repent for her mom. Then elaborated on that horrific event at the terminal and how he quickly shielded her to safety. The more Larissa goes on about him, the more uncertainty is detected within her tone. Lyric expects her to be glad which is why she's confused.

"You good, sis?" Lyric asks.

"I just be thinking sometimes, why?" she confessed. "Why he even fucking with me? Guys like him at our school aren't usually fond of darker girls, they usually wanna holla at girls like you. And there ain't much about me from the jump. But he still pursued me, did this stuff for me."

"Looks like you got a real one. Sis, it ain't that deep."

"I know but he too good for me. I think he knows that. Maybe that's why he doesn't fret over someday losing me."

There was a brief breeze that soared through them. Lyric gazed up at the sun, glad that Larissa suggested the shade on the steps. It's hard for Lyric to argue against how most boys from their school rather prefer herself instead. Or to defend Chase's perspective when Larissa knows him better than she does. Yet, she knows her best friend a lot more. Larissa contemplates an alternative.

"Unity." Larissa suggests. "Dark-skinned girls like me need a spot to escape in order to vent and embrace all parts of ourselves. I'd even invite girls with lighter complexions too if they had self-image issues. Good vibes only, black people need unity regardless of whichever shade y'all are."

Lyric simply shrugged. "Well, I ain't trying to throw no shade but ain't no greater place to spot race unity no more than a mixed bitch like me. Sis, I'm everything. Niggas can't even tell what the fuck I am." she gloats, then composes herself. "But real talk though, that boy fucks with you 'cause he's into you." Lyric reassured her.

The insecure look Larissa shows doesn't seem like she believes her, even when she tries to conceal it.

"You're a sweetheart, sincere, caring and hopeful." Lyric adds. "And he finds your complexion sexy too, it ain't no hurdle. You don't need no group to make you feel good about yourself. Hell, at least guys don't want you just on your looks alone."

Lyric elaborates how boys don't even really try to invest in her besides her appearance. That they expect her to be soft since they assume darker-skinned girls are less feminine or more ghetto. Whenever she divulges her black origin, guys automatically dismiss that.

"Guys act like I'm sweet. Like I ain't gonna buck if you come at me wrong. When they dismiss my black side, it just makes me wanna go off and keep acting ratchet. That's why I don't be taking them seriously, just use 'em for free shit or just act out. There even be times when I don't want to be doin' too much and they still don't put me in my place. Just goes to show they're too bitch-made to see through me."

"Must suck then, huh?"

"Only 'cause of their intent but I still love the attention of just how thirsty these fools get. They like how my skin glows, but they ain't really interested in me." Lyric scoffs at her friend's unison idea. "You don't need no group to get you gassed up. I honestly be a homebody sometimes, be taking time by myself to decipher who *the fuck I am.*"

"And who is that?" Larissa genuinely asked.

Lyric's lips pursed. "I dunno. Others only check for my looks, I checked for myself and it wasn't that deep." her tone lowered. "So at least someone's invested in who you are. And if not, fuck 'em! You got so much going on for yourself that you don't need no unity, Chase, or your mom for you to be at peace. Just gotta value how great of a person you already are, queen."

Larissa's self-doubt began to uplift. She's never heard her friend talk like this before.

"Y'know, there be times where I don't even bother mentioning my black side. They don't care nothin' about that or about me. Maybe that one guy who might be '*the one*' won't wanna fuck with me 'cause of it."

"Remember you told me it's no hurdle." Larissa said.

Lyric shook her head not thinking it applies to her, yet hearing Larissa out.

"Like, I got no beef with you not acknowledging your black side as long as you not rejecting it neither." Larissa encouraged. "Just embrace all of yourself, including them African features since that makes you, you." She sees Lyric begrudgingly nod. "But honestly though, ain't none of that shit matters. Because I know you. And your individuality alone stands out more than all those things that makes you, you. And that's what makes you glow."

After all of that, her friend looked at her hopeful. Larissa knew she had gotten through to her. Not much more needed to be said. The sunshine started to release more into the shade. Lyric seemed to not care; Larissa decided to not move. Lyric sprung up with her arms embraced out, absorbing the heat, letting herself be brought to light.

"You see this, sis." Lyric proudly announced, she hands Larissa her phone to take a picture. "You see how I'm glowing right?"

Larissa smiled and nods. "Ok, I see you. Radiant." She captured Lyric in four pictures with her posing.

"Don't be scrolling through my photos now."

"*Please…*" Larissa huffed. "It's them damn texts I should be more worried about."

The girls began playing Woke Knee-Grow's new soundtrack. Blasting his song as Lyric unapologetically dances on the steps. Larissa watches her moves as she sings along with these ungodly lyrics. Lyric encourages her to dance along. While hesitant, (*the music, joyous vibe shared, and most of all… Lyric*) she felt the uplifted urge to baffoonishly dance along. Both happily hollering. Larissa embraces that she's joined the choir.

† Chapter 16: *YO, THEN PULL UP!*

Jovanny Gibbs is sitting on his couch at home on his phone. Solanda Wright is coming from work soon. He's thinking about his friend Essie. Neither one of them have reached out since her incident, he's wondering about her well-being still.

A car alarm goes off outside. Jovanny ignores it since he's too relaxed as of right now. Then the sound of glass shatters are heard along with repeated banging. He hopped up off the couch with sheer confusion and rushed out to the window. Jovanny couldn't believe what he was seeing. There was someone outside wearing a red hoodie smashing his truck windows with a crowbar. Without hesitation, he runs downstairs to the first floor, rushes out the front door to intervene.

"YO, THE FUCK IS YOU DOIN', MAN?!" Jovanny barked, keeping a safe distance away from the assailant. The person turned quickly. It was a furious black woman firmly gripping the crowbar with both hands. Jovanny's eyes widened, he recognized her. "Tonya?" he gasped.

"Long time, no see, nigga." Tonya sneered, moving forward towards him. Jovanny extends his arms out then frantically hurried behind his truck. "Oh, don't act shocked now, bitch! You thought I was sweet, thought I wasn't finna clap-back, huh?!" she waves the crowbar around.

Jovanny's eyes lock on her every movement as she screams obscenities. He feels the crackles of glass remnants at the heel of his feet. The alarm is still roaring causing Tonya to scream with greater force. There's nobody in sight as Jovanny searches around.

"Chill, just cool out!" he pleads. "Jesus!"

"After how you fucked me over!" she smashed his right taillight out. "I'm going to hell because of you!" she sees the perplexed look on his face. "I slept with niggas like you, just to get dogged out. You said you were different. Then you go and pull the same shit." she rambles on about how letting him become intimate with her body before marriage has now destined her to hell.

"Girl, you gotta stop this before my girl pulls up."

"*GOOD!* Let her see then." Tonya said, then swarms around to take a swing at him.

Jovanny notices from afar that Solanda's car is arriving. It comes to an abrupt stop, having Solanda jolt out running to them. Tonya observes her getting closer, the alarm noise grows louder as she gets near.

"What the fuck—" Solanda yelled.

"You must be his new white bitch?"

Solanda halts and observes the crowbar being pointed at her. Tonya showed no fear, nothing but rage on her face.

"Who are you?"

Jovanny announced that she's his ex-girlfriend. That she's mad at him and warned her to not get close. Solanda pulled her phone out then began recording.

"You trying to be on video!" Solanda threatens. "You want the police here? *YOU BETTER LEAVE THEN!*"

This ultimatum settled with Tonya there silently contemplating her next move. While acknowledging that crowbar, Solanda holds her position recording her from a distance, Jovanny's paralyzed behind his truck. They're both tense from what might transpire, it's all on her. Tonya grunts and flees down the street.

"This bitch." Jovanny groaned, seeing the damage done to his vehicle. Solanda sprints to him, hugging him tight. "I'm good, it's all good. Let's just head inside."

While they're in the living room, Solanda presses him about what happened between them. Jovanny told her how Tonya was his girlfriend a few years ago. She experienced a few abusive relationships prior to meeting him. Many of the men Tonya had encountered back then wanted her only for her body and discarded her shortly afterwards. Some guys verbally broke her down or physically assaulted her, resulting in those guys eventually leaving her. Tonya ended up having a reputation of being a slut, no man was going to take her seriously. Jovanny had later dated her. They were intimate quickly which lasted for months; until she went to jail for unauthorized use to commit credit fraud.

When she finally got released from jail, Jovanny contacted her after initiating zero contact at all during her jail sentence. He invited her to his place to watch a movie and catch up. Tonya was thrilled since she'd been under house arrest. However, the terms were that she was allowed out but had to return back home before 7 o'clock. Jovanny had talked her into it, promising that he'll pick her up then drop her back in time without breaking parole. That day, he drove her to his home at 2 o'clock, she still had on her bulky, surveillance ankle bracelet along with sexy attire. Tonya divulged how awful her experience was and how glad she was to be out. Once they settled in, she requested for him to buy her Chinese food, claiming how much she was craving it as opposed to what she was served with. He didn't want to, Tonya repeatedly pleaded but Jovanny still refused her that privilege. This caused her to have an attitude, she went moody in a way that resembled a child.

Jovanny still wanted to sleep with her so in order to lighten the mood, he put on a movie that she missed in theaters since she got locked up. When it started, they sat on his couch in the living room. Tonya refrained from snuggling close with him by sitting on the opposite end of the couch. Jovanny figured he would eventually warm up to her. After an hour, she had finally laid up on him. As he caressed her, he leaned in for a kiss, she declined. Then after a while more, Jovanny initiated again, this time she accepted. Once the movie finished, she searched for another and found one to watch. Jovanny was getting irritated by the amount of time being wasted but he was accommodating. Ten minutes into the film, she went back to cuddling with him. Sensing he'd make a future move had her tell him that she was trying to improve herself. Tonya was attempting to not repeat past mistakes of getting sexually active so casually by being celibate; and that's when Jovanny Gibbs tossed her out.

"That's right," Jovanny said. "I remember she claimed that she was now 'born-again', so I simply picked up the remote, paused it, and then leaned close to her ear and whispered for her to *get out*."

Solanda laughed. "*WOOOOW*. I'm dead."

"And believe me, she wasn't havin' it. She wanted for me to drop her back. Like I'll waste gas money for her wasting my time. So I pulled my phone out recording her in case she wanna call rape. Then this bitch started undressing, suddenly wanted to fuck in exchange for a ride. I was so over her at that point that I just told this bitch to kick rocks."

"*SAVAGE*." Solanda encouraged. "So, that's it?"

"Well, with the time she wasted here, she couldn't rush back in time to make her curfew. Then went to prison for violating probation, last I heard. Ain't never thought I'd hear from her again. She should've been glad she ain't pull that shit with them dudes she used to fuck with, 'cause they don't give a fuck about your 'no'. See, I did the gentlemanly thing and just thrown her ass out."

"Looking for someone to accept her flaws."

"Exactly, she knew what she was doing. Her body count is mad high but now she wants to make me wait even though we fucked before. Apparently, she a reformed hoe now. I swear, half the time bitches be quick to forget."

Solanda snuggles on him. "Being a fucking tease. Baby, I don't blame you. Good thing I pulled up too, huh?"

"Now I gotta go get my shit fixed, shit."

They both relaxed on the couch watching TV.

† *Midtown Mall 5:37 P.M*

Today was a new day, Icarus McGrew had embraced. He's sitting on the upper floor watching people. Checking around while eating his fries and chicken tenders. An hour has gone and he hasn't had enough drive to approach a woman yet. The harsh rejection had been boggling his mind lately. He remembered Chet Lopresti telling him to lay off women and that there are plenty of guys who chase them. Icarus sees a tall man walking over to a lady on her phone; the two adults shake hands. She was smiling and the guy pulled a seat next to her. Icarus doesn't mean to stare but they haven't noticed. He sees them exchange numbers then the girl gets up, waving him goodbye. As she passes by Icarus, she turns her head the other direction. Icarus wasn't looking at that point but noticed her passing. The lady's neck looked like it was almost stiff the way she avoided being seen by him. After he's out her sight, she faced forward again.

What was that? Icarus thought. *I wasn't even really looking at her. That's strange. Guess I know not to approach her then.*

Seeing that man boldly introduce himself and attain her number had emboldened Icarus to try once more. *Come on, man, think positive. Sure, it's been a bit tough, but you'll get one soon. Even that older, nice lady believed I could. Icarus, you got this.* He spots a Hispanic woman leaned on the wall looking blank at her phone. *Ok, let's try her. She's cute. Oh, wait, she's got her headphones on. I don't see her talking, probably listening to music, guess I could ask her which song sh—no, no, anyone listening to music isn't trying to breakdown every lyric, artist, genre of it.* He's getting closer to her. *Look, look, look, it's no biggie, ok? Just introduce yourself, it won't be bad.* "Excuse me." Icarus softly said. She doesn't hear him, still facing down on her phone. Then he cautiously waved up his hand nearby. Her head finally checked up; she didn't remove her earbuds. "Can you…" he hesitantly began, confused if she can hear him. "Wait, can you—?"

"No." she replied, then went on her phone.

"No? I don't—wait, no what?"

"I said no!" she firmly repeats, as she stared down.

Icarus just leaves, eating more of his fries. *She could've just taken out one earbud at least.* He looked around to see if anyone witnessed that, nobody did to his relief. *I hope I didn't creep her out. Maybe she did hear me and got annoyed that I didn't speak up. Oh well, onto the next.* As he walks, there's a woman browsing alone crossing his path. Icarus doesn't really care but notices her staring at him looking skeptical. The moment he glimpsed over at her, she delved her whole head down, her blonde, straight hair hangs down. *Is she seriously doing that to hide from me?* Icarus watched her instantly return to normal after she passed. *She stared at me first. I hadn't even watched her long when I caught her.* Icarus fixated; he tries to shrug it off as he explores the upper floor. *I know I haven't approached her before, she's not that attractive. Acting all weird as if I was gonna shoot my shot. She just universally shot me down for no apparent reason, I wasn't trying to even do anything. No matter, you didn't want her anyways so...* As he heads down the escalator, an Asian woman is by the vending machine. He casually comes over to her.

"Excuse me." He said, she acknowledged him. "I was just passing by, if you don't mind me asking what ethnicity you are."

"I don't understand."

"I meant like where are you from, you seem of Asian descent."

She appeared puzzled. "How's that even relevant?"

"I mean, it's not irrelevant." He nonchalantly said. "We weren't discussing anything different before so it's not like I suddenly went off on a tangent."

"Korean." She bluntly answers. "Why?"

Icarus was starting to realize this casual talk isn't progressing things. It's best to just be more direct. "You just caught my attention really." Icarus points at the escalator all the way he got off. "See, I saw you from over there and thought you looked pretty cute."

She skeptically checked where he pointed. "From down there, huh?! Ok…" she nods her head and moves away.

"Oh no, I wasn't following you." He said while following her. Then he stopped himself, then leans near the vending machine, checking around for any women. That section starts to get crowded with people.

While looking around, his mind begins to trail off. *Do people think I'm watching them? I usually mind my own business until I introduce myself. And even then, I'm not in suspicion of a person near me. Like that lady from before, that was a huge overreaction.* He begins to sense everyone's presence moving close. Turning his head scanning the area as the flow of adults cruise straight, some were turning their face the other direction. A guy glimpsed at Icarus and looked down at his phone. *Geez, man.* He thought, his head starts to weigh down. The area is compressed with more incoming shoppers. Music blasts aloud from his left causing him to peek. It was from a teenage girl's enormous headphones. She detects him then tilts her head forward at her phone while moving faster pass him.

Icarus grunts to himself and he moves around instead. *I don't think I look sketchy or anything like that, do I? Well then again, you are at the mall alone by yourself. You are here a lot, doesn't help that you just stood in a corner neither.* A white woman just cut around the corner, Icarus observed her presence in front of him. She moved with her head held high, her bare shoulders swung back, back straight with breasts bouncing. Her face seemed extremely tranquil as well, she moved powerfully like she claimed this territory. Icarus politely waved to her while showing a grin. The woman slows down then faced him to a complete halt.

"Hi, I—" Her scowl cuts him off. He feels swelled up but already has her attention and doesn't want to waste her time. The look she shoots implied *WHATEVER YOU WANT, THIS BETTER BE GOOD!* Icarus then smiles. "We just made eye-contact, I just thought I'd say hi." She immediately sped away without a word. This momentarily boggles him as if it seemed surreal. Icarus turned around, unable to detect her, she just vanished. *She wouldn't have liked you anyway. YOU'RE GONNA DIE A VIRGIN.* Icarus thought as he faces back forward to a few incoming people. *Shit! Did they see that? Her just dash away like that? I hope they don't assume I said something or stare at me, judging me. Or worse, not look at me at all. Probably because they think I'm off somehow or monitoring them by now.* Two girls passing closer stretch their necks the other way. A man blankly walked then looks at his phone, Icarus catches a glimpse of that. *Great, even he gets uncomfortable. My sight wasn't anywhere directed at him. Watch him act normal once I pass by. Actually, you know what, let's test this.*

"Excuse me, sir?"

"Yes?" the guy replied.

Icarus didn't expect him to be polite. "Sorry. Do you know what time it is?"

He checks his phone again. "Five-fifty." Then he left.

Icarus felt reassured afterwards. *Nice, ok. Guess it wasn't exactly because of me. Or maybe, maybe—wait, why didn't he know this prior to me asking? The guy was already on his phone, I saw him. He was most likely faking it. Who doesn't know the time right off the bat when checking your phone? So, whenever I'm in sight, does that signal for men and women to now delve down in fucking unison? God, am—hey, stop, stop!* Icarus sat down for a minute to clear his thoughts. *You're at the mall for a reason. Ok, do not torture yourself.* He remained down for a few minutes calming himself with taking a breather.

A black lady is spotted going up the escalator. Icarus wasn't entirely well yet but refused to let her disappear. He charged and sprinted up the escalator, she's seen going into Purity. Once he's inside, there are women exploring around. She's seen in the back looking at exfoliator products. Her braided hair was the highlight of her. As he gets the urge, the thought of that Korean woman and the last woman struck his head. *Ok, you'll just compliment her hair. Simple as that. If she doesn't seem all that engaged, I'll just leave her be.*

"Hi." He cautiously begun, she faced him. "Sorry to bother you, I really like your braids. They l-look nice."

She squints her eyes. "Yeah, Thanks." There was a brief silence so he started to leave. "Hey, hey!" she called him back. "You don't remember me?"

"Sorry?"

"You met me last month, at this very mall, again in this store." She stated. "You told me you liked my style."

His chest throbs by his pounding heartbeat. "*Oh, ok.*"

"Mm-hmm. Just to be clear, you should be aware of how you come off to women, ok?"

"I didn't— did I offend you?"

"No, you didn't. But if you sprinkle your compliments around to the wrong one, I promise you you'll get reported by mall security. It might not be me but best believe it'll be by someone else, understand?" she discreetly said, Icarus nods. "Good, you have a nice day."

Dumbfounded Icarus McGrew leaves the store, and he

tries remembering meeting her. *When, when had I met her? Last month, really? Does she think I'm just going around trying to pick up females here?* Icarus recalls the Korean girl to mind then the Hispanic one. *She probably saw me go to them too. What if other people see me around knowing my intent from the get-go? At least she was nice kinda, even if it was a warning. How do you forget someone like that? I bet you won't forget her now. YOU'RE GONNA DIE A VIRGIN!*

Icarus went down the escalator with his thoughts circulating until he recognized a woman. It was the mother who screamed at him. Her head tilts down as she'd foreseen him from ahead. His muscles started growing tense, he didn't want to make her feel more discomfort by his presence. Turning his head to his left pretending to be window shopping to avoid staring. There was a minor pain from holding that position, his tightened vision held steady, his eyes were strained just itching to resume back to normal. Icarus then relinquished himself, the two locked eyes which made her instantly nosedive down at her phone. That sends an enormous plummeting feeling in his chest causing for him to haul himself to the seats.

Drooping in the seat, his mind focused on nothing but the awful interactions he's endured. A series of women's uncomfortable reactions echoing inside his head were beginning to consume him, especially the single mother. *After the way we chatted up in person and messaged each other just for you to wind up a creep in her eyes. Didn't even sleep together, didn't get a kiss, YOU'RE GONNA DIE A VIRGIN!*

Icarus remained slouched in his seat; his energy oppressed by a pound of self-doubt. He stared off into oblivion until his sight caught something peculiar. In a crowd of people crossing his direction, there was a woman walking with her entire body completely bent down. Icarus was bewildered at the sight of this woman's whole upper body sunken forward. While watching her, he noticed an owl tattoo on her left arm.

I don't believe—are you serious? Icarus thought while watching her pass. He continues to stare until she finally resurrects herself back up. It was confirmed as the same Indian woman he approached last time. *She was honestly that afraid to be seen by me. All I did was mentioned her tattoo, I didn't even follow you afterwards. Wouldn't even have recognized you until you did all that just because of me.* "Fuck you." His poor voice lowly croaked. *You should just head home.* After a few more minutes of remaining there, he got up to leave.

Icarus kept analyzing every angle of his interaction with that woman, who didn't involve her responding at all. He recalled her just nodding. *She seemed calm when I talked with her. Oh, who're you kidding, it wasn't a two-way street, she was probably just praying for you to leave her alone. Probably saw me around earlier and thinks I'm lurking for girls now. She was so on edge that she almost tipped over. Even that mother…* his thoughts amplified. *She was so agitated, wondering if you'd harass her, that she had to act like she's on her phone. YOU'RE GONNA DIE A VIRGIN!* His thinking expanded to where he hadn't noticed his surroundings, pushing forward as the

Korean lady from before had cut into the crowd. As she walked, she turned around detecting Icarus. She kept peeking behind at him appearing anxious. The woman randomly halts in the middle of the collection of people. He's perplexed at her statue-like form, she still peeped back.

Is she scared I'm following her or something? I'm going my own way. She's just standing there. Should I say something? He had gotten closer. *Just forget it.* Icarus just kept walking, he had noticed a short, redhead, white woman next to him.

"Excuse me." He said, she looked. "You're looking nice today." He managed to choke out, hoping others couldn't overhear him.

"Thanks." She groans. This has Icarus' eyes veer around the mass of adults around. "Can you quit following me!"

"Huh?" Icarus blurted, puzzled. A guy in front checks over at them. She firmly repeats herself. His muscles began to stiffen then progressively lingered behind her. The woman checks over her shoulder at him shooting a hard, stony look. A ginormous weight stamped on his chest.

I wasn't following you to begin with. God, I hope nobody else saw that. A swarm of incoming shoppers had Icarus become more self-conscious. His vision went narrow in attempts to deviate himself from causing discomfort. In general, Icarus could notice everything in sight from all angles at ease. Now the more people passed, the more he felt gravitated to turn but instead choose to look the other way. Eyeballs trembled, it hurt like a twisted rooted irritation, resembling an agitation strain, stretched close to catching glances. His neck is an adjusted wooden shaft, hoping stranger's heads won't dip down. Pretending his vision couldn't observe the widespread of everyone in sight wasn't neutral, resisting to give into temptation, he's just aligned aimlessly.

This isn't you; this isn't you one bit. Icarus faced a brief detachment. *Just relax, no one's concerned about you.* His mind rapidly recollects the Indian woman bent over, the mother pretending to check her phone, the Korean lady holding back. Females consistently reacting as such has Icarus feel placed into a particular void desolate of acceptance. Those passing thoughts begin to engulf his spirit. Now flooded with wandering thoughts as to what purpose is being served coming here. Recollections of women concealing their faces echoes more. *YOU'RE GONNA DIE A VIRGIN!* His body started to lack walking momentum; he feels drained as his sight began to branch off slightly. A black girl appears in front of him, her head took a sharp turn at the ground. *Of fucking course she'd think I'm stealing glances. I wonder how many people know my routine circling the mall and stores for women by now. This whole time.* All this analyzing stirred his emotions with more unsettling doubt.

Icarus escaped the mall, he's outside his parked car. He stood there motionless with the cool breeze surf his face, bringing some relief. He contemplates whether to just go back inside and try to gain at least one number. The sight of that woman, who scowled at him earlier, showed her leaving the exit. Icarus watched as another man waved her to stop. All traces of anger vanished when talking to him. It baffled Icarus as to why. Her face had turned brighter, shaking this stranger's hand. Icarus stood locked again inside that desolate realm, watching that her entire demeanor had changed, instilled with the harsh reality of never having this chance. Her not at all paralyzed with unpleasant, sketchy thoughts about him or him not eroding a questionable aura made Icarus forgo even more isolation. Both adults exchange numbers, with her initiating. Then they separate.

Alas, his head dropped in surrender. *YOU'RE GONNA DIE A VIRGIN!* Icarus went in his car and drove off.

Richez Shrive 8:10 P.M.

The bar isn't packed tonight, Jovanny is mostly checking his phone searching for the cheapest repair mechanic. Seething still from yesterday, he pours himself a drink. Icarus McGrew comes up to the counter, Jovanny automatically served him a strawberry daiquiri. The two were quiet until Icarus asked how he's been. Jovanny told him about the whole Tonya situation, including their past. Icarus unfolded about his struggles at the mall today and the woman he tried to give another chance to.

"I'm telling you, I haven't felt this self-conscious for a long time." Icarus said. "I've been turned down before but addressing this now makes me feel almost skeevy."

This confession had Jovanny groan that he warned Icarus about how females aren't sympathetic, are led solely through emotions and that he shouldn't have been attached to anyone of them. "At least you ain't argue with that crazy chick, I'll give you that. Believe me, there's a surplus of sluts outside these streets, son."

"Ok, sure but what point did it make, still felt horrible afterwards. I only didn't get mad because I wasn't trying to creep her out more and it didn't even matter."

"You shouldn't even value a bitch's opinion since they fickle as shit. Second, you should give yourself permission to be creepy." Jovanny states while Icarus seems confused. "Like, you already risking approaching 'em, not doing weird shit, so just refuse to give a shit. I know you don't be remembering the ones who curved you respectfully…" Icarus instantly thinks of the black woman at Purity. "… so ain't shit to gain from remembering no shitty ones."

Icarus shrugs. "I guess. I just hate to make people around me uncomfortable, you know. Just being *myself, I guess*." He said weakly. "I just treat people equally, just wish they'd treat me the same."

"See, that's your problem. You don't treat the opposite sex like we're alike." Jovanny mocked. "Women fall for men that're better than them, so you might as well not treat 'em as equals. They either wanna be above you to have her validation or beneath you. It's all a power play and you, my friend, have dropped yourself to a position of weakness."

Jovanny served him another drink with a sense of concern. Icarus remained quiet, fixating over how little progress he's made in his head.

†

Joy Pluss rehashes today's objective with her client. Grant smokes a cigarette as he listened. They're both arriving at his old high school in downtown Holksdale. As an alumni, he is donating money to the theatre program. The school named it after him once he became famous. The teens attending summer school will witness this charitable event. The company Take-Late is delivering musical instruments to the school. She insists that he takes pictures with any fans of his.

Knowing that Grant loathes donating his money to any organization makes it just the more maddening. Grant argues about how lower income organizations or communities just wait to be saved. They don't effectively form as a collective to build their society. Joy suggests that this is a good contribution that can help his career. Informing him that the funding for constructing the bridge is going well. Donating to this school really infuriates him. Grant hated his high school experience.

"And don't forget where you came from." Joy said. "You are still human regardless of your success. You gotta watch how you treat others, Grant."

Joy reminds him of the time he had paid for an airline ticket to fly this exotic woman out to meet him. She had been a huge fan of his. Grant had flown her from Massachusetts to Los Angeles. She had suggested that he treats her out somewhere expensive, but Grant refused. But instead led her to his house. Gave her leftover Italian food. Things were going well until she refused to be intimate with him. Things were spiraling too fast from her logic. Grant coldly kicked her out. Rage unleashed from this scorned woman. Especially, with him refusing to buy her a plane ticket back home. She ranted about how he thinks he is better than her and that he's entitled as well. Grant still kicked her out.

Grant snorted. "Her asking of me to devalue myself to act as if we're both equals is dehumanizing in itself. Take-Late has the best return policies, as do I." Proudly stating that he refuses to let lesser individuals waste his time.

"That backwards kind of logic got that woman making an allegation towards you."

Grant shook his head. Belittling the actress, Tatum Maxwell, about how shy she was when they met. Tatum was just a background actress. She would have been complacent because she is scared of rejection. Mocking her fear of failing an audition. Until he encouraged her to follow him in order to be a well-known actress. "I provided a bountiful supply of wisdom, and look what I get. People just perceive kindness as weakness."

"I don't." Joy protests. Once they get out the car, she opens the trunk. She presents this portrait that was sent to Grant from a fan. It is a painting of Holksdale from a bird's-eye view. The clouds in the foreground of the portrait are slowly gliding. The cars and pedestrians *(that appears as dots)* are individually moving haphazardly. It is on a repeated loop.

An emotionless look painted Grant's face. As they observed it, Joy complements the portrait. She insists that he handles it with extreme caution. Grant shrugs it off then flung it in the car.

As they're in front of the school, the Take-Late truck is outside. It contains many instruments (*flutes, drums, microphones, violins, trumpets, guitars, saxophones and pianos*). Joy hears a sound. A soft, relaxing musical ambience. The dreamlike sound came from the homeless lady playing her harp on the sidewalk. This warm look swept across Joy's face as she admired the woman. This prompt Joy to drop five dollars in her hat. The lady gave an appreciative nod. Joy encourages Grant to give some money, but he simply walked off. The lady still wishes him a blessed day.

The newest principal, Mr. Fury, rushes outside. He gladly shook Grant's hand, introducing himself. Mr. Fury expressed how much the faculty and the theatre department appreciates this blessing. Grant begrudgingly smiled. Joy added how it was Grant's idea. Mr. Fury escorts them inside to the gymnasium. Joy tells Grant that she set up for him to give a speech to the kids doing summer school. This overwhelming familiarity wave consumes Grant as he roams down the hallways. The passing employees stared at him in shock.

Once inside the gym, here is a plethora of teenagers circling around. Loud chatter amplifies the longer they stayed. Mr. Fury excuses himself to set things up on stage. Joy accompanies him and insists that Grant waits back. His eyes scavenged around at students. Many of them stare in disgust, playfully announced his name, or left the gym. However, his vision latched with one young man. He was a sixteen-year-old sophomore. This kid had an angered look directed at Grant. In response, Grant had a small, mocking smile. This kid approaches him.

"You know you're not welcome here, right?"

"Well, your principle says otherwise. I'm here to donate."

"But nobody wants you here still." The kid said. Including his sister feeling uncomfortable with Grant's appearance due to this allegation. The boy points out his sister's blatant discomfort from across the gym.

This left Grant perplexed. His sister was a boy wearing lip-gloss, earrings, a blonde wig, and long eye lashes. The boy reveals how celebrities like him sickens his sister. Grant bluntly says that is a boy.

"That's my sister." The boy firmly declared. "She's transgender."

"He's a boy wanting to become a girl."

"No, she's my sister. And as a progressive, born-again Christian, she doesn't even like those kinds of labels."

Grant condescendingly nods. "Right, right. Does that rebirth include him being a born-again female too?!"

The boy stares at Grant speechless. Trying to disguise his anger but can feel his face exposing it. The student senses Grant's inner satisfaction from this. The boy's tone tries remaining stern as he tells how his sister feels uncomfortable even talking to Grant.

"You mean him?"

"Her. She's transgender now."

Grant shook his head. "He's transgender now. He is now a 'she'. Meaning prior to now, she was a 'he' back then."

"So, he's a woman now!" the boy hissed.

"You said it best. He is a woman now. And I don't fetishize over men."

"She's no man."

"Look, you don't have to worry about me pursuing after your brother."

"MY SISTER!"

"You should just accept who he really is if you're that concerned for her safety."

Witnessing this kid visibly peeved had Grant appeared stoic. The boy's fists were bawled, and his fiery exhales grew. He could tell this kid would have impulsively fought him. Knowing the world, he would not want to get demonized for fighting a minor. Instead, Grant decides to taunt one last time, then deviate himself elsewhere.

"Let me guess," Grant began, observing the boy's frustrated body language. "Your sibling's gay as well?"

"Not that that's any of your business but no." The boy said, irritably. His sister had a girlfriend and is now dating boys instead.

Grant skeptically nodded his head. "Huh. I guess the scissoring just couldn't cut it. *Buh-bye now.*"

He left the kid seething still. Then searched the halls for the school theater dedicated to him. A freshman directs him to the theatre while admiring being in the presence of a celebrity. As they approached the door, Grant stopped. His eyes stared at the sign: Theatre.

The sign used to read: Grant Critchfield Theatre. The freshman boy was confused until he realized the abrupt halt. Praying there would be no follow-up questions. Grant was displeased to learn that parents were complaining about it being attached to an actor now facing an allegation. The theatre department finally removed it.

A sunken, shrill feeling had spiraled through him instantly. The kid was staring at him with a look of anxiousness. However, this vague expression crossed his face. Grant reassured the student that he was fine. His phone is ringing; Joy was calling. This meant either she was wondering where Grant went, or it was time to get on stage.

Once back in the gymnasium, everyone was sitting on the benches. Joy gestures for Grant to come up on stage. Before he complains about the theatre, Joy cuts him off abruptly. She urges for him to say nice things about his experience here. To say how being an alumni made him want to donate. To answer any questions. And to motivate the students with an inspiring speech about achieving your goals.

Principal Fury urges for the students to silent down. Joy encourages her client to act humble. Mr. Fury proudly introduces Grant Critchfield. All that cycled through Grant's mind was the removal of his name. As if it was a disgrace. This dragging anger lengthened even more at the thought of blessing these ungrateful students. That one boy and his sister/brother reminding him that he is not welcome back here. This stuffed anger is on the verge of breaking loose as he stares back at these students. Nothing he preaches will have any impact on them. They have already chosen what they believe. All anyone is fixated on is what Grant is providing instead. Everything rushed through his head as he stood on stage.

His agent sensed that something was amiss. She knew her client all too well. Grant excused himself then left the stage. Everyone watched as he exiles the gym. Joy rushes to announce that her client will be right back. Then she chases after him. After spotting him down the hallway leaving, Joy yelled out for Grant.

Grant was talking to the trucker parked outside. Then he returned to the car. Joy went to the window. Grant protested donating these instruments after this newfound knowledge about the theatre. Joy apologizes for his disappointment but urges for him to come back. Grant told the trucker to return everything. This infuriated Joy.

"What're we supposed to tell the faculty now?" Joy barked at him. "These students?"

"That I don't want to overstay my welcome! Now get in!"

"Goddamn you, Grant!" Joy blurts, then hears the principal calling for them from the entrance. Grant frantically waves his hand for her to come in.

"IT'S TIME TO ABANDON SHIP! LET'S MOVE!" Grant yells. Joy hopped inside still aggravated at him. Then they sped away.

† *York Avenue 11:23 P.M.*

Tonight, was the night Larissa's been looking forward too, the opportunity to finally see the miracle firsthand while being escorted by Chase. Essie is in her room struggling to fall asleep. Larissa receives a text that he's outside, reading this has her excited. She quietly maneuvers through the apartment then heads outside. Chase is seen waiting for her on the steps. Larissa dashes at him giving a huge hug, inhaling more of his enticing apple cologne. Then they took the nearest bus to their destination.

They eventually arrive closer, Larissa seemed a bit cautious being this far from home this time of night. However, Chase grabs her hand, reassuring her that she's secured and to follow his path. She hears several voices up ahead, there's laughter too. Chase mentions it's only his friends gathered there too. Larissa shrugged it off, willingly open to meeting them. Her smile widened as they emerged closer to the edge of this. Looking down had shown the presence of other teenage boys and girls. There was a fire made to create light. He pulled Larissa's arm down with him, down this enormous crater which extended far. Maintaining her balance at the bottom of the pit, she observed the widespread of it all. The multitude of teens from either her grade are exploring, laughing and goofing around. He introduced Larissa to some of his teammates from track.

His Dominican friends Kevin, Jake was the first to talk

with them. Then Mike and Alex, two black sprinters. Lastly, Craig, a Caucasian, long distance runner. Larissa felt warm inside having Chase introduce her as his girlfriend. He tells them it's her first time being here.

"For real though?" Craig said. "Yo, that's wassup." His other friends looked embarrassed for him.

"Yea, well, it's crazy." She replied. "Like, we just got here and I ain't even find my name yet."

"We on the hell side." Chase clarified. "Guys, we gonna search where her spot at."

The two walk around the area. Larissa watches other teens orbiting together smelling of weed, the scent grows stronger. There's a group of girls taking photos and recording videos together around the fire, they're also drinking alcohol.

"Your friends seemed cool, even your boy Craig."

Chase snorts. "Don't mind him. Dude acts like he's black when we got other white kids on our track team that he hangs with too."

"Be nice. Probably just finding himself."

"I mean, he's cool and all but still…" he remarked. "So how you like it here so far?"

"I like it, ain't know people were gonna be here." she said as she looked at the names engraved into the dirt. "Y'know lightning produced all this, right? It's pretty lit."

"Yea, yea. I bet we passed your mom's name back from where we left off."

Larissa shook her head. "Oh, I see you got jokes, huh?"

They've both been scanning the ground by alphabetical order. There's remnants of colorful silly strings circulated around; she automatically recalled how Elijah must've been here earlier. The endless strands of curiosity had lead for them to arrive at her name: *Larissa Sheppard.*

This attendance has Larissa stare at it in awe. Seeing it on the website on her phone seemed miniscule compared to this moment. Larissa kneels to it, she runs her fingertips through the rough exterior, this seemed way too surreal.

"Now imagine my mom being right with me." She said.

"You really want for her to wind up with you? Like, even while enjoying this, you still think of her."

"The thing is," Larissa began. "It makes me feel hopeful that I can make this happen, almost self-assured. Even when people tell me this whole phenomenon ain't real, I still got enough faith to just keep it pushin', y'know? It's still goals."

Chase sees how much this meant to her and remembered how far she's willing to take this. A random ambush of silly string struck Larissa's face, she jolts back wiping her face. While completely blindsided, childish laughter is heard. Instantly knowing this is Elijah Atwood.

"I got you." Elijah laughed. "Didn't expec—" Larissa charged at him, tackling Elijah for the spray. Elijah light-heartedly withholds it but she's relentless. Chase tries to intervene but refrained himself since she's wrestling him for it. Elijah's continuously smiles it off until a deepened, razor-sharp bite sinks into his forearm. Larissa's wrath wouldn't end, then he releases the silly string can.

Chase immediately grabs the can, then helped Larissa get up. Her fingertips slowly massaged her right eye, it was irritated. Elijah finally got up, checking the marks on him.

"Hey, bro, you play too much." Chase said.

Elijah chuckled. "My bad. I was just playing." He checks for Larissa, she's still attentive to her stung eye. "Larissa, are you okay?" he asked sounding worried. "I didn't mean—"

"JUST GO SOMEWHERE, ELIJAH!" Larissa yelled. "Don't nobody want your apology, you mad childish!" she turned her back to him. Elijah tapped her shoulder, he extends his arms out for a hug once she turned. *"NO!"* she repeats, then faced Chase.

Elijah remained paralyzed in that spot, pouting, it became evident to Chase. Staring now at Larissa's uncooperative back. Chase shook his head, Elijah took the hint and finally disappears.

"It's all good, he's gone now."

"Good." She groaned, still applying pressure to her eye.

"C'mon." Chase pulled her towards a large rock. Larissa sits there and leaned her head back. He pulls his small unopened water bottle from his pocket. "I'm about to wash your eye out, alright? Try not to flinch."

The cold sensation slowly stung at first. Her right eyelid closed shut but eventually opened back up. After a few more drops, the irritation in her eye began to dissolve. Chase held her hair up to prevent getting wet. As he tends to her, Larissa boldly complains all about Elijah Atwood. Ranging from him constantly messaging her, to begging for them hangout alone, or just bombarding her presence whenever he catches her walking. Chase just listened the entire time and nodded. He checked her eye, it was a little red but wasn't agitating her anymore. Larissa rubbed it still.

"Good looks." She said gratefully.

"No problem. And Elijah sound like he's into you. He's putting you up on that pedestal." He sees her nod in frustration. "But seriously, I don't want you to fall into that same trap. You get me?"

Larissa's confused. "You accusing me of cheating?"

"Nah, I mean with your mom." Chase explains. "Like, I ain't trying to put down this miracle for you, I mean look at where we're at, I just think you've gone all out for her. And from what it sounds like, she don't even appreciate it."

"Again, like I said, good looks." She replied politely.

They returned back to Chase's friends, they had a laugh about Elijah's foolish mistake. Larissa found his friends pretty entertaining. Chase noticed how all his friends kept cracking jokes more so than usual, making her laugh a lot, but maintained himself. He watched Larissa enjoy herself as she flourished in this energy.

"Shit!" Craig announced. "Bro, you see that shit!"

Upcoming from the distance was a group of guys their age who they all recognized as their rival track team from the high school in uptown Holksdale. Seven sophomore boys dived where everyone else is. Chase led his friends to march in their direction, Larissa hesitantly follows hoping for it to not escalate. The seven boys consisted of four white guys and three black guys, they all storm forth. All boys halt at the lightning strike crack separating heaven from hell. Other teens were watching their standoff that became the center of this place. Both sides stared with intensity.

The Caucasian boy from uptown, Jacob, had smirked at them. "I didn't expect to see any of you here. We just came to check on some names up-close engraved for heaven. Plus, I heard kids come out at night sneaking to see this thing. What about you guys?"

"What about it?" Chase asks skeptically.

"Well, I searched up your names on that site advertising this." He replied, shrugging his shoulders. "Kinda fed into my curiosity and saw that some of your teammates, including yourselves, are too far gone to even make it into heaven." His friends laughed. "So why the fuck are you even here?"

Most of these kids from uptown Holksdale who were entitled into heaven had become emboldened to act out without a thought of any backlash. This miracle has been closed off from entering due to being vandalized with graffiti, hosting feud between believers versus nonbelievers and the constant loitering. The miracle located uptown is always available for entry to residents to view their placement without any blasphemous tension. Some of the vandalism had come from the kids uptown, doing that just for fun, contributing to it eventually being restricted.

"Your town kept fucking with ours, that's why we're here." Chase said. "And I'm not about to go around in circles with you about this."

"Good, keep that same energy for when you lose against us at our next track meet."

"Say what?"

"*God,* you really can't keep up." Jacob mocks. "Can't blame us, we're the good ones heading to heaven."

"Y'all think you're better than us—" Craig began.

"We are." Jacob's black friend, Louis said. "That's why we're elevating in not just life but even in the afterlife."

Other kids are recording these boys bickering at each other, some are instigating to have a fight erupt.

"And what the fucks up with you, Craig?" Louis called out. "You talking different like you've grown up in the hood. I know you been watching way too many black sitcoms, bro, 'cause this ain't you." They all laughed, Craig gets mute. "What next, you watch a film of some dude who's mentally fucking ill now on the come up gonna make you put all your eggs in that one basket case too."

"Jacob, I'll tell you like this." Chase threatened. "Y'all keep running y'all mouths and we're gonna fight. Nobody gives a shit about this 'cause it ain't real, so keep talking that shit and I'll run my foot up your ass."

Jacob and his friends huddled together like troops preparing to rush. Then outpours a hurl of insults amongst them. Kids watching begun an uproar of cheering, causing each side to refrain from backing down. Chase's friends keep supporting him while Jacob's does the same. Larissa feels the tension buildup but isn't nervous, she absorbed the booming volume of her boyfriend's tone, she knows he's in control. Her attention is completely invested in where this'll escalate into. The unknown mushrooming thought of how he'll handle those boys boiled within her engaging heat.

"Now, y'all are at a crossroads right now." Louis warned. "Whether it be with your morality at stake here or with your boy Craig who stay thinking he black. Y'all don't wanna catch this fade."

"YO, THEN PULL UP!" Mike provoked, the rest of his followers repeated. *"PULL UP, PULL UP!"*

"CROSS THE STREAK RIGHT NOW," Jacob yelled as he stomped close to the strip. *"LET'S GO THEN!"*

Louis chimed in. *"WHAT, Y'ALL THINK WE SWEET? DON'T THINK JUST 'CAUSE WE HEADING TO HEAVEN DON'T MEAN WE WON'T GET UNHOLY IN THIS BITCH!"*

"Y'ALL NOT ABOUT THAT LIFE, FUCK OUTTA HERE!" Chase snaps. *"YOU'D CROSSOVER THEN!"*

Louis faced Jacob. *"BRO, YOU STILL ARGUING WITH THESE SATANIC HOE-ASS NIGGAS. THEY AIN'T SHIT!"*

"Guys, guys." Craig gently intrudes. "How's about we just let this shit slide, huh? Let's not escalate—"

"MAN, SHUT THE HELL UP, CRAIG!" Jacob screamed.

Chase snaps at him. "Craig, who's side are you on?"

"Bro, I don't wanna get flamed. I'm trying to crossover, bro." Craig cried.

The commotion stirring was fueling more, their ongoing hollering dominated the entirety of this area. Both sides are about to lunge forward. The ferocity of their screams ceased at the roaring noise of a police siren from a mile away. The boys froze, other kids dashed off leaving behind their empty beer bottles. All kids scattered, most dug their nails into the dirt, tearing at the earth trying to climb out of there. Chase yanks Larissa's wrist urging her to haul ass. He and his friends agreed to disperse separately. Larissa's chest drums harder as the siren strengthens, consistently checking over both shoulders overhearing teens warning others. Some kids struggle to climb out of this mess. The two dart into the other direction, Larissa's breathing amplifies to where Chase feels it strike his neck. Then her heavy breathing evolves into a joyous smile that unbeknownst to her soon turns into laughter.

"What?" Chase exhales. "What's up?"

Larissa came to a stop. She's filled with such a thrill running through herself. Her eyes widen, merry smile refuses to settle and her presence appears utterly fearless.

"It's a rush, I get it." Chase encouraged. "That's right, I see you. Feels good don't it?"

Larissa's only response is her extreme exhales while focused on him. Then she targeted Chase, locks herself onto his face and seizes his lips. She passionately kisses him, not wanting this powerful wave to settle. He wrapped his arms around her waist.

She finally released his face, still speechless. Then by an unspoken agreement, she ran off, implying to race him. Chase accepts her challenge and laughed trying to keep up.

† Chapter 17: And I wish to make peace.

Tensions amongst both genders have increased all around Holksdale. Many men have recently faced legal troubles due to accusations made from women. More celebrities have been exposed by the media and are shamed by the public who only know thé bare minimum. People have mercilessly slandered the accused to where males grow extremely weary on how they interact with females. Anxiety festers within the workplaces throughout Holksdale since most male professionals don't want to be accused of any forms of harassment by female co-workers. Some men are refusing to partner solo with them as well, especially located uptown. These factors have instilled a huge gender divide.

Officer Lambeth and officer Colthirst are doing their daily patrol around the city. They recently got called into settle a domestic dispute located downtown. It was reported that the woman requested police to remove her partner from the apartment. When they arrived, they were immediately buzzed into the building. The two are already prepared depending on how dangerous the male assailant is. The couple are located on the fourth floor, both officers went upstairs. Once on the floor, they cautiously proceed to the right door. They're eavesdropping only to detect furious arguing from behind the door but no trace of any aggressive physicality. The woman is screaming aloud, the man's voice tore through the walls. Officer Colthirst ponders on if there are any weapons this man owns, or an exact estimate of how many adults are inside. Officer Lambeth knocked on the door, he announced they're the police department. The man went silent but the woman kept yelling at him still.

"Hello?" the man politely spoke as the door crept open.

"Hello, sir." Officer Lambeth greets, then glanced at both his hands. "We got a call from a lady inside reporting arguing. Everything ok?"

"Yea, we good here." he instantly replied. "What can I do for you, officer? Because nothing bad—"

"Nah, nah!" the woman interrupted. "Officer, please haul this nigga up out my place!"

"Your place?! This my crib. I don't stay with you, you live with me, alright? I got my own lease, bitch!" he yelled, blocking her path.

"Sir, she tipped us off." Officer Colthirst affirmed. "We can't see her with you in the way and we could hear y'all two arguing. We need to check to see if she's all good."

The man went stiff, unable to formulate a proper excuse to keep them outside.

Officer Lambeth observed his entire stance. "Listen to us, sir. We can't view her right now, we're concerned that she's injured. It's clear there was a verbal confrontation and we need to check on her welfare if you don't mind."

The guy steps aside. Both of them cautiously walked inside. Inside the residence was bombarded with items. A tower of toilet papers positioned by the wall was built up to hit the ceiling. There's a flash of red illuminating its entirety through the living room by an enormous lava lamp bigger than any of them. There's a gigantic glass piggybank jar half-empty with a variety of coins that's costing them half of the living room. There are many other items sprinkled everywhere. Neither officers detect anything bizarre, nor any signs linked to physical abuse. They're concentration gets ruptured from the couple arguing again.

"That's right, look around, officers." the guy said. "She a goddamn hoarder. Had me purchase all this stupid shit!"

"You told me to put it on your card!" She responds. "So now you wanna act brand new?!" she turned to the officers. "He always flip-flops and shit, he don't know what he talkin' about. Like, he always be on about me being into thugs or cheating with them, then this nigga stay trying to act hard. You not about that life, he practically begged me not to call y'all. You not about that life but you wanna punch holes in the wall."

Three holes were pointed out towards the window. Officer Lambeth emerged at them.

"I ain't do that!" he quickly defends. "She did that shit! Plus, you do be cheating on me with herds of niggas every chance you get, multiple fucking dudes. Just be out sharing ass like it ain't nothing. So yea, you not into no thug, you just partake in these gang-bangs."

"ENOUGH, ENOUGH!" Officer Colthirst screamed. Then forced himself closer, the two began arguing about finances. The guy's enraged by how he supports her and his trembled tone goes vocal implying she's not different from

his ex-girlfriends who used him for financial gain. It gets more heated between them.

She crossed her arms. "It's sad the amount of times you be thinking bitches just fight over what's in your inner wallet. Which ain't much."

"Not as sad as the amount of fools you let slide up your inner walls."

Officer Colthirst pries between them. "Well, her sexual proclivities aside, I'm gonna need for y'all two to separate."

"I'm glad y'all pulled up." she said. "I need my son safe, I be trying to create a safe space for him here."

"Now you tell me how the hell he'd have any free rein of this place with it cluttered in this clusterfuck of a mess, hoe?!"

"WAIT," Officer Colthirst announced. *"THERE'S CHILDREN INVOLVED HERE? HOW MANY PEOPLE LIVE INSIDE THIS RESIDENCE?"*

The man startled at his voice. He informs him that him, his girlfriend and their son lives here. Their son remained inside his room like they told him. Officer Lambeth checks up on his safety, the couple are told to each sit on both opposite ends of the couch. Lambeth cautiously opened the bedroom door to find a black ten-year-old boy curled on his bed watching a video with his headphones on. The boy sensed him and pulled them out his ears, Lambeth reassures him that everything is fine and he's only hear to speak with his parents. He tells him to just wait in here while they sort things out, the kid understood.

Returning back to the living room, Colthirst informs him that he checked for their identification. The tall black man's name is Deon Howard, he was a tall twenty-nine-years old with black wavy hair. His girlfriend, Crystal Newton, a light-skinned twenty-seven-year old with three slashed bruises on her right arm. Crystal stretched her arm for Lambeth to see, she also had small cuts around her knuckles. Both officers turn to Deon, observing him suspiciously.

"Nah, nah!" Deon squawked. "She did that shit to herself 'cause I caught her in a lie."

"Bullshit!" she yells. "What I gotta lie about?! Y'all see how he presses me on everything when I give him my all."

"She don't do shit around here."

"I wash and fold your laundry, wash up all them damn dishes, cook for—"

"Since when you cook?!" Deon overrode.

Officer Colthirst orders them to be silent. Before they proceed to more investigating, Lambeth tells them their son is most likely eavesdropping. They're going to question them individually. Lambeth escorts Crystal as she limps into their bedroom, Colthirst remained with Deon in the living room. In their room, she pulls out their foldable bed mattress from the wall. While descending out, a powerful glow emits from within, brightening the room. Crystal grabs rubbing alcohol off the dresser, Lambeth helps apply it to her wounds. Crystal tells how Deon was pressuring her to do more housework because she's unemployed and then became enraged at the thought of her cheating that he targeted the wall punching three holes. She describes it as if he got possessed with a demon in him. Then claimed Deon pulled out his pocketknife and cut her arm. She promises Lambeth that she's faithful to their family while attempting to conceal her tears. Crystal even showed nine missed calls and texts from him wondering about her whereabouts. While treating her wounds still on the bed, Lambeth studies her stiffened posture wearing a black metallic belt. She then adds that he kneed her in the leg, explaining her limping. As he scoots over closer, a tough object was felt within the pillow. Lambeth dug inside only to unfold a kitchen knife, his bewildered look shows he's waiting for an explanation. Crystal confides that she's been sleeping with it close for her and her son's safety out of paranoia that this would happen.

Lambeth patted her leg. "Don't worry, ma'am. We'll handle this. You and your son are safe." Crystal gives him a hug. As she's hugging him, her phone received a text behind her from a contact named Trey messaging *'Where you at?'* Lambeth dismissed it and tends to the wounds.

In the living room, Colthirst hovered over Deon, interrogating him. Deon claimed that Crystal got fed up about him suggesting she gets a job that she started an argument. He told his son to go to his room. Deon tried to be accommodating at first but she wouldn't stop verbally emasculating him. His insults caused her to furiously puncture the wall three times. Then demanded him to get out and threatened to call the cops, he admitted he wouldn't believe she'd do it until both officers actually arrived. Deon urges that she stormed out the living room then returned with her arm bleeding.

"Officer, I'm real understanding." Deon softly spoke. "I don't press her about her business, always pay for her and encourage her to get back to work. I even gave her an allowance. She just want me gone to get more money from me off child support, Crystal just wanna gain control."

"Well, from what it sounds like, she's never had it." Colthirst replied. "You just mentioned how you're so understanding. However, you been accusing her of cheating. Why would she need to contact the police then? Has there ever been a physical altercation?"

Deon sucked his teeth. "Man, ain't no—"

"You're gonna watch that tone." Colthirst urged. "I ain't your son. Sure as hell ain't your girlfriend neither because with her present I've seen how you get reckless with the mouth."

Crystal limped out with Officer Lambeth shadowing her. Her right arm is wrapped in cloth for now. Lambeth tells his partner he'll check on the kid. Inside the room, the boy lies on his bed staring at him. He then waved.

"Hey there." Lambeth softly greeted. "Can I ask you something, son?" the kid nods with a confused look. "Has your father ever frightened you or your mother before? Maybe did something that made her seem uncomfortable?"

"*Nuh-uh.*" The boy answered, uncertain.

"Son, what's your name?"

"Myles. I'm Myles."

"Alright, Myles. I'm officer Lambeth. My partner and I just want to make sure nothing bad goes on around here. I'm not targeting you, ok? I just need you to be completely honest about anything strange happening at home."

"I mean, there's this monster." Myles sheepishly admits, Lambeth looks concerned. "I could hear him but can't see him and it scares me every time. He stomps all around here. I hear him at night when I run to the fridge for leftovers mom cooked. I'll just run away back to bed. When dad comes home, that's when he always pops back up."

Lambeth surprisingly makes a connection, then patted Myles' shoulder. He asks Myles if he heard which parent had initiated today's argument from his room. Myles shrugged, saying he had his headphones on the whole time.

"I do everything for him, officer." Crystal explained.

"*Please*. When's the last time we fucked, huh?" Deon turns to Colthirst. "She ain't fucked me in a month but she pushing me to wife her up. I ain't marrying no cheater."

"I satisfy him every night. So what about my desires?"

Deon hissed: *"YOU DON'T EVEN SUCK DICK!"*

Colthirst quiets them down then his partner returned. Lambeth hovered over Deon with his arms crossed.

"Your son Myles told me something about a monster appearing whenever you come home at night. Care to explain that?"

"The fuck? I dunno what that boy be talking about."

"Also, Crystal told me you cut her arm earlier."

"That shit was self-inflicted." He choked out.

"He did it with the pocketknife in his pocket." Crystal cried. Everyone shared an uncomfortable silence afterwards. Colthirst commands for him to stand up.

Deon stood, appearing annoyed.

"Go ahead and turn around for me if you don't mind." Lambeth requests. Deon does exactly that. "We're just gonna pat you down for any weapons. Please hold your fingers tight together behind your back."

"Man, I swear to God…" Deon mumbled while barely grasping his fingertips.

"Swear to God, huh?" Colthirst said, yanking his wrist. "Get on your knees, get down!" Deon collapsed to his knees, making him agitated. "Now interlock them fingers like you're praying!" Deon listens, then Colthirst cuffed his wrists. "Good, you go ahead and pray to God then."

Officer Lambeth's fingers perused his entire body. His pants pockets were cleared but his shirt pocket wasn't. He whipped out the pocketknife from there.

"Is this yours?" Lambeth asked, dangling it.

Deon's bewildered stare didn't even merit a response. *"Yes."* He hesitantly confirmed. "Yes, that is but I have no idea how that got up on me."

Colthirst applied pressure to his shoulder, preventing him to raise up and escalate things. Neither officers look convinced nor was there a response.

"I swear, I usually keep that thing locked somewhere, I ain't cut her." Deon's body started agitating, then stretched his neck upward repeating louder. He started coming off as a threat and both officers bent down to keep him restrained. Lambeth gripped his cuffed wrists and Colthirst seizes his shoulders to get him pinned down. Deon's face plummets into the ground resulting in groans.

"STOP RESISTING! RELAX, RELAX." Colthirst urges.

His whole body calmed down. After two minutes of no aggression, they got off him. Lambeth told him to remain down then patted his back. A random noise came from the ceiling. The rush of scattered footsteps transfers to the wall, an unknown source shuffles around like cockroaches. Everyone ignored it, both cops checked on Crystal. They question her about any other physical abuse from the past. Deon is overheard by them, praying to himself. His voice grew louder, Lambeth worried about Myles overhearing him, so he went over to examine him. His upcoming footsteps alerted Deon; a tangled mess of nerves clenched at his stomach. The walls erupt into a stampede thundering to the ground, everyone's focus targeted Deon instead. The volume of his prayers loudened; Lambeth told him to quiet down. Crystal repeatedly announced that he shouldn't be here around Myles. The recent predicament he's in, being pinned beneath Lambeth's gaze and the powerless taunting web of scenarios scribbled inside him. Muscles in his face twitched. Deon's mouth twisted into a nerve-racking smile which then croaked out strangled laughter. They all cringed while witnessing the entirety of his body convulsing with blatant laughter.

A door crept open with Myles peeking at his father until Lambeth raced to block Myles view. He encouraged him to remain inside with the door closed, Colthirst charged at Deon before he gets up.

Colthirst leaned into his ear whispering. *"You need to calm your ass down, you're scaring your son."*

This realization had Deon try to stop but he couldn't resist. He whipped his head at his son peeking at him through the officer's legs, then buried his face into the floor. His forehead pressed flatly down until he hears the bedroom door shut. Deon releases a shaky exhaust. Colthirst relinquished him once Deon's body became numb. Both officers collaborate to the side.

"Look, we need to haul him outta here." Lambeth urges. The rumbling perused the walls again. "God, I'm getting tired of this nonstop movement."

"I'M NOT RESISTING, LOOK!" Deon announced.

Colthirst agreed then observed their suspect.

"Crystal," Deon pleads. "Crystal, don't let 'em do me like this, please." Crystal just ignored him as he groveled.

Both officers walk over to him instructing that he needs to come with them.

"Wait, wait." Deon cries out. "Let me tell Myles bye right quick. Allow me to say goodbye to my kid."

A brief silence was shared between officer Lambeth and Colthirst as they contemplate his request. They hesitantly agree. Deon politely requests for them to remove his cuffs so his son doesn't see him like this. They lifted him up trying to help him get steady. Officer Lambeth removes his handcuffs. Colthirst instructs him that he's got exactly five minutes to go in his room and hug him goodbye. Deon went and shuts the door. Crystal limps over but Lambeth halts her, insisting it's better for them to be alone. She begrudgingly complied. After five minutes passed, Lambeth approached Myles door.

"Deon, it's time." He said, there was no response.

"Let's go, Deon." Colthirst added. "You don't wanna make a scene."

There was still silence, even from within the walls. Lambeth tried the knob, the door was locked. He banged on it. Crystal watched looking perplexed. They repeated themselves, hoping for a response. Colthirst kicked the door with brutal force, it flung open revealing they were gone. Both rushed inside, they were shocked. Lambeth spotted the opened window above the AC. His head overstretched out catching him maneuver through the fire escape with his son being fastened onto his back.

"DAMN!" Lambeth blurts as he bolted pass Crystal, she immediately chased after him. Colthirst quickly accessed the fire place to catch them. Lambeth raced downstairs then made it outdoors. His head whipped all around trying to locate Deon. The noise of a car accelerates from around the corner, it's them. Lambeth dashed towards the vehicle. Deon drove with Myles sitting in the passenger seat. Lambeth knew they were too far away straight down the street, he couldn't accept this to be beyond his control, Deon

had to be stopped. With no other alternatives around this, Lambeth's narrow vision locks onto the vehicle. The crime of kidnapping triggered him forward to intervene firsthand in the most effective way possible. Officer Lambeth jerked out his firearm from his waist, targets the car speeding straight, then fired four fierce gunshots. The bullets flooded the inside of the car. An uncontrollable swerve landed their car into a grassy yard and collides into a tree.

The collision caused a loud honk to keep blowing, smoke from the hood could be seen rising to the sky. Lambeth darted over hoping Myles wasn't harmed. Lambeth arrives only at the sight of Deon's blood splattered on the windshield. His neck is overstretched resulting with him face down in the puddled surface of blood discharged off the dashboard. There were shards of glass from the back window sprinkled in all directions of the backseat. A huge airbag had compressed Myles to where he appears stuck. Two bullets were lodged into Deon's back, with the back of his skull that devoured the last two. This grisly sight flashed officer Cliff Lambeth's mind to where he's unable to process this, leaving him completely befuddled. His jaw clenched shut, his chest swelled, he couldn't choke out any words. He almost fell as his foot took a woozy step back, uneven to the ground, using all his strength to help reclaim his balance. The ongoing honking blazed his hearing; the car smoke had blasted up his nostrils. The shock of this calamity had pulsed through his armor leaving an embedded severe frequency causing for him to descend into numbness.

MIDTOWN HOLKSDALE: 10:34 A.M.

Icarus McGrew has been locked inside his home for a few days. He's hunched over at the edge of his bed focused on these recent failure approaches. Constantly analyzing each memory had him seething. Beyond his control, his head inflates bad memories within his thoughts leaving an intense concentration, leaving him brooding in bed.

I'M GOOD, I DON'T WANT TO GIVE MY NUMBER OUT! His mind recalls. *Ok, what're you yelling for? We've already met so what's your fucking problem, huh! If you showed up the first time than we wouldn't even be here. In fact, I have no problem leaving you and your son alone. GOOD, YOU GO THEN!* The image of her scowl jutted out from the back of his mind. Her sharp tone recycled in his head. *And for some reason you've still got an attitude, I didn't even do anything to you. I would've been long gone by now but you just wanna create a huge scene.* The vision of the crowd staring him down from the kiosk filled his head. He shook his head in frustration, his breathing intensifies. Icarus keeps fixating on the thought of those customers' judgmental stares. He slouched over more, pressing the heels of his palms against his eyes as his mind whirls to the incident with the woman at the gas station. *PLEASE GET AWAY FROM ME!* Rattled his brain, then recalled the short, redhead woman: *Can you quit following me!*

"I wasn't fucking following you!" Icarus mumbled to himself, this thought orbiting his psyche. Infuriated at how he passively let her bark at him like this, her vicious stare was refreshed in his head. "You don't know what you're talking about. Judging me, being that fucking arrogant!" he snapped. His thoughts trailed off to the Korean woman in suspicion of him following her. "You don't have to wait there just for me to pass you, like there's something strange about me." Icarus stood up enraged, pacing around. Then becomes more beside himself with anger from the stony stare from the woman scowling at him. The pure disdain still baffles him, and he swelled with embarrassment from trying to be cordial. Icarus can't sever that moment from his head of looking and sounding eager by tone. "Fine, you can go! No point of you stopping just to have a bitchy attitude." He bawled then hectically shooed his hands. They forcefully wave more by the stare from that man at the mall making him feel more shameful. A mass effect of women's unsavory opinions fused to his shallowly perceived image that chafed his psyche. "You couldn't even be polite to me. I don't get spiteful in the slightest. I don't yell, disrespect in any way, can handle rejection. I can even accept that you're not obligated to grant me your attention or that I'm not entitled to sex. And I'm still looked at as a fucking creep."

There's this inexplicable chain binding him to these godawful internalized results. Icarus plummets to his bed, he sulked as anger circulates while still lying in an uneasy position. No matter which direction he turns, it's impossible for him to feel satisfied with himself. His body ached a little with this cloud of disgrace engulfing him. Icarus hasn't had enough energy to motivate himself into approaching women. His appetite has decreased tremendously, and his hygiene has decline. Icarus hasn't showered for a few days. His bedroom is messy with the dusty dresser, his untucked bed, and his piled garbage bin. As for his novel, he hasn't focused on finishing it either, being only thirty pages typed.

The sunlight starts to shine through his pulled curtains, it's hard for him to take a nap. He trudged downstairs to the front window to observe across the street. The sunshine flashes his weakly eyes, he sees a few cars pumping gas. That woman who bent over to avoid being seen by him recycles nonstop. *That's how uneasy women get around you.* Icarus' thoughts dwelled. *Just how those other girls sense how much of a creep you must be.* As he stood by the window, he tries to focus on anything positive, searching for any guidance. He tries recalling the advice Jovanny had given. Especially when Jovanny mentions there's a surplus of them. Or how Chet advised for him to stop pursuing them. Icarus had considered doing this.

A white woman comes out her car to pump gas. She was blonde with a robust chest that slightly jiggled as she leaned on her car. Her thighs were large and were accentuated in her jeans. The spotlight was on her, Icarus felt the urge to run and introduce himself. She looked to see him watching from his window but didn't react. There wasn't a sign of discomfort from her, she just looked then her eyes trail off into oblivion. After her tank is filled up, she drove off. That gorgeous female was enough to nudge him with hope that he could attain one girl's number at the minimum. Icarus brushed his teeth then rinsed his face.

Ok, ok. Two hours. I'll roam around a bit and then I'll head home. No mall this time. No luck there. You're not a creep, Icarus. He drove off on his quest. Circling around the block, the sight of how bright it's become really coaxed him into keep going. After forty-five minutes of cruising around midtown, there wasn't anyone he could find. It was also difficult to concentrate by his mind being flooded with flashbacks of horrible approaches. Icarus parked in front of a wide dollar store to scope out any attractive women going inside or coming out. There weren't many female customers coming that he found attractive and had refused to settle for someone unattractive. There was an attractive Caucasian woman who walked inside. Icarus immediately went inside, he checked around for her. She pushed her cart down the aisle with several snacks. Icarus lurked in the aisle and recognized her; she attended the same college as him. He maneuvered around her a few times as she observed the food on display. His nerves began to spiral the closer he moves in, causing for him to consistently halt himself. Embarrassing past interactions occupy the halls of his mind. The lady noticed his presence from the distance.

"Icarus?!" she cheerfully said. "Icarus McGrew? Hi, how are you?"

"*Hey*." He cautiously replied, his tone sounds uncertain.

"It's me, Lindsey Cartwright. From our criminal justice course." She clarifies as she hugged him. "Wow, look at you now, you haven't aged much."

"Thanks, you haven't aged much either really."

"Yes, I get that a lot." She proudly said. "I remember you being so quiet back then." Icarus seemed a little standoffish now to her but it didn't impact her friendly demeanor. "Well, you take care now."

Icarus plastered a smile. "You too, Lindsey." Then walked off not wanting to ruin her perception of him. *Come on now, you followed her up to this point. She even called out to you, Lindsey clearly saw you as a decent guy. You should see it through at least.* He returned back to her aisle; she's packing candy in her cart. His nerves were still scrambling as he walks back since another lady joined the aisle.

"Lindsey!" he quickly called, she looked shocked that he's back. She gradually smiled again. "I forgot to ask but…" the other lady was within earshot of them. "… but how did you do in that criminology class?" his voice unnaturally lowered.

"*Uh*, I got an A." Lindsey replied, perplexed.

"Cool, cool." He awkwardly said, the lady had gotten closer causing his words to gush out. "I don't remember that professor's name but I thought he seemed nice."

"It was a woman." She flatly replied then turned to the snack shelf.

"*Right. That's right. Seemed that long ago.*" His words overflowed as the lady left the aisle skeptically staring back at him. Lindsey sensed something peculiar about his behavior but didn't ask. "*So, who was that professor again?*"

Lindsey kept staring at the snacks on the shelf.

"So, you got a family now? Any children?" he asked.

She just stared at the shelf with a neutral face and lacked a response. Icarus felt his own random presence intrude, he suddenly deflated.

"Well, nice running into you again." his voice weakens, Lindsey turned her back at him pushing her cart forward. Icarus trudged out the store back to his car. He buried his face in his palms, lacking the drive to continue.

Great Icarus, you scared her off. She was even nice to you. Lindsey just bluntly ignored you and that nosy lady just watched you. You ruined it. YOU'RE GONNA DIE A VIRGIN!

As he sulks there, a young black lady was seen across the street sitting at the bus stop. He knew it would seem odd to offer her a ride or let her see him in a car. Then recalled when Jovanny encouraged him to lie to women, especially now. Icarus leaves his car that's parked further from her and jogged over before her bus comes.

"Excuse me." Icarus said, she looked at him with an innocent stare. "Hey. You're waiting for the bus too, huh?"

She nods. "Heading to the mall. Don't wanna be late for work. You?"

"Just went for a walk, sure is nice out today. Thought I'd take myself a quick rest. Where do you work?"

"I'm an employee at a perfume kiosk." She said proudly, then looks up. "You right, today looks nice out."

"Yup, so do you." Icarus said. "What's your name?"

"Alicia." She answered. "Nice to meet you."

"Likewise, likewise." He calmly replied. "I'm about to walk off but how's about we exchange numbers?"

Alicia smirked, squinting her eyes. "How old are you?"

"I'm thirty."

"Do you know how old I am?" she calmly asks. Icarus couldn't tell. "I'm fifteen."

"Oh, I did not know that." he replied sounding oblivious. Alicia held in her laughter as she watched his shocked face. "See ya around." He instantly said, Alicia laughed. Icarus walks off realizing how comical that was.

"Hey. Hey, you!" a deep voice called out, Icarus turned around confused. It was a big white guy. "I was just waiting by the bus stop. You trying to pick up underage girls?! I overheard you, you rapist!"

Icarus was shocked as he emerges him. He veered around to detect if any pedestrian could overhear.

"*No, no, no, no.*" Icarus nervously bursts, his lips formed a trembling, uneasy smile. "I didn't know she wasn't legal. Trust me, man, I'm no pervert or anything." The guy closed in on him. "Her and I both laughed it off, simple misunderstanding, alright? It's nothing to take seriously."

The guy looked at his car behind him. "Thought you said you went out jogging." he skeptically said. "So, you just parked over here this whole time watching for her. You're out here stalking young girls, creep!"

The silence lingered with just them in the parking lot.

Icarus froze, his skin began to crawl at the theory he formulates. His face is furious, Icarus can feel the fear show on his own. Icarus can't even conjure a decent lie since this guy took away his guilt at face value.

"No, look, I see how this looks—" Icarus cautiously began. The guy pulls out his phone then starts recording. "Please, don't record me." Icarus shielded his face with his hand. "I'm leaving, okay? I'm going."

"That's right, everyone." He announced for the video. "I caught us another man creeping around harassing females out here. He tried pursuing a fifteen-year-old girl just out minding her own business. Fucking creeper!" the guy proceeds to follow Icarus. "What's your name, huh?"

Icarus tried opening his door, but the guy forced it back shut. Then repeats his question louder.

"Don't bother me!" Icarus demands. The guy shoved his camera more in his face. "Get that camera off me!" Icarus swatted it out his hands.

A sharp hit to the face sends Icarus crumbling to the ground, followed by a kick to his ribs. Icarus instantly rolled over then jolts to his feet. He wobbles with his fists shielding him. The guy dodged his first few swings, Icarus pushes him back. His forearm blocked the attempted punch from Icarus, then slapped him. Icarus kicked him. The guy latched onto his ankle with a fastened grip. He uplifted it causing Icarus to take a nosedive to the ground. Icarus gets stomped on repeatedly until a woman watching screams. He ceases, then spits on him and picks up his phone recording him sprawled on the ground. The man proudly runs off. Icarus feels burning wounds as he's motionless.

DOWNTOWN HOLKSDALE 5:30 P.M.

A week later since the death of Deon Howard, Cliff Lambeth had made the news. Many people were outraged by this due to the increase of several corrupt incidents involving the police in this city. The highlight of this case was the current state of ten-year-old Myles Howard going into a coma after the car accident. Myles hasn't shown any signs of recovery. This fueled many citizens to rally at the downtown police department in protest for an indictment. There are several citizens chanting outside of there to where they almost overtook the street. Officers are standing guard at the doors of the department watching them all. They could be seen in a troop stance in preparation of any chaos. Multiple adults showed up with three types of posters. One with Deon's face saying: Justice for Deon Howard. Another that said: Salvation for Myles Howard. The final one has officer Cliff Lambeth plastered saying: Cliff Lambeth is the antichrist. They've been at this for about six hours now.

"INDICT HIM!" the crowd continuously chants. They're furious, the pain in their voices is felt. Posters are risen higher; fists are pumped in the air. *"SAY THEIR NAMES!"* their yells evolved. The main goal of this peaceful protest is to ignite a chain reaction of amoral officers to be held to justice for future crimes. The multitude of citizens started to silent down as a black man emerged before them all. He uses a microphone to announce for everyone to remember this is a peaceful protest. He encouraged that they're able to

make a difference in Holksdale, that they will receive justice. The plethora of people cheered in hope of this. An excess of applauds and screams soar everywhere.

Breaking News on TV had the chief of police at the podium about to make an announcement. People in the crowd had checked their phones for the recent update. He first extends his deepest sympathies to the families and loved ones of Deon Howard. Then acknowledges the gathering of people in his honor anxiously awaiting news pertaining to this. Before he continues, he cautions everyone that regardless of how they feel about this information that they are expected to conduct themselves in a civil manner. Everybody was silently eager to know the outcome. The chief of police calmly informs that after a thorough review of the domestic dispute involving Deon Howard that there will be no charges at this time. Then includes that officer Lambeth will be suspended on paid leave.

The flood of protestors erupted in a fury. More officers emerged outside. Cliff Lambeth walked out the department, their yells furiously amplified. Lambeth held his head high in the face of intensity from everyone outraged at his egregious behavior. They waved their posters higher, skyrocketing as they resume chanting again. Lambeth understood how they feel. He had a yearning to grab a microphone to acknowledge that what transpired had gone awry. That he regrets causing the death of Deon Howard and the tragedy of Myles Howard. Unfortunately, he knows it wouldn't alter the severed trust between police and citizens.

That they desired to witness him unfold on his knees in tears and facing a harsh prison sentence. Lambeth conducted himself in a stern manner.

Officers help to escort an elder black woman to him. The crowd knew of Lambeth but not her. She introduced herself as Deon's mother, Elizabeth Howard. He didn't know how to begin and was at a loss for words. Elizabeth faces the crowd with a microphone, everyone had quieted down.

"Good afternoon." Elizabeth said. "We're all gathered here today in honor of my son and my grandson who's in my prayers and hopefully in yours." Her voice was extremely blissful. "I have suffered a tremendous loss that no parent should endure. However, I hold no animosity towards officer Lambeth today. And I wish to make peace."

She stretches out her feeble arms summoning Lambeth. He slowly comes forth and she wraps her arms around him, he does the same. The crowd still barks at Lambeth but not as intense as before. Lambeth slowly gets a warmth uplifting feeling. Elizabeth nests her head on his shoulder.

"Now you listen to me here well, officer." Elizabeth whispers in his ear. *"The only reason I am turning the other cheek is to help to ease tensions between citizens and the police. Can you hear them? Do you hear these protestors?"* Lambeth was speechless but nods at the chanting from people. *"That's the devil fueling them to act out like this, hopefully most will become enlightened by this scenery since our higher power of law enforcement can't rectify this situation themselves. This is to prevent the wickedness that already bedevils here, to soon possibly*

spread had I refused. But at the end of the day, you took away my son, a father, and harmed my grandson in the process. Regardless that he's now in a better place, his place here was perfect for raising my grandchild. I am not forgetting that. You will be condemned by the masses for this, and God's reckoning is now upon you." She uplifts her head from his shoulder then pats him on his back.

Cliff Lambeth couldn't believe it, there was no justification he could conjure up, he was powerless. Everything stung deep even more from the crushed expectation of her embracing him. It was almost a relief hoping she wouldn't harbor any ill will towards him. The realization that she, alongside everyone else, has now identified him as no different as these other corrupt, gun-toting sadists that patrol Holksdale had killed his spirit.

MIDTOWN PENITENTIARY 6:00 P.M.

Larissa came alone to visit her mother; it has been way too long since their last visit. Her mom hasn't called her in a while. There's so much that she wants to tell her mom. She eagerly awaits behind the glass window for her presence.

Danielle Sheppard is seen being escorted by a prison guard; this brightens her daughter's face. As she draws closer, her mother has some bruises on her face. Danielle's left cheek has cuts, several bruises are located on her forehead, and her right eye is slightly red. Larissa's shocked and immediately picked up the phone, Danielle stares at her with a scowl before finally getting the phone.

"Ma, what happened?" Larissa's voice croaked. *"Are you alright? Who inside did this to you?"*

Danielle silently watches as her daughter almost broke into tears. She still looked serious withholding any explanation. Larissa shut her eyes tight to prevent any overflowing tears.

"Where the fuck Essie at?" Danielle firmly asks. "She ain't drop no money up in my commissary or drop off that dish she was supposed to weeks back. I know that accident ain't kill her."

Larissa was confused. "She's at home, recovering still."

Danielle nodded seeming frustrated. "Of-fucking-course. Next time don't pull up her without her."

"Mom, what happened?" Larissa pleaded.

"I finally did what you begged my ass to do. I confessed about what brought me up in here during my last group therapy. Some females in here, turns out they got kids too, and found what I did pretty fucked up. One of them lil' heifers from therapy that ain't like me snitched to they homegirls and they cornered me about it. Got my ass sent to the infirmary for about two days."

Larissa got a hard knot feeling in her chest at the thought of them targeting her mom.

"Because of you, I got my ass whooped. See, I knew I shouldn't had listened to yo' little hard-headed ass!" Danielle snarled, both her fists bawled in rage at her. "How many times I done told you not to annoy me with that dumb shit about redeeming myself?! All 'cause you believe in that baffoonish shit around the world. Nah, nah, my biggest sin in this world was giving birth to your stupid ass! I should've terminated you the first chance I got! Then I wouldn't be in this mess."

Larissa's eyes swelled up; she repeatedly wipes them.

"Go cry to that heifer, Essie. Don't bring that shit in here and if Essie don't come next time, don't even bother showing up." Danielle barked then hung up the phone.

The guard escorts Danielle away back to her cell. Larissa is glued to the seat finally relieved to let out her cries.

Jovanny's place 7:16 P.M.

Jovanny Gibbs and Solanda Wright are together in their bedroom discussing the recent update on Deon Howard's protest. They're both upset that officer Lambeth received no charges. Solanda thought it was sweet of Elizabeth to forgive her son's killer on the air; Jovanny didn't believe it to be a genuine response but couldn't figure out why she committed with it. Everyone knew that most officers in Holksdale are sentenced to eternal damnation once they die. There has been countless corruption escalating ever since, leaving those policemen cleansed of any guilt, absolved from all punishment. On the news, they announced that the peaceful protest had went into a frenzy after officer Lambeth was escorted from the crowd by police. More officers had to get involved. Then Lorell St. Louis had later come with her enormous group of followers at that protest with her own agenda. Jovanny played the link for them to watch. It started with her giving her condolences to the mother of Deon Howard. Then she spoke to the crowd as they began to simmer down. Lorell declared that Deon agitated those officers and that's why this misfortune had transpired. The horde of people backlashed against her. This hadn't prevented her from continuing about how men are the catalyst to these problems. Claiming that Crystal Newton had been abused in their relationship and that her assailant shouldn't have took advantage of his power. Some women in the crowd started pondering her speech, others did not. Men were booing Lorell St. Louis, the only ones who advocated her were the male feminists in her group. Outraged protestors began lashing out at each other, some men diverted their aggression at Lorell's group chanting that today's men are toxic. Arguing heightened by this new conflict that the crowd's focus shifted away from downtown Holksdale's questionable police department. Lorell's male oppressing speech had inflamed everyone's feelings that resulted into a whole brawl. The video finished with screaming being made.

"I don't believe this." Jovanny said. "This bitch instigated a whole struggle just to promote her fucking feminist agenda. People out here getting hurt because of her. This shit's crazy."

"It look like she almost sided with the police." Solanda added. "Like, I know she went on about men being harsh but you see how she swayed everyone's attention from why they're all there, from the shit they tried accomplishing. Like, I seen how she played them women at that event I was at. She knew they'd argue, she knew what she was doing."

On the news, people are causing havoc tonight on these streets as retaliation at Lorell's manipulative stunt and the unjust treatment officer Lambeth received. It's getting darker outside. A bunch of people are heard yelling, this sent Jovanny to check his window. Adults dashed down his block evading upcoming police cruisers. They're seen hauling items that they've stolen. As Jovanny's eyes veered outside, he detects someone crouched down scratching at his truck. Solanda hears him scream at whoever's doing it. He races outside, it's a lady keying the words in his door:

PEDO

Jovanny recognized her as another ex-girlfriend getting back at him. She was a black women named Kia. She stared him down completely unfazed.

"What the hell, Kia?" he screamed.

"Yea, that's right. I know you ain't forget me. I hope people parked next to you catch sight of that door."

"You carved my truck outta some petty shit?!"

"Petty?!" Kia blurts. "My name's carved into the fucking ground destined to hell after getting fucked over by dogs like you! You did my ass dirty, nigga!"

Solanda rushed outside, she scanned the area to confirm it's safe. Kia stared her down only to realize she's with him.

"Girl, do yourself some good and keep away from him before he rape you like he raped me."

Solanda had frozen on the steps in disbelief.

"Baby," Jovanny said. "Baby don't listen to her, this bitch crazy. Look what she done did to my car door."

Solanda glanced to see his vandalized door.

Kia laughed. "Yea, mark this like how you marked me."

"Ain't nobody violate you!" he yelled. "You tried using me for free dates, talking about '*I was assaulted before, I'm not too comfortable engaging in sex that fast or being alone with a guy*' but you quick to be alone with me if I was treating you out to places."

Jovanny had invited her to his place after being exclusive with Kia for four months without any intercourse. At the time, he felt she was acting superior since she withheld sex and laughed him off when he brought it up. Kia finally decided to tease him a little, soon things had escalated into intercourse at his place. Jovanny never contacted her again and ignored her calls and messages.

"You were selfish in bed." Kia said. "I was mad uncomfortable that night and you didn't even try to pleasure me. You heard me sobbing afterwards, you knew I wanted for you to stop. After investing four months with you, I caught the raw end of the stick over some dick that ain't even that good."

"All you did was act mad arrogant, especially when I tried to fuck. You took such pride in rejecting my advances, withholding the pussy like you a prize. You ain't had no job or car but wanted to leech off me. Hell yea, I was selfish that night, you ain't had shit else to contribute."

"SHUT UP!"

"I swear, you always brought up your rape, and wore that shit as an identity. You only used it as some excuse to justify in keeping them legs closed. Plus, you survived so you should've been recovered. Shit, I would've."

Kia turns to Solanda. "Sis, I promise you, this nigga—"

"Bitch, if you don't go somewhere with that bullshit!" Solanda overrode her. "You wanna remain celibate, go fetch yourself those chastity belts."

Kia had stood speechless. Sirens were heard ahead. Two cars accelerated down the street. Kia and Jovanny jumped out the way, Kia fled to her bike and rode away. Jovanny noticed Solanda looking relieved that she's gone. She comforts Jovanny by wrapping her arms around his waist, insisting they retreat inside before things get too dangerous.

York Avenue 7:42 P.M.

Chaos outside increased as the night went on. Police have arrested adults for loitering and fighting. After the protest went awry, some men had gotten brutally harmed during the fights. Few women had been injured while in the crossfire. Essie watched it on the news as they detail how mayhem has escalated into the streets. Footage of people engaged in this turmoil or of them being hospitalized from tonight had Essie's mind spiral about Larissa's whereabouts since she isn't home nor has picked up her phone either.

Essie hopes she isn't searching for an attempt to save Danielle again. She then texts Yanie Juergens and Jovanny Gibbs. There was no response from Jovanny but Yanie called her. Yanie has no clue as to where Larissa is, Essie becomes more anxious. Then there's an uproar heard from outside. A group of men are beating this one guy on the ground; stomping his ribs and neck until he's unconscious. There is smoke arising from a fire detected from the corner of her eye far down the block. Essie contemplates Larissa's well-being to her own, then tells Yanie to come get her.

As she awaits for Yanie, she prayed for Larissa to show up beforehand. Essie constantly checked her phone for any missed calls or texts; Larissa still hasn't replied. Many horrible scenarios about her condition run through her head causing for Essie to pace throughout the kitchen feeling unsettled. Her phone rings, she quickly checked only to see it was Yanie who finally arrived. Essie rushed downstairs then came to an abrupt halt at the door. Her surroundings increasingly squeezed the closer she emerged to slip out the door. Not having set foot outdoors was really a choice to remain away from insanity. The realization of having been isolated for so long, losing focus of Larissa, has planted her now in sanity. Essie's Christ-like compassion conceived this urge to leave, then she walked out the door.

Yanie's eyes glowed up. "Yes, hallelujah. She finally left her home." She unlocked the door, Essie jumped in.

"I know, I know. Believe me, I'd rather be anywhere else then out here."

"Like back indoors." Yanie mocks. "For weeks you been off the grid." They drive off in the truck patrolling the area. "Still no call from her?"

Essie groaned. "No, nothing yet. Jovanny hasn't returned my text either. Where the hell is she?" she veered outside for any sight of her.

Outside was dark with screams around the corner. A car was seen abandoned after colliding into a building. Car alarms from several vehicles go off after they're windshields got broken; their tires are now missing too. Police cruisers accelerated passed them. Yanie sees a group of men sitting aligned on the sidewalk in handcuffs with two officers supervising.

"Ain't she with her friends, maybe?" Yanie asks.

"I don't know. She's been hanging out with some boy, Chase, who I don't really know too well. Hope she's okay."

The streets have garbage cans spilled over. There're delis that have been vandalized with broken windows. People are escaping from one deli with snacks, soda and liquor. Sirens ahead forced them to scatter. Signs made for the protest are littered on the sidewalks. Yanie sees a vehicle parked with fire burning the inside. Men are running away from it. Essie detects two teenagers spraying graffiti on a building wall. They drove around more until they got to a street filled with adults brawling. Essie's shocked at this upfront disaster; then her phone rings from Larissa calling.

† Chapter 18: Sorry, I'm not interested.

The contact on her phone made Essie's chest drum. She blurts to Yanie that it's Larissa. Yanie appeared relieved that she's alive. Essie quickly answered. The screams from people fighting had prevented her from hearing Larissa. Yanie rolled up all the windows as Essie repeatedly asks for Larissa's whereabouts. The call ended.

"What happened, what she say?" Yanie eagerly asks.

"I-I couldn't hear a thing."

"You think she's back home?"

"Larissa better be! Better there than here."

"Text her." Yanie urged.

"No, she normally picks up quicker. I need to hear her voice." She observes people fighting. "We gotta leave now."

Yanie attempts to reverse until heaps of people were blocking there way. They were fighting too. Essie looked behind them to notice there's another empty car now on fire.

"*Jesus!*" Essie shrieks. "Yanie, I think these people behind us are arsonists. They're setting more cars on fire."

"Shit!" she mumbled, then honks for people in their foresight to move. They're not budging. What had got people's attention was the roaring sound of propellers from a news helicopter that shined a rotating spotlight on everyone. Yanie spots a nearby alleyway on their right. The helicopter propelled her to swerve into it causing for the force to throw Essie sideways.

"Quick, stop!" Essie said, the truck had stopped directly in the center of the alley. Essie browsed for Larissa's contact then called. Larissa didn't answer, Essie was worried.

On the street filled with a plethora of assailants and arsonists had drawn the attention of more people. These group of men wearing steel helmets, heavily body armed vests and extending their ballistic shields are marching forward. The SWAT team had captured the attention of everyone. They halted in an aligned block with their shields. A police officer spoke through a blow horn. "I hereby command those on this street to exit the roadway. You have four minutes to disperse, or you will be detained or subject to arrest." These words caused people to shout, some people fled, and others recorded on their phones.

Alleyway

"You think she's hurt?" Essie asks, she calls again. "Why didn't she answer?"

"Essie, I'm sure she's fine but did you hear that?" Yanie checked over her shoulder.

"Essie?" Larissa answered.

Essie's voice rejoiced. "Larissa, honey, where are you?"

Yanie had a satisfied grin. "Told you she's fine."

"I'm home. Where you at? Was that Yanie?"

"Good, you stay there. And yeah, Yanie's here."

Yanie left the truck to see what was happening. She spots everybody rioting at the SWAT team. The possible violent outcome had her retreat to the truck. Essie detected

Yanie's worrisome face. Essie puts Larissa on hold.

"What going on?"

"Fuckin' SWAT!" Yanie warns. "Things are gonna get wild and I ain't trying to get caught up."

Essie noticed that if they move forward down the alley, it should take them back to York Avenue. Yanie agrees and Essie took Larissa off hold.

A grey Mercedes had emerged in their pathway. Irritated Yanie honks for it to reverse out. It stopped momentarily with its headlights shining, annoying Yanie and confusing Essie, who's monitoring her tone while speaking with Larissa still. Someone leaves the driver's seat, their presence is a silhouette slowly incoming. Yanie honks again, Essie bewilderedly stares. It was Nneka Barshak proceeding forward with a scowl. Yanie rolls down her window. "The fuck is you doing?"

"Get out the truck!" Nneka commands.

"Who's that?" Larissa asks.

Essie hesitates. "They're not talking to us, don't worry." She looked to Yanie.

Yanie shrugged then whispers. *"I dunno."*

"The fuck out the truck now!" Nneka repeats.

"Essie?" Larissa asks more anxiously.

Essie hints for Yanie to honk or to do something else. Nneka shoots the stink eye directly at Essie causing for her to instantly tilt her head away to the window. Yanie honked again, yelling for her to leave them alone. Nneka maneuvers to Essie's side. Larissa sounds worried while requesting for answers on what's happening. Essie's voice rattled, her tone sounding now shaky.

"We're fine, Larissa. I'm abou—" Essie's cut off at Nneka's hard pound at her window.

"I see you, Beverly. That's my fucking truck!"

Yanie was shocked, her alias being shouted had sent an electric wave to scrabble inside. Essie's head flicked back and forth between Nneka and Yanie; completely confused as to who Nneka believes she is. Essie nervously shook her head every time she was called Beverly. Nneka griped the door handle, unable to get it pried open, enraging her more.

"We don't know no Beverly." Yanie calmly announced.

Nneka kicked the door, imprinting a dent. "Open that goddamn door now, Beverly!"

"Who's Beverly?" Larissa asks. "Essie, are you alright?"

Nneka kicked the door again. This yelling had attracted two incoming masked guys that escaped from the crowd. One arsonist and one with a baseball bat. Yanie starts her engine but noticed the two guys. The men conspire for one to set Yanie's truck on fire then smash it with the bat afterwards. However, neither women notice their presence.

"Everything's alright." Essie instantly replied. "We're ok, we're just on our way back home."

Frustrated Nneka digs in her pants and whipped out a pistol, waving it directly at them.

"HOP OUT MY FUCKING TRUCK!" Nneka growled.

Yanie became tongue-tied, Essie's body had paralyzed in fear. That arsonist had a bottle filled with ignitable liquid in preparation to throw. The crowd is screaming. The SWAT team commenced to throwing tear gas. One of them spirals into the alleyway. His partner is about to heave the bottle at them. The man with the bat quickly grabs the tear gas, tossed it up high with the goal to hit it back out, a swing and a miss. It rolls further out dispensing fumes in the alley.

"Honey, I'll be home soon, bye." Essie's tone dropped to an alert, strained farewell, then hung up.

The tear gas exploded with smoky fog expanding, the combustion noise startled Nneka, who in the blink of an eye, fired at the arsonist's bottle causing for him to combust into flames. Yanie launched her foot on the gas pedal. The truck catapulted forward almost hitting Nneka, who delved behind the dumpster. Yanie clashes them into the Mercedes. Cries of torment from the arsonist trail off into the street with him rattling into people. Essie and Yanie are still horrified by the foggy outcome. The truck can't push back the Mercedes, Essie raged for her to reverse. Yanie pitched it in reverse, the truck accelerates into full swing, bulldozing the man with the bat unconscious.

They're in the middle of the street. It was much clearer; they were exposed to a horde of people escaping the street. Explosions punctured people's eardrums. It was from the SWAT team hurling flash grenades. These men marched with their shields reflecting bricks, rocks and other items being launched at them. The police officer repeatedly announces that anyone caught will be subject to arrest. Some officers pinned down men, cuffing them on the street.

A man records the chaos that ensued. On footage there's people being arrested, men getting viciously beaten by nightsticks and police leaving a flash grenade skipping nearby that erupts in his wake. The arsonist spirals out still burning heavily. Cars, bushes, and certain people had caught on fire crossing his path. He finally collapsed onto the road. Hands had clapped on the truck, in attempts of reducing getting hit. A brick smashed Essie's window causing for them to drive faster. Coughing from everyone was chaotic as the smoke engulfed people. They shielded their mouths and noses with their shirts. Essie caught a whiff of it on her side. She tore off her shirt trying to fan it outside. Yanie honked, commanding others to move aside. More cruisers pulled up down the street with regular officers, including officer Colthirst. A stampede of scared adults darts at them away from the SWAT team. They clashed into officers. Officer Declan Colthirst commands for them to go home until he's unknowingly tackled by three men. Followed by a plethora of people forcing their footsteps on top of him in attempts to escape over him. His body absorbed the heels of everyone resulting to his unconsciousness. Other officers rushed to his aid.

Essie harshly rubs her eyes. She carefully slides the glass remnants into her shirt then hauled it out the window. More flash grenades exploded; everyone scatters to somewhere safe. Yanie hands her a white shirt hiding beneath her seat. Essie quickly wears it only to notice it's worn out. It has multiple holes located at her chest, stomach, and shoulder. Another incoming call from Larissa was heard, Essie informs her that she's on her way back home.

"Who was that?" Essie asks, bewildered. Checking behind to see if she's following them.

"I dunno. She just pulled up outta nowhere."

"I know but she kept calling me Beverly. Who the hell's that?! Then accused us of being…" Essie looked cynically at Yanie. "…in her truck."

Yanie spots her look. *"Wassup?"*

"Yanie, did you steal her truck? Is this her vehicle?"

"No, no, no, Essie. I don't got that job no more. I'm straight. Plus, she was accusing you, calling you outside your name. She clearly mistook you as some bitch named Beverly, trust me. I bet she was trying to rob us since people tonight are acting out."

"So in other words, you bought this on your own?"

"Yup, which I volunteered to help you search out for Larissa in, which was a waste since she at the crib."

Essie hesitantly believes her. Things haven't changed much outdoors in her eyes so that woman most likely was lying. Yanie's mind boggles as to who exactly that was. She ponders how she was traced since she knew her alias. Hoping her former boss didn't snitch but recalls his obsessive phone calls afterwards that she ignored. Yanie began to worry for Essie's safety since she had a gun.

"Hey." Yanie gently began. "You a real one for risking it all to get her. I am glad you finally left, choo-choo."

This aroused a tranquil look upon Essie's face.

"Me too." Essie said. "Actually, I've been struggling to even contemplate getting out." she divulges her nightmares, her ongoing anxiousness and her terrifying flashbacks to that fateful day. "I noticed they're recurring during the day whenever I'm exposed to bright light."

Yanie chuckled. "Who is you, a vampire?!"

"All I know is I've been fearful a lot of that."

"I get it. Me and Jovanny should've come pay visit. I'm wrong for that but I got you."

Essie slides out a big exhale in relief. "Thank you."

As soon as Essie gets inside, she instantly calls out for Larissa. Larissa was already waiting for her in the living room. The sight of each other's concerned looks get exchanged. The reassurance of Essie's safety drove Larissa into the arms of her guardian. Essie absorbs Larissa with a warm, acceptance hug. Larissa wrapped herself into Essie. A half hour passes, Larissa confessed about visiting Danielle in prison. Her being upset led her to reach out to Chase. They were at his house for a while then he walked her home. She didn't get Essie's calls because her phone died. Larissa asked about the insanity happening over the phone. Essie warned her about the riots happening tonight. She tells that she was in earshot of a homeless person harassing the driver next to them for a ride to deviate from the craziness. Her story seemed very bizarre. However, Larissa didn't overthink it because she trusts her guardian wholeheartedly. They kept inside for the rest of the night.

The following day, it was announced on the news that last night's riot downtown of Holksdale had a major impact. Arson was brought on multiple vehicles and stores. Multiple stores had been robbed of merchandise. People had been arrested that night. Officer Declan Colthirst is now hospitalized for internal injuries after being charged at. Including the death of some adults being caught on fire. The streets are littered with rubbish and vandalism was evident.

Larissa sits on the front steps observing the aftermath of her street. Essie is inside on the couch. She receives a text from Jovanny Gibbs apologizing for not responding; admitting he was handling something else. Being forgiving, she responded that Larissa was okay and informed him that she's been okay too. Yanie stopped by to check in on Essie.

"Wow." Yanie said. "They done finally fuckin' lost it."

Essie nods. "And you wondered why I locked myself inside. Especially that insane lady who could've shot us."

"Don't fret, you're safe now, Beverly." Yanie mocks. "I was actually thinking after dropping you off. Thinking how it's a struggle to bring yourself out during the day."

"Yes, resulting with me retreating back to my bat cave. What's the point?"

"The point is I got you. There's this big party tonight in midtown being thrown by someone celebrating going to heaven. I figured we go together." She suggests, seeing Essie's uncertain face. "Look, look, it'll be fun. They'll have drinks, dancing, you name it. And no riots carried out there from yesterday. Nothing'll have you triggered."

"Sounds fun." Essie said. "But after last night, I—"

"Essie, I get it." Yanie interrupts, knowing her friend's struggle with being decisive. "Last night was crazy but you made the choice all on your own to contact me, and go through hell and back to save Larissa. Compared to that, this ain't nothing. It's all about living your best life."

†

Larissa sat on her front steps. Chase's shadow emerged over her, she got startled but was glad to see him. They both discussed the mayhem that transpired.

"I'm sorry about your mom. How you feeling?"

"Still shitty. Like, I thought she was doing better and apparently it's on me."

"Ain't shit on you." He reassures. "You didn't put her in there so don't think like that."

"Thanks." She said, then became reluctant to recall their hangout last night. "By the way, I know you wanted to take things further but I don't think I'm all for that yet."

As Chase was consoling Larissa over her mother; he had used it as an opportunity to persuade her to get intimate. He sent sensual kisses down her neck while caressing her thighs. While Larissa was melting in his arms, the thought of the miraculous list popped up. Premarital sex would definitely deter her chance into heaven. She put a halt to it. Her excuse was that her guardian was probably worried where she was (*especially with her phone uncharged*). Chase took it in stride then walked her back home.

Larissa hugged him and kissed his cheek. They both relax on the steps. Chase notices Elijah Atwood from down the block. He warns Larissa that they should probably go inside. She groaned but doesn't seem to feel unease. Elijah sees them and comes nearby. Chase suggests he could tell him to go away; Larissa rejects the idea and goes on her phone instead. Elijah finally arrives.

"Hey… Larissa." Elijah cautiously said. "How you doing?" he watched from the steps as Larissa just ignored him while on her phone. "I'm sorry about the whole silly string joke. *I sometimes play too much*." His voice got weakly. Chase awkwardly watches him pleading to be seen. He has a look of pity for him that he subjects himself like this. Larissa still silently scrolled through her phone. Elijah sadly trudged off.

Larissa glanced to see him leave. She has a faint grin emerge. "Thank God, he finally dipped."

Chase nodded. They converse as if nothing happened.

Jovanny's place 12:10 P.M.

Jovanny Gibbs arrives to his apartment building after taking his truck to a mechanic. He's annoyed about the aftermath of dealing with those bitter women. There's a white man who awaits on the steps; he stares at incoming Jovanny Gibbs. This has Jovanny thinking he just got locked out and needed his help.

"Excuse me..." The guy said. "Are you Jovanny Gibbs?"

Jovanny was reluctant but replied: "Yea, what's good?"

"I'm Earl." He introduced himself sounding stern. "I believe you know my wife, Brittany."

The realization that this guy came to confront him about a woman he possibly hurt had him frozen. However, Jovanny doesn't know (*or at least remember*) exactly who Brittany is. He calmly denies knowing her. Earl skeptically nods while introducing a married photo of them. Jovanny suddenly recognized her as the Indian woman that he kicked out. The one who Solanda had invited to his place.

"Right, right." Jovanny gently began. "I knew her as B. Look bro, I ain't know she was married. Plus, you ain't gotta fret over me wanting her, my girl—"

"So you got a girlfriend and still sought after my wife."

"Nah, my girl introduced us first." He elaborates how Solanda met her at a bus stop then brought her to their bed. "Plus, let's not act like she ain't consent."

"You slept with my wife then?" Earl pressed.

"No, no. I had her consent but she refused to consent on paper, so I asked for her to leave. That's it."

Earl scoffed. "Well, she told me you offended her and physically…" he tries to suppress his anger. "… physically threw her out after being intimate with her."

Jovanny veers at his plain hands. "Bro, as God as my witness, I ain't fuck your wife. Ain't nobody ever lay hands on her neither. Believe me, had I had proof we smashed, I'd pull out her damn signature. Hell, I keep my receipts."

Earl expresses disbelief.

"And why should I trust anything you say, huh?!" Earl

replied. "You lied about not knowing my wife. Then your girl brings my wife back to your bed?"

"I ain't lie, alright. I just ain't remember who—why would you trust your wife at this point?! Bitch is a liar—"

"Hey! Don't call the mother of my child a bitch or liar!"

Jovanny scoffed. "Well, she revealed her loose pussy to me claiming she had no kids, so we both stretched the truth a little."

Earl stares at him quite speechless. Jovanny and he shared an uncomfortable silence. Jovanny looks tranquil as he shrugged his shoulders waiting for Earl's rebuttal.

Then Earl shook his head. "You know what, I hope whoever your girlfriend is, I pray she comes to her senses. And I bet she will since my wife is now pregnant by you. You clearly mistreat women. But that's okay, there will be hell to pay."

"I hope you come to your senses." Jovanny taunts. "I ain't ever fuck her so it must be yours. Your wife wanted for me to go in raw. Like, I can't tell where this bitch been. It's clear your wife clearly broke you down."

"IT'S YOURS!" Earl raged. *"I GOT A VASECTOMY!"*

Jovanny laughed. *"AND JUST LIKE THAT, THROUGH THE GRACE OF GOD, YOU'VE NOW BEEN FIXED!"*

The two barked at each other, hollering so loud that Solanda rushed downstairs to intervene. Both men were emerging closer as their argument got heated. Solanda crowbarred herself between them preventing a physical altercation. She tries calming Jovanny down, he informs her about whom Earl is and why he's arrived. Earl kept yelling trying to provoke a fight.

"Sir, sir." Solanda sternly said. "My man didn't know she was married, I did, ok?"

Earl sneers. "So because this guy treats you like shit, you wanna fuck up our marriage now?!"

"Your marriage was already fucked up." She declared, then showed him her phone. "Your wife messaged me on this dating app." She gloats about his wife requesting to get intimate when she's free, excluding Jovanny. Bragging about how his wife loved the attention from other guys online. "Your wife sure as fuck is molding a syndicate of simps out for herself. So, blame her."

Earl's face looked shocked almost on the verge of appearing heartbroken. He stood silent, contemplating any excuse to absolve his wife but couldn't conjure anything.

Solanda waves her phone closer at him. "Exactly, so don't blow up at my man. It ain't his fault you ain't perform your daily due diligence and properly vet that hoe out first. And then you go wife her up."

Earl glanced at Jovanny, who grins at him, then silently stormed off. Solanda mocks him about his wife revealing he struggles getting an erection. "I met her on her way back from church. She probably pulled up there on her knees praying to help resurrect that limp-dick."

Jovanny slowly smiled and nods at her. Solanda truly appreciated it. Not often had he shown much gratitude, so this rare time felt like she was truly doing God's work.

†

Yanie Juergens arrived to Essie's apartment to take her out for the night. They're going out to a party in midtown. Yanie called Jovanny so he could tag along. Seeing Essie finally comes out to her truck had Yanie's face light up. Yanie wore make-up concealing her whole face, a long red wig, and long fluttering eyelashes. Essie wore a nice outfit with perfume on. As she's arriving, Yanie has Jovanny Gibbs on the phone.

"*Choo-Choo!*" Yanie happily screams, both ladies hugging each other. "I ain't seen you in a minute. Where you been?" Essie dismissively rolled her eyes. "Just kidding, I know you been on lockdown."

"Essie?!" Jovanny sarcastically asks. "Nah, hold up! Is you finally out the crib?"

"Yes, ma'am." Essie playfully replies. "I'm not Danielle, I could leave whenever I want."

Yanie tells how she's trying to persuade Jovanny to come out with them tonight. Jovanny admits he's tired. He uses the fact that his truck is getting repaired as an excuse. Both Yanie and Essie try to lightheartedly pleas him into coming out tonight. Jovanny was still inflexible. Yanie mentions that sexy women are going to be there. Essie reminds her of the chastity trend. Yanie responds with for him to just look at.

"I don't gotta draw out my sword..." Jovanny said, hinting at his crotch. "…and slay these hoes."

"Sword?!" Essie snickers.

"Right?!" Yanie agreed. "Boy, don't nobody want that pocketknife between your legs."

Essie reminds them of the transgender Jovanny told them about. Proposing a scenario of him meeting another one tonight. "He's probably scared to get into an actual sword fight instead."

Jovanny dismisses their jokes. As they're laughing, Jovanny deflects onto Essie finally coming out.

"Right?! You can't be a homebody all your life." Yanie said.

"I'd rather be that than damn near homeless or jobless." Essie replied.

"I been busy makin' boss moves." Yanie protests. Essie and Jovanny didn't believe her until Yanie elaborated.

Ever since she got fired, Yanie's been doing webcam work. She signed up for a website where she exposes her body to her thousands of subscribers. Sometimes she'll be naked. Most of the time, Yanie is half naked usually wearing lingerie, bikinis or simple undergarments. All of her male followers pay to observe her tempting content. Guys donate money for special requests. All of the messages stroke her ego (*sometimes is more valuable to her than the money*).

This reveal had Essie shocked. She silently conceals her judgmental look. Jovanny encouraged it. He even envies that she gets to work from her own home.

"Nigga, I been inside grinding. Getting this bread." Yanie proudly gloats about the money she gets. Mentioning that four of her exes even subscribed. That each subscriber pays 5.99 a month. "Blessings on blessings."

Jovanny tells her to take advantage of her youth while she can. Yanie's physical image is better now. However, the older women gets, the less attractive they become. Her looks will begin to fade. Yanie shrugs it off. Jovanny tells that it's called "The Wall" that every women will experience as they advance in age. Then tells Essie that it applies to her as well.

"You think Donny subscribed too?" Jovanny asks.

"I don't give a damn if he does. I never claimed him." Yanie hissed. "Wasn't even a man I could fall back on."

"You know what faithful companion you could always lean on…" Essie mockingly adds. "*…the wall.*"

All three went into in a hysterical frenzy. Jovanny hung up. Yanie pulled out some vodka pouring Essie and herself a glass shot. They clinked their glasses and simultaneously gulped it down. Being outside with her friend felt like a breath of fresh air.

"Looks like it's just ladies' night." Yanie cheered, playing loud energetic music. "Tonight we 'bout to get lit!"

Essie cries ecstatically: *"LOOKS LIKE IT'S JUST YOU, ME AND DENIIIIIISSSE!"*

The truck took off, music blasting out the window. Yanie singing along with the song. The sight of her friend happy to have her out filled Essie with a refreshing, electric feeling cycling through her. This aura is sensed by Yanie, who then encourages Essie to dance along to it. Both ladies rejoice.

"WE OUTSIIIIIIDE!" Yanie joyously announced.

†

Later that night, Grant Critchfield had begrudgingly arrived at the hospital. His agent, Joy, has been waiting for him in the lobby. Joy had set up a special guest appearance for this young patient diagnosed with muscular dystrophy. This is a seventeen-year-old male named Mikey Green. Mikey had messaged Grant for four years with fan letters. He's been following Grant Critchfield on social media, defending him from these accusations and keeping Grant in his prayers.

Mikey's condition slowly grew progressively worse to the extent that he can't move not one single muscle below his neck. His parents had reached out, requesting for Grant to make a special visitation to their son (*while he's still got time left*). Joy had agreed through email that Grant would be thrilled to come. Through insisting that this would make Grant appear good in the eyes of the public (*including the eyes of the beholder*), Joy was able to persuade him into this.

Grant Critchfield appears with a birthday cake for Mikey. His birthday had been a week ago. However, this was around the perfect time to see him. Grouchy about having to purchase a cake for him (*with custom icing decorating*), Grant appears looking irritated. Joy detects him from afar, having her playfully gesture for him to smile.

Grant sees this and turns around. "*Buh-bye.*"

"Oh no you don't!" Joy demands. Causing Grant to come finally. "Glad you're here. This'll be good for your career."

This nice reassurance for his former acting career had Grant nod. Joy rehashes the planned visit. They're going to spontaneously walk in Mikey's room after the nurse leaves. Grant will be holding the birthday cake; Joy will give balloons. As they enter, they'll be singing Mikey a happy birthday song. Grant will pleasantly (and patiently, she asserts) answer any fan questions Mikey may ask. They will be here for over an hour minimum. Lastly, Joy will take a few pictures for Mickey to cherish forever. Grant reminds her that they'll be uploaded for the world to view too.

The nurse just walked out, blankly staring at Grant.

Grant lets out a brief exhale. Trying to build the tolerance for this. "Alright, let's wish Mickey a happy birthday."

"Mikey." Joy clarifies.

"Same shit."

"Wait, wait!" Joy halts him. "What'd you write on his cake then?"

The two entered in the hospital room with the birthday cake: *HAPPY BIRTHDAY MICKEY!* Joy joyously sung; Grant sang in a monotonous voice, looking confused. Mikey, who's head was facing the opposite wall, had his father instantly turn his head towards them. Mikey's dreary eyes had lit up at the appearance of Grant Critchfield. His father smiles at them both taking pictures. His mother sat in the corner with her arms and legs crossed. She displays a blatant look of disgust towards Grant. Mikey slowly forms a lopsided smile as the singing continued. Mikey's father began to sing along. He tries getting his wife to join but she remained silent. Alas, the song finally ceased. Joy commenced clapping, cheering for Mikey.

"Yay." Grant flatly said. "No need for the applause. However, Mickey you're automatically excused."

"Mikey." Joy impulsively corrects, then her attention went to Mikey. "You gonna make a birthday wish?"

"It's already come true. In the flesh." Mikey humbly said. He was laying on his back in a hospital bed. Mikey's skin was pale, his upper body was pipe-thin, skinny with his scrawny arms flopped to his sides. Strands of his black, floppy hair dropped to his face. His mother gently brushed them aside. Mikey's smile was seen through this clear, oxygen facemask hooked into a respirator. There were hospital monitors besides his lifeless body.

This moment was disrupted by the heart monitor chaotically beeping. Everyone's eyes darted at Mikey. His father was about to yell for help until Mikey erupts in laughter. Mikey then clarifies that his heart is rumbling because he's excited. "No need to call in nurse Benn." He politely said. The whole room was relieved.

Joy had sweetly introduced herself, shaking both parents' hands. Grant greets them both. The father happily shook Grant's hand in appreciation for showing up. The mother tends to Mikey's legs. She adjusts them properly from sliding off the bed. Mikey wishes to speak with Grant privately. His mother politely protests with her son that perhaps they should supervise. However, his father gives Grant their blessing to engage with Mikey solo.

As the parents discuss this across the room, Joy pulled Grant in another direction. Through his peripheral vision, Mikey's staring admiration could be detected.

Joy detects this too. "You see that?"

"Can't help but see it."

"This young man is dying to interact with you." She softly said. Grant snickers. "You know what I meant. Just be nice."

"I will."

"Good. Say something sweet too. Like, *'if I could trade places with you, I would.'* Kind stuff like that. Give him a memory for him to always cherish."

"We'll be fine, Joy." Grant firmly states. "His mother appears to be the only issue here."

Joy informs Grant that his mother is somewhat uncomfortable with the allegations in the news about him. Then reminds him that they messaged him before any of this. Seeing Grant give Mikey's mom, a repulsed look, had urged Joy to remind Grant to still be nice. Grant nodded.

Both Mikey's parents held hands while leaving the room. His mother's eyes stare directly pass Grant's entire being. Her hand grip clutched more with her husband as she's passing him. His father quietly mouthed out, *thank you*. Lastly, Joy took one picture with them alone. Her hopeful smile was expressed at Grant. Now everyone had left. It was now Mikey Green and Grant Critchfield.

The admiration bestowed on Grant had him satisfied. He tried to masquerade his stubbornness of having to make the trip. Grant sat alongside Mikey, who seemed still pleasantly surprised. Mikey requests for Grant to remove his face mask. This had Grant almost refuse due to not wanting to be perceived as responsible for his death by the public. However, Mikey assures him that he doesn't always rely on it. Grant's eyes glanced at the door, then he cautiously removed Mikey's oxygen mask. His weakly smile was more present. Mikey reveals his mom thought Grant wouldn't come. Grant tells him that he cares about his fans and would go out of his way for them.

"If you didn't, I'd be fine." Mikey said, in an unsteadily tone. "I've had a lifetime of disappointments. I just put on a strong face for my family."

"That's all you can put on."

Their space fell into this deafening silence once that was said. Mikey then blurted laughing. This surprisingly prompts Grant to begin chuckling.

"I'm glad at least someone who enters my room can crack wise." Mikey laughed.

As they're together, Mikey started naming his favorite films starring his idol. Started quoting Grant's memorable lines that he's clearly recited many times alone. This has a bubbly, relief flowing through Grant the more praise he gets. A warm smile had genuinely formed on Grant. This led Grant to indulge him by wanting to know what Mikey thought of Grant's online posts, interviews or just on cinema in general.

Mikey liked the interview Grant did where he walked out on the interviewer for asking ridiculous questions. The two agreed that the interviewer was just trying to expose Grant for a public dispute. His questions were irrelevant to the film. Mikey loved the nonchalant attitude of Grant just leaving in the middle of it.

Mikey remembered a social media post Grant wrote about most summer blockbuster movies being uninspired. That there was no eagerness looking forward to summer films anymore. Mikey rants about how characters act out of the ordinary usually to advance some commotion for stirring the conflict for the plot. Grant wholeheartedly agreed.

Grant, now feeling fully engaged, asks Mikey how he felt about his situation. Mikey shrugs his eyebrows. Revealing that he's accepted it. He's even accepted not remaining on earth long. However, he fears everything he'll leave behind.

"Leaving your parents?"

Mikey forced a smile. "Mm-hmm. Both my parents and very few friends that remained since childhood." Then told of how when he was in his teenage years, he would complain about his disability. He would annoy his friends since it had grown worse. Expecting them to feel sorry for his misfortune. Unfortunately, they had grown tired of him moaning about his troubles. Those close friends had eventually cut contact. Mikey reveals he didn't realize how much of a sorrowful complainer he was being until it was too late. "I don't need to always vent about my problems. When I'm gone, I want to be remembered fondly. Y'know?"

"No. There's no justification for that shit." Grant bluntly

said. "Life dealt you a bad fucking hand. Your friends were selfish for leaving in your time of need. Then causing you internal suffering from criticizing yourself. And never fester over wanting to be a good memory. Opinions usually change, harshly anyway."

This entire speech cycled through Mikey's head. Cycling through his lifeless body, having his chest heaving. Nobody has ever introduced that perspective to him. This clarity presented to him by a famous actor he's idolized has overflowing sensations drenching him. Mikey's eyelids flickered nonstop. Tears raced down, flushing hurt memories of blame from himself. Mikey, staring teary-eyed, graciously nodded at Grant Critchfield. *"I felt that."*

"Did you?!" Grant mocked, causing the two to laugh.

There was this blissfulness shared between them. One that both can detect that the other really needed. Mikey senses that Grant must've experienced this long ago. Probably took more time to even let that feeling resolute. Grant sensed that Mikey had the urge to ask how he relates to this just from the silence alone.

"Back in high school, I had a former friend who had me questioning myself. Getting in my head." Grant reveals, with a stone expression. "I didn't do anything wrong to make him act different towards me. And yet, I still felt I was wrong somehow. By putting his feelings above mine."

"You two never made up, huh?"

Grant coldly shook his head, shrugs his shoulders. "No matter. I hardly even remember his name."

"Well, I still want my parents to cherish memories of me." Mikey sheepishly said, sounding hopeful. He brought up that miracle, happily stating how he's destined for heaven. As accepting as he is, Mikey tells of how dying will devastate his family. Despite any godsend, there's no true salvation without his loved ones.

This miracle brought peace to Mikey's mother. Knowing there's proof that her son would be beautifully secured somewhere. Mikey admitted that he wasn't sure if it was legitimate when it was announced. His mom kept preaching daily about how it was real. As skeptical as Mikey was at first, he refused to disrupt his mom's beliefs.

The more he elaborated on this, the more silent Grant was becoming. Grant was occasionally nodding. A small, forced smile was smeared. His eyes began to steer another way. There had been this vague, detached look now across his face. It slowly registered to Mikey that his idol was declared to hell instead. It had slipped his mind completely. Then he remembers the accusations.

"Sorry." Mikey utters, his voice shaky. *"I forgot you—"*

"Don't be, just don't. It's nothing to me."

"You don't believe in it?"

Grant shook his head. "I did a lot of good things that people tend to forget. I even mentored a young aspiring actress. Then she chooses to make a false accusation."

"I heard about that too." Mikey timidly said. His voice felt clogged to request any further explanation. *"You seem just fine to me so far."*

"Thank you." Grant said, sounding satisfied. He describes her as a huge fan of his just like Mikey. That she desired his knowledge due to his past career experiences. Gave her insight on how Hollywood works. On how she was timid but eager to be famous. That he read her original manuscript for a romantic film. Bragging about boosting her confidence so she wouldn't be complacent as a background extra. "And this is how I'm now valued." Grant said, disgusted.

"It's messed up." Mikey politely said, his tone attempting to steer the conversation elsewhere. "I appreci—"

"Exactly." Grant blurted. "Me not worthy of reaching the promise land. That certified my belief on how false this is."

This prompts Grant into unfolding how Hollywood consists of many negative aspects from all sorts of people. The worst actors with bad tantrums, cycles of sexual harassment, addiction problems, and entitled attitudes on set. Or directors overworking actors. The unreported animal abuse when training in preparation for films. Grant rants on all these worse aspects that don't compare to him.

"I have personally worked with actors who are claimed to be saints that don't deserve it. Believe me, this isn't real."

The more Grant continues, the more Mikey became uncertain. Mikey's eyes impulsively wandered. This stuffed discomfort brewing inside him. Everything Grant said had gripped Mikey's ears. A picture tries to form inside Mikey's head for an afterlife.

"Then where do you think they'll go?" Mikey wearily asks.

"Most likely nowhere. Nothing. Honest to God." Grant hollowly said, with a blank stare.

As hard as Mikey tried to imagine somewhere nice or just somewhere for his soul to rest, he could not. That's exactly where his mind went, blank. This defeatist acceptance was shown across Mikey's face. Grant finally detected this. Mikey's eyes averted him, lips kept trembling until it ultimately forms a pout, his entire being seemed soulless.

There was this disconnect between them now. Grant thinks about how Joy wanted this to go well. Encouraging Mikey not to seem upset. That him coming shows that he's a good person and not to alter his fate. Then an idea came to mind on uplifting Mikey's spirits.

"Hey, Buddy." Grant nicely calls. Mikey faced him with unease. Observing his fan's paralyzed body. Grant kindly expressed: "Believe me, if I could trade places with you, I would."

"YOU WANT ME TO BURN IN HELL?" Mikey blurts, his voice struggled, eyes bugged out.

"No, no, no!" spilled out Grant's mouth, watching Mikey's head squirming both ways. "It's not even real, Mickey. Alright? It's not re—"

The door flings open. Both Mikey's parents rushing inside. Fear overcame his parents, wondering what all the commotion was. Joy lastly followed inside. Her eyes trace to her client, expecting an explanation. Mikey yells at his mother that she lied to him about an afterlife. His mother attempts to hug him but he kept stretching away his neck.

"There is no heaven, there is no God!" Mikey fiery roars, a sunken inflow of disappointment now formed into boiling anger ripped out.

His mother was trying to resolve this. Mikey's raging had overridden her. Then her warm demeanor abruptly ceased. Her eyes now trained of Grant Critchfield instead. She began yelling at him that he's programming blasphemy into her son. Grant tried explaining that it was a misunderstanding while trying to maintain his sizzled anger. She kept yelling while Joy and Mikey's father tried to settle this situation.

"This was a mistake." She turned to her husband. "We shouldn't have let Mikey engage with this pervert."

"Fuck you!" Grant yelled. "Your son was looking like a fucking desolate vegetable until I arrived. Me even showing up may as well be the second coming of Jesus for Mickey here!"

Once he's done, all hell breaks loose. Mikey's mother charged at him. Her husband restrained her, firmly trying to talk her down. Joy interjects between them attempting to calm down Grant. Both hollering at each other.

"Get out now!" she yelled; her husband still seized her.

"Okay, buh-bye." Grant said, smiling.

This leads to Joy apologizing as her and Grant retreat. Grant told her what happened. Joy was furious, reminding him of the plan that he shouldn't have gone off script.

"I get it. I should've remembered how much of an influential icon I am." Grant gloats, then they both leave.

Downtown Holksdale 9:00 P.M.

Lorell St. Louis had orchestrated a gathering in a huge parking lot outside the small shopping center. There's a plethora of women and some men who are listening to her preach on stage about her perspective on men. She speaks to everyone with such passion about how men need to become better. Women applaud the loudest in the parking lot. Her many male feminist followers stand on the sidewalk proudly holding signs for passing cars to observe. Signs saying, *Fuck the Patriarchy*, *Ordering women around is sacrilege*, and *Honk if women deserve recompense*. Cars honked multiple times passing through. Other people were joining her sermon. Her midget assistant joined holding a sign, *Stand tall for female rights*.

"You women of Holksdale deserve so much more." Lorell announced. "I am proud to see you've all arrived wearing your chastity belts. And I hope the empty spaces around here are supporters wearing your ghost cloaks." The crowd laughs. "We have come far in our efforts to be taken seriously by resisting temptation by the opposite sex. Because we know our worth. We've gotten reports that intimacy has dropped down significantly. Men need to comprehend that their actions have brought us to this breaking point." Applauds are made again. "They need to repent for causing us to be oppressed. For tempting us to submit causing our fate to be altered for hell."

Everyone silently listened to her elaborate more of how

women are saints, misogynists will speak blasphemy and how they will prevail under her guardianship.

"HEY!" an unknown voice was heard. *"HEY!"*

Lorell acknowledged the man interrupting her sermon in the background of the crowd. It was a big bald dark-skinned man with a smooth-shaven clean face, an oversized belly wearing a black long-sleeved clergy shirt with a white collar around his jumbo neck. It was Pastor Marques.

"Yes, I couldn't help but overhear this tomfoolery here that's all wrong." He protests. Everyone turns their heads over at him. "The hell kinda bullshit is you preaching?"

Lorell held her composure. "Sir, I am enlightening everyone to the ugly depths of your gender. The oppression you have started."

"Oppressed by us for what?!" he mocked. "For God making us born with a dick and balls? Miss me with that bullshit. In this day and age, men ain't got the power to oppress y'all bitches."

The crowd were shocked at this language escaping a pastor's lips. Lorell tries to resume her speech, but he still interrupts with his powerful tone captivating her audience.

"Men be treating women like goddesses. Y'all got manginas, simps and low-key misogynists stocked up on y'alls pedestal." He recalled how our superiors bring out the devil inside us. "They force us down to hell from the jump. That's why we need to quit this damn supplication to women." People began recording him, including the men holding up signs. "And not just y'all virgins out here but the law, the frikken media and these goddamn male feminists out here!"

He speaks with such conviction that infuriates Lorell St. Louis who remains stoic.

"Lorell is a false prophet, y'all." He denounced. "She's no different than the propaganda in the media boasting females, particularly the ones targeted for you teens, or in your early twenties. She's as dangerous as these thirsty guys y'all hate so damn much because she wants to catch you when you're young, naïve and don't really know no better."

"Alright now, that's enough!" Lorell bursts.

Pastor Marques looks at the young women in the crowd. "You young girls get easily influenced. And y'know why girls get so gassed up in their goddamn already ego inflated airheads?! It's because of feminism, it's having women believe you're more superior than y'all actually are. Placing you high up but you out doing all this desperate groveling so y'all can avoid forever torment in hell. Y'all need to come back down to earth, real talk!"

Everyone's silent while he recites the scripture from the miracle. The scripture enforcing to take your power down. Reminding them of how they're stupidly going against God by creating a gender divide while taking advantage of their female privilege. Even creating enemies in the process. For not holding themselves accountable.

"Oh, but God forbid anyone tear me down off my pedestal built off female privilege and fueled off blatant misandry and simps. But don't worry… God got something for that ass!" he said. "Especially men of color, they ain't got no power to oppress nobody. Lorell knows this but she wants to brainwash you into believing men are the enemy."

He reveals how Lorell St. Louis has only preached around downtown and midtown due to believing residents here aren't informed enough to know this already. That they think underprivileged people are easily manipulated into following her agenda. Marques exposes her reframing from going uptown due to them being more educated on this. And how the city of Holksdale is so divided that uptown refuses to inform the other two towns.

"She's been sent by the government to promote feminism to help dismantle the family unit. That's why she keeps playing off on y'all females' emotions to separate you from most men so you can pledge an unwavering allegiance to her control. Family members form this undying loyalty that supersedes the demands, power and influence of feminism. And she knows this."

Despite captivating his audience, some were reluctant to believe they were double-crossed. However, it all made sense to them once he makes the correlation of their past actions leading up to the government wanting to seize control through these tactics. The citizens looting, causing havoc due to knowing their fate and the discrimination towards Muslim residents prior to now. People looked either dumbfounded or embarrassed by this.

"If we wish to surpass this," Marques suggests. "Then we all must come together to undermine their control."

"This is ridiculous!" Lorell said, in attempts to sway her listeners back. "You make it out as men being victims. Women aren't obligated to entertain you."

"Entertaining and having enough common decency to acknowledge a guy are two completely different things. And if that's the case, then us men don't owe y'all women who fucked these no-good-ass dudes that had babies outta wedlock, we don't owe y'all nothing either. Hell, the reason there's so many thirsty men out here is because y'all are depriving men of sex. You started all this and are too proud to admit your role in all this." Marques recalls how our society absolves women mostly. "These male feminists won't contradict you because of their pursuit and in hopes for inevitable pussy. All these factors have given y'all a false sense of fuckin' entitlement. Believing us men owe you an apology, so we'll get in your good graces once more. Despite y'all bringing nothing but trouble to the goddamn table like Judas himself. But don't nobody owe anyone anything except for human fucking decency and respect."

Pastor Marques concluded by walking away knowing everyone's absorbed his wisdom. Lorell, slightly thrown off, tries to continue. After a few minutes, some people left the parking lot. The men holding signs before were gone. Her crowd started decreasing the more they contemplated what they've heard. There are women realizing things have been worse off since they embraced Lorell's advice but remained still out of pride. Others accepted they're sins being verbally announced and decided to leave.

York Avenue 12:23 P.M.

Essie and Yanie had arrived back from that party. Both laughing and tipsy from their drinks. Essie and her conversed about their lives once they got there. They had drinks bought for them and danced the night away. It was a huge relief to be in another environment where she didn't feel closed in. Yanie felt proud to finally get her friend to embark with her tonight. The joy Essie showed wiped her conscious clean about the other night. Essie gets out of the truck and Yanie drove off. Feeling loose on her way inside, she decides to momentarily sit down on the steps. Essie looks up at the sky glad to not experience any bizarre episodes nor any fight-or-flight response. Only a moment where the breeze can be felt, and the silence remains bliss.

"Ma'am?" a voice called to her. "Excuse me, ma'am?"

Essie slightly groaned to see it was a homeless man at the bottom of the steps. He was a forty-year-old Caucasian whose face was engulfed in a messy grey beard. His shirt was torn with many holes and wore sandals.

"Are you ok there?" he asks.

"Yes." She immediately replied, her eyelids closing down more. "I'm doing fine."

"You've just been sitting there for ten min—"

"I don't have any change."

The man looked offended. "I'm not asking for no handout, just seemed concerned. Usually it's a little girl I see sitting by these steps."

The realization that he watches Larissa, unbeknownst to her, everyday relaxing had alerted Essie.

"Sir, do not watch my daughter!"

"I see her around, nothing weird about that. There ain't nothing perverse about it. Seems like a good kid."

There was this draining feeling circulating in Essie's body. Her muscles were numb causing her to subside towards the upper step. Essie hoped Larissa wouldn't catch her like this; she hoped this guy would disappear.

"Sir, don't you have somewhere better to be?!" she groaned. "I'm not in the mood for this right now."

"I don't, I just make my way arou—"

"Well, leave then!" she barked. "Unless you want me to call the police? You wanna wind up in a coffin tonight?!"

"OR MAYBE THEY'LL HAUL YOUR DRUNK ASS TO THE DRUNK TANK! YOU DON'T FUCKING TALK TO ME LIKE THAT!" the man snapped. Essie is surprised by him hollering about how people ignore or mercilessly scream at him. *"IT'S ALWAYS FREEZING OUT AT NIGHT. HELL, AT LEAST A COFFIN'S WARM AND SOMEWHERE TO REST. I'D LIVE FOR THAT!"*

Essie observed this man's attire again only to be reminded how she mistreated him. He could see it on her face that she regrets it and he decides to walk off.

"Keep warm tonight, sir." She said.

"Don't worry." he responds sounding irked. "To where my fate lies, I'll rest warm at home soon enough."

Essie struggled inside after watching him disappear.

MIDTOWN 1:12 P.M.

The next day, Solanda Wright had driven to one of the community colleges to meet up with someone. Solanda had requested to meet with a girl through a dating app who was physically attractive by her boyfriend's standards. Her name was Chloe Miller; she was a student taking two summer classes. Both women were talking for a week and Solanda had sent pictures of her and Jovanny together. While walking around, Solanda noticed how almost empty the campus seems during the summer. Chloe had sent a message to meet her at the school coffee shop.

Once she arrives, Chloe waves at her, then the two greet each other. Chloe was a slim Caucasian twenty-eight-year-old. Her hair was dyed purple with such a youthful bright face. She had small breasts and a big butt. Solanda bought coffee, Chloe had bought herself a bottle of water. They both sat at a small table close at the window.

"Here we are." Solanda said cheerily. "You look good. Like, I'll be honest with you, I'm glad you actually exist."

Chloe chuckled and nods. "I get what you mean. Just glad I haven't been catfished yet either. But when I saw your photos, I knew it was the real deal."

"Believe me, I'm not dangerous. So how often you use dating apps?"

"I have a couple times." Chloe confessed. She tells about how she's met a few creepy guys. That some older men had cut contact once they'd been intimate and how she wants to give it a chance with females now. "And I'm sure you're fine. I just feel safer meeting strangers somewhere public."

"Ok, that sucks though." Solanda said. "Some guys are like that. But full-disclosure, I'd want us to have an addition of my boyfriend."

Chloe was suddenly quiet, looking as if she's trying to conjure up an excuse. Solanda senses her discomfort.

"I'm not upset or nothin'." Solanda gently said. "I just thought you'd know from the photos and me bringing up my boyfriend constantly over texts."

"Jovanny." Chloe quickly added. "Jovanny Gibbs."

Solanda was surprised but confused.

"That's right, except I ain't never mentioned his name. So, you already know him?" Solanda skeptically asks. Chloe begrudgingly nods. "You two dated or something?"

Chloe scoffed. "No, never. But he did date my sister."

Solanda already assumed the worst based on these few weeks. However, she sat silently drinking her coffee as Chloe elaborates. Years ago, Chloe's older sister named Miranda, had a yearlong relationship with Jovanny Gibbs. Miranda had been approached by him in a dollar store, she was instantly charmed by the guy. When she introduced him to her sister, Chloe sensed a bad aura while around him. Miranda never listened and continued dating him. Jovanny refused to pay for dates, meet with their parents nor even say he loved her (*if he ever did*). She had caught Jovanny cheating twice but still forgave him. Miranda had confessed to Chloe about him coming home late and always ignoring her calls when she moved in with him. This sent Miranda in a constant state of paranoia about him cheating. One night, they had an intense argument; resulting in him severing the relationship and kicking her out. Chloe revealed her sister had to move back home. Miranda was heartbroken for months. Her whole positive demeanor had changed into a pessimistic one. She alienated herself in her room from her family every time she'd arrive from work. Chloe struggled breaking Miranda out of this funk but eventually she encouraged her sister to date a kinder guy.

Miranda met a good man who treated her right. They became engaged after two years together. Her spirits uplifted, but she still felt tethered to Jovanny Gibbs, who never called to work things out. Just completely cut contact. Chloe urged her to not reach out to him. However, Miranda sent him her wedding invite as one last attempt at closure. Jovanny's presence at her wedding made her the happiest woman in the world. She admitted how much she missed him once they were in private. This had emboldened Jovanny to persuade Miranda to not follow through with her wedding. Miranda had left her fiancé alone at the altar.

Solanda was fully engaged and perplexed by the story.

"So, they just fled away together?"

"Yeah." Chloe said. "She called our mom and told us she couldn't move on from her ex. Her ex who didn't even try to meet our parents."

"Look, I get it, that's shitty." Solanda admits. "But your sister made that choice. Jovanny couldn't force her."

"I know." Chloe begrudgingly said. "I know. I just couldn't believe she'd hurt her fiancé like that, all just for him. But I can blame him for how he treated my sister afterwards." She sensed Solanda's nervous demeanor. "Not only had Jovanny still cheated on my sister but convinced her to quit her job because the company was moving across the country. He convinced her that our parents were just shaming her and didn't want what's best for her since she went back to him. Causing for her to ghost them."

"Chloe—"

"But the worst thing was when she called me late at night after months without hearing her. I remember I had a friend on the other line discussing some other shit. My sister was crying over the phone about how Jovanny had gotten her pregnant since he was annoyed with using condoms. That he forced her to get an abortion. And once she did, he kicked her out." Chloe was boiling. "She couldn't bring herself to come home, to face our parents, she just needed someone to talk to that night. We talked for a while, but she couldn't afford to stay anywhere else. She told me not to worry, that she'd figure something out." Chloe was momentarily trying to gather her words. Her lips quivered as her face slowly goes red. Then she finally manages to choke out: "Three weeks later our families called to identify her body at the morgue. Autopsy revealed a suicide overdose. My parents were devastated, I was haunted with guilt. That I couldn't do anything. By how much I knew about their relationship, I still failed her."

It was extremely uncomfortable having all of this told about the man Solanda loves. Chloe's genuine reaction expressed that this wasn't just some random woman lying about him. Solanda placed her palm over Chloe's hand.

"I'm so sorry for your loss."

"Thank you." Chloe's tone struggled.

Solanda was still perplexed. "I've gotta ask." She politely began. "Why'd you accept to meet with me then? With everything you knew about him? What's the point?"

Chloe gulps her water. "Because this is a warning from someone who's still suffering from the aftermath of knowing this man. Leave him." Chloe urges. "Cut him off through text or fucking ghost him. Because he doesn't truly respect or even care about the women he's with. Jovanny will one day end up locked alone in a room by himself with no choice but to self-reflect. So, when I saw him in your pictures, I knew I just had to reach out."

"Well, thanks. But him and me—we're good. Like, I'm sorry for your sister but I don't need to be saved." Solanda respectfully said, then sips her coffee.

Chloe nodded. *"Okay, I understand."* She sulkily said, then gets up. "You can always message me if anything just so you know."

"Sorry, I'm not interested." Solanda firmly said, then continues to drink her coffee.

Solanda watched as Chloe left. She's still processing everything she just revealed. Then her thoughts recalled whether he was honest about his other two ex-girlfriends.

† *Newly Avenue 1:55 P.M.*

Elijah Atwood has been waiting in the grassy landscape by the sidewalk. He rests under a shady tree; tall weeds and grass bombard him. While outside, he notices the usual black man setting up his truck in order to sell watermelons. Elijah sees another Christian handing out more flyers advertising their church. The watermelons would be tasty to eat right now but he didn't want to give away his position. Elijah was waiting for Larissa Sheppard.

This boy has been obsessed with her since his eyes noticed her in their biology class freshman year. He noticed how friendly she was the first semester and introduced himself. Elijah normally was quiet, but his attitude changed whenever Larissa's beautiful face appeared. He requested her on social media. Elijah liked every post, viewed her stories and messaged her to hang out together. Throughout the school year, he would go out of his way to interact with her. Sometimes by walking alongside her after their class was over. Always cracking jokes that occasionally made her giggle. Even forcing a conversation in attempts to build rapport with her.

Unfortunately for him, Larissa never dated him. A whole summer apart would kill him. Catching up with her on this avenue was the highlight of his summer thus far. He hadn't realized him constantly pursuing her had driven her further. The night of their fight had been replaying in his head. Also, a student from their school had recorded it from afar and posted it on social media group chat for their entire grade to see. Students mocking him online about it had increased his humiliation. It stung more watching himself sulking on camera after being beaten by a girl. His pride was obliterated by how meaningless Larissa recently treated him at her front steps. Especially since her boyfriend silently watched. She unfollowed him from social media; then soon blocked him when he tried to rectify it online.

The embarrassment was ingrained deeply. Elijah kept recalling what happened with scenarios of other things he could've done to rectify that night. This kept him infuriated but couldn't release Larissa from his mind.

Elijah had gone to explore the sketchy parts of Holksdale and had encountered Nneka Barshak. She hadn't cared about his age. Nneka sold him a pistol; Elijah refused to accept her offer on how to fire it. All he needed to know was based off what he's seen on TV. Television was the same basis he used for lessons on love, relationships and happily ever after. Elijah scans the area for a while more until Larissa appeared walking with her headphones on.

"LARISSA!" he yelled. She had turned to realize it was him then kept moving forward. *"LARISSA!"* his voice echoed the street. Seeing her continuously move on had him grow annoyed. Elijah's fists balled up. His pistol is held to his waist. While observing his target, he reached at his pistol. The street went silent as a gunshot went off.

† Chapter 19: *Shit, who am I to play God?!*

At killip's Quarter's, the club is filled, male customers have recently been increasing each night. This is from the sexual decline spreading throughout Holksdale. Solanda Wright has enjoyed seeing some regulars and they're always enthused to seek her. However, after her interaction with Chloe, she's been contemplating Jovanny Gibbs.

Solanda's on her break with Latoya. Latoya has been getting adjusted with being pregnant. She's been saving her money while implementing the advice from Lorell St. Louis. Latoya brags about being treated by many guys on dates, having men buy her baby essentials (*crib, diapers, food*) for her upcoming child and gaining this all without breaking a sweat (*nor her belt*). As for Solanda, she confided her boyfriend's past to her, including Miranda Miller.

"Damn." Latoya said in disbelief. "She took her life?"

Solanda reluctantly nods her head. "She actually warned me about him. Implying he'll hurt me next. Like, I knew he had a falling out with some of these girls, but this here, that's way too much."

"How you not leave him after his ex's pulled up calling him out on his shit?"

"Because he told me how they fucked up. Told me how crazy they were and it don't help they pulled up at our spot starting bullshit, showcasing it neither. But I'm starting to wonder if he was keeping it real with me."

"Ghost his ass!" Latoya said. "This fool ain't shit."

"I can't, at least I don't wanna just jump to conclusions."

Latoya urges for her to move in with her instead. Encouraging her that she doesn't deserve to tolerate this. She even recalls the feminist's advice about believing she's the prize; that men like him don't appreciate good women.

"I can't just up and leave—I love him too much."

"He ever tell you that?" Latoya asked. Solanda's speechless. "Has Jovanny ever told you how much he loves you?" she firmly repeats.

"Never…" she confessed, her voice croaked.

"You deserve better. I know you deserve better. You can get—listen right quick!" Latoya said as they grew silent. The men started howling over the strippers performing. "I done seen so many thirsty dudes write they number on bills they be sliding you. You can literally get any man out there."

This insight was nothing new to Solanda. She appreciates them feeding off her beauty and even sometimes advice. However, she felt bind to Jovanny Gibbs.

"I'm only sprung on him." Solanda confirms. "I'm not trying to get hurt again. But with these patterns of women being done wrong by him… *I dunno."*

"Then put your foot down, girl. Or better yet, close up shop. Ain't no more fucking until he proves himself. I can lend you my spare chastity belt, sis."

"That shit won't work. I love sex as much as him. Plus, I don't want him thinking I bought into this whole feminist agenda pulling that tactic. Either he'll leave me or he won't care about me leaving him. I want him to change for me on his own, showing he really does love me."

Latoya reminds her about taking back your power.

"Extract the best of the best resources from him." Latoya reassures her. "Only way you gonna get that boy to behave is to have the upper hand. Like, say if you get knocked up."

"Say what now?"

Latoya had a devilish grin. "You heard me. One puny hole in a condom, he'll do whatever you say for the rest of his life."

"What if I just end up like one of these single baby mommas out these streets?"

"You just threaten his ass with child support. Then he'll do everything to keep y'all situation going. You'll have all the power the way God intended, he won't wanna pull no goofy shit. That first expensive child support payment gets due, he'll be wishing to burn in hell."

Solanda's actually contemplating this theory. She knows how deceitful this is. Latoya encourages how it'll save their relationship. Then her mind whirled with the memories of his ex-girlfriends who were hurt by him. Knowing she doesn't want to be in their position.

"I mean," she mumbled. "I'm doing this to save us."

"Exactly." Latoya said as she resumes to her job.

Solanda Wright knew that she wasn't always great at choosing men. All this worrisome reminded her of being impacted by her longest boyfriend. Her worst relationship was a few years ago with a guy named Oscar. Solanda had let him move in with her around the time they decided to make their relationship more serious. Both were living fine together for a while. Solanda was still working as a stripper; Oscar had a job at a packaging company. Eventually Oscar had lost his job and struggled while searching for work. Days had gone with Oscar being supported off Solanda's money. She paid all the bills, bought the food and bought him stuff. There was this domineering attitude that she slowly developed. It inflated her ego whenever Oscar would politely request her to buy him something. Unfortunately, this dynamic led to their mutual respect being subsided. Whenever she was upset about something small, she would verbally disrespect Oscar. It could've been a mistake he made or even forgetting something. She would exaggerate it and go off on a tangent about him not working, commanding him around without hesitation. Solanda enforced rules for him to obey. If Oscar had stood his ground, she would kick him out her apartment. Oscar would be sitting outside until he'd eventually grovel back apologizing. It became routine for him to submit.

One time Oscar was playing videogames on the couch. He hadn't showered for a few days since Solanda didn't feel like being intimate that week. Intimacy was only shared on her terms. Horny Oscar was slouched in his funky, crisp boxers. He could overhear her on the phone with her friends complaining about Oscar still being unemployed. Solanda wasn't even slightly fazed by his upset presence. He wanted to speak up but there was no exception to interrupting her while on the phone. Then she hung up.

"Babe," Oscar sheepishly called. "What you doing going out telling my business for?"

Solanda sneered. "Business?! *You got a startup plan, nigga?!* Last I checked, entrepreneurs have businesses. Not no broke bitch sleeping up on my couch, taking up all my damn space. You ain't got no privacy up in here. Everything you do is my business."

Oscar deflated, slowly resuming to his game, praying that she doesn't instigate more issues.

"Everything you got, I paid for." She reaffirmed. "Best believe that! Then you got the audacity to ask for some head last night. Fool, you ain't shower for—what, three days now—but got the nerve to beg for me to gobble up them salty nuts. You got me fucked up. Turn that game off!"

"Nah, c'mon." he pleads. *"My fault, my fault."*

"I ain't gonna ask twice." She repeats. Then watches him obey. "What you need to do is you need to peel your ass up off that couch so you can peel them damn skid marks out your drawers." She watched Oscar trudge over to the laundry basket. "And make sure you wash my damn clothes first too while you at it!"

Life for them living together was like this for months. She would dictate anything that goes on under her roof (*food, TV and phone privileges, curfew, and sex*). Oscar felt that Solanda was his goddess who he could depend on since she provided for him. He pedestalized her despite her egregious behavior.

Even whenever he had the urge to search for a job, his spirit was so crushed by his girlfriend's mistreatment that he had developed this slothful mentality.

Then one night, Solanda had granted Oscar his small allowance for the week. While unemployed, he took his chances with the lottery. He had won twenty-six dollars off of a scratch-off ticket. Oscar was ecstatic to where his girlfriend detected this.

"What you so happy about?" she asks.

"I got it, I got it."

"A job?!" she mocked. "You got your own shit, got your own place finally?!"

"Nah, the matching logos." Oscar cheers, as he showed the ticket. "I can't believe this."

"Me neither. How much I won?"

Oscar slowly grasped the question. *"Wait. Say what?"*

"Nigga, you deaf?!" she said. "How much I won?" she studies his perplexed face. Then began to laugh at him. "Oh, you thought we were gonna split that?! It was my money that bought you it." she said, then extends her hand out.

"Baby, I won twenty-six bucks off this, c'mon now." Oscar politely said. "And it was my allowance, remember?"

"Don't make me ask twice."

He got irked at her for attempting to take this from him.

"You can't just do me like this." Oscar protests. "I'm sick of you trying to renege on me."

"And I'm sick of you living under my roof, eating—"

"STOP! YO, CUT THAT SHIT OUT!" he hollered. Then he rants about how she allows him those privileges. *"YOU CAN'T JUST ALWAYS USE THAT AS LEVERAGE!"*

"I SEE YOU PRETTY BOLD SINCE YOU GOT A LITTLE

POCKET CHANGE! THAT'S NOT GONNA SUPPORT YOU OUT THERE ON THESE STREETS, NIGGA!"

The couple have an intense argument. Solanda threatened to kick him out again if he refused to give up the ticket. Oscar randomly being defiant had increased her wrath. This sent her to ridicule him for remaining unemployed, lacking ambition, begging for everything and all his past mistakes. Oscar discriminates her job as a stripper; labeling her as a slut.

"YOU RELY ON MY CHECK STILL, WHICH BOUGHT YOU THAT TICKET, YOU JOBLESS BITCH!"

"AND YOU TAKE SO MUCH PRIDE IN THAT SHIT!"

"YET YOU STILL CALL ME GODDESS AND SHIT." she screamed. *"JUST KEEP PUTTING UP WITH IT. YOU'RE NOT NO FUCKING MAN."*

"SHUT UP! SHUT YOUR FUCKIN' MOUTH, BITCH!"

"I HAVE TO CARRY THIS RELATIONSHIP, JUST HOW I GOTTA CARRY AFTER MYSELF." She announced while gesturing towards her vagina. Then she roared: *"WITH YOU, I HAD TO FAKE ALL MY ORGASMS. YOU AIN'T—"*

Oscar furiously gave her a crisp face slap. Her whole body twisted the opposite direction. All that superiority had escaped and been replaced by terror. Fear of how he'll react next once she slowly faces him. Oscar's whole demeanor changed as his body was erect; his stern face observed her whole being struggling. Her face and spirit felt a lasting stung that she refused to accept. Solanda called the police to report domestic abuse. They arrested Oscar after examining her swollen cheek. That was the end of their relationship. After Oscar, she hadn't really been too invested in other guys until Jovanny himself. She remembered that Oscar felt emboldened to hit her since he believed he received a slither of control. She pondered about Jovanny potentially harming her like Oscar if she didn't have complete control. This realization solidified her choice to go through with it.

Kental Avenue, 2:15 P.M.

On this day, Icarus McGrew had arranged to pick up a young lady who agreed to go out with him for a date. He had met her last weekend at the pharmacy when he was buying bandages for his recent bruises. She noticed them and they conversed about the craziness that transpired. She laughed at the misfortune as he was cracking jokes on himself. They exchanged numbers and were talking since then. Icarus was surprisingly receiving texts back but was still anxious that she may change her mind. Now he's parked at the address of the house she gave to get her.

Icarus rings the doorbell. To his surprise, a fifty-year-old Puerto Rican man answered the door.

"Hello, can I help you?"

Icarus nervously began. "Hello, sir. I'm here—"

"I know." He firmly said. "And why's that?"

"Does Natalia live here?"

The man crossed his arms, scanning Icarus from head to toe. "Who wants to know?"

Icarus softly explained that they agreed to go on a date to a restaurant within the area. There was an uncomfortable silence between them. The man had introduced himself as Natalia's father.

"I'm Icarus." He blurts then quickly extends for a handshake.

"Woah, wait! What're you reaching for?" he said, taking a step back, covering his groin.

"No, no, no. Don't worry, I'm not like—not gay."

"What's off about being gay?" he asks skeptically.

Icarus can feel his entire upper body tensing up. It's evident how shaky his arms were now. He was tongue-tied.

The man laughs. "Got'cha."

Icarus nervously joins in the laughter. Her dad reassures him that he knew the whole time and that Natalia is busy getting ready still. Icarus had a huge relieved look. In attempts to keep the friendly vibe going, Icarus informs him more about himself. About his age, his profession and how they first met. Her father introduced himself as Hugo.

"So, what're your intentions?"

"Just getting to know each other over some food."

Hugo nods. "Good, good. Keep her safe."

Natalia comes to the door. She's dressed in a blue summer dress, carrying a small purse. Icarus absorbs the beauty of this twenty-two-year old Puerto Rican girl. She even worn her glasses. She gives Icarus a sweet hug, then promises her dad they'll make her ten o'clock curfew.

"It was nice to meet you, Icarus." Hugo said. "You seem

like a good guy."

"You too." Icarus cheerily said. "Actually, since we're all here, let's meet her mom."

Hugo was still at the door. Natalia insists that they don't want to be late for their reservation.

"It's okay, I'll get us there in time. Don't worry." He reassured then turned to Hugo. "Your daughter told me she'd be here with her parents so I may as well get to know her mom too since I'm here, right?" Icarus chuckled.

A small silence occurred as Hugo stood at his front steps without breaking eye-contact with him and announced: "Honey, someone's at the door for you."

They all quietly wait a couple seconds until a forty-five-year old black man appeared answering: "Yea, what's up?"

†

They arrived at the restaurant on time for their reservation in midtown. Natalia selected the table by the window. Icarus pulled her chair out for her; she silently sat down checking the menu. Icarus couldn't decide his dish.

Icarus turned to the waitress. "Can you please give us a minute? We might take a while."

"Excuse me." Natalia sternly protest. "I know what I want. I just kept weighing my options first."

Natalia firstly orders an appetizer of nuts. Icarus didn't expect to pay for appetizers but remained silent. It's his treat. She follows that order with two plates of food. Fried chicken tenders and fries; barbeque ribs with fries and corn.

She even orders pineapple soda. Icarus concealed his shock with a neutral expression. He could afford this but it seemed costly. Then attempts to search the menu; still indecisive about what he craves. Natalia encourages the waitress to leave now since her date was taking forever. The waitress says she'll get him a glass of water.

They're now paired alone. Icarus smiles at her; Natalia decides to look at her phone instead.

"You look pretty."

"Thanks." She said flatly, still scrolling her phone.

Icarus begins pondering. "You're dad seems nice."

"Which one?"

"Um, the black one?" he said, she looks at him. "Hugo seemed nice too. Didn't catch his husband's name though."

"You mean the black one?!" She scoffed. "It's Isaiah." She returns to her phone.

Icarus stretched his eyes over at her phone. "So what're you doing there?" he asks in a light-hearted tone.

"What happened?" she asks. He softly repeated. "I'm just seeing who's liked my most recent post."

"That's cool. Posted about our date?"

"Nope."

Icarus didn't want to seem too eager to force a conversation. He let Natalia have a moment of some silence to herself. The incoming footsteps of the waitress had brought Natalia's head up. They received one water, one pineapple soda and a bowl of three nuts. The man-sized nut filled up the bowl; each was the size of a tennis ball.

The waitress asks if Icarus knew what he'd like yet. He decided to have the small hot chicken wings with fries. Once the waitress left, Natalia grabbed a handful of the nut.

Natalia shook her head after one bite.

"You don't like it?"

"No, why'd you let me order this?" she growled.

Icarus shrugged his shoulders. "I honestly don't know what to say." He warily said.

Natalia tries washing the taste down with her pineapple drink. "*Great!* They brought me the wrong one. Can you go up to her?"

"On it." Icarus said. He finds the waitress walking with someone else's order. "Hey, excuse me." he gently said. "My date says she got the wrong order."

"I didn't bring your food yet."

"No, no. Her drink. Pineapple soda."

"Yeah, she's got it." the waitress confirms. "She's the only one who's ordered that today."

Icarus was flabbergasted at her response. He thanked her; leaving away confused. Once he returns to his table, he sees Natalia's gone. Icarus sits down thinking she went to the bathroom until he checked over at her drink. The glass was halfway empty. Then looks over at her chair to see her purse wasn't even rested on her chair. A negative scenario came to mind. He wondered if she left him. Icarus quickly eliminates that and thought: *No, she wouldn't just leave me. I wouldn't do that. It didn't go that bad, we literally just got here. She probably got a bit nervous and had to escape to the little girl's room for a quick second. Yeah, yeah, that's it.* His phone vibrates. It's from his date. She just messaged him that she was annoyed with the appetizer, the drink and the waitress taking too long with her food. She says she decided to go. Icarus looked around to catch sight of her. His head whipped at the window but couldn't find a trace of her. Icarus sits wooden in disbelief; he feels his face descend into a small pout. The waitress is coming with the food.

"Here's her plates." The waitress said. "Yours will unfortunately take a little longer."

Icarus feels exposed, then confessed: *"Ma'am, she's not here. She's left."*

"No I didn't." Natalia laughed. Icarus was perplexed at the sound of her voice. Her head appeared, still laughing. "I didn't leave you, my food ain't even come yet. I've been here this whole time. I was wearing my ghost cloak."

Icarus was shocked. Not by her being invisible but from her revealing her true intensions. The waitress excused herself then left. The ghost cloak reminded him about what Jovanny had mentioned involving a feminist encouraging her supporters to abstain from intercourse. Icarus purposely knocked down his phone. When he bent down to get it, he detected Natalia wearing a chastity belt under her summer dress. Icarus revealed his head at the table now looking irked. Natalia noticed his silence; he's just staring outside.

"What's wrong with you?" she judgmentally asked.

"Nothing." He sighed.

She watches him while eating her ribs. After there being

no talking for several minutes, she decides to engage.

"So… how old are you again?"

"Thirty."

"I went out with a guy in his thirties once. Took me to some concert, then dinner afterwards."

"Did he bring you here to eat?"

Natalia chuckles. "No, somewhere nicer than here."

"Do you normally date older men?"

She shrugs. "Depends. I used to get asked out by a bunch of older men at this restaurant I used to work at. They'd slip me their number at the cash register."

"You're a cashier."

"No. I was until I got fired." She said. Then elaborates about how some woman lied about her meal which led to an argument. Then resulted in a physical altercation. "She thought she was 'all that' since she was going to heaven."

"Customers' always right." Icarus added. She looked at him annoyed. "I'm joking. Just joking."

"Mm-hmm. Actually my last date was with an older guy in his late twenties that took me for coffee earlier." She said, snickering. "Hell, this is my second date today."

Natalia persisted with asking more about him. His food hadn't come yet, but gulped his water. Icarus tried to politely decline answering some questions (*about his finances, what kind of home he lived in and how many women has he been involved with)*. She looked eager to know these essentials; her eye contact was held as she consumed her plate. Icarus said he dated four women and had never tried to cheat.

Natalia had an envious look. She confides that most of her ex-boyfriends had cheated. That she forgave them but they didn't change; and proudly admits that she ended each relationship on her terms. Natalia gets approached by men constantly which raised her ego.

"Bet you're glad I gave you a chance, huh?"

Icarus shrugged. She looked offended.

"I mean, you haven't really tried getting to know me."

"Yes, yes I have." She condescendingly said.

"Asking about how much money I make isn't getting to know me." Icarus bluntly said.

Natalia looks stupefied. "Well, excuse me. I just didn't want to come off too strong."

"By asking how many women I've been with?!"

"I was just wondering your body count. You don't look like the type—"

"Type?"

"The type to get women. Like, I did you a favor giving someone outta my league a shot. I could've flaked, y'know."

"You may as well have." Icarus snapped. He brings up about her spending the beginning on her phone, acting obnoxious and pulling that childish prank. "And also, what makes you think you're such a prize to begin with?!"

"My genetics." She proudly said. "My face and body." She ostentatiously pointed at. "I keep attracting guys. Whether they're up to my standards or are guys like you."

"But all your boyfriends cheated for another pretty girl. There's not much to you other than your looks."

Natalia begins seething. Icarus rants about her being unemployed. Other customers were glancing at them.

"Unlike you, I've got a job. My own home without having to leech off daddy, or shall I say daddies. And a car."

"Who the hell are you to judge?!" she roars. "You don't know a thing about me!"

"And who's fault is that?! You've mostly been on your fucking phone. I've got more to offer than you do!"

"Y'know what else you got that I don't—money. Because you're gonna pay for this right?"

The waitress had come over politely requesting for them to lower it down. They're table was uncomfortably silent. Natalia was veering her eyes to see if customers were still staring. Icarus didn't care, he was peeved. His annoyance inflates realizing that his food still hasn't arrived. He settles for eating one of the nuts. Natalia could hear his aggravated crunching. Seeing how she's had this much impact on him actually made her feel important.

"Icarus." She said. "You've never dated much, have you?" His silence answered her question, and he knew it. "I could tell. Have you ever been intimate with a woman?"

He was too drained to either lie or deflect. They both already knew.

"So how about this?" Natalia tempted. "You seemed to make a good first impression with my dad, so I'll give you one last chance to show me how good you are. And maybe, just maybe, I'll let you show me this home you were telling me about." she offered. Icarus looked curious. "You buy me another drink, give me some of the fries off your plate then pay the whole bill. And maybe tonight you'll get to count your blessings. Sounds good?"

Icarus appears transfixed by this. She clutched tight to her purse with a belief that paying for her share was considered sacrilege. Then realized she's most likely as good as it gets for him. He shamefully nodded.

The waitress had finally brought his plate of food. Icarus ordered his date another pineapple soda, sending a big grin on Natalia's face. Once the waitress had left, Natalia immediately grabbed some fries off his plate. Then the two were silently eating. Icarus noticed the two nuts left (*including the one with a huge bite his date took*) and began eating the other one. As he remained still, his thoughts raced over the women who've offended him. That this is what he must resort to in order to have sex. This is the closest thing to a miracle he's ever going to get. Jovanny's advice about dates and women had infiltrated his head. All these criticisms that've been rattling him had resurrected.

The waitress brings them their check, then left. Natalia tells him to go ask for something to package her food in. Icarus got up. Natalia's promise replayed in his head; the possibility of intimacy almost sounded worth it. But at the cost of him losing more of himself, after everything she did today. At this moment, he didn't obsess over why he failed with women or about chasing women. Icarus finally decides to go his own way. He veered around and didn't detect any employees; Icarus flees the restaurant, regaining himself.

†

Grant Critchfield prepares himself at his house for this interview. He's dressed well in an expensive suit. This was set up by Joy Pluss, who urged for him to not be combative. That the audience can have a more positive outlook on him based on this. She informs Grant that many celebrities have been on there. Cherry Stockdale is the hostess, with a female audience. She is known to extract information from all her famous guests. However, she is sternly direct, blunt, argumentative, and was always in a state of collectedness. Or when she'll create a feeling of comfort, only to steer guests into a vulnerable, inferior position.

Knowing this beforehand, Grant wanted to refuse. Joy reminds him of ruining the other alternatives. Grant protests that his money funded the bridge construction still. Joy advises him to answer the questions civilly (*not condescendingly*) and to refrain from divulging too much. Joy strictly repeats herself, then makes Grant repeat it. She encourages him to think positively about the outcome.

His mother is heard watching TV in the living room. Grant felt compelled to converse with her. Since he has returned home, she has been lukewarm towards her son. Violet's face remains emotionless whenever he's nearby. Grant decides to tell her about the interview.

Once Grant's footsteps are heard, Violet's eyes latch onto the TV screen. He greets his mom, she didn't respond. As he drew close, Violet then crossed her arms. Grant wants for her to view his attire to at least ask why he got dressed up. However, Violet stared intently at the screen. The lack of interest did not deter Grant from continuing. He tells about this interview his agent set up for him on "The Cherry Stockdale Show". Violet nonchalantly nods, still plain.

"Mom," Grant hesitantly began. *"About this situation involving me…"* he watched as Violet got up off the couch. His sight flows in her direction as she poured herself some tea. This feeling of withdrawing distance had tugged at him. "Alright, mom." He then shrugged. "I'll be home soon."

"Which situation?" Violet skeptically asks.

Violet's tone ceased Grant's movement. He knew what she meant. Their eye contact with each other would not break. Silence fell between them.

"I'm sure you're well-aware of me, mom."

"Which part?" Violet patronizes him. Bringing up Grant's past movie roles, TV roles, controversial online posts.

"My recent circumstances." Grant bluntly replies.

"And again, which part?" she brought up his past drunk driving incidents. Taunting about him lashing out at the paparazzi. Lastly, she announced how his relationship unfolded with Tatum Maxwell.

"She was just someone I mentored." He hissed. "I di—"

"Countless times I've heard your name make notoriety. As famous as you are, you're recognized for something as horrendous as this. How could you disgrace the family name, Noah?!"

"Huh?" Grant responds, sounding unconvinced. He goes

on about how his mother returned to her maiden's name after his father died.

"Your father would've understood, Noah!" Violet blurts out. Her tone grows frail at the mention of his father. Then deflects that he would not understand how his own son could commit these terrible transgressions. "You were drunk, weren't you? Or on drugs? Or both?"

"Mom—"

"I don't want to hear it!" Violet barked, her voice trembles unsteadily as a sly hurt pinched at her throat. "*You were such a sweet boy, Noah. Then the more popular you became, the more craziness about you I overhear.*"

Just that confession alone had sent this spiraling inflow of sorrow to clog, just awaiting to burst loose. Drumming through him, intensified by the pressure of her words. Lastly, gushing out in the form of an unsettling frown.

"Well, how's about you pray for me then?!" Grant said in a snobbish tone, in attempts to feel superior. "Better yet, try splashing me with some holy water." His eyes trailed off to the wooden cross on the wall. "Or convert me with this?"

"You disgust me, Noah." Violet coldly said.

"Grant!" he asserts. "My name is now Grant! The world knows me, identifies me as such."

His mother's sorrowful eyes observe his face entirely. Searching for a trace of something familiar. "*Well, Grant… I don't recognize you. I haven't for a very long time now. Sometimes I just wonder what goes on in that head of yours.*" She left him. Then Grant just left Noah behind on his way out.

Downtown

"LARISSA!" Elijah yelled. She had turned to realize it was him then kept moving forward. *"LARISSA!"* his voice echoed the street. Seeing her continuously move on had him grow annoyed. Elijah's fists balled up. His pistol is held to his waist. While observing his target, he reached at his pistol. Elijah firmly grabs it causing for the gun to fire off.

The gunshot echoed that street causing most adults to flee. Larissa had frozen; her wooden neck reluctantly turned to find Elijah Atwood collapsed onto the pavement. She rushed over to him as well as the man selling watermelons.

"HELP!" Larissa bawled, trying not to step in his blood.

The man attempts to pull him up, revealing the pistol drenched in blood. Elijah's face looks weakly. His eyes barely keep open, high-pitched piercing cries escape his quivered lips, and his muscle strength sunk.

"Cover your eyes!" the man warned Larissa. She obeyed by facing the opposite way. "What happened?"

"I-I" she stammered. "I heard him calling me but I just kept it pushing. Then I heard the gunshot. I think he did this to get me to acknowledge him. *I don't know.*"

"It's okay." The man said to them both. "Call 9-1-1!"

Larissa immediately does on her phone. She informs them about what happened and what avenue they're on. Elijah stares at Larissa's back. She couldn't bring herself to leave until the ambulance arrives. Elijah Atwood had bled to death before anyone arrived.

At Chase's house, Larissa confesses this whole ordeal to him. She was shocked that Elijah would do this to himself. The image of his bloody form marinated her mind.

"What'd his folks say?" he asks.

"I dipped after the ambulance pulled up too late." She confessed. "The man there said that I should get home."

Chase could sense just how guilty she feels.

"You think this was about y'all fallout that night?" he gently asks. "About what you did?"

Larissa sighed, leaning into his arms. "I honestly hope not." She got wrapped in his arms. "I never should've did all that. It was all just a stupid joke."

"You want a drink?"

"I shouldn't be drinking. Let's just chill."

They both relaxed on his bed. Chase lets her rest on his chest. Larissa sulked, thinking about Elijah. Thinking of his parents coping with losing a child.

"I know he's in a better place." Chase assures her.

"Yea?" she hopefully responds.

"Yup. He was a good person just like you." He said. Then he kisses her. She passionately engages; he slides his palm on her back. His shadow emerged once he rolls on top of her. Larissa's slightly surprised but didn't let it bother her. Gentle kisses travel her neck which runs this tranquil sensation through her body. His mischievous fingers attempt to explore her thigh region—she halts his hand.

"Nah, baby." She declined. "I'm not really feelin' it."

"You looked like you were. C'mon." he softly said, then kissed her again, now trying to lift her shirt.

"Chase, chill with that!" she said sounding irked. "You doin' too much."

Chase ejects off the bed in frustration. "Don't tell me you fell for that whole feminist agenda crap. Or is this about you not wanting to offend God." He mocked.

"It's about me not—like, I don't have to. And it's weird you say that after saying Elijah's—"

"Elijah's fucking dead. Ain't nowhere else for him to be. I don't even buy into this miracle bullshit."

"Well, I do!"

Chase scoffed. "Oh, I know. Gave your ass a sense of purpose, huh? Like, you ain't think it's sad that you're trying so hard to get your mom into heaven? She treats you like shit. Just like you treated Elijah like shit."

"Screw you!"

"Worst part is you're busy looking dumb as fuck regardless of it being fake, just 'cause it has your ass feel self-assured." He proudly said. "And I'm glad you feel bad over Elijah, because you did that kid dirty." Chase mentions how she ignored him when he passed by her apartment. "You took such pride in watching him beg for your attention. And I know why you ain't have no issue letting him come over that day. All 'cause he boosts you up since you don't feel good about yourself."

Larissa's spirit was crushed, she knew he could see it. There wasn't anything she could think of in her defense.

"We're done." Chase firmly said. "Lose my number!"

† *Richez Shrive, 8:56 P.M.*

The bar has some people drinking tonight. Many were talking about Pastor Marques speaking out against that feminist that's been trending online. Icarus comes in to order his usual strawberry daiquiri. Jovanny notices his bruises after him being absent for a few days.

"Bro, the fuck happened to you?"

"Some guy did this to me." Icarus said. "Thought I was a creep coming onto a minor."

"Damn. You put up a fight at least?"

"I tried but it didn't work out too great."

"Well, what else is up with you? I noticed you been off the grid." Jovanny said.

Icarus told him about how bad his date with Natalia went earlier. Jovanny protested about him spending money on her. Then was surprisingly proud that Icarus abandoned her with the bill. Icarus even mentioned her proposal.

"Good thing you ain't follow through with it." Jovanny said. "As easy as she sounds, you'd likely end up catching herpes." He then confides about an angry husband confronting him about almost being intimate with his wife.

"And she lied about you getting her pregnant?"

"Yup. I swear, bitches create way too many theatrics."

As time passed, Icarus decides to order beer instead to relieve the memory of that godawful date. Jovanny groaned about his truck still being fixed. Icarus was consuming a lot more beer, listening to Jovanny. Natalia called Icarus seven times since he came to the bar; causing for both of them to just laugh about it. Icarus read her several text messages saying that she couldn't pay for her meals and drinks. That she had to call her dad to come take care of it. Then saying he made a huge mistake not taking her up on her offer.

Jovanny laughed. "Good on you, bro. Keep them texts for some shit to look back and laugh at."

"Yeah, yeah." Icarus cheerily agreed. His face started feeling numb as he ran his fingers across his cheeks. Jovanny detects his drunken state. Icarus gulped more of his drink. *"I actually might withdraw myself from dealing with women from so forth. No point in dealing with the same results."*

"Believe me, they love wasting your time."

Icarus sighed. *"Not in my case. They don't even like me around apparently. Refusing to reply to my texts, getting stood up, and being ridiculed no matter what the fuck I do."*

Jovanny's forced laugh showed his discomfort. "Icarus, I think that's that liquor talkin'. You've had yourself one too many, bro."

Icarus wildly shook his head. *"Nope, nope, nope. I've had awful results with females all since high school. Nothing's changed. Years down the line, still the same way."* He recalled how students talked bad about him, how other girls were always alert around him and how bad his friendship with Lori Timmerman was severed.

During his senior year, Icarus sat with Lori in the cafeteria for lunch. Lori had felt sorry for him being alienated from others; she's also upset about her best friend not being around her too often. Kimberly wasn't feeling comfortable enough sitting with her, knowing that Icarus would be there. She'd acknowledge Lori's presence but always remembered how obsessive Icarus had acted. Including her other friend, Helen Fair, who felt uneasy around him just by the sight of him. Lori didn't admit why either one felt creeped out about him. At lunch, she would sometimes glance over at Helen and Kimberly sitting with their group of girls talking and laughing.

Icarus noticed one day how reserved Lori was acting during lunch. She passive aggressively mentions how Kimberly refused to sit with her. Icarus knew it was because of him; but was surprised Lori would be that insensitive. Then she complains about him not moving on after Kimberly rejected him. Icarus claims he did, and they remained friends until she acted cold. Lori erupted at him about how deluded he was; Icarus lashed out because she kept criticizing him harshly.

"All you did was act fake whenever Kimberly came around." Lori snapped. "Constantly cracking jokes, acting upbeat, she saw right through you! She told me herself."

"We were friends, I could joke around if I want."

"No, you tried always impressing her. You didn't move on, even after she said she had a boyfriend. She had no clue what your intent was at that point. You scared her off."

"Her just being around made me happier." He warily said.

"It wasn't genuine. You were infatuated, you didn't know her on a personal level like I do."

Her sharp tone embarrassed Icarus. He knew she was right and even attempts to admit his fault, but Lori had no mercy. Lori's harsh voice thundered the cafeteria.

"I felt sorry for you since everybody's on edge being around you. Even Helen, the school whore doesn't want you. *YOU'RE GONNA DIE A VIRGIN!"* she proudly yelled.

That whole rant obliterated his fragile self-esteem. Lori snatched her lunch and walked off to the other table with Kimberly and Helen. Her words marinated in him, especially with other students staring at him afterwards, probably speculating that Icarus scared her away. Lori's laughter captured his attention; the girls were mocking him for being alienated from everyone.

Jovanny finished hearing his troubled story. Watching Icarus drunkenly attempt to maintain his pride.

"So, it's official." Icarus said, his tone faltered. *"I'm a certified creep."*

"Man, anything you're ashamed of, just bury it deep down. Then onto the next chapter of your life."

Icarus shrugged. *"I guess, but I'm on my thirtieth chapter now in life and it feels like I'm stuck on my seventeenth still. Lori was my only friend back then, I made it my mission to be a perfect gentleman. After that day at lunch, she never acknowledged my existence again. Spread rumors about me being creepy and I never gained closure with her before we graduated. She cut me deep. That's how she'll remember me."*

"Listen to me." Jovanny sincerely said. "You don't need no closure from her. Being validated is for women only, not for men. Even if she sees you how I see you, it ain't gonna do much for your life. Like, why's it matter?"

"I know. I know. I just would've been happier if I hadn't been treated that way." Icarus said. He brings up Lori's last words, labeling him. *"To this exact day, I remember her saying I'd die a virgin. That the school whore didn't even desire me one bit."*

"Icarus—"

"I wanted to lose my virginity to prove to myself that I could ever since then. That I wasn't creepy, that I'm capable of attracting the opposite sex all on my own. And as far as what Lori said, I'd always remind myself of that, believe it or not. Whenever I'd approach someone new, if she rejected me, it wouldn't matter. No rejection would be as hurtful as what Lori told me back then. However, it hasn't helped me much lately. It's been crippling me inside actually. I can just feel how women won't like me anyway, so really what's the point?"

Jovanny didn't know how to help him. He felt that maybe Icarus just needed to pour his heart out. There was a deeper issue that Jovanny had sensed but just couldn't detect. Icarus excused himself to the restroom.

In the bathroom stall, Icarus fell to his knees over the toilet as a messy turmoil poured out of his mouth. His throat felt burnt, a headache ensues and there's this sharp puncture in his stomach. He stuck two fingers down his throat to make him vomit more. Icarus buckles himself onto the toilet seat. He's slouched on the toilet; staring around the stall. There's a lot of blasphemy on the wall. His mind is struck with bad approaches causing him to hunch over feeling more drained. Icarus spots this odd writing on the wall: *in need of a guardian angel, call this number...*

Icarus was befuddled at this but simultaneously curious too. He first trudged out the stall to scan if anyone else came inside. Once it was clear, he dialed the number.

"Hello?" An angelic male voice immediately answered.

"Hi." Icarus replied with uncertainty by how quickly he picked up. *"I hear you could possibly help me, maybe?"*

There was a brief pause.

"What seems to be the problem?"

Icarus seemed a little cautious but continued. *"I'm not feeling too great lately. Kind of shitty actually."*

"I understand, you're not at peace. What's your name?"

"I'm not prank calling you or anything." Icarus immediately replied. *"I found your number written somewhere—you know what, I apologize. I'll leave you alone."*

"I'm not upset." The voice reassured. "Who have I got the pleasure of speaking with tonight?"

This question had Icarus feeling nervous. Whoever this was, they're beginning to pry, but it wasn't from frustration. Icarus couldn't just be rude and hang up; he felt stuck.

"My name's Matthew." Icarus warily said.

"Ok, Matthew. What exactly would you like to confess?"

Icarus was already hesitant to engage any further. Then the realization that this person on the other line has no clue as to who exactly Icarus was. No matter what Icarus unapologetically admits, he won't be identified as a creep. Perhaps he'll gain a better perspective. Icarus unfolds about his high school experience, from being fixated on Kimberly to Lori's final words and how it impacted him. He reminisces about the awful approaches he's recently initiated and how self-conscious he's now become. The man on the other line occasionally nonchalantly responds with "*mm-hmm*" to show he's still listening. Icarus reveals how he wanted to lose his virginity to confirm that he's not a creep. Then tells how hopeless it is for him at this point.

"*So, what do you think?*" Icarus asks.

"I think that you have been hurt." He replied. "I believe that this goal of yours, this temptation, is doing you more harm than good. How often do you advance toward women, Matthew?"

"*Always, pretty much waste most of my days except recently. I took a little hiatus because it was too much.*"

"What was?"

"*My thoughts.*" Icarus sulkily said. "*I can't help but feel burdened by the frustration. The embarrassment of feeling exposed for trying to proceed with a woman. For still being labeled creepy after all these years. That how after high school, I wasn't a Casanova like I envisioned I could be. Or that I could still obsess over what everyone thinks even after not feeling natural. After what Lori said.*"

The guy asked Icarus to elaborate more about him feeling unnatural. This request actually surprised Icarus.

"*Um, well, I haven't felt natural interacting with a female I've liked for a long time now. I think it started with Kimberly at first, I just became so infatuated by her that I acted way different. And*

I admit that. Back then, I thought feeling that happy was better and that I shouldn't let my peers ruin more of that. Even though I wasn't me."

"Why did you still embrace this persona if it wasn't who you really are?"

Icarus pondered on how to explain it. The guy encouraged for him to take his time.

"I spent most of high school alienated from everyone because I was nervous about how I was perceived. I was mostly an introvert until I met Lori, then Kimberly. So after I got this creepy reputation, it felt relieving to shift the blame onto how I acted. It was a liberating feeling to have this newfound shell shield me like a barrier instead. Those misplaced judgements weren't identifying me because I wasn't me. This shell would shield my heart from any future harsh rejections, and for years it did. But lately it hasn't helped much. These bad outcomes, nasty looks and repulsed reactions are beginning to creep in more, having me feel like I truly am one deep inside. I don't even think straight anymore."

After that entire confession, Icarus gained some tranquility. Never has he ever been this expressive to anyone before. Icarus awaited for his response.

"Matthew, you are not spiritually at peace. Your pursuit for intimacy has had you inadvertently pedestalize women in attempt to validate yourself that you're not creepy. You need to be authentically you. And you must relinquish the past in order to overcome this detrimental cycle."

The man spoke with such an understanding tone. Icarus somewhat knew this but it felt refreshing to hear.

"Your entire identity shouldn't be based on how women see you. It shouldn't dictate how you maneuver through life as well. If you embrace yourself, then you'll get honest results. Everything leading to this point was disingenuous, so tonight is your rebirth. What people think about you are their beliefs, not yours."

Icarus absorbed this honest genuine criticism that felt like an unexpected dawning. There was this amazing clarity that flushed away his self-doubt.

"And most of all, don't give up. Do not lose faith in finding a woman in your life, just don't make it a burden on your soul. I hope I was able to help you."

Icarus smiled. *"Thank you, thank you so much."*

"You're welcome, Icarus." He replied, then hung up.

That response left Icarus stupefied. He quickly dialed him again but the call went to a Chinese restaurant. The annoying cashier lady kept urging for an answer but he just ceased the call. Instead of being paranoid, Icarus remembered the man's helpful words. This made Icarus think of the draft of his manuscript that he's been procrastinating due to him prioritizing chasing women. His head began to gradually cleanse; accepting that most bad outcomes originated from his inability to truly act organic.

Icarus returned to Jovanny, appearing more serene. Jovanny assumed he may still be drunk. He gave Icarus a glass of water to help regulate him. As Jovanny served other customers, Icarus was thinking of his positive traits. Recalling how naturally he felt while chatting with Jovanny.

The fact that he refused to supplicate to Natalia and abandoned her with the bill. This compels him to reread her angry texts; sending a smooth grin of his face.

He feels clearer. As he looked around, he noticed a cute Caucasian female having drinks alone. She had a neutral expressionless look, wearing a purple sundress. Even though he didn't feel obligated to initiate just for an agenda, he decided to express his genuine self instead. No ulterior motives; just wanting to convey how in control of himself he feels. Icarus calmly introduces himself; they shook hands. Then without asking, he pulled himself a seat.

Jovanny's place 11:24 P.M.

Jovanny returns with a heavy weight circulating his being. Feeling exhausted, he splashes his face with some cooling water. Then he throws himself on his bed. Solanda hears him from behind the bathroom.

"Jovanny?" she called out. "Baby, is that you?"

"Yea." He blurted out.

"You ok, baby?"

Jovanny released a huge yawn. *"I'm good. Just tired."*

"That's too bad." She seductively said. Then opened the door, revealing her completely nude in an alluring pose. "I thought we could have a bit of fun before bed."

His head springs up, nodding for her to come. Solanda took his shirts off as they were kissing.

"Quick, I'll grab us a rubber." Jovanny said.

"No, we're good. I got one right here." she suggests, pulling one out.

"Where were you hiding that?"

"Y'know, strippers got our own tricks up our sleeves."

"Since when do you ever buy them though?"

"I was just in the mood, I thought ahead."

Jovanny was momentarily silent then shrugs it off. Solanda kept kissing him. Her hands were rubbing all over his body. She then proceeds to give him a blowjob. During the act, Jovanny ponders why she aimed to purchasing a condom when Jovanny normally would. Solanda hands him the condom to wear so they can continue. Before he does, he asks for her to quickly get his phone charger from the living room, so it can recharge in the meantime. Jovanny noticed how she rushed for it. Solanda checked around the living room but found nothing. As she comes back, Jovanny sat upright on the bed holding out the condom.

"The fuck is this shit?" he firmly asked, exposing the condom.

"What's wrong, babe?"

"Why's there a hole in this shit? Did you puncture this?"

Solanda contorts her face. "No. Wait, you sure? I can't tell really. Looks fine to me, so let's not make—"

"Look!" he demands, forcing it close at her face. There's a puny hole directed at the center. "And I checked the wrapper, it has one too."

Solanda silently shrugs, unable to justify it. Jovanny elaborates how odd it was that she even purchased one that she kept suggesting they use. Solanda could see him not falling for it.

"Actually, I'm not in the mood anymore." she deflects.

"Nah, nah! Why'd you poke a hole in this?" he pressed. She was unable to conceal her guilty look. "You trying to get pregnant?"

"Yes." She groaned. "I wanted to get knocked up."

Jovanny nodded, knowing his suspicions weren't false. Solanda marched for her robe. She crossed her arms, sitting on the opposite side of the bed.

"Why would you wanna purposely get yourself pregnant?" he asked. There is a brief silence. "Did that bitch, Latoya, from your job talk you into pulling this shit?" There's still no response, frustrating him. "*SOLANDA!*"

"No!" she cries. "Nobody talked me into doing this."

"Then why? This ain't you, this not what you want."

"What would you know about what I want? About what the fuck I ever desire? You ain't never asked what I want."

Jovanny is confused. Her indirect replies just annoy him. Solanda senses him starting to grow distant from this.

"Who's Miranda Miller?" she asks, staring at his perplexed speechless face.

"*What?*" he mumbled. "Who you been talking to?"

"Who is she, Jovanny?" she firmly repeats. "Hmmm? Is she another one of your crazy ex-girlfriends who'll pull up here? She some fling you had back then? She someone you impregnated and then made her terminate y'all child?"

"Hey! Who the fuck is you talking to, huh?" he snapped.

"Where you even hear this shit? 'Cause I ain't put a baby in nobody. You doin' too much."

"Don't fucking lie to me! At this point, I honestly don't know if you've ever been upfront with me."

Jovanny tries emerging closer but she distant herself.

"Yo, don't try to deflect the shady shit you pulled tonight!" he said. "So this is all because word on the street is I did something that ain't even fucking happen?"

"I met Chloe Miller this week." She revealed. Then elaborates on how Chloe informed her about how toxic their entire relationship became due to his selfish actions. Including fleeing her wedding, kicking her out and pressing Miranda to abort their child. Warning of how Solanda may end up hurt next. "And do you know where Miranda is in life now?"

Jovanny nonchalantly shrugs.

"She's dead. Fucking dead 'cause you told her to kick rocks and she ain't have nothing left. Poor girl overdosed, it destroyed her family. But you don't even care, huh?"

"Well, maybe it was just her time to go." He casually said. "*Shit, who am I to play God?!*"

Solanda shook her head in disgust, still distancing herself. Jovanny releases a vexed exhaust.

"Fine. Miranda and I got off on bad terms. Who giv—"

"Not just Miranda!" she interrupts. "But those two other crazy bitches who you clearly did wrong. God knows how many more. And then you try to lie about Miranda."

"I ain't want no fucking kids back then."

"I don't know if whatever you say is true or not. There's clearly a pattern you don't see or choose to play blind to."

"So, what the fuck do you want then, Solanda?" he yelled. "You wanna leave then since you that paranoid?"

"No, I don't wanna leave." She shouts. Then admits that she felt uncertain if he'd hurt and leave her. That fabricating the idea of a child keeping them together would allow him to become more loving. "I just wanted to keep you around."

"Bullshit!" he defiantly said. "It wasn't to keep me around. It was 'cause you wanted to keep me underneath. You would've called all the shots and felt entitled. Knowing everything would fall in your favor."

"I was trying to fix our relationship. All I ever do is give and give." She brought up the women he desires, her cooking and her loyalty. "This was the only way to have you committed to me. You always have this attitude like you don't care about me being around. Like you could leave any moment. Never put me first, there ain't never been an even exchange, just like your past relationships. You're selfish!"

Jovanny smirked. "Firstly, the other women in the bedroom, that shit was mutual. So don't act like I was the only one getting something outta it. Secondly, our relationship didn't need no fixing until you pulled this shit. Our situation was fine but you done turned it into a power struggle. You love it when men act beneath you." He mentions the desperate customer who assaulted her after being bamboozled by her. The male customers desiring her that she gets the opportunity to reject. He mentioned Oscar assaulting her because she mistreated him. The Oscar defense infuriates her.

"I took care of that man, showered him with everything and look how he hurt me after he won a bit of money."

"You weren't no saint! You fucking pushed him around 'cause you loved how inferior he was to you. Same shit would've happened to me. Lock me on child support, keeping me powerless, using it as leverage to keep me in line." He yelled. She couldn't fabricate an excuse. "But you ain't ever consider that because ain't nobody hold you accountable. Especially, not those simps who listen to whatever the fuck you say, who got you all gassed up. You even be acting like you better than them strippers. But you still be exposing yourself up in there like how I'm exposing your ass right the fuck now. I tell you what, you could bless me with all the food and thots I want. But the last thing I want from you is to bless me with no bastard-ass kid."

"I'm outta here."

"That's right, just leave. You all leave eventually."

Solanda abruptly halts, slowly facing him, processing what he just said. Jovanny eagerly awaits another flimsy rationale. The scowl on her face transitioned into a pitiful one as she remembered his ex-girlfriends.

"Is that what this is about?" she warily asks. "You think I'll leave you regardless, huh? That all that investment I put into us was only for me to inevitably leave?" Jovanny's quiet. "That's why you cut off and disrespected those poor girls. You must got some serious issues with yourself."

"Nah, I'm a savage. You weren't gonna like me in the end no way. Y'all ain't shit."

Solanda feels her throat constricting. *"You know you never said you loved me? Or showed you appreciate me?"* her tone dropped, observing his unfazed demeanor. Then settles her tone. "Your past relationships don't work out, not because it's female nature to abruptly leave you, it's because of you. Your misogynistic scared ass."

"Then leave!" Jovanny said, his tone sharp. "Because you got yourself the wrong one."

This had Solanda tongue-tied, realizing her urge to maintain things wouldn't have rectified anything. Jovanny feels dominant due winning the argument and to not being flexible. Almost like he was gloating and Solanda could sense this. She couldn't force herself to apologize for her conniving plan; and didn't appear upset nor disappointed. All she did was put on her clothes and pack her suitcase with more clothes. Then Solanda escapes to the door instead. This irrational side of her tries to maintain faith that Jovanny would prevent her from leaving as he watches her. That he'd show something that verifies how much he appreciated her. Jovanny wouldn't budge.

"I'll be back tomorrow for the rest of my things." Her voice strained, then she left.

† Chapter 20: Be careful what you wish for.

It's late in the night, Icarus McGrew is accompanied by the woman from the bar. They're both joyously intoxicated at his house. Her name is Bianca, she's holding onto his waist, resting her head on his shoulder.

At Richez Shrive, they conversed for two hours. Bianca was nonchalant at first, engaged with his casual demeanor. Icarus had felt entirely present within that moment. There wasn't any fixation whether or not he'd attain her phone number, maintain her attention nor attain her at his house. The advice he received had marinated; making him embrace himself wholeheartedly (*with the help of liquor flowing*). He kept making Bianca laugh and had her feeling comfortable enough to divulge more about herself. As time passed, they shared a desire to leave together. Without being concerned about Bianca's opinion, Icarus initiated for them to go to his house. She gladly agreed.

They're kissing in his room right now. Both are caressing each other in his bed. Bianca closes her eyes; Icarus observes her drunkenly gleeful face. Icarus couldn't believe this was actually happening. He gently massages her breasts. Bianca jumps to her feet and pulls off her purple sundress. The seductive visual appearance of her in her undergarments had Icarus mesmerized. Bianca wobbled back onto the bed. His heart is pounding; hoping she won't instantly feel his chest. She rests on her back, uplifted her legs to glide off her panties, and then separates them. Icarus maneuvers his way up to her bare breasts. They were average-sized but enticing enough for him to suckle on them. Bianca pressed his head down more onto her sensitive nipples. He gives them teeny bites; then licks the soul of them. This results in Bianca's trembling moans.

Icarus gently rubs his fingers on her soaked vagina. Her moaning deepened, desiring for him to do the same. He stripped off his clothes. However, his penis was now flaccid. Icarus grasps it with both hands, yanking it. To distract her, he nervously rubbed legs. Bianca's eyes are shut, slowly nodding her head, smiling. Icarus excuses himself to the bathroom; she encouraged him to hurry back.

He massages his entire shaft, mumbling for himself to straighten up. It was still softened. His hairy testicles sagged despite his efforts to stimulate them. With no other option, he dropped to his knees and prayed over the toilet.

"God, I need your help, father God." Icarus pleaded. *"I'm in need of a miracle. I don't want to disappoint my foxy, lady guest tonight. Like they say, 'you can do it all through Christ', so I need your guidance please. Just one stroke of luck. Amen."*

There was silence. No sign was made. Icarus slowly rises with an aching in both knees. He returned to the room to find Bianca asleep. Seeing her angelic snoozing, appearing seemingly helpless, had finally gave him an erection. Icarus tries shaking her shoulder but she groans. Then rolled to her side. He could tell she's too intoxicated, so he covers her body with a blanket, tucking her in. The conquering urge remained but he suppressed it. Then fell asleep beside her.

†

In the morning, Grant was asleep next to someone. Both clothes were off. Her slim arm was wrapped across his chest. Last night after the interview, Grant avoided Joy. He went nonstop drinking. Bought the most expensive liquor and blacked out. There's a tingling sensation once his eyes weakly open. This throbbing in his head drummed repeatedly. The realization of being on an unknown bed struck him. Grant's eyes flickered at the woman next to him. The only thing visible was the back of her head. Her black afro hair was tickling his cheek. There was this uneasy oozing in his stomach. Grant studies the black woman. Her dark-skin glistened everywhere. This familiar scent came from her. The lady's skin felt smooth.

Grant slowly reaches her back to cautiously wake her up. His head filled with questions such as who she was, where they were, how they met. She wouldn't flinch. Her entire body was lifeless. Grant thought that perhaps she was still hungover. Then he heard the door slowly creek open. His heart galloped as his attention was directed towards the door. It was Pastor Marques greeting: *"BAM!"*

The appearance of this guy had shocked Grant. The exact shock most people show when they see Grant Critchfield out in public. Grant has seen him make notoriety on the news with his public rant. He was left speechless.

"Don't worry, she's not real." Marques laughs. "Lord only knows you need more allegations involving these women."

"Who is this?" Grant slurred out. *"What's her name?"*

"Anything you want. Them hoes are expensive."

Marques gestured for him to take a look. This prompt Grant to flip her to her back. Her face said it all. The googly eyes were glassy, her mouth was open with a small microphone down her throat for audio. The lips were plastic smeared in lip gloss. She was a customizable human resembling sex doll. This relieved look swept Grant's face. Knowing that she's not just this sex object but also legal.

She began making this robotic moaning sound. It sounds like a digitalized recording from another woman. There was this awkward silence as the sensual audio continuously looped. Marques realized it was her morning alarm. He firmly squeezes her breasts to turn her off. Grant stared at her snoozing option perplexed.

"Why'd I purchase this thing black?"

"Well, you were the highest bidder at this year's slave auction."

"No, I didn't mean it like that. No offense." Grant quickly responds. "I just normally prefer real people."

Marques chuckles. "Now we're not considered people?"

"No! Just not attracted to you people!"

This interaction made Pastor Marques laugh at how frustrated Grant became. Claiming that he knew what he meant. Then offers him a glass of water. This offer seemed skeptical to Grant, he politely refused.

Once Marques placed it on the dresser, he calmly explained what transpired last night.

Revealing that drunken Grant was found in his car. His car was parked on the curve in front of Marques' house. Grant ran into the trash cans. Marques brought him inside to avoid any publicity who might recognize him.

"After that interview you did, I figured you wanted to release some tension with her." Marques laughed as his eyes trailed to the doll. "Sunday church donations don't even get me shit like this. She smell like cocoa-butter too."

Grant rubbed his already irritated eyes. "Fuck, you saw that interview?"

"Yup. Just like how everyone and they mama witnessed my ass in action too. It's all good."

"It's not. I'm a famous celebrity." Grant groaned, then flopped back to bed. He began thinking about how aggravated his agent probably is. Then began mumbling her name while he shook his head.

Marques slowly slid the glass over to him. Urging that Grant should try sobering up. He begrudgingly accepted the water. The cool liquid washing his teeth had almost made Grant nauseous.

"Look, try sleeping it off." Pastor Marques said as he walks out. "I'll let you two be alone for a bit."

Thoughts stampeded Grant's mind as he tries to reflect on last night. He remembered the anger fueling him into storming from the studio. Then began wondering about Joy's reaction, his mother's embarrassment, and the fate of his pending career.

York Avenue 9:12 A.M.

Essie and Yanie had spent the night together after they arrived back from another party. They've been at it for a while now. Essie's nerves have decreased tremendously. She only went out at night due to preventing exposure to sunlight. Yanie was glad she was feeling better. The first to awaken was Essie, overhearing Larissa moving things in the kitchen. Yanie instantly woke up. They both relaxed in her room discussing last night. Essie blushed about the older man who flirted with her on their way out.

"He was too handsome." Essie said. "I don't know why he couldn't just ask for my number."

Yanie shook her head. "Nah, he must've been scared to go all out since feminists been acting crazy lately. Got these men shook. I used to get guys buying me drinks. Now men get all choked up when they come across me."

The thought of how Essie didn't insist on exchanging numbers had her somewhat regretful. Yanie brings up Donny Bedford; bragging about how their sex was amazing. All the positions, the kissing and their laid-back relationship brought a loving smile on her face. Essie sensed how great of an experience that was, keeping her intrigued.

"What happened to you two?" Essie asks.

"I broke it off." Yanie proudly said. "He had two kids and issues with his baby mama. It was getting outta hand." Yanie recalled when she had to fight Taivy and Donny recorded for evidence as a way to help him out. "He wasn't shit anyway. Dude just wanted evidence for the court to see his kids even though he ghosted them years ago. He thought being a father would keep him from going to hell."

"Him too?" Essie asks, sounding irked. "Idiot. Did it work for him at least?"

"Who knows? I cut him off." Yanie shrugged. "But what about you, *choo-choo*? Girl, what's your body count?"

A brief pause occurred as Essie processed that question.

"I've never." She flatly said. Yanie's smirk changed into a perplexed look. "Never really tried to. I've gotten offers but nope."

"You still a virgin?" Yanie genuinely asks.

"With work and looking after Larissa, I just never went through with it—you've known I've been single for years."

"Yea but I thought you were low-key with it. Maybe doing one night stands or a side-dude. And working at a hospital is the perfect excuse for you to have something casual. Especially being isolated at home these few weeks. I thought you'd have more company over besides Larissa."

"I get it but there's always porn to watch. And I'll only watch it when I'm really in the mood."

"What kinda porn do you like?"

Essie laughed about liking videos of missionary sex with men and women. Also, reading the comments sometimes. Yanie insists on watching videos of a fake taxi manipulating women into intercourse whenever they can't pay the guy.

"I love the ones where the guy goes recording a sexy bitch passing by." Yanie cheerily added. "Like, she doesn't know there's a hidden camera inside his hat or wherever. Or they do know and try to ignore it. *But they know.*" They both laugh imagining it. "They could just sense they're being followed but don't wanna make a huge scene."

"Refuse to make a scene—just leave it to that guy."

"Exactly. One of my favorites." Yanie expressed. Then she whipped out her phone insisting to show Essie something. *"Look, look!"*

"Yanie, it's too early for that."

"Nah, it's something else." She urged. Essie peeks at it.

There was an advertisement on this website that networks community pages. Registered members create content such as links, images, and pages to join or comment. Yanie mentions this recent post submitted on the dark portion of the website. It is a free invite announcement for *ANYONE* allowed to this sex party. To meet attractive individuals to become intimate with. There will be condoms, liquor and drugs present. Any sexual preference is allowed. It is being hosted two days from now in midtown. No recording is allowed there. The party will start at nine o'clock and go on all night.

That whole invitation from an anonymous source sounded extremely suspicious; causing for Essie to seem apprehensive. Yanie detects this but figures she could persuade her friend otherwise.

"It ain't as sketchy as it comes off." Yanie reassured.

"You ever been to one of these before?"

"Oh yea. They're cool. It's all consensual."

"So no one ever forced themselves on you there? Man or woman?" Essie skeptically asks. "Or tried getting you drunk or high?"

"Best believe they'll try." Yanie proudly said. "Have you seen me?! But all jokes aside, they've got security at these things. And the hosts are usually nice."

Many scenarios infiltrated Essie's thoughts. Multiple red flags kept popping up. The host could be a pervert who possibly abducts women. Or a man or woman forcing themselves on her if she rejected them. Maybe it's a hoax for a hidden camera show exposing those that're foolish, and post it online. Yanie persisted her even more.

"Hear me out, Essie. It's just one night. I promise you that everyone's easygoing there. We could crash at this motel nearby and drop Larissa there until we get back. I know you don't wanna leave Larissa here since you'll be too far from her." The inclusion of Larissa's safety eased Essie a bit. "You can meet a cute guy there, swipe your V-card and have a good time. Then we'll make it back soon."

"I just don't know, Yanie." Essie nervously laughed, contemplating all of this. *"What's the dress code?"*

"Nada." Yanie laughed. "Plus, it even starts at night, so you ain't gotta worry about getting flashbacks or nothing." She sees Essie beginning to go along with the idea of it. "All you gotta do is just put yourself out there that night and just let 'em shoot their shot."

Hearing Yanie's past experiences being there and an opportunity to take a risk had Essie reluctantly say: *"Sure."*

Yanie could sense this Essie still having misgivings. That there's more to her indecisiveness.

"I can tell you gotta vent real quick. What's up?"

"I just get this bad feeling." Essie said. She clarifies that she's had this feeling for a while since summer began. That Essie could inexplicably predict when horrific things. A premonition of unforeseen disasters that orbit herself.

"Wish I had that." Yanie envies. "No telling when shit might pop off."

Essie shook her head in protest. "This feeling transcends pass familiarity. It's almost as if I've experienced going through this myself." Confessing that this force overwhelmed her prior to the time those patients had flooded the hospital, the church riot and that plane crash. Certain settings she's never entered or images she's never seen beforehand just surpass familiarity. "And just reality in itself… *seems unbalanced.*"

Yanie nods. "Reality been outta wack since 2012."

"Not just that." Essie said, excluding the mayhem from people this summer. Her dreams (*before the nightmares*) used to be of things that she's never done but she vividly remembers them. Dreams of skydiving, exploring exotic places worldwide, bull riding, crowd surfing at concerts. That she could still grasp the energy of something that wasn't actualized. Yet, somehow is more fulfilling than their world. "Just feels thinly disconnected from what I'm supposed to be. That there's a superior, alternate version of myself somewhere. And I'm just an outsider in this realm."

The bizarre aftermath of this miracle being unveiled to the world makes this feel like a dream sequence to her. Surviving the plane crash, staring up at the sun was almost an awakening to all of this. This led to Essie bringing up how helpless she's felt since then. Even while confined within the safety of her home, there's still entrapment. She choked out that there's various infinite possibilities of her embracing life unsealed elsewhere. Outside of her apartment but repressed within her dreams. The harsh reality was that her life leaves her deeply unfulfilled.

A lingering dissatisfaction submerged within Essie Chu. No matter if she witnesses stupidity from her patients, or crazy citizens causing mayhem or comparing herself as not as dysfunctional as others. It still didn't uplift her spirits. Essie's genuine, wild spirit is a whirling itch stuffed inside her subconscious just wishing to burst loose. A tender bubbling of tears pooled her eyes. It brews more as Essie admits to being the most high-spirited and joyously expressive when she dissociates from this nightmare.

Yanie nodded, showing a concerned look. "Continue livin' your best life. Make these dreams your reality then. And stay woke." She sweetly said, seeing Essie absorb this advice. Then reassures Essie that the current version of herself can be upgraded but she must restore herself first.

"Thank you." Essie exhales, wiping away her tears.

"We're both priceless." Yanie proclaims, hugging her.

"Until men access you for 5.99 a month."

The two laughed, still holding onto each other's value.

MIDTOWN HOLKSDALE 9:44 A.M.

Nothing but silence lies in the home of Icarus McGrew. The light shined through the window curtains, brightening his room. Icarus was already awake; unable to force himself to move. His head was pounding, an ache had circulated his stomach. Almost a prickling feeling edging his belly. Bianca's slight movements had him turn his head. To his amazement, he attracted a woman enough to come home with him. An exhale of satisfaction is made while he remembers kissing her soft lips and sucking her breasts. Her desire for him, her moans from last night; the erotic thoughts send a stimulated rush to his now formed erection.

He slowly maneuvered himself out of bed. His dizzy journey to the bathroom inevitably had him vomiting down the toilet. Then continuously shoved his fingers down his throat to excrete more, this fueled a burning sensation in the back of his throat. Icarus tears up a little. A few minutes pass as he catches his breath. Then he rinses his face with cool water from the sink.

In the kitchen, he boiled some tea. Icarus wonders if Bianca would still wish to get intimate after a failure one-night stand. He's still erected from thinking about her body. Icarus returned to her with two cups of tea. She's still snoozing. As he stood on her side, he noticed some of her vomit oozed off her edge of the bed, leaving a mess on the floor. Icarus gently rubbed her blanketed shoulder; causing her to groan for someone named Eddie to stop. This baffled

Icarus for a moment, then continued. She peeked at this unknown naked man hovering over her with an erection. Bianca's eyes widened with shock; the entirety of her body stiffened. Icarus detects her strange demeanor.

"Good morning." He sheepishly said, taking a step away. He watches her appear speechless. "Sorry to wake you up, I was just going to offer you some tea." She began to scan the area with a perplexed look. "You okay, Bianca?"

"How do you know who I am?" she shrieked. Then feeling her body tangled in a blanket. "Where the hell are my clothes? Who are you?"

Icarus finally realized she must have blacked out last night. Unable to tell if her memory loss began exactly once they left the bar or returned to his house. Bianca began to recognize Icarus, as her mind slowly formed him as the stranger from the bar last night.

"We met at the bar last night, we were chatting for a while, and had a couple of drinks. Then I invited you here."

That reveal had Bianca press her face into her palms out of shame. Exasperating a huge sigh of disappointment.

"Look, don't be upset." He encouraged, observing her hunched body. "All we did was kiss and fool around a bit."

"What?" Bianca gasped, quickly adjusting the blanket concealing her body. *"What'd you do to me last night?"*

"Nothing, nothing without your consent." He instantly said. "We never got fully intimate, you passed out." He could see the terror in her face still, then offers her the tea to relieve her. "Here, take a sip."

"Get that shit away from me!" she hissed, rushing away to the opposite side of the bed. "I don't want what's in that."

"It's clean, I swear. Look, look!" Icarus urges, sipping from his cup. Then showcased his mouth to reveal he actually swallowed it. "See, it's not drugged, alright? It's fine. Everything's fine."

"No, no, no, no. This cannot be happening. Why me?" she muttered to herself, averting her eyes from him. Overhearing him repeatedly claim its fine. "Everything's not fine. I have a boyfriend." She snapped.

That left Icarus staring at her trembling body with pity. She searched around to find her purple sundress and panties on the ground in the corner. She swept them both up. Icarus tells her where the bathroom is; Bianca escapes to it with her things. Icarus understands her guilt of cheating on her boyfriend. Trying to formulate the best advice to help ease her guilt, he hears her rumbling in the bathroom.

Bianca flees the bathroom fully clothed after flinging the door open. Icarus awkwardly asks if she's feeling better but she ignores him on her way back to his room. She veered around his room. Icarus followed to see her furiously check through his drawers for something.

"Please don't do that." he politely said. "I didn't take anything from you if that's why—"

"Where's my fucking phone?" she growled. She stared him down in revulsion with her arms crossed.

Icarus shrugs. "I could help you find it if you want?"

"Yeah, you do that!" she said, her tone sharp.

To avoid any more issues, he checks around for her property. Bianca kept a distance from him as she watches him closely. Icarus is a little upset she invaded his room but maintains his composure.

"I hope you're feeling better."

"I'm fine." Bianca firmly said. "Because I know I didn't do anything wrong. You used me last night. Probably dosed my beer too. Now you want to offer me some tea."

"I didn't drug you. We both bought our own individual drinks." Icarus said crouched down, then pulled her phone from under the bed. "And I never took advantage of you. You were too drunk—" she snatched her phone away, he follows her to the living room. "Look we had a good time but not too good a time."

"What's this address?" she asks.

"Why?"

"Because I don't believe you. You're telling me I woke up naked under your sheets without you sleeping with me? Bullshit, you fucked me last night. So I'm calling the police."

Icarus stood there tongue-tied. His skin trembles at the possibility of law enforcement getting involved. The drumming of his heart hits stronger at each pound number she pressed.

"B-B-Bianca," he stammered. "You were way too wasted so I didn't pursue any further." She proceeded on her phone. His tone dropped to a pleading one. *"We were just kissing and feeling each other—"*

Bianca got agitated at the thought of them kissing. "You

fucking pervert. I would never want your touch. You're lying. And I always see you at that bar talking to other women. You've probably done shit like this before."

"YOU'RE THE ONE WHO TOOK YOU'RE CLOTHES OFF!" Icarus barked, sounding like it ripped fresh from his throat. *"I COULD'VE FORCED MYSELF BUT I DIDN'T!"*

Bianca flinched. "Don't get any closer!" she squeezed out, alarmed by his bawled fists. "I don't believe you."

Icarus jerked forward, gripping her phone. Bianca screamed. Both wrestle for her phone. His tightened grip overpowered her. She instantly yanked at his wrists, defiantly screaming *"RAPE"* aloud. Her shaky, shrill voice was ear-scorching to him. Icarus covered her mouth causing for Bianca to viciously bite the palm of his hand. That pain made Icarus jolt. The two lose their balance, sending Bianca to crash into the glass coffee table.

The shattered noise thundered through the room. A long stretch of silence occurred. Icarus was alarmed and rushed to her aid. Bianca was sprawled on the floor with her body pierced in glass. The intense, sharp pain prevented her from hollering. All that was heard was her gasping for air. Icarus quickly tries attempting CPR. He pumped her chest as much as possible then blows down her throat. Her blood pastes to his lips afterwards. Panic gripped at his stomach tighter as she didn't respond. Bianca's gasping became shallower, then was hollow after ten minutes. His actions were now futile as he curled himself up terrified. Bianca's blood appears on her purple dress as red spots now oozed.

York Avenue 10:22 A.M.

At this time, Yanie Juergens had left, leaving for Essie to check in on Larissa. She noticed that girl hadn't made much noise this morning. Normally, Larissa would be eating something or raiding the refrigerator for something to drink. Not a teenager in sight. There weren't any plates in the sink, so Essie knew Larissa hadn't ate yet. Assuming she's in her room, Essie called her phone. Larissa answered.

"*Morning, sweetheart.*" Essie greets. "I didn't hear you get out of bed yet. You want me to make you some bacon and waffles?"

"Nah, I'm fine." Larissa replied tiresome.

"You okay?"

"Mm-hmm. I just ain't got much of an appetite. Thanks though."

"You sure you're alright?"

"Yea." Larissa answers flatly.

"Ok." Essie hung up, still wondering about her.

Essie simultaneously heated up some waffles and fried strips of bacon. She couldn't hear any trace of Larissa's footsteps moving around upstairs in her room. The thought of her maybe feeling sick lurked in Essie's mind. This propelled her to boil up a cup of tea.

A gentle knock was made by Essie, requesting to enter. She discovers Larissa lying on her side in bed facing the wall. The window blinds were closed, behooving the both of them. Essie placed the small plate of three syrupy waffles alongside four bacon strips and a cup of warm tea down at her dresser. Larissa could smell the food but didn't budge.

"Thanks, Essie." Larissa said.

"You're welcome." Essie realized something had bothered her but didn't want to pry—at least not yet. And could sense that Larissa wants to be alone to herself. She'll allow Larissa to eat first and keep alienated for a while. "I'll be downstairs if you need anything." She softly said, her shadow guiding over Larissa's curled body, yet couldn't bring her any relief.

Larissa heard her guardian leave. She didn't want to bother Essie last night, especially overhearing her and Yanie enjoying themselves. Everything Chase had said echoed in her head since she left his house yesterday. Elijah being deceased after their confrontation had her feeling restless. The realization of taking advantage of Elijah's admiration reminded her how unvalued she is. It's worse how apparent it is that Chase could see it; believing why it was easy for him to get rid of her. Chase ignored her double texts and call, feeling more embarrassed to even try rectifying things.

His whole rant about her attempts to actually getting her mom into heaven. Larissa feels exposed after revealing she felt a sense of purpose while believing in this miracle; only to be ridiculed afterwards. Feelings of inadequacy lurks over her as the thought of her relentless pursuit to have her mom saved was most likely fueled by her low self-worth. Larissa fixates on the idea if he just wasted his time just for coitus. Pondering if that's all she was worth to him.

It weighed her down more, almost causing for salty tears to escape her eyes. The fact that Chase could easily move on to another girl (*based off his social media*) had ignited a hot flare trapped inside her. Larissa's thoughts whirled back to him coldly bringing up her mother's mistreatment.

All that past unapologetic hurt Danielle inflicted on her began trickling in her head. This has her start silently crying. Not just from the hurt, but from the possibility that she may never change. That she's beginning to lose faith—not just in Danielle—but including from within herself. It burdened Larissa more that Chase's gloating could've been right.

Knowing her mother would feel indifferent towards anyone else's opinions or plight in life had almost made Larissa want to embrace that path. To relieve herself from the guilt over Elijah Atwood; to be dismissive over Chase's viewpoint on her. She ponders if her mom, stuck inside a box day by day, has ever questioned her actions while bombarded by her own shadow. She questions herself as a person each time she thought of Elijah. Justifying ignoring Elijah isn't working because she knew that she could've been nicer and forgiven him for his mistake. Accepting Elijah's praise—only for her to discard him harshly afterwards—had her feeling bad. However, embracing her mother's mindset would only prove that Chase was even more right about Larissa being like her. Which really struck a nerve. Larissa felt as if there were two devils on each shoulder with only one choice being the lesser of two evils. She knew the only deliverance was to embrace this hellhole.

Figure Pines 11:13 A.M.

Figure Pines is an enormous forest on the outskirts of downtown Holksdale. It inhabited various woodland animals. Hikers rarely ever explored around there; even though it was permitted.

Icarus McGrew had driven his car into the forest while alone on the road. He didn't want any possible ongoing drivers detecting him. The vehicle cruised for a few minutes deeper inside. All Icarus could think about was Bianca. Her impaled corpse from his living room. The instant regret she felt realizing what could've transpired last night. Even her boyfriend who'll never see her again; confused exactly as to why. That his girlfriend is stuffed inside this trunk.

The forest has a plethora of trees. Trees stretched up to the heavens. Some trees are curved diagonally, branches twists into other trees. Leaves above conceal any brightness from emitting. Icarus detects a family of geese swimming in a pond. The pond mirrored the dangling leaves and trees. As he journeyed forward, there are few colorful mushrooms the size of gnomes rooted in the grass.

Icarus finally parked his car in a grassy spot underneath a shady tree. Then slightly rolled his window down to hear of anything peculiar. Chirpy birds and flapping wings were all he heard. His veering eyes didn't find anyone. No hikers, hunters or homeless around. Icarus steps out his car, feeling more isolated, like he's trespassing. The enchanting ambience of this place had rarely been disturbed.

The humid weather couldn't fix his icy, trembling fingers. Icarus remained still beside his car. Pondering whether he should proceed from this point or just confess to the police what had transpired. The repercussions of killing a woman has him feeling numb. All of this happened even when he wasn't desperately chasing a female. Icarus was honestly himself last night. Now look where that got him. The trunk contained Bianca's corpse and a shovel. She was wrapped in two large, black, plastic garbage bags. Each end connects at her stomach, held by duct tape. Her bodies twisted based on the angle of the bag. The sight of this added a stronger layer of crushing weight.

Icarus convinces himself the sooner he covers this up—the sooner he'll feel better. He took a glance around the proximity of where he's at, then grabbed that shovel and slowly began to dig. As he commenced to digging, an itch started at his ankles. Then his neck started itching. Icarus intensely swatted at the mosquitoes. The itching caused him to scratch himself. Icarus started getting sweatier. Under his neck, armpits and his lower back. The wave of heat is slowly engulfing him. Pellets of sweat begin trickling down to his chest. Repeatedly wiping his neck and forehead with his shirt. He finally whipped off his shirt to wipe everywhere. After rubbing his eyes, an increased brightness strikes his face. The sunlight poked through the tree leaves. Icarus shielded his eyes with his shaky hand. Emitting light solely on Icarus makes him radiate guilt. His eyes panned around the environment as he started getting jittery.

Icarus immediately returned to digging. His back started feeling sore as he scooped up each pile. The dirt grows more harden. Almost as if the dirt gripped itself back to its roots to remain more grounded. He groans as he pierced into the dirt with enough force. His frustration had his mind flood with memories of Bianca. Her seductive figure, her alarmed look, her screams. An ache had clutched and sharply twisted his insides. It's getting tougher for Icarus, the deeper he digs himself into this.

He started profusely sweating again from getting devoured by the forest's heat. This has him take in a long stretched, deep breath to help steady himself. Exhaustion had him almost stop entirely to bring himself some relief. Then the stirring fear of being caught ripped through, pushing him past it. Icarus tore into the dirt faster. A breeze sweeps by him, attempting to pull him back. The sound of leaves and branches rattled as the force strengthened. Icarus focused completely onto digging her grave.

The hole is done. It stretched enough for Bianca's corpse to fill in that void. Tiresome Icarus climbs out. He brushes off the dirt from his legs. After all that digging, Icarus hunched over to catch his breath. A sound crept nearby.

"Shit!" he gasped, feeling a small jolt of panic at the crackling sound of leaves sat on by a random fox.

After detecting this, he realized the fox had been watching from afar. It had sat upright far away from him. Positioned in a dominant frame that wasn't affected by the forest itself. It had orange fur. The fox's triangular ears had occasionally flickered; that was the only movement this statue-like creature made. It had a flattened skull. Icarus felt agitated being watched like this. Staring with its slightly upturned, snooty snout; pointing Icarus out on patrol.

This presence made Icarus hesitant about burying Bianca. He wondered how long it stayed there and if it would leave. The fox never budged.

Icarus turned towards the body in the trunk. He could sense himself still being watched but commenced to handling her corpse. Icarus glanced over his left shoulder to detect the fox's narrow vision still. Minutes finally passed until he tenderly pulled Bianca—which gripped at his stomach—with the most graceful handling. He opened the bag to look at her face one last time. Bianca's eyelids refused to shut, staring back at her assailant. Icarus cupped her cold cheeks with the palm of his unsteady hands. Then finally slowly places her within the hole.

The dirt gets tossed back inside. Icarus struggled to continue the moment her face was the only part of her left not concealed in dirt. Bianca's frozen expression reflected her barefaced fear. Icarus piled the remaining left back in.

Afterwards, Icarus stood over her grave, giving a silent prayer. Both his eyes closed and his hands together. He knows the fox is still staring him down. Part of Icarus hopes this is enough to convey how deep his sorrow and remorse truly was. When he finished, Icarus reluctantly stares the fox back. His saddened eyes along with the lines running through his cheeks didn't affect the unshakable fox.

†

Footsteps are dragged from the other room. Pastor Marques watched Grant slowly enter his kitchen. Once Grant sits, he's given a mug of ginger tea. Its warmth is felt in his hand as he took a sip. The tea slowly coursed through him. Grant's mind began to become clearer.

"How'd you two sleep?" Marques asks, smiling.

"Better, now knowing she's not real."

"A one-night stand with someone like her. That thought might not age well. Can't trust that algorithm."

"As long as her software's over eighteen, I don't care how she's aged."

The two smirk as they're silently drinking tea. Marques confirms that he didn't spread this interaction online. Grant appreciates it. He asks if many people recognized Marques after that video went viral. Marques proudly nodded. Grant tells him to enjoy that feeling momentarily; hinting that it won't last very long. Marques inhaled deeply. He exhaled a satisfying confirmation of notoriety. This tempted Grant to reveal that fans treated him like royalty. Now everyone criticizes him over an allegation, try prying information, and refuse to work with him.

"Pretty much demonize you."

Grant nods. "Exactly. It's just nice sitting with someone who doesn't have any ulterior motive."

"Just helping another man out. It's a cold world we're trapped in. But men gotta look out for each other."

The recovering sluggish look on Grant Critchfield had Marques mention something he forgot. That Marques agreed with what Grant said on that show. Those words being heard had the audience's disagreements flush out of Grant. In response, Grant admitted to liking that viral video of Pastor Marques. For a famous person to have listened to him preach had Pastor Marques feel even more powerful. Both men having a triumphant gulp of their ginger tea.

"It's always been a dream of mine to have one of my sermons witnessed worldwide. Even if it wasn't at church. And miss me with these allegations. Before all this shit, you were living the dream too."

"I've actually been having this reoccurring similar dream. Had it last night too." Grant admitted. The dream from last night was him looking at the public. Passing adults not even glancing at him nor acknowledging him. Everyone was seen from the inside of himself being secured. There are stretched, metallic fencing wires cutting him off from the general public. The barbed wires feels like they're guarding everyone else. Then there is this locked exit. The key for it lies in Grant's hand, but he doesn't put it to use. "And I've had dreams like this for years."

Marques shrugged it off. "Believe me, it ain't that deep."

This confirmation of his dreams being meaningless was slightly disappointing to hear. The thought of this pastor possibly shedding light for a deeper truth had formed in Grant's mind. It had him eager. However, Grant didn't show it, and instead became straight-faced.

"You should be sleeping just fine with women. Or last night with every man's dream doll."

"Believe me, having fame isn't that tempting." Grant bluntly said. "You have to become more selfish, more relentless in pursuit of being well-known, you always have to sever from who you once were to actually become someone. And there's always this realization."

"Of what?"

"It entirely depends on you." Grant said, his eyes latched with Marques. "This awareness that disrupts whatever you genuinely hoped to accomplish through Hollywood. It alters your perception, your original objective, and then you find yourself down this alternative course. It feels like you normalize living in some other realm, until you're finally accustomed to it. Then this dream finally fades."

"*DAMN.* That's tough." Marques blurts. "What was yours then? Your main goal?"

Grant exhaled deeply. "I really can't remember myself."

"C'mon man, yea you do. What was it?"

A brief silence fell.

"To create something new. It could've been anything that had everything. Something unique, something that matters, something that creates a pathway for others."

"Goals change as you do but will endlessly cycle back." Pastor Marques states. To his belief, as actors or people progress, they can lose track of their ambition. More paths will open to make things more accessible. People's mindset changing isn't always bad. He urged, while his eyes directly clicked with Grant, an alternative option. "If you're devout enough to your goal, then it'll eventually get resurrected. With an even better perception of how things work."

This disagreement did not enrage Grant. It slightly annoyed him that it contradicts his current reality. He politely disagrees but refused to argue about it. Especially since this man helped him out. Grant politely excuses himself to freshen up in the bedroom. Then sluggishly left.

Richez Shrive 3:19 P.M.

Jovanny Gibbs is mostly relaxing due to a lack of many customers today. He earlier patrolled Solanda and Latoya packing up all of her belongings; making sure they weren't stealing anything of his. No words were exchanged between them. Solanda returned her spare key and then left.

While being on his phone, he didn't notice Icarus McGrew come inside. Jovanny makes him the usual strawberry daiquiri. Icarus was still coping with what he'd done hours beforehand. He was in a new change of clothes after taking a long shower to cleanse himself. There was this swollen mass constricting his boney chest.

"By the way, congrats." Jovanny said, handing him his drink. "I saw you leave with Bianca last night."

Icarus was speechless. His hands grew wobbly, unable to be settled. His pale skin crawls, hoping nobody else saw.

"Man, I knew you could eventually pull a bitch, Icarus. Even though she got herself a man, you still finessed her."

Icarus shook his head, trying to keep a steady tone. "I didn't. We didn't have sex last night. She had second-thoughts and went home."

Jovanny looked baffled. "Really, she reneged on you? She looked like she was down to head back to your spot."

"Seriously." Icarus assured, tilting his head more down at his drink. "Nothing more happened between us."

Jovanny shrugged it off. However, he observed Icarus looking guarded. Then Jovanny remembered the rant about his awful history with women and believed Icarus was disappointed about Bianca leaving.

"Don't worry about Bianca. You wouldn't wanna fuck with her anyway. I hear her man's crazy. Plus, women be crazy jealous too. See, look over there." Jovanny points to a couple sitting in the back.

A chubby guy, named Jake, was with his slim-thick girlfriend, named Nicolette. Since Nicolette was insanely paranoid about getting cheated on, she subjected Jake to wear a blue, dog cone whenever they're out in public. This was too prevent him from looking at other women. Jovanny mentioned that Jake confided this to him. Everyone at the bar (*including Nicolette*) knew that she was way out of his league. Jake was willing to do anything to keep their relationship going. The couple clinked their shot glasses. Nicolette gulped her drink; Jake raised his glass, pouring it down his cone.

Jovanny shook his head in revulsion. "If only he could see himself now. Plus, I just cut my girl off last night."

"Sorry to hear." Icarus said. "You're fine with it?"

"Oh yea." Jovanny casually said. He told Icarus about her insane plan to trap him. Then proudly mentioned winning the argument that ensued and kicked her out. "So trust me, you're in a good place right now. Don't be Jake."

"*Thanks man.*" Icarus choked out. His mind still went to that ungodly act. Wondering to himself if Bianca had any children of her own waiting for her to return home. Icarus began getting numb as his head raced.

York Avenue 5:49 P.M.

Larissa's been asleep for a while now. She'd eaten her waffles and bacon. Her cup of tea was almost finished. The knocks on the door slowly woke Larissa up. Essie discovered her inside still sprawled on her bed, rotating over to her. The exhausted look on Larissa's face showed she wasn't in the mood.

"You okay, honey?" Essie softly asked. "You've been upstairs all morning. Are you feeling sick?"

"I'm ok."

"No you aren't." Essie said as she sat on the edge of her bed. "What happened? Is this about your mom again?"

Larissa shook her head.

Essie asked her about how her little friend, Chase, was doing. This had Larissa release a frustrated exhaust while shrugging her shoulders. Essie didn't want to annoy her so she encouraged that Larissa could talk to her about it whenever she's comfortable. Larissa stopped her as she was on her way out. Everything about Elijah's death, Chase, and her mom getting beaten had poured out of Larissa's mouth. Essie silently absorbed all of this. She appeared stoic, refraining from any signs of judgement.

"I feel nothing but guilt over what he did." Larissa cried. "I never would've been that harsh if I knew *he'd take his own life.*"

"No, don't!" Essie protests, giving her a hug. "You aren't responsible for any of that. That's awful but that's out of your control. Sure, you shouldn't had fought him but it was in self-defense. Remember that. And Chase shouldn't have said that to you."

"That's the thing though, he might've been right about my mom though." She begrudgingly said. "Ma hasn't showed no signs of becoming better, for getting into heaven. And I ain't sure if she ever will."

"Remember what I told you before? When I showed you my old yearbook?" Essie asked. Larissa's baffled face couldn't recall it. "Don't spend time worrying over nonsensical things. Elijah and Danielle—they're their own worst enemies. They're choices shouldn't have any bearing on your life. And as for Chase," Essie urged. "Don't ever let anyone get inside your head."

"I just wish I could've showed him how sorry I was before he did what he did. Or show my mom that what I'm doing actually matters for us both."

Essie had gotten a text from Yanie asking if she was still down for the sex party. Encouraging Larissa to move forward had Essie reflect on how she's put her patients and Larissa before herself. This feeling liberated her into taking the risk. Essie types a text verifying that she's still willing; then sends it at six o'clock. She follows up with Larissa: "Be careful what you wish for." Essie encouraged. "You'll never know when your last breath is gonna be."

York Avenue, two days later

Tonight's the night of their upcoming sex party for Essie. Jovanny was invited to tag along after revealing his relationship ending. Yanie offered to drive them there in her truck since Jovanny's vehicle is still getting fixed. Essie's embracive attitude showcased that she's still willing to explore. Larissa is upstairs; getting ready to go out with them for the night. Essie told her that they're going to a party solely for adults.

To make sure Essie wouldn't change her mind, Yanie verifies that everything was taken care of. She reassured Essie that she found a motel in midtown for Larissa to stay safe for the night. That nothing allowed happens without their consent and that they're free to leave whenever they choose to.

Larissa comes downstairs with her backpack on. She puts up a neutral expression for Yanie and Jovanny. However, Essie still detects her guilt. They both shared a mutual heartwarming smile. All four of them left outside to Yanie's truck. They drove off.

† Chapter 21: Karma's come to collect.

They had arrived in midtown a half hour before the party begins. Yanie arranged for them to stay at a cheap motel for tonight. Essie, Larissa and Jovanny wait inside the truck while Yanie handles the payment at the front desk. Being unemployed for a while now, Yanie decides to try out one of the credit cards left behind in Nneka Barshak's truck instead. She figures that it'll be just for tonight at this average motel. The transaction was approved and Yanie gladly received her key to room *121*.

Everyone went to the room. Their room contained two beds, a small bathroom, one window and a nice TV. The adults weren't worried too much since Jovanny and Yanie planned on staying at the party overnight. Essie doesn't mind sharing space with Larissa either. Larissa only packed another set of clothes in her bag. She then lies on the bed while being on social media. Yanie and Jovanny are both eager to leave already. Essie senses this, and also has this unsettling aura while looking inside, unnerving familiarity.

"Essie." Yanie called her over. "Larissa's all good where she's at. We ready. Jezebel spirit's in full-effect."

"I'll just check on her before we go."

Yanie groaned. "Fine. Me and Gibby will wait in the truck." The two leave the room.

Essie observes Larissa's sad expression after hearing the door close. Then pulled out one of her headphones once Essie comes over.

"How are you feeling, honey?" Essie sincerely asks.

"Not really." Larissa sighed. "But don't worry about me, I'll be fine. Go have fun tonight."

"Are you sure?" Essie urged. Larissa nods. "Are you positive?" Larissa nods again. *"Are you surely positive?"* Larissa snickers at Essie's playful tone. *"Are you entirely—?"*

"I'm sure I'm good, I'm positive." Larissa laughed.

Essie nods with a serene smile. She's almost certain to leave after getting Larissa to finally smile since their last talk. Before Essie goes, she quickly informs Larissa of the guidelines for being unsupervised for a while: *That she is not allowed to open the door to let anyone inside. To not leave the room to go exploring around this area at night. She could leave to only get snacks from the vending machine on this floor. And lastly, that her curfew is at midnight.* Larissa would rather stay up later than midnight but reluctantly agrees.

Two texts are sent to Essie's phone. It's Yanie telling her to hurry up. Then heard the honking from outside.

"Okay, I'm heading out. Call me if anything. Love you."

"Sure, love you. Goodnight." Larissa tiredly expressed while she returned to her phone.

Essie rushes out the door only for Yanie to still be honking. She gets in the backseat reassuring them that she's ready to go. As she looked back, she discovered Larissa watching them leave from the window. Essie waved her goodbye. But Larissa missed it by checking her phone for Chase's posts, then left from the window. Jovanny notices Essie's concern and reminds her that Larissa will be fine. Yanie immediately drove off.

† *MIDTOWN HOLKSDALE 8:34 P.M.*

While at home, Icarus McGrew sulks in his bedroom. He's been under his sheets for hours today. There's nothing to encourage him into getting up. All that goes through his head was killing and burying Bianca in the woods. Icarus hasn't eaten anything since this morning. His eyelids heavily weighed down, facing the wall.

What's this address? His mind recalled. *You're telling me I woke up naked under your sheets without you sleeping with me? Bullshit, you fucked me last night. You fucking pervert. I would never want your touch.* He began clenching his jaw. *Don't get any closer!* Her shaky, shrill voice swells his head. The image of Bianca's blood oozing through her purple dress as red spots had flashed his thoughts. Icarus feels this sharp inhale run through him the more his focus latches on him gripping for her phone earlier. All his fingertips massage the bite mark she left on his palm after trying to conceal her screams for help. *I swear I didn't mean for this to happen. You kept accusing me, threatening to report me. You were way too wasted so I didn't pursue any further.* That vision of Bianca's frozen expression was now buried deep within his psyche. *I'm so sorry. If I could take it all back, I would. I'm so, so sorry.*

These thoughts began to escalate towards the past women who've been alarmed by him. *I'M GOOD, I DON'T WANT TO GIVE MY NUMBER OUT!* Had infiltrated his mind. Remembering that mother causing a scene at the mall then transitioned to the plethora of sour looks from people.

Including that white guy who scowled at him. *This fucking guy. Judging me. GOOD, YOU GO THEN!* Flicked his thoughts. *She was that anxious around you. Didn't get no relationship, no kiss, and no date. Just that creeper she detects from a mile away.* He remembers her instantly nosediving down at her phone. *Anything to fucking avert your eyes from me, huh? That's YOU, Icarus. YOU'RE GONNA DIE A FUCKING VIRGIN!* This tangled mess of a woman stringing him along binds with the Indian woman bending herself over once foreseeing him. *Literal backbreaking work just to not be spotted around your presence.* Icarus deflated more, his scrawny legs coiled up to his boney chest, which swelled to his knees. These thoughts orbited towards the incident with that woman at the gas station. *PLEASE GET AWAY FROM ME!* Remembering as he scrambled away. *Can you quit following me!* Rattles his brain of the short, redhead woman from the mall. *Nobody—absolutely nobody feels comfortable around you. No one whatsoever. How many people get frantic whenever you're nearby?! Men and women at the mall, boys and girls from high school. Helen. Even Helen, the school whore doesn't want you.* Began devouring him. *That's the last time Lori spoke to you, your only friend back then. The class creep is how she'll always remember you. YOU'RE GONNA DIE A VI—*

Police sirens from outside severed the chains binding him to his own personal hell. Icarus jolted his neck forward. That panic gripped at his stomach the more the sirens amplified. Icarus dashed to the window. A police cruiser pulled into the gas station across the street. Two officers go inside together. Relinquishing Icarus of any future fugitive scenarios. The cops come out with coffee in both their hands. Then they drove off.

"Don't!" Icarus defiantly muttered to himself in attempts to not focus on before. He took a deep breath. *Your entire identity shouldn't be based on how women see you.* He thought, then exhaled. *What people think about you are their beliefs, not yours.*

Icarus decides to escape outside on his front steps. Sitting there watching the cars drive through. Watching vehicles stop for gas across the street. Happy, the cashier, gives him a goofy wave as he's taking out the trash. Icarus sees a woman come to a halt at a red light. Through the corner of her eye, she notices Icarus from his steps. She's in his line of sight and doesn't budge. The lady slowly lowers her front seat all the way backwards. Icarus annoyed by this scene. She is completely out of sight from her window, then proceeds to drive forth.

That is almost enough to have him revert to his negative thinking. Almost retreating indoors to his sanctuary, he halts himself, remembering that phone call. Reminding himself that he shouldn't give up hope on finding a woman. *Do not lose faith in finding a woman in your life, just don't make it a burden on your soul.* He internally recites. This gradually gives him more clarity.

Icarus McGrew goes to his car. While starting his engine, he began having second thoughts. However, Icarus decides to take a leap of faith. He drove off to the mall.

MIDTOWN HOLKSDALE PARTY: 9:09 P.M.

In the privately gated residence of this area inhabits a large house with multiple cars by the front. The music soars through the walls. The lights can be seen flickering to different colors inside. Essie, Yanie and Jovanny emerge to the front steps. While checking her phone, Essie hadn't received any missed calls from Larissa. Yanie reminded her that they can't have their phones on them to prevent recording. All three turned off their devices. Essie rang the doorbell, which made a feminine moaning noise.

A man who looked to be in his forties had joyously opened the door. A brightening light had blasted out the entrance. He was a handsome man with muscular arms who introduced himself as Sir Lynch. They're all inside his huge living room where it's filled with adults. Many adults were nude or half-naked. People were having sex on the floor, passionately kissing and licking everywhere on their bodies, drizzling food on body parts, including much more. A man was in the corner making love to a realistic-looking female sex doll. The guy's eyes moaned closed while the doll's lifeless pupils targeted Essie. There was a nude couple swinging and hollering on a sex swing. Then Jovanny points out a nude woman making love to a sheep in another room. Gripping at its fur, grinding her hips against the back. While Sir Lynch shows them around, he notices their perplexed looks. Sir lynch chuckles, as if their reactions are a common occurrence around here. He calmly clarifies that this is indeed a sex party, but this summer's event is more different for a separate occasion. He recalls of the phenomenon making its mark. Just this reminder has Essie, Yanie and Jovanny share an unspoken irritation. Tonight's party offers a warm welcome to everyone who'll burn in the afterlife. And even inviting and tempting to corrupt some saints. The goal is to provide a sanctuary scapegoat that includes many temptations that society may consider taboo.

Sir Lynch cheerily nods. "This is a place where all sinners, queers, dykes and homos can escape to both freely express and inflict their perverse, sexual desires without any fear of shame nor criticism." Then continues about finding himself loving to be submissive equally as much as being dominant.

Essie looked concerned. Yanie gives her a gentle look to reassure that everything will be fine. Sir Lynch opens a door to grab his homemade pamphlets to help explain things more. Inside the room exposes a motionless man with a noose tightly gripped around his neck, dangling above the ground.

"OH, MY GOODNESS!" Essie's cries tore fresh from her throat. *"HELP HIM!"*

"He's alright, he's alright." Sir Lynch laughed, then mentions that the guy's favorite kink is auto-erotic asphyxiation. He explains it involved hanging himself while simultaneously pleasuring himself.

The guy inside gives a thumbs up showing he's okay; his other hand's preoccupied while facing the opposite way.

Still feeling jittery, Essie is consoled by both Yanie and Jovanny. Yanie adds that this is her first time involved in this. Sir Lynch understandably hands them all his pamphlets as a guidance to enjoy many of tonight's options.

Scream to the Heavens was the first one: of being tied down with your privates stimulated; hollering until you reach deliverance. Dominatrix Nun involves a woman in an erotic nun costume having you abide by her every commandment. Taking in every word she spoke as gospel. If unable to commit, then her slave gets punished.

"What's 'Fornication with Crucifixion?'" Jovanny asks.

"We strap you down. But instead of a dildo, we penetrate you with a cross."

"No nail through my hands?"

"Only thing getting nailed is your ass." Sir Lynch explains. "It also includes 'Working for Indulgen-sins', which is everyone's favorite."

Fap-tism Choirboy Circle-jerk is when a group of men dressed in choirboy attire surrounds you, ejaculating everywhere on you. Lurk Almighty is basically being watched during the act of intimacy because the lord sees everything. There are plenty more that they haven't read.

"I will leave you all to explore." Sir Lynch said, excusing himself to entertain his other guests. "Just remember, leave your phones in that room and here we cast no judgement."

"He's cute." Yanie adds, watching Sir Lynch maneuver around the room. Then turned to Essie. "So how you feeling? You good?"

By now Essie's jitters had ceased.

Her discomfort silence showed she was contemplating on leaving. Jovanny senses the ladies should talk in private. He left to find a woman.

"Don't worry about nothing." Yanie said. "Ain't nobody finna enforce you into that choking hazard. Plus, there's other things on this pamphlet you probably ain't never heard of. Minus the weird shit."

"I see, the devil is in the details." Essie groans. "I'm just not sure I can go through with this still."

"Remember about taking risks." Yanie urged, then swiped away Essie's pamphlet. "Living in the moment. You been blessed with this crazy opportunity tonight to just let loose like you've been doing with me for a while now." She sees Essie considering this. "Just browse for a bit. See what you like. Tonight's about getting you some dick, that's it."

Essie watches as every other person engaged in a sexual act. Then noticed the liquor, drugs and condoms scattered on a separate table. Two women snorted cocaine off each other's engorged breasts. A gay couple had invited another male to accompany them on their pursuit upstairs. Jovanny was seen already kissing with another woman. Essie reflected on her choice of being cooped up inside her home after being so scared to leave outdoors. Then choosing the courage to search for Larissa.

She glimpsed at her phone, seeing no calls or messages from Larissa, then turned her phone off. Goes to secure it in the next room while Yanie does the same.

"Okay. Let's have some fun." Essie agreed.

†

Pastor Marques watches content creators discuss the whole Grant Critchfield scandal. He was never a huge fan of Grant but couldn't help but search him up. His rant during that interview was talked about everywhere. The clip from the show had Pastor Marques laughing.

There was a knock on his door. Pastor Marques opened up to Grant himself (*smelling like cigarettes*). He was slightly perplexed. He asks if Grant had left something behind.

"You leave something behind?"

"No. No, I—"

"Or someone?" Pastor Marques mocks, jogging his memory about the sex doll.

"That's right. You can have it. You could sell it online, say it belonged to a celebrity."

"*Great.*" he sarcastically said. "Just pass her off to the homies with your autographed seed on it."

Not wanting this to escalate, Grant suddenly claimed her. Reassuring that he'll take her with him. Marques thought perhaps Grant wanted to verify if Marques had gone online with this. After letting Grant inside, he told Grant that he didn't and neither did she. Grant was not here for that neither. Marques sat down, skeptically flicks both eyebrows up, awaiting for him to speak.

"You said you saw that interview?" Grant asks.

Marques nods. "Yea, man. It's surfing all over the web."

"*I know this already.*" Grant irritably sighs.

The blatant frustration increased. Marques consoles him by liking the points that Grant made. Grant tells him that his agent was screaming over the phone about that toxic interview. Telling him that she has more work to do to prevent him from getting cancelled. Grant's mother called him but he didn't answer. The online comments section gripped at him as well.

Marques spoke with ease about the many other people online who agreed with him and supports his message. Then shows Grant his phone with those messages. This was leading to online debates. Fans versus trolls. Grant tries to feel better but worries he might get blackballed.

"If you're here to confess your guilt over this—"

"I'm not here for that." Grant said, prideful.

"Ok, good. The crib ain't no confessional booth."

"I came here to proposition you something." Grant said.

This had Marques lean a bit forward. Grant tells him about the people praising Pastor Marques online. The many people agreeing with him. Loving the edge of a man in clergy attire being vulgarly, outspokenly honest. Him delivering a sermon that gripped people collectively. Hearing this began fueling Marques' ego as he grew a grin.

Grant offers helping him gain more popularity. This eagers Marques. Grant suggests helping him by offering him a podcast. A bought small studio, microphones, including hiring someone to edit everything. Just to help him gain more followers to preach to. Grant adds that they will even send him money online.

There was this small plea in Grant's tone. Almost as if there was an alternative reason for this that benefits him. Grant concludes his pitch. He is waiting for Marques to accept. The room fell silent.

"What'chu trying to finesse me out of?" Marques asks, sounding suspicious. "Make it make sense."

"Nothing." Grant then quickly said, hoping to accept. Justifying it as his bona-fide offer for helping him. Claiming that Marques just has to keep preaching the truth to acquire all of this.

"This doesn't involve me coming up out my pockets?"

"I'll handle the financial aspect of this." Grant said, then his tone sounded graceful. "All I ask is that you defend me on your podcast? I'll need your support."

This request had it all unravel. Grant Critchfield wanted a recognizable face (*gone viral*) to come to his defense. To tie this miraculous and empowering movement with his allegation. That those are the reasons the public eye views him different. To steer his audience to a different perspective. Pastor Marques does not believe Grant is guilty but sees right through him.

"Follow me." Pastor Marques said. Grant appeared confused. "Join the show. You pretty outspoken yourself. Fans will tune in just off you, increasing our views." He added, to help boost Grant's spirits. "And maybe other celebs will want to donate or just collaborate with me."

"Okay then. Sure." Grant said, being the vessel to speak that gains attention prompts him, even while uncertain.

Midtown Mall 9:21 P.M

Tonight is crowded as usual with people accompanied by their families and friends. Icarus McGrew sits at a table in the food court. He keeps trying to think positive about getting a woman while eating his churro. Still reciting the advice he was given over the phone. His eyes scanned everywhere for a potential female present. There was a pretty, blonde woman by herself on her phone. Icarus was glued to his seat; taking glimpses at her. She soon threw on her purse, got up and left.

After sitting down for quite some time, he finally decides to leave elsewhere. The halls are filled with multiple people walking by. Icarus cautiously veered around at some in hopes of not making anyone uncomfortable. Walking around began to get tedious as time passed. Then he made his way to the beauty shop, Purity. Many women were on line. There were few with their daughters that're browsing around. Icarus notices the same pretty, blonde lady from the food court. The more he observes her sweet face, the more he halts himself.

What people think about you are their beliefs, not yours. He reminds himself, beginning to move forward. *You can do this, man. Just embrace who you are.* He finally approaches her.

"Excuse me." He said. She instantly makes space for him to get through. "No, no, you're fine where you are. I thought you were looking pretty tonight. Pretty enough to where I remember you from in the food court earlier."

"*Ok…*" she replied, sounding repulsed. "What're you following me?!" then she walked away to another aisle.

Icarus shrugged it off. As he turned around, he detects the tall employee who stocks shelves, silently staring at him. The man's arms are crossed. Icarus stops near him.

"Yes, can I help you?" Icarus politely said.

"I'm just watching." He judged. "You know you're a regular face in here, right? Never purchasing anything, always seen chatting with customers, maneuvering around our aisles. For months, we've seen you. We know why too."

"And why's that?"

The man arrogantly shook his head. "You know why."

His passive aggressive breakdown of Icarus appearing in the store slowly had past thoughts creep in. Reminders of the previous man who scowled at him when he got yelled at. Or the man who overheard him approach an underage girl. These memories almost engulfed his mindset as Icarus observes the employee's condescending face. All that criticizing Icarus has already self-inflicted didn't change how others perceived him. Anymore added would've gave that man the satisfaction. Icarus had slowly begun to convert himself, believing he's good enough. Not to let any other identity creep in. His faith would've been momentarily shook but instead he replied: "Keep on patrol for me then. I'll be lurking back again soon."

The employee seemed slightly annoyed watching Icarus take one more mocking gander around the store. Then Icarus made his way out. As he walks around still, the feeling of clarity lasted longer. The vision of that employee seemingly irked. Including the unshakable belief within himself that nobody else could alter.

Icarus boldly walks into the wave of incoming people. His head held high, shoulders swung back and leaving his back straight. Feeling in complete control over himself. He turns to see everyone in front of him. A woman turned her head the opposite direction. Another woman, who recognized him from months ago, had tossed on her ghost cloak. There was a female who got closer walking alongside him. He looked at her momentarily; she withdrew herself back. Each reaction hadn't affected him. It only made him feel more powerful that he could unintentionally cause this. This liberating newfound energy of having no attachment to how he's labeled by the world. Baffled as to what possessed him to think that harsh before. Even the miracle that's plagued the world couldn't deter himself.

What people think about you are their beliefs, not yours. Had orbited his mind. It inflated himself more as he analyzes the blatant agitation, alarmed or shaky responses stirring inside some people. His vision tightened more unto strangers he'd foreseen from afar. Monitoring everyone in sight. Few men avert their eyes. Other women dipped their heads at the ground. Someone shielded her face with her hand. A man in a wheelchair tilted down his head and kept it pushing.

Icarus McGrew embraced the domino effect of heads that bow down to him. Having him thrive like a God as he makes his final image known.

MIDTOWN HOLKSDALE PARTY: 9:30 P.M.

More people have shown up to the party since it started. Already getting intimate with the first stranger that catches their eye. Essie hasn't found anyone she's interested in as of yet. Jovanny was groping two women in the bathroom. Yanie hasn't had sex with anyone yet. Instead, she's drinking more before she pursues anyone first. Essie continues observing everyone. A few minutes ago, she and Yanie engaged a conversation with these friendly triplets who arrived here together named Houston, Gale and Lily. She sees a small naked woman boldly parading around, occasionally poking people with a dildo bigger than her. A guy keeps popping out of nowhere watching people getting intimate by concealing himself with his ghost cloak. The sheep from earlier is maneuvering around. There's a huge TV on the wall playing pornography. The genre switches after each video. Before it was lesbian porn; now it is foot fetish porn. Essie grabs a bottle of wine then heads to the bathroom to try to loosen up in private. Once inside, she sits on the toilet and commenced to drinking.

"What the—" Essie blurts out, alarmed at hearing a sharp clap on the shower glass. Then hearing heavy, stretched moaning from two women fucking in the shower.

Essie escapes from the bathroom. Then sits beside a young man who appeared as tense as she felt.

"Hey, how are you?" she began.

"I'm okay." He said softly. "You enjoying yourself?"

"I just got here not too long ago with my friends. So we'll see. Did you come here with anyone?"

"Nope. All by my lonesome."

"So what's your name?" she asked.

"My name's Kenleigh Foster. And yours?"

"Essie." She said, shaking his hand.

Kenleigh was a dark-skinned twenty-year-old. His face looked younger than his age though. The guy had skinny arms and a slim stomach. His body was slouched over his chair. With everything happening, he appeared very timid.

The two began talking about what craziness they've witnessed thus far. Kenleigh admits that he came here to try something new since he's never had sex before. His lamblike demeanor had Essie feel comfortable enough to confide the same thing. She offers him some of the wine but he politely declines.

"Here's honestly the best place you'd rather stay sober at." he encouraged. "I don't really know too much about here."

"I just feel much more relaxed after a few drinks. Almost sound like a different person myself."

Kenleigh warned her about some guy got yelled at for spiking someone's drink here. He hasn't seen him around since. Essie notices a handsome Caucasian man leaving the kitchen. Kenleigh acknowledged her interest.

"His name's Jensen. You think he's cute or something?"

"Maybe. You think he'll be interested."

"Well that depends. Are you dead inside?!" he jokes.

"What do you mean?"

"I had overheard him earlier claiming to be into necrophilia. Sleeping with deceased bodies."

"What kind of sick freaks are at this party?" she gasped, sounding tipsy. "Don't tell me you met him yet?"

"No, I'm not gay." He laughed. "Just haven't really initiated anything as of yet."

"How come?"

"I don't know. I've just been sitting here alone with my thoughts. I sometimes get lost in my head."

Essie couldn't trace not one issue with this guy. She asked if he was destined to burn in hell on that list. Kenleigh says he's going to heaven but doesn't take the list too seriously. Essie tells him about being isolated in her home for a while, only to come out and end up here after being convinced by her friend. That this party seems too out of her comfort zone. Kenleigh suggests that she shouldn't take her friend's lead even if her intentions are pure. That she should choose what is best for herself. Essie realized what he said was true. Essie felt the pressure of breaking her routine so much and not knowing what more she desires for herself that she let Yanie misguide her here. This place doesn't feel like where she should be. But Essie didn't want to ruin the fun for Yanie and Jovanny. Instead, she decides to stick around until her friends are ready to leave, she may even change her mind the longer she's there.

Essie politely excuses herself to go wander around upstairs. A door with a crucifix on it had intrigued Essie into thinking that maybe it was a room to get some privacy to herself. She opened the door to the triplets from before. All were laying sideways naked on the bed. Houston using a vibrator on his sister's clit, Lily was sucking Gale's erect dick, and Gale's tongue massaging Houston's asshole. Essie was completely shocked that she almost lost her balance.

"Essie, nice seeing you again." Houston nonchalantly said, observing her disbelief. "Hard to believe right? But this is our thing."

"I'm sorry." Essie managed to squeeze out, tilting her head down.

"You should be!" Lily hissed. "Don't you know not to barge in a room with a crucifix hanging off the door?!"

"Don't worry, Essie." Houston said. "We're not mad. Lily just wants me to finish. As would I. My brother on the other hand is a little tongue-tied right now. So won't you please excuse us?"

While still averting her eyes, Essie instantly shuts back the door. They could still be heard from the other side. Houston stimulates his sister so intensely that she's heard moving away.

"Oh no you don't! This time I got you by your feet, so we don't all get separated like at birth." Houston yells.

Essie retreats downstairs. Genuinely cautious of the next ungodly thing she might stumble into. Kenleigh is still by himself, so she returned. She tells him what she just walked into, wishing she hadn't.

"Not even step-siblings? Kenleigh asks.

"Biological from when they introduced themselves."

"Really?"

"You want to catch a glimpse upstairs for yourself?"

"*Sheeeeeeit!*" Kenleigh defiantly said, his voice in a high-pitched mocking tone. "I'm good. It's clear they prefer to keep it in the family."

His unexpected response and his sudden transition had Essie erupt with bloated laughter. Her nerves finally having settled. Kenleigh looked seemingly joyous.

"Who are you?!" Essie laughed. She gets up while Kenleigh switched back to being silent. "I'll see you."

†

Yanie Juergens was drinking still. Her tolerance was too high so she's mainly sober. While getting accustomed to here, she was kissing another woman, sucked a guy's dick and got herself randomly fingered by a man who blatantly requested to. She began checking for her friends. Jovanny was nowhere in sight. There were people gathered around doing more drugs. Many adults ended up digesting ecstasy.

Washing it down their mouths with liquor. Yanie knew things were about to get crazier soon. As her eyes panned the area, she notices a shirtless guy with lashes on his bareback coming downstairs. This got her interested as she races upstairs hearing guys either hollering joyously or screaming for mercy. There's a room with those men being brutally whipped by a sadist in an erotic nun outfit. All of their backs were marked, oozing blood while tied down.

Yanie deviates from that room unnoticed. She panned to a room with a man being surrounded by different ethnic woman. All these ladies were kneeled down naked; aligned in a circle around this man. He had ferociously gripped at his genitals preparing to ejaculate all over them. Glanced down at each anticipating female. He insists they all beg for his sperm, exactly the way he likes it. All the women surrounding him had closed their eyes and clapped their palms together in prayer. Simultaneously saying:

"Our daddy who art in heaven, who made us scream thy name. Thy made us cum, thy will be done on earth as it is in heaven. Give us this nut, our daily train and forgive us our pettiness. As we don't forgive our fathers who tried to control us. And lead us straight to temptation and deliver us from protection." They conclude their prayer by sticking out their pierced tongues. "*Awwwwww-men.*"

The stirring sensation within his aching balls ripped through in a wave of heat that devoured them all. Sperm sprinkles (*like a geyser orbits around*) on each submissive girl.

Yanie just left to explore some more. She began getting frustrated that she hasn't had sex with anybody here yet. Her mind recalls the handsome brother she talking with before, Gale. She thinks she hears his voice in the next room. The door with a crucifix on it. Before she opened, Essie yells for her. Yanie is ecstatic to see her again.

"There you are." Yanie gleefully said. "Don't go in some of these rooms up here. *Sweet Jesus!*"

"Including this one." Essie warns. "I made that mistake

earlier. It's not pretty."

Gale's moaning progressed inside that room.

"I bet it's that cute brother from before." Yanie suggests.

"It's not."

"You sure? Sounds a little like him tho—"

"No, believe me, it's unrelated." Essie quickly adds.

The two returned downstairs to a table where they can drink. Neither of them had seen Jovanny anywhere. Essie goes on about how she hasn't found anyone here attractive but had conversed with Kenleigh Foster. Yanie encourages her to go for him but Essie refuses. Claiming that Kenleigh was cool but seemed a little weird.

Sir Lynch noticed Yanie staring at him from across the room seeming enamored. He smiled back at her then continued chatting with his voluptuous guest. Essie still looked around for any sign of Jovanny. He was nowhere. Instead, she just assumed that he took a lady to one of the rooms. Essie's mind begins wandering about Larissa's well-being in that motel.

MIDTOWN MOTEL 10:49 P.M.

Being locked in the room all this time, Larissa stayed on her bed. The TV plays as background noise while she's scrolling her social media. She could feel herself desiring a snack from the vending machine. Remembering her guardian's rules has her wanting to make this a quick trip. Larissa cautiously checks for anyone that might seem weird outside. She finally makes it to the vending machines in the lobby. The first thing she purchased was a water bottle. Instantly took a sip while pondering on what snack to buy. The man at the front desk has been on the phone before she came. His friendly voice from checking them in prior now sounded serious and concerned. Then he mentioned room *121*. Being in earshot, Larissa almost turned her head but kept facing the machine. The man addressed the person over the phone as "officer". Her eyebrows sharpened, using her peripheral vision to glimpse over at the counter.

The employee mentions that the woman who paid for the room doesn't fit this description. Also including a description of the other people accompanied with her. Once he began describing the minor, a gut-punching rush had Larissa almost turn her head over at him. To not be detected, she had to resist the temptation. Inside of Larissa's throat starts flaring up, growing her more parched. Then there was a mention of law enforcement on their way. She begun to replenish with more water as things began to correlate in her head. The reminder of Yanie's sketchy job, the unknown source of Yanie's truck, being at a motel, and all of them being unidentified.

A powerful ding echoes in the lobby, making her aware.

"Young lady!" the employee called from behind the front desk. "Excuse me. May I speak with you for a second?"

Larissa instantly took a step toward but *HALTS*. The water bottle made a crackling sound the firmer she gripped at it. Frozen at the vending machines. The man sternly repeated himself louder. His eyes appeared skeptical as to what she's doing. He then realized that she must've been eavesdropping. Rising above his seat sends Larissa running for outside.

"WAIT NOW!" He demands. The noise of his chair moving back made her escape faster to her room.

The room door slammed shut. Larissa turns every lock with force. Then whipped her phone out, instantly calling for her guardian. The phone's ringing. Larissa's pacing around hoping to reach her. Her eyes keep twitching at the door. Larissa sucks her teeth in frustration once she's sent to voicemail.

"Essie, it's an emergency!" Her words eject out. "Or a misunderstanding I hope—" *TWO POUNDS HIT AT THE DOOR.* The man orders for her to let him inside. "I think Yanie did something. That dude at the front desk is busting at our door." He yelled that the police are coming. This sent Larissa in a frenzy, lowering her tone. *"I wish you were here."*

She hung up. Larissa swipes her phone charger and bag. The man announced that he's getting the room key. Larissa called for Yanie to try clarifying things. The more the phone rings, the more she fears her not answering. It went straight to voicemail. Larissa targeted for the window, then climbed out quick. There is no sign of that man outside. Even though leaving could make things worse, Larissa runs far. She's scared of getting spotted as a cold criminal. Instead of being recognized as an innocent, warm teenage girl in the flesh.

MIDTOWN HOLKSDALE PARTY: 11:15 P.M.

Many of the guests are now feeling the ecstasy kick in. Some people were so relaxed that they were slouched on top of one another on the living room couch. Women were excessively dancing. Grinding up on guys, wildly swinging their arms to the blasting music (*off beat*) and one lady was performing splits everywhere. Sweat had oozed down many foreheads and bodies. The sweat drips were blatantly seen on their chest and armpits.

One guy was chatting with Essie. The whole interaction was getting uncomfortable as he was extremely upbeat. Almost as if he was overcompensating for something. He was in her personal space to the point where she had to keep reminding him. His pupils appeared dilated. She excused herself to go find her friend. Essie went for her phone instead and headed for outside to check on Larissa. She saw that she had five missed calls from Larissa. This had Essie immediately listen to the whole voicemail. She rushed back for Sir Lynch to let her inside. He offers her ecstasy, but she politely refused. Essie searched around for Yanie but couldn't find her nor Jovanny. Her adrenaline worsens the more she thinks about what Yanie has involved them all into. Essie decides to just leave to settle this. Sir Lynch halts her at the door. She quickly tells him that she's leaving. Then rushes to Yanie's truck. Even though Yanie said it wasn't stolen, she doubted that Yanie started it with a key. Essie sees the weird contraptions in the glove compartment, this confirmed her fear. Essie used it to start the engine and drove out of there.

Yanie runs into Sir Lynch asking if he's seen her friends. He informed her that Jovanny was seen upstairs with a woman and that Essie had just left.

"How?" Yanie asks, perplexed. Then she ran outside to see her truck was gone. This infuriated Yanie that Essie car-jacked her. "Can't believe this bitch took off." She groaned. "She over here acting like she dodged a bullet."

"Everything's fine." Sir Lynch reassured. "Because the life of the party has just arrived." He said, lively. Gesturing toward the window where nine vehicles arrived.

He opened the door where Yanie had a closer look. There were hearses parked outside. The confused look on Yanie's face had him clarify that nobody's attending a funeral. Sir Lynch had made reservations for dead bodies to satiate the necrophiliacs here. The drivers had helped bring inside the coffins. Jensen is joyous in the background.

"Settle down now, Jensen. Settle down." Sir Lynch said.

†

Inside a separate bedroom upstairs inhabits Jovanny Gibbs with a pale-skin lady named Sam. Sam had long blonde hair down to her backside. Her skinny legs were crossed. As they were kissing, her luscious lips left a moist, red lip gloss print on him. Sounds of seductive moans had Jovanny's erection harden more.

Sam smelled angelic with whatever perfume aroma she carried on. Jovanny requested for more to happen but Sam insists that she's waiting to involve another girl. This elevated his interest even more. Jovanny agreed to be patient and pours them some more liquor. Then Sam starts asking him about what his fetishes. Jovanny lied to keep the conversation seductive. Claiming he likes bondage, involving toys and roleplay. Sam seemed pleased then admits to loving being dominant. Jovanny tries changing the subject asking about her tattoo on her forearm: *WE'RE ALL MADE IN GOD'S IMAGE.*

Sam smirked. "I got this years ago, back when I was finding myself. I actually want to get it removed soon."

"No, it ain't bad."

"I'm gonna go freshen up really quick." Sam excuses herself to the bathroom.

The coffins were set up in the basement where several necrophiliacs could satisfy themselves. Sir Lynch returned to talk to Yanie. He admires how nonjudgmental she was once the bodies arrived. She noticed a woman in her fifties admiring over at him.

"You gonna get at that?" Yanie asks.

"No. She's a bit too old for my taste. You?"

Yanie shook her head. Then spoke of her sexual escapades while here. She leans closer, smiling on how she hasn't had intercourse yet.

"It'd be nice to hop on a body that's alive." She hints, giving him seductive eyes.

Sir Lynch invites her to accompany him in his bedroom where there's more drinks. Yanie gladly follows.

The two started stripping their clothes once they reached his bedroom. He begun kissing her neck; she commences to rubbing his cock through his pants. Yanie remembered him revealing his dominant and submissive fetish. She insists on starting off dominant over him. It's almost like she answered his prayers.

Yanie was riding on top of his raging erection. Sir Lynch lies on his back with the most ecstatic smile. The bed rocks immensely while she gyrates her hips. Sir Lynch requests for her to grip at his throat. She grappled around his neck without question. He urges for her to squeeze tighter, so she does. It wasn't enough, then it gets tighter. Now he's closer to being fulfilled. Yanie's moans amplified as she's reaching climax. Sir Lynch's hardly muffled sounds could be heard over her stranglehold. A masculine moan is heightened from the corner.

This has them both quickly stop. Both staring at the empty corner, leaving Yanie confused. Sir Lynch recognized that sound. Then took a moment to again catch his breath.

"Thomas!" Sir Lynch yelled at the empty corner. There was no response. "I know you're there."

A small blonde, olive skin man appeared after removing his ghost cloak. Shirtless Thomas had his pants down to his ankles with his hardened penis gripped in one hand.

Yanie was annoyed by this lurker. Sir Lynch ordered for him to leave. They both watch as Thomas drags his feet with his pants still wrapped around his ankles. Dick still hard, pointing him his way out. They both continued afterwards.

A truck comes to the front yard as the parties still going. It had a red colored cabin with a white shipping container. The shipping container stretched out long. It was a little rusty but still secured. The two men leave the cabin to release the locks off the container.

†

Jovanny Gibbs pulled out his phone while waiting for Sam to finish up. Once it's activated, it showed he had four missed calls from Larissa. He texted her asking if she's alright. Then he contemplated whether to call her. Sam finally walked out smiling. Two glasses of wine were in her hands. Jovanny gladly accepted and put his phone away. They cling glasses then Jovanny gulped down his.

"I see you're all good now."

"All better now." Sam agreed, setting her glass on the floor. *"So, I was in there wondering..."* she sweetly began, one leg stretched across his lap. *"...if you didn't mind being tied down?"*

"Baby, I'll tie you down soon after this party. Be wifey and everything." Jovanny laughed.

"No silly. I meant to the bed for me?" Sam clarifies. "You said you were into bondage anyway so that's fits well with my dominatrix fetish."

"Nah, I'm good."

"Why not?"

"I'm just not in the mood for all that but we could still get it going. Ain't no big deal."

"Okay." She nonchalantly said. "I did ask you nicely."

Hearing Sam utter these words had brought Jovanny some relief that things wouldn't deter this. In fact, Jovanny feels too relieved. His vision was slowly getting blurry. An almighty wave flooded his internal organs. The muscles in his body softened like mush. There is a tingling sensation spiking through his toes rushing up his legs. Helpless Jovanny Gibbs crumbled on his back like glop. The only muscle active of his remaining still is his erection.

No sounds could be vocalized from his loosened lips. He couldn't scream nor speak. Both tiresome eyes settled directly on Sam, who watches him with an arrogant sneer.

Sam runs her hands down his chest. Then snickered at how fast his heart rate is beating. She removed off his shirt, shoes, and pants. Jovanny watched as Sam digs into her purse to withdraw two handcuffs. Both of his wrists felt twisted as she seized them to the wood frame. Sam once again manhandles them to get them properly reinforced.

"You've committed the cardinal sin of accepting drinks from strangers." Sam teased whilst softly kissing his forehead.

Hovering over his motionless body had made Sam feel superior. Jovanny's stretched arms extended opposite sides, his lifeless chest, untethered legs and crossed barefoot. To Sam at least, he almost resembled being crucified. Then Sam wrapped tighten a blindfold over him.

All Jovanny could hear was Sam's footsteps leaving the room. His head swells with any possible way to escape out of this before whatever is to come. None of his muscles can move still, infuriating him more. Praying that Essie or Yanie would somehow put a stop to this. The door slowly opens then clicked shut. Sam's familiar fingertips began to loosen the blindfold. Jovanny is petrified for whatever is to unfold.

The pitiful look on Sam's face forms once seeing Jovanny's eyes shut tight. Encouraging for him to open his eyelids to see for himself.

The realization that nobody can save him slowly demolished him. His eyes opened to see a preteen Asian girl. This reveal sent this uneasy icy, pinning gnawing down his spine. Leaving his body entirely frozen. Sam elaborates on how the party finally received the awaiting shipment of human trafficking. These enslaved children are to satiate the pedophiles invited tonight. Including that these foreign kids are reluctant to be the most docile.

This girl's rosy cheeks slowly shake. Strands of her black unkempt hair run down her back. Her slim arms and legs both shivered in the ripped garment of sheet she drags. As Jovanny looks over at her with such Christ-like compassion, the girl's innocent eyes averted elsewhere (*mainly at the ground, hoping someone will answer her prayers*). Strands of her black unkempt hair run down her back.

Sam began to slowly undress. Jovanny tries to move any sort of muscle. Once the dress is gone, Sam revealed her veiny, gargantuan penis. Jovanny's anxious breathing heightened along with Sam's unyielding erection. He couldn't help but stare down this unholy sight. It was like a wolf in sheep's clothing (*or in this case, a protruding dickhead masquerading as a pulsating clitoris*).

Sam chuckled at this struggle. "Don't worry you. You'll get your turn. You're not going anywhere." Then directs her gaze at the girl. *"In the meanwhile, I'm gonna be in my happy place… you."* Sam merrily said, while manhandling her.

MIDTOWN MOTEL 11:39 P.M.

On the path to the motel, Essie was entirely anxious. The thought of Yanie getting them in trouble with the law and having to drive this stolen vehicle all the way back, had her on edge. Larissa getting involved is what circulated the most. Unable to answer her phone after calling back multiple times now.

She monitored how fast she was moving to prevent getting pulled over. Once she drove nearby, she stopped. Checking the outside of the motel. There weren't any patrol cars or flashing lights in sight. The absence of police brought Essie a brief of relief. After parking outside, Essie rushed out the truck, heading to room *121*. As she's at the door, she gripped the doorknob, forcing herself forward inside.

Inside was a complete void of darkness. Nothing was detected. Essie's hands frantically felt the wall for a switch. She called for Larissa as she moved slowly for the light.

The room spontaneously brightened from the corner by the lamp. Sitting nearby the lamp was Nneka Barshak.

Nneka's sudden appearance had Essie shriek then freeze. Essie's nerves go rampant throughout her skin. Now instantly recalls the night Nneka swarmed at her and Yanie at gunpoint. Barely escaping with their lives intact.

It was unsettling being scorned at by her. Nneka sat with her entire body sitting upright with her thick legs crossed. Her wrathful eyes latched with Essie's petrified ones. Larissa's inexplicable absence left her wondering what Nneka had done. There was nothing but stillness in the room. Nneka's vision intensifies, leaving Essie unable to look away.

"I'm the woman whose truck you stole." Nneka firmly states as she unslings her .45 caliber pistol. "Shut the door!"

The rate of Essie's heartbeat almost ripped through her chest. Her whole back pressed at the wall. Nneka then gestures the gun at the door. The trembling arm of Essie's cautiously slides the door until it closes shut. Essie felt her tense neck strain as her throat dryly clicked. Lastly, she slowly turns back around to face her. As she turns, her eyes trailed off in hoping that Larissa wasn't held hostage nor dead in here. She still wasn't detected.

Nneka's gun was still directed at her. She never moved an inch. Essie staggered back at the wall. The sharp stare held amongst them had Essie's eyes feeling glassy.

"You're quite hard to find, you know that?" Nneka said. "Had to interrogate your boss, who gave your ass up in a heartbeat. Slipped away during that riot. Now here you are at the mercy of my gun."

Then she follows up with the credit card company contacting her about an unusual charge at this motel room. Remembering her cards were in there confirmed that she'd catch the person responsible for stealing her truck.

Nneka shook her head. "You're already in debt for jacking my truck and wasting my gas that brought us here. You seem to have got yourself paying a hefty price now." Then sharply unlocked the safety from her gun. "Karma's come to collect."

This mixed feeling of fear and rage towards Yanie cycled through her. She struggled to fuel inward enough strength to speak. Her unsteady lips mouthed out nothing. At last, her feeble tone forms something mumbled.

"SOUND OFF, BITCH!" Nneka barked.

"It wasn't me. It wasn't, I swear."

Nneka shoots a skeptical look of disbelief. "Then who?"

Silence clouded the room. It took everything for Essie to not blurt out Yanie's name, description, entire lying existence. Her teary eyes just quickly scavenged for a saving grace. Then reluctantly focused on Nneka once again. Too alarmed to blink, her eyes could open to the flash of an unannounced bullet. All those possible outcomes of dealing with the police seemed miniscule compared to her now circumstances. Hell hath no fury like a woman scorned.

All that's fresh in her brain is Larissa's well-being. Her jumbled thoughts kept leading to that one concern.

Essie sheepishly began: *"What happened—"*

Three fierce gunshots fire off. Striking Essie's body, catapulting her to the wall. One bullet punctures her shoulder, another tore at her stomach, the final blow ripped through her chest. Essie flopped to the ground. There were blood spots splattered on the wall.

An unsettling groan leaves Essie's mouth after that sloppy fall to the ground.

Nneka Barshak slowly got up from her chair then loomed over her. Her lips formed a devilish smile after having proudly witnessed the fall of Essie Chu.

After hearing Essie's harsh breathing, Nneka then crouches over her.

"Come on now. You could make it." Nneka softly taunts, watching Essie's struggle. *"Have yourself a bit of faith. Don't give up, don't go towards the light just yet."*

Essie's eyes are slowly gushing tears of hopelessness. Her dying breath sorrowfully spills: "La… *Lar… Larri…"*

Both her eyes slowly close.

Nneka then threw on latex gloves and goes through her pockets for anything worth of value. Avoiding the blood slowly oozing on the ground. The only thing she pulled out was her wallet and phone. After yanking money from it, she checks her driver's license. Nneka stared at the name on the license. Afterwards, she searches for any forms of identification. Then found her medical I.D.

This sends her mind into a blank state. Realizing that her name's not Beverly. Essie's excuse of not stealing her vehicle came to mind. Nneka then remembered last time during the riot, Essie was in the passenger seat. Another woman was behind the wheel. Piecing the clues together that Essie was unaware of being driven in her stolen truck. And that Nneka just shot an innocent woman. Her arrogant attitude changed as she registers what she's just done.

MIDTOWN HOLKSDALE PARTY: 11:52 P.M.

Children are taken to separate rooms to be violated. The remaining frightened kids are still chained up in the locked container.

Exhausted Larissa finally made it to the party using a tracking app for Yanie's phone. She was full of rage. The possibility of law enforcement getting involved had her bang on the door. Larissa waits for a moment, growing more eager for someone to answer. The door crept open, revealing a man's serious face. This has Larissa feel unease.

"Young lady, how old are you?" he skeptically asks.

"No, I'm actually here for—"

He began snickering. "I'm just kidding, we welcome all ages here." Then fully opens the door.

The guy's body was in a submissive leather suit. Larissa's eyes stared at him stupefied. He galloped away to his boyfriend in the kitchen. The music loudened as she watches any nude adults in this place. She's baffled as to why Essie would ever go somewhere like here? Averting her eyes from their genitals as best she can, she maneuvers around in pursuit of Essie, Yanie or Jovanny. A sheep spirals out of the kitchen with its fur disheveled. Timid Larissa repeatedly excuses herself as she bypassed guests (*doing everything to not come into contact with anyone*). The atmosphere began getting warmer due to adults being within close range. Larissa fans her face with her hand. Sweat form down her forehead, making her more anxious.

"Fuck, it's hot." She mumbles.

"Then get out those clothes, kid." A guest encouraged.

Larissa fled upstairs, praying that person didn't follow her behind. An upsurge of moans is heard as she passed by certain doors. She keeps moving passed the ferocious barking behind one other door. Then her ears recognize Yanie's familiar loud tone from two doors down. Larissa quickly knocked while checking for anybody on this floor.

"Yanie!" Larissa yelled. "Yanie, you in there?"

This announcement had Yanie shocked. The door flung open, having Yanie yank her arm inside. Sir Lynch was in the bathroom taking a shower.

"Yo, get your clothes on! We got company." Yanie announced to him, then turned to Larissa. "The fuck is you doing here? You crazy?"

"I'm here 'cause your fucking credit card was reported stolen." Larissa snapped. Mentioning that the man at the front desk was calling the police. That he gave descriptions of them and that nobody picked up their phones. Telling her that she tracked them down all the way here.

Yanie's heart drummed so fierce. This had her realize why Essie had left early unannounced. A possible sequence of events involving law enforcement rattled her brain. Larissa looked to her for answers. Studying her whole frozen demeanor, forming scenarios to why she's wearing a robe in a place such as this.

Yanie finally snapped out of it, noticing her. "What?"

"What is this weird-ass place?"

"You shouldn't even be here. Plus, we're leavin'. Essie already dipped out. Now we gotta check for Jovanny's ass."

Larissa nods, cooperatively. "What we finna do about the whole situation back there?"

"We'll figure it out." Yanie said, sounding irked.

The bathroom door creaked open. Both heads instinctively turn to shirtless Sir Lynch in a pair of pants. He was fastening his belt. Yanie silently gestured for him to grab on a shirt.

"What's the matter?" he asked. "Our final guests have finally arrived."

"Fuck is you talkin' about?" Yanie replied, seeming perplexed. "She a minor."

"Of course. I ordered for minors to satisfy some of my guests. Didn't expect for an African girl though, the shipment was supposed to handle solely Asians."

The confused look on Yanie quickly transitions to an expression of disgust. Her arm extends as a guard for Larissa's well-being. His eyes trained on Larissa, having her paralyzed in fear. The blatant look of discomfort had his face brighten with a smile. His easygoing attitude left Yanie and Larissa speechless.

"It was on the pamphlet I handed you. Don't act surprised. Remember, *no judgement here.*" Sir Lynch said.

Yanie jolts upward, blocking Larissa. Sir Lynch slowly scraps his feet towards them. The room fell deafly silent.

"Don't come at us like this." Yanie demands, trying to hold a steady tone. She feels her shaky throat, almost having her voice fall flat. *"Don't make me say it again."*

As he unfastened his belt buckle, blowing a kiss at Larissa, he commences lurking forward.

"I won't come at you, Yanie. We've already had our fun. And I respected your wishes, gave you my consent of basically being submissive." Then his eyes again hunted for Larissa. "Now it's my turn to be on top."

"HEAD FOR THE DOOR!" Yanie urged.

An alarming clang from the belt buckle slamming on the ground was echoed. Larissa hauled the door open to—

Sir Lynch forces it back shut. His hand slaps Yanie's face, having herself descend onto the floor. Larissa hollered for her as Sir Lynch's grisly hands seizes her forearms. His almighty grip fuels for a rush of screams to rip out from her throat. Larissa's devotion to escape had her body twisted for the door. This powerful force dragging at her arms, yanks away at any escape. Her whole body gets thrust to the bed. Yanie's cheek still stings. Larissa's wrists get pinned backwards causing her to lose all willpower. The sound of her deafening screams puncture Yanie's eardrums. The view of him towering over Larissa ignites a powerful rage inside of Yanie. Sir Lynch directs his entire focus on Larissa's petrified face. Her legs were pedaling blindly for freewill. Having him pressing deeper onto both her wrists had her heart thunder inside her chest. Any ability for her to maintain a firm rhythm of speech or tone was now gone.

Tears begun to pool her wide eyes as her thoughts fumbled in her head for what to do next.

SIR LYNCH'S HEAD JERKED BACK.

His claws releases Larissa, hoisted away, now spiraling in the air. He's now *madly* gripping at a strip of leather latched onto his neck. Yanie fastened her swung lasso loop of leather to secure around his throat. A loudened choking escaped from his mouth. This intense rage had Yanie clench down her teeth the more she chewed at his neck. Larissa huddled at the corner of the bed away from the madness. She gripped at the sheets as she watches Yanie handle him. Shaky grunts are heard at the top of his lungs. His elbows repeatedly missed Yanie as she curved to the opposite side. Forcing her knees deep amongst his spine, jerking back against his windpipe.

Both his frantic arms spiral the air for something as leverage. Nothing was made useful. He impulsively cocks his head from side to side. Eyes scavenge for anything. Yanie still clutches at his own belt onto his tightened throat. Sir Lynch rushes backwards into the walls. He kept slamming her back into the walls. A mirror loudly broke causing for Larissa to gasp. The adrenaline wave racing through Yanie didn't have her fazed. Yanie only gripped tighter, now latching her legs around his stomach with each collision. Both were grunting as he torpedoed into the walls.

Everything in sight begun to form blurry. His prior high-pitched squeals are now inaudible. The weight of the situation had him fall to his knees in front of a smashed mirror. Showcasing the remainder of himself squirming in the remnants of shattered glass. There was no loophole for him this time. The realization of her being dominant earlier, only to now latch onto that control still, had him suffocating more. Instead of fighting a losing battle, he refused to grant her nor Larissa the satisfaction of watching him feeling inferior as she's cutting off his airway.

That defying grip on the strip of leather had graciously unfolded. The ongoing struggled pawing against her robe had finally ceased. He locked eyes with Yanie's in their reflection. Sir Lynch's trembling lips formed a cold, devilish sneer. They both plummeted as he takes a nosedive at the ground. All that rage within Yanie slowly begun to dissipate. The leather belt strap finally unfastened from around his neck but her grip on his belt remained. And just like earlier, Yanie Juergens had come out on top.

Larissa remained statue like on the bed. Staring at Yanie heavily breathing while looming over him. Sir Lynch's smile deceased face creeped her out. The fresh belt-mark loop fused into the flesh of his neck has her teeth still chattering. Yanie runs over. She could tell Larissa wasn't eager to be touched but understood that she still needed a hug. Larissa's shaky skin felt so warm to Yanie. Her forehead buried in Yanie's chest, trying to prevent tears from flowing. Yanie caresses her head.

"La-la, I want you to wait here right quick." Yanie said, as she reaches for a cardboard box underneath the bed.

The sight of Sir Lynch is still traumatizing for Larissa. All the madness slowly still registers in her head. Larissa is still shocked. Her eyes focus on Yanie digging through the box.

After Yanie slept with him, he'd mentioned how he had a box of toys for roleplaying. There are dildos, ball gags, vibrators, invisible blindfolds, handcuffs, and a fake pistol. Then Yanie changes out her robe in the bathroom. She bursts out in regular attire holding the pistol and the belt.

The sight of Yanie gripping the gun had startled Larissa. Yanie reassured her that it's fake. Larissa looked baffled.

"We're getting the fuck up outta here." Yanie said, waving the gun, sounding ruthless. "Ain't no one stopping us. I'll find Jovanny, you wait here."

"What about them other kids?" Larissa choked out. Then mentioned that they were all Asians. "We can't just leave 'em behind. I know I won't. So, what's the moves?"

Yanie reluctantly nods. "Let's get it."

They head for the door. Larissa cautiously steps over Sir Lynch; Yanie presses her foot on his neck. The two escape the room.

Moments later, the door silently crept opened. Nobody was seen coming inside. Not a soul was detected, not even Sir Lynch's. All that was left of him was his corpse. Thomas then appeared, removing his ghost cloak. He observed Sir Lynch just lying there dead. Feeling so surreal after he had just kicked Thomas out not too long ago. Then Thomas heads for the door.

"JENSEN!" Thomas hollered. *"WHERE YOU AT?"*

†

Yanie kicked in a few room doors. Most were unlocked, in case someone wanted to join in. Larissa kept a lookout. Six doors later, she finally found a shirtless pedophile who had pinned down a nine-year-old boy to his knees. The man quickly throws his hands in the air at the sight of her gun.

"Please don't shoot." The man begged. "Are you with the cops?"

"*C'mere, little boy.*" Yanie softly called, not realizing how predatory that sounds. "It's all good. I got your back, kid. I ain't one of 'em."

The boy slowly maneuvers over to her. Yanie asked if he understood English; the boy hesitantly nods. She asked how many kids are now inside. He waved up seven fingers. Hoping that the others could understands, the boy sadly shook his head. Yanie instructs for him to follow her and to translate to them that they're being rescued.

"Who the hell are you?" the man asked, perplexed.

"Don't nobody need to know that." Yanie shouts, directing the gun at him. Then demands that he gets on his knees with both arms stretched together behind him. She calls for Larissa to tie his wrists to the bedframe using the sheets.

The man watches Larissa, looking baffled. "How are you going to look down on me when you've got a minor of your own? Mine's just from overseas, ya' hypocrite."

"She's with me."

"Okay, now I see." He mocked. "Can't have one of your own, so ya'll want to abduct."

Yanie walks over. Swipes off a pillowcase and ties it tight over his mouth. They leave in pursuit of the rest.

After being drugged and powerless, Jovanny Gibbs is still deflated on the bed. Sam had left twenty minutes ago with her stuff. The room inhabited Jovanny and the girl. She is huddled at the corner with her shivering legs pinned together. Knees pressed to her chest. The rags on her are torn off, leaving her bare. Tears of violation heavily downpour her shaky cheeks. Sam had raped her. Then had forced the girl to be penetrated by Jovanny's erect penis as Sam watched and masturbated. Lastly, Sam had uncuffed him to flip him on his stomach. Then had drilled his anus with her erect penis until Sam climaxed on his back. Sam had cleaned him off with a towel, kissed his forehead and left. The drug was slowly waring off. Even with the ability to move some muscles; Jovanny remained naked and still.

His ripped anal sphincter burns like holy water. The floodgates of blood had felt like crusty paste glued from his anus to his inner thighs. A blanket of Sam's dried sweat is puddled underneath him. Sam's grunts and moans are stirred in his head. These ongoing thoughts has his lower back feeling constricted. Helpless screams and cries from the girl had his chest bend inward. Remembering how he closed his eyes as she was violated because he just couldn't watch anymore of it. Jovanny started feeling this tidal wave of guilt. Getting raped by Sam had kept his head throbbing.

Attempts to divert his thoughts failed. His thoughts get more jumbled as he persists. His whole body is drained of all energy to get up. Both of his tired eyes blankly stared at the wall. The girl's sniffling is heard from across the room.

"I'm so sorry." His voice broke, still unable to liven his tone and spirits. The drug effects haven't worn off yet.

The door got kicked in. Yanie barges in then her relentless energy just fell flat. She stared at Jovanny's bare ass and the girl in the corner. Jovanny's eyes glowed with horror by the sight of all this. Yanie stared at him in disgust. Not hearing Yanie yelling yet had Larissa poke her head in disbelief. Both couldn't believe what Jovanny had done. Yanie told Larissa to wait outside. After slamming the door, she marched over to Jovanny.

"Yanie, listen…" Jovanny weakly tries.

"NIGGA, HOW COULD YOU!" she yelled. A sharp sting strikes her chest.

Fists start striking his back. Jovanny's mouth feels wired shut. Each attempt to speak felt like a tear in his jaw. Slowly waving his right arm to try calming her down just has Yanie deviate from him. Yanie calls in the boy to speak to the girl about what happened. The boy asks if that man on the bed had sex with her. She nodded her head as more tears flush down. Yanie slowly covered her body with the blanket on the floor. Rubbing her back, helping her up.

From the look of him, Yanie could tell that Jovanny must've been under some type of substance. Her first thought was ecstasy or alcohol. But having the boy translate the truth of what happened shattered any excuse that she could conjure for him. They escape the room, leaving Jovanny behind. Pitiful Jovanny watches them all go.

Then extended his woozy arm as a plead for help.

That was the last girl brought inside. The other six are trailing behind Larissa in a group. Yanie tells the boy to translate that they're leaving. As he does, Yanie runs downstairs flashing the pistol in the air. The guests started freaking out. Some drop to their knees, others throw their backs at the wall and many just froze.

Yanie announced for everyone to make way for them. Nobody tried stopping them. Larissa was the first to hold the door for everyone, aiding their escape.

The driver of the truck gets held at gunpoint as Yanie throws him out. After having Larissa cuff both the drivers to the mailbox, Yanie returned to the truck. A burst from the door got flung open, as the sheep had run out of the house.

Inside the shipment container are the other children divided into two pairs. Females chained by one side, males on the opposite. All huddled themselves tightly against the other nearby. Many squirms in terror as to wherever their fate lies. Sniffling, uneasy breathing and stomach growling is heard from the darkness within. Then the harsh noise of the latch opening occurred. Their precious hearts had hysterically rumbled. The entire void is black. Some impulsively search for a sign as to which way it's coming from. Others have lost faith in anyone coming to their rescue. As the doors slowly cracks open, a dim light sparked everyone's dreary eyes. The rusty squeaks of them opening had become a slow burn on those children. Light slowly blooms into a golden glow within, igniting a stirring fear.

All heads aligned with each other facing outside. Trembling legs fastened together, hands clutched with each other's, and some hoping for a Hail Mary of sorts.

Their eyes squinted as the powerful brightness chipped away at them. However, the angelic, silhouette figure from afar was different than what they were exposed to prior. Yanie calmly extends out her arms, raises both hands out, displaying she's no threat. The boy translates loudly everything she instructed for him to announce. That she understands that they've been kidnapped and that she's rescuing them. Her eyes read the room. Some were in disbelief. Yanie then presents the other rescued children to help further convey this message. One girl chained in the back hollered something that Yanie couldn't understand.

"What she say?" Yanie asks the boy.

"Where will you take us?"

"Anywhere but here."

The boy reluctantly translated for all to hear.

Yanie, Larissa and the boy are in the front.

"What about Jovanny?" Larissa asked, concerned.

Yanie angrily states. *"Ain't nobody checking for his ass!"*

The engine igniting slightly triggers the children, yet they remain calm. Even without reassurance of where they are heading, they gladly follow Yanie by default. As she is now seen as their savior (*of these children of God*).

They all finally exiled this Godforsaken place.

† TO BE CONTINUED... †

Ian Ramsay

grew up in Long Island, New York. Has a passion for great storytelling. Most of his inspiration has derived from cinema and television shows. Hopes to create more.